DECEIT

A NOVEL OF LIES, DUPLICITY, & FRAUD

To Marsha,
Take A walk on the
wild side when I lived
on the dark side of the
Moon.

by John Austin Sletten

Outskirts Press, Inc.
Denver, Colorado

To Ellen

You were always there.
Johnny Sletten

The secret source of humor itself is not joy but sorrow.
Mark Twain

Acknowledgements

This is a book about the individuals and institutions that abuse power ... and the collateral damage to the innocents. So let me thank my family, beginning with my wife, Ellen, and my children: Kelly, Chad, Joseph, Daniel and Christopher. And to my grandson, Ethan, who makes me so happy. I thank all of you for putting up with me.

As a writer, you can only be as good as the readers you share your first drafts with. They are my conscripted friends who were forced, by horsewhip, to read various drafts and to give in-depth boosting commentaries. I want to give special thanks to my Aunt Mary Ann Jensen, who has always been such an inspiration to me, for her encouragement: and to three out of the ordinary friends, whose opinions I value so much - *men of true grit*: Norman Ritter, Harold Gavaris, and Bruce Jones. Thanks to all of you for your candor, comments, and suggestions to help make this a worthy read.

The characters in this book are real. Their names have been changed to protect the guilty. The venues have been changed to protect the unknowing.

A special thanks to Kelley Colbridge and Jay Sletten for editing the original manuscript through its fruition. A big round of applause for Dennis Gillen, who designed the cover and jacket as well as for Nichole Sletten for keeping the project schematized.

And for Mary Shanahan, *Here's looking at you kid.*

John Austin Sletten
Philadelphia, Pennsylvania
February 1, 2011

Preamble

My book is story, not history or biography or autobiography. It is, nonetheless, true. It is written in the form of a novel. It is a graphic expose of white collar crime and how the FBI miss-uses their staggering powers to barely touch the surface of the case's real essence. So, what is the why? Why is why never explained? And, who's agenda? The schema here is simply my recollections.

J. Edgar Hoover, the most powerful lawman in America for over fifty years, was also the country's most controversial and feared public servant. His career as director of the Federal Bureau of Investigation spanned nine different presidential administrations and survived a dozen attempts to sweep him from office. During that time, Hoover completely reshaped domestic law enforcement as he expanded the reach of the FBI and transformed his G-men into an elite national crime fighting division. Despite his contributions to the criminal justice system, Hoover fell from favor soon after his death, the victim of rampant rumors and innuendo. Later it was determined Hoover had a long-standing alliance with the Mafia.

Against a background of the Watergate scandals, Jane Fonda files, and the ensuing demoralization of the Bureau's leadership, I came to Washington D.C. with my college degree in accounting and psychology in tote. I was a naïve twenty-seven-year-old young man hailing from the Midwest thinking I was going to make a difference. As I was taxied from National Airport to the Department of Justice Building, located on Pennsylvania Avenue, it was a bright, sunny September day, in 1971. I was not thinking about my new job with the Bureau. Rather, my eyes were fixed on all the famous buildings, monuments, streets and sights. I couldn't believe I was in Washington D.C, let alone going to be working here. I was excited. Here, right in the nation's Capital.

Of course, I had no idea what I was getting myself into, all that glitters is definitely not gold. Instead, I was about to be coerced into an audacious undercover operation to break up small business operations teetering on grey lines. I would be working undercover for the Federal Bureau of Investigation. And, undercover work in white collar crime had not yet been tested, let alone defined by written rules. In 14-plus years as an undercover agent, I would infiltrate top echelons of white collar crime business operations. I would dine with them, sleep in their homes, and visit with their families. And, in the end, if I did a good job, I would put them in jail.

Along the way, I learned everything about the nefarious ways and thinking of those pursued and the actions of the Federal Bureau of Investigation. In order to do so, I had to become those criminals and understand their thinking and the purposes of my bosses to avoid becoming their target. Rules of engagement were made up as the scrutiny went along. To effectively do all this meant talking, acting, and even thinking like them. The stories are sometimes funny, surprising, repulsive, revealing, and shocking. However, they paint an authentic, entertaining, and complete picture of an illegal high life on both sides of the fence.

In reality, these law-breakers are not uncivilized thugs, criminals, and killers. They live by their own strict code of ethics and actions that both reflect and refute the ways of the so-called honest business world, of which, there is no such beast. These high-lifers have their own take on loyalty, laziness, opportunism, food, friends, confrontation, intimidation, information exchange, hiring practices, office politics, revenge and more. So does the FBI. And, perhaps the Bureau has learned a thing or two from these enemies.

Through it all, and in the end, I attempt to deal with the self-serving rigidity of the FBI bureaucracy. After accepting the wisdom of my final assignment, which a mission accomplished has simply been a ruse with a whole different purpose; I was in fear of my own life. I knew too much, especially with the Department of Justice looking into the affairs of the Federal Bureau Investigation and its higher-ups. Special Agents, like me, were simply a method for their means. In the end, I felt like the hunter hunted.

When my career ended with the Bureau, I realized it was a line of business that caused me to raise one fundamental question. Who is to be held responsible for the clandestine operations of the FBI and its unconstitutional practices concerning white collar crime? What's the difference between the tactics of the Federal Bureau of Investigation and the people they so casually take aim?

Prologue

Route 95, slightly north of Baltimore, Maryland
Saturday, January 14, 1984

It was a partly cloudy afternoon. I was driving my 280Z to my home in Philadelphia. I hadn't been home since Christmas and I was looking forward to spending some time with my wife and children. With a sleek body and 145 horsepower, the Z car begged to be driven and it just felt good to goose it a little when I was certain there were no olive green patrol vehicles in sight; those Maryland State Troopers.

When I exited the Fort McHenry Tunnel I noticed a flash in the sky and a loud sound, like an artillery round exploding. I was traveling sixty-five to seventy-five miles an hour, so the sight and sound were simply a blur and a pop at that point in time. Ordinarily, the flash and the din wouldn't have even made an impression on me. Because it was from the direction it came that got me thinking. So much had been going on at Atlantic States Surety recently, especially with the Board of Directors.

Just before Christmas I was summoned to Paul Gordon Charles' lavish office. He was the CEO and majority stockholder of Atlantic States Surety. His private office was colossal, with its marbles and granites. The walls were mirrored, except for the one behind his desk. PGC's chair was turned facing that wall when I entered. Richard Corrigan, Senior Vice President sat me down at a long leather black couch in front of a stretched mahogany table. Corrigan stood and motioned for me to stand. Gordon, as he preferred to be addressed, said, in a clear, well enunciated voice, "Gentlemen we have to do something about Tom."

Tom Harvey is a very successful, black businessman in the

District. He has connections with the District of Columbia's mayor and religious evangelist Jessie Jackson. He supposedly has the right links to the President, Ronald Reagan. He has invested heavily in PGC's surety company. Recently, he has been bored with the goings-on at Atlantic States Surety or A.S.S., as he usually refers to it. He wants more perks to keep him feeling good about himself."

I said, "Mr. Charles, I just arranged for a new Mercedes for his girlfriend, Angel."

"Not enough," says PGC, loudly. "He wants more to keep his damn mouth shut!"

"What now?" shouts, Richard Corrigan, deridingly?

"You know Tom," PGC says, dragging out the *m*," is a pilot. He wants an airplane, a nice one."

"Who does he think he is; *the Red Baron or Eddie O'Hare?*" asks Corrigan.

Gordon smiles, saying, "Jack you have to arrange financing for an airplane for Tom. He wants a four passenger. A *Cessna* or some flying machine like that." There was a long pause. "Something like that," Gordon says again.

Between Christmas and New Year's, I'd arranged for a new *Cessna* for Tom Harvey. He seemed quite happy, although a little reticent to accept such a gift from Gordon.

"You really know how to fly this thing?" I had asked him.

"Come on, I'll give you a ride, Jack."

"I don't know if you can fly this thing or not, Tom, but I'll go up with you."

Tom and I took off out of Friendship Airport in Baltimore, and flew up to Pennsylvania and back. He seemed to be a terrific pilot and I really enjoyed the trip. He learned to fly in the military. He flew in Korea. He seemed to be a really good guy and highly skilled.

I pushed thoughts of Tom Harvey out of my mind, putting music on the radio. When I pulled into our driveway all the kids were in the yard ready to greet me. After spending moments with them and listening to their stories, Ellen came toward me and gave me a hug.

"John," she said. "I think something is going on. The phone has been ringing off the hook the past two hours. Joe Neverson left a number. He said it's important.

Joe Neverson is the only one who had my telephone number in Pennsylvania. I didn't know exactly who Joe was, other than a mighty fine lawyer and friend. He didn't know who I was either, but he and his wife and children had just spent Christmas with us at our house in Glenside. We made it work for the children, but Joe and his wife, Nancy, couldn't speak to each other without fighting.

I took our portable phone into the back yard and dialed Joe's telephone number, which was actually my number in Maryland. After the Christmas fiasco, Joe moved, supposedly temporarily, into my recently rented apartment.

"Jack," he said. "Tom Harvey is dead. His plane exploded over Maryland somewhere. He and his son were killed. You need to get back here."

"What happened?" I asked.

"Guess?" Joe responded.

After I shut the phone down, I just sat there staring into space, wondering if Gordon Charles really did arrange a plane crash. Good God almighty!

"Are you alright, John?" Ellen inquired, while walking up to me. I gave her an abbreviated version of what had happened. She was stunned, asking, "What are you going to do?"

"We'll watch the news tonight to see if anything is being reported. Hopefully, it won't be here in Philadelphia. I'll go back to Washington, tomorrow."

Ellen picked up the telephone, saying, "You've got ice in your veins."

"Ellen, I spoke out loud, "What the hell do you want me to do?"

"Resign! Resign that fucking job!" She screamed out while walking back in the house.

I sat down at the picnic table and lit up a cigarette. To murder was not as simple as it appeared, especially to blow up Tom

Harvey's plane in mid-air with him in it. Too many people would have to be involved, but Gordon had the ability to get it done. He would have to go outside his empire for help. Someone on the inside would have to have given him an assist, though, because he never puts himself in harm's way. No, murder was simply too problematic, or was it?

Deception had become my stock-in- trade. Like water that seeps into a crack and later freezes, expanding the crack into a fissure, deception had found the cracks in my character and exposed them. Deception, at the beginning of my career, made me uneasy. But by this time in my line of business my capacity to deceive defined who and what I was. I didn't think of myself as a liar. Lying was simply what I did to do my job well. Nevertheless, I was a champion liar. I not only lied to my suspects, but I lied to everyone I knew, including myself. I'd been undercover for too long, and my experiences had altered me in some basic and dark ways.

I put out my cigarette and looked into our house where I could see Ellen putting an early supper on the kitchen table. The boys seemed happy we were all together. "She's right, I've got to give it up," I'm whispering to myself as I walk into the house.

"Hey," I shout. "Save a plate for me. How about we go to a movie tonight?"

"Yeah," the boys shout in unison. Meanwhile Ellen is shaking her head with a forced smile. She says, "You'll never change, Johnny. You are always the life of the party!"

I shrugged saying, "What can I do?"

What Is Past Is Prologue

Montevideo, Minnesota
Tuesday, January 27, 1959

It is a wintry Minnesota morning, although warmer than usual for late January. Mounted just outside our kitchen window is Dad's weather-worn thermometer; typically standard equipment for a northern community home. It reads five degrees and there are a few snowflakes floating in the air.

"I hear the singers are staying at the Hunt Hotel," mother says, with a smile, while putting four pieces of buttered toast on a plate between my brother and me. The Hunt Hotel is owned by our neighbor's landlord, Judge Hunt. My father would often comment on how old Judge Hunt is as crooked as the day is long. The other story about the judge is he's been very instrumental in Minnesota's Senator Hubert Humphrey's political pursuits. The hotel is located on Main Street and is a very swanky place for Montevideo.

"What singers?" Dad growls, while turning a page of the Minneapolis Star Tribune. He folded the front page of the paper in quarters and handed it to Mom commanding, "Save it!"

"For crying out loud, what for?" was her response.

"There's a picture of Nixon on the front page. Put it in the toilet so I can wipe my ass on it the next time I take a shit." Dad replies, with a hee-haw.

I finish my toast and exclaim enthusiastically, "Buddy Holly and Ritchie Valens. Oh, and Dion and the Belmonts," I add, while my brother takes his third slice of toast.

"Big Bopper too," Ricky chimes into the conversation.

I am a freshman and my brother is a sixth grader. I go to

Central High School, which is located roughly a mile west of our house. We live in a neighborhood called Burns Addition on the southeastern side of town. My brother, Ricky, goes to Alexander Ramsey Elementary, located about two miles north of our home. Ricky rides a Simon Olson school bus to and from school. When it's really cold, bone chilling, I catch a ride with Dad to the corner of Black Oak Avenue and Third Street. Most days, like today, I just jog or walk the distance.

I'm zigzagging through the smaller streets, which run adjacent to Black Oak Avenue. I'm bobbing and weaving, like I often do, with a stiff arm here and there, pretending I'm running a winning touchdown for the Minnesota *Golden Gophers* in a Rose Bowl game. The truth is I have plans to meet up with my buddy, Augie, to discuss our plans to get into the Winter Dance Party tonight.

August is a year older than I, but we've been good friends since I was in 7th grade and he in 8th. We both love music and sports, although August can't carry a tune. We had agreed to meet at the Hill Grocery, which is kitty-corner from the high school, to plan our strategy for getting a peek at and hearing the singing stars.

Montevideo is considered a relatively small town by most standards, but it is the biggest town for many miles around. Area teenagers come to "Monte" to drag the main, visit the bowling alley, the roller skating rink, or the back alley of Main Street. The biggest attraction is the Tuesday night teen dances at the Fiesta Ball Room, formerly Gladys, until the Big Swing Bands faded out. It was Elvis Presley who was the man responsible for the emergence of rock 'n' roll. *Hound Dog, Don't Be Cruel and Love Me Tender*, were some of his first hits that had set the tone for change.

The décor of the Fiesta reflected the tradition of Montevideo's sister city in Uruguay. Colorful sombreros, maracas, and Latin musical instruments grace the ballroom's walls. Waitresses wear gaudy skirts and peasant-style blouses. The ballroom's logo has a sombrero jauntily perched on the "F" and a scarf trails behind the word. When ballroom owner, Clarence Burns, first started his teen dances, he required his young patrons to provide a parent's permission slip before entering. Once a teen was admitted, they couldn't leave the building until the show was over. Burns didn't allow smoking in the Fiesta during teen dances. The restrooms were patrolled by employees to make certain teens were not drinking or smoking. If a teenager was caught, he or she would be detained in the office until a parent arrived to claim the offender. Or, so that was the way it was suppose to work. Did it? No! Even back then, teenagers were a little bit more resourceful.

August Eng met me in front of Hill Grocery, a place where students congregated with snacks before school each day. August and I are about the same height and weight. We are five feet eleven inches tall and weigh one hundred seventy-five pounds. I have light brown hair and brilliant blue eyes. I have more of an athlete's build and I'm charismatic. I'm told I have a natural way about me, whatever that means. August has light brown and bluish-green eyes. He is a good sized guy and a good athlete. I am Norwegian and August comes from English-German descent.

August is shy around girls. I'm diffident around everyone, although I prefer being alone. I'm more of a guts act. When August and I aren't talking music and sports, August is fantasizing about seeing some girl naked. August really has no hopes of this happening but I, on the other hand, never dwell on anything I don't think possible. I believe, with all my apple-cheeked, athletic good looks and ornamental charm, I can make anything happen.

For instance, my aunt, Mary Ann, is a beautiful young woman. She is only five years older than me and was spending last weekend at our house because she had a date. I had told August I had a surprise for him.

"What!" he'd asked.

"We're going to see my aunt naked," I said, with a devious grin. "You know the big tree next to my parent's bedroom? That's where Mary will be staying. She has a date at six o'clock. So we'll climb the tree about five fifteen and wait for her to come out of the shower."

When Mary Ann exited the shower and came into our full view, she was wearing nothing but a towel around her head. We were in the tree at eye level with the window. We had a full view when Mary put down the towel and walked over to pull the shades down. When she saw us, in the tree, peering at her, it was like that scene from Bonnie and Clyde, years later in the movie, when the birds all flew out of the trees just before the bank robbers were staring down the lawmen with shotguns. Here we were, just August and I, looking at my aunt's naked body from our perch. Of course, she got mad as hell, but never said a word to my Dad, her older brother. Yes, right then and there I learned I could be a rainbow maker while August creamed his pants in a tree.

It seems this year, for the first time, girls were approaching me, especially the older gals. As August and I meandered the block toward the high school, I said, "I told you Diane B will get permission slips signed for us. She's in my Latin class and flirts with me for some motivation. Sometimes I let her copy my Latin homework assignments. Maybe that's why she flirts, I don't know. She looks like Liz Taylor, but they say Diane B is wild as the wind?"

"She'll sign a slip for me too," August queried?

"Of course," I followed, vociferously. Diane B was one year older than August, but he didn't seem to know any of the girls. He liked to look, and, dream. "Would I leave you out, Jackass?"

August was smiling, now, saying, then singing, "Okay! .....*if you knew Peggy Sue......*"

I usually sit in the back, on the left side of the room. I was sitting there when Diane B plopped down next to me. She had a stenographer's notebook and a sheet of ruled tablet paper. She smiled like a girl with a secret. And when she did, I was thinking she's the sexiest girl in the whole world. She was chewing gum, in a provocative way, when she asked: "How do you spell your last name, John? And, what's your mother's first name? And, your buddy's information?"

While handing me the permissions slips, Diane B asks me slyly: "Do you want to play pocket pool?"

"What?" I queried, while studying her intents. She took my hand and squeezed it. She was mischievous and flirtatious as she was lovely.

She laughed, saying, "*Maybe Baby.*"

I met August on Black Oak Avenue at 11th Street, which was one block from my home. The Fiesta Ballroom was close by and with the permission slips in our shirt pockets, we were eager to see the show. When Diane B saw us about an hour later, she invited us to her booth, which was located directly in front of the bandstand.

"How did she pull this off," August pondered out loud. I simply shrugged my shoulders while Diane B hobnobbed with the celebrities. Meanwhile, we focused on the stage, where Buddy Holly, playing his sunburst Fender Stratocaster, and his band, the *Crickets,* sang out "*Peggy Sue;*" Ritchie Valens sang "*Donna,*" then ripped out "*LaBamba;*" The Big Bopper, J.P. Richardson, mimicked a ringing phone and shouted, "*Hello Baby!*" Then, Dion and the Belmonts sang a love song, "*Teenager In Love.*"

Diane B pulled me onto the dance floor and got real close. She danced so secure I could feel her breasts rubbing up against my chest. She didn't say a word and I hoped she didn't feel my erection. I didn't know what to do, so I just followed her lead. When the song was over, I thanked her for the dance, and hesitantly asked, "How do we get out of here? It's almost ten o'clock."

"That's right," she said. "You have a curfew." Then, she stopped Waylon Jennings, a young country singer who we'd watch croon and twang his guitar. Diane whispered something in his ear. She pointed us out to him and then walked back, saying. "Just follow Waylon, he'll let you out the back. Hey," she said, "There's a party at my house afterwards. They'll all be there, pointing at the entertainers. "If you can get out, you're invited. You better get moving." Waylon motioned for us to follow him.

He let us out the back door, where the entertainers entered, and as we walked away from the jam-packed parking lot, the Fiesta Ballroom loomed in the background. It looked like an armory with its huge rounded top. A summer or two ago, I had tried to lay out a baseball diamond in the vacant grounds in back of the ballroom. It didn't work out, but it kept me busy that summer. August and I used to look at Playboy magazine there, where nobody would ever catch us. It was just a vacant field with rugged rutted terrain and weeds growing at random. We called it the desert.

When I arrived home it was ten to ten. Mom and Dad were getting a snack and getting ready to watch the late news, weather, and sports. I announced myself with a simple, "Hi" and went to my bedroom. I took off my clothes and sat on the edge of the bed studying a ticket stub I'd picked off the table while sitting with Diane B. There was a picture of the Fiesta Ballroom on top. Printed below it read:

Call AM 9-6100 for Booth Reservations
Tues, Jan. 27 TEEN HOP
Coral and ABC Paramount Artists
Buddy HOLLY & The Crickets
With such stars as
BIG BOPPER, Ritchie Valens and Dion and The Belmonts

I put the ticket in my sacred baseball card box and went to bed.

Chapter One

Lutheran Theological Seminary
Philadelphia, Pennsylvania
Wednesday, September 7, 1983

"Hey, John!"

I recognized the voice. I turned my head toward the whine and sure enough, it was crybaby, Jay Larkspur. He had just exited the large red doors of the Krauth Memorial Library and was making his way down the steps. I was at the circle, in the front of the building, where five sets of sidewalks lead different directions onto the fourteen acre campus. I paused at center circle allowing Jay Larkspur to catch up with me.

"Hey," Jay said with a nervous twitch on his lips. The human mind will sometimes grasp for straws when you're in over your head. No one knew that better than me. Jay was looking for an assist. Yes, Jay was the perfect seminarian with the perfect wife and children looking for help from the one everyone looked down upon. My family and I didn't make any sense to this bunch and their Sunday school education of the scripture.

"John," he said, wryly. "You mentioned an Old Testament sermon you wrote this summer on First Samuel. You know, with all my kids, wife working ..." I stopped him right there, thinking privately I'd mentioned the sermon two nights ago when Larkspur came over to our apartment complaining my son, Joe, had sucker-punched his son, Jimmy, in the stomach.

"Jay," I said, "if you want to use my sermon , it's okay with me. I could care less."

"Okay," he said, sheepishly, "Some people have a problem with these kinds of things." He followed his remarks with a joke and a few guffaws. I laughed politely. I've never liked jokes and the pretentious laughs that follow. In Jay's defense, the past ten years had turned me into a disparaging asshole.

"Drop by tonight, Jay," I said. "I'll give you the sermon."

While I watched Jay walk toward the quad, I picked up on a guy in a brown suit who was donning a pair of sinister dark sun glasses. He was leaning against a tall tree, which was displaying beautiful yellow-golden autumn leaves. My eyes followed the leaves some forty feet into the sky, I guessed. It was a beautiful day. Then, my gaze drifted to the bottom of the tree, knowing full well the man standing there was looking for me. All I could think was he was so out of place here. Why the mysterious glasses. What happened to discreet?

I noticed passersby's looking at the interloper with the aviator sun glasses. I didn't want my fellow classmates seeing him single me out for a little chat. I'd been an enigma here and my first year at the Lutheran Seminary at Gettysburg, Pennsylvania. I was older and imagined I didn't quite fit the role of a parish pastor candidate, mostly by my out-of-classroom diplomacy. And, of course, let's not forget my negative attitude toward the female supervisor during my Clinical Pastoral Education, or CPE, at Allentown State Hospital. But she gave me a great report on my internship, which balanced the books. Although, in my opinion, I didn't think most of my classmates fit as a minister and leader of a congregation, either. For the most part, I thought them too young and naïve.

I was thirty-six and most of the others were right out of college when we started this journey together in the autumn of 1980. We came from all over the country and all walks of life. Perhaps, we all came seeking some type of refuge. I certainly didn't think I'd be running into such a beer-drinking crowd. Nor did I expect to encounter the brilliant minds of these young people. They didn't deal in mathematics and concrete concepts; rather in philosophies and those things left to deep thinking and uncertainty. Most seminarians had a basic Sunday School knowledge of the Bible, which frustrated them to no end when professors taught the Bible proves God exists and that He doesn't, as well. Faith alone will set you free.

I looked at the Special Agent standing under the tree, while he looked at me. Knowing what was certain, something not so new and predatory came to mind. Before 1972, when the FBI Academy opened in Quantico, Virginia, we were trained on the top floor of the *Old* Post Office Building in Washington, DC. Here, I was schooled in the law, the violations that come under the FBI's jurisdiction, proper procedures and techniques of interviewing people, and conducting all types of investigations. I was trained in self-defense tactics, proper procedures and techniques of car chases and making arrests, and in the use of every type of firearm the Bureau uses. No I'm not a theologian, psychologist, or a social worker. I'm a Special Agent with the Federal Bureau of Investigation.

"John, the agent exclaimed as I headed down the adjacent sidewalk which leads to our apartment. I stop and look at him intently. He forces a smile and walks across the grass between the two paths. The Bureau never plays proper politics. He was a special agent on a mission.

"John," the agent says, smiling and extending his hand, "You're wanted in Washington Monday morning, 0800 hours."

No way was my immediate thought. "What, this coming Monday?" I laugh heartily.

The agent grins. "Look, John, I'm only the messenger. Be at 935 Pennsylvania Avenue, 0800 hours this coming Monday!" He flashes his credentials, extends his hand and departs. It's the way it works. It was like this when I left Virginia Beach, Virginia. Here one day, gone the next without explanation.

The unreality of it was beginning to sink in, realizing there were no choices. I became emotionally attentive, but unavailable and distant. I was crawling back in my single-handed mode, wondering what I'd be doing. Who would I become this time?

I had been enjoying seminary days. I'd applied myself and was getting straight A's. As long as I graduated before turning thirty-nine I could join the Navy and become a Chaplain. This was my plan; obviously not the Bureau's. Fleeting thoughts of finishing my Masters of Divinity degree were coming and going in my mind.

Then, everything became surreal. There would never be a record of me ever being here or anywhere else. I kicked a pine cone across the sidewalk.

Once again, there would be a new resume of companies I've worked for, which of course no longer exist, but are covered with phone numbers. I knew the game and I was sick of it. The action was no longer exciting. My prayer was just to be able to be one person, truthful and straightforward again. I wanted deception, lying, cheating, and stealing out of my life. This most recent nice-to-see-you-but-I'm-too-rushed-to-stop-and-talk-just-now meeting really upset me. *Just do what you are told*; a Hoover mantra, I was thinking when Professor Lull crossed my melancholy.

"John," great paper," he said, while tapping me on the shoulder, with a smile, as he walked on by.

I don't exist, I'm deliberating, watching Lull pass by. I envied him, thinking he must be content and happy. He has a wife and three boys like me. The difference between Lull and me was the professor was in control of his own destiny. Jay Larkspur interrupted my thoughts as I saw him approaching.

"Hey, John," he shouts in his Virginia southern drawl. He's rubbing his hands together like he's anticipating great excitement or an event. "Do you suppose I could get that homily now, so I can start working on it this afternoon?"

Although his persistence was pissing me off I realized it would be better to just give it to him. I would certainly be drunk tonight. "Sure," I said, motioning toward our apartment house.

You won't tell anyone now will you?" He gargled, like an asshole.

I felt like punching him, but replied nicely, "Who would I tell?"

I wondered what Jay Larkspur would do if he had my problems? Yeah, commit suicide, most likely. He thanks me and away he goes with my First Samuel sermon. I went directly to our bedroom, to my side of the bed, and lifted the mattress up. Here I plucked two twenty's and a ten. I fixed a Lebanon bologna sandwich, with mustard, and ate it on the way across the street to the beer distributor. I bought two cases of Budweiser and while walking back all I could think of was itineraries, travel times, and flight numbers. I'd have to master a new made up history, a biography. From what college or University I graduated was just the tip of the iceberg. I'd be covering something up, escaping something, taking on a new identity. I never knew for sure. There is really no way to anticipate what was coming at me next.

How ridiculous and what a stranger he is who is surprised at anything which happens in life. **Marcus Aurelius**

What Is Past Is Prologue

Hershey, Pennsylvania
Saturday, August 15, 1959

We began our first and only family vacation August 12, 1959. We arrived about noon on Saturday. It had been a long drive across Minnesota, then Wisconsin, and south into Illinois, on Day One. And, as much as I had protested against this vacation, once we got going it was interesting. We had a 1957 Plymouth, fire engine red, which Dad bought from Grandma Austin after Grandpa passed, May 3, 1958. Most of the time I sat in the front seat with Dad, playing my Big League Manager baseball game as we motored down the highway. I got such a kick out of being able to get a Milwaukee Braves game on the radio while passing through Wisconsin. And, it was even better picking up the Cubs and White Sox games as we passed through Chicago.

When I requested my front window be closed because the wind was blowing my baseball scorecard around, everybody acquiesced for about ten minutes. Mother had taken the hump in the back seat between my brother and sister. It was getting hotter than hell in the car, being absent of the cross breeze. When Mom shouted out, "This is ridiculous…" I put away my game and rolled down the window.

"Warren you better stop now before your daughter pees her pants. Do you hear, Warren?"

Dad shouts back, in his Archie Bunker voice, "Jesus Christ, do you want me to pull a Skelly oil station out of my ass?" Dad pressed harder on the accelerator as we roared down the road sixty-five miles an hour. Soon enough a Sinclair oil station appeared in the distance. When Dad pulled along the gas pump an old timer waddled up to the car, inquiring, "Fill er up?"

"Restrooms?" Dad asked.

"Don't work." replies the old timer, pointing to a falling down shed.

"That works!" he says with a hoarse laugh.

Mom screams out: "Our daughter can't go in that shed."

Meanwhile the old timer fills the gas tank and seems to be enjoying the family feuding. Dad had us make a circle around our sister, facing away from her of course. She peed. Dad, Rick and I went to the shed to relieve ourselves.

Mother had just begun to fight. She took the front seat and I jumped in the back, putting my sister in the hump seat. Mom held her need for twenty miles, until we arrived at a truck stop near the Wisconsin and Illinois line.

We stayed at a cheap motel just east of Chicago. We were all pretty tired from our travels on Day One. The constant wind blowing through the open windows and the beating of the red hot sun in our faces seemed almost unbearable. Along with the family bickering and complaining, I really thought several times Dad would turn the car around and head for home. He didn't and Day Two went by relatively uneventful as we crossed Illinois, Indiana, Ohio and to a few miles west of Pittsburgh.

Dad picked out a motel with a swimming pool. So, we relaxed and later watched Harvey Haddix of the Pittsburgh Pirates best Joe Nuxhall of the Cincinnati Redlegs on television in nearby Pittsburgh. I was starting to feel like a big shot. But, I figured if I told my friends about it, I wondered if they would even believe me. Or, would they just call me a bullshitter?

Early in the morning, we travelled the Pennsylvania Turnpike. We didn't have roads like this in Minnesota, two lanes running parallel in each direction. The tunnels were fascinating as they bored through the Allegheny Mountains. When coming through to the end of a tunnel, huge valley's loomed in the distance. The scenery was magnificent and with the advent of each tunnel, it kept all of us busy just looking and anticipating what was coming up next. When we took the Harrisburg exit off the turnpike, Mother started preparing us for our first stop by telling us a story.

"Martha and Benny Focht kind of adopted me in Wilmington, Delaware. Your Dad was flying all over the world and I was in Wilmington, and very lonely. I met them on the church steps one Sunday and we became very close friends. After you were born, John, we were sent to Presque Isle, Maine. Your Dad was stationed at the Army Air Corps base near Mars Hill. I didn't see Martha again after we left Wilmington, but we corresponded at Christmas time over the years. Funny, about two years after we left Wilmington, Martha signed her Christmas card *Martha, Benny and Ellen.*"

"So Ellen must be my age." I said.

"Must be, maybe a year younger," Mom replied.

"Keep your eyes peeled!" Dad said, as we crossed into Hershey, Pennsylvania's city limits.

An aroma of chocolate filled the air. The street lights looked like chocolate kisses and coming up on the left was the Hershey Chocolate Factory. A huge hedge near the front of the building spelled out: *"WELCOME TO HERSHEY"*

"Is this where they make the Hershey Bar, Dad?" My brother asks, licking his chops for a taste.

"You bet," Dad replied. "You bet!"

"We're in Palmyra," Mom announced from the back seat. "Did you see the sign, Warren?" Mom usually called attention to a sign after we already driven passed it.

Mom had Martha's letter out, "says here, you come to a V in the road. Stay left and make a quick left on Miller Avenue. Says here, Miller Avenue looks like an alley… go to the last house on the left, 125 Miller Avenue. Says here …"

"Mom, were here." I said. "Look, their back yard is a cornfield."

"Just like home," my brother, Rick, says with a smile. He loved corn on the cob and I'm sure he's licking his chops again.

As we pile out of the car I couldn't quite imagine how we were all going to fit in that small little house. It was very small white, stucco home. Also, it looked like nobody was home as Dad approached the front door. Before he could knock he was greeted through the screen door by Ellen, whose arms and apron were covered in flour. "Come in," she says. "My parents will be here shortly. They went food shopping. I'm trying to bake two cherry pies."

Dad motioned us forward, allowing my mother to take charge. She has great social skills and introduces everybody as we enter. I had positioned myself in the back of the line. When it was my turn, Ellen's beauty stunned me.

I got my first rapturous glance at Ellen Jane Focht. She was a spellbinding, improbable true brunet beauty. Her natural charm captivated me. Just her presence, standing their covered in flour, suggested a carnality that took me to the borderline of sinful thoughts as I stood there and gaped at her. To me, it felt like no appreciation of mere loveliness, but some corruption of covetousness or gluttony. Her green eyes drank me in, and I noted flecks of gold.

Hello," she said. "You must be Johnny? My name is Ellen." She took my hand and squeezed it. She was lovely and I fell instantly in love.

Those who act receive the prizes. **Aristotle**

Chapter Two

Lutheran Theological Seminary
Philadelphia, Pennsylvania
Wednesday, September 7, 1983

We live at Gowan Avenue, right on the campus. It's a large house with one family on the first floor and our spacious apartment on the second. There is a third story as well, which houses two single seminarians. After bouncing around in Gettysburg, my first seminary year, between trailer houses and a basement apartment; we really have appreciated our housing at the Philadelphia Lutheran Theological Seminary.

In every place I've lived, since being married to Ellen, there has been a designated drinking place. Here it was our kitchen, away from the children's bed rooms and the rest of the apartment.

I'd been stewing since the Special Agent and Jay Larkspur had departed. It was my family whom I was concerned about. When pack-it-up-time came about it was more confusing every time. We always thought it would be the last time; it was a theory or lie I proposed to my wife. I kept telling her good work was moving me up the ladder. It made sense, too, only because she was busy taking care of three boys. Four, if you want to add me to the list. I'd been visible the past three years.

It was five-thirty in the afternoon when Ellen came through the door with a bag full of groceries and our toddler close behind. We pretty much bought groceries by the day to make sure not to run out, like we did once in Gettysburg. We had once lived on scrapple for two days. The first thing my wife noticed was the Budweiser. She asked sarcastically, "John what's up? Is there something wrong?"

She knew me better than I knew myself and I could feel the dread roiled her stomach. I'd seen the same expression on her face before. The other two boys trickled in before she could say more, which gave me time to get my story together. When you're with the FBI the truth is never the first response or consideration.

Ellen fixed the boys grilled cheese sandwiches and a glass of milk while she listened to them chatter about their day. Meanwhile I sneaked another beer, noticing my maneuver had not escaped her fleeting look. While she changed into jeans and a sweatshirt, the boys settled in front of the television set. When my wife joined me in the kitchen her stare was unwavering.

"Well," she queried. There was the smile again, even when she was angry, she made me grin. Actually she was proud of me, she told me many times we may not be together forever, but I'd always be her most memorable character. Whatever that meant, it was good enough and endearing to me.

We had just seen the movie *Poltergeist*. I said, "They're back!"

"Shit!" she said, loudly. "It's what I expected. What? So we've had almost three years of a peaceful financial train wreck?"

We had been derailed. By family and peer opinions, we are successful. We both have Master degrees in Business and Psychology. We both passed the CPA examination. People used to look at us as a power couple. We are bright, educated and good looking. What happened? They didn't know the half of it!

"Are power and money ever enough?" Ellen asks. "What now, John? I'm tired of this crap. Whatever happened to my dream of being the first woman appointed to the Supreme Court? Everything in our life seems so bizarre. I'm terrified life is quietly becoming intimidating and menacing. Sometimes I really think I want out. Is that even possible, John?"

"I'm to report to 935 Pennsylvania Avenue on Monday, 0800 hours," I say.

"Wonderful! Is it going to be D.C?"

She is listening in speechless astonishment, in a dull, almost vacant state of horror and disbelief when I tell her I don't know anything yet. I know she loves Washington, so I give her a maybe.

"You poor thing," I say, with a smile. "What would you do without me?"

Ellen opens a cupboard and pulls out a half bottle of Jack Daniels and a cheap bottle of gin, "Well, let's do this right, Johnny. Let's get shitfaced!" Once again she is mollified for the moment. Tomorrow will be a different story.

The most exhausting thing in life is to be insincere. **Anne Morrow Lindbergh**

What Is Past Is Prologue

Gettysburg Battlefield
Gettysburg, Pennsylvania
Monday, August 17, 1959

I'd heard about the Battle of Gettysburg, in my 8th grade American History class. Mr. Terry, our teacher, liked me because I was his best athlete and he was the coach of our 8th grade football and basketball teams. Dad and he had fought in the Korean War, and he asked me to bring in Dad's slides when I told him about the pictures I'd seen over and over again.

He assigned a paper due on one of the battles of the Civil War. I chose the Battle of Fredericksburg, which surprised him. When he asked me why Fredericksburg? I simply said, "The South won the battle!"

"The South," he said. "Why?"

"I grew up in Alabama and Oklahoma." I said, looking for him to be surprised. "Aah, like maybe Camp Rucker and Fort Sill, eh? I get it, okay research what happened at Fredericksburg. It was a significant battle." He patted me on the back and walked away.

I was relaying this story to Ellen as we sat down on the Minnesota monument. "I see," she said. "Are you still a rebel, Johnny? You seem so serious about the Civil War." She queries while seemingly studying me.

During the weekend Ellen and I were inseparable. Saturday night we went to Hershey Park, where I had my first roller coaster and ferris wheel ride. Actually, I didn't like the ferris wheel. It was like sitting on a cliff. But, I bucked up to show that I was afraid of nothing by rocking the bucket slightly.

We accompanied Ricky and my sister, Chrissy, to other rides

while holding hands. The tunnel of love was the grand finale. I coerced her into giving me a kiss on the cheek, with my brother and sister looking on.

On Sunday we went to church in the morning and washed her dog, Boots, afterwards. In the afternoon, my whole family and Ellen went to the Hershey Factory. At the end of the tour we came out of the building with Hershey Kisses shooting at us from every direction.

After supper, I asked Mom if Ellen could come with us to Gettysburg. She got Ellen's mother's approval and here we fell in love; at the spot marked where Lincoln gave his Gettysburg address. Here we made promises to each other to write once a week and made plans for me to fly out next summer for a visit. We exchanged friendship rings we had purchased at the park. It was something to hang on to, even if it was puppy love.

My sun sets to rise again. **Robert Browning**

Chapter Three

30th Street Station
Philadelphia, Pennsylvania
Monday, September 12, 1983

I walked into the Amtrak train holding nothing but my ticket. I was wearing an out-of-date suit, shirt and tie. I looked like anything but a fastidious Hoover man. Since entering the Lutheran Theological Seminary at Gettysburg, in the fall of 1980, there certainly had been no funds available for new clothes. In fact, it took two months to finally get my government paychecks squared away.

I had them sent to PO Box 13, in Biglersville, Pennsylvania, a small hamlet seven miles down the road from Gettysburg. Then, the CPE training during the summer of 1981, at Allentown State Hospital, was even more problematic.

When we transferred from Gettysburg to Philadelphia, in August of 1981, my wife got a higher paying job. The financial noose really tightened again, because it took a month to get my paychecks coming to PO Box 39, Glenside, Pennsylvania. Glenside was only a three mile jaunt from the seminary. Ellen's job was with a CPA firm in nearby Jenkintown. We seemed set, once the checks started coming. So I really didn't care about the status of my attire, because I was not trying to impress. I wanted out, not a new government assignment.

As the train grinded and groaned to a smooth roll I peered around the car noticing most passengers were dozing or sleeping. This train had originated in New York City, with stops only in Philadelphia and Baltimore. Its destination was Union Station, Washington, D.C. The name of the train was the Metroliner. The fare cost more but it was the fast track from Philly to D.C., a one-hour-twenty-minute ride. I was tired, but I didn't feel like sleeping. I was on overload, wondering what was in store for me.

While passing through Wilmington, Delaware my mind drifted to all the stories my folks told me about their time here. In fact, I was born here on June 13,1944, at Wilmington General Hospital. Now it was thirty-seven years later and circumstances were as uncertain now for me as they must have been for my parents in the middle of World War II. At least they knew who they were back then and, if they survived the war, they knew where they were going. I'm musing when a conductor shouts, "Baltimore is next. Baltimore is the next station stop."

My mind drifts momentarily, thinking about the conductor. I wondered how he likes his job, telling passengers what's the next station stop all day long. If one has ever ridden the train on the Northeast Corridor, it doesn't take much effort to know the stations stops. Oh, well, not important. Who am I? Who'd want to be me and have my career?

I'm thinking no more than a handful of people in the world know who I really am in real life. Not even my own family knows who I really am. I become remorseful about lying every day, and that I'm still living a lie. Why? For me, it wasn't for a high moral purpose anymore, if it ever was: to help the United States Government. In my previous undercover work, everything, including my life, had been riding on the lie. Collect and gather the information and testify. In court, it should be a problem, too, because I'm a professional liar. But it isn't, it's fixed.

Who's going to believe me? When the case is made, everything would be riding on the truth. What a joke! In fact, everything I document is from memory and sometimes it is a drunken memory. For me, there would always be testifying to do. Without credibility I have nothing; a certifiable conundrum? Huh? They fix it.

"Union Station is next. Union Station, Washington DC is next." The conductor bellows. There the man goes again with his useless information.

So there will be no record of me or my accomplishments. I

can forget my Masters of Divinity degree, earned honestly, first at the Lutheran Seminary in Gettysburg, second at the Lutheran Seminary in Philadelphia. Not really honestly, because they did not know I was an undercover agent hiding out in their angel factory. Once again, I would be coming from some trumped up job, verified by phony telephone numbers answered by Bureau personnel. There would be no recorded payments of Social Security Wages, no filed income tax returns and no credit history. I felt angry as the train came to a stop.

I checked my watch. It is 7:15 a.m. We had arrived slightly early, so I'm in no hurry to push myself through the train car. Should I walk or take a cab to the J. Edgar Hoover Building, I'm contemplating this when I feel a hand on my shoulder.

"I have a car waiting for you out front," a voice says, firmly. I recognize the voice, he is the same guy or agent I met Wednesday, at the seminary.

"Traveling light," he laughs with a smirk.

"Fuck you," I mouth back.

"No longer the religious type, John?"

"Asshole," I whisper, loud enough for him to hear. "Did you spend the last five days in Philly to make sure I show up today?"

A seemingly long silence passes, after my last remark as we make our way through the car to the exit door. Once on the dock, I give him a withering look of contempt.

"What's with the super-secret clandestine techniques?" I ask moving toward the terminal. I didn't like it because I was beginning to feel like a criminal with an appendage. Disgust seeped into my voice. "Who are you, really? It's never worked this way before, following me from the rear with covert surveillance. I think your tactics are strictly junior-varsity."

Once outside a Plymouth K-car pulls up where we are standing. My shield opens the back door on the passenger side, and I pile into the seat. He goes around the car jumps in beside me. The driver, whom I'm sure is another agent, glances in my direction, looks in the rearview mirror and pulls into traffic. Nary a word is spoken as we travel around the Capitol Building and turns onto

Pennsylvania Avenue. There it stands, a place I had spent little time, the *Puzzle Palace*. The J. Edgar Hoover F.B.I. Building, for which President Richard Nixon signed the entitlement two days after Director Hoover's death. On September 30, 1975, President Gerald Ford dedicated the building. I was here that day, along with many other agents I would never hear from or see again.

The building has an open mezzanine and courtyard, but access to the courtyard is limited, and most of the first floor is closed to facilitate security. Recessed panels along the ground floor are spaced to give the illusion of two-story columns, thus producing an arcade-like façade. Also for security reasons, no stores were included on the first floor. The main part of the building faces E Street, retaining the idea of a central core of files. Here's where we got out and walked into the entrance. The Special Agent, who had been dogging me, stopped at a receptionist desk. He said: "Special Agent in Charge (SAC) Bennett's 0800 appointment is present." He immediately departed, having delivered the goods. Me!

They kept me waiting in an outer office for half an hour. The ash-blond receptionist kept glancing over at me furtively, like she was trying to catch a glimpse of a grisly car accident while trying to keep her eyes on the road. When I was finally ushered into Bennett's office, I was surprised. The SAC was a tall, dark-haired, good-looking guy, a veritable chick magnet. This wasn't your typical G-man. Or was it, now? I didn't know.

"Someone needs to take you clothes shopping, "was the SAC's first remark, snickering. "Do you smoke," he asked. Of course, a guy like this would never ask a question he didn't already know the answer to, I was thinking when I responded honestly. "Yes, I do smoke – Kool 100's – lung busters, three packs a day."

"Smoking is out on this assignment. It's a filthy, disgusting habit and it indicates a lack of self-control, just as getting drunk is a sign of weakness." He follows.

"On the other hand, "I retaliate, "Standing around smoking cigarettes is an excellent way to cross-pollinate, connect with people in different places, and obtain useful intelligence."

"Are you not an athlete, John? I can tell it's in the way you walk. It's the way you carry your body. I like it. But you're not synchronizing." I don't like this and his bullshit, I'm thinking. I smile.

"Was," I argue. "I'm not an athlete anymore." I laugh. "Synchronize?"

"John, we're sending you on a very important mission. These are high class people, a special group close to the President of the United States. You have to synchronize. Mirror! If they lean forward, you do the same. If they lean back, you lean back. If they cross their legs, you cross your legs. Watch the tilt of my head, and mimic me. Even synchronize your breathing with mine. Just be subtle. Don't be blatant about it. This is how you will connect with people on a subconscious level; make them feel comfortable with you. People like people who like themselves. Are we clear?"

"Special Agent in Charge Bennett, may I ask where you are sending me; into what lion's den?" I was thinking about my family now, and myself. I didn't want to be away from my wife and children for long lengths of time. Of course, I couldn't tell Bennett my thoughts. He would have called me a pussy, the way things seemed to be going.

Bennett stood up from his desk, turned and looked out onto Pennsylvania Avenue at the Capitol Building, I presume, and spoke matter-of-factly; "John, you are moving into a life of luxury.

"The people in whom we are interested spend money like drunken sailors. Of course, the money they spend is stolen and gained by fraud. They are the masters of white-color-crime. We are working with the States of Maryland and Virginia on this investigation. Neither state knows what the hell they are doing, so we have to step in to make them heroes and wipe the egg off their faces."

I fidget, while Bennett continues. "When you leave here a car will take you to our Baltimore field office. You will meet the Special Agent in Charge and others. You will set up your time tables. You will go through days of tutoring and indoctrination by types. Your head will be stuffed with all kinds of useless information important to make you believable. You will never be late again," he scolded. "You will not have a problem with punctuality. An electronic paper trail will be created. You know how it works, John." He smirks.

This was more than I expected. He was treating me like I didn't have a family or life at all. "John," Bennett interrupts. "You're a quick study. Just always know the depths of your own incompetence. Remember what we've taught you. Your job is to collect information; raw data based on requirements. Activities such as interviews, technical and physical surveillances, human source operations, searches and liaison relationships result in the collection of intelligence. The FBI is recognized for its excellence in collecting information."

What Bennett left out was the how? Anytime you're working undercover, who you bring into the operation is a crucial choice. It has to be somebody you can trust with the job and your life. I had to establish a new identity that would stand up under whatever kind of examination that could arise. Everybody is suspicious of everybody else until you prove yourself. Suddenly, I felt a surge of energy, just thinking about the action! It's what I'd missed most.

Courage is resistance to fear, mastery of fear, not absence of fear.
Mark Twain

What Is Past Is Prologue

Simon Olson School Bus
Baseball Trip
Montevideo to Willmar, Minnesota
Thursday, May 14, 1959

I'm staring out the bus window thinking about Buddy Holly, Ritchie Valens and the Big Bopper being killed just one week after they'd performed in Montevideo. Their plane had crashed soon after take-off just north of Clear Lake, Iowa. The pilot and three singers were killed upon impact with the ground.

Everybody had heard about it on the morning of February 3, 1959. Rumors had been floating about the big party at Diane B's house afterward. She had even told me, in Latin class, Buddy, Ritchie, Big Bopper and Dion had autographed her bedroom wall. "If you don't believe me, John, come over and take a look."

I'm having a difficult time dealing with their deaths. I had seen them in their glory and a week later they are gone forever. After so much early success, the world has simply gone on without them. I can't imagine the world going on without me. Especially when I think that I'm going to be 15 years old in a month, getting a driver's license, and I'm already the starting third-baseman on the varsity baseball team. My dreams are coming true, as well. Yes, I'm the starting third baseman for the Montevideo Mohawks varsity baseball team and I'm only a freshman. It's good beginnings.

My reverie has made the bus trip to Willmar very short. There is nothing but blue sky, miles and miles of it, disturbed by cotton ball clouds that drift across a horizon as flat as a tabletop tiled by plowed fields. A John Deere tractor groans in the distance while it pulls a disk smoothing out the dirt getting ready for planting.

The bus has stopped near the backstop and everyone is piling out. As each of us push toward the front I'm getting slaps on the back, "Come on Johnny, this is the big game. We regulars got to be sharp to beat these guys. Let's hear some chatter at third." Ronny Anderson, our senior first baseman, encourages.

Our time on this planet is too short, I'm thinking as I find my bat. The last thing I say in my prayers each night is for the Lord to help me be a professional baseball player. It seems I'm getting a good start, having cracked the starting lineup as a freshman. Coach Hoffman posts the batting order on a hook in the dugout. I look. It says I'm batting 2nd. I smile for the first time since I stepped on the bus for Willmar.

One year ago, Coach Hoffman had me dress for the varsity game against Willmar, I was only an 8th grader and it was a sad day for me. My grandfather Austin had died, but I still wanted to dress for the game. Grandpa would have wanted me to do it.

I wondered how I would do today. Dad told me to know what the future might bring a fellow he has to understand what has happened in the past. Last year I got one at bat, and I struck out. Today, I smacked Willmar's pitcher's first fastball over the leftfield fence.

"That a fire!" Coach Hoffman kept yelling as I turned the corner at third base. Yes, I like good beginnings.

Success is never final, failure is never fatal, its courage that counts.
Winston Churchill

Chapter Four

The Inner Harbor
Baltimore, Maryland
Monday, September 12, 1983

Baltimore had certainly changed in eleven years. What was once an ugly harbor town full of dirty warehouses, dilapidated tankers, and strip joints had become a lovely boardwalk of restaurants and chic Shoppe's. The water slapping up against the piers was now fit for humans to engage in water sports. The ship *Constitution* stood stately in the distance, as if it were protecting the many walkers peregrinating their ways in the new harbor.

A huge glass edifice rose toward the sky beyond the *Constitution*, I would find out later it was Baltimore's new aquarium. Here swam, in addition to every fish and reptile thinkable, a Great White shark and several whales. I was impressed with what I saw and thought about what a great place to vacation, at least for a long weekend with my family. Reality then hit me. I was here for a particular raison d'être. It was an underpinning completely unacceptable for a family man.

The temperature scrolled across a neon sign across the way. In that direction was a large sign displaying Domino Sugar. The nearer neon sign read sixty-two degrees. During the intervening time, I purchased two hotdogs and sat down on a concrete wall to enjoy a sunny, delightful September day. For now, my mind wandered and reminisced.

On June 2, 1970, Ellen and I were married in Juarez, Mexico at the United States Consulate office. Why Juarez, Mexico. Simple, it took three years to get a divorce in New York versus one day in Mexico. Jim, Ellen's first husband, Ellen and I drove to Juarez via

Minneapolis to Santa Fe, New Mexico. There were two beds in
the hotel room and we argued about who was going to sleep with
who. Since they were still married they slept together and I took
the other bed. The next day we drove to El Paso and played the
same game. Jim was two for two. On the third day, we crossed the
Rio Grande where I paid for Ellen and Jim's divorce. Afterwards,
I drove Jim to the airport.

It was a hard moment for both of us. Ellen still loved Jim and
I did too. We had done everything together the past three months.
However, we stayed the course and got married that afternoon,
anxious to start our new life together. Of course, there was much
more to the story. *Now for the rest of the story*, as Paul Harvey sets
the intrigue, *well, it will come later.*

Three months later, I resigned my job with Larsen, Allen and
Weishair (Certified Public Accountants), a Minneapolis CPA
firm. I accepted what I thought would be a big step forward with
Nicolette National Bank. Here, I was assigned to the accounting
and auditing department. I was happy to be back in banking, but
I hated leaving the friends I had with the CPA firm. Additionally,
I didn't like spending so much time footing and ticking work pa-
pers, knowing intuitively a step up here may be a year or two away.
And, I'm not a patient guy, accepting wisdom that I'm smarter
than anyone else.

It didn't take me long to figure I'd made a terrible mistake.
When I gave my two weeks-notice at LAWCO (Larsen, Allen
and Weishair), Marquette National Bank acquired a travel agency.
When I reported to work on Monday, September 14, 1970 an
entire different agenda was waiting for me.

"John, welcome aboard!" greeted, Dave Maxwell, my supervisor. "Since we hired you," he dragged out the u, "we acquired Sathe
Travel Agency. And, they are losing money," he finished, dragging
out the *y*. "John, we need you to find out why?" He hesitated, waiting for my response.

"Okay," I said. "Where's the agency?"

"Good," says Maxwell. "It's right here in this building. The
books are kept manually by a bookkeeper, who is an elderly gentle-

man. I want you to computerize the accounting system. We have software I think you can use. It was not designed as a general ledger package, but I believe it will work. But, what I really want, John," dragging out n, "I want to see what the hell is going on down there with the agency?"

The bookkeeper was a charming old Irishman named Christopher Kilkenney. He posted the journals, general ledger and reconciled bank accounts. He had white-gray hair, a ruggedly handsome face with a flow of red and a kindly smile. His laugh was raucous.

"Money isn't something you spend. It should be like Green Stamps, something you never use." Chris preached. I would shrug in tacit acknowledgement, but I didn't pay much attention to what he was saying. Touché, when I asked certain questions, he seemed to have selective hearing. "Aah, boy!" he'd go on about.

Working with Chris for a month, I sensed he was becoming somewhat nervous showing me the ropes. At first, I thought it was because he didn't want me to take his job, but there was more to it, as I would find out soon enough. It became obvious to me that escrow funds were paying unauthorized expenses for the Chief Executive officer. I told my favorite mentor, Chris Kilkenney, to resign before I exposed this information. He seemed relieved, saying blithely, "Take care, son! Don't let problems linger. Don't trust anybody. I wouldn't want a young fellow like you getting in trouble."

My up-stairs office was in a cubicle, in the middle of a cube farm. It was called the open-plan system. I checked into my cube first thing in the morning and then traveled via elevator downstairs to the travel agency. In fact, I successfully dissociated myself from the accounting and auditing department to which I was attached. I'd see them at coffee break and chat some about how the agency was doing. Monthly, I'd give them a convincing report showing progress being achieved under my financial tutelage. For all the reports I was generating I was being considered a brainpan, rather than the maniac I was becoming. Actually nobody was really paying any attention to what I was doing. The higher-ups in the bank were only concerned about their personal travel plans, which was comped. They were kissing the ass of Mr. K, the CEO, who was ripping them off. I found it all so fascinating and chose to sit and watch how it all played out.

I kept telling myself I knew how to be the star of the team, a big man on campus, a good-looking guy all the girls wanted to go out with. I told myself that anyway, and I guess I believed it. I decided to play the roll and it was working well with the sexy-looking gals, in their mini-skirts at the agency. Applying some learned principles in Psychology, I knew to be any good I'd have to be willing to corner a person and close the easy exits of escape when it hurts. Life's problems are supposed to hurt. Having experienced a divorce from my high school sweetheart, I couldn't imagine anything more painful. So, I had all the girls at the travel agency eating out of the palms of my hands, giving them hope I might ask them out for a drink. In those days, I was beyond charming. I could sell anything to anybody, especially myself. I was a really a fine bull-shit artist. And, I wanted to see how far I could push this thing without putting myself in jeopardy. It was a game; a game I was enjoying, to see how it might end. I had gathered everything on all the big shots. Thieves!

With my adrenaline-fueled anxiety, I kept moving forward with my plan to see how far I could take this thing. It was an act of stupidity, but, why not? Maybe I can write a book about it someday? The whole thing was too easy; there were no internal controls. I had access to the bank's computers and I had the authority to move money from the travel agency accounts. Everything in the travel business is based on escrow and trust. I kept the agency's books, controlled the bank accounts, and submitted all transactions to the bank's computer; what I deemed necessary to track. I knew the new account gals and they thought it was a privilege to set up a new account for me.

Phony financial statements were easier, giving the big shots what they wanted to see. I surmised nobody looked at them anyway. During coffee breaks, I'd ask certain questions trying to find out if any had perused the documents. It was a joke, especially the higher-ups, who were supposed to be monitoring me.

Months passed by quickly. I was having fun moving money around into different accounts and back again. Why I was maneuvering the money, I'd ask myself all the time. The only answer was I could. Then, one morning I was asked to report to Dave Maxwell's office. En route I was a little bit nervous, but I knew all the money was there. Dave greeted me, "Good morning," then motioned me to sit down in one of the chairs in front of his desk.

"John," he said. "We want you to start training Harris Mix to take over the accounting in the agency. We have another project for you." This floored me because I hadn't prepared for such a sudden move. I had money in ghost accounts. They were in the name of the agency. However, only I had access. I had a slight problem! "We're moving you up-stairs," I was told. "Good job!"

My nuts were numb when I received the news of my so-called promotion. I didn't know how to play this hand. I realized this time my audacity could cost me dearly if I couldn't get a few things squared away. Seemingly, my overconfidence and effrontery was like a weakness for alcohol and broads. Dad always told me there were no shortcuts in life. For instance, if I'd spend as much time studying, rather than trying to figure out how to cheat I'd be way ahead of the game. "But, it wouldn't be as much fun," was always my silent response.

I figured I needed two weeks to get everything back in place, knowing my actions were more serious than robbing the office supply cabinet. I decided just to play it straight. Boot camp for boot lickers was what I was thinking. No more fucking off, getting in at nine or ten and sneaking off directly to the travel agency. No more drinking lunches, and, of course, I'd have to cover up. Covering up, of course, was the easy part as dumb as Harris Mix appeared to be. He would simply do what he was told. In fact he was my back up system. If anything was found out, it would be some kind of a foul up Harris Mix bungled.

The Baltimore field office is adjacent to Route I-695, the highway that encircles Baltimore. I thought it strange because traditionally FBI offices are located in or near Federal Courthouses so that agents will be close to prosecutors and the courtrooms where we testify. Baltimore has a poor transit system. So, I guess it made more sense for the field office to be located near a major highway, so agents could easily drive to interviews.

I was rationalizing and kind of scared. I couldn't quite figure what was going on. I was relieved when we arrived at the cream-colored brick building, located in an industrial park, approximately ten minutes early. An attractive redhead greeted me and showed me into a rather bland conference room, where I was greeted by a man obviously expecting me.

He wore his hair short, perhaps to de-emphasize balding, I'm thinking. He studied me, and then opened a file, while I studied him. He motioned for me to sit down next to him at the end of a short conference table. Slowly, his eyes lifted from the file and he looked at me directly, saying, "Here's the deal!"

I shrugged in implicit acknowledgement, perhaps trying to push his buttons by seeming indifferent. Of course, I was wondering if this guy would be trying to yank my chain. I peered around the room and at his person, looking for any live surveillance devices. I had been taught well, nothing is what it seems. Who do I trust? Only myself. Remember, everything is a test. I am no better friend, I am no worse enemy!

"Cleon Tomko," he said, extending his hand and giving me one of those unnecessarily bone crushing handshakes, grabbing my knuckles in such a way that I couldn't shake back. His handshake was a crusher and it pissed me off badly.

"We have a serious situation in Maryland and Virginia. We've been watching this guy for years, but we can never get anything substantive on him. Just maybe he's fucked up this time. We already have agents on the inside. He needs a new Controller, because the old one, for some reason, up and quit. You will be called by an agent setting up an interview for you. This call will come tomorrow. You will arrange an interview, immediately, and accept the job they offer you. Understand?"

My first assignment with the Bureau had placed me in Northern Virginia. Where the Beltway crosses the Potomac River, a traveler enters Maryland. I knew this area well. I was wondering how they were going to get me in the mix this time? I always worried about the façade. Then, I adopted a calm, voice of authority, brisk but cordial while asking, "When?" I felt a prickle of defensiveness, maybe just a gut instinct. "Where and why?"

Cleon Tomko took a slurp of cold coffee and said with a desperate tone, "This man is stealing people's money across state lines. He's getting insurance licenses and bonding powers predicated on false financial statements. He's collecting high priced premiums from contractors who shouldn't be getting bonded in the first place. He's taking premium dollars to live lavishly, knowing claims are sure certain to come and the reserves will be gone. Your job, again, will be to prove what we already know."

"Un-varnish the numbers," I say.

"Yes," he said. "And, time is of the essence."

I gave him a cocky smile, "Who said you can't put toothpaste back in the tube?"

Cleon Tomko looked very uncomfortable. "I suppose you're right, John. What's been done can't be undone. But let's stop the bleeding!" There was a pregnant pause.

"John from what I've read and heard about you, you were born to do this job!" There was another pregnant pause.

"So," I responded slowly, "The torch has been passed."

"Yes sir," Tomko replied at a snail's pace. "It has been passed, John. It is being passed to you and good luck." He said, guardedly.

"I gather I'm not going back to Philadelphia tonight. So, when's my interview?"

"Tomorrow," says Tomko. "1700 K Street, sixth floor."

"They occupy the entire sixth floor!" I reply.

"The whole sixth floor," he added. "The number 6 is his favorite number. There you will meet with Richard Corrigan, Senior Vice President in charge of Underwriting."

"Is he one of us?" I query.

"No, he's been with Paul Gordon Charles for many years. He's a yes man! You'll know soon enough, I think, who's on the team. You figure it out. As you know it's the only way undercover works!"

"Yeah," I say. "It's the old cloak and dagger routine."

"Thank God, for your sake, for our ways!" he fires back, with disdain.

"So, where am I staying tonight?" I ask.

"The Hilton, under Jack Oleson,"he says. Then, he hands me an envelope, which appears to be filled with cash. "John," he says diminutively, "buy a nice suit, long sleeved white shirt, conservative tie and black shoes. This guy is like our former director, J. Edgar. You must dress for success."

Then he looks at my hands, uttering, "get yourself a manicure too." He added, while fidgeting with my file. "I'll meet you for dinner at 8 sharp tomorrow night, at the Hilton's Sky Top."

As I was taxied around and through Baltimore to the Hilton Hotel I was thinking how only a week ago I was involved in a new semester and all was quiet and peaceful in our home. I was now in about the last place I wanted to be, buying choice clothes to present myself for an interview already set in stone. Tomorrow night I'd have dinner with the balding one to tell him how wonderful the interview had gone and, yes, I got the job. What a big surprise? Then, if I'm lucky, I will get to take leave from this strutting asshole, SAC (special agent in charge) Tomko, to go home to spend the rest of the weekend with my family.

For three years I'd retreated into a life of sloth, and, now I'd be back on top. I wondered where I liked it best. Perhaps, where it is more superlative? That was the anomaly! There seemed to be no place in-between for me.

Accept things as they are not as you wish them to be. **Napoleon Bonaparte**

What Is Past Is Prologue

Saloon Restaurant
Philadelphia, Pennsylvania
Thursday, April 24, 1986

I was having dinner with a friend at an upscale eating and drinking establishment in Center City Philadelphia. It's been exactly a year since my wife, Ellen, passed away. I was painfully feeling her loss as I waited for the check. My friend and I were heading to the Spectrum to see a Neil Diamond concert. My late wife loved Neil Diamond and told me once the only damn thing she had left to do in her life was to see him perform. My friend must have sensed my psyche drifting, when she queried, "Are you okay?"

"Yeah, it's a sad day for me." I say. She pats my shoulder, saying, "She'll be right there with us tonight." I took the check and paid it with cash. We mosey out to the street where a limousine is waiting for us. En route my friend says, "You ought to write a book. You know, dealing with the hand you've been dealt. Just tell your story. All you need is to tell the truth."

I smile thinking what Susan doesn't know was I wouldn't know the truth if it came up and slapped me across the face. She knew nothing about me. I'm a well trained professional liar, a spin doctor. Oh, I've enough life experiences to pen a dime novel or a mystery thriller. Some would like to read about my so called attempt at playing *Mister Mom*; what a great comedy or tragedy it would gyrate. I could tell stories about the nefarious ways of how real business is done in this country. I could tell stories about the iniquitous ways of the Federal Bureau of Investigation. However, my pledge has been to listen, watch, and keep my mouth shut, in that order. No, the timing is all wrong and my children are too young, which is always a good excuse not to do something or make a diversionary maneuver.

I had put some feelers out and received tickets for Neil Diamond's concert. The seats were front row, directly in front of the stage. Some of my connections owe me some favors, but who knows how long these perks will continue. But, I play the cards as long as I can. Anyway we could've reached out and touched the great artist we were so close. Susan was extraordinarily impressed as she loved Diamond's music, too. As the concert played on, my cerebrum drifted with the music. I wondered why I found the truth is always negotiable. Why did I wander to places where there is absolutely no peace of mind? Tears came to my eyes when Diamond played: *"Love on the rocks ... ain't no surprise ... pour me a drink ... and, I'll tell you some lies ..."*

"Are you okay, John?" Susan asks.

"I'm good," I say, with a smile.

She grabs my hand and holds it. It was a caring, kindly gambit. While the concert played on I thought about what she had said to me. "Just tell stories." I thought, I have always liked telling stories and have lots of stories to tell.

As I continue my thinking I recognize several major obstacles. Those being the hazards of memory, inevitably influenced by selectivity and hindsight, and the habit of modesty because of the use of the first-person pronoun with which I have always been comfortable. Perhaps because I remember the wisdom of that quintessential American philosopher, baseball great Jerome "Dizzy" Dean: "If you done it, it ain't braggin'."

When the concert ended we stood and gave Neil Diamond a grand ovation. When he was coaxed back to sing, *"Only in America ... Land of Opportunity,"* I thought, yes, maybe. But, there were the obligations of loyalty, which for me outweigh all pressures to cast prudence, privacy, discretion, and the secrets of others aside; and finally, the limits, both of time and space, requires me to avoid redundancy and the temptation to meander into every detour and byway.

Susan nudges me and shouts, not too vociferously, "What a

great concert! Thanks so much for taking me. I think I love you, John."

Back in the limousine I'm thinking, while Susan makes us a drink, that paranoia has a normal state of mind. We are all guilty of something. Perhaps, I would paint life as I would like it to be if I'd write a book. Some questions are best never answered. Life is a gift. So, make each day count. Is there anything better in the world?

I'm in deep contemplation when Susan hands me a drink. "Are you okay," she asks again. I smile and whisper, "I think I love you, too." She kisses me.

Doubt is not a pleasant state, but certainty is a ridiculous one.
Voltaire

Chapter Five

1700 K Street
Washington D.C.
Tuesday, September 13, 1983

The offices of Atlantic States Surety occupied the entire sixth floor of an office tower with a curved façade of glass and stainless steel of slate spandrels. They are located at 1700 K Street, in Washington D.C. K Street, as everyone knows, is the Champs Elysees of Washington lobbyists. When I approach the elevators two other well-dressed gentlemen enter before me. One of them presses six, for the sixth floor, and we ride sixty seconds in silence. When the elevator doors open, I follow them to the left and watch them disappear between two huge glass doors. Atlantic States Surety Company is handsomely lettered in navy blue coloring, across the frontispiece.

Just before the double doors, I see a sign for restrooms. I stroll casually into the men's room, simply to tuck in my shirt and tighten my tie. Suddenly, a distinguished looking man with gray hair, slicked back on both sides, comes out of a stall and saunters up to the wash sink next to me. While we wash our respective hands I catch him staring at me. I return his gawk.

"Jack," he queries, with a smile. "Jack Oleson? How do you spell Oleson?"

"Mr. Corrigan," I answered, smiling back. "It's spell it O – L – E – S – O – N."

"Richard Corrigan," he introduces himself boldly. "You're here for the controllership position, right?"

"Yes sir," I reply. "My interview is set up with you."

Corrigan laughs a hearty hoot. "Great place to get acquainted," he says. "Right here in the crapper, eh?"

We departed the bathroom and walk between the double doors into the sanctuary of Atlantic States Surety. He introduces me to Mary Robinson, the receptionist, telling her to get me whatever I want to drink and seat me. "Give me ten minutes, Jack," he says, as he moves along.

Mary is very classy, a very pretty light-skinned black woman. I guess her in her mid-forties. She has a beautiful smile and a voluptuous, curvy body. "So, you're here for a job interview, Mr. Oleson," looking at her diary.

"Yes," I reply. "I'm applying for the controller position." The lies were already rolling out of my mouth. *Applying for a job? Right! I'm thinking.*

"Umm," she mutters with a smile. "I see." There was a long pause while I imagined wheels spinning her head. "Just be careful, Mr. Oleson. Stuff is crazy around here, lately. Things are not always what they seem. The last controller just up and quit. Did you know that, Mr. Oleson?" She says, looking at me very seriously.

Here it comes, I'm thinking. She is to interrogate me and give Corrigan a full report on my responses. I go into my defense mode and give her very little back as she questions me. Finally Corrigan buzzes, asking Mary to escort me back to his office.

"Mr. Oleson," she says, rapping on Corrigan's door. "Take care!"

"Thanks," I say, with a chuckle, offering a kindly smile. She waits with me until Corrigan opens his door. When the door opens, Mary says again, "Take care, Mr. Oleson." I thank her.

"Come in, Jack," Corrigan greets me enthusiastically, pushing his door closed. I am surprised to see another suit sitting in a chair next to where I suppose I'll be sitting. When we walk toward Corrigan's desk the other fellow stands up and introduces himself, "Jerome Bitterman."

"Jack, Bitterman has been our controller since the company's inception. He's moving on, but has agreed to spend a week or so with us to help with the transition of finding a suitable replacement. So, he'll be asking you some questions. Okay?"

I hand Corrigan and Bitterman a copy of my resume. It is

impressive, in fact, I'd just read it at the hotel this morning while drinking a cup of coffee. Corrigan just sits his copy on his desk, without even looking at it, and asks, "How old are you, Jack?"

"Thirty-nine," I quickly respond.

"Perfect!" Corrigan exclaims. There was too much vigor in Corrigan. His personality was trained, he took a used-car salesman approach to life. Meanwhile, I noticed Bitterman pouring over my resume. It made sense, as I was certain he wanted to see by whom he was being replaced.

"University of Montana," Bitterman queries with interest. "What in the world are you doing on the East Coast? Shouldn't you be rustling cattle?" he asks with, a gleam in his eye.

"Big Sky," I answer back proudly, like a real Texan would react to his state. "Missoula, Montana is a wonderful place. It's the hub of five mountain valleys, you know," I say, being factious. "Sometimes you wake up in the morning and there are snow caps on the mountain tops, but it is fifty degrees down below."

My country-boy façade is working, though, Bitterman is looking at me like something was seriously wrong. For him things weren't quite adding up. "How did you get out here," he asks?

"I married a woman from Hershey, Pennsylvania."

"How in the hell did you meet her, in Montana." Bitterman wonders out loud.

"I didn't," I said, liking that I had him going. He was desperately fishing for information. If you're dead wrong, avoid or confuse them! It is axiom number one.

"It's kind of a long story. Is it important? The story, I mean, Mr. Bitterman?" I ask respectfully and deviously.

"Hell no," Corrigan blurts out, "Let's cut to the chase here. Jack, you've been recommended very highly by one of our officers. Ned Larson is a Vice President with Atlantic States Surety and a Commander in the Navy with an outstanding military record. Jack, he says you are one crackerjack accountant. And, that's good enough for me. Plus, I like the way you handled yourself in the outhouse."

Jerome Bitterman looked perplexed, confused and pissed off. I could tell he didn't want to be so easily replaced, especially by some cowboy hailing from Montana. "Jack, what do you know about insurance accounting?" He asks me, smugly.

Before I could answer, Corrigan interrupts, "What he doesn't know he'll figure out. Jerry, Jack is an experienced accountant."

I realized, right there and then, the interview process is over. Funny though, I thought, as we walk down the narrow halls of Atlantic Surety, he never asked me if I would accept the position. And we never discussed salary or a compensation package. Every deal was done differently, but this one had me bewildered. What had my colleague and friend, Commander Ned Larson, done to wield this much power? Why was it all so confounding this time? I was full of conjecture as I followed Corrigan and Bitterman into a private office.

"This is the claims department," said Corrigan. "Joe Neverson, meet Jack Oleson. Joe is our claims attorney, Corrigan continued. "Jack will be our new controller." There he goes again, I'm thinking, saying I'm already on board.

"Come on Joe, we're going to the St. Regis, shouted Corrigan raucously. "Maggie, come join us." Maggie was Joe Neverson's secretary, who referred to them as the *A-Team*, replete with a placard in front of her desk reading same.

I had been wondering what that *A-Team* sign was about. All I could think of was about *Mister T* on the television series, *A-Team*. Okay, it made sense. "You guys that good, huh?" I ask.

"Jack, meet Maggie Little, Joe's secretary. And, a good one, I might add." Corrigan, says cheerfully, but in a hurry now.

"I'm an administrative assistant, Mr. Corrigan. Come on, please flatter me." Maggie Little responded with a simper of confidence and a killer smirk. She was strikingly attractive with glassy black hair, milky white skin, and caramel brown eyes. Her lips pulled down at the sides when she smiled. She was a beautiful and elegant woman. I sensed another side to her, though, when she said to Bitterman: "It didn't take long to replace your Jew ass. When did you resign, yesterday?"

She looks at me and winks. "Not bad, Jack!"

"What," I ask?

"Your ass," she says. "Not bad at all."

Joe Neverson is a fastidious dresser and a handsome man. He is kind of short but makes up for it with a stunning grin and an arrogant way of behaving. Actually, he is very charming. He is ready to roll as he gets up from his dark mahogany desk. He tells Maggie, "Let's go!" He lights a cigarette and we are off.

I survived because I was tougher than everyone else. **Bette Davis**

What Is Past Is Prologue

Missoula, Montana
Monday, May 9, 1966

I graduated from Concordia College, Moorhead, Minnesota, on May 1, 1966. I had been hired by First Bank Stock Corporation during my senior year. First Bank Stock is a holding company for ninety some banks and they were hiring new college graduates to participate in a management training program. I was thrilled with their offer and the opportunity to start my career in picturesque Missoula, Montana.

Today is my first day on the job. Woody Johnson, the Operations Officer, spent a good portion of his day introducing me to the officers, tellers, bookkeepers and other support staff. Everyone at Western Montana National Bank seemed friendly. But I could tell most of them wondered whose job I was going to steal. A management training program didn't make a lot of sense. I sensed these people were just a non-pretentious bunch. Most of them probably led a quiet life, came to work, did a good job and went home to their families. It was exactly what I had pictured for myself.

My wife, Beth, and I were married on February 1, 1964. She worked at a bank in Moorhead, Minnesota, while I finished the last two and one half years of college. We lived parsimoniously, but so did everyone else we knew. Playing football paid my tuition and books. To supplement Beth's income at the bank, I had a job with the Athletic Department passing out jocks, socks, and towels to the Physical Education classes. My junior and senior year, I worked three hours a day as a bookkeeper for Carl Dommer's accounting firm in Moorhead.

At the end of fall semester, 1965, we found out Beth was pregnant. The baby was due at the end of August, 1966. We were thrilled and couldn't wait for graduation. And commencement came soon enough. On the day we left for Montana, Beth's father shook my hand saying, with tears in his eyes, "Go west young man, go west."

With college days behind, a good job leading to a strong future, a beautiful wife, a child on the way and an outstanding Rocky Mountain view from our porch, what could be better?

What could be better than Montana? What could be better than Big Sky country?

Still round the corner there may wait a new road or a secret gate.
J.R.R. Tolkien

Chapter Six

The St. Regis Hotel
Washington D.C.
Tuesday, September 13, 1983

The hotel was one square down the street located at 16th and K. As we approached the building, it rose majestically from a vestibule floor, which housed the restaurant. When we entered, it was, as I expected, a very posh restaurant with marble walls and stately standing pillars. Hanging crystal chandeliers were strategically placed over antique Persian rugs and burnished fruitwood tables. The establishment had a hushed elegance, reeking from old money. There was even a prim, middle-aged British hostess.

"Mr. Corrigan," she acknowledges, "Your table is ready!"

"Thank you," Corrigan says, grinning, handing her what I guessed was a fifty-dollar-bill.

We followed a maitre d' to a circular table backed up against a wall giving off a good view of the adjoining *Library Lounge*. It was a place that caught my eye with its old and new books surrounding a long *Chicago-style* bar and tables. I quickly noticed Corrigan being seated by a member of the staff serving our table. Richard was in the catbird-seat, with his back against the wall, having the best view of the lobby. Bitterman sat on Richard Corrigan's right and I on his left. Joe Neverson positioned himself next to me and Maggie Little sat next to Jerome Bitterman.

We had formed a half moon sitting like we were, with all of us in position to view the front entrance. We ordered drinks and made small talk. We ordered another round as small talk continued. I didn't say much while listening to them talk about certain problems, of which the gist seemed to be they would have to be settling on some pending claims in the near future. Actually, I was doing more observing rather than listening to what I didn't know enough about to render an opinion.

What I noticed, mostly, was the way these folks were drinking. Corrigan was drinking double Vodka Gimlets and Neverson, double Scotch on the rocks. Little and Bitterman were sucking down beer, one after the other while I was trying to pace myself with Jack Daniels and charged water. After five or six rounds, an hour or so later, five more people appeared at the table. One I recognized right off as that tall-drink-of-water, Ned Larson. Commander Larson, I thought. The last time I'd seen Ned was when he was helping me move a refrigerator onto a U-Haul truck in Virginia Beach. Four years had since passed. Actually, I'd kind of forgotten about Larson. I glanced at him and the other newcomers while Corrigan introduced me.

I knew Ned was one of us. We'd worked together before, but I was certain nobody else at the table would fit the role, save maybe Margaret Little. I wondered if she was a sleeper, a mole. Again, she was attractive, a pretty face with ample bosoms and a tight ass. However, she had a mouth like a sailor and walked like a truck driver. It was also apparent she was very knowledgeable about the claims matters they had been discussing. Most likely, she was Joe Neverson's right arm. Yeah, she could be one of us. So could Neverson.

One of the new people who'd just joined us, Raymond "Red" Bertrand, was built like a square, with a military-style crew-cut, who barked some orders at Art and Jim, whose last names I didn't catch, only that Art was in charge of collateral and Jim was an underwriter. I would find out what all that was about soon enough. Red politely introduced himself again to me and acknowledged everyone present while Corrigan, who was laughing loudly, again at Bertrand's orders, called for another round of drinks!

These people are crazy wild, I'm thinking, wondering if this was a routine day. There was a sea of glasses at our round table, when I caught the eye of a beautiful, tall, woman, maybe six feet tall. She was dressed perfectly in very expensive-looking clothes donned with lavish-looking jewelry. She smiles at me when she notices me eyeing her. I thought she looked and presented herself as eloquently as the restaurant we were patronizing. I nodded and lifted my glass suggesting a simple toast. She did likewise as I wondered what her part was in this make-believe scenario? Just then, Joe Neverson nudged me.

Everybody seemed to be avoiding the real issue, which I thought was the hiring of a new controller, with booze. Or, I wondered, was my hiring even an issue. Corrigan, who hired me, appeared to not even have read my resume. Bitterman had skimmed through it with some personal interest before Corrigan told us we were going to the St. Regis. They didn't seem to know anything about me or care to know. Ned Larson had recommended me and the bullshit resume followed, creating my new legend. It had created my biography; a student-athlete, a graduate from the University of Montana with degrees in Accounting and Psychology; five years with Price, Waterhouse (a Big Eight accounting firm), nine years as a sole-practitioner in Portsmouth, Virginia with a recently sold practice, looking for a corporate life.

"Jack, it is Jack isn't it?" Neverson slurred when I looked in his direction. "What the hell are you doing here? Where the hell did you come from ....." Corrigan interrupted him. "Joe, that's enough. If you want to read Jack's resume ....." Neverson interrupted Corrigan now, "Where is it? I want to read it!" Then Joe knocked over his drink, spilling it across the table into Red Bertrand's lap.

"God-damn-it Joe, sons-a-bitch, you drunkard!" Bertrand growls, after wringing out the sleeve of his coat.

I say nothing, but it is difficult not to laugh at the shenanigans. I notice Ned Larson and the tall blond, smiling kindly at me. Or, I wonder, is she feeling sorry for me.

Joe Neverson is stone cold drunk, but none of that was enough to overshadow his brilliant blue eyes, chiseled features, and perfectly sculpted albeit short body, even though short, let alone his infectious smile. He was beyond charming and I sensed he could sell ice to an Eskimo. Right now, Joe had his Scotch goggles on, yet wanted to continue as most of us do when we are drunk. The round table was temporarily silent when Joe, looking at me, announced: "Jack, you don't understand this business!"

"Joe, back off!" Richard Corrigan shouted blithely with his hearty laugh. "Jack hasn't even started with us yet." Corrigan scolded, while he motioned to the maitre d' for menus. Red Bertrand, who looked aghast and still pissed about his suit coat being drenched, parroted Corrigan, "Back off, Joe!"

When the menus came, Joe ordered another drink. After taking a long swig he looked directly at me and then around the table saying rather calmly, "If Jack is going to help, we have to give it to him straight. The real stuff," he slurred. "We can't keep pushing the envelope. Bitterman buttered up the numbers to keep our friends in high places from coming down on us. This must change," he roars, while falling out of his chair and puking on the carpet.

A long silence ensued as staff hauled Joe Neverson off to a men's room. I suspected the rest of them had seen Joe in action before. I also sensed able and caring men and women who wanted to make this company work. Their livelihood depended on it. I'd seen this before, capable people being reduced to gofers and errand runners for a trumped up cause. Again, that was it, it was the glitch. Hard-working people trying to make a company work, but the dog-and-pony show would defy it.

It was the old boardroom ritual. The higher ups, who call the shots, who have invested their monies for a high-yield return, plus perks, read the financials the way guys grab the sports section and devour the baseball box scores. The same old story, Chairman of the Board wants unreasonable results yesterday, whatever it takes for his expediency and insatiable wants. In order to accomplish the task, the standard procedure is to give out as little information as possible, in case a withheld detail could help. This was the situation I thought I might encounter here, and I knew full well I'd be chasing the truth for some time.

The inebriated one intrigued me the most in this bunch. He had an imperious way about him, adamant in all his opinions. He seemed sadistic, conceited, and predatory. I suppose, like most lawyers. I suspected he felt like me. That excuses aren't explanations; rather there is an explanation for everything.

It was 9 p.m. when we poured out of the St. Regis Restaurant. Joe Neverson looked like a whipped puppy bouncing off walls and stumbling out of the bodega. Corrigan told Maggie Little to take Joe to the company apartment, which was on the 6th floor of the St. Regis. PGC's favorite number is 6, somebody mentioned as they hauled off the drunk. I couldn't help but notice how certain people were telling others what to do. They were like barking orders. As Corrigan spoke with Little, Joe looked like a guy holding a sign. After they departed, Richard Corrigan extracted an envelope from his inside breast coat pocket. He handed it to me, "Jack, look it over. If you're satisfied you're on board next Monday. We need you right away. Call me in the morning."

We shook hands and he, like everyone else, disappeared into the night. I looked at my watch realizing I had forty minutes to meet Tomko at the Hilton Sky Top. As if on cue, a cab arrived at the curb. I wondered if the balding one would even be there when I arrived with the proposition.

The driver was not overly friendly and I sensed a tremor of unease. I wondered if he was an agent because he seemed to appear out of nowhere when I needed a ride. As we motored toward Baltimore, on the Baltimore-Washington Parkway, I pulled out the envelope from my vest pocket. Since I entered the taxi, I'd been lording over the little box of dirt, like the tyrant of a terrarium. It said welcome to Atlantic States Surety Company. The offer was a full controllership at a salary of $60,000 per annum plus a new car of my choice, and a generous expense account. The offer was more than twice what I received as a Special Agent. Once again, my thoughts were to quit the FBI and take a job like this. But, of course, that wasn't possible. Or, was it?

Traffic is traffic, one of life's levelers. I didn't arrive at Sky Top until 8:45 pm. Of course, Special Agent Tomko wasn't there. He knew what happened though. I just knew he knew because I wasn't there or somebody somewhere had called him. I sat down at the bar. I felt kidney-punched. It was all I could do to order a drink. I wanted to take advantage of the quiet time for a few minutes to gather my thoughts.

Actually, I felt like I needed a sabbatical, not a new assignment. I'd never felt this way before. Rather, I'd always prided myself on my ability to endure pressure that would crush most other guys. I have too much fiction in my life, I'm thinking. We keep lying to ourselves because it's the only way we can get through the day. A time will come, I know, where the lies will get to me and I'll say fuck it and quit. Really, flat quit! And, I want to quit now! However, one more time, I'd try mustering enough intestinal fortitude to do this one last job.

My mind is rambling as I sit at the bar drowning my thoughts. I decide to call Corrigan at 9 am to accept his offer, with a start date Monday-a-week. I will check in with Tomko, then taxi to Amtrak for the trip back to Philadelphia. I have a lot to do in very few days. I want to talk with the Dean of the seminary so I may complete my last semester by correspondence in order to graduate. I realize nobody but I care about that situation. It is just time to make the best out of a bad situation. My life seems to lack such purpose. I wonder for the one-thousandth-time how all this happened. All I wanted to be was a math teacher and a coach. My life's purpose seems to be only a cautionary tale for everyone else. At 10 p.m. I charged my drinks to the room and went to bed.

In the morning, I make the phone calls and taxi to Pennsylvania Station in Baltimore. As the Metroliner is rolling across the Susquehanna River, nearing Philadelphia, I become apprehensive about seeing Ellen and my boys. When we approach 30th Street Station in Philadelphia, I feel like I have just swallowed ice.

Opportunity is missed by most people because it is dressed in overalls and it looks like work. **Thomas Edison**

Chapter Seven

Ellen and the boys meet me at the gate. The kids are annoying the hell out of her as we walk out of the terminal and heap into our 1970 Ford Maverick, a vehicle I'd purchased from a fellow seminarian for fifty bucks. It was a black and white two-door sedan that looked like it had been painted with a broom. But, it started and ran. What more could a married couple with children want?

"Well," she queried, cocking a brow provocatively, but saying nothing. Before I could respond, fortuitously a fist fight broke out in the backseat of the car between the two older boys. While I was breaking up the brawl, Joe, my oldest son, kicked the rear window out of the car while Ellen was trying to get into the right hand lane of the Schuylkill Expressway.

"Jesus, what was that?" She hollers!

"Your son, Joe, just kicked the rear window out of the car! No problem, we didn't need that window anyway." Ellen was so mad her face was turning a shade of deep purple.

"This damn car won't go more than forty miles an hour and what ever happened to power steering? I remember, not so long ago, when we were driving Lincoln Continentals. Is it me? Where did I go wrong?" she started to laugh, while approaching and making our exit onto Lincoln Drive.

As we plowed onto the beautiful parkway, with high, stately stone bridges arched over the roadway, I started to laugh. So, I ask. "How was your week, Ellen?"

She turned, giving me her are-you-out-of-your-fucking-mind look. "Do you not worry about anything, John? You know I've made a couple of attempts to start a conversation, but it's like striking a wet match. What the hell is happening?" she spelled out slowly.

"I got the job," I replied softly. "It's D.C."

"I know you got the job, John. What? It is D.C.? She barks, snidely. "Are we going to live there? I've got a lot of questions, buddy? We're big kids now!"

An implacable hush permeated as we met Allen Lane. She turned right to Germantown Pike, then a left and a quick right on Gowan Aveune. When she pulled into the parking lot and she turned off the engine, the children were clamoring to get out of the car. I opened the door while Joe and Dan crawled through the space where the back window had once been. I grabbed Chris before he tried the same ploy. The children race off to the playground just adjacent to our house.

We both breathed a sigh of relief as we amble to a park bench. Now we can talk, watch the boys, and enjoy some fresh air. My thoughts were all over place. I'm thinking one thing and I know, intuitively, she's thinking about what happened to my ambition. We've had this conversation before. When she first met me, I was an enthusiastic, fired-up, a sky's-the-limit kind of guy. Perhaps she sees me now as deceitful, deceptive, dour, cynical, and bitingly sarcastic.

"Johnny," she said, while lighting a cigarette, "You were once such an optimistic person. It was this personality I fell in love with. What a toll we've paid since you joined the Bureau. I had no idea it would be this way. Did you?"

"I know I've said it before, but expect good things to come." I lit one up, and continued my speech. "You might think I lost the fire in the belly, but I haven't lost my spark. It hasn't been that bad the past three years. We act and feel like poor people, but we know better. This will be my last case. I'm going to make that happen."

Ellen let me ramble because I hadn't been saying much lately. "With what I know, I'll go into private practice and make a fortune. All is well that ends well, right?"

"If it doesn't kill us first," Ellen replied mordantly. "What other woman can say they went to pick her husband up at the train station and came back with her rear car window kicked out and missing? Huh?"

"Look," I said. "We'll have retirement income, a practice and a beautiful home somewhere in Virginia. We just have to get though this move. It won't be that long. I say less than two years."

Somebody was crying on the playground. A little girl had fallen out of a swing and her mother had raced to help her, while our boys barely took notice.

"Whatever," she said, matter-of-factly. "Honestly," Ellen whispered with a smile. "I'll keep expecting another hailstorm."

"Keep your rubber poncho and galoshes close by, "I reply, grinning.

She nudges me while lighting up again. She puts her hand in mine and squeezes. "I'm counting on you big fellow."

While she took another drag off her Winston, I say, "Hey, let's take the kids for pizza and a movie."

"Pizza and a movie," Ellen chuckles. "Are you crazy, what did we hit the lottery? There was a pause, "Oh, I forgot you just came back from Washington. Did you get a little expense money, darling?" she asks contemptuously. "Like maybe we can sneak in a couple of beers. Maybe?"

"As a matter of fact I did. An envelope full of cash and a new resume," I pulled it out of my left pants pocket, flashing it.

"God, I love the way the Bureau cracks the whip," she chortles.

We corral the children and go to our apartment. After washing up we depart for nearby Chestnut Hill for pizza and a movie. *The Natural* is playing and as we stand in line for tickets Ellen comments, "Just what I need, a baseball movie."

I retaliate with, "You can handle Redford, right?"

She prods me forward saying, "Oh yeah, I can handle him."

"But can he handle you," I ask, paying for one adult, one student and three children.

"Who's the student," Ellen solicits with a laugh.

For the moment everything is working, but it is all happening too fast. And, tomorrow is another day. So enjoy the moment.

The absolute truth is the thing that makes people laugh. **Rob Reiner**

What Is Past Is Prologue

Missoula, Montana
Friday, May 5, 1967

This last day working at Western Montana National Bank in Missoula, Montana, has brought tears to my eyes. It has been quite a year living here at the junction of two great trout rivers. It is a place where the Blackfoot rivers meet the Clark Fork and move upstream to the Bitterroots in Idaho.

I'm standing now at the Clark Fork River, which pretty much parallels Interstate 90. About one year ago, Big Jim, a University of Montana student who worked part time at the bank, took me to this exact spot. Here, he taught me the art of fly fishing. I watched him cast in the waters and then tried my skills at it under his tutelage. What I remember most was the pure beauty of the scenery and the power of the water slapping against rocks in the near distance. We were only here once because he liked fishing the Bitterroots better.

The Bitterroot River flows northerly through the Bitterroot Valley which is magnificent country. It's like being in a wonderland and it was here I caught my first trout. These few fishing trips were a lifetime experience. Today I want to visit this spot one more time, to reminisce a little about dreams come true and some put on hold. Tomorrow, Beth and I and a dream come true, our daughter Kincaid, will head back to the Minnesota. We will leave Montana behind.

As I walk away from the river, I think about the party there will be for me this afternoon. Everybody will sign a card and wish me well. I'll be leaving co-workers and friends and after a day or a week or two, who will even remember me? Who will remember us? But I think I'll remember it all.

Here I started my banking career; I'm thinking it will be a long and prosperous one. In Missoula, our daughter was born August 30, 1966. During the year, we took many rides to the majestic Mission Range, Flathead Lake, and Glacier National Park. We were involved with our church, teaching Sunday school, and playing music. Beth and I gave guitars lessons and played a few night clubs to earn extra money.

In Montana I learned how to hunt deer and elk. I did a lot of duck and goose hunting. The best part of our year here was we had really good friends because we lived a normal life. Our year in Montana had passed too quickly. I really didn't like leaving our friends and putting the past here behind.

Teach us to delight in the simple things. **Rudyard Kipling**

Chapter Eight

1700 K Street
Washington, D.C.
Monday, September 26, 1983

"Hello Mary," I said. She was sitting at her desk, which was perched, an extra three feet off the floor for an effect of control and power, I suppose. She was dressed to the nines in a sharp gray pant-suit, a ruffled white blouse, and all the appropriate trimmings. She smiles.

"I heard, through the corporate grapevine, you'd be here this morning, Mr. Oleson. Have a seat," Mary said, pointing to a row of expensive looking chairs along the wall. "May, I get you a cup of coffee or a Perrier?" she asked, politely.

"Coffee, just black," I replied.

"Black, like me," she winked, stepping on by and into an adjacent room. One minute later, she was back with a cup of black coffee on a saucer, replete with a coaster and napkin. After which she positioned herself at her desk and picked up a ringing telephone line. I couldn't help thinking there was something more subtle and far more powerful going on here as I watched the comings and goings of people. It was nine in the morning and suddenly this place had come alive. My gaze drifted to a commotion at the front entrance. Mary's eyes watched the goings on as she quickly transferred to whom she was talking with to somebody else.

Two huge men passed through the gateway first; one I estimated about six-foot-two with an athletic strut, and the other about six-foot-five, lean and sinewy. It was Commander Larson. I hadn't recognized him at first during the confusion. Ned was one of us. Following Larson was a more elegant masculine man, with deeply tanned skin and a full head of jet black hair, combed straight back. His eyes were dark, nearly black; a *Wayne Newton* look-a-like. He kept his head down and followed the other two men to the right along the corridor of power. Following them was a red-headed woman with a smoking hot body and two security guards. It was like the President of the United States arriving, minus the Marine Band playing *Hail to the Chief.*

Mary looked at me, smiling, in askance. "Uh, uh, that's PGC." I sensed energy between us. I didn't know what it was but it was, but it was kind of a mother-protection thing, a lion protecting her cubs. Maybe PGC was too scary for me, treading too close to the scorched earth he created. It was like *get the hell out of here before you get hurt.* Shoo, go away!

I'd read PGC's file. He was popular, played basketball at Phillips Andover and Yale – the complete package. He had been one of fifteen classmen tapped for the Order of Skull and Bones during his third year at Yale. It was the ultimate referral network, twenty-five hundred of the most powerful people, including Presidents. These people were trained from childhood to pretend to be something other than what they are.

Mary is busy answering phone lines as I sit in a wing-back chair thinking. Skull and bones is a secret society. It consists of the guys who run the world for fun and profit, be it oil, drugs, or criminal ways. What a person wants does not dictate how that person should behave. That's the nature of being part of something greater than oneself, I'm brainstorming from memory. The bonds between members override any other responsibility to family, to the law, anybody, including self.

Mary must have noticed my moments of a meandering mind. "He's here today to meet you, Jack." She smiles a synthetic smile when the intercom buzzes. She turned her head, speaking softly to the caller. Meanwhile, I was feeling like a deposing suspect waiting to meet God on the thirteenth floor that didn't exist.

"Okay, Mr. Oleson, Mr. Charles is ready to see you. Please follow me."

The office is a maze, leading back to the inner sanctum, giving me opportunity to gather strength of mind. Mary keeps opening and pulling doors shut as we pass through the halls. We eventually arrived at the Executive Secretary's desk. Here sits the beautiful tall blond I'd met at the St. Regis on interview day. On her exquisite marble desk was absolutely nothing but a telephone.

She extends her right hand, saying, "Hello, Jack." She drags a wet middle finger across my palm as she slowly lets go.

"We've met," I told Mary.

"Very well, then, I leave you two to carry on." Mary replies, exiting the office.

"Believe it or not, nothing is really formal around here, except when addressing Mr. Charles. And once you're recognized, he'll have you call him Gordon. Please have a seat and he'll be with you shortly." She smiles warmly, reminding me of a Stepford wife. She seems like a different person from that first night.

"And what do I call you," I ask.

"Charlotte." She says, as the intercom buzzes. Like *Hush, hush sweet Charlotte*, I think to myself.

While I wait, my mind wanders. I'm thinking, as long as I have the benefit of inside information, I'll be okay. But, what happens when I don't? Not to worry, I'll figure out how to handle it. I am scared; scared because I am about to cross a line, doing something risky at a whole new level. I feel nervous at the thought of poking around here where I so clearly don't belong. I don't want to be caught doing something I couldn't even begin to explain. It was pre-game jitters, I knew, as the double doors to his office suddenly open.

Richard Corrigan and Joe Neverson come through the double oak doors. Neverson doesn't even acknowledge me. Corrigan greets me cordially and ushers me into Mr. Charles' office. It is colossal and pristine. The walls were mirrored, except for the one behind his desk. PGC's chair was turned facing that wall when I enter. Meanwhile, Corrigan sits me down at a long black leather couch in front of an elongated mahogany table. He sits himself directly across from me. When we are set, Mr. Charles exits his desk chair and walks slowly toward the end of the table. Corrigan stands and motions for me to stand. While seating himself in a comfortable black leather chair between Corrigan and me, Mr. Charles says, in a clear, well enunciated voice: "Jack, welcome to Atlantic States Surety."

"Where's your pad and pen, Jack?" With the pleasantries over with, they are the next words, he utters to me, in a scolding sort of way. Like, *you dumb shit!* Before I can respond he tells me, "Don't ever come into my office without a pad and pen."

"Richard," he drawls, dragging out the h, what did Al Capone say?"

Corrigan parrots: "You get a lot more done with a kind word and a gun than with a kind word alone."

Don't go to war without your rifle, I'm musing, while PGC barks into an intercom.

"Charlotte, where's Jack's legal binder and writing instrument?" Who is this guy? Adolf Hitler? I'm meditating. Everything is an order or a command.

When one of the double doors opened, Charlotte emerges carrying a leather-bound binder and a small box. She hands both to me saying, "Enjoy, Jack." She, too, had a deceitful look in her rather dark eyes, as if to say, *she-knew-something-I-didn't-know.* It was a look-o-kiddo kind of gape.

I stared at the binder and was amazed to find my initials emblazoned in gold lettering on the bottom right – *JO.* I opened the folder, and found a bound yellow pad. I close the slip and open the small box. Inside is a black pen with a white top, a Mont Blanc. I open the pad and write down the date. I look intently at Mr. Charles with a level gaze, saying, "Thank you."

PGC dismissed Corrigan and got up, motioning for me to sit down in front of his big oak desk. I feel compelled to comment on his first rate office and furnishings, but instantly decided against such small talk. It would be like commenting on the weather outside which he would not know about or care about. The picture windows were completely covered with ceiling-to-floor drapes. He kept his office very dark. There were no overhead lights. He had expensive looking brass lamps strategically placed in case illumination became necessary. I saw nothing personal, like family pictures or any special curios which might carry a story. His mammoth private office is cold and gave me the chills.

Paul Gordon Charles whispers into a device located in the center of his credenza. While he is dictating, I take another gander around the inner sanctum. His office is expensively, but sparsely furnished. It has the feel of temporary occupancy, a place that could be vacated on the spur of the moment. Lonely is the first word that comes to mind. Again there are no pictures of anybody. There is nothing warming, whatsoever. Suddenly Mr. Charles swings his chair around, glaring directly at me with piercing eyes.

"Pick your poison, isn't that what they say, Jack?" Paul Gordon Charles asks with a sardonic closed-mouth grin. When I didn't respond he began fidgeting with his signet ring. It was engraved with the distinctive seal of Yale University, carrying the Hebrew text *Urim v' Tumim* and its Latin translation *Lux et Veritas*, which means light and perfection. I was told he always wore that ring and I'd studied pictures of it during my brief orientation.

The silence remains, as I'm not answering his question, if it was to be interpreted as one. Then, "Jack," he said, in a Bostonian accent, "I want you to make a list. Tomorrow, report here at 8 am sharp to tell me what you found out." I noticed he had a habit of looking at you longer than you expected after he spoke, as if to catch your true reaction to what he had been saying. Yet, his gaze was unsettling. He knew how to use space to create life. He held up his right index finger, saying, "There's more."

"Jack, you have one shot at this. Know what your duty is and do it without hesitation. *Blessed are warriors who are given the charge of a battle like this, which calls them to do what is right.*"

This guy is crazy, I'm thinking. *Pick your poison, supposedly quotes from Al Capone and the last maybe from Napoleon?* Or, I wondered, was he really just being myopic. He adds, "The Potomac River is always moving. It is the one true constant." He says as he punches a button on an eight-track tape player. Meanwhile I'm thinking baseball is the one true constant, and then Handel's Messiah plays away just above a whisper.

"Jack," he says. "Are you ready?"

I had my Mont Blanc pen in the ready position, nodding in the affirmative. "I want you to tell me what you know about this list tomorrow morning. *The management company ... the operating company ... the leasing company ... the banker ... Fripp island ... Potomac place.*"

I grin at Charlotte as I pass by her empty desk. What does she do all day? I'm thinking.

"Jack," she whispers like she is surprised to see me. "Did you get your first homework assignment?" She laughs an evil laugh while I stare at her slightly bewildered. I smile back waggling my leather bound notebook.

"Okay," she said. "Good boy!" The evil cackle again. She was so much different from that first meeting. I determine I'll ask Ned Larson about her. I look back and she is gone, without a trace. There was a beautiful, young, brown-skinned woman at her desk. The once empty desk is now filled with papers. *What the fuck?* I think. I shake my head to clear my brain. Am I seeing things?

While I'm meandering down the halls of power I'm trying to figure what's really going on. Why is Charlotte fucking with me? Is she imaginary? My mind is racing. Yeah, money is how they keep score. And money never sleeps. It appears to be kick-ass-management, as everybody's nose is to the grindstone displaying stone masks, while Scrooge Mc Duck vaults day after day. The company's heartbeat is the regular thud of the thousand-ton behemoth, which was sending vibrations up my spine. *Embezzlements, bribes, kickbacks, cover ups, fixes with PGC as well defended as a medieval castle.*

The new is coming off the crystal chandelier. It is time to get to work. As I enter my new private office, Duke Ellington's *Mood Indigo*, is playing softly on the commercial elevator music feed. My desk is empty, completely void of everything but a single telephone. I feel a swell of resentment, of resolve.

Just roll the dice, I'm thinking. I stride confidently out of my office, and for the first time in a long while, I feel a palpable sense of relief. I know what I am going to do. Who better than Jerome

Bitterman to tell me about the things on the list? Bitterman is suppose to be around this week for introductions and to discuss work in process. I believe strongly in first impressions. I read anger in Jerry Bitterman's eyes. I figure Bitterman has a lot of stuff to get off his chest. Only he could tell me the way things are or point me in the right direction. Or, who really is Jerome Bitterman?

I walk to Mary Robinson's perch. She is just hanging up the telephone. "Well," she says. "Today is orientation day, huh?" She smiles warmly at me. "What can I do for you Mr. Oleson?"

"Jack," I say. My father is Mr. Oleson."

"Alright," she says. "What can I do for you, Jack?"

"Jerome Bitterman. Is he here today?"

"I think you'll find him in the coffee lounge." She points to her left, while laughing.

"Thank you, Mary." I reply with a smile and walk back toward my office. I can see the coffee lounge door, it is closed. When I enter my office I'm stunned. There is Charlotte sitting behind my desk in my swivel chair.

"Are you looking for Bitterman, Jack?" She has changed from a dress into a pant suit. She throws both her legs up on my desk and points to the coffee room. "Do you want a cup?" She asks getting up on her feet and walking toward the door. "See you," she says, with a sneaky finger wave.

"Charlotte," I yell after her. I walk toward her. "It's Boyer. Charlotte Boyer."

How she knew I was going to ask for her last name, I don't know. She smiled and just disappeared. What the fuck? I hadn't thought and wondered so much about things since I was a child. I push open the coffee room door. Sure enough, there's Bitterman reading the Washington Post's sports section.

"Hey, Jack, looks like your Phillies are going win the NL East."

"Maybe it's one last hurrah for a bunch of old pros." I reply. It was the first normal statement I'd encountered today.

"Grab a cup of coffee and I'll take you around to introduce you." He looks at his watch. "We have lunch with a banker at noon, in Baltimore, so let's get moving.

I'm thinking to know what to do in the future I must understand the past. And to be cautious, well, it's the greatest risk of all. I nod sagely to Bitterman, accepting the wisdom that if I don't succeed I run the risk of failure. I can't lose or fail! It's not in my nature and the attitude goes way back. Just give me the ball!

"Let's go," I say.

Wise men talk because they have something to say. Fools talk because they have to say something. **Plato**

What Is Past Is Prologue

Benson, Minnesota
Friday, November 4, 1960

The story goes something like this:
It is a bitter cold Friday night. The glaring lights shooting from the top of the old light poles bounce off the snow that has been plowed into drifts around the perimeter of the gridiron.

Coach is trying to dig his spikes into the frozen turf around the thirty yard line at the north end of the field.

"No way," Coach mutters, out loud, as he kicks into a small line of snow that's been furrowed by a snow plow. He shakes his head in disgust while peering toward the south end of the field. He sees school buses unloading Montevideo students who have traveled to see their Mohawks do battle for the West Central Conference championship. He glances toward the bleachers noticing they are beginning to fill with parents, local supporters, students, and even college scouts.

"Damn scouts," Coach speaks softly, hoping the scout's presence won't affect any of his senior's devotion to a team effort. He stands for a moment silently contemplating the possibilities of the game. He watches like a ghost as fans start going through their rituals, preparing for the upcoming event. Each one, after locating the most available strategic vantage point, is scraping snow from iced planks. They spread out two Army blankets across their space. They pull another set of Army (a bunch of World War II veterans in this crowd) blankets across them wrapping the ends under their legs on each side. Most of the men are wearing Army parkas they probably brought home from WWII or Korea. Once settled, couples and groups push closer together, shifting continuously for warmth.

Coach smiles; as he senses the excitement in the air as parents and other spectators greet each other with vigor. It is obvious they were ready to weather the inclement conditions for the big competition. Coach wonders seriously, will his players be so game?

Coach is a formidable looking man. He keeps himself physically fit. He has a rough looking, but handsome face. He is a religious man whose approach to life is very basic and old fashioned. His crew cut conveys this image. Tonight, he wears a wool stocking cap pulled over his head and an old Army parka too. As he ambles toward the locker room, he stares down at his unbuckled overshoes. He's pondering over whether or not he has prepared his team enough mentally for the night's encounter. "Yes," he thinks out loud. He will fan the flames of his charges one more time before taking the field.

This is Coach's second year at Montevideo. Here, he had accepted a real challenge. Prior to his arrival, the Mohawks had been a football doormat. The student population is drawn from lower and middle class families. This group coupled with the surrounding farming communities, provide the players. The Mohawks poor football record in the past was always blamed on poor coaching and foolish discipline.

Coach was immediately disgruntled when he found nearly every player had a car they drove to the athletic field. Coach's first rule was no cars were to be driven to practice. This axiom had caused him a great deal of grief when the players invited him to a meeting protesting his action. They tendered him an offer. If the players walked eight blocks to practice, he walked too. He agreed to their solution and his abstinence won the battle. He didn't like being dictated to in this manner, but whatever it took to have a winner. He had a plan, a three-year scheme to move on to the college ranks with Montevideo as a stepping stone.

Before accepting the position of Montevideo's football coach, he had been lured by the school's athletic director talking about the talent on the Junior Varsity. Coach had watched the JV films and concurred there were players in this bunch. The up and comers did look promising. So, as Coach approached the doors to the locker room he wondered if his program had peaked too soon.

Last year's Mohawks were youngsters. There were a few seniors, but sophomores and juniors were the team's nucleus. They had won five and lost three, finishing second in the conference. Their record this year is six wins and one loss. Tonight's game would determine the conference champion as their opponent, the Benson Braves, is sporting an identical record. It was winner-take-all, whether or not Coach's program has prematurely peaked or his players were better than he thought. Whatever, forty-eight playing minutes would decide a champion. Coach wanted it badly!

When Coach arrived at the locker room doors, he paused for a moment to collect his composure. He didn't want to appear eager or apprehensive, but calm. When he pushed open the doors, cold air rushed into the warm locker room, causing all eyes to shift toward his direction. The warm air and smell of the analgesics caused his eyes to water.

"It's cold out there boys!" Coach shouted. "The turf is frozen near solid. Footing will be tough."

After a short exhortation, coach began pacing across the locker room, allowing the players to see his intensity. The players are anticipating the shouting would soon begin, but there was a *spooky* kind of silence instead. Some are getting taped and others are staring blankly into space. The players know only the cracks of the pads on the first play would break the tension, ridding their stomachs of the butterflies.

Coach walks over to the table where his junior fullback was about to be taped. The trainer looked at Coach saying, "Here are some ankles." Simultaneously, he stretches a roll of white tape across the fullback's foot and around his ankle. He pulls the tape tight as the player winced, whispering "Too tight. It's too tight."

Trainer looks him straight in the eye, saying, gruffly, "When I get done I want to see those toes turn purple!"

Seeing his fullback's discontentment, Coach said, "You're going to need that extra support out there tonight, big boy," slapping him on the back.

The player gave Coach a slight smile; he then began wiggling his toes. He argues, "I'm telling you, it's too tight!"

"Now there's a tape job," the trainer announces. "No sprained ankles for my boys! You'll feel great once you're out there, son!"

"Okay," The fullback says, with a shrug, "I'll give it a go!"

When he slid off the taping table he gingerly put his weight on his feet, reiterating, "Damn, it's so tight. It's cutting off the circulation to my feet!" The fullback always disliked his ankles taped. Once he hit the field, however, he knew everything would loosen up.

Coach shook his head as he watched his fullback walk bull-legged over to his locker. He whispered to his trainer. "There's going to be a lot riding on that kid tonight. We won't able to get Jimmy outside as the track's too slick. We're going to have to go straight at them. Yep, we're going straight at them!"

"He's our biggest and strongest running back, coach. This should be his kind of game."

Coach slapped his trainer on the back and entered the small office made available for visiting head coaches. He began looking through the papers attached to his clipboard: kicking team, receiving team, punt team, defense and offense. We have to grind it out on the ground, Coach thought. It will have to be the offense. He kept staring at the fullback position. This damn weather, he muses. A big game like this shouldn't be played in horseshit weather.

Coach has built his offense around two fleet-footed senior half-backs with a strong blocking fullback. At the beginning of the season, their exceptional outside speed coupled with fullback plunges had been an awesome attack. Then, at midseason, the left halfback gave way to injury. Coach thought again about his fullback and what a great job he has done, with his blocking, deceptive speed and hard running. The offense would be carried on his back tonight for sure.

Coach got up from his chair to journey back to the locker room. He stopped in the doorway. Coach peruses the musty old confines for a moment. Coach thinks back to his playing days, remembering the tension that builds within before game time, especially for a game of this enormity. He wonders what is going on in his player's minds. He hopes the game is as important to them as it is to him. His thoughts still center on his junior fullback.

Coach watches him lace up his cleats, with the player showing little emotion. Coach is meditative over whether he should have started him as varsity fullback last year as a sophomore. He was a better player than the senior he had in there, but it was only fair the way he did it. Although tonight Coach wishes his fullback had that extra year of experience.

His fullback seems the quiet type who never has much to say. However, he seems to be relatively popular among his teammates. And, his practical jokes are becoming legendary. He is five feet eleven inches tall and tips the scales at 185 pounds. He keeps his light brown hair cut short and his blue eyes convey gentleness. When in competition, however, those eyes are as cold as ice and can beam right through an opponent. He has a determination Coach has never seen before in an athlete's presence.

He is that rare football player who comes along every ten years, fearing no personal injury. He takes every opponent head-on, regardless of physical advantage or disadvantage. He is polite and respectful to everyone. Coach understands his nature as he, too, had been brought up in a disciplinary, military environment.

Coach walks over to where the fullback is sitting. He can't help but notice how the young man's trunks were split on the sides of each thigh. The circumferences of his thighs were larger than the leg holes of his trunks. "That's a real fullback." Coach muses.

"The game is really on your mind, huh Coach?" The fullback queries when he detects his coach standing there. He doesn't like anybody crowding him.

"You're on my mind, big boy. I figured next year would be your year, but happenstance has certainly changed things. I'm wondering if you know what you're in for tonight."

The fullback shrugs, saying, "We'll win it! This is our year, right?"

Coach smiled, saying, "They're going to jam the middle on us. It's too slick to get outside."

"I'll just have to run over them, then," interrupts the fullback.

Coach slaps him on the back saying, "I guess you will, big guy. I guess you will at that."

Coach walks to the chalk board, looks around the locker room, and shouts, "Okay men! Let's gather around here. It's post time."

There was shuffling of equipment and clicking of shoulder pads as the team jostled for a position around the coach. Suddenly, a dead silence ensued. The coach turned from the blackboard saying, "Well this is what it has all come down to. One game! Forty-eight minutes!"

After a pause, he continues, "Remember the devastating August heat? Some of you were *puking* your guts outs because you weren't in shape. Now, it's the cold of winter. We'll see what you are made out of tonight? I'll find out if I did my job.

After another pause, he continues, "There are a lot of folks out there counting on you. They are your classmates, parents, towns-folk, and me. Oh yeah, I know, a girlfriend or two might be out there for you to show off your athletic prowess."

Coach laughs, sarcastically, before he continues.

"I didn't expect to be playing for the championship this year. But, now that we're here, let's get after it. For most of you seniors you may never have another chance like this. The last game you play is the one you will remember the most. It's the one you'll remember the rest of your life. Just ask yourself when you go out there tonight; do you want to be remembered as an *also-ran or a Champion.*"

Silence prevailed among the players as Coach walks away from the blackboard. He looks back shouting, "It's up to you!"

The pre-game hype is over. It is time for the slow walk to the playing field. The Captains jump out front and lead the way as the processional begins, with cleats clicking against the concrete floor.

When the players exit the building, the cold air stings their hands and feet first. Everyone begins rubbing their hands and running in place keeping their circulation flowing. The Mohawks are a quiet bunch as they peer into the distance at the lights hovering over the battleground. Once at the gate of the playing field, the team begins slapping their thigh pads in unison. The Captains charge "Mohawks," and the players run onto the field.

Everybody exercises vigorously just to keep warm. Passing, punting and catching the ball is like dealing with an anvil. The balls are near frozen. As the clock ticks towards game time, Coach huddles his team.

Coach prays, "Father you have brought us this far. We ask you to protect both teams from injury and give each of us the courage to play to the best of our abilities. Amen."

The Captains race to the center of the field for the coin toss. Montevideo wins the flip and elects to receive.

As the receiving team headed toward the playing field, the coach hollers at his fullback, motioning for him to come to the sidelines. "John Sletten," he says, "I want you deep with Jimmy. Tell Billy to move up. I need sure hands back there tonight. DO NOT fumble the ball."

I ran to Billy's position. He was a sophomore running back filling in for super speedster Larry. I told him to move up to my position on the 20 yard line and I was taking his spot. He looked a little confused, but said nothing.

Our superstar, Jimmy, looks over at me asking, "What are you doing back here?"

Grinning, I say, "Hey, Coach told me to line up beside you to make sure you don't fumble."

Jimmy smiles and shakes his head, saying, "Same old Sletten, full of shit!"

The referee blows his whistle and Jimmy signals ready, but the wind blew the ball off the tee. As the Benson Braves regroup I look into the stands for Mom and Dad. They were easy to spot all wrapped up in their OD-colored Army blankets. I smile as the referee blows his whistle again.

The pigskin flew end over end directly toward me.

An honest tale speeds best being plainly told. **William Shakespeare**

Chapter Nine

1700 K Street
Washington, D.C.
Monday, September 26, 1983

The entire office is a huge rectangle. Mary's counter is center square. A wall of private offices extends from behind her perch all the way to the east end of the building and then across to the other side back westward to Mary's desk. Continuing past Mary's station, the private offices go all the way to Mr. Charles'complex. Crossing over in front of his facilities and turning left the offices continue eastwardly back to Mary's reception desk. There is a magnificent conference room adjacent to the accounting department. It's located directly in back of Mary's posting. I estimate forty private offices in all, not including PGC's expansive set up. The first stop is the accounting department.

"Hey Jerry," says an attractive woman I guess in her mid-thirties. She is very proper and reminds me of my eighth grade English teacher who I'd had a crush on in those days.

Bitterman said, "Nancy Sullivan, this is Jack Oleson, my replacement."

She extends her hand saying, "I'm very pleased to meet you."

"Likewise," I say as Jerome Bitterman interrupts.

"Nancy," he says, "takes care of the payroll and the bank reconciliations."

"Whatever I can do to help?" She says before being interrupted by another.

"Jerry, I have to speak with you. Neverman needs some checks cut."

"McKenzie this is Jack Oleson, my replacement."

Looking surprised, McKenzie introduces herself as McKenzie Gillen, head bookkeeper, aggressively. "I'm very pleased to meet you, Mr. Oleson."

Bitterman says, "Jack's from Montana."

"Really," said McKenzie. "What are you doing out here?"

Bitterman is being an asshole, and he senses my slight anger at such an unnecessary remark. He announces for all to gather around. There are ten people who gather, including McKenzie and Nancy.

"I'd like to introduce Jack Oleson. He is my replacement. Jack's starts today and I'll be around for a couple of weeks to help make the transition."

Nothing happens by accident, I'm thinking as each member of the bookkeeping department greets me individually. They say their names, but I don't pay much attention. From what I could gather, they all reported either to McKenzie or Nancy. The latter two report only to Jerry Bitterman and now to me. I sense Jerry is having second thoughts about resigning or, I wonder, did he get fired? The hard way is the only path to true certain knowledge. Maybe Charlotte would tell me the real story, or an explanation, thereof, in riddle form.

"It runs itself." Jerry barks proudly. "The numbers I need everyday are the cash balances and projected collections. The payables are all paid within thirty days. Each check is signed by two officers, except Mr. Charles. He rarely signs a check, but his signature trumps all."

He shows me the conference room. It is huge with the largest conference table I've ever seen. "Each month, you'll give the treasurer's report to the Board of Directors, a piece of cake." Bitterman says.

"Who's on the Board of Directors?" I ask, while wondering why the treasure's report is a piece of cake.

"A sordid cast of characters," Jerry replies with a chuckle. "You'll be surprised."

The next stop is the collateral department. Here I am introduced to Art Aamot and his small staff. Bitterman says, "You'll be dealing with Art often in the near future."

Aamot looks nervous when I ask, "What kind of collateral do you hold?"

He says, slightly stuttering, "All kinds." I don't say anything as I watch his eyes dart around the perimeter of the room. The power of observation is everything. When I first joined the bureau one of the assignments was learning to observe. They'd give me an address, which was usually a bar. I was to pick three people at the bar to scrutinize. I was not to write anything down, only give a verbal report of my observations. I was certain some of my subjects were plants. Why did such unruly characters show up on my watch?

Bitterman helps Aamot by saying, "We secure high risk bonds with cash, certificates of deposits, checking accounts, deeds of trust, whatever a contractor can put together in the form of assets. Art and his crew monitor the accounts, maintain the logs, and secure the collateral. When we need to draw down on collateral, Art makes the arrangements."

I nod in Art's direction. I notice he doesn't seem to have much of a sense of humor. Bitterman is right, though, I'd be seeing a lot of Mr. Aamot. In him I see a weak link in the chain. Finally, he speaks. "We are very meticulous here. There is no room for errors." Perhaps, I'm thinking, the only mistake he will make is getting caught.

Next up is Risk Management. Bitterman walks into a private office as the door was wide open. A rather large, muscular man is standing at a drafting table, reviewing construction blue prints. Jerry introduces him as Matthew Ferrone, a former United States Marine helicopter pilot. "He did three tours in Vietnam." Jerome Bitterman proclaims as if he'd done them.

Matt seemed distracted, so our chat was short. Then Bitterman reminded me we'd have to catch the others later as it would take an hour plus to make Baltimore. "We have a meeting with the banker at noon, Matt." Matt looks directly at me saying, "Good luck, Jack."

On the way to the parking garage I ask Jerry what exactly Matt Ferrone's job entails. "He's PGC's construction manager. You know, when we have to go in to clean up a mess. That's the function of Risk Management, trying to limit our losses by getting the right people into the right position to complete a performance bond."

It made sense to me, not having a chance to visit long with Matt Ferrone. However, when Bitterman added Matt was PGC's enforcer and he spent most of his time doing construction on Mr. Charles' personal residence and beach house, my eyebrows raised.

"Enforcer," I ask? "What does that mean?"

Bitterman laughs. "Matt works over anybody who writes a bad bond, leaving the company to pick up the slack."

I didn't respond, realizing I was becoming privy to the translations of all its opacities and secrets. Jerry was finding it difficult to surrender himself to the code of discipline. It is a disgraceful breach of confidentiality. You rapscallion, I thought. You just try to take advantage of my enfeeblement. Jerry, Jerry, Jerry what would you do if you knew about me? But, you don't. And, you won't.

The difference between fiction and reality? Fiction has to make sense. **Tom Clancy**

What Is Past Is Prologue

Benson, Minnesota
Friday, November 4, 1960

T
he story goes something like this:
I catch the ball on the dead run sidestepping toward the center of the field. The players on the kicking team are staying in their lanes as I break up the middle of the gridiron. I surprise would-be-defenders, breaking away from the pack into the open spaces. Only the kicker stands between me and the goal line. I lower my head and run through and over the player who stood between me and pay dirt. I run the last fifty yards untouched. The Mohawk fans go wild. Benson is stunned. Jimmy kicks the extra point, Montevideo 7, Benson 0.

Benson's first possession is successful, culminating with a 33 yard touchdown pass and an extra point. The first quarter ends in a tie, 7-7. The second quarter is a defensive battle. Yet, both teams manage a touchdown with the half ending in a tie, 14-14. The Mohawks true test of character was still ahead of them.

The warmth of the locker room was a welcome atmosphere. The temperature has dropped considerably since kickoff. Each player seems more concerned with thawing out than they did with the task ahead. Coach suddenly emerges shouting.

"I know it is miserable cold. I'm cold too. But there's still a job to be done. Twenty-four more minutes. The truth is I'm proud of what you did out there the first half. We can win this thing. I want to see some intestinal fortitude now! Blood and guts is what it takes! Do we have it in us? Do we want it bad enough?"

"Mohawks," the team shouted in unison. "We are the Mohawks!"

Coach grabs a piece of chalk and goes to work. The entire team gives him undivided attention. The team is ready and the coaches can feel it. The anticipation of being cold was gone. The players race onto the field as if they were involved in *Pickett's Charge*.

Montevideo kicks off to Benson. It was three and out for the Braves. After Benson's punt the Mohawks take over on their own forty-yard-line. Coach sends in the first play, Bobby, the quarterback, calls it: "234 on two … on two. Let's go!"

My time to shine, I'm laughing to myself, as I position myself three and one half yards from the line of scrimmage. Thoughts begin to race through my mind. Just before leaving the locker room, Jimmy, the fleet-footed all-state candidate, told me this was my game. The slick turf had taken the game away from him. I rocked on my feet as I set down in my stance. The play called for Jimmy in motion right to left, fake a dive play to Billy and give to me, the second man through, the ball on a cross-buck into the four hole. It was simple play, but had been good for long gains during the season.

With the frozen field, I suspected they would stack the middle, not being too concerned about Jimmy going in motion. On the other hand, Jimmy was so good they had to watch his every move. Bobby called the signals. Jimmy went in motion trying to draw a linebacker or two. The snap came with me taking a jag step waiting a second for Billy to fake into the line. Bobby slammed the ball into my gut as I tore through the line.

The linebackers had not moved with Jimmy and as I broke through the cross blocks I ran right into them. I hit hard splitting through putting them on their vestigial tails, moving into the secondary where I simply outran their fastest. Jimmy kicked the extra point. The Mohawks were on top, 21-14.

Benson was unable to move the ball again, but punted to Montevideo's thirty-yard. Coach sent in another play, screen pass right. Bobby took the snap then faded back with the entire Benson Braves line in pursuit. Bobby tossed the ball to me waiting behind three linemen. I caught the pass and raced untouched seventy yards for another touchdown. Jimmy kicked the extra point.

Benson fumbled the ensuing kickoff and the Mohawks recovered on the twenty-five-yard line. Jimmy quickly burst through the line on a dive right and ran the distance for a touchdown. I kicked the extra point. The third quarter ended with the Mohawks leading, 35-14.

In the fourth quarter Coach played all his seniors and they held their own against the Braves. The fourth quarter was scoreless as the teams played the game out between the two forty yard-lines.

I was uncomfortable standing along the sidelines in the fourth quarter accepting congratulations from my coaches and teammates. It was also a strange feeling knowing this might never happen to me again. This might be my big moment and I felt I was letting it get away from me. I did keep peering into the stands, however, trying to get a read on my Dad's mood and reaction. I supposed he was wondering why I wasn't playing in the fourth quarter to pile up another touchdown or two.

After the game the locker room was bedlam. It had been twenty plus years since Montevideo had won anything. Present were school officials, local reporters, parents, scouts, and many others. I was fielding all sorts of questions as I removed my shoulder pads. I didn't give much response to anybody. Coach surmised my discomfort and came to the rescue, saying, "Please folks, let me have a moment with my fullback."

When the crowd dispersed Coach said to me, "I was proud to be part of your performance tonight, son. I hope you can say that about me someday. You played a hell of a game tonight, kid."

I managed to say, "Coach, we were lucky. We *ham and eggers* have a great line."

He smiled, saying, "Good. Good enough, I see I taught you well. Always remember the line first, you *ham and egger.*"

The team bus was quiet as the players waited for the driver to take off. I sat next to a friend who hadn't seen a minute of playing time all season. Ronny was a sophomore who fashioned himself as a real ladies man. We had become acquainted because our respective girl friends were best friends.

Ronny says, "Kate ought to be nice to you tonight. You played a great game! I shrugged my shoulders. I had great games before and the last time she didn't even see the game because she was making out with a Sauk Centre hood who had driven to the game as a spectator. So, I didn't know what to expect from cute little Kate. My mind was wandering anyway, wondering if I'd ever have this moment again. It was simply frightening that the season was over. The season itself had given me an identity. As the bus moved toward home, my mind remained at the field.

When the team bus pulled up in front of the Windom Building in Montevideo, there was a crowd of people waiting. The cheering and chanting removed my semi-depression caused by realization of the season being over. Coach greeted the team bus and for a first time he showed some emotion as he addressed the assembly. After the short rally, the crowd dispersed. Ronny and I walked toward his 1951 Ford. Ronny jumps in the driver's side where Lucy is waiting in the front seat. I hop into the back seat where Kate is waiting.

"It's celebration time!" Ronny announces. "Let's go park."

Kate looks at me and hugs me, saying, "John, I'm the envy of every girl in school tonight. How does it feel to be a hero?"

"I'm not a hero," I said. "My Dad's a hero. He was awarded the Bronze Star Medal for bravery, while in Korea."

"Whatever," Kate said. "You're my hero."

Kate was my dream girl. She was a sophomore, five feet tall with auburn hair. She is very moody and consequently opportunistic. She would like being with a football hero or any kind of hero. She could do that whether she liked you or not.

She grabbed my hand, putting it between her legs. I felt a little awkward but I was enjoying the activity. She put her head on my shoulder and turned her head for a kiss. She was a real flirt and cockteaser, leaving her best for a possible future encounter. Ronny and Lucy got in some kind of an argument and our romantic night ended rather abruptly. I arrived home at midnight. There was a note on the kitchen table. It read:

John, I was proud of you tonight! Mom and I went to Rosie's Supper Club with friends to celebrate the occasion. How about meeting me at Stampson's Café tomorrow for a doughnut? Say ten o'clock.

Dad

I reread the note as tears came to my eyes. It had been a great night.

What a wee part of a person's life are his acts and his words! His real life is led in his head, and it is known to none but himself.
Mark Twain

Chapter Ten

1700 K Street
Washington, D.C.
Monday, September 26, 1983

C harlotte Boyer caught up with Bitterman and me at the elevator. "A little field trip, boys," she says, winking at Jerry. "Where are you staying tonight, Jack?" Her question takes me off guard as Bitterman answers for me. "Jack's staying at the company apartment."

"Nice," she says. "You boys have fun!" She smiles at me and walked off with a swagger.

"What's her deal," I asked Jerry. He smiles, answering, "You'll, find out soon enough. You can't even imagine, Jack? You have to see for yourself."

As Jerry whips his 280Z around tight turns in the parking garage, I wondered if anything or just one day is routine at Atlantic States Surety. Bitterman drives like a race car charioteer through the streets of Washington and then levels out on the Baltimore Washington Parkway.

"Where exactly are we going?" I ask.

"Baltimore." Jerry said.

"Where in Baltimore," was my reply.

"Light Street," he says with a laugh. "We're going to a new bank. America's First something or other. The banker we're going to see used to work for big one, Maryland National. He is the head commercial loan officer at America's First something or other. He's pretty much agreed to loan Atlantic States twenty million dollars if all the bank's conditions are met. I've been working on this deal for some time."

Jerry fiddled with the radio while my mind is racing. I ask: "Why does Paul Gordon Charles need ten million dollars? Is the company in that much trouble? And who's guaranteeing this loan and what is its purpose?"

Jerry ponders for a moment. A big grin appears on his face. "Everybody on the Board of Directors is going to sign. The purpose is for Gordon." He answers snidely, as he makes his way into the center of Baltimore. As we approach the tall buildings from Charles Street we turn right to Light Street and we park on Water Street in an outdoor parking lot. When I get out of the car, there it is: American State Bank of Maryland. I wondered how Bitterman could not remember the correct name of the bank. The building displaying the sign looks run down. Jerry points toward the back of the bank and says, "We enter here," never addressing the real name of the bank, as if it might make a difference.

We go in through the back door. I realize there will never be any normalcy at Atlantic States Surety. "They're going to give us ten million bucks and we're back door customers." I say, laughing out loud.

"Sssh," goes Bitterman cupping his right hand over his mouth.

Jerry presses a buzzer. Seconds later the door opens, like it's an old fashioned *Speak Easy*. Bitterman motions me forward like he is leading a charge for the 7th Cavalry. Once inside, the place is laid out beautifully. Thick red carpet leads to a reception area. "Henry Peter Fleck," Jerry requests, with authority. "Yes, Mr. Bitterman," she replies.

We sit in two wing-back chairs in front of her desk. We wait a good ten minutes before double doors open and out walks banker Fleck. He is dressed to the nines in a green silk suit. His imposing height, about six feet two inches; a rich baritone voice; a full head of jet black hair turning gray at the edges, but made less so with judicious use of darkening highlights; and a bespoke wardrobe draped nicely over his lean frame. He seems a complete and potent package.

"Gentlemen," Henry Peter Fleck says with a slight bit of southern drawl. Normally, I would have an immediate dislike from a showboat like this, but there was a hint in his smile that told me he was acting. I could grow accustomed to his starchiness until I got the final read on this guy.

"Jerome," he says.

"Hank, I'd like you to meet my replacement, Jack Oleson." Mr. Fleck extends his hand toward mine.

"Jack," he says. "You're going to be filling some big shoes. I look forward to working with you."

I made a decision, spur-of-the-moment kind, to see where this was all going by agreeing. "Yes, I do have big shoes to fill from what I've seen so far." I fake a nice smile, realizing Jerry thought he was introducing me to a special passionate kind of young man I never dreamed even exists. Not in Montana, anyway.

"We're going to the Union Club, Judy," Henry Fleck told his secretary. Then, he turns to us saying, "Let's beat feet, guys."

It was a city and a club that knew exactly who it wanted and I sensed Jerry and I didn't quite fit the bill. At least not the way we were dressed. Everyone was taking our measure, but we got in on the coattails of Henry Peter Fleck but more likely, American State Bank of Maryland. The table we joined was not a happy one when they saw us arrive. They were older gentlemen engaged in a heated argument about something. They were drinking martinis and it was the alcohol that was talking with one of the conversation participants. We sat down and they left when the one with too many alcohol-fueled words, told the other to quit talking redneck.

Our table was immediately cleaned up and this is when I got my first rapturous glance at a Maryland southern beauty. She was a spellbinding, improbable blond beauty. She asked, "Can I get you gentlemen something from the bar?" Henry spoke right up, ordering a double scotch, up. Jerry ordered a beer and I a Jack Daniels on the rocks.

"So, Jack, did Jerry explain to you what we're trying to accomplish?" Bitterman intercepts the question. "No, Hank, I thought that it would be better coming from you."

"Fine," Hank said, then explaining the deal in length. By the time he had finished we had ordered our third round of drinks. Of course, the way the banker explained things, the money was being used for expansion. By expanding, they obviously could write more business, which would require them to have more cash reserves. Which was American State Bank of Maryland's objective? It would be their largest deal ever and it would enable them to increase their demand deposits not only by having Atlantic Surety's account, but also having all the joint accounts used for collateral. What were Henry Peter Fleck's reasons to do the deal, a major kickback, I'm certain.

First came the soup. Veal Marsala was the second course with a mound of ghastly mashed potatoes and carrots cooked to lifelessness as accompaniments. It did us all good to concentrate on eating, letting the atmosphere around us decompress before the conclusion of the meal.

When parting the gentility that is both the bedrock and the quicksand of all social endeavors, brought grace and quietude to the last act of the meal. We shook hands, but there was no love loss among us three participants. The purpose of the meeting was to test me. I was agreeable, in my opinion, as if I had set the bar too low for myself.

Driving back to Washington, we were both very quiet. I'd been sensing Jerome Bitterman didn't really want to leave all the action. He was a big player with power. I, on the other hand, was thinking as I did on every job how people are so willing to trust me with such lethal information. I found it amazing. Nothing happens this fast. I was wondering if I was being set up. It was just too easy.

"What do you think" asks Jerry.

"I thought Hank was an impressive young banker. He's on the ball." I say.

"No, I mean of the deal. How it works!" Jerry redirected.

"People have to make a lot of commitments, especially the guarantors." I spoke cautiously, while anticipating the question he really wanted to ask me.

"What do you think of 3% for Henry for putting the deal together?"

Jerome Bitterman just answered two questions. He was splitting the kitty with his buddy Henry Peter Fleck. I act like I'm thinking it over.

"It's not an unreasonable broker's fee, if you are indeed a broker." I say.

"So, you agree? This deal is paramount for the company." Jerry says, enthusiastically, hoping for my support.

"What does Mr. Charles and the Board of Directors think about this broker's fee?" I ask?

"Look, Jack, my job is to make this transition smooth. Are you a player or not? Jerry queries with a slightly raised voice. I hesitate before I confirm. "I'm a player, Jerry!"

"Okay," he smiles as he pulls the 280Z into the parking garage.

Twenty years from now you will be more disappointed by the things that you didn't do than by the ones you did do. So throw off the bowlines. Sail away from the safe harbor. Catch the trade winds in your sails. Explore. Dream. Discover. **Mark Twain**

What Is Past Is Prologue

Montevideo, Minnesota
Sunday, February 5, 1961

It's a gloomy Sunday afternoon. The sky is cloudy, roads are filled with slush and snow, flurries are in the air. My friend, John Norman, and I are driving up and down Main Street, in his mother's 1950 Pontiac, looking for something to do.

We are bored as nobody seems to be around, so I suggest, "Let's go bowling."

"Okay," Jim says, never being one to disagree much. Instead of making a u-turn to go back up Main, he drives straight across the railroad tracks and turns left on Highway 212. A minute later he turns right into the bowling alley parking lot. We amble to the bowling alley, pay for one game, two balls and shoe rentals.

We are directed to lane twelve, "It's the last one on the right," yells the huckster. We put the bowling balls on the rack and lace up our shoes. I sit down at the scoring table to set up the score sheet, saying, "You're up, Jim."

While Jim Norman threw his first ball I noticed her on lane eleven. I knew instantly she was the one for me. She was wearing auburn and green plaid slacks. She wore a red sweatshirt displaying *Clarkfield Cardinals* across the front. She gave me a gleaming, wide smile as she walked back to her scoring table. She had golden blond hair just touching her shoulders.

She was with a girlfriend, who was also pretty and one overdeveloped redhead. She pushed out her perky breasts in an attempt to redirect my attention. Her friend never had a chance, though, after she swept her beautiful blue eyes up toward my face, seemingly searching for my eyes.

"My name is John," I say.

"Hi John, I'm Beth Ann and this is Nancy."

"And I'm Jim," Jim Norman chimed in, adding, "I got a spare, Mister Scorekeeper."

As we bowled our games, Beth Ann and I made small talk. I'd take my turn, firing the ball down the alley with extra super speed. When I hit a strike the pins flew like they had been struck with a charge of dynamite. My buddy, Jim, couldn't help but notice my being smitten. Meanwhile, Beth Ann seemed very composed. When Beth Ann was bowling, her friend, Nancy, gave me some solicited inside information.

"Beth," she said, "is a popular girl in our high school. She's friendly, but not outgoing, attractive but demure. She's very, very punctual. She does her homework and plays tenor saxophone in the band. She goes to church every Sunday and does her chores. She never steps out of line. She never argues with anyone. You know, always like agreeable."

"What are you two talking about?" asks Beth Ann.

"You," I say with a smile and a laugh. "I'm gathering information about you from Nancy. So, I hear you're the farmer's daughter?"

"I guess I am," she says. "We need to go, Nancy. It's starting to snow pretty hard now."

They had just finished their game while we were in our eighth frame. As they were gathering their stuff I asked, Beth, "Do you girls want to get a hamburger and a cherry coke next door at Anderson's Super Service?"

She told me she'd like to but they really had to get home before dark. Her parents didn't want her driving in the snow after dark. "Unless," she said. "You guys want to drive to Clarkfield, and we'll have a hamburger and cherry coke there.

"Okay," I say. "I think I can get Jim to drive over. He's the one driving today."

"What's your address?" I ask, preparing to write it on the score sheet.

"Hazel Run," she said, laughing when she saw me writing it down.

"Hazel Run, what?" I ask.

"Hazel Run, Minnesota." She expresses kiddingly.

"John, when you get to Clarkfield, just ask anyone where we live. We just live a mile from downtown Clarkfield. It's called Hazel Run. Really, just ask where the Harper farm is located. They'll tell you."

I look at my watch, it is nearing 3 p.m. "See you around, say five?" I suggest, watching them dodge slush puddles to their car.

"Okay," she shouts back with a smile, and a quick wave.

It took a little talking him into it, but Jim finally agreed to the drive to Clarkfield. When we arrived, we stopped at a little corner store and saw people our age. I got out of the car and asked a girl I thought was about our age if she knew Beth Ann Harper. It seemed everybody did as all eyes seem to focus on me. When I asked where she lived, all eyes focused on the girl I'd asked the original question.

"It depends on who's asking," she responds.

"He's good," a voice says, coming from the back of the store. I look and thought I recognized him, probably played against him in basketball a couple of weeks ago. I say nothing.

"If Bill says you're okay, you're okay with me. Hi, I'm Lavonne. I'm Beth's classmate." She volunteers the directions.

We turn left instead of right at the designated cross roads. Sure enough, there is a farm we thought was the right one, with several vehicles parked in the driveway. Jim pulls in front and center and parks near the side door.

"There you go, John, I'll be waiting right here

"Oh..., good luck," he chortled.

I make my way through the snow to the door of an old farmhouse. There is a lot of noise coming from the inside. Music and laughter pierced the air waves, when I asked a young boy if I could speak to Beth Ann. He quickly disappears and leaves me standing there feeling like an ass. A couple minutes later, there she was again.

I remember *Wonderland by Night*, by Bert Kaempfert was playing on the radio when she walked toward me, appraising me with her blue-flecked eyes. I'm wearing jeans and a pull-over OD green Army sweater. Over that ugly color, I have my Montevideo letter jacket on, with my football letter centered on the back.

"So, this is where you live." I say for something to say. I'm feeling very uncomfortable and think everybody is watching my every move. "No this is Nancy's house. We live the next farm up." She says, smiling cutely.

"Oh, where we turned left we should have turned right." I guffawed. "But you're here anyway, so it's a good thing we made the wrong turn," shrugging my shoulders.

"Come on. I want you to meet my parents. We walk into another room full of people. I see a couple sitting on a sofa. There is an attractive man wearing a suit and tie, and a pretty woman sitting on his left. The man looks kind of like Clark Gable, with a penciled in mustache and the woman an Ava Gardner look-a-like.

Beth says, "This is my Dad, Ken Harper." He looks at me like I'm an interloper. "You from Montevideo," he asks?

"Yes sir." My name is John Sletten.

"You're not related to those wild Sletten's in Wegdahl, are you?

"My Dad is from Wegdahl."

"I'm Betty; Beth's mother." I shake hands with her, while she asks? "What's your mother's name?" I thought it was a strange question, but I told her. "Idamarie Sletten."

Betty smiled, saying, "Idamarie Austin. We lived in the same apartment building with each other. We were such good friends. Your mother is a very good person. I heard she married some aviator during the war. I didn't know who, but I would have never guessed a guy from Wegdahl. Huh, he must have been good looking." She took a long swallow from her beer.

"He still is good looking. Dad was a navigator in World War II. He was from Wegdahl. It's not much of a town, but it did produce a few war heroes. Dad was just one of a bunch."

"Are you a football player, John?" Mr. Harper asks. "I see the letter on your jacket."

"Yes, in fact we had a pretty good year." I said proudly, feeling some common ground now.

"Montevideo did well this year. What position do you play?" He asks.

"I'm the fullback." I say, when Beth interrupts me. She whispers. "Let's take a walk.

I turn to Mr. Harper, extending my hand, saying, "It was a pleasure to meet you."

Looking at Betty, I say, "I'll tell my mother I met an old friend of hers. It was a pleasure meeting you."

Betty smiles, while Ken Harper keeps looking at me with jaundice eyes. Beth led the way as we walked through the farmhouse to the outdoors where Jim was still sitting in his car with the engine running.

"Beth Ann, I would like to see you ….. " She interrupts me again, saying, "I know – me too." She hands me a piece of paper and says, "Call me, John."

"4893," I say, When?"

She says, "Wednesday night, say, eight o'clock."

It snowed all the way back to Montevideo. I dominated our conversation with making plans to see Beth again. I had a basketball game on Friday and Saturday night. "The Friday game is home with a *sock hop* afterwards." I'm telling Jim, while talking with my hands. "The game Saturday night is at Appleton."

"So, take her to church on Sunday," Jim says as he pulls up in front of my house.

"Oh, I'll figure it out."

"I'm sure you will big guy!" He drove away laughing with gusto.

I dwell in possibility. **Emily Dickenson**

Chapter Eleven

1700 K Street
Washington, D.C.
Monday, September 26, 1983

It was nearly four o'clock when we entered the doors of Atlantic States Surety. Jerry continued through the offices with a basic meet-and-greet formality. I met a bunch of secretaries, underwriters, and administrative assistants. When we reached the eastern end of the building, there was a gathering. Jerry said, "It's happy hour. Let's have a drink."

"Only officers and directors are allowed here during happy hour," Bitterman says cautiously, while popping the top off a Budweiser. "Help yourself," he suggsts pointing to a half gallon of Jack Daniels.

This office has narrow windows on both sides of the doors so everyone can always see inside. There really is no privacy here, I'm thinking, when I see Richard Corrigan enter the suite. He is gesticulating wildly with his hands to another suit who I had not met before. "Who's that with Corrigan," I ask Jerry?

"He's a new guy who's heading up the casualty insurance department. His name is Larry Leopold." Jerry has no more than spit this information out of his mouth when Corrigan gives me the high sign. He and Leopold are on the move, heading in my direction.

"Jack," Corrigan barks asking about my first day. Then, he introduces Larry Leopold to me with vigor. Larry's in charge of our casualty insurance department. Larry, Jack is our new controller."

I extend my right hand, saying, "We're new starts together."

"Nice to meet you, Jack," says Larry.

Larry looks tired as I watch him survey Corrigan while talking to Bitterman. His eyes are set deeply beneath a low Cro-Magnon brow. He has a large head, a double chin, and a ruddy face that reminds me of a glazed ham, with deep acne pits on his cheeks. His dark brown hair was another *Just-for-Men* victim, I assume. It is cut in a layered pompadour. Everything he wears is monogrammed with an upper case script *LL*.

Thank God Larry's administrative assistant, Sandy Adams, arrived. She is a sweet, pretty woman, very tall, with long brown hair, perhaps ten years younger than me. She apologizes repeatedly for being late. She offers to get me another drink as we make small talk. From what she is saying, her main job seems to be apologizing to everyone for what Larry forgot and her taking too much time to finish what he didn't start.

My first reaction to Larry Leopold was to be unimpressed. He probably always got away with everything. He kind of reminded me of the unctuous Eddie Haskell in the old *Leave It to Beaver* TV show. It seemed the company didn't care if its representatives were particularly smart. The people I'd met today sure weren't any Phi Beta Kappas. I pictured Larry as the guy who took prospective customers out to lunch or dinner all the time, ate well, drank a lot of beer, and didn't have time to exercise. But, Larry didn't like to lose, especially in a dog-eat-dog kind of world. He thrived on competition, probably a used-to-be athlete, used to punishment and abuse too. Or, he could pass as the outgoing, naturally affable type; the chairman among college frat guys. He was the one who lined up the entertainment and beer. And, now he is a buff on *St. Elsewhere*, a T.V. series.

Soon enough, Sandy was back with my drink and one for herself. She apologized it took so long. But, the liquor station was very busy. As we shared a drink together she tells me she graduated from Harvard, but on financial aid. Her family tried to keep everything a secret, as WASP's do, but everyone figured out the truth eventually.

"So what do you think of Larry," I ask Sandy.

"He's a little dorky, in my mind, but he's taught me to never use the word cost or price with a customer. Insurance is an investment, not a contract; that contract is a scary word. That paperwork or agreement is a better way to present insurance work. You endorse copies and okay agreements. The big thing Larry has taught me is to believe in myself."

"Dorky," I say. "What makes him dorky?"

"You know, like the dry-to-wet rule of table setting. He doesn't know the water and wine is placed to the right of your plate and the bread and dry things are on the left. Larry was born with a plastic spoon in his mouth."

I like Sandy and her down-to-earth sense of honesty. I see why Larry liked her, too, as she was bright and anxious to please. Choosing a guy like Larry as a mentor probably was a mistake, but the thing that counts is how many times you succeed. For the more times you fail and keep trying, the more times you succeed.

"Sandy," I predict, "Expect good things to happen."

I pick up on Joe Neverson out of the corner of my left eye. He motions for me to meet him in the hall. With beer and liquor flowing, everybody is laughing loudly, exuberantly, narrating their stories about the day's events. I duck into the hall where Joe is waiting, sipping on his drink.

"Where are you staying tonight?" Neverson asks in a whisper.

"I'm staying next door, in the company apartment." I reply.

"Good," I'm staying there too. We need to talk." Joe replies.

"Okay," I say.

"I'll meet you in the Library Lounge at St. Regis, Jack, in a half hour. If one of us gets detained, just wait. We need to talk." Joe Neverson says, with a sense of urgency. .

Joe Neverson is sipping brandy from a snifter when I arrived slightly later than I had anticipated. I had been detained by Corrigan as he introduced me to more key players, some who I'd already met. But, I was learning it wasn't official until Corrigan made the overture.

"Come," Joe said, tapping the bar stool next to him. He did it in his best personal way, yet challenging me to overcome his disdain for everybody. I suspected Neverson, like everyone else in the Washington power structure, had a public persona and a private personality and, as often was the case with these people; the private personality was rather less attractive than the public persona. Publicly, he was smooth, self-confident, erudite, and witty. Privately, he was often self-contained, impatient, and egoistic. Drunk, he was an asshole. One thing he never was – bland. No one ever forgot him. No one mistook him for somebody else. Joe Neverson defied categorization. This was my read on him, so far, which was always my first assignment, getting to know the dramatis personae.

I sat down at the bar. "Sorry to be so tardy," I say. "Corrigan ….." Joe put up his right hand, "Stop," he says. "I know this is your first day, but I need some answers."

"What happened at the bank today?" Joe queries dryly. His question puts me in an awkward position. I really don't know if Neverson should know what happened at the bank today, or if I knew what actually happened. If I did know, why would I share the information with him? So I answer him by saying, "I met the banker. He seems like an aggressive man who knows what he's doing."

Joe smiles at me, ordering another drink, while I ordered a Jack Daniels on the rocks. There was a moment of quietude as Joe tended to show some contempt for me. I thought he might do this to anyone he didn't consider his intellectual equal, which probably included everybody. My answer brought his façade down. He was uneasy now. The tension was there. It was palpable.

"Listen, Jack. I have to settle a claim at the end of the week. I need to send out a check for $150,000. I've been stalling this outfit for nearly six months. This one has to be done or they're contacting the Insurance Commission." Joe finishes his speech and downs another snifter.

"Joe, let's look the paperwork over in the morning and if that's what has to be done why not send it tomorrow? Or, is there more to it?" I ask.

"Okay, we'll sit down in my office at 8 a.m. and I'll show you the file. By the way, Jack, your suspicions are well-founded. There's always more to it at Atlantic States." Joe Neverson says, cautiously. "There's always more to it."

While Joe ordered another round, I contemplated what was really going on here. Was I being set up to take a fall? Joe Neverson was a bold, clever man. He seemed the type to cover his tracks quite shrewdly and a person who'd manage to do what he did all but under the noses of those who would be concerned. Being discreet is presumably his stock-in-trade; ironically, it's mine, too. Forethought, of course, is a useful cover for indiscretion.

"How about Bitterman," I ask? "He seems to know, Fleck, the banker pretty well?"

Joe lit up a cigarette and ordered another round of drinks. "You mean, Jack, would Jerry be subject to inducements?"

"He certainly would not be alone, not in this town." I respond.

We were playing verbal volleyball with each other. We were like two prize fighters feeling each other out in the first round. Again, he was bold and shrewd. He was intelligent and knowledgeable. He had considerable style and no question he would take inducements with panache. It is Ditto for me, perhaps.

I check my watch. It is 10 p.m. I tell Joe I need to get my suitcase from the car and get some sleep. "It's been a long day."

"See you upstairs, Jack." Joe says, tiredly.

"Say," I ask, "What's the deal with Charlotte Boyer?"

My question made him cock an eyebrow. "Be careful," Joe says, with a tone of watchfulness. "Some say she's a vampire! Now you see her – now you don't?"

"Get the hell out, Neverson." I respond with a laugh.

"Oh, Jack, I wouldn't use the phone in the apartment, unless you don't mind PGC hearing all that you say." Joe is just giving me a fair admonition.

"Thanks!" I yell back, while walking away. Of course, what Joe doesn't know is I only use phone booths. And, I try not to use the same one twice.

All things considered I like Joe Neverson, I'm thinking. There's no lying with Joe, although he is as devious as me.

Nothing in the world can take the place of perseverance. Talent will not; nothing in this world is more common than men with talent. Genius will not; unrewarded genius is almost a proverb. Education will not; the world is full of educated derelicts. Perseverance and determination alone are omnipotent. The slogan "Press on" has solved and always will solve the problems of the human race. **Calvin Coolidge**

Chapter Twelve

It had been a full day and night. Yet, it isn't over. It is my youngest son's sixth birthday. I picked out a phone booth earlier that morning. It is in a pharmacy across the street from where I am staying. I call the red line, which rings only in our bedroom. Ellen answers. "John, are you okay?" She asks, answering on the third ring.

I had a lump in my throat, just hearing her concern, then say, "I'm good. Did Christopher have a Happy Birthday?"

"He really did, but he was asking about his Daddy." My wife was struggling with words, too, "And," she continues, "the Seminary is looking for September's rent." Part of being undercover was to be normal, like being past due for things. It was horseshit. But it was the way I sometimes would justify our situation.

"Come hell or high water, I'll be home Friday night." I assure her.

"I'm not kidding, John, you better be home." She hung up on me. I always hate it when she does that or slams a cupboard door. She is right, though. This was no kind of life for us, and especially for our three boys. Maybe I was losing her. Maybe enough was enough for her. The job has certainly lost its glamour, if it ever had any.

I tried to call her back, but she didn't answer. I would try her tomorrow, or would I get a chance? I was determined to be there Friday night, thinking she would acquiesce once again to my job. Would she? I wonder as I walk back across the street to get some sleep.

Joe was not there when I arrived. It was nearing midnight. I put my briefcase down on the kitchen table and my suitcase in the last bedroom down the hall. There was a balcony and I stepped out on it. I wasn't particularly fond of heights, but I loved views. I thought about the Capitol Building being right there with a full moon as a backdrop. I wished Ellen was here enjoying a gin and tonic with me in my reverie. In reality I was looking at the back of another building, overlooking a huge dumpster. Why did we make our life so complicated with children and wild jobs?

Just then there was rumble at the door. I stepped back into the bedroom to see what was going on. I figured Joe was just drunk and probably had a whore. Instead, I saw Joe fly across the living room in mid air. I saw this huge white guy go for my briefcase on the kitchen table. My FBI credentials were inside, plus my service revolver. I sprinted toward the interloper and hit him on the dead run with the old college bull rush. He went right through the wall and the brief case flew back into my suite. I grab the briefcase, protecting my identity, as he escapes through the neighbor's front door.

"Jack," Joe shouts. "Let him go!"

"What the hell is going on," I ask.

"You really don't know, do you, Jack," was Joe's response, laughing. "Ooh, it hurts to laugh. I think I have a broken rib or something, Jack."

Realizing anybody else's first day on the job would've ended right here, I had to make out like this event had really bothered me. In fact, I was a fairly nice guy, but not when threatened. "What now, Joe," I ask?

"Cool it," he said.

Suddenly a man and woman appeared at the hole in the wall. They were in night clothes, shrugging their shoulders. "What happened," the man asked?

"Troublemaker," Joe says, trying not to laugh.

"The wall," the neighbor says in astonishment. He shrugs his shoulders again.

"Our apartments just become one. Go to sleep sir. We'll take care of it." Joe assures him.

When they walked back through the framing studs, I couldn't keep from laughing.

"What do you have in the briefcase, Jack?" Joe asks, with a grin?

"There is absolutely nothing in it, Joe." I reply.

"You protest, too much, Jack." Joe responds and laughs heartily.

"Fuck you! I return, emphatically, walking back to my bedroom.

Joe poured another drink. I went to bed.

If you are going through hell, keep going. **Winston Churchill**

What Is Past Is Prologue

Gettysburg, South Dakota
Friday, August 22, 1969

What do you do when your wife is having an affair? Things happen to people that changes them. It happened to me. Although it's difficult not to look back at the past, to try figure what went wrong. At the time, I realized I had to stay focused on the future. It and it alone, was a place I could still do something about. My future is a place where my each and every action needed to be smooth and efficient.

"This tragedy will pass," I say out loud, while looking in the mirror I see the reflection of myself. This can't be true – no not to me, I'm thinking. My life had been perfect, everything running right on schedule or so I thought.

We had moved to this little hamlet from St. Paul, Minnesota, in March of 1968. Why I don't know, other than I was trying to move up the banking ladder quickly. I had been flying back and forth, traveling from Escanaba, Michigan to Missoula, Montana doing computer conversions for First Bank Stock's affiliate banks. I was just being recognized by my peers as doing a good job, by getting glowing reports from the affiliates where I was making these adaptations. Also, I'd been introduced to the American Express card.

It was the American Express card that first opened my eyes to white collar crime. The first person the affiliate bank sees is the correspondent banker. There were guys like *Mister Basketball*, George Mikan. George would go out in a fancy suit, an ex-NBA great, who played his entire career with the great Minneapolis Lakers. He was armed with a credit card or two, and always took the bankers out to a big evening to get their *yes* on the deal. I was up next, a nobody, to make the manual-to-computer transition as painless as possible.

The bankers had been spoiled, however. They were average people making a poor salary, but commanding respect. The first day I arrived all they wanted to do is go for drinks and dinner. I was told to give them the first class treatment. The trouble was I didn't have any idea what first class treatment meant. I followed the bankers lead, doing and ordering what they did. The tabs were outrageous, so I thought, but I didn't care. I was doing what I was told.

Having read computer manuals over and over again, taking three-hour-lunches, playing cards (*Hearts*), watching time click off the clock, I finally was put out in the field. They must have read my mind because I was so bored, re-reading what I thought were pretty simple applications, in the first place, I thought about joining the Army and going to Vietnam. Instead, I asked the personnel director, who had recruited me, for a transfer. Once on the road, though, I was beginning to enjoy my work, but, of course, then the call came from First Potter County Bank in Gettysburg, South Dakota. Quagmire! I really didn't want to leave all the action of the Twin Cities. I was having fun, hob-nobbing, drinking and enjoying dinners out on the town.

When the call came we had just bought a house in St. Paul and times were moving along quite nicely. However the opportunity was in South Dakota and I was never one to turn down an opportunity. We sold our house and moved to the middle of South Dakota where I began what I thought would be an opportunity to move into banking management quickly. At the tender age of twenty-four years old I was the Cashier and Installment Loan Officer of a descent sized bank in South Dakota.

We were welcomed into town like celebrities. I was the young new banker with the pretty wife and adorable daughter. Beth Ann looked terrific even being five months pregnant. We settled into a little house we rented for $75 per month. I became active in the Jaycees and bowled with the bank's bowling team. I also put a 3-piece band together and played baseball for Potter County. I spent most of my spare time putting together sets of music, practicing and playing gigs at bars and country clubs in the area.

It was a Thursday evening, April 4, 1968. I was watching an episode of the Virginian when the program was interrupted with the news Martin Luther King had been assassinated in Memphis, Tennessee. Living out on the prairie, I virtually knew nothing about the man. Whenever his name came up it seemed to be associated with some kind of protest. I thought he was some kind of a rebel rouser and was irritated they'd interrupted my program. Little did I know his assassination would set off a nationwide wave of riots, in more than sixty cities.

I was closing the bank's booth at the Jaycees Summer Sidewalk Festival, on June 4, 1968, when word came Robert Kennedy had been shot by an assassin after his victory speech in the California primary. On June 5, the following day, everyone was listening closely to the radio to get any news update about Kennedy. It is just after midnight, on June 6th, when the news came that Robert Kennedy was dead. I finished closing the booth, and walked over to the Legion Club to get a beer and the scuttlebutt.

On Saturday afternoon, June 8, we watched as Kennedy's body was carried by a funeral train from New York to Washington D.C. Perhaps a million people lined the tracks and millions more watched the television at home. It was right here, in front of the television set, I was determined to serve. I didn't know how or doing what, but I felt the urge to go to Washington to see if I could help.

Life went on and my schedule was full and soon enough Beth Ann delivered our son on July 13, 1968. With a good job, beautiful wife and two adorable children, Kincaid and Charley, I felt like I was on top of the world, but the seed to serve had been planted in my cerebrum.

With the race riots going on in the big cities, we were quite content living in this small town, so quaint and seemingly perfect. However, I didn't know it, but it was not so picture-perfect. Here I learned that people, places and things are not what they seem.

My plans were much bigger now and there was just a false sense of complacency about this place. Let's say, it was unsettling, dark and violent. And there were no tall buildings, which was my original concern.

The final year of the obstreperous *sixties* had seemed relatively serene. I was more involved with the daily operations of the bank. I also was spending considerable time chasing Indians, on the Sioux Indian Reservation, trying to collect payments on new cars and pick-up trucks. I'd travel in the big brown bank car out to some bluff, which sat on the banks of the Missouri. I knew they saw me coming so I'd learn to expect anything. It was Tuesday, the 8th of July, 1969. It was a nice day and I felt like taking a ride. I told my boss I was going out to the bluffs to collect a couple of payments:

When I arrived it went something like this:

"Are you Bill Lends His Horses," I ask.

"No."

"Do you know Bill Lends His Horses," I ask of a gathering crowd."

They all shake their heads negatively. "Is that the bank's pick-up," I ask, pointing at the vehicle.

"No, that's Bill Lends His Horses' pick-up."

"I thought nobody knows Bill Lends His Horses." I say, moving toward the vehicle.

All were quiet as I opened the door to the truck, noticing a key was in the ignition. I check the vehicle identification number, making sure it matches. Then, I walk around the truck checking for damage and notice a rag being used for a gas cap. How do you lose the gas cap to a new vehicle, it made no sense? I get in the pick-up cab, which stinks like a stale beer bottle.

I start it up and push in the clutch to put it in reverse. The truck starts moving forward so I slam the brake pedal. I slam it once, twice, three times as the pick-up starts rolling down a short, but steep embankment. *Smash!* The truck comes to rest almost perpendicular to the bottom of the hill. I crack my head on the top of the steering wheel. I'm pissed off really badly.

When I try getting out of the truck I have to lean on the

driver's side door and as a result bend it back flush with the left fender. I slid off the door and virtually crawl up the hill because it is so steep. As I become visible, crawling over the lip of the cliff, all of them are hee-hawing.

"No brakes," said one of them. *Ha-Ha!*

"Tell Bill Lends His Horses I'm sending a wrecker out for his truck!" I say, fiercely with an attitude. I got in the bank car and squealed off the bluff.

It was a typical day. I loved having the ability to get out of the bank. I'd check wholesale at the various dealers we were floor planning. And, of course, make collections as I saw fit. Nobody monitored my time or what I accomplished day to day. It was really a great job, but I was bored.

Today I was contemplating what my keyboard player had told me en route to our gig last Saturday night. He had told me to be careful. Life at home might not be what I think. I just told him Beth Ann and I had something special between us. He dropped it but I was still thinking about what he had said, because I had sensed some irregularities myself in the recent past.

On Sunday, July 20th, 1969, Beth and I with the children went to our friend's house for a cookout and to watch the landing of Apollo 11 on the moon. After all the turmoil a good thing was finally going to happen before the end of the decade. Then the unthinkable, the major television networks interrupted their live coverage of astronaut Neil Armstrong's scheduled Moonwalk to deliver a news bulletin: *Senator Edward Kennedy had been involved in an automobile accident on a remote island off the coast of Martha's Vineyard. The senator had survived when his car plunged off a bridge into the water below, but a young woman riding in his car had died.*

Regardless, the *Eagle* landed at 3:17 p.m. Central Daylight Time, Sunday, July 20, 1969

My high school sweetheart and wife had become a charlatan. Suspicions were confirmed. She was leaving me, when I thought she was the one who liked certainties with things settled? To make matters worse she was leaving me for somebody else, my so-called best friend, a real fraudster. My heart was broken, not knowing what was going to happen next. I feared it would not be good.

I guessed I'd really blundered, which wasn't like me. Usually I was somewhat circumspect, careful, particularly with somebody fragile. I knew I could get her to open up soon enough, just like a clam. And then I might get somewhere with her, because I held no malice or guile. It was just that she made me feel like I had missed the track to Saginaw. A real solution seemed light years away.

Everything had seemed to go so smoothly during the early-to-mid-late *sixties*. Or, they did for me anyway. While I received my college education, she was waiting in the wings for our so-called better life. It came for me, but not for her, evidently. Was it simply all about me? Or, simply, did she need an activity other than being a mother and housewife? Or, was it I was too overwhelming for her? I wondered if I'd really under estimated her, not realizing the sparkle plenty days were gone.

The resolution: We went our separate ways, stupidly and without forethought, giving no concern to our two lovely children. She had to have her guy, and me? I needed *to get the hell out of Dodge*, leaving everybody else to mend their own broken hearts.

Loneliness and the feeling of being unwanted is the most terrible poverty. **Mother Teresa**

Chapter Thirteen

240 Berkley Road
Glenside, Pennsylvania
Friday, September 30, 1983

Jerry Bitterman had taken me to Union Station where I took the Metroliner to Philadelphia. I asked Corrigan for Friday off, telling him I had to get some of my affairs squared away. Also, I needed to gather some clothes and other things I need day to day. Of course, Corrigan had no idea what I really needed to get done. First, getting my family moved from the Seminary to a house she found for rent in nearby Glenside, Pennsylvania.

Bitterman had arranged for somebody to meet me at the gate at Pennsylvania Station in Philadelphia. He told me she would give me a car and that I could just keep it until I got my wheels squared away with the leasing company. A pretty woman named Harriett met me at the gate. I followed her outside to a parking lot just outside the terminal building.

Sitting there was a new 1983 Chrysler New Yorker, with Maryland license plates. It was dark blue with a gray leather interior. I dropped Harriett off at the 555 Building on City Line Avenue, on the Main Line. Atlantic States Surety offices encompassed the entire fifth floor of the building which is perched on a hill off the Schuylkill Expressway. The view of Center City Philadelphia, I imagined, was panoramic from their vantage point.

I met Ellen at 240 Berkely Road in Glenside, Pennsylvania at 6 o'clock p.m. She was sitting in the Ford Maverick, one house down from the rental property, when I pulled up in my new car. When I got out she just sat there. I walked over to the driver's window, where she was sitting. "What's wrong," I ask?.

"Do you want a list?" She replies. "What's wrong, you dare ask?"

Just then a stranger shows his face. "John and Ellen," he queries. He's speaking with a far-eastern-India-accent. "My name is Chauhan. Professor Chauhan," he exclaims. I introduce myself, while Ellen exits the Ford Maverick. "You have two cars," asks Chauhan?

"No?" I quickly reply, "We're dropping that car off for a friend of a friend. The new Chrysler New Yorker is our car." I point at the car.

"That is a fine automobile," Chauhan says, while looking it over.

We rented the house for $850 a month. We signed a year's lease, giving him a check for two months, first and last. Chauhan wished us well as he departed. During his exit he took a few minutes to look over the New Yorker one more time.

"You see, John, I don't know what I would've done if I'd been here alone driving that piece of shit car." She lit up a cigarette, arching a brow.

Smiling, she says, "I did notice how you jumped right in there to defuse the situation. Who is this friend of a friend?"

"You know what I was worried about," I snickered, "that he would ask about the Maryland license plates."

"What," Ellen says, "the car has Maryland license plates. Why? But, then again, who would be looking at license plates except somebody like you." She says, loudly.

We walked around inside the house; picking the places we were going to put things and whose room was going to be whose room. We'd done it so many times before. Then we walk out the front door and sit down on the stoop.

"This is a good home for a year. The case I'm working on isn't going to last that long. I already know the problems and I've been there less than a week." I say, encouragingly.

"If it goes longer, well, we can buy a house in Northern Virginia. You like it there, don't you?" There was a lengthy pause, as Ellen fidgeted while lighting a cigarette.

"John, I love you. I'm so proud of you. And, you're my most memorable character. But ..." she stammered, grabbing my hand securely, "I can't do this anymore."

I squeezed her hand, "Sure you can." I say, assuredly.

"No!" Ellen Said, emphatically. "I want out!"

"What do you mean, you want out?" I ask, fearfully.

"D-I-V-O-R-C-E, like the song spells out," she says, angrily.

I know better than to push her on this right now. "Here are the keys to your new car," I say, handing them to her. "I'll get the check, you just wrote, covered on Monday, with a wire transfer. Where are the kids?" I ask?

"On the way to Hershey, my mother picked them up for the weekend so we could get moved." She said.

"Let's go to Rudi's," I suggest. "Good food and a great piano bar."

"Have you forgotten we're moving tomorrow?" She queries.

"I'll get a U-Haul truck and round up some seminary guys, who always need a few extra bucks."

We were headed toward the car, when she asks, "Whose car is this?"

"Your car," I say.

"You mean the government's car?" She responds.

"No," I said, "it's your car."

"I see," she says. "Until it is not my car anymore, am I right?"

I parked the Ford Maverick in the driveway and we drove less than a mile to Rudi's Restaurant.

We had a steak dinner, while I tried to explain how this case would be my last no matter what. She wasn't interested so I stopped talking.

"John, let's just enjoy the evening." Ellen said, with a smile.

Sitting at the piano bar, I ask her, "Sing *Here's that Rainy Day*, for me."

"That, I can do, John. I can do that!" Ellen says.

Failure is only the opportunity to more intelligently begin again.
Henry Ford

Chapter Fourteen

Union Station
Washington D.C
Monday, October 3, 1983

J erry Bitterman picks me up at Union Station at 7:20 a.m., as
agreed upon. He looks slovenly, like he'd spent a tough weekend drinking. His brows are thick and march above his eyes like a
large caterpillar. His eyes are shit brown, a similar shade to his car,
and it looks like he is wearing a cheap brown toupee. It must have
near killed him to get up so early to meet me at the station, if he
ever went to bed in the first place.

"Did you have a good weekend," he asks, with a slur?

"It looks like you did," I guffawed, while looking him over one
more time. I have been trained to answer every question with a
question of my own. "Is that a Bloody Mary you're sipping on?" I
ask, testily.

He turns his brown-eyed gaze on me, his eyes appraising and
unreadable. "I have to sneak up to the room, clean up and get some
sleep. PGC will be back from Fripp about noon. He's coming back
to see you. Let me go over the list so you can answer his questions."

Jerry Bitterman came to pick me up either to give me advice I
don't want or to tell me something I don't want to hear. His guile-
lessness is the only craze I might admire, because of his need to tell
his version of the truth. Other than those seeds of despair, which
may have already frayed any intimate connections, I assume he is
a quiet, intuitive man; the times he gets out of control is when he
becomes too talkative and trusting because of the drink.

"A.S.S, Associates, the management company owns the operating company. The operating company is kept clean as a whistle,

because it must be dirt free. All the bullshit goes on in the management company, A.S.S, Associates. You'll have to find out about the bullshit on your own. For now, it's just important you know the operating company, Atlantic States Surety, is owned by A.S.S, Associates. PGC owns 51% of the A.S.S, Associates stock, but really a lot more because his players each own shares which he really controls." What a life of lies, I'm thinking, knowing all investors has already lost their money. Jerry pauses, takes another drink of his Bloody Mary as we wait for a green light near the Columbus Circle. When the light turns he pulls around the circle jumping on Massachusetts Avenue.

"The leasing company," Jerry continues. "The C is Charles, the B is me. C&B leasing is a partnership. I guess nothing will have to change." Jerry smiles as he pulls around Scott Circle, onto 16th Street then pulls into the St. Regis' parking lot at16th and K Street Northwest.

"Is there a partnership agreement," I ask.

"Oh, yeah, imagine how it reads and in whose favor." Jerry says, with a negative outlook.

"C&B Leasing leases everything PGC needs. Let's see: say 101 cars from Chrysler to Rolls Royce, computers, furniture, houses, offices, and the futures are airplanes and yachts." Jerry says.

"Who does he lease this stuff to," I ask.

Jerry laughs again as he looks around the parking garage. "The operating company, the management company, but mostly it's for himself. It's how he takes money out of the operating company, funneling it upward through the management company, funneling sideways through C&B, the leasing company – *tax frees* we call it."

"Listen, I have to take a shower and clean up before anybody sees me. You need to get at your desk. The banker you've met. You just have to finish up the deal. You need say only what you know; it's just financing to put more money in the operating company. Fripp Island, is his home away from home. It's a fabulous place located on the South Carolina coast near historic Beaufort and a short distance from Charleston, Hilton Head and Savannah,

Georgia. Legend has it that many pirates plied these waters and that Captain Fripp himself buried treasure here. And, PGC loves pirates, treasures and that kind of shit. He also loves Stephen King novels." Jerry laughs again, mouthing, softly, *Cujo*."

Jerry peruses the garage again, saying, "I have to get out of here before anyone sees me. So," he says, "hundreds of thousands of dollars are being poured into Fripp and Potomac Place. Potomac Place is a mansion in Maryland he calls his personal residence. It's right across the street from Jimmy Hoffa's house. Jimmy's not home much anymore?"

He pours the rest of his Bloody Mary out the window onto the pavement. "Let's go," he says.

I lean on the trunk of the 280Z, watching Jerry Bitterman waddle into the St. Regis. He looked like a man not to be trusted, easily swayed, willing to say or do anything to reach a goal, legal or illegal. It wasn't mentioned, but I knew his banking scam was the only thing that mattered to him. I wondered what he was going to do the rest of his day. Sleep?

To me, life is nothing more than a series of decisions. You make good ones and things go pretty well, barring a calamity over which you have no control, you know, an earthquake or a plane crash. You make bad ones, well, things don't go so well. Jerry was about, or maybe had, made a bad decision, one he'll have to live with. It is up to him to straighten out his life. No one could do it for him, including me. I suppose I was becoming angry again at being lied to all the time. And then I would just even the score, by lying back.

When I entered the office Mary Robinson motioned me toward her. Standing in front of her desk was a short, compact man; no more than five feet, six inches tall, with a chiseled face, his posture erect, and gaze steady. He wore a crisp white shirt and a wrinkle-free tan safari jacket. His salt-and-pepper hair was in a buzz cut, the sides of his head shaved close. He announced that he was career military, Army, retired, his final rank, a Two Star General.

Mary said, "General Jurgens, this is our controller, Jack Oleson."

"General," I say, shaking his hand.

Mary said, "Mr. Charles suggested General George Jurgens come by this morning to ask you a few questions about the company. He's meeting with Mr. Charles at 10:00 a.m."

I couldn't be more unprepared for a Q & A. "Surely," I said, looking at Mary smiling. I check my watch, it is nearing 9 a.m. "Coffee," I ask the General. He nods in the affirmative. "Mary," I say. "Java is coming right up, Mr. Oleson." Mrs. Robinson interrupts.

My meeting with General Jurgens went well. I was honest with him, telling him I was the new controller, giving him some of my prior experience. Did I say honest? Rather I gave him a new line of bullshit that corresponded to my new resume. He told me he had been approached to be on the Board of Directors and a shareholder. He wanted to see the financials to discuss the direction the company was taking.

I told him I had a meeting with Mr. Charles at noon and if he directed me to send him the financials I would be happy to do so. Furthermore I'd be happy to meet with him again for analysis. The hour passed quickly as we got to know each other. I was certainly impressed with him and hoped he was with me. It was so good to meet with somebody with character, rather than the lowlifes I'd seen so far.

With all the fanfare again, save the Marine Band striking up *Ruffles and Flourishes*, Paul Gordon Charles entered the doors of Atlantic States Surety at exactly 9:55 a.m. I knew what the commotion going on was all about, but I didn't want the General to see the entourage entering with PGC in the middle. So I handed him the most recent Atlantic States Surety newsletter. As he skimmed through it the lobby cleared.

Ten minutes later Mary was rapping on my door advising General Jurgens Mr. Charles is available to see him. We shake hands, with him saying, "I hope to see you soon, Mr. Oleson."

"It's been my pleasure," I say, looking over his back shoulder directly into Mary Robinson eyes. She winks, knowing full well what an awkward position she'd put me in.

Men freely believe that which they desire. **Julius Caesar**

What Is Past Is Prologue

Syracuse Hancock International Airport
Syracuse, New York
Friday, October 3, 1969

The flight had been a scheduled milk run. Minneapolis to Rochester, Minnesota; Rochester to Madison, Wisconsin; Madison to Milwaukee, Wisconsin; Milwaukee to Detroit, Michigan; Detroit to Buffalo, New York; Buffalo to Rochester, New York; Rochester to Syracuse, New York. The lift off from Minneapolis was at noon. Arrival time in Syracuse was estimated at six o'clock Eastern Standard Time.

While making our approach into Milwaukee the plane kept going down, down, down into the cloud cover. Suddenly it pulled up, seemingly reaching a perpendicular status and shot above the cloud cover. All the stuff from the overhead luggage racks was flying all over the cabin. When the plane straightened out and blue skies were glowing, the pilot spoke softly, "The visibility in Milwaukee is near zero. We are returning to Madison where continuing Milwaukee passengers may board buses for Milwaukee. For the rest of the passengers, continuing eastward, remain seated. We will fly directly to Detroit, Michigan as soon as we get clearance in Madison. We are sorry for the inconvenience."

When the Eastern Airlines *whisper jet* finally landed in Syracuse, New York, everybody departing was thoroughly pissed off. I put on my sport jacket and meandered down the steps of the plane. I looked around but didn't see anybody I knew, until I got inside the terminal.

"Johnny," I hear a voice from my right side. There she is even more beautiful than she was ten years ago. She was all smiles as I walk her way. "Better late than never," I said, shrugging my shoulders.

"I've been here since 5 o'clock mister," Ellen says. "You better take me to dinner, sir," she demands, before putting her arms around me. We give each other a long kiss, much better than the one we sneaked in the tunnel of love boat, in 1959, at Hershey Park.

"God," she says, Do you see that fellow there? I thought he might be you." The man probably is our age, but he's completely bald and overweight. "Thank God," she says. "I've never been on a blind date, but I've heard some stories."

We hold hands for a moment. I am a little nervous and I suppose she is too. Ten years is a lifetime when you're so young. What did we know about each other, really? We'd met when were just kids, in high school, full of dreams, hopes and positive expectations. And, we'd seen each other only for four days. However, we wrote many newsy letters during those high school days, until I married somebody else during second semester of my sophomore year in college. I always thought about her though, wondering how she was doing.

I was surprised how small the airport was in Syracuse. I thought everything was big on the East Coast. Although Ellen told me this was Upstate New York, not the East Coast, but I thought it seemed very east. I had a whole new language to learn, and I didn't know it yet. We picked up my bags and headed to the parking lot. When we got to her car, a 1968 red Volkswagen *Bug*, she opened the front end of the vehicle, which was the trunk, and pointed. I threw my two bags into the sachet, while Ellen handed me her keys, asking, "Do you want to drive."

"As long as you navigate," I reply. "I have no idea where we are or where we are going." I had another problem I didn't mention. I didn't see well at night without my corrective lenses, but I was too vain to say anything about it. Instead, I left my prescription sunglasses on telling Ellen I had trouble with the glare from other headlights. She didn't question me any further as I could see just fine.

Just before we got on the New York Thruway Ellen suggested we stop at a place just ahead and have a drink. I didn't drink much, but I said "sure" not knowing where she lived or what she had planned. It was a great bar named *Elmer's Tune*, with live music and we were seated in the middle of the room where we had a good look at the entertainment. When the waitress came Ellen ordered a gin and tonic, without hesitation. I hesitated, then ordered a Budweiser. Then she really surprised me, she lit up a Winston cigarette and took a long drag, blowing a ring of smoke in the air. I didn't smoke either.

"So, Johnny," she asks, "What's your nanny look like?" Her question bowled me over so much all I could do was grin. "Oh, she looks a little like Brigitte Bardot. Maybe a little bit more stacked." Ellen sat back in her chair, crossed her legs, sipped her drink and said, "Is that right?"

Ellen lit up another cigarette, saying, "She's better looking than Brigitte Bardot, huh? She seemed a little nervous when I talked to her on the phone today, wondering if you we're going to show up?" I wondered what Ellen was up to, if she was asking questions to trip me up, or just making conversation. Or, was she fucking with me?

"She assured me you were on the way and that you were real excited to see me. But she sounded really jumpy." Ellen said, taking another puff off her cigarette and slugging back another drink.

"Maybe, I better call home to make sure there is no problem with the kids." I respond with an air of concern in my voice, knowing full well Beth wasn't going to be home today.

Ellen expressed amusement at my quick responses. "You passed," she chuckled. "I didn't talk with your nanny today. I called but nobody answered. Then I checked with Eastern Airlines and they said your Northwest flight to Milwaukee was sent back to Madison because of fog. They tracked you to Detroit, saying you were put on an Eastern flight to Syracuse. Here you are sitting in Syracuse getting tipsy with me."

I should have of told her the whole story right then and there, but I didn't. We talked about current events, the Vietnam War,

Charles Manson's murders, Woodstock, and Hurricane Camille. We updated each other about the past ten years, staying away from talk about our spouses. Yes, she and I were both married. She was unhappily married and I was still taken aback from the happenings of the last three months.

"Let's go," she said. It is ten o'clock and we were just finishing our third drink. The band is playing Stevie Wonder's version of *For Once in My Life*. I asked her to dance. I say, while dancing, "October 3rd will be our first date and this is our song."

"Okay," she said, bringing her head next to my shoulder as the song ended. As we walk out of the bar, hand in hand, she says, "Hey, did I tell I was at the Woodstock Festival?"

Nothing happens that is meaningless. **Pat Conroy**

Chapter Fifteen

Union Station
Washington, D.C.
Monday, October 3, 1983

They say behind every great fortune there is a crime. It had been a stressful weekend at home with Ellen telling me she wanted a divorce. Then, it was the move. I could only find one seminarian around to help and he was filled with questions. *Why? Why? Why? Are you quitting the seminary? Why? Why? Why?*

I finally gave him fifty dollars to help me move and fifty dollars to keep his mouth shut. It worked and we were able to get it all done. My mind now was totally preoccupied with Ellen, and her farewell message, *we need to talk*, and worried about what was going on in front of me. *We need to talk* are the scariest lexis in the English language.

What does General George Jurgens want from this lot? Whose he pissed off at? Things aren't always the way they appear from the outside. There's usually more to the story. Life can only be understood backwards, but it must be lived forward. I think General Jurgens has his own motive, or, is he one of us? I am thinking, when my thoughts are interrupted by Joe Neverson.

"Do you always start a job, and then go on vacation," he says with a raised voice.

"Bitterman told me not to pay any claims until I talk with PGC. I'm meeting him at noon today. Do you want to go over any details, particularly?" I ask, defensively.

"No, we have time now. They filed a complaint with the insurance commission. I didn't want to do it that way, but it buys a lot of time. It just makes me look like a jerk, and it sets me up to take the blame, when it all comes down." Joe Neverson says, looking disgusted and dejected.

I motioned Joe to come into my office. I sat down behind my desk and Joe sat directly across from me. "What's going on here? You're not shallow, and I sense you have courage. Also from what I have gathered you can be very ruthless and predatory. Why are you here?"

Joe Neverson sat quietly, asking me, "Why are you here?"

There it was a question to answer a question. Joe had been a young lawyer working his way up in a Washington firm, where he had self-respect. What had turned him and the apparent rudeness say of PGC, to defend the crimes of this organization? He was angry. He was so very angry. "What did he promise you?"

"What did he promise you, Jack Oleson? Let me see, he's looking for a few people with a special sense of commitment. He said, huh, you are circumspect and, you must agree to work for him, will support him while you are with him. In other words you will do what you're told and keep your mouth shut. Huh?" He smirks at me. "Did I cover the essence of it?"

"He didn't say any of those things to me." I reply, seriously.

"He will at your noon meeting today. Let me ask you something, Jack. Have you had any problems in your past? You know a bankruptcy, divorce, infidelities or whatever?" A rambunctious Joe Neverson asks.

"Nothing significant," I say. "Why?"

"Jack, everyone who works here are capable and willing people. We're here because we need money. Money PGC is quite willing to pay for a price, turning all into a bunch of *gofers*. Of course he's not really paying us with his money, we get the money that we arrange for him to steal from the officers, directors and the general public. If you want a new house, car, educations for your children he'll have you make those arrangements. If later ever comes, he will say you stole the money and he didn't know anything about it. Albeit, Jerry Bitterman."

There was a knock at my door. Joe reaches over and opens it. Mrs. Robinson was standing there, saying and nodding in Joe's direction, "Hello, Mr. Neverson." Joe gets up and smiles at her. "It's PGC time for our new controller, Mary?"

"Exactly," she says, grinning at Neverson.

"See you at five o'clock in the Library at St. Regis," Joe calls back.

"Did he mean you or me, Mary?" I ask.

"Don't start any rumors by trying to be cute, Mr. Oleson. Here's your pad and pen" she says, handing me the two work instruments.

"Where did you get that stuff, Mrs. Robinson?" I ask, in astonishment.

"Where men put everything," she says. "You slung it over in the corner, on the floor!" She points slyly. I say, "I'm going to take you to dinner."

"Hmm," she mouths. "I'll remember you invited me to dinner, Jack. Will you?"

She giggles as she motions me to follow her to the inner sanctum.

When we approach, Boyer, Jurgens, Corrigan and Paul Gordon Charles are assembled in Charlotte's reception suite, sipping drinks and munching on chips and nuts.

"Welcome Jack," announces Mr. Charles, enthusiastically.

He always impresses everyone with his self-assurance, his reserve and calm. He works with a self-conscious, artificial briskness. He has the pose of an official investigator not that of a first class criminal.

"Jack, dig in!" encourages Mr. Charles, while Charlotte hands me a Jack Daniels with a charge.

"Jack," she says, running a wet middle finger across the palm of my right hand.

"Jack," says PGC, "I understand you and General Jurgens visited. He told me you explained the company's mission well and was impressed with your grasp of Atlantic States' business in a very unpresumptuous period of time."

My god, I'm thinking, who is this General Jurgens? He must be one of us? What I'd discussed with him was what I didn't know and I had a grasp of nothing. As I smiled at the General, I noted the man's defined hardnosed impatience and unforgiving. Who is this guy? I thought again, wondering why he was here and for what reason.

Suddenly another man entered Boyer's office. He was reed thin and not tall, wore a tweed jacket with leather elbow patches, a pink button-down shirt, knit tie and wingtip shoes. He appeared to be a gentleman on the liberal side.

"Ted," greeted Paul Gordon Charles, enthusiastically. "Gentleman and ladies, of course, I present Theodore Rex Masters, our new General Counsel."

Ted moseyed around shaking everyone's hand not remembering anybody's name, I'm sure. As he moved away from me I studied Theodore Rex Masters. There was something compelling about his calm and seeming gentleness. Actually, he was probably about ready to go insane and this group will push him over the edge. He seemed intelligent as he talked about his background.

Then, in my opinion, Theodore Rex crossed the line when he said, drinking his second scotch on the rocks, "The government's run by a bunch of morons who only care whether they get reelected, big money from lobbyists buying their votes, etceteras, etceteras."

"Charlotte, get Ted another drink." PGC bellowed, earnestly, looking directly at Master's eyes. "They are morons, Ted. They're there to be taken advantage of."

General Jurgens looked a little pissed off. I supposed he was a difficult man by any standard, crusty, cranky and opinionated, incapable of accepting any views that didn't mesh with his true my-way-or-the-highway personality.

Mr. Charles, sensing tension, speaks up. "Ted is a good man who has been in a lousy job. He was an Assistant General Counsel for the Virginia Insurance Commission in Richmond, Virginia, before joining us. Before that he saw too much of the underbelly of society, responding to those who commit grisly murders and brutal rapes, young punks killing one another over a marijuana cigarette, or a bag of pills, or a pair of sneakers as a Public Defender.

"Ted is a Vietnam veteran, General!"

"Hey Ted," General Jurgens reacts with a good-buddy routine. How long was your tour?"

Theodore Rex Masters seemed sensitive, as the smile he flashed was as white as the monogrammed shirt he wore. "My tour, sir was one day. The first day on patrol I was shot in the ass and they sent me home."

"I see," said the General. Charlotte started to giggle and the rest of us were about to burst out in laughter. At least, I was. Meanwhile the General was looking pretty grim. He didn't respond verbally, although anything he might say would be negated by the knowing expression on his deeply tanned face.

"That's what we like about Ted," Corrigan chimes in. "He speaks the unmitigated truth. He'll be a great General Counsel."

I noticed Charlotte staring at me, waiting, I suppose, for me to put in my two cents. I had nothing to add as Corrigan had stirred the pot turning the conversation to underwriting. After a few minutes or so I sensed Mr. Charles growing tired of the banter and motioned to Charlotte.

"Freshen everybody's drinks and move us to the long oval table in my office."

SG (Sarah Gonzales), the beautiful, young, brown-skinned woman I'd seen playing switch-a-rooney with Boyer, that first day, was helping Charlotte set up the table in Gordon's office. This was my first good look at SG. She had a slender figure and full breasts, and I like the way her lip curled into a smile while she was busying herself with work she really didn't enjoy. Her eyes, when she looked directly at me, were penetrating. Scary! Like a pleasant façade changing to stone.

When we were seated, with fresh drinks, Paul Gordon Charles called the meeting to order, by having each of us introduce ourselves. After which, the real purpose of the meeting was put on the table.

"Gentleman, we are about to put ten million dollars into the company. The purpose is to expand into ten more states which, of course requires more reserves. The money will be borrowed from a new bank in Baltimore, which Jack will be making final negotiations within the next ten days. How are the negotiations going, Jack?" Mr. Charles asks, looking at me.

I feel like somebody threw a brick at me, with the question. Now all eyes were looking at me. "Everything is on schedule," I say.

"Good, Jack," PGC jumps in.

"Jack," the General says, "Tell us about this loan. How does it work?"

I look at Mr. Charles, wondering if he wants me to speculate. He signals with his right hand to continue. I notice the new general counsel opening his leather note book and turning his Mont Blanc to the ready-to-scroll position.

"The management company is borrowing the money from American State Bank of Maryland. The management company will guarantee the loan as will the shareholders, jointly and severally. The money will flow from the management company downstream to the operating company. The reserves have to be maintained in the operating company." I say and paused, looking around the table for further questions.

You could have heard a pin drop in the room. General Jurgens had a serious look on his face, giving the impression of being a stoic Don Rickles. I saw Theodore Rex studying me, like I'd left a major portion of my speech unsaid. The meeting went on for another hour. I wasn't asked any more questions. I just listened, but learned nothing new. My ears perked up some when PGC got on Corrigan's ass about the casualty insurance division. Gordon told Corrigan that Larry Leopold better start producing. It made me think about Leopold's assistant, Sandy. She has great credentials, but not much to work with in Leopold. I'm thinking about this when PGC concludes the meeting, asking me to stay.

He motions me to sit in a chair in front of his desk. He says, "I have my sources and the word is you've jumped right into the fire and are getting involved. Good," he affirms. He asks me about everything he told me to investigate. I gave him the Bitterman answers of which he made no comment. I'd already picked up from him and others he only dwells on bad news. Good news was always expected.

We discussed C&B Leasing last. He explained pretty much what Jerry did except for the fact he received any benefit from the partnership. He told me about Charley somebody in the New Orleans office wanted a Cadillac Eldorado. "Get 'em one!" he said. "And," he continued "pick wheels out for yourself and one for your wife. Those New Yorkers are nice, but if you want a Corvette, or something like it, go ahead."

"Fripp Island," he said. "The day we close the loan I want you to join me at Fripp to spend the weekend going over the budget for 1984. Your wife is welcome to join us, if she has the time available."

"One more thing, Jack, I think Masters might be a plant. I want you to tell me whether he is or isn't within ten days. I have a real need for a General Counsel, and I can't give him things to do until I know he's not a spy. Good?"

I nod and he spins his chair around to load his tape deck. I say, "Good Day," and walk out of his office closing the door behind me.

Charlotte Boyer is filing her nails as I enter her area. Everything is cleaned up, pristine and not an item on her desk. I ask what time it is. "You haven't received your Rolex, yet? I've been hearing glowing reports about you."

I smiled, tapping my left wrist. "It's 2:37 p.m, Mr. Oleson."

"Thank you Ms. Boyer." I say with a smirk on my face.

"See you tonight, Jack."

I shrug my shoulders and walk down the long corridor. I'm thinking this whole place is crazy. My head is spinning. I've got so many damn assignments I don't know where to begin. I haven't even checked in with the accounting department. I'm hoping it really does run itself. I stop at Mary Robinson's desk to see if she has any messages for me.

"Charley Rivers, he called from the New Orleans office. He wants to know when his new Cadillac Eldorado will be ready to pick up." She hands me the telephone message, saying with a smile. "You better get on it." I cocked an eyebrow, saying "I'll get right on it."

"Sure you will," Mary says, softly, "Sure you will."

As I approach my door I wonder why it is closed. I know I wouldn't have closed it, because I hate closed doors. I turn the knob and push the door open. Charlotte Boyer is sitting at my desk talking on the telephone. I sit down in one of the chairs in front of my desk. She hangs up the phone a moment later. "Hi?" she says.

I ask, with a serious look on my face, "What's going on?"

"I have to go, Jack. See you tonight." She stands up and walks out, leaving a pair of pink panties on my chair. Just as I pick them up, Ted Masters arrived. I slip the panties in my middle drawer, while he just stands there watching.

"Yes, Ted," I say, with an irritated tone.

"Jack," he says, "I would like to sit down with you to go over the corporate structure."

"I don't know the complete picture. But I'll give you what I have, and hopefully together we can make sense out of everything. How about tomorrow, say 10 a.m." I reply.

Ted smiles, "Sounds like a plan. Oh, don't forget about those panties in your middle drawer."

Where am I, I'm thinking as I watch Theodore Rex Masters walk away from my office. The whole thing seems like a comedy, a complete farce. I sit down at my desk to make up a list of things to do. Where's my damn leather notebook and Mont Blanc pen. I open my middle drawer and the only thing there are those pink panties. I open my right hand top drawer, finding my notebook and pen. I stick the panties in between my notebook covers and head for Charlotte's office. When I arrive SG is sitting at Charlotte's desk.

"May I help you Mr. Oleson?" She asks curling her lip.

I shake my head, negatively, smile and leave. When I get to the front door I exit and walk into the men's room. I go into a stall and hang the pink panties on a hook in the back of the door. Fortunately, the bathroom is empty when I enter. I wash my hands and leave in a hurry. I amble toward Mary's desk. I give her a quick wave and she puts up a stop sign with her right hand.

"Jack," she whispers "Charlotte Boyer is in your office."

I broke out in laughter and thanked her. I re-routed myself to the accounting department to see what was going on there. The hell with Charlotte Boyer, reminding myself I'm a special agent with the FBI. Even more interesting, now I'm a double agent, investigating Theodore Rex Masters as a mole, for my first subject, Paul Gordon Charles.

When I entered the accounting department everybody is busy doing their jobs. I wonder what they all think. I haven't seen any of them since I was first introduced by Bitterman on day one. They must think I'm some kind of boss.

McKenzie Gillen must have noticed my entrance because she came out of her office to greet me.

"Mr. Oleson," she greets me with a friendly voice and kindly smile. "We've been wondering when we were going to see you again."

"I apologize, but Bitterman and Mr. Charles have been keeping me very busy."

"I know," she acknowledges. "We hardly ever saw Jerry. C&B Leasing took up most of his time."

"McKenzie," I ask, "I'd like to get the cash balances, projected receipts and the general ledger as of the end of September as soon as possible." I'm thinking tomorrow.

McKenzie opens a file folder she is carrying under her left arm. She extends the file in my direction with her right hand saying, "Here are the daily cash balances and the projected monthly receipts for October, November and December." She grins, seemingly looking for approval.

I open the folder to see neatly hand written sheets with the numbers by location and totaled. "Thank you very much," I say. "And the general ledger," I ask, expecting her to simply run a copy. Instead, McKenzie Gillen looks embarrassed.

"We've been trying to set that up but no one is quite sure where to begin, including Jerry. We're hoping you will help us get it done?"

As she talks I'm not surprised there is no general ledger. I'm sure Jerry Bitterman knows nothing about a general ledger. If he did I'm not sure he wanted any such permanent record of the transactions, which would leave an audit trail.

I ask, "How does Jerry prepare the monthly Treasure's Report?"

McKenzie Gillen looks like she is going to cry. "Mr. Oleson, let's go into my office."

As we approach I say hello to Nancy Sullivan. She smiles while McKenzie points toward her open office door. I enter, sitting down in front of her desk. As I wait I figure her back wall is adjacent to the right side wall of my office.

When she sits behind her desk I ask, "Looks like we're closer neighbors than I thought. Isn't my office right next to your back wall? I query.

"Yes," she says.

"Are the walls paper thin?" I ask.

"No," she adds. "Not unless somebody is shouting." She replies.

"So," I say. "Don't say anything dirty, huh?"

"Yes, Jack, don't say anything dirty." She guffaws.

"The Treasurer's report," I ask. "How is it prepared?"

"I prepare the Treasure's report, Mr. Oleson. I have the premiums written and collected. I keep the cash disbursement journal and pick out the appropriate expenses and post them to the report. I accumulated the year-to-date numbers and give it to Jerry. And, he makes his adjustments, which I never see."

There was a pause as I watched McKenzie collect her thoughts. Then, I say, "Okay, there is no general ledger. Rather it's simply your compilation of raw data in Treasurer's report form? I see. Is your report the one Jerry presents to the Board of Directors?" I ask.

"No, it's his report after his adjustments. I never see his report." She says.

"What happens to Jerry's reports?" I ask, quizzically.

"They're destroyed," she says, angrily. "They are picked up after the meeting and burned."

"Who collects the statements? Burned? Where are they burned, in what?"

"Charlotte," she says. "SG gathers them and Charlotte Boyer burns them in the incinerator at the Watergate." McKenzie says as she screws up her nose.

"Why the Watergate, you mean Nixon's Watergate?" I say to confirm.

"Yes, Nixon's Watergate. She lives there, you know. So do all his other Ex's." McKenzie says.

"I'm always finding Charlotte going in and out of my office. Do you know what she is doing?"

McKenzie chuckles, saying, "She's probably bugging it."

Changing the subject, I say "We'll start working on that general ledger next week. Thank you."

As I walk out of the Accounting Department I check my watch. It is nearing five o'clock and I want to meet Joe Neverson at St. Regis.

When I arrive at the St. Regis I spot Bitterman and Neverson at the Library Lounge bar. They look like secretive people set to drink all night, while talking in hushed voices.

"Jerry—Joe," I greet them. Neverson pats the bar stool between him and Bitterman.

"Still drinking I see," needling Jerry.

He retorts, "I slept most of the day, stopped by the office to find you, but was told you were in a meeting so I went to Claims to visit with Joe. How was your day, Jack?"

"That's a loaded question, Jerry." I respond with an attitude. "First, I meet this Major General, Retired Army. He wants me to explain the mission of the company. Then, I meet this lawyer who had a one day tour in Vietnam because he was shot in the ass. The General's name is George Jurgens and the lawyer is Theodore Rex Masters. He's our new General Counsel."

Neverson takes a swig of scotch, smiling. "I regurgitate what you told me, Jerry, about all the companies and their purposes, including Fripp Island, but not Potomac Place."

I take a break to taste my Jack Daniels, which tastes like I swallowed a stone. "Then, I find Charlotte Boyer in my office talking on my telephone. She leaves rather abruptly, leaving a pair of pink panties on my swivel chair." There was no reaction from Jerry or Joe.

"While I'm examining the panties the new General Counsel arrives to set up an appointment with me. While I'm stuffing the panties in my middle drawer, setting a time with him tomorrow, he cautions me about not leaving the pink panties in my drawer."

"Bring us doubles," Joe Neverson tells the bartender. "Is there more, Jack" Joe queries, lighting a Marlboro.

"Yeah," I say. "I'm pissed and I fish the panties out of the middle drawer and put them between my notebook covers and walk directly to Boyer's office. Of course, there, I find SG at a cluttered desk working her pussy off. I nod and she acknowledges knowing full well I was looking for Boyer. I do an about face and charge back up the hall, exiting at the men's room. I hang Boyer's underwear on a hook on the back door of one of the stalls."

"After leaving the bathroom I walk through the reception area toward Mrs. Robinson's desk. She puts up a stop sign to tell me Ms. Boyer is in my office. I had a good laugh with Mary Robinson and went into Accounting. McKenzie tells me Boyer is probably bugging my office."

Jerry and Joe had listened to me rant and rave for a half an hour, interrupting me only to egg me on. Neverson usually asked specific questions, delivering them with the sharpness of a surgical knife.

"It's working, Jack."

"What's working Joe?"

"They're starting to get to you!" He laughs, smugly.

"Yeah," says Bitterman.

We talk no more business. We were all tired and left the bar at 8 p.m. Bitterman to wherever his destination, Joe and I head to the company suite. En route somebody shouts out "Joe!"

The caller was a strong, beefy man, tall and solidly built, with brown hair tinged with red and just the right touch of gray at the temples. Everything about him was oversized; I supposed Joe, who was now on the receiving end of his handshake, was getting the crusher form the size of his enormous paws. He motions for Joe to sit down as I meander to the elevator.

When I arrive at the room door I just stand there, I feel an eerie presence coming from the inside. My credentials, holster and pistol are under the seat of my so-called company car wrapped in a towel under the passenger's side back in Pennsylvania. The only thing in the apartment is my empty briefcase and a few clothes. I shrug and put the key in the keyhole, turn it, and push the door open slowly.

As I close the door a voice came from the kitchen: "Hi Jack." Her voice startles me as I reach for my gun, which isn't there. Now she is standing in front of me with her drink, dressed like she was ready to go to the Kennedy Center for a show.

"Charlotte, what are you doing here?"

She smiles, puts her drink down on the table and lights one up. "Bugging the place," she says, with a sardonic laugh before handing me a drink. She is wearing a tight black skirt, showing lots of leg, and a ruffled white blouse. She takes her drink and sits down on a sofa, crossing her legs so the skirt rides up high all the way to her bush.

"I left my panties in your office, Jack. Did you find them?" She asks slyly, exposing that bush. With this contrive, the room's quiescence was deafening.

Finally, I say, "What's going on Charlotte? Everywhere I go, you show up!"

She smiles, focusing the dark pupils of her eyes on mine. I look away from her penetrating eyes while she hikes her skirt above her waist. She starts undoing the buttons of her blouse, spreading her arms upward and out.

I stare at her, noticing her beauty and perfect figure, when she asks with that sardonic grin again, "Do you want to do the mess around, Jack?"

Great people are not affected by each puff of wind that blows ill. Like great ships, they sail serenely on, in a calm sea or a great tempest. **George Washington**

Chapter Sixteen

Schuylkill Expressway
Philadelphia, Pennsylvania
Friday, October 7, 1983

In the distance I can see the Good Year Blimp hovering over Veterans Stadium in South Philadelphia. It's the third game of the National League Championship Series, best three out of five.

I have the game on the radio (WCAU 1210). It is the top of the fifth inning and the Phillies are leading, 4-2. The Philadelphia Phillies won game 1 and the Los Angeles Dodgers won game 2. This is the pivotal game of the series for the rights to play in the 1983 World Series.

I was excited about spending a weekend with my family and watching the Phillies earn their way into the World Series. Ellen didn't seem as enthusiastic about my coming home for the weekend. It was like she had other plans, which left me feeling empty. She told me she had not changed her mind, about wanting a divorce, saying, "You've always been a wonderful provider for me and our three children. It's just me, John, I can't live with all the *helter skelter*. For you, Johnny, the glass is always half-full, and that's a good thing. For me it's the other way, it's always half empty. I'm sorry." It had been a very depressing phone call for me.

As I drove down Allen's Lane past the seminary I became anxious about getting home. There was so much going on that I was not a part of anymore. My oldest son was playing in a football game Saturday morning, and, I was looking forward to watching his game. Ellen told me I should take the other boys with me as she had things to do. In fact I felt I had been dictated to during our telephone conversation. I had always been a man who took long pauses before responding to comments or questions, a calculated indication of my nature. This was different being it was simply an impotency of my inability to act while getting kicked in the gut.

When I pulled up into our driveway the Ford Maverick was gone. The 1983 Chrysler New Yorker was parked in the center of the parking space, instead. It was quiet, nobody seemed to be around. When you get to know people, you can size them up in seconds. Trust me; Ellen knew dissent would be both futile and inflammatory in dealing with me. I check the car door of the Chrysler New Yorker. It is open. Ellen is not very good about locking doors of any kind. I lay across the front seat of the car and reach under the passenger's seat. I feel around and fish out my service revolver and credentials. I feel a big sigh of relief.

My whole life these days is perverted. I'm living a life of lies, but at what price now I'm thinking as my son Dan yells "Daddy. Is that our car?"

"Do you like it, Danny?" I say, walking over to show him the new Cadillac Eldorado I'd bought for Charley Rivers. I didn't tell my son that or that Charley Rivers was no longer with the company. Rumor had it that Matthew Ferrone took Charley out of the picture because he'd pocketed an exorbitant premium he'd collected and promised to the company.

"Keep the car," Matt had told me. "You won't see Charley no more."

"The show must go on, huh?" said Ellen from the top stair of our stoop. She walks down the steps with a smile on her face.

"Hi, Johnny," she says, putting her arms around me. "Don't embarrass the Bureau, right." She adds. It was J. Edgar Hoover's mantra, and God help any agent who violated it. We had laughed about his proclamation, in many of our ugly situations.

"Never," I agree. "Do you want to take a ride in my new Cadillac convertible, sexy lady?"

Her laugh was dismissive, saying "Honorable men don't always see the reality of things."

"Maybe," I semi-protest. "Let's drive Danny around the block."

"He won't layoff until we do," Ellen agrees.

"Taking me to dinner, tonight, honey? I have a babysitter." Ellen teased, with a kiss on my lips.

"I'd love to take my wife to dinner, Ellen." I reply.

I took Danny for a spin and, at his request, to the, 7-11 store so hopefully he might see a friend or two to see him exit the Eldorado. It is wonderful to see the perpetual smile on my son's face.

Afterwards Ellen fixed the boys supper and when the babysitter arrived we went to Rudi's Restaurant, which was less than a mile away. Rudi's is our favorite place because of the piano bar and the regular crowd. We went to the bar first, "Tell me Johnny, what's going on down there amongst the rumormongers and the powerful?"

"The fat-cats, you mean," I replied. "They're all crazy! I mean really crazy, *E*. Ellen barely reaches five-feet-tall, and I started calling her the *Big E*, after Elvin Hayes the 7-foot basketball player. Why, I don't know. I guess she always stood that tall in my eyes. Meanwhile the bartender has poured shimmering red wine into our glasses, and we touch rims.

Milt, the piano player, who I estimate is in his mid-eighties, starts playing *Smoke Gets in Your Eyes*. Milt, the piano man, smiles at Ellen and me while tickling the keys so gracefully. We nod in acknowledgement thinking it is an appropriate song selection for us.

The owner is Italian, a middle-aged man, his face fleshy, his mouth weak. I suspect he was a tough old bird, with leathery skin, a broad chest and muscled arms. He patrols his restaurant, while his overweight wife works her ass off cooking food and waiting tables.

"Can you believe that pompous ass," Ellen says.

"Are you talking about Rudi?" I query, with a laugh. "It seems like he has it all under control. He collects the money and has all the fun, showing everybody his tricks. His wife does all the work! What's wrong with that, *E*?"

"Try it," Ellen replies, while lighting up a Winston. "He's the kind of man who mows his lawn and finds a car." She guffaws, giving me that not-interested-but-trying-to-fake-it laugh I know so well.

It's the way our nights out usually start, small observations and quips about what we see. We are people watchers. The second glass of wine did a better job of allowing our feelings to surface and tongues to loosen before dinner.

"Okay, Sletten," she says. "Enough smiles and pleasantries, what's going on?"

"They're nothing more than a bunch of lowlife punks living high off the hog. You know, living a hypocritical life!" I report to Ellen, being careful not to say too much.

"Snafu, then, huh?" she says, after taking a major swig off her wine.

"Yep," I say. "Situation normal, all fucked up!"

"How long," she asks, with a sour expression on her face. Again she knew dissent would be futile and inflammatory. I took a long pause before responding, getting a break when the waiter brought us another glass of wine, to her question, a calculated indicator of a thoughtful nature.

"E, this will be my biggest case and hopefully, it will be my last. I just know there is more than meets the eye here, every day I learn something new. Yet, it's just too easy. I could nail the target with so many offenses right now it would put him away for years. Again, I sense there is more going on. I just can't figure out what they want me to do, it's day by day." I say with concern in my voice. "This bunch is fucking crazy!"

Ellen said nothing, which was typical when she didn't understand my business. Finally she said, "The Grand Finale, huh. You've spent enough time on the streets, kid, and you get to know people, can size *em up* in ten seconds. Don't tell me you don't know. You're scaring me!"

"You cannot believe the cast of characters I've met already, Ellen. Some of them seem like extraterrestrial aliens. They come and go, appear and disappear. Also, he has his staff stacked with high ranking military men." I reply, laughing.

Her laugh has become mocking, she is the one who always knows how to make the most out of a bad situation. "I should have never had that last glass of wine, Johnny. Get me a gin and tonic, please."

Although the prohibition era was long gone, Rudi ran his place as if it was a speakeasy, palling around with customers, doing favors, slapping backs and making everyone feel like a high roller in a posh casino. It was Glenside's answer to *Toots Shor*. The décor was an electric mix of old Philly, huge prints of Phillies baseball stars, sharing the walls with black-and-white photos of nearby towns and saloons.

Rudi was working the crowd now, wearing an expensive custom double-breasted suit that slenderized his body. He looked like a youngster donning Dad's suit..

"John and Ellen," he greeted. "Are you singing for us tonight?" He drops off a plate of salmon with a dollop of horseradish sauce on crackers, and hummus on toast points.

Ellen's eyebrows go up, when a slightly obese man wearing a navy double-breasted blazer, gray slacks with a razor crease, a pale blue shirt and a solid burgundy tie sits down next to her. His smile seems perpetual.

I'm talking to Pete, one of the wisecracking bartenders, when Ellen squeezes my hand.

"Are you okay," I ask, in a whisper. I'm looking around, thinking she hasn't been this affectionate to me in some time. Lately she's been talking divorce. It's been confusing?

She looks at me smiling, saying, "Don't ever leave me. I feel so safe when I'm with you, Johnny."

"So I'm good for something, huh? I say suggesting, "Let's have dinner," while motioning to Rudi.

"Yes," Ellen replies. "Dinner sounds perfect," she says as I watch the guy next to her watching her every move.

While I paid the bar tab, I began to study the character who'd been sitting next to my wife. I wanted to slap the smile off his face. I threw down a twenty and a ten and backed away from the bar. When I turned toward the dining area Rudi was already seating

Ellen. A few seconds later, after I joined my wife, I positioned my-self in the chair which had a direct view of the stranger at the bar. I had a suspicion about the fellow, but dismissed it as implausible.

I think and think for months and years. Ninety-nine times, the conclusion is false. The hundredth time I am right. **Albert Einstein**

What Is Past Is Prologue

Allentown State Hospital
1600 Hanover Avenue
Allentown, Pennsylvania
Monday, May 4, 1981

I t was difficult leaving my family in Gettysburg this morning. We are still living in our basement apartment, near the seminary, but at the end of the month we'll be moving on campus to better our digs. I am determined to be home each weekend to help Ellen with the boys. I just hoped the old black and white Maverick is up to the 200 mile jaunt each week. Oh well, I'm thinking, we have been living day to day since we began this theological contrive.

The transition has been difficult, leaving our home in Virginia Beach, Virginia in August, 1980. When I told my *FBI handler* in May, already a year ago now, that I could start wrapping my current case up in Portsmouth, Virginia he asked me for the lead time. When I told him a month to six weeks, he said, "We've got to get you out of there!" Adding, "We need to send you somewhere really safe. Think about it, John."

I had become intrigued with studying religion during my college days. Concordia is a Lutheran college and religion is a required subject all four years. Additionally, I had taken religion very seriously while growing up. Although I do not attend church regularly now, the intrigue is still there. Also, since I'd been with the FBI, I feel everything I am doing is totally against my religion. If nothing else, perhaps a little redemption would help.

"I think I'm going to apply to the Lutheran Seminary." I told Ellen. She was busy with the kids and wasn't paying much attention to me. "Don't you think I'd be a great parish pastor?"

She laughed. "Right," she said. "Don't you have something better to do than think of shit like this; parish pastor. Are you going to wear your gun to the altar?"

Nevertheless I filled out the paperwork, even though I was discouraged by everyone not to bother to apply. Religion, nobody goes to church anymore unless it's a *born again* scenario. I proceeded with the process anyway. Of course acquaintances and friends didn't know my situation; that, soon I had *to get the hell out of Dodge* again.

Six weeks passed quickly and the federal marshals came to close up the chemical and coating factory I'd been pursuing for nearly two years. I had been hired by this paint manufacturer as an accountant to take charge of the accounting department, payroll, accounts receivables and payables. In my analysis I found them double billing the Government in different exercises. Sometimes they billed them for the paint twice. They would also bill for product not delivered and acknowledgements as received by Government purchasing agents, for a nice kickback, of course. Most of the shady shipments were sent to Seattle, Washington.

I was especially suspicious about the so-called empty containers, because the weight still tallied up. Maybe they were moving drugs, but I didn't know and that was for another department. I listed my qualms in my report, however. So when it went down, when the contractor bit the dust, I would be arrested as well as the others involved. Only my arrest was to be evidence for my disappearance. The idea was the others would be so tied up in legal problems they would soon forget about me.

Prior to the confiscation of the chemical and coating company, I'd relocated my family to Biglerville, Pennsylvania. I hadn't been accepted at the Lutheran Seminary yet, which was in Gettysburg, seven miles away, but I was sure certain I would be as my transcript from Concordia checked out and I passed their psychological evaluation. I received good reports from my bogus references, set up by the Bureau; one of them noted I needed more pew time. *Your app can't be perfect, you know, yeah?* Of course I would get in the pew time, at a *point in time*, I assured all during my Virginia Synod snooty higher-up's interrogations.

We found a trailer house located on top of a mountain near Biglersville, Pennsylvania to temporary house us while I stayed on in Norfolk testifying. During the first week of August I'd wrapped up what I needed to get done and headed for Pennsylvania. I was approved to go to seminary, during the cool down period. I could operate as any other student, work jobs and whatever; but, I would make myself available to do temporary assignments or paperwork when they needed me during this sabbatical. This time frame could be tomorrow or for years. So for now, I'm John Sletten, the seminarian. Yet, I had one more test to pass before I was accepted by The Lutheran Theological Seminary at Gettysburg.

I was invited to a summer retreat at Luray Caverns, in the Blue Ridge Mountains, to meet with Virginia Synod endorsement committee. I met a bunch of great people and several were starting at Gettysburg. At the end of the day, Saturday, August 16, 1980, after a grueling Q and A by the committee, I was endorsed to be enrolled.

The first academic year went well. I received good grades and did things I thought I'd never do, like conducting church services, preaching sermons, and wearing a clerical collar. I found being an older student to be quite an advantage. I had some real life experience to draw from, unlike the 22 year old kids who were my classmates and trusted in their Sunday School knowledge on the subject of their faith.

Ellen took a job as a staff accountant with a local CPA firm in Gettysburg. At night I taught guitar lessons at Ziegler Music. Joe and Dan went to George Meade Elementary and we found good and reasonable day care for Christopher. By Christmas time our life had settled down. Although during the school year we kept hearing stories about this summer's session of CPE. How they would try to break you down. Make you cry. Strip away all you defense mechanisms. So, I had mentally prepared myself for this encounter mostly by talking with the upperclassman. It sounded like a bunch of horseshit to me. Pussy time for pussies.

These are my thoughts as I pull into Allentown State Hospital. I enter onto a long tree lined boulevard. About half way up I see the building I'm supposed to report to on this sun- spanked May morning. I'm a few minutes early so I continue past the building, which looks like a huge mansion, and go to the top of the hill. Here there is a large rectangular building with a clock centered atop. I see bars on the window, it looks like a prison. There are hardly any people around, but a few sitting on benches. They look normal, not crazy. I'm thinking as I loop around and make my way down the other side of the boulevard.

I circle around the bottom of the thoroughfare and head back up to the house where I'm to rendezvous. I park my car at the curb and make my way to the front steps of the building. In the center of four pillars are a huge set of double doors. I open one and walk in as a huge Grandfather clock is chiming nine times. I'm on time, but certainly not early.

I see coffee, donuts, and several young people gathered around. I walk over to pour a cup and to find out if I'm in the right place. I no more than get my cup poured when I hear a female voice demanding attention.

She looks like she's from the psychedelic sixties. She has on a long *hippie-style* dress which goes all the way down to her ankles. It is colorful and fits snugly around her waist. She wears a loose-fitting blouse which houses, I guess, a small pair of tits. One thing for sure she is wearing no brazier. She has long blond hair and a beautiful face.

"I'm Chloe Mercer," she says. "And, you are Emma Johnson, Adelaide Harrington, Hannah Hanson, Henry Wilson and John Sletten," pointing at each one of us while clearly enunciating our names. "I'm your supervisor for this fourteen week session. I'm a Baptist pastor hailing from Texas." She extends her thumbs and little fingers while waving her hands and saying, *"Hook 'em horns."*

I was certain I was the only one in this group who knew what *hook 'em horns* meant. It didn't seem to be my kind of group and I already wished this summer session was coming to an end. But, of course, I listened. I had nothing better to do.

"John," she queried. "Why are you wearing those aviator sunglasses?"

"They're prescription. I can't see without them." I reply. It was lie number one to Choloe, the Supervisor.

She didn't like my quick response and began executing a cold professionalism with unshakable sanctimonious piety. She looked at me and I looked at her, but we really didn't look at each other. She was pissed and I knew it.

"Henry, what do you think of John's sunglasses?

Henry Wilson looked like he'd just won student of the year *award* and he was not about to say anything negative about me. He squirmed, not saying anything immediately. Now Chloe was writhing in anger. She had fucked with the wrong seminarian and she knew it.

First, I am 36 years old, muscular, in good physical shape and a good looking man. One punch would have knocked boy Henry back to Tupelo, Mississippi. She said, "John, are you one who doesn't quite fit into this world so you distract the truth by shocking people with misbehavior?

"There you go," I say.

What's her fucking problem, I'm thinking. Now I had to reel in my anger. On first impression I was always the person everybody liked, not the one anyone would try aggravate. Thank God I'd been trained by the best, *things aren't always what they seem,* and so, I just smiled, pleasantly.

"Is something funny, John Sletten?"

"I heard somewhere that psychiatrists are the knights of reason and order saving clam sols from the proliferating dragons of the mind." I knew I shouldn't have said it as soon as I did. But, I was already so fed up with her shit the words just fell out of my mouth.

Her manipulative skill and ability to destroy by insulation seemed to be working on the rest of them. It was her infuriating and insidious tool I had exposed. The qualities of piety and command concern that had been taught to her as a woman, in a man's profession, had been defeated by me in front of the group. The instrument of power to keep men in their place had had the reverse effect of emasculation.

At 3 p.m. she dismissed us for the day. "Group session starts at 8 a.m. tomorrow. Then you'll start spending your first day on the wards. So, get yourself organized for a difficult 14 weeks." When she said difficult she was looking directly at me.

"John Sletten, shed those glasses. I'm sure you brought another pair along. Nobody reads with sunglasses."

"Okay," I said. "Thank you."

"John," a female voice shouted behind me, as I was about to cross the boulevard.

"You were great! I'm Adelaide Harrington. Just call me Ade. Hey, try to understand Chloe. She's a PK."

Ade was short, about the size of my wife, Ellen. She was very pretty and had long brown hair, with gentle unguarded eyes. She had a beautiful smile.

I asked, "What's a PK?"

She looked at me in amazement. "You don't know what a PK is and you're here?"

"So," I asked again. "What's a PK?"

"I'm a PK," she said. "A preacher's kid!"

"Oh," I said, "I'm not!"

"You're kidding me," she laughed.

We had crossed the boulevard and approached the dormitory we'd be staying in for the duration. We walked into the building to the second floor where our rooms were right next to each other. We checked them out. There was a bed, a dresser, a mirror and a window. There were bathrooms and showers down the hall. Nothing was marked *Ladies* or *Gents*.

After ten minutes in our solitude, Adelaide knocked on my door. "It's the Biltmore," she says with a laugh.

I reply, "Hannah Hanson commutes, Henry Wilson commutes, and Emma Johnson commutes. We live here. I wonder if anyone else lives in this fortress."

"Don't know," says Ade. There was a pregnant pause. "This place gives me the *creeps*, though. I'm surely glad you're next door."

"Let's get out of here, I saw a bar at the end of the boulevard …" She interrupts me.

"So did I," she says with giggle.

"Henry's …. O'Henry's, something like that," I recall.

"Let's go, John."

En route I asked Adelaide, "Why did the *Super* assign me to the criminally insane ward?"

Ade said, laughing, "Chloe loves you John."

We walked a few more paces and I say, "This is crazy!"

"What's crazy?' Adelaide asks, with a grin.

"Everything," I say. "Let's play the jukebox and get drunk!"

She grabs my hand, saying, "PK's like music and getting drunk too."

When we walked into O'Henry's it was like walking into a movie theatre out of the bright sun. It was pitch dark and took a few seconds to get oriented. When we did we saw an oval bar with a juke box playing some crazy song. There were no other customers so we sat down at the end of the bar that faced the TV set. The bartender was singing with the juke box and watching something on the television. "May we get a drink, sir?" I shout. He doesn't move. I look at Adelaide and she starts to laugh.

"I see you got some pull around here, John." She says.

I start to laugh as the same song replays on the juke box. *I'm a gonna breaka yo face …*

Suddenly the bartender turns and walks toward us. "What can I getcha?"

He was an *Edward G. Robinson* look-a-like. He looked like him, talked like him, a real tough guy attitude. We each ordered a bottle of Budweiser and he set them down, without asking about glasses, and returned to his television watching.

When that song started up again I took four quarters off the bar and moseyed over to select other tunes. When I did the barkeep looked annoyed. I picked out four songs, starting with *Love on the Rocks*, by Neil Diamond and ending with *Bette Davis Eyes*, by Kim Carnes.

Ade and I toasted each other's beer bottles and for the first time today we relaxed.

"So," Ade said, "You're married with children."

"And you," I answer with a question of my own.

"I'm married, but I just caught my husband in an affair."

"I'm sorry," I reply. "It's the most difficult thing to deal with and I don't know if one ever really gets over it."

"You sound like you've experienced what I'm going through?"

"It was a long time ago, Adelaide and I still don't like to talk about it." I respond, while ordering us another round of beers.

"Yeah," she agrees, "I don't know what I'm going to do about it. Coming up here for fourteen weeks will certainly give us a break where he hopefully can determine what he wants to do as well. Great song selection, *Love on the Rocks!* Appropriate though."

"Of course I didn't know. I like all of Diamond's music. You know, Ade, the fate of every infidel is to eventually get trapped by their own actions. In my case, which was my first marriage, she couldn't resist the temptation to strike through her inscrutable mask and deprive her claims to authority and purity." I speak knowingly and the master of remembering certain lines so well spoken or written.

"Wow," Ade says, "So she had an affair on you?

"Yes and it was with my so-called best friend, of course. I was devastated, and I played it out all wrong. I should have punched him in the nose and stood my ground. But, I was so young and foolish. And, personal pride gets in the way. Then, there is the hurt. Why wasn't I good enough for her? So, I had to leave. I entrusted my children to her, knowing above all she was a good mother. It still hurts, though! I suppose it always will be an empty spot." I suggest.

"Your story sounds like it's from a Greek tragedy, maybe Antigone? The depiction of the consequences of the refusal of the individual to submit to the orders of the establishment...."

"Or, say, Oedipus. What?" *You will kill your father and marry your mother!* I ordered another round of beers from *Edward G.* "It was much simpler than all that!"

"Or, was it?" Ade said, smiling. "*The Greek Myths.* John, we could get in real trouble here, a whole summer together drinking and discussing literature?"

I grinned, saying, "I love beer, music, women, and the Greek Myths. Have we sinned yet?"

"Not yet," she said laughing. "So far, we're good."

The best time to make friends is before you need them. **Ethel Barrymore**

Chapter Seventeen

I had a meeting set with PGC and Henry Peter Fleck at 10 a.m. We met in Gordon's office sitting at a magnificent conference table. Fleck and I had been ushered in by Charlotte Boyer. She was very business-like today and it was like her scene a week ago never happened.

"Henry Peter Fleck," Gordon Charles greets as he enters from our rear. "How was your trip from Baltimore?" He asks for something to say. I detected from day one PGC didn't like dealing with anybody one on one.

"The deal is sealed," said Fleck with a smile. Paul Gordon Charles looked at him with those piercing, dark eyes. "Is everything exactly the way I want it, Henry? You know this is a great opportunity for you and the bank." He tells him.

"I have drafts of all the documents here." He opens up his brief case and takes what looks like a ream of paper. "It's voluminous," he says, "but everything that needs to be signed is here. Have your people read everything and we'll set a closing date, which can be as soon as next week. Also, part of the deal is to open your collateral and joint accounts with us. When you are ready I'll send over two or three new accounts people to fill out the documents. These accounts must be opened before we disburse the monies."

"Sounds like you've got your ass covered pretty well, Henry. I don't like any ring around the collar, either. So, leave the documents with Jack and we'll get everything on our end moving. Jack," he asks. "Have you cleared everything with General Counsel?"

"Yes, I wanted to talk with you today about General Counsel. In short, it's an all clear." I say.

"Are you positively sure, Jack?"

"Yes, positively." I reply in earnest.

Peter Fleck and I walk right past Charlotte Boyer without saying a word as she is moving toward PGC's office. We walk down to my office and I usher Fleck into my quarters. He lays his paperwork on my empty office desk and smiles. "Are you cool?" He asks.

"Well, Henry, there is a lot more to this job than meets the eye. I'm cool so far, depending on what cool is, of course. In reviewing these documents I suppose I'll get Jerry Bitterman involved. Jerry can fill me in on whatever I should know. My position is whatever you agreed to with Bitterman and in behalf of PGC, I'm going along with the program."

Henry looks a little perplexed, even nervous, as he reaches in his vest pocket. "I hear you're a big Phillies fan, Jack." He extends two tickets toward me. "Tomorrow night," he says. "Here are front row mezzanine seats for the first game of the World Series."

I've listened to or watched every World Series game since 1952 and this would be the first one I'd see in the stadium. "Thank you, Henry. This is quite a thrill for me. I suppose you're pulling for the Orioles." He smiles, saying, "I am and I'm sure you will be pulling for the Phillies."

"Thank you again. May I buy you lunch, Henry?" I ask. "I have another appointment. Let me know right away if you have any questions with the loan papers." He shook my hand, saying, "Enjoy the game."

I walked Henry Fleck to the main door. As I returned to my office Mary Robinson gave me a kindly wave while fielding a telephone call. Charlotte Boyer was not in my office. I sat down behind my desk and started paging through the papers. Most of it appeared to be standard language. The first page that really interested me was the list of guarantors.

Everyone on the Board of Directors, including Paul Gordon Charles and General Jurgens, were guarantors. I thought about all kinds of scenarios, but I was hoping Jurgen's decision hadn't been entirely based on what I'd said. It's the part I disliked most about my job, gaining people's confidences knowing full well they'd be fully taken advantage of in the end. I didn't care about the ones in because of greed. I did care about the ones, like Jurgens, who was getting involved because he just wanted to be back in the arena again. But, I didn't know much about the General. Becoming a General was often political, too. Who knows maybe General Jurgens has a little greed going as well. I thumbed through the rest of the paperwork before I'd put my feelers out for Bitterman. Although, and I didn't tell him, he knew I'd be receiving these documents today.

When I was through scanning the loan documents I stacked them neatly and put them in the top drawer of my file cabinet. I locked the cabinet and went down the hall to the coffee lounge. Here I found Maggie Little putting a tray together to take to the Claims department, I assumed.

"Jack," she says, taking a sip of coffee. She smiles asking, "Are you getting used to things around this madhouse?"

"A madhouse, indeed," I reply. "Mary, have you seen Jerry Bitterman around lately?"

"Try my office," she says. "He's bullshitting with Joe about something."

"Thank you, Maggie. Hey, do you know anyone who would like to go to the World Series game with me tomorrow night?" I ask.

Maggie put her coffee down and slowly walked toward me. She put her arms up and gave me a romantic hug and squeeze. "Me," she said. "I'm the number one *O's* fan. Are you kidding, you have tickets."

"You know I'm a *Phillies* fan" I reply.

"That's your problem," she said, adamantly.

"You're not fucking with me, are you Jack?"

Going to the game with Maggie could be an interesting experience, I'm thinking. She's sexy, witty and a baseball fan. Oh yes, she still talks the talk and walks the walk, but I liked her the first time we met. Also, during the six hours we'd spend together I could find out about a lot of people and things. These are my thoughts as I pour a cup of coffee.

"Of course, I wouldn't fuck with you. Not about baseball, the only unvarying in my life. Are we on?"

"We'll leave from here." She says. "Shall I tell Jerry you're looking for him?"

"Yeah, tell him to come to my office as soon as possible. And Maggie, I'm looking forward to tomorrow night. Go Phillies!"

She picked up her tray, and whispered in my ear, "Go Orioles!"

Jerry Bitterman appears in my office ten minutes later. "What's doing?" He asks. "Maggie says you're looking for me."

"Jerry, I want to schedule a time to go through these loan papers. Henry met with PGC and I this morning and says we can close next week if we get everybody signed and in the right position."

"No time like the present," Bitterman says.

"My dentist used to make that statement, Jerry." I warned.

"Well, at least this won't be painful." He guffaws.

According to the way I thought, borrowing ten million dollars is an admission of defeat. PGC would say it was an opportunity. Jerry Bitterman and Henry Fleck would say it all makes sense, if they get a cut. Only time will tell I'm thinking as Bitterman and I spend the rest of the day going over the papers in the Board of Director's conference room.

When we were finished Jerry extracted a sheet from his in-side vest pocket. "Here are the disbursements" He says. The sheet of paper was a letter to Henry P. Fleck at American State Bank of Maryland under Bitterman's signature, which was now crossed out. "You're the Treasurer now, Jack, you need to have this letter retyped under your autograph."

I said, "I see."

The directions to the bank were: *first, to deposit of $9,700,000 to the new checking account, to be set up at American State Bank of Maryland, in the name of A.S.S. Associates, Inc.; second, a cashier's* *check in the amount of $300,000 payable to C&B Leasing; third, in-structions under my signature as Treasurer of Atlantic States Surety Company.*

Jerry was drumming his fingers on the conference table as I read. "If anything goes wrong, it will be my fault, huh? I say laughing. "Is that the idea, Jerry?"

He keeps drumming his fingers, a little louder now. "Is there a problem, Jack?" Jerry asks nervously. "Are you sure I'm not supposed to guarantee the loan, too." I say with an attitude.

"Hey, Jerry, don't you think the $300,000 to C&B Leasing is going to raise some eyebrows?" I ask with a tone of incredulity.

"Ordinarily," he agrees. "But, the only people present at the closing will be PGC, Henry and you."

"And, we're all on the same page? Does PGC know everything about what's going on, Jerry?" I ask determined to get him to commit.

Jerry started thwacking his fingers with both hands. I always like to see the guilty squirm, especially if they think I'm just looking out for myself. This loan maneuver is big; it will implicate who we want to point the finger at. PGC is our target, I think.

Jerry knew what I was trying to do, but he didn't know the purpose. I'm sure Henry and he were doing 50-50, or 60-40 with the C&B proceeds. I also knew I'd have to make my move now for it all to work.

"What's my cut, Jerry?"

He was really thinking now. About 30 seconds of silence passed, when I suggested, "I'll take 10% of your's and Henry's kitty."

"Thirty grand, Jack, done!"

"I should have asked for 25%." I say.

"But you didn't," Bitterman said, with a gleam in his eye. PGC will be pleased."

"He will be pleased bout what?" I ask.

"He told me if you didn't ask for a cut, you were not the man for the job." Jerry guffawed.

"So, he is running this loan conspiracy." I say accusingly, trying to get Jerry's dander up.

When Jerry didn't respond I ask. "How do I get the signatures of all the Board members? And, when is a feasible closing date?" I shrug my shoulders.

"I'll get it done at the Board meeting next week. I'll be there to introduce you and pass the torch. Before the meeting I'll greet each member and tell them I need signatures on the loan documents that day. They all like and trust me so it won't be a problem."

"Just like that, Jerry." I say with a grin.

"Just like that, Jack. You see this loan has been in the works for about a year now. We just had to find the right banker." Jerry said, very smugly.

"When's the Board meeting?" I ask.

Jerry said, without looking at a calendar, saying succinctly, "The 20th."

"The loan can close after the 24th." I suggest, knowing Jerry, Henry and PGC were in a hurry. "I'll check with PGC and you check with Henry?"

"Okay," says Jerry. "Good job, Jack." He shakes my hand saying, "I'll see you at the Library Lounge. I'm ready for more than a beer."

I checked my watch, it is 4:30 p.m. Now it was all about Theodore Rex Masters.

I had given my *FBI handler* Masters name asking them to check him out. Over the weekend the handler called me in Philadelphia and told me he is who he says. He's squeaky clean, but does seem to have a marriage problem. That he left the Virginia Insurance Commission for personal reasons, which always raises eyebrows. Especially, when he joins a company the Commission is investigating.

I needed to talk with my handler again concerning this loan. I knew the money would allow PGC a lot of liberty to move forward on all his personal projects at the expense of the company and its shareholders. So getting the go ahead to proceed would be easy. But, the rules were clear about any such decision involving myself. With those thoughts in mind, Ted Masters shows up in my office.

"Jack," he says. "Charlotte Boyer told me you were looking for me."

"I laugh. "Why did she tell you I was looking for you?"

Theodore Rex gave me a rare grin. "I don't know, Jack. She just told me you were looking for me."

"Actually," I say, "I was about to go find you, but it has nothing to do with her."

"Okay," he says. "I'm here. What's up?"

"I received the loan papers today; you know the ten million dollar deal. I need you to review the language, terms and conditions. I read through all the documents, but it was not for fine tuning purposes."

I handed the papers to Ted; he tapped them on the corner of my desk to make sure the pages were true with each other. "I'll get at them tonight. I'm sure PGC wants this cleared as soon as possible."

"Like yesterday." I respond.

"Ted, do you have a few minutes?"

"Surely," he says.

I ask Masters to sit down. When he did I warned him about my concern of my office being bugged.

"By who?" Masters asks, quizzically.

"It's just innuendo, but I've been told to look out!" I say, cautiously.

"Charlotte Boyer hasn't bugged me for a few days, but at first everywhere I showed up she was there first. Several employees have told me she's been bugging my office." I say, feeling a little bit foolish.

"Me too," Ted responds. "Although she's just starting some of the same stuff with me, hanging out everywhere I go. I haven't gotten the pink panties treatment yet, though." He replies laughing.

I told Ted about all the events that had happened to me, including the attempt to steal my briefcase. He told me he had heard something about that, but nothing in particular. Then I complete the panties story. How Charlotte had been waiting for me in the hotel room when I'd come up from the Library Lounge. I told him how she wore her dress hiked up so far I could see her bush. How she tried to seduce me when she asked if I wanted to *do the mess around.*

"Yeah, it's a Ray Charles song." I affirmed.

I said I was certainly tempted, but before I could make a decision she stood up with her dress still hiked, saying look what I found. She pulled pink panties out of her purse and pulled them on. She headed for the door saying, "See you."

PGC interrupts our session. "Jack, Ted," he greets. "Jack, may I see you a minute, alone?" Ted took the cue and stepped outside my office.

"Ted," PGC shrugged. "Is he okay?"

"For certain," I confirm. I checked him out through the Virginia Insurance Commission. He's squeaky clean, but does have marriage problems. So, they say. He left the insurance commission citing personal problems."

"Your story checks with mine." PGC said. "He'll be checking the loan documents, I suspect, shortly."

"He's starting the project tonight," Mr. Charles.

I had a feeling PGC had already checked Theodore Rex Masters out and was just testing me to see if I did it. Paul Gordon Charles left my office seemingly ecstatically happy.

Masters stepped back in when he saw PGC leave. "I'll see you tomorrow," Ted says.

"Okay," I agree, with a wave.

I am not proud of many of the things I have done and I often felt that for the sake of my parents, career, and the FBI, these things are best left behind. But this deal is totally different because it will affect a lot of innocent people. Or, will it? Everyone I talk with since I have been here seems to be crooked or strange. I really don't feel sorry for anybody. So, I determine this is just another day at work. This is my job, isn't it.

Now there is another person standing in my doorway. Her face is open and lovely, framed by hair the color of burnished copper. Her five-foot-seven-inch figure, which was my estimate, is nicely proportioned. Most appealing at this our first meeting is her ready, wide smile and a seemingly sincere interest in me. She is an impressive package.

"Hi, Jack, my name is Madeline Haycock. I'm the company's auditor."

With every question she asked, I sensed she already knew the answer. She asked about family, past employment, wife and children, the whole gambit of things. I had noticed she was always in the PGC's entourage. She was not only the auditor, but Gordon's number one squeeze. Charlotte Boyer had been the one before her. I'd found this out through Joe Neverson.

All her questions and moves seemed pragmatic. She seemed very matter-of-fact, a no-nonsense, and down-to-earth type. I couldn't keep my eyes off her huge breasts and I suspected she knew it. Yes, she was one of the staff who traveled with PGC, kept pace, eyes straight ahead, smug authority dispensed with each step. I suspected Madeline was on Gordon's own personal list of those who'd prospered through his generosity, and she owed him.

"I have to scoot," she says. "I just wanted to meet you. I've heard nothing but good things about you so far. If there is anything I can do to help you just let me know. See you later, Jack."

There was no end to the players. I'd been around long enough to know that casually sharing information with anyone, even those who presumably were in your camp wasn't prudent. So, I did what all savvy people do. I reply to questions without offering anything they didn't already know.

On this gig I hadn't met anybody born to a privileged family with the inherent advantages that situation creates. Madeline was bright, built and pretty. Her face was unblemished and glowing, a fit and trim figure, solid and firm. At maybe 35 years of age, I guess she was just playing out her hand. All the rest of them here seemed to be doing the same thing.

I'd had enough for the day. I needed a glass of bourbon and some good conversation. Hello *Library Lounge*. I picked up my empty briefcase and headed for the door.

You gain strength, courage, and confidence by every experience in which you really stop to look fear in the face. **Eleanor Roosevelt**

What Is Past Is Prologue

Allentown State Hospital
1600 Hanover Avenue
Allentown, Pennsylvania
Tuesday, June 2, 1981

It is the fifth week of the syllabus and everything has fallen into a daily routine. A typical day is, first, a chaplain group session, 9 to 10 where one or all may share a story from the day before and listen to the opinions of the supervisor and other chaplains present; second, off to the wards, 10 till noon, where we read patient files to become familiar with those who we are scheduled to interview; third, meet the other chaplains for lunch in the common cafeteria to discuss any ward problems.

Fourth, after lunch each of us go to our second ward and spend 1 to 3 meetings with patients. The two wards I was assigned were at opposite ends of the spectrum. The *criminally insane* was the morning bunch. *Stepping Stone* was the afternoon horde. Those at *Stepping Stone* were not completely crazy, their next step was society but most didn't want to make that leap. They were happy being institutionalized. Fifth, a verbatim group session is from 3 to 5. Here one of us presents our weekly verbatim subjecting it to review by the supervisor and the other four chaplains. A verbatim is the recalling of an interview with a patient and a listing of the questions and patient responses. I simply made up all my verbatims, like I was writing a screen play. Perhaps Chloe was superstitious of me with all my correct responses, I thought, but she was too busy flashing her bare legs in my direction.

This morning, on the criminally insane ward, I had asked for a young man's file. His name is Vince; last names weren't used on this ward. I had noticed Vince was always hanging around while I was working the floor. He was a good looking young man standing at least six feet three inches and weighed some 225 pounds. He looked so normal, but there was obviously another side or he wouldn't be here. So, when I sat down at the nurse's station to peruse the file a supervisor kept staring at me very circumspectly.

It only took a few moments to find out why. Vince had killed his mother with an axe. Now I was the one who was wary, wondering if I should go into a private conference room with such a maniac. So my guard was up when the security sentinel escorted Vince into a cage.

"If you need me, chaplain, I'll be right outside the door." The guard said, assuredly.

I smiled and waved him out. "Vince," I said. "How are you today?"

"Good," he said, while walking toward the window.

"It's a sunny day. It's a good baseball day." He added.

We talked about those Philadelphia Phillies. I told him I moved to Pennsylvania in the summer of 1980. Here he interrupted me saying the Phillies had won their first World Series that year, giving me all the details. He told me he was a great baseball pitcher in high school, saying he threw a one hundred mile per hour fastball.

"Wow," that's fast!" I reply.

"I would've played for the Phillies," he said. "But I axed my mother!"

I must have looked very chagrinned, having asked him why?

"It's okay, chaplain." Vince said. "Everybody asks why? It was easy; she just pissed me off when I was in a bad mood. But, you came right out with it just like that!"

I shrugged my shoulders in tacit acknowledgement. It seems the worse I do the more popular I become. I'm thinking quietly, when suddenly Vincent's personality changes. He asks, "Preacher can we play catch."

I got up from my chair and walked to the window. I see a rough baseball diamond and a wooden back stop. I'd noticed the diamond before wondering if they really put balls and bats in these people's hands. But, a ball, I'm thinking, I can catch anybody's fast ball, so why not?

"Okay, Vince, I'll see if I can round up a glove for you, a catcher's mitt for me and I'll have you pitch an inning or two. How about tomorrow, say 11 a.m."

Vince clapped his hands, saying, "Thank you chaplain, yeah, thank you. I can't wait to show you my fast ball."

I gave him a big thumbs-up.

What a botched interview I'm thinking while leaving the ward for the cafeteria. As I walk down the corridor twirling my big ring of keys, I realize it's only the keys that separate me from one of them. Yes, just the keys.

The food isn't bad at the common cafeteria, but eating alongside the patients was tough. It was especially hard-hitting when the geriatrics ward came to the table, which was right at high noon. Most of them were physically handicapped, grotesque, slopping their food everywhere attempting to eat without any teeth. Actually, I was only eating lunch there now. I have never been a breakfast person, unless it is late night or early morning, after a late evening of drinking. I usually have a cheeseburger at O'Henry's for supper. So, it was just lunch. I figured out if I got there ten minutes early I'd get served and be finished by the time the wards started filing in single file.

After lunch I walked to my second ward assignment. It was down the hill from the Administration and Cafeteria building. En route I encountered a woman named Mary who was sitting on a bench perched on the hill overlooking beautiful mountain scenery.

When she looked at me, her mouth screwed up and shouted out, "Fuck you, preacher man!" It was our turned around white collar and black cleric vestment that seemed to set her off.

The first time it happened it was unsettling. The second time I responded, "I love you, too, Mary." She followed, "You cocksucker."

Today, I say, "Merry Christmas, darling!"

She was all smiles when I gave her that comeback.

I liked going to *Stepping Stone*. Most of these patients were just misfits. The State Hospital gave them refuge from the real world.

The patients really liked me on this ward, mostly because at the end of each day's stay I played guitar and sang. One of the guys, Bob Dawson, we called him *Disco*, always handed me a pool stick when I walked into the building.

"I racked 'em up," he said. "Hit 'em preacher!" Bob shouted, eagerly. "Break 'em up!" he urged me on with a big, *"Ya Ha!"*

A few gathered as I readied to hit the ball. *"Smack!"* I hit the cue ball squarely and so hard that four of the balls went in pockets and one through a window pane as Bob stood there with eyes shimmering in amazement, and chanting, *"Ya Ha ... Ya Ha ... Ya Ha!"*

"How did that make you feel, Bob?" I ask.

He started his disco dance, singing out of tune, *"I like the night life ... I like to boogie ..."* he didn't know the rest of the lyrics, but he just kept on dancing.

I knew I was doing it all wrong. I was supposed to be talking to the patients, preparing them and applying preparation *H* for them to be meeting the world on the outside. I, on the other hand, had not seen anybody yet who could make it on the outside. I was killing time so why not entertain them and myself. Why not? All this crap about how-do-you-feel and what-are-you-thinking about was dog shit to me. These people are just fucked up.

The ward staff liked me because I got most of their bored patients off of their backs for an hour or so. And, that was enough to get lustrous reports from them. So, when Bob stopped discoing I asked, "How did you like that break?"

He kind of stood at attention and yelled out, "It makes me feel like *God the Father Almighty, maker of heaven and earth ... Ya Ha,* preacher, *Ya Ha"*

It was a typical day at *Stepping Stone*. And, it was the way they liked it. About 2:45 p.m. a larger crowd gathered waiting for me to play the guitar. *Roger Miller* tunes went over well with this outfit.

Dang Me was their favorite. And it was Bill Madison who yelled out *Dang Me* as a request.

Bill was a big fellow, standing more than six feet tall and weighing I suppose some 250 pounds. While Bob Dawson was ssleeping one night, Bill pulled Bob's two front teeth out with pliers. Bob was snoring too loud or something like that. When I asked Bob what happened, he replied with a *"Ya Ha, yeah!* Bill Madison pulled my front teeth out!"

I played the song, and everyone joined in with the chorus, *"Ought a take a rope and hang me."*

I played one more request, *Great Balls of Fire* by the *Killer*, Jerry Lee Lewis. They loved all my tunes! I bid them goodbye until tomorrow as those who were able gave me a standing ovation. As I walked by the Nurse's station, Amy, the nurse Superior, leered at me saying, "God, I wish I had a minister like you."

I laughed knowing full well what she meant. She was about my age with sandy brown hair, blue eyes and an ass that looked like two pigs in a gunny sack.

En route to the mansion I realized I didn't have a verbatim ready. A verbatim was a required document to be prepared to read in session. One a week was required, and we didn't know who would be called upon each day.

My job as an undercover agent required no notes. Everything I reported to my handler was from memory. Again, sometimes, it was from a drunken memory. So, I thought as a possibility I would say I lost my verbatim and request to ad-lib it. I would use the Bob Dawson story about his teeth being yanked by Bill Madison. If I got called upon, I would make it up as I went along. I mean nobody was a better bull shitter than me, I thought as I entered the *Great Room*.

All were present at 3 p.m., fixing their usual cup of coffee. Adelaide Harrington whispered to me, "O'Henry's, afterwards?"

"Yeah," I said.

Chloe called us together quickly. We circled up with her. As usual she positioned herself directly across from me. I don't know why, although her posturing was quite apparent. She always crossed her legs and they were tantalizing. I think she loved me eyeballing her.

"John," she said. I have some rosy reports about you. You are well liked on both wards."

"That's good news," I reply. "I'm trying." I say, with a simper.

Ade pulled down her half-glasses and looked me directly in the eyes. She gave me that you-are-so-full-of-shit look.

"Now, Hannah has something she would like to share with the group." Chloe, says.

Perfect! I thought, knowing Hannah would take up the entire session once she got rolling with her breakdowns and crying. If necessary I could even throw a question or two into the hat. So, I was home free without my verbatim today!

Adelaide and I bellied up to the bar about 5:10 p.m. We ordered our beers and watched the regular crowd shuffle in. We were now regular, too. We were part of some Angel Factory, I thought.

Ade squeezed my hand. I squeezed back asking, "How was your weekend?"

She shrugged, saying, "He needs time, so he says."

"Time for what?" I ask Adelaide.

"It's over, John. He says he loves me, but he also loves her." She says softly.

"How about you? What do you think?" I ask.

"I feel nothing. I'm indifferent. Thank God I have you to talk with, John. I only look forward to seeing you and being with you, John." Ade, said, while putting up two fingers for another round. "And, I know our relationship is just temporary. And, that really scares me!"

To change an uncomfortable subject, I announce: "It's my eleventh wedding anniversary today. Ellen and I were married in Juarez, Mexico eleven years ago today." I say. "We celebrated with the boys at Pizza Hut in Gettysburg on Saturday night." I add.

"And, I'm sitting here with you tonight." Adelaide says, with kind of a guilty tone in her voice.

"Yeah, she has the kids and I'm drinking with you on our 11th," I say smiling. "I always seem to get the better end of the deal. Ellen would vouch for me on that," I speak with a suggestion of guilt in my right to be heard.

"John, she has a pretty terrific guy. She really does." Ade tells me, while reaching for my hand again.

"Thank you" I kind of whisper. "But, I'm certain she would debate you on the *terrific* part."

I ordered another round while Adelaide goes to the bathroom. When she comes back she put her arms around my neck from the back of my bar stool. I turn and she kisses me softly on the lips.

"Happy Anniversary, John, I really mean it. I want to meet Ellen sometime." She kisses me again as *Edward G. Robinson* looks on suspiciously.

Suddenly the door opens with a gust of wind and a crash. Two persons pushed through the door barely able to close it behind them.

"What a storm," one of them shouts. I think it's a tornado."

I put my arm around Ade's waist, pulling her next to me. "Tornado, shit!" I reject the assumption. People around here don't know what a real tornado is like. If it's a tornado it's not like the ones we get in the Midwest. A tornado there would blow this building and the people in it to New Jersey." I suggest.

"Hopefully not to Princeton," Adelaide retorted as the lights went out.

Everything was momentarily quiet, and then sirens were blaring. Quickly it started getting very hot in the bar. *Edward G* opened the two doors. Surprisingly, the sun was shining and all was tranquil.

"Good God," he said, "all kinds of trees are down."

Adelaide and I take a look outside. It appears a tornado or a very strong wind had hit with great force. When I saw *Edward G* go behind the bar I walked in quickly and asked if he would sell me two six packs to go, saying if the lights didn't come back on the beer would get *skunked* anyway.

I gave *Edward G* twenty bucks for two six packs, and met Ade in the doorway where she had been watching me negotiate.

"You certainly have a way with words, John." She says as we

walk across the street, dodging fallen tree limbs. When we get to our building we climb the upstairs steps on the side of the building and just plop down. I crack two beers as a slight breeze is blowing now and it feels good sitting on the concrete veranda. We finished a six pack on the stairs as we watched storm clouds gather again. We decide to get the windows open in our rooms.

We end up in my room, because I have a radio fueled by batteries. We talk and listen to music until it is dark. With the beer gone we decide to go to bed. Adelaide went to her room and I stayed in mine. As I tossed my shirt and pants over the chair, I sat on the bed wishing the electricity would come back on so I could get the news on television. Then suddenly thunder was roaring and lightning was cracking across the sky. I walked over to the window and watched for awhile. As I walked back toward my bed there was a knock at my door. I opened it up and there stood Adelaide in her nightgown, with her bra and panties outlined underneath. She was carrying two bottles of red wine and a corkscrew.

"John, I'm scared. All this thunder and lightning and this spooky building, may I spend the night with you?"

"Of course," I reply, grabbing the wine bottles. "Are you really scared?" I ask.

"Yes, I am." Ade said, quietly. "It seems like my whole world is coming apart. But, I really want to be with you, too, John."

I gave her a hug, saying, "We haven't done anything wrong."

"*Yet,*" we said in unison, somewhat laughing at our situation.

I opened one of the two bottles of wine and poured it in two room glasses, which were probably filled with dust. We toasted each other and continued the night. After finishing a bottle of wine we were both relaxed and a little loopy. We set down our glasses and sat up on the bed.

Sitting next to each other, in our underwear, Adelaide said, "I've put off a lot of stuff that I shouldn't have, assuming there would be time for it later. I regret that."

"You shouldn't live that way anymore," I encouraged.

She laughs, "You've got, what, fifteen years on me. You can skip a lot of mistakes."

I speculate out loud, "Life is what happens while we're making other plans."

"I suppose," she says.

I reach out for her saying, "Come here."

She came to me deliberately. I took her in my arms and lowered my mouth to hers. I kissed her to offer comfort, to distract her from recent sad memories, to fill a lonely corner of her heart.

I kissed her slowly, deeply, savoring the taste of wine on her tongue, drinking in the feeling of her body against mine. She melted into me, surrendered willingly, accepted what I had to give her, and gave back in return. Gradually comfort gave way to desire, distraction to sharp focus and keen awareness.

We made love by turns both slowly and urgently; without words, but in full communication in a language of gasps and eyes locked on each other. Our bodies moved together, arched against each other, tangled and tugged and stroked. We went over the edge together, reality giving way to bliss. I hadn't felt anything so satisfying and right in a long time.

After the loving, we polished off the other bottle of wine and fell asleep in each other's arms.

I like living. I have sometimes been wildly, despairingly, acutely miserable, racked with sorrow, but through it all I still know quite certainly that just to be alive is a grand thing. **Agatha Christie**

Chapter Eighteen

Maggie came to my office exactly at 4 p.m. She was carrying a small duffel bag as she asks, "Ready, Jack."

"You going dressed like, huh, to the nines?" I ask.

She taps her bag, urging me on. "Let's get going, traffic is going to be a bitch." Maggie announces, loudly.

"Okay," I agree, "and, I thought I was the baseball fan."

"Not like me," she says. "Not like me."

"I have to change my clothes," I say.

Maggie simply closed my door and locked it. Then, she began taking off her clothes as I stood in wonderment watching. When she was down to her panties and bra she looked at me, saying, "Well, are you going to change or not?"

As I stared at her milky skin she pulled a *Baltimore Orioles* sweatshirt from her bag. As she pulled it over her head I took off my shirt, pants and shoes, saying, "What the fuck!"

Maggie smiles as she puts on a pair of jeans, white socks and sneakers. I pull on my *Philadelphia Phillies* sweatshirt, and then put my Phillies cap on my head. Maggie puts her *Baltimore Orioles* cap on her head, saying, "Come on, Jack, move it."

I finish dressing adding jeans, socks and sneakers to my sweatshirt. We put our clothes on hangers in my office closet and exit the office. No one was present or taking notice of our departure, with the exception of Mary Robinson. "Enjoy the game you two," Mary encourages, with a grin.

So here I am driving up the Baltimore – Washington Parkway

heading to my first World Series game with Maggie Little. Every day gets crazier than the day before. Who is this Maggie Little, I'm thinking as we cruise the parkway.

En route Maggie tells me her life story. She has two boys by an ex-husband who has been at large since the divorce papers were signed. She told me she had been sexually abused by her uncle when she was fifteen. *"He fucked the hell out of me,"* is the way Maggie put it.

That, she had run away with her ex-husband after he worked over her uncle with a tire iron. They lived with his parents and she went to secretarial school in Baltimore. After graduating and delivering her first baby she took a job with large law firm. That now she lives in a apartment in Silver Spring, Maryland with her two sons.

She talked non-stop from Washington to Baltimore telling me one story after the other about the times of her life. Now I knew she wasn't one of us. She talked too much about herself. I had successfully not spoken a single word, even edgewise.

When we entered Baltimore there was excitement everywhere, even though a misty rain was falling. As we traveled up Charles Street Maggie and I were both wondering, out loud, if the game would be played. Then, there it was - Memorial Stadium, looking like a space ship with lights flashing in the dark. As we walked from the parking lot to the gates we could see the rain drops falling through the lights mounted on the towers.

When we arrived at our seats we were pleased to be in the covered mezzanine level. However, the rains had seemed to subside and just then the *Phillie Phanatic* came out of the Phillies dugout wearing his rain gear. It made me feel at home. As he lumbered around doing his act, I thought of home, my wife and children hunkered down on our sofa ready to watch Game One of the World Series. While I'm contemplating Maggie had gone to a concession stand to get us a beer.

By the time Maggie got back it was time for the singing of the Star Spangled Banner. She grabbed my hand and leaned her head on my shoulder, whispering to me, "Thank you, Jack, I'll never forget being here tonight."

A light rain fell throughout the game. Phillies ace John Denney gave up a first inning homerun to Jim Dwyer, but that would be it for the Orioles on the night. With the score, 0-1, in the top of the sixth, 40-year-old Joe Morgan tied it with a solo shot off Oriole's ace Scott McGregor. McGregor would comment after the game that Howard Cosell, cantankerous sports broadcaster, disrupted his rhythm when prolonging an interview with President Reagan after the fifth inning. We could see the interview being conducted to our left.

In the top of the eighth inning Garry Maddox led off with a solo homer off McGregor for the final margin, 2-1. Al Holland closed it out in the ninth for the Phillies.

The victory put me on cloud nine, taking me away from my ugly world for a few hours. And, I was there. Maggie was not quite so pleased, but did say, "The O's will win four straight now. But, I'm happy for you Jack. Make no mistake about it!"

"Okay," I agree to disagree. "But, perhaps you are not that happy if you are a real baseball fan. I can't stand to lose. I want to win every game."

"I'm happy for you Jack is what I said. Otherwise it was a bad night for me from a baseball fan point of view. Only the game, though." She adds.

I smile, saying, "Thanks for clearing that up for me, Maggie."

Now she smiled, saying, "Get out of here!"

While the traffic cleared, Maggie and I stopped at a little dirt bar along the street near the stadium. Maggie told me to take my Phillies cap off or I might have to take a beating.

"I'm not taking this hat off tonight, what do you think I'm a turncoat. No, I'll take my chances." I told her.

"Don't say I didn't warn you, Jack!" Maggie warns.

We had three beers, and other than a couple of jibes, everybody was calm. After an hour we made our way to the car, with a cold six-pack.

En route back to Washington we drank three beers a piece and talked about what was happening at Atlantic States. She told me huge claims were coming and we're just on the brink of needing lots of dollars. Hopefully we'll get them from the new loan. But, Joe Neverson says PGC won't use of dime to satisfy claims.

I got the picture and quickly changed the subject to Charlotte Boyer. I asked Maggie what she knew about Charlotte. She hesitated somewhat, but came straightforward.

"She's PGC's ex. He keeps her around to do dirty tricks and surveillances. For that she maintains her high salary, her Watergate apartment and a new Mercedes. Be careful, Jack. She'll say or do anything to please PGC."

When I asked about Bitterman, she said, "He's a crook! Jack, don't trust him or believe anything he says. Hell, he stole one hundred thousand from his mother's estate. Yeah, PGC bailed him out."

"How about your boss?" I ask Maggie.

Maggie announces with pride, "Joe is the best lawyer. He really knows his stuff. He cares!"

"If so," I question, "Why is he working for Paul Gordon Charles?"

Maggie cracked the last beer and took a gulp.

"All Joe wants is to be an honest and descent man again. He hates all the deceit, lies, duplicities and fraud. He got himself in trouble when he tried a construction project. He lost everything, including his wife and family. He looks at Mr. Charles as his way out. He wonders now if PGC will be his complete undoing – losing his license, even jail time."

With this tidbit of information I pulled into the office parking ramp where I parked next to what I thought was Maggie's car. Also, it appeared to be the only car in the parking lot.

"Well," I say. "It was a great game and you were excellent company."

She moves closer to me, looking into my eyes. She put her arm around my right shoulder and reached her lips to mine. We kissed, stopping when a police car rolled into the parking lot. It pulled behind us with flashing red lights. Police officers appeared on both sides of the car.

"Everything all right," the officer on Maggie's side of the car asks.

"It was until you guys got here." She smiles, kiddingly.

"You a Phillies fan, sir?" The officer on my side of the car inquired.

"We were at the World Series game. We work together. I'm dropping her off."

He looks around the car and sees nothing. Maggie has parked the empty beer cans under her seat.

"Be careful," the officer cautions. They both walk back to their squad car and drive away.

I walk Maggie to her car. She gets in and starts it up. "See you in the morning, Jack. Thanks again."

"Yeah," I say. "See you."

Success is going from failure to failure without losing your enthusiasm. **Winston Churchill**

What Is Past Is Prologue

Allentown State Hospital
1600 Hanover Avenue
Allentown, Pennsylvania
Monday, July 13, 1981

It is the eleventh week of the core curriculum and each week becomes more monotonous than the week before. Ade and I have never spoken about the night of the tornado. The day after her husband showed up for an unscheduled stay. I wondered if Ade had called him or maybe it was just good instincts on his part. But, it surely changed things. I spent a lot of time alone, which is my way if I can't associate myself with someone I like.

I took my guitar one day to a place called the Wine Cellar in Bethlehem, Pennsylvania, which is located just a few miles east of the hospital. My purpose was to audition as an entertainer. Hired on the spot after performing only one song, I now sit on a stool playing and singing *oldies* and current *top 40* songs in front of a small dance floor. The crowds are small, but those who come drink a lot, dance and tip well. I play Tuesday, Wednesday, and Thursday nights. I started the gig the last week in June and the entertaining is saving my sanity. It is only baseball and music which sustain me, when my life seems out of control.

I manage to get home every weekend to see Ellen and the boys. I didn't dare suggest I stay weekends so I could play music on Friday and Saturday nights. I had a pretty good following after just a few weeks and the owner tried persuading me to play weekends. In fact he even threatened to find a musician who could play all five nights. I simply told him to do what he had to do, but for the summer I'd have to leave it to three nights. Ellen would have never approved of me playing guitar in a club on the three nights I was already was doing. She always said music led to drinking and therefore it was a bad influence on me. True, but I tended to keep Ellen on a need-to-know basis when it came to things I knew she wouldn't agree with and I was already was doing.

Ellen and I had gotten into it over July 4th weekend. After her complaining about my dedication to the Bureau, rather than my family, she was driving me crazy with her verbal assaults and bombardments.

Finally, I shouted: "So with what you say, it should impact me to the extent that I give up my career after nearly 12 years of service? It makes it difficult, especially when you work side-by-side each day with the criminals. I understand your concerns, but I question whether this is unique enough to send me fleeing the Bureau in search of something less volatile and crushing." She had my anger up. "Just throw it all down the drain, and the retirement benefits I'm building. Is that what you are saying?"

"Not a bad idea, John. You're still a young man, with credentials." Ellen replied..

"Yes, Ellen, I suppose the Bureau is my life, and despite its occasional *slips*, it is still an organization to be looked at with pride by every man and woman. It is, after all, nothing more than a gathering of human beings who happen to work in law enforcement, rather than in banks or advertising agencies, the post office or a computer giant."

She countered. "What are you afraid of John, that I'll say something nasty about your precious FBI? Huh? *Don't embarrass the fucking Bureau!* She laughed, then, coughed. Her laugh was forced. "I didn't choose to marry a servant of J. Edgar Hoover and his whims! I chose you, a handsome, caring, charming kind of guy. I just wanted an ordinary life. I was happy to be married to an accountant and a fellow who could play guitar and sing. You were what I dreamed about my whole damn life."

She was on a roll. "John, it's your living the undercover life with impunity from your family. Think about it. Meeting people at bars and restaurants, becoming familiar faces in communities, hanging around accepted and trusted. Yet, you are never comfortable on any assignment too long. You just cut and run, with me and the kids tagging along with you.

"You walk around with unlimited cash in your pocket, you tell me, your wife, you'll be away for a few days, which sometimes becomes a month, on official business, but don't ask any questions, darling. It's for our country and for your own safety. You run with all sorts of women, supposedly agents, but God help your wife for questioning it. It's always official business. It's like little boys and girls playing cops and robbers and being paid for it."

Ellen cleared the counter and pulled a bottle of gin out of the cupboard. She took a glass, filled it and started drinking it straight. "Now this ridiculous set up. God, yes God, it is sac- religious pretending you are a man of the cloth. You are anything but a man of the cloth."

"John, we've just been going our own ways for years now. I've always hoped it would change. We could teach school, deliver mail anything but killing ourselves with this exaggerated subsistence. I really thought there was some hope when we were at Gettysburg. You said what you did about going in the Navy as a chaplain. You could do it as long as you could meet the requirements by age 39. It was my last hope, and a real one until this CPE bullshit."

"I'll do it, Ellen," I said, meaning it. "I'll do it. Don't be so bitter. I really want the same things you do. I'll do it!"

I stepped over to put my arm around her, while simultaneously she turned her head, pushing me away, pouring herself another shot of gin. "We'll see?" she said, offhandedly. "We'll see?"

She was right. In fact, she was always correct. My best intentions never quite made it. I was too self-possessed and never should have been married or had children. I never thought of the FBI as my life at the expense of everything else. I liked being married and being a father. They gave me a home front. They gave me a sense of belonging.

Whereas the FBI gave me the freedom to basically do what I pleased. I could always say what I was doing or where I was going was classified. At times we would live beyond what a FBI agent brings home in a paycheck. There were always business deals on the side. When Ellen would find a few extra thousand dollars in a pants pocket she would ask where it came from. If she caught me in a good mood, I'd give her a few hundred or so to buy her a new outfit. Otherwise, I would tell her to mind her own business.

"Oh, now the truth comes out." I say. "You want me going from dark secrecy to total disclosure. Just throw in the towel! Huh?"

"John," she says. "When we're out with a group or around a bunch of people you're the life of the party. When you are home or working you are a loner."

"I like being on my own." I reply. "Maybe that's why I'm good at my job. The job requires being a loner, using disguises, staying away from this bureaucracy as much as possible. I keep it low-key with no fanfare then, *get out the hell out of Dodge.*"

"By sundown," Ellen said, with a snicker. "Johnny you're just so unknowable, an enigmatic person marching to your own drum. It's not even like you're with the FBI and the bureau's prevailing philosophy – *TEAM – TEAM - TEAM*, with little room for individuality. You just don't fit that mold. It's as though you work for an agency within an agency, and under a different set of set of laws. Yeah, it's your rules!"

"You are right, Ellen. The FBI sells one thing to the public, deals another way with its own people. Remember how gung-ho I was at first. I worked 16-hour days and weekends on my first assignments. I know now how that ripped at our marriage. I gave it everything and look where I am now? Probably a wife and three children down the drain. And, for what, a lousy letter in my file that gives them the right to walk all over me.

"Screw the FBI!" Ellen says, loudly. "Screw the FBI!"

As the program began to wind down I started playing Chloe's game with her. During our one on one's I would make up a situation with which she would help me deal. Of course, I'd give her a scenario I knew would keep us busy for the hour. I found she was actually very intuitive and understanding. She gave me some good advice for the state of affairs I'd painted.

I played catch with Vince once a week. He could really fire

that baseball and when we were through each day the palm of my left hand burned. Since I started playing guitar at the club I put a sponge in the catcher's mitt to absorb his power.

By accident I found out the library was air conditioned. It was open until nine o'clock so I'd spend a couple hours there reading the newspaper and doing paperwork on Monday nights. I was busy every night of the week, which solved my being lonely. The week after the tornado Adelaide moved to the far end of the hall, I expected it was her husband's request. After the 4th of July weekend ten young nurses started a training program. So the whole second floor was now occupied by Ade, ten nurses, and me.

Today had been relatively scheduled. It was really hot and I decided to go to O'Henry's for a cold beer after our verbatim session. Chloe, thinking she had me under control, didn't sit directly across from me anymore. Today I found Hannah Hanson with her legs crossed, looking directly at me. When I caught her gaze she was smiling at me. I nodded. Hannah had a dynamite figure but I hadn't paid much attention to her during our training because she wasn't my type. She was a Moravian, who dressed very plainly and wore no makeup. Today she was paying attention to me, which I didn't understand. Other than in sessions we'd barely spoken to each other.

We were doing Henry Wilson's verbatim today. A patient had stood him up wielding a sharpened pencil and he had screamed for help. *Did I handle it correctly?* Henry asked the group. *Like the pussy you are,* I'd thought, so, I couldn't wait to get out of there and left abruptly when the session ended.

When I sat down at the bar *Edward G* put a bottle of Budweiser in front of me. I drank it really fast and he brought me another one. I fired up a cigarette and took a long drag. *Slow down,* I told myself. While I was thinking about conversations with Ellen and my last time here with Ade, I saw Hannah walk in the door. She was just standing their letting her eyes adjust to the darkness of the room. There was no place to hide so I pretended not to see her. But, she saw me when her eyes attuned. Slowly she walked around the bar while I ignored her approach.

"Adelaide told me you might be here. Hello, John!" Hannah said.

"Actually, I was just getting ready to leave." I reply.

"Let me buy you a beer, first," she offers.

"No, because then I have to buy you one and it will get late. I have a lot of paperwork to do tonight. Thank you, anyway." I respond.

Edward G walked over. Hannah said, "He'll have another and I'll have the same." She laid a ten dollar bill on the bar.

We talked for a couple hours about everything. She had graduated from Moravian College and Moravian Seminary, in nearby Bethlehem. She was going into the Navy to be a chaplain once her CPE training was complete. She had all the details and I was interested in what she was telling me. If nothing else, I would have something to report to Ellen this coming weekend, liked I researched the possibility.

Hannah did all the talking while I listened. It was exactly the way I liked to get to know somebody. Listen to everything about them and tell them nothing about me. The only information she got about me she already knew. That, I was a second career Lutheran Seminary student, married with three children. She couldn't handle the truth!

It turned out to be an interesting evening, but perplexing. Her plans about joining the Navy were very interesting and informing. I was at a loss as to why she wanted to talk with me. But, sometimes I can be so naïve. Everybody has an agenda and my first task is always to find out who the protagonist really is and what they know or want? I was trained to suspect everybody and trust nobody.

Outside of O'Henry's, Hannah Hanson slid into her 1968 *Army staff car colored* Dodge and drove into the night. I stared across the street looking at the double march of tall trees that led up to the dormitory. It was so different six weeks ago. Tonight I felt very ill at ease, feeling nothing about the night. Zilch is always a troubling state of mind.

Think you can't or think you can … either way, you will be right.
Henry Ford

Chapter Nineteen

1700 K Street
Washington, D.C.
Wednesday, October 12, 1983

I couldn't believe I was going to miss Game 2 of the World Series, especially since the *Fightin's* had won game one. However, once a month PGC took his troops to the St. Regis for dinner. It would be my first outing with Paul Gordon Charles in attendance.

It had been a very busy day. I met my handler at the *Ellipse*. We met walking around the historical site. The first twenty yards he told me I had to keep in better touch. That, I was not flying solo. I told him the big loan would be closing soon. That for me signing the papers and exercising the kickbacks I agreed to be paid thirty thousand.

My handler was a short, fit man in his late forties. He had slicked-back hair and cool blue eyes. He was articulate, unapologetic, and prickly. He didn't hesitate to lecture, even scold if he thought the situation called for it.

"Not enough," my handler speaks. "Ask for fifty."

"Are you serious," I ask.

"Do I ever say anything I'm not serious about?" He says.

"Okay, fifty it is. I'll see what they say." I reply.

"It's not about the money, it's a mission. They'll think more of you the greedier you play it. This is a story about human weakness, of hubris and greed and rampant self-delusions; of ambition run amok."

We had reached bottom of *The Ellipse* at Constitution Avenue. "Keep in touch," he says, as he takes a left on the famous boulevard.

I was in my office shortly before nine. Mary Robinson congratulates me on the Phillies victory. "Look out for Maggie Little, Mr. Oleson. She's mad as a wet hen!"

I look at Mary, confused. "I thought she had a great time last night. Women?"

"Perhaps she had too good a time last night, Jack. Perhaps she didn't know you are a happily married man?" Mary gave me the shame- on-you maneuver with her two pointer fingers.

I shrug my shoulders upward, saying, "I give up."

Mary Robinson laughs. "The banker and Bitterman will be here at ten o'clock."

I no more sat down at my desk when Maggie Little barged into my office. "Good morning Maggie." I address, with a cloud nine smile. "Go Phillies!"

"Why didn't you tell me you are married?" Maggie asked challenging me, with mocking half hysterics.

"You never asked me. Actually, I thought you knew. We were together to see a damn baseball game. Is that so wrong?" I ask.

"I'm sorry, Jack. I really like you and I thought maybe I found someone, oh, you know what I mean. Hey, let me get my clothes out of your closet. We wouldn't want your wife to find them there." She said, giving me a hug.

She left my office and I sat down at my desk to take a telephone call from the Kansas Insurance Department. While they were giving me a list of financial information required for application for an insurance license in their state, Bitterman appears at my door and I motion for him to sit down.

"Has anything changed with Fleck?" I ask.

"Everything is a go. We're ready to close after the board meeting. Has anything changed with you, Jack." Jerome Bitterman queries.

"Yes," I say. "It's too big of risk. I need fifty-thousand to cover my end. That's all!" It's the first time I saw Bitterman thunderstruck.

"I'll talk with Henry before we meet. I'll take care of it, Jack. Please just don't bring what you asked up again with anyone. I'll see you in a few minutes."

I knew right then I got the fifty and the difference was coming out of his end. How about my *handler*, it was what I was thinking when Mary buzzed saying Mr. Fleck had arrived.

We met in my office, exchanged pleasantries with Henry Fleck asking, "How did you like those tickets last night."

"Thanks again, Henry. The seats were great and the game was better. How about those Phillies?" I reply.

"I'm happy they won one game. They won't win another." He said convincingly.

"I'm thinking sweep," I say.

Henry Fleck laughs. "Okay," he guffaws. "Sweep, that'll be the day."

We agreed on Friday October 21st to close the loan. Bitterman agreed to have all the signatures of the guarantors. We set the time for 10 a.m. I was told the disbursements to the significant others would be done that day as well. "So bring the C&B checkbook, Jack!" Bitterman says, licking his chops.

"See you then," said Henry. He and Bitterman exit together, leaving me standing there wondering when the day would come when it would be so simple. And the fifty thousand I'm getting, what am I going to do with it? Ellen and I had looked at a house in Jenkintown, Pennsylvania. She wanted it badly, calling it her *Gingerbread House*. The realtor wanted an answer by Friday, with that *time is of the essence* shit. The asking price is $95,000 firm. Maybe I'd stick $45,000 down on the house and five in my pocket for change. Just a thought, I'm thinking. I still have my corporation open, yeah, I'll just make my check to JASCO, my corporation and nobody will care. My mind is racing when Mary Robinson appears in my office. She says, "Mr. Charles is requesting your presence in ten minutes."

I grab my leather bound legal pad, Mount Blanc pen and head toward power row. When I arrive at Charlotte Boyer's reception area she is at her empty desk filing her nails. She knows it's me and doesn't look up. "Jack, please sit down. He'll be with you momentarily." She says continuing to file her nails, totally ignoring me.

A few minutes later Charlotte's phone buzzes. She gets up and motions for me to follow her into PGC's office. As usual his back was facing me as he was writing something on a legal pad setting on his credenza. "Jack, have a seat. I'll be right with you."

As I wait Charlotte reappears with a covered silver platter. She carefully unwraps what looks like tuna and turkey sandwiches, placing them on fine china. Whereas everybody else I knew put their sandwiches on deli paper.

I'd been told Paul Gordon Charles was one of the 4.0 guys who had some street sense, whereas most 4.0 guys were a bunch of savants. Gordon is an inveterate collector of relationships. At each major stop in his early life, he forged bonds that lasted for decades. These weren't only personal acquaintances. Time and again, he would tap his growing network. For a job, for a favor, or to surround himself with those he trusted. This skill propelled his climb. It was always inevitable that he would be a man of wealth. And at each of these early stops, he received a taste of life at the top.

Although PGC insisted that other businesses he chaired failed simply because of the brutal cycle of business life. *Shit happens*, he liked to say. We were just a victim. But, in all cases, rarely has there ever been such a chasm between corporate illusion and reality. Scrutinizing his affairs exposed more epic business scandals none more than the tales of cooked books, which was certainly his way allowing him to live a lavish life.

PGC turned around in his chair. His dark eyes were trenchant. "I hear you've satisfied the bank's needs and the loan is ready to close." Mr. Charles stated. I had not yet figured out who all his sources were but he never made a statement, or asked a question that he didn't already know the answer.

"Yes, we're closing the day right after the board meeting." I reply.

"Have you told Henry how you want the proceeds distributed?" Mr. Charles asks, with an imposing tone in his voice.

"Fleck has his instructions. I don't anticipate he'll do anything but what I ask." I answer, unassailably.

"And, C&B, do you have any problems there?" He queried.

"Bitterman has given me those instructions, which I passed on to Henry Fleck." I register water tightly.

"Jack, does your job live up to what you thought it would be? Does it meet your expectations?" Mr. Charles asks.

"And, then some." I reply.

"The next six weeks we have a ton of work to accomplish. I want you to make a list to include the following:

1. Treasurer's report as of September 30 – for 10/20 Board Meeting
2. Loan closing – Henry Fleck – 10/21
3. C&B distribution – 10/21
4. Financing – Yacht I
5. Financing -Yacht II
6. Financing – Cessna for Tom
7. Financing - Jet for PGC
8. Financing – Restaurant
9. Liquor License for Café Sebastian
10. Fripp Island for Thanksgiving – dinner and annual budget- invite your wife to join us

"That's a long list and a big Job, Mr. Charles." I emphasize.

"Jack, this isn't a job. It is an opportunity. You don't just go to work here. It becomes a part of your life, just as important as your family, or, more important than your family, or, the best thing for your family. And, depending on how it plays out, it may reach a point where it puts you on top, or, it's not worth sticking around."

I stared at PGC trying to sort out exactly what he meant. It was true what I'd heard about him. He was a hard man not to like, if he liked you. If he didn't like you he was an easy man to hate. He made a point of serving drinks to his subordinates along for the ride on his flagship corporate jet. He built a deep reservoir of goodwill among those who productively worked for him. He remembered names, listened earnestly, and seemed to care about what you thought. He had a gift for calming tempers and defusing conflict.

But this style, soothing though it may have been, was not necessarily well suited to running a corporation. He had the traits of a politician; he cared deeply about appearances, he wanted people to like him, and he avoided the sort of tough decisions that were certain to make others mad. His key people understood this about him and viewed him with something akin to contempt. They knew that as long as they steered clear of a few sacred cows, they could do whatever they wanted and he would never say no. On the rare occasion when circumstances forced his hand, he'd let someone else take the heat or would throw money at a problem. PGC didn't like to get his hands dirty.

"See you tonight, Jack. Oh, give me a daily report on your progress with the list." PGC ordered.

"I will and I look forward to dinner. Thank you."

When I approached Charlotte Boyer's desk, she gave a sly look. "See you tonight, Jack."

"Okay." I reply and walked on by.

Far better is it to dare mighty things, to win glorious triumphs, even though checkered by failure ... than to rank with those poor spirits who neither enjoy much nor suffer much, because they live in a gray twilight that knows not victory nor defeat. **Theodore Roosevelt**

Chapter Twenty

I worked late spending a good deal of time in the accounting department going over reports McKenzie had given me. I mostly worked on verifying income with deposits and reviewing the expenses. What I found was what I expected. The total deposits in the bank were less than the income reported in each of the nine months Treasurer's report. I found the expenses paid were much more than those reported on the Treasurer's report. In final analysis the Treasure's report grossly overstated its profit every month.

As I walked from 17th to 16th Street I was thinking about the numbers. The results were no surprise. The degree of the financial discrepancies was extraordinary. Talking to others the focus was claims, big claims to pay. The Treasurer's reports reflected only a light percentage of possible claims. Yet, with these phony reports they'd coerced successful businessman into investing large sums of money into the company. And, now a ten million dollar bank loan was on the table, approved and ready to be disbursed. Its approval all is based on not genuine financial statements. And, some of the checks I saw, not recorded on the Treasurer's report, was crazy. Like, *six-figures* worth of expense advances. I was getting delusions of grandeur, thinking I was closing in on this operation as I walked through the spinning brass door of the St. Regis.

I turned to the left where I saw several of the players had gathered in the Library Lounge. It was 6:30 p.m. Joe Neverson was drinking, smoking and talking to a short, balding man with an endearing resemblance to Elmer Fudd. Before I got to the bar I heard a commotion behind me. It was the entourage and we were all ushered back to a private dining room, where a long oval table is centered.

Paul Gordon Charles is escorted to the far end of the table, to the *catbird seat* where he can watch everybody. Seated on his right flank are Tom Harvey, followed by Richard Corrigan, Ray *Red* Bertrand, Matt Ferrone, Larry Leopold and Charlotte Boyer at the opposite end. On his left flank sits Madeline Haycock, Elmer Fudd (who I learned later was Dr. Sandusky, a board member), Ned Larson, Joe Neverson, Ted Masters and me, sitting on Charlotte Boyer's right. There were thirteen of us, PGC's 2nd favorite number. It was PGC and his twelve disciples.

The first round of drinks was delivered without much ado. He seemed to know everyone's call drink, or, at least Charlotte knew. I saw it right away; here Mr. Charles was in his element. Also, I noticed he was not drinking liquor. It looked like a Coca Cola, and he drank it pretty quickly. I noticed his eyes darting around the table observing each person, eyes dropping on some of the different conversations going around the table. He kept a smile on his face during his deliberations. I wondered what he was thinking and I supposed he was unsure what each other person was dwelling upon.

Every fifteen minutes a new round of drinks came and when the fourth arrived, PGC shouted out. "Ned, drink your drinks. Nobody else can have another sip until you drink your drinks, Ned."

The chattering started up again as I saw Ned Larson dump two of his in a flower arrangement. I looked at PGC, who was busy talking with Madeline Haycock. Now Ned took his first drink, which he'd already drank half of and took a drink. He toasted PGC when he got his attention.

Mr. Charles clinks his wine glass with a spoon and announces, "Ned drank his drinks now everyone else can enjoy theirs."

I was amazed how much control he had over these people. Everybody simply began drinking again and conversations got back to normal. "What's the score," I asked a waiter?"

"Philadelphia, leads 1-0, after four innings." He replies, quickly.

"Yes!" I shout, thrusting my right arm upward, drawing everybody's attention.

"Jack, you have good news to share?" Mr. Charles says, with an affable grin.

"I apologize," I say, feeling idiotic. "The Phillies are up 1-0, after four."

PGC tells our server, who is always within easy hearing distance of our *leader*, "Another round to toast Jack's *Phillies*." Then he looks directly at Ned Larson, saying, "Drink your drink, Ned."

We continue to talk back and forth amongst each other for an hour or so. The waiter, for a *Grant*, keeps giving me updates on Game Two of the World Series. The last report was Baltimore leading, 4-1, at the end of seven innings. Then suddenly, Joe Neverson, who was hammered, yells out at Ned Larson, "You are the weakest man I know!"

Ned had been bragging about the large increase in premiums written and Joe negatively countered with the recent extraordinary claims coming in from all over the country. While they argue I kept watching PGC and noticed how he seemed to be enjoying the conflict. I also sensed Joe was expressing real concern about the real financial position of the company and its inability to pay these claims. Of course, I knew Commander Larson was simply fueling the fire to get more and more out on the table. Ned was one of us and his job was to stir the shit storm.

Tom Harvey, who only cared about getting a new Mercedes and a new Cessna was twiddling his thumbs and seemed half asleep. Doc Sandusky, the psychiatrist who indeed looked like Elmer Fudd, was so drunk he just rattled on about increasing the Director's fees. "Gordon," he asks, "When are we going to eat?"

While Joe Neverson continued to rage both Harvey and Sandusky passed out. *"Bill of Fare,"* PGC orders. While we're looking, bring us another round of drinks. I toss my drink into the plant, with Ned Larson noticing and laughing at my scheme.

Everybody ate a full course meal and somewhat sobered up.

Joe Neverson kept staring at me. I wonder what he is thinking as I'm sure he was wondering who is that Jack Oleson. And I wonder what this night is really all about? It seems to be such a big waste of money, without purpose. I don't see anybody who I think is really enjoying themselves, other than PGC. Maybe?

It also seemed Gordon was pitting certain people against each other. Or, did he just want to expose weaknesses. For instance the two on the Board of Directors, Harvey and Sandusky, as two who couldn't hold their liquor; Corrigan and Ferrone against each other as a favorite protector; but never in a million years would I have thought Commander Ned Larson to be PGC's man servant. When Mr. Charles is on the road, Ned leads a detail with a can of Lysol into every city to completely fumigate the room where the leader will be staying.

PGC loves employing high ranking military officers to do dirty deeds for him. He loves ordering them around. Bertrand is the observer and Matt Ferrone the muscle. Leopold, nobody talks much to him knowing he will be the next person fired. I don't think Ted Masters could quite believe what was taking place here tonight. All he wanted was a real job, which would keep his wife's complaining mouth shut. PGC and I watch each other. I think he is hoping I'll get drunk too loosen my mouth. I couldn't and wouldn't let that happen.

Charlene and Madeline, the old and the new, keep an eye on each other as they know full well PGC likes them quarreling for his attention. Then, finally the purpose of the night arrives on a jeweler's cart.

Paul Gordon Charles clanks his glass until he has everyone's attention. "Richard Corrigan, would you please step up next to me."

Corrigan makes his way and stands next to Gordon. "Richard has been with me in several different endeavors. He's been a leader and a work horse under my command for twenty years. Therefore I'm making him a gift to show my appreciation. Madeline, would you bring the gift to Richard."

Corrigan opens a very snazzy box, which is holding a Rolex

watch. "This is too much, but thank you very much, Gordon, you shouldn't have." He says, extending his hand to PGC.

When the PGC entourage leaves the building I confirm that the Phillies had lost Game Two of the World Series, 1-4. And Neverson, who had sobered up some, pushed me toward the Library Lounge. "Finally," he said, "it's just you and I."

"Jack, I understand we're closing on the ten million dollar loan on October 21st." Neverson is looking for corroboration.

"This is most certainly true," I confirm.

"Jack, I can only try to reinforce to you that we must pay some claims." Joe says, emphatically.

"Joe, give me a number?" I ask.

"Six million is the short list, Jack."

"Jesus," I reply.

"I can spread it out, but I need at least three million within a six month period." Joe says, in a hush. "And if you don't reserve the funds, PGC will spend them."

I sense his concern and sincerity. He is serious, but I know nothing of the numbers other than the fraudulent Treasurer's reports, which are seriously understating claim contingencies.

"Huh?" I go.

"Jack," Joe says. "You have no idea what the real problems are," ordering us two drinks. Just then Ted Masters and Charlotte Boyer join us.

"What are you boys talking about?" Charlotte asks.

"Baseball," I reply, wishing they hadn't showed up..

"Sure you are, Jack. In fact I hear the O's beat the *Phillies* tonight. Disappointed, Jack?" She asks with her sardonic grin. She has a way and is so good at it. I suppose she is taking a crack at Theodore Rex Masters now. Poor guy!

"Actually, Charlotte, I'm pissed off." I reply. "I don't like to lose!"

Ted was now talking to Joe about the procedure of getting a liquor license. Meanwhile Charlotte has dragged me out to the dance floor. She is an excellent dancer. Her right knee spent most of its time jiggling my balls.

"So," she asks. "I hear Maggie Little is infatuated with you," as she poked one of her long legs between mine, drawing me close, and whispering sweet nothings in my ear. I spin her around to get free as the song comes to an end.

"Thank you," I said. She stood in place looking at me with her mysterious eyes.

"Well," she asks? "You are such a stud!"

"You mean a real thoroughbred." I recommend.

We both laugh, while rejoining Ted and Joe as last call was announced.

Mistakes are part of the dues one pays for a full life. **Sophia Loren**

What Is Past Is Prologue

El Conquistador Restaurant
Canal Street off Military Highway
Chesapeake, Virginia
Monday, February 4, 1974

I'm sitting at the bar of this dumpy beer joint listening to a half-assed musician strumming a guitar and trying to sing Wilbur Harrison's great song, *Kansas City*. He is terrible and I am thinking about asking him if I can play and sing a few numbers while I wait for the new owner of the establishment to make her appearance.

But just as I order another beer a vivacious blond sashays into the bar room, looking around for me I suppose. Following close behind is a good looking man, a *Clark Gable* look-a-like with a pencil thin mustache, dressed in a fashionable suit. He doesn't seem to belong in this dive and I wonder what is up?

"John," the pretty woman asks, while *Clark* looks on with unfocused but inquiring eyes.

I stand up and shake her hand, while she introduces her lawyer, Bobby Doyle. Then, she says, "Bobby this is my new accountant, John …..What's your last name again?" She asks in a pronounced southern drawl.

I moved to the East Coast in September, 1971, and nobody can spell or pronounce my last name here. "It is Sletten … S L E T T E N, a Norwegian name," I reply.

"Norwegian," asks the lawyer. Where are you from, Norway?" He asks, snooping.

"I'm from Minnesota. Most Minnesotans' are Norwegians or Swedes. The good ones are Norwegians. We kill, pillage, rape, steal and cause all kinds of unnecessary problems."

Shirley states with a southern belle charm, "I don't think I've ever met anyone from Minnesota?" She giggles, while adjusting her rather ample breasts in my direction. "So," she says. "You're my new accountant. Honey Fitz recommends you highly."

I look at the lawyer who is waiting for her to slow down so he can get a word in edgewise. I suppose he is wondering why she would hire somebody she knew nothing about to keep her books. But, he wasn't. Instead, he asks me what I charge. It was a good question with great timing on his part.

Honey Fitz owns the Chesapeake Lounge and I charge him $75 a month. I knew Fitz wouldn't divulge such information, so I said I'd do it all for $100 per month. A big grin appears on the lawyer's face. He tells Shirley to get us a drink. "I need to talk with the *boy* accountant here."

While Shirley wiggles her ass around to the back of the bar, the lawyer put his left arm around my back. He puts his face real close to mine and says, "I own a dozen places like this. I buy them and sell them. When I sell them I usually get them back in about a year or so. The owners spend any excess cash personally and don't care that much about making the business work. Other than it being a cash cow, for a while they have no long term goals. I get enough front money for the business so I'll make out, even though I may have to take the joint back again. In the meantime I collect rent for the building, which I always continue to hold. Get it?" The lawyer asks, quizzically.

Get what, I'm thinking, wondering if he is going to fix my prices in exchange for having the opportunity to acquire several more accounts. Would I also be expected to keep him posted on these business' he owns and finances for the buyers that he knows are doomed before they commence operations. Shirley certainly seems to be no rocket scientist. *Honey, I'd always dreamed of having my own place. Why, I'd give up my first born for it.* Shirley had said to me.

"What exactly are you recommending, Mr. Doyle?"

Robert Doyle, says, "Call me, Bobby." He slaps me on the back again. "Make it fifty dollars a month. If they make it, move 'em up to sixty, you know what I mean?"

"Okay," I say. Now I was smiling. "When do I get my first new account?" I ask.

"I like your style kid. Is tomorrow soon enough?" He looks at his watch. Meet me at my office on Granby Street, in Norfolk tomorrow. Call first to make sure I don't have to be in court, unexpectedly." He hands me his business card.

Shirley comes back with two beers. She must have been watching us because she arrives shortly after our conversation ends. "John," she queries. "Honey Fitz tells me you are a good musician. You can play guitar and sing? The guy playing tonight really stinks. Customers are complaining and want me to turn on the juke box."

"The lawyer's ears seemed to perk up when Shirley mentions music. "Let's hear you!" Bobby Doyle shouts, loudly, giving me an encouraging slap on the back.

"I just happen to have my guitar in the car." I say.

"Well, go get it. I'll tell the guy he's done." The lawyer says, without proviso.

I hope the new nick name, boy accountant, wouldn't stick. I had a hard time with my age as it was. I'd be thirty years old this year, but I looked more like eighteen. It's a Norwegian thing, looking young, even past middle age. To be one's accountant you want to look older so they think you have some experience. In my eyes I had plenty of experience, but it was difficult to convey because of how young I appeared to be.

In fact the Bureau didn't know quite what to do with me at first. I was an easy hire, being a naïve mid-westerner with good grades and good looks. I was also a collegiate athlete, which made it easy for me to meet their physical requirements and show leadership skills. I breezed through New Agents Training, since the Academy at Quantico hadn't opened yet when I joined in September, 1971, the training was too easy.

My first assignment, after training, was at the DOJ (Department of Justice Building), working Selective Service cases. Disappointingly, it had proved to be a monumental bore. I had been assigned to a Selective Service squad, where I was relegated to the position of record checking at the numerous draft boards throughout Prince George's and Prince William's Counties, in the surrounding Maryland and Virginia suburbs. It was as interesting as looking numbers up in a telephone book.

I was hoping to be assigned to a criminal fugitive squad where there was always plenty of action, little paper work and virtually no involvement in moral judgments. Instead of developing evidence for potential prosecutions, they were concerned with only locating and arresting fugitives so that they could be returned to the appropriate state of federal jurisdiction to stand trial. The fugitive investigations seemed incredibly interesting. But, again it seemed I was too young and inexperienced to be one of those guys, leaving me reading Jane Fonda files and working Selective Service with fifty other agents.

For some reason my supervisor, Joe Ramsey, took a liking to me. Joe Ramsey, who looked a lot like the unkempt *Walter Matthau*, was an amiable, unassuming individual admired and respected for his fairness. When he found out I did not want to hunt and harass guys of approximately my same age, for not keeping in touch with their draft board, he understood my reticence. That my evasiveness perhaps was simply I had too many classmates who were doing the same thing.

Unlike many supervisors, Joe had not forgotten his lengthy career as a street agent; consequently, he recognized that many of the archaic rules and regulations were impossible to operate under if followed to the letter. In the maze of bureaucratic regulation, Joe demonstrated the ability to differentiate between the chicken salad and the chicken shit and allowed his men to function accordingly.

Joe Ramsey also had a lively sense of humor, but when the Inspectors descended upon the office for their annual charade, he was all business. Instead of rolling over to the Inspectors and following the example of other supervisors whose primary concern was to "cover their ass," he defended his men. He didn't offer up a youthful candidate to help fill the prearranged quota for *letters of censure*, he took the letter himself. Ramsey was one of the few supervisors who would stand up to the ruthless, dictatorial tyrant who serve as Special Agent in Charge (SAC).

Since Joe Ramsey and I had always spoken candidly with each other, he was aware of my current dissatisfaction. He was the one who told me, when I was trying to figure out what to do with idle time, to go get a haircut. "Goddamn!" he had exclaimed. "You don't get your hair cut on your day off, son. If your hair grows on Bureau time, you ought to damn sure get it cut on Bureau time. Hell, the weekends are your time. Get out and enjoy yourself."

He offered to lobby for my transfer to the bank robbery squad, but that was no simple matter. In the meantime, however, there was increasing speculation that a new squad would be formed to intensify looking into white collar crime. If formed, it would be Joe Ramsey being considered both a likely and willing prospect for the new desk. When I asked Ramsey about his possible upcoming appointment, he told me he would take it if offered. If so, would I like to go with him? He asked enthusiastically.

So here I was about to play a few songs at the El Conquistador, an establishment that I would also be keeping books for and preparing income, payroll and sales tax returns.

During the summer of 1972, Joe Ramsey sent me to Portsmouth, Virginia to work with Edward M. Hargrave, a Registered Public Accountant. He was eighty-two years old and his staff was in their sixties and seventies. Ramsey told me the Big Eight firm of Peat, Marwick and Mitchell was trying to put an audited financial statement together to make a filing to go Public. Edward Hargrave was the local accounting firm who kept the books for the outfit trying to go Public. Joe Ramsey understands that the books were at least two years behind.

"John," Joe said, "here's the shot you've been looking for, sport."

Joe Ramsey and I were looking at each other across his desk. "There are four men that formed a joint venture, here in Washington, who are acquiring music companies across the country for the purpose selling, mainly, pianos and organs. These four individuals have acquired another organization called *Guaranteed*

Keyboard Learning Centers. The course comes with the purchase of a new organ or piano. Supposedly, if a designated student cannot learn to play using this method they can return the piano for a full refund within a six month period.

"Sales had taken off big time and the joint venture had purchased twenty-two stores in the Washington D.C. and Tidewater, Virginia areas. So, they're taking their sudden good fortune and are packaging it to go public. It's the music stores in Tidewater for which we need the real numbers." Joe finally took a breath, allowing me to talk.

"So, I fly to Norfolk, Virginia and report to this accounting firm in Portsmouth, Virginia. My job is to post the books for the last two years, obtaining trial balances, so Peat, Marwick, Mitchell and Company can put together an audited statement for the purpose of filing for an initial public stock offering, an IPO."

"There you go," smiles Joe Ramsey. "John, as you will find out over the coming years, what we are really looking for you'll never really know. You're job is to gather the information we request. For example, as this outfit moves organs and pianos across interstate lines its seems a bunch of their tractor trailers get high jacked. Like I say you never really know what the designated goal of the Bureau might be. Just keep your ears and eyes open and your mouth shut."

"Who will all these people think I am?" I ask, shrugging my shoulders.

"You're the new accountant for Edward M. Hargrave's Registered Public Accounting practice. We've made certain arrangements for you to take over his practice, soon enough. It will put you on the map in the entire Tidewater area. It will put you on the inside as certain investigations come up in the near future. Meanwhile, you simply report to the intersection of Court and High Street in Portsmouth, Virginia next Monday morning. They will all be expecting you." Joe Ramsey smiles deviously, saying, "Be careful what you wish for, John."

"Just fit into the community," had been Joe Ramsey's final instruction. "Just be yourself and carryon like your only mission in life is to be a successful public accountant in the Tidewater area of Virginia. Collect your fees, pay your related bills and if you make a profit good for you. If and when we want you to do a special assignment, you'll do it. In the meantime, in your own mind, pretend you do not work for the Bureau. Of course your paycheck will arrive timely at your designation."

Having met the lawyer, Bobby Doyle, I was conjuring up all kinds of new successes in my mind. In fact I was hoping, *if and when*, would never come. The Bureau had set me up nicely, or did they? I was thinking as I re-entered the beer joint. *Be careful what you wish for John*, the aphorism was now ringing in my ears.

The one who had been playing the guitar was sitting at the bar with a pissed off look on his face. How embarrassing for him, I thought. I suppose he was drinking his remuneration for his performance.

I plugged my guitar into the house public address system. I played my version of *Kansas City* and then Ray Charles' *What'd I Say*, and *"Ain't no Sunshine When She's Gone*. When the singing and clapping was done, the lawyer walks over to my spot. He takes the microphone, saying, "how about, *I Get a Kick out of You?*"

I'd had had a band out in South Dakota and we played music from the *40's* and the *50's*, and he was amazed when I suggested the key of *Bb*. We played and sang two sets, together before we called it a night. Bobby told me this was how he had paid his way through Law School at the University Miami. He was the front man for two or three strip joints. He had an older fellow playing the piano back then and as the girls stripped he sang *old standards*. We forged a bond together that night with our music, *fuck the accounting*, I thought.

When I arrived home my wife, Ellen, is provoked. "Did you at least find one client; you've been gone all night?"

"I found at least a dozen," I say. I told her the story and she was unimpressed saying, "Tomorrow night I'm going to take my flute and see if I can get so providential. I hate that damn guitar, it always sidetracks you."

"Let's watch Johnny Carson," I suggest.

"Yes, let's do that," she says, snuggling up to me with a cup of coffee. Between sips she says, "Good ole Ellen, forgive and forget."

"I'm meeting Bobby Doyle tomorrow at his office for lunch."

"Are you bringing your guitar?" My wife says, snidely. "Where's his office?" She asks.

"It's right downtown, on Granby Street." I tell her.

"His office must be near the Federal Building, John?"

"Oh yeah," I agree. "I'll have to careful."

"No shit, Dick Tracy!" Ellen speaks softly and slowly. "How do you do it? How do you justify or defend the activities of the FBI? *Joe Blow America* would be shocked at the goings-on. Someday somebody is going to ask you how you, a government agent, of purportedly high moral character, who has undergone a thorough background investigation, could consciously violate the very laws you have sworn to uphold. How will you explain the influencing factors?"

I turned off the television and fix Ellen and I a drink, saying, "I graduated from high school, college, passed my CPA, and earned my MBA. Even though I was playing music in clubs and for barn dances I never had a drink or smoked a cigarette. I was brought up in a military family with a conservative, patriotic background. And, it was a background that left me unprepared for the life-style we've now encountered. For you, too, but at least you were at *Woodstock*."

Ellen lit up a cigarette and poured us another drink. "Yes I was," she smiled broadly. "Don't you wish you'd have been there? She leaned on the bar ready to listen.

"When I graduated college in 1966, I was aware there was a war going on in Vietnam but in all honesty, at the time; it wasn't of paramount importance to me. It seemed only real when I heard friends from high school and college had been killed serving there. I felt so guilty hunting Elk in Montana, while my classmates and friends were being killed in the jungles of Vietnam. Actually I figured once I graduated I'd actually be in Vietnam with plenty of time to learn about that issue. I never even considered any other course of action. If the draft board said go, which they surely would, I thought, I would just go. It was simply my duty as an American to answer my country's call like my Dad and grandfathers had done. Never once did I stop to think that perhaps the war was illegal, immoral, or unnecessary."

"During my senior year in college I applied for Officer Candidate programs, with the Air Force and the Navy. I passed their tests, academically and physically. I qualified to fly but then talked with my father and he said, much to my surprise, *no*. What he said I never questioned. When I said I would probably get drafted, he told me, *nobody's going to draft you without checking with me first*. They were powers that belonged to a war hero, who is still serving.

"So enthralled by Kennedy's Camelot, and remembering his challenge in his inaugural address: *Ask not what your country can do for you, but ask what you can do for your country*, it seemed the thing to do when the opportunity was right. So, as you know, I applied for the FBI after we got married. The trouble was everything I applied for I got accepted as a candidate. After a few stops along the way, here's what we've become."

"You mean," says Ellen, "It's what you've become. Not me!"

The unexamined life is not worth living. **Plato**

Chapter Twenty-One

1700 K Street
Washington, D.C.
Thursday, October 13, 1983

"So, it was a tough night," Mr. Oleson. She asks, knowing I feel like a freight train is roaring through the middle of my head.

I wave her off as I go directly to the coffee bar to grab a strong cup of java. Mary Robinson watches my every movement as I move toward my office. I'm finding her obsessive observation of me very strange. When I open the door Charlotte Boyer is sitting behind my desk in the swivel chair.

"Hi Jack, did you enjoy dancing with me last night?" She asks, facetiously.

"What?" I ask, annoyed by her presence.

"Did you enjoy our dance last night, Jack, you bad-ass thoroughbred." She queries again, while flashing her naked vagina. "See what you're missing, Jack?"

"Get the hell out of here, Charlotte. I'm meeting with an auditing firm in a few minutes." I say rather stridently and callously.

"You don't think I know your schedule, Jack." She smiles deviously as she walks by me. "See you tonight, Jack"

"No you won't!" I bark. "No, you won't."

I sit down behind my desk and pull out last year's annual insurance report and audited financial statement out of my briefcase. I had never really looked at either of them. Now I was in charge of producing this year's audited statements, knowing full well last year's were completely bogus.

Looking at the balance sheet I would guess the cash included the collateral accounts. The accounts receivable didn't exist because premium receivables shouldn't exist, according to insurance accounting standards. The investments were certainly questionable, thinking they were simply cash advances for PGC's whims. I was certain the prepaid expenses were travel advances to PGC or C&B Leasing. I was speculating about all this information, without even feeling a need to look at supporting documents. And, I was sure certain there must have been serious payoffs to last year's auditors.

Of course there are no liabilities showing, but the equity section looks as strong as the electric chair. PGC has mastered the principle of putting numbers in front of even smart people's eyes and deceiving them. For the most part, people don't look at the numbers because they don't understand them. Some may look at the bottom line, but they don't understand it, either. What they believe is the spin the leader puts to the story.

In my conversations with those who know him best, in addition to our FBI files, in describing Paul Gordon Charles they just don't use the word *smart*. They use phrases like *incandescently brilliant*, or the smartest person I've ever met. Plus Gordon is a strikingly handsome man to add to his breathtaking mental agility. He can process information and conceptualize new ideas with amazing speed. He can instantly simplify highly complex issues into a sparkling, compelling image. And he presents his ideas with a certainty that borders on arrogance and brooked no dissent. uses his brainpower not just to persuade, but to intimidate.

But, for all his brilliances, I have already found dangerous blind spots. His management skills, *kick-ass*, are appalling, in large part because he really doesn't understand people. He expects people to behave according to the imperatives of pure intellectual logic, but of course nobody does that. People will do things just because they're people. What seems to thrill PGC is the intellectual purity of an idea, not the translation of that idea into reality. He is the designer of ditches, not the digger of ditches. He is so sure of himself that anyone who disagrees with him is summarily dismissed as just not bright enough to be a player. And, his most dangerous blind spot of all is that he is so sure he can beat all odds.

As I flip through the footnotes of the audited report my intercom buzzes. "Mr. Oleson, a Mr. George Edwards and a Mr. Robert Franta have arrived for their appointment." Announces, Mary Robinson.

"I'll be right there Mary, is the Conference Room available?"

I immediately leave my office with the financials tucked under my arm. Mary Robinson introduces us and shows us to the Conference Room. She is back in ten minutes with a silver chalice of coffee and three China cups replete with coasters. She also brings in a tray of pastries on a silver serving dish. She pours each of us a cup of coffee, giving Franta his requested cream and sugar. George Edwards and I drank our coffee black.

As we drank coffee and eat pastries I began feeling sorry for these guys. They were perhaps my age and feeling pretty good about themselves being a major cog in a large local firm, in Washington, D.C. Bob Franta is married with four children. George Edwards seems to be a playboy of sorts. They are dressed to the nines and very pompous. We all get along well enough and they make all the right promises about a speedy audit to meet the insurance commission's deadlines. I assure them I am impressed with their presentation and would get back to them soon. What I didn't tell them, if they were lucky I wouldn't call them. That the accountants conducting this audit were probably going straight to jail.

The auditors left with a smile on their face thinking they had landed the golden goose. And, I had already determined they should have been smiling. I was going to use last year's firm, Ruth, Cobb, Greenberg, and Foxx. I didn't want to hurt anybody new and I was interested to see how Bitterman pulled off last year's certified audit. I would be certain to ask Jerry really soon, like before the loan closing, how he used the back door of the accounting firm.

It seemed I could never get a break as Ted Masters appears at my door. "Did you find the right accounting firm?" He asks. His question was confounding?

"No," I reply. "How did you know I was looking?"

"Word travels fast in these halls." Ted says.

"Who the hell is interested in what auditing firm we are using this year?" I ask. Ted shrugs his shoulder and changes the subject. "Have you seen Charlotte?"

"Yes, I've seen Charlotte." I reply.

Ted closed my door. "I think I'm in trouble, Jack. I fucked her last night."

"Where," I asked?

"We did in my *K* car, right in the back seat." Ted Masters says, clenching his teeth.

"Jack, do you think she'll tell my wife?"

"Probably, if you don't do what she tells you to do?" I laugh. "God, how could you be so stupid. And her telling your wife is the least of your worries." I caution.

"I think I'm getting sick, Jack." He raced off toward the men's room, moving like a man who had just shit his pants in mixed company.

I walk outside my office to look around. Mary Robinson asks, "Anything new, Jack?"

"Is there anything that's not brand new around this place, Mary?" I say with a goaded tone in my voice.

"Just checking, Jack," Mary says, with a cackle.

"I'm going to take an early lunch, Mary."

"Have a good one, Jack. Maybe you should invite Maggie Little." She added. I hesitated and started walking toward the Claims Department. I turned looking at Mary who was in good spirits.

"Maybe I should. Yeah, maybe I will"

I wondered if Mary Robinson is with the FBI and her job is to monitor me.

With ordinary talents and extraordinary perseverance all things are attainable. **Thomas Buxton**

What Is Past Is Prologue

Robert Doyle, Attorney at Law
Office Building @ Granby Street
Norfolk, Virginia
Monday, February 5, 1974

When I walk into Doyle's office it reminds me of one pictured in a movie. It was cluttered and seemingly undersized. A receptionist, who didn't seem too bright, was struggling with an out of date copy machine. I state, " I have an appointment with Mr. Doyle."

She smiles, asking, "What's your name?"

"Boy Accountant," I answer.

She took a stenographer's pad from under a stack of papers and wrote down *Boy Accountant.* Your first name is Boy and did I spell your last name correctly?

A C C O U N T A N T. She spelled it out loud.

I was feeling badly about confusing her, while she told me Mr. Doyle would be back from court about noon. As I was checking my watch the door opens and in walks the lawyer with an attaché case.

He grins when he sees me, greeting, "John."

"Mr. Doyle, this is Boy Accountant. He says he has an appointment with you." His secretary informs him.

The lawyer laughs, while shaking his head, saying to me, "Okay Mr. Accountant come into my office. I followed him. He sits down behind his desk, after moving a dozen files or so out of a chair, I sit down in a chair facing him..

"So, this is it." Bobby says. "As you can see I keep expenses low. The easiest way to make money is not to spend any. I share this office and the secretarial expense with another attorney, Zeke Uggla, a real estate attorney."

I noticed a family picture on his desk, various diplomas on the wall, and a newspaper clipping picturing a rather large boat in flames. What's that clipping all about, one of your cases?" I ask.

"No. It's my boat. The whole damn thing went up in flames. I keep the picture on the wall to remind me never to get frivolous again."

"What happened," I ask.

"Don't know," Doyle says. Luckily, insurance covered all my losses. No more boats or yachts for me." He said, with emphasis.

You know I have a boat story, it happened right out there on the Elizabeth River. In the summer of '72, when I first arrived in Tidewater, I was working with Eddie Hargrave, a RPA in Portsmouth, to pull together a trial balance for an audit. Sam Barnes was the lead auditor with Peat, Marwick, and Mitchell. He popped pills all day long for some nervous condition. At any rate he lived at the Portsmouth Marina on his house boat. I was living next door at the Holiday Inn.

Sam was single and I was alone in Portsmouth, so we would stop at the Holiday Inn lounge during their Happy Hour. In fact I think Sam ate most of his dinners, non-gratis, because they really set out a nice selection of food.

It was a Friday night, and we'd been at the Holiday Inn for three or four hours, when Sam told me about a party in Hampton Roads. He said we could take the boat from the Portsmouth Marina right across the channel to Newport News. I didn't know the area so I asked him how long it would take. He assured me no more than a half an hour. When I asked him if he could operate the boat in his current condition, he said, *a piece of cake.*

I usually flew back to Washington D.C. on Friday nights to spend the weekend with my family. But, they were really putting the pressure on me to get a trial balance so I decided to put in a long weekend. So, I agreed to make this jaunt. What a mistake!

Once we got out between the buoys Sam Barnes told me to take the wheel. He said he was going to the toilet. He had not given me any instructions because he said he would be right back. It was a beautiful evening and I was enjoying the cruise as I watched the Norfolk skyline. Suddenly I saw what looked like stakes sticking out of the water. I intuitively slowed down the speed, trying to steer away from the protrusions. I was also screaming out for Sam, who I found sound asleep on the toilet. I pulled him up the stairs by his hair, telling him to look at the stakes in the water. Now, even though I'd shut the engine down, the drift was taking us right into what appeared to be disaster.

"My *God, it's the coal pilings.* Sam shouted. *We're doomed!* He started the engine to try back out of there, but as he eased it in reverse a stake pushed through the bottom of the boat. My head smashed through the windshield cutting me deeply above the eye. *The boat is sinking! The boat is sinking! The boat is sinking!* Sam Barnes bellows.

"Blood was gushing out of my forehead. I tightened up my life jacket, kicked off my shoes and dove in the water. I could see a dock some hundred feet away and my goal was to swim there and hope the Coast Guard or somebody would pick me up.

"The salt water seemed to stop the bleeding when I reached the dock. Sam, who'd been yelling out, a *Captain can't abandon his ship,* had swum by me like a fish as I had done the dead man's float to my destination. Soon enough a Coast Guard boat with four men aboard scooped me up and took me across the channel to the Norfolk Naval Hospital.

"I was fine. They sewed a dozen stitches above my eye and said I could go home. The next day I was working on the books when Sam Barnes stumbled in about noon, handing me my shoes. They had fished his boat out of the water and he was returning what belonged to me

"I never saw Sam Barnes again after the boating accident. Peat, Marwick, and Mitchell saw fit to put another CPA on the job. I suspected it had nothing to do with the accident, but rather he wasn't getting any work done because of his pill taking and drinking."

Robert Doyle hadn't said a word during my story. When I was finished, he said, "You survived some story, John. So, I gather you bought Eddie Hargrave's practice and moved it to Citizens Trust Bank building?"

Doyle had done some homework. That's exactly what I had done. When I had completed pulling the trial balances together it was late August. The government set me up with an SBA loan to buy Hargrave's duplex on Court Street and his accounting practice. The only condition was I'd pay Eddie $150 per week until he died and he could live in the house, rent free, until that day.

"The house appraised for $50,000 for which I paid $20,000. I received a $20,000 first mortgage on it, and an additional $20,000 working capital from the SBA, who also secured the house. I did move my office from the corner of High Street and Court Street to the Citizens Trust Bank. It did seem like I was set until I found out most of my clients were near or the same age as Hargrave. I still had my job and salary with the FBI, but I was always on call. It was a confusing time and I never knew what was really going on. In August, Ellen resigned her job at the Pentagon and we moved to Portsmouth, Virginia, Ellen, Joe and I.

The story all flowed nicely. I just left out the biggest part. That, I was an undercover agent for The Federal Bureau of Investigation. When I told Robert Doyle the line about most of my clients being as old as Hargrave, he laughed like hell. "Well, that we can fix, but only because you're a great musician. The first person I want you to see is a friend of mine named Chris Kevatas. He was a trainer with the New York *football* Giants. I talked with him this morning."

Bobby wrote a telephone number on the back of his business card. "Just call him, John. He has a little place about twenty miles from here, in Moyock, North Carolina. A joint, he sells beer and sandwiches. Set something up and I'll ride down there with you. Let's go get some lunch."

Our problems are man-made, therefore they may be solved by man. No problem of human destiny is beyond human beings. **John F. Kennedy**

Chapter Twenty-Two

Archibalds
Between 1500 &1600 K Street
Washington, D.C.
Thursday, October 13, 1983

Maggie Little and Joe Neverson couldn't wait to go to lunch as they'd been so harassed by claim calls they were ready to give up. "Let's go to Archibalds," Joe suggests.

"Are you okay with that, Maggie." I ask, knowing what her answer would be.

"They have cold beer and nice tits bouncing for the guys. This means I can look at the young, good looking studs drooling over those tits, knowing I, too, can offer up a pair." Maggie replies, analytically.

"Okay," I agree, "Archibald's it is."

Archibald's is underground. It's rectangular with a long bar. The short width of the place is expanded by mirrors facing each other. We are about a half an hour ahead of the lunch crowd so we find a place in a secluded corner, saying to the hostess we have business to discuss.

A lovely topless young lady takes our order. Joe can't take his eyes off her bodacious breasts. Maggie is looking at me, saying, "it is the beginning."

"Is the loan still on schedule for next week, Jack? I mean, I don't know how long I can keep the wolves at bay." Neverson whines.

"It's still on and I have no reason to think it won't stay the course. In fact Henry Fleck is coming to Philadelphia on Saturday for the World Series game. He's bringing a girlfriend. We're going to the game and then Old Bookbinders for dinner. So, if anything is going to hold the loan up I'll know this weekend. But, I don't think so," I say, positively.

"It's serious, Jack. PGC just keeps assuring me we'll have the money soon. I know better, but to keep my own sanity I just give him the benefit of the doubt, hoping he'll do the right thing." Joe says.

"You know accounting games are never meant to last forever. But, now we're faced with auditors again and I'm really in a position to simply bring back the ones from last year. How much was kicked back to Ruth, Cobb, Greenberg, and Foxx last year? I haven't even looked at the hard numbers, yet I see the setting up of off-balance-sheet partnerships and joint ventures.

Regenerating cash flows through prepays and showing cash collateral accounts as accumulated cash reserves, well, that dog don't hunt. How can big-time auditors miss these things unless they are getting greased? In PGC's mind, though, there is no way he is going to fail." I say, now negatively. "So fix it, Jack!" Huh?

Maggie ordered us another round of beer while Joe Neverson speaks, "Jack, it seems you have picked up on things pretty quickly. Maggie and I have one problem. You have many. I haven't even thought about the auditors and all the fake frosting on the cake. I need to pay claims or they will shut us down. I can't worry about anything but claims."

"PGC doesn't have the patience to do it right, does he?" I ask. "This company is such a beautiful idea and a needed equalizer to the giants. It gives everybody a chance at good work. But he's using it for personal gain only. He sees everything in split second economics. This loan we're talking about is no more a huge tool to show the cash flow where they need it. It really is just a disguised loan that analysts won't know about or find. If they did Atlantic States Surety would have a junk rating.

"The same goes for off-balance-sheet debt, which doesn't get shown or found. Can we make a more confusing annual report? The off-balance-sheet debt, the structured finance, nonrecourse debt and guarantees make the non-reporting of these items criminal. Somebody, accountants, management are supposed to be scrutinizing these audited financial statements and annual insurance reports. Does anybody even read the footnotes, which are not correct anyway? Instead the Controller's job here is to fool the auditor and fool the banker. However, neither really has to be fooled because they are being paid off. There are no watchdogs in this organization."

Maggie and Joe seem to be stunned by my regurgitating of the facts. Maggie grins saying, "Shall we have one more and order a sandwich? It sounds like we have a lot of work to do."

It's the first time I ever saw Joe Neverson speechless. After a long pause, he extends his hand to shake mine. He admits, "Jack, I really under estimated you. You do understand the business. Now tell me one thing, where the hell did you come from?"

"Mars," I say. "None of what I just said leaves the table. If it does I'll know the source."

Maggie and Joe gave me a thumb's up.

I tell you the past is a bucket of ashes, so live not in your yesterdays, not just for tomorrow, but in the here and now. Keep moving and forget the post mortems; and remember, no one can get the jump on the future. **Carl Sandburg**

Chapter Twenty-Three

Interstate 95 - Northbound
Somewhere between Wilmington, Delaware and
Philadelphia, Pennsylvania
Friday, October 14, 1983

I had spent most of the day in the accounting department assembling bookkeeping information to prepare for the upcoming audit. With the Board of Director's meeting coming up in a week, I wanted to be familiar with all the numbers and what they meant. The whole accounting department was very cooperative, especially McKenzie Gillen and Nancy Sullivan. I sensed a great deal of edginess from both of them; however, it was as if I were auditing their records. In a sense, I suppose I was doing just that.

Mary Robinson told me PGC had jetted to Fripp Island, South Carolina to look at a yacht he wanted to purchase. Mary always had a way of giving me more information than I really needed. Sensing she wanted me to comment, I was indifferent and silent. I just smiled and told her I would be working in the accounting department most of the day.

When she asked me if I was going to Philadelphia for the weekend I replied, "Sounds like an excellent idea to me. It's the home of those *Fightin' Phillies*, too. I have four tickets for Saturday's game. I'm taking my wife and the banker and his girlfriend to Veterans Stadium for Game Four."

She'd responds with, "How'd you get those tickets?"

"I have friends in high places, Mary." I said.

"I bet you do, Jack. I bet you do!" Mary Robinson says, displaying that sexy smirk of hers.

It is relatively quiet the rest of the day. I actually worked diligently in the hush confines of the accounting department. It had become quite apparent to me that no one in the company, especially the Board of Directors, knew how Atlantic States Surety was getting their spurious financial numbers, but as long as they met their quotas and kept the right ratios, everyone seemed quite willing to simply accept the exaggerations of the facts. Or, should I say fail to examine the reports. They worried only about increasing Director's Fees and perks. When it falls, I thought, no one will be able to put *Humpty Dumpty* back together again.

This assignment was a whole dissimilar kind of ball game. Normally I just move into a business, make my maneuvers, gather information and move onto the next arrangement. This time I saw what a viable idea this man had and how he was about to destroy what he had so cleverly began. I wondered why investors were so willing to guarantee, jointly and severely, ten million dollars and entrust it to their fearless leader. How well did they know him? Why would they trust me to give them the numbers to support this loan endorsement when the majority of them hadn't even met me yet? Here were intelligent men with noteworthy credentials, military honors who were willing to personally guarantee ten million dollars worth of money owing.

It was the preparation of the Treasure's Report and it's delivery to the Board of Directors next Thursday that really bothered me. I knew the reports would be rubber stamped and the loan deal would get done. Normally an accountant would have to defend his numbers and answer questions. Not with this bunch. Plus what did I have to be concerned about; I'm an undercover agent with the FBI. And everything we do is bullshit, lies, and spin.

As I near the Schuylkill Expressway I can see the *Good Year* Blimp hovering over Veterans Stadium. What a grand site I'm thinking. The World Series is being played right under that balloon, and I'll be in the stands tomorrow. Then reality hit me. I'll be in the stands with the banker. He is a dedicated Baltimore Orioles fan who was about to fuel the big rip-off machine.

Game Three is going well for the Phillies as I drive the expressway north. Our perennial ace, Steve Carlton is pitching, with "Gary

Matthews and Joe Morgan already lashing solo shots homeruns, respectively in the second and third innings. When I exit my 280Z car into our driveway the Phillies are leading the Orioles, 2-0, after five innings.

Ellen is happy to see me. She gives me a hug and kiss when I arrive. The children are all excited chattering away and throwing punches at each other. "I thought we'd order a pizza," said Ellen. "I know you are going to watch the Series."

"Terrific," I say. Ellen has the TV set already tuned to the game, as I quickly noticed the Orioles had scored in the top of the sixth. The Orioles scored two more in the seventh as we finished our pizza. I wasn't too upset, because the Phillies had two more at bats. But, no cigar!

Jim Palmer picked up the win in relief, shutting down the Phillies. This win by Palmer, along with his first World Series win in 1966, marked the longest span between World Series wins for an individual pitcher in major league history.

The boys went to bed. When Ellen came downstairs, she fixed us both a drink and we sat down at the kitchen table. I put on a Neil Diamond album and we were calm, just listening to the music.

"Thank you, Johnny." Ellen said, breaking the ice.

"For what," I ask.

"For not getting barmy when the Phillies lost." She said, almost inaudibly.

"Aw, they'll win tomorrow. They wouldn't dare lose when we are going to the game." I reply.

We make small talk for about an hour, listening to the Diamond music. I update her on some of things happening in Washington and she tells me about the children's activities. Our conversation was so peaceful and the house seemed to be hushed. Everything seemed poles apart like there was an ambiguity about the house. Like maybe important things were being unsaid?

"Are you okay, Ellen, you're so quiet – laid back. Is something wrong?" I pose. Then, I regretted asking her if something was off beam. Something was always wide of the mark and my questions usually gave her reason to express her melancholy.

"Okay, who is he?" I ask, not wanting to hear an answer.

"I didn't want to do it this way, Johnny." She replies.

"There is no good way to do it. Who is he, Ellen." I ask again.

There is a pause as I grab us beers. I pop the top off both of them and push one toward my wife.

"Harvey Fienstein." She says. "He's handsome. He's successful, bright, and funny."

I homed in on Ellen when she told me about Harvey, but I couldn't be too hard on her. I had set myself up for catastrophe. I had made a lifetime making a series of false assumptions and wrong moves. Not intentionally, but it just happened that way. So once again I was finding myself in danger and peril because of the choices I make. I realize I'm only thirty-nine years old and the worst is not yet behind me. The worst is ahead of me because I know I have to live the memory of my fate and history for the rest of my life.

"Harvey *fucking* Fienstein, are you kidding me? Why that fucking pussy? Isn't he the guy I plowed into at second base during last summer's firm's picnic softball game? Remember he called me a big bully as he limped off the field.

"So, what are going to do with him?" I ask, with a tone of disbelief."

"How the hell do I know?" Ellen says. "I feel so boxed in," she says with tears seeping out of the corner of her eyes. "I guess the real question is what are you going to do?" She asks, cautiously.

"Ellen, I've been suspicious of an affair for some time. I had no idea with whom. What's the matter with you? Harvey *the jerk* Fienstein, who outfits himself in leather pants. He's your boss for Christ's sake. He's a Jew! He's married isn't he?"

Ellen didn't respond. "Have you come to any decision, yet?" I ask, while crushing an empty beer can. I mean about us – about you – about him – about the end of the fucking world as we know it." I query.

"Johnny, quit it." She says, firmly.

"Has he told his wife yet, Ellen?" I ask. "That's the big one for him. "Telling his wife he's leaving her for a married gentile woman with kids. He'll never do it!"

"He's thinking of telling her next week." Ellen pronounces, softly.

"Bullshit. He's playing you like a piano." I say sharply, with an astringent tone in my voice. "He's using you, Ellen."

She just stares at me. I say, "Ellen, I want you to be my wife. I want to be a better husband to you; honestly, I'll do anything you want. I'll fuck you on the kitchen table and cover you with whipped cream and lick it off slowly. I've figured a lot of things out lately and one of them is that I love you very much and that means I'm going to fight to keep you."

"I don't know, Johnny." She says. "Are you going to fight, fairly?"

"What do you mean, fairly? I only know one way. I play to win. I don't lose." I shout. "To answer your question, only pussies fight fairly."

"Johnny, what you say sounds wonderful. But it would be nice if you could say it without all the cleverness and all the jokes. You know, I don't believe you've ever told me you loved me without making a joke out of it." Ellen says.

"Really? That's not true, Ellen, and you know it. I have told you I love you often, maybe it is with sheepishness and embarrassment. I'm not good at confirming something I believe you already know. But, I've done it any number of times. And, although I may have done it clumsily, I mean it."

"Harvey tells me all the time, Johnny. He's never sheepish and he's never embarrassed. He says it simply and sweetly and sincerely. Ellen says, refuting my attempt to simply smooth everything over.

"Ellen, please take your time with this decision. Think about it hard." I say, getting up from the table.

"I rarely think of anything else, John." She says, in a whisper.

"I'm going to try to get some sleep. Remember we have a big day tomorrow. We have to pick the banker and his girlfriend up at 30th Street Station around 10:00 a.m. You will like them. We'll have a good time at the ball game. We're eating at Old Bookbinders afterwards.

"Good night," I say simply and sweetly and sincerely into the darkness of that empty room, without all the cleverness and without any jokes. "I love you, Ellen."

One day in retrospect the years of struggle will strike you as the most beautiful. **Sigmund Freud**

Chapter Twenty-Four

The day dawned bright and sunny. We took the boys out to breakfast at the New Kenyon Diner in Glenside, a place we often frequented. The boys ordered pancakes and devoured them easily. They seemed so happy when we were all together and they had so many stories to tell. I caught Ellen just looking at me and she caught me looking at her. When we were getting ready to leave my son, Joe, asked me why he couldn't go to the World Series game. "Mom, doesn't even like baseball, Dad." He pleads.

The past two years we had gone to a lot of Phillies games. We went together and had grand times. The kids knew the names of the players and loved eating hot dogs and drinking Coca Cola during the game. We had a lot of fun and I really wanted to take Joe to the World Series game, but I couldn't. "It's a business thing, Joe." I tell him. "It's always business, Dad." My son spoke back disappointedly.

Ellen and I arrived at 30th Street Station at 11 a.m. Henry Peter Fleck and his girl friend were standing by the swinging doors on the City side of the Station. Henry recognized me when I pulled my Chrysler *New Yorker* along side of them. They jumped into the back seat and we were off to Veterans Stadium.

Everybody introduced each other as I drove down the Schuylkill Expressway. While Henry and I talked about the Series, the women got to know each other with small, girl talk. When we took the Broad Street exit you could feel the excitement in the air. A sea of red was walking the streets of Philadelphia. You still think you have chance with a crowd like this, Henry," I ask, glowing with exhilaration and confidence. For the first time since I'd left for this tour in Washington I felt like a real human being. Baseball was always my old standby; it was the only constant in my life. When I was a child and things weren't going so well, I would wander up to the ball yard, look around and dream of someday seeing the old stadiums on the east coast. I'd sit in the dugout and imagine Duke Snider, Willie Mays or Mickey Mantle hitting a home run. Or, there would be Brooklyn Dodgers running around the bases, scoring a victory over those New York Yankees. It was in my own little fantasy world where I found peace. Now here I was in Philadelphia, Pennsylvania, a long way from the middle of nowhere, and, I was finding peace again as we entered Veterans Stadium.

I had been to the stadium many times and knew where the seats were located. The Bureau did a terrific job in accommodating those whom it made sense to provide accommodation. Once in the stadium, Ellen walked with me and Henry with his girlfriend, Joy, followed. When I pointed downward, Henry said, "You've got to be kidding me. Are we going to be sitting right behind the Phillies dugout?."

"Fifth row," I said.

"I'm impressed, Jack," Henry says. "I mean really impressed!"

Every time the beer man came around, Henry bought the beers. We must have had six or seven beers a piece. Henry had a few more as he polished off what Joy couldn't drink as well. As usual Ellen hung in there with the boys. As tiny as she was I never could figure out where all that beer went in her body.

The game itself was scoreless until the fourth inning when the Orioles Rich Dauer singled in two runs off Phillies ace John Denny. The Phillies got one back in the bottom of the fourth. When the Phillies scored two more in the bottom of the fifth on a RBI double by Pete Rose, Henry had his Baltimore Orioles cap doused with beers by *Fightins'* fans. The moments of glory for the Phillies faithful didn't last long though as Baltimore scored two runs in the top of the sixth and added another in the seventh. I knew it was over and it was before a crowd of 66,947, which was the largest crowd for a World Series game since 1964.

We arrived at Old Bookbinders restaurant around six o'clock. We had reservations made by those same people who had set us up with the good World Series tickets. While working for the Federal Bureau of Investigation, things just happened. You never knew how. You didn't need to know how! You just had to show up. But their influence was always impressive.

We were seated at a corner table in the main dining room. We were all surprised to see Howard Cosell and Steve Carlton sitting at the table next to us. There were two other guys with them, who we didn't recognize. We had spent an hour at the bar before our table was called, so everybody was in a really good mood, even me considering the Phillies had lost. After a couple more rounds of drinks I told Henry I was going to introduce myself to Howard Cosell.

I stood up and stepped over to where Cosell was sitting. He looked at me while I said, "Howard, I'm Jack Oleson, a real Phillies fan." There was a pause before he drawled, "So."

I felt like an ass, then said, "I just wanted to meet you." He shook my hand and I retreated to my seat, like a dog with his tail tucked between his legs.

"Wow, he was impressed," Ellen guffaws. Henry and Joy doubled over in hilarity.

Ellen tells us, "Let me show you how it's done." She stepped over to Cosell, whispered something in his ear, bringing a smile to his face. She kissed him on his lips. She squeezed his hand and returned to our table with a smug look on her face.

"What did you say, Ellen?"

"I asked him if he wanted to get laid. He told me he would settle for a kiss."

Henry and Judy roared again as our dinner arrived just at the right time. We enjoyed our meal, including desert with lots of coffee. Afterwards we drove Henry and Joy to 30th Street Station for their return trip to Baltimore.

As we drove home to Glenside we were very quiet. We had had a wonderful day, despite the Phillies losing, and now all of our problems would be waiting for us at our home. The boys were already in bed when we arrived. While I paid the babysitter, Ellen went upstairs to bed. I turned off the lights, locked the doors and retired myself.

The best thing about the future is that it comes only one day at a time. **Abraham Lincoln**

Chapter Twenty-Five

240 Berkeley Road
Glenside, Pennsylvania
Sunday, October 16, 1983

E llen is up early making breakfast for the boys. When I wander downstairs they are just finished eating. "Do you want an omelet, John?" She asks with a pleasant smile.

"Are you joining me?" I ask as she hands me a cup of coffee.

"Of course," she whispers

"Then omelets would be superior," I confirm.

"Like okay for a Sunday morning." She supposes, with a kindly grin.

"The Phillies will probably lose it today, with Charley Hudson going against Scott McGregor. It doesn't look good." I allege.

"Good God," Ellen says, tossing my omelet down in front of me. "With all that's going on the only thing you can talk about is the fucking Phillies? She barks, snappishly.

"What do you want to talk about, Ellen, a divorce?" I snap back.

"I'm going to church. Keep an eye on the children." She demands as she heads toward the front door.

"Church," I question. "Are you going to church or the synagogue?" I ask as she exits, giving me the finger.

She had been gone for two hours when I tuned in the World Series game. The first person I see is Howard Cosell giving his take on the series and Game Five. What I noticed most is how his hands are shaking while holding his microphone. It seems impossible only a few hours ago Ellen had walked over to his table and gave him a kiss. We were having such a good time then, and now veracity had taken over again.

Ellen arrived home during the sixth inning. The Phillies were losing, 5-0, with Eddie Murray hitting two homers and Rick Dempsey one. I had determined that was it for a great Phillies season. With each pitch the angrier I got as hopes for a victory faded away. Simultaneously the madder I got about Harvey Fienstein, the fucking infinitesimal little Jew who might be fucking my wife. I decided I would stay home tonight so I could have a chat with him in the morning.

"Long service," I ask Ellen.

"I went shopping, I knew you'd be watching the game." She says, glibly.

"You're not a good liar, Ellen." I say.

"But you certainly are, in fact you're the best." She follows.

I had never won a game of verbal volleyball with *E*. She was the master of the game. I flipped the baseball game off. "Ellen, we need to talk honestly. I'm really under a lot of stress right now. I need your support. We can't spend much time together right now, not as much as I want too. I really mean it. But, let's see what we can do. Wasn't it you that said you never leave someone for somebody else?"

"Don't you want to watch the rest of your game?" She asks.

"No! I want to talk about us. By the way I'm staying here tonight. I'm leaving for Washington in the morning." I announce.

"Why," she asked, ardently.

"I have somebody to talk to in the morning." I tell her.

"And who might that be?" She asks, quizzically.

Before I could answer the boys came running in the house. My son, Joe, says apologetically, "Dad, I'm sorry the Phillies lost."

"You know what's good about baseball, Joe, with baseball there is always next year." I say with a smile.

"What's for supper, Mom?" Dan asks.

"Well, John, since you'll be here tonight, how about grilling some steaks."

The kids chant in unison a big, *"Yeah!"*

I go out the back door carrying charcoal and lighter fluid. I scan the yard for the grill and find it where I'd left it the last time

I grilled steaks, which was probably on the 4ᵗʰ of July. It was a Weber and the top of the grill was missing, leaving the bowl filled with mud, tree twigs and fallen autumn leaves. I turned it over, dumping the contents on the ground under a nearby tree. I poured charcoal into the pit and fished the grate out of the rubbish I'd dumped under the tree.

After pouring lighter fluid over the coals I tossed a match into the works. There was a slight explosion for a second before the charcoal caught fire and began to burn slowly. I asked the boys to find the top for the grill, and a few minutes later they arrived with it in tow.

Danny says, "It was in the basement. We are going to paint it and use it for a sled when it snows." I laugh, taking the lid and shaking off the dust. Joe and Dan were now tossing the football around. I saw Chris and Ellen, through the dining room window, sitting at the piano. Ellen was already teaching our youngest to play. He seemed to have a natural talent. Children are amazing, I thought. And so is my wife, I'm thinking as I stare into the flames glowing from the grill pit. My thoughts were running rampant. As I often do, I started philosophizing and jotting down my deep thoughts on a blank page in my Day Timer.

There are no verdicts to childhood, only consequences, and the bright freight of memory. I wonder now of the sun-struck, deeply lived-in days of my past. I am more fabulist than historian, but I will try to give myself the insoluble, unedited terror of my youth. I betray the integrity of my family's history by turning even sadness, into romance. There is no romance in my story; there is only the story.

Again and again, I think of Ellen and our children. I have married the first woman I had ever kissed. I thought I had married her because she was pretty, blessed with horse sense and sass and unlike any other woman I have ever met. I had married a fine and comely girl, and with brilliance and craft and all instincts of self-preservation jettisoned, I succeeded over the years, through neglect, coldness and betrayal, in turning her into the exact image of somebody I didn't deserve. You see I am not comfortable with anyone who is not disapproving of me. No matter how ardently I strive to attain their impossible high standards for me, I can never do anything entirely right so I grow accustomed to that climate of inevitable failure. In Ellen, I had formed the woman who would be subtle and a more cunning woman. Yet I sense she has come to feel slightly ashamed of and disappointed in me.

There are last things to say. Ellen has awakened something in me that has slumbered far too long. Not only do I feel passion again, I felt the return of hope and a clearance of all storm warnings in the danger zones of my memory. No one understood better than I the reason she had to find love outside our home. But, no, I don't give up. Never!

"John," Ellen shouted, startling me. "Are you ready for the steaks?" She asks, with a pleasant tone in her voice.

"I'll be ready in ten minutes." I answer back.

"Okay, I'll bring the steaks out in ten minutes." She says. "Are corn, peas and garlic bread good?" She asked.

For the first time in a long time we all sat down at the dining room table as a family. We all enjoyed the meal and the children talked about everything. Even our six-year-old chimed in with a few remarks. I helped Ellen clean up after dinner. She told the boys that if they went upstairs and put on their pajamas we'd all watch a TV program together. And, that she had just made a pudding pie with a graham cracker crust which she would serve everyone a piece while we were watching TV.

The boys went to bed at 8:30 p.m. It had almost been a perfect day, if the Phillies would have won. Ellen and I drank coffee and talked until 10 o'clock. I told her about all the significant things about to happen in Washington. She talked some about her job and how the children were doing in school. Then I introduced the main topic of the weekend, it was about our marriage.

"Ellen, we've been through so much. We have to make this marriage work. If not for ourselves, we owe it to the children. If we're going to make it you have to stop seeing your friend. I mean now. You must tell him tomorrow. Or, I'll tell him. Either way he's history." I said, insistently.

"I know," she said. "It's going to be difficult not talking with him. He helps me clear my head. He always says the right things.

But, I'll do it tomorrow. He might not like it, either. He could fire me. Who the hell knows?" Ellen shrugged her shoulders.

I grabbed Ellen's hand, softly. "No, he won't fire you. He won't get mad, either. You will be doing what's right."

"John, you're going to talk to him – aren't you?" She asks.

"Of course," I am. "It will solve any future problems." I say, pulling her close to me.

"Hey, is that house you like in Jenkintown still for sale?"

Ellen's eyes lit up. "It is," she said.

"Let's buy it next weekend." I suggest.

"Really, John, "You'd buy that for me with our circumstances seemingly so up in the air"

"I'll be home Friday about noon. Set it up with the realtor. Don't you know I'd do anything for you?" I assure her.

"Including being a better husband," she asks with a smile. "Including, resigning from the Bureau, after this case." I nod in the affirmative, saying, "Count on it!"

Now let me do something for you. Let's go to bed." She says, provocatively.

The best way to predict the future is to create it. **Peter Drucker**

Chapter Twenty-Six

Jenkintown Plaza
Jenkintown, Pennsylvania
7 a.m.
Monday, October 17, 1983

I said my goodbyes to Ellen and the boys and drove to a nearby 7-11 store for a cup of coffee. The convenience store was always busy in the morning and I even ran into a friend I'd coached Little League Baseball with the prior spring. While standing in line we asked each other *what was up* and bid farewell.

I turned right on Glenside Avenue and drove the two miles to nearby Jenkintown. I crossed the small bridge that went over the railroad tracks and turned right on Runnymede Avenue, pausing at 220 to take another peak at the house Ellen wanted to buy. She was right, it looked like a little gingerbread house as she referred to it. I continued onto the stop sign and took a right on West Avenue and then a left on Greenwood Avenue directly in front of the train station. I took an immediate left into the parking area and drove around to the back building where I knew the firm's employees parked their cars.

I pulled into Harvey Fienstein's private parking space, which had his name stenciled in black on a white sign. It was 7 a.m.. Ellen wouldn't arrive until 8 a.m., so I was hoping Harvey, the hard working early bird, would arrive soon. And, he did, with an attitude. He pulled behind me and started honking his horn. Then he leaned on it, making an annoying blaring sound which started to attract people's attention.

I touched my gun, which I had holstered on my left shoulder. *One false move*, I was thinking as I stepped out of my vehicle.

Harvey had his palms upside down making that shrugging gesture of, *what the hell?* He looked at me and I at him. "What's your problem," I asked at his open window?

"John," he queries. "What are you doing in my parking spot?"

"Waiting for you, asshole." I say, pushing my suit coat back slightly so he could see my gun.

"What are you doing with a gun," He questions.

"What are you doing messing around with my wife?" I quizz back, while reaching into his open window and grabbing him by his neck tie. I drew it up tight around his neck and pulled his head to where it was sticking out the window. "Roll it up!" I ordered. When he didn't, I tightened the tie around his neck and said, "Roll it up, asshole or I'll choke you to death."

Slowly Harvey inched the window up, tightening on his neck and choking him into a cough. His head was beat red and I could smell urine coming from inside of Harvey's car. He was so scared he'd pissed himself. I noticed two more partners now turning the corner and heading toward reserved parking. "Roll it down, Harvey." I order, while drawing and pointing my gun at his forehead. Harvey obliged, quickly. When the window was down I gave my nemesis a straight right, knocking him down on the seat. I jumped into the driver's seat and drove his car to the other end of the parking lot.

I pulled a handkerchief from my breast pocket and threw it at Harvey. "Sit up asshole," I demanded, bad-temperedly. "Here's the way it's going to work. You will not tell anyone about our little meeting this morning. You will not fire my wife. When she quits, and she most definitely will, you'll give her the highest of recommendations. Other than what is absolutely necessary concerning work, you will not talk to her again. I don't know what the extent of your relationship is with Ellen, but it has ended other than work. I'm not interested in the past, but if I find out today or ten years from now you had sexual relations with her I'll kill you."

Harvey Fienstein appeared to want to say something, but he didn't. "Harvey you don't know who I am, nobody does, but I can squash you. That's all you need to know. But be assured you are being watched. Be assured if you fuck up again there will be no more warnings. If you have a future, remember, people aren't always who they seem."

Harvey started to apologize as I bounced his head off the dashboard. "Don't you ever speak to me again, or to anybody concerning me? Now go home and get cleaned up. You look like shit for a big shot partner in such a supposedly high-status firm."

I walked across the wide-ranging parking lot to my car; it was 7:45 a.m. When I reached my vehicle the senior partner had just exited his new Cadillac. "John," he greeted me with a firm handshake. "What are you doing out and about here in Jenkintown on a Monday morning?"

"I was home for the weekend. I'm just heading back to Washington now. It's good to see you, Walter."

"Have a safe trip, John."

I nodded and entered my vehicle. *Asshole*, I thought. I was sure all the partners knew about Harvey's fling with my wife. I started becoming angry again when I saw Ellen pulling into the parking lot. She didn't see me so I thought I'd simply slip by her so she wouldn't be anxious about what had just happened. When it comes to marriage most controversial things are better unsaid and known. So, I cranked my automobile onto Greenwood Avenue and headed for the Schuylkill Expressway.

I can't go back to yesterday, because I was a different person then.
Lewis Carroll

What Is Past Is Prologue

Outdoor Movie Theatre
U.S. Route 212
Two miles east of Gettysburg, South Dakota
Thursday night, August 7, 1969

We are watching the end of the movie *Paper Lion*, while our children, Kincaid and Charley, have just fallen asleep in the back seat. My wife, Beth and I had said nary a word to each other during the entire movie. We had placated the children with hotdogs, lemonade and popcorn. It was nearing 10:30 p.m. and they had just dozed off.

I had spent most of the movie thinking about what had happened earlier in the evening. I was watching the children when Sissy Gooch pulled up in our driveway, in a cloud of dust and rocks. "Where is your wife," she shouted.

"At the Country Club, it's her turn to host. Why? Is something wrong?" I ask incredulously. Sissy was crazy. I'd seen her do crazy stuff, like jumping in a mud puddle wearing a white pant suit. She had stabbed her husband, Tommy, in the back with an ice pick and she'd tried to scratch his eyes out. God only knows what else she had tried to do. And God only knows how Tommy provoked her with his drunkenness.

"John, she's not at the Country Club. She's with my husband! They have been secretly meeting for a long time. What's wrong with you? Are you blind?" Sissy bellowed, loudly, catching the attentions of my neighbors.

I am surprised, but not shocked. I have been suspect for some time, but I trusted Beth Ann implicitly. Although she had quit playing in my band, I thought there was no more to it than she was just tired of it. And, every Sunday morning when I woke up I found Tommy sitting on our sofa talking with my wife. I usually didn't get home until early in the morning on Sunday after Saturday night dance jobs. His continual being there on Sunday mornings made me mistrustful and it was annoying. Also, there were the unexplained shopping trips to Aberdeen (90 miles away), where Beth never bought anything. I couldn't check the mileage because the speedometer didn't work, but again, I trusted her unreservedly.

"Okay, Sissy, stay here with the kids and I'll drive out to the Club to see if she's there. If she isn't I'll ask around. I'll find her." I assured her of success.

Sissy sat down in a lawn chair to watch Kincaid and Charley play in the backyard. I fired up my 1966 Mercury Marquis four-door sedan and headed for the golf course. Everything in this one-horse town is, at the most, a mile or two away. It was another reason I didn't believe Beth could be having affair. I was well known in this little hamlet. I was Assistant Vice President at the bank and everybody knew me.

Elmer, my piano player, on the way to a dance job just last week alluded to the fact that something might be going on I didn't know about with our marriage. *That what's really going on in a relationship may not be what it seems.* Again I explained to Elmer how I trusted Beth Ann without proviso, and above all we had something special in our rapport.

When I arrived at the Country Club she was not there. Although I did find out Beth had been there earlier. She had brought two hot dishes by around four o'clock and left rather hurriedly. I received this information from the women she was supposed to be hosting with and who now seemed aggravated she was not present. The other hostesses were now giving off the impression of words unspoken. I thanked them for the information and took off for home.

When I arrived, with the little information I had obtained, Sissy left in a cloud of dust and a shatter of rocks. She had no more than left when Beth pulled into the driveway. Kincaid, Charley and I were sitting on the back stoop. Beth slowly got out of her car. She wore a white jump suit, which was much wrinkled. For one who was always so fastidious, her outward appearance was completely disheveled and out of character.

She gave me a kiss on the cheek and went into the house. I followed her asking where she had been and that Sissy Gooch was looking for her and Tommy. Beth did not respond. Instead she walked into our bedroom and changed clothes. When she came out she said she had brought two hot dishes to the country club. I told her I knew about that and queried about where she had gone when she left. That, three hours had passed.

"I took a ride." She said. "I drove across the Missouri River and next thing I knew I was in Eagle Butte. I got an ice cream cone and came back. When I crossed the Missouri again I turned off on the overlook and sat for a spell looking at the River."

I didn't buy her tale but rather than get into it I suggested we go to the drive-in movie. She seemed relieved and said she'd pop popcorn to take along. I gathered the kids and told them what we were going to do and they were excited. Beth Ann made a pitcher of lemonade and we were off to the movies like a big happy family. Little did I know it would be the last time we would ever be together as a happy family again.

When the movie ended I backed out of the parking spot and entered the exit line. The egress was slow, but as soon as we turned west onto U.S. Route 212 what looked like a pick- up truck came out of the ditch and rammed our car in the rear jarring the children to the rear floor. I looked into the rear-view mirror and saw the heads of Tommy and Sissy Gooch. I stomped on the accelerator and sped the two miles into town, making a left turn into the hospital parking lot.

Tommy and Sissy arrived seconds later. They bailed out of the truck, leaving his mounted shotgun in place. I got out of our car, telling Beth to stay in the car with the children. Tommy was so drunk he could hardly walk or speak. "Sissy told me you were going to kill me. How?" He asked, clinching his fist in my face.

Tommy and I were about the same size, but I had lightening fast reflexes. He was drunk and I was completely sober. When he clinched his fist he was too close to my face to have any power. If he punched I would have blocked it and then would have applied a forearm flipper under his neck and punched him underneath the nose driving a bone into his brain. With my anger, which always garnered extraordinary strength, I probably would have killed him instantly. Bethany's scream stopped such an engagement before it started.

Sissy was trying to pull Beth out of our car by her hair. Tommy directed his attention to his wife by slapping her to the concrete pavement. I made sure Beth was alright and tried to settle the children down, who were now screaming over all the negative goings-on. Next I raced over to help Sissy who was being kicked in the gut and the ribs by her husband.

He didn't pay any attention to my yelling telling him to stop kicking his wife. So I took a few steps back, zeroed Tommy Gooch in, and was about to give him the old football bull rush when the town cop pulled up. He knew Tommy, they had been high school classmates, and told him to stop or he'd have to arrest him. He told me to back off!

I watched and listened to the cop getting Tommy Gooch settled, telling him everybody knew about his affair with my wife. I couldn't believe what I was hearing.

I never asked Beth how, when, and where she began her affair with Tommy – this is not the sort of information I wanted to hear in detail – but it was something that remained missing because I did not know. Not that it matters decades after I divorced her.

In legal terms, I charged her with irreconcilable differences, in lieu of adultery, and she never admitted to such disloyalty, either. I never pressed her, but I simply didn't want or require any details or explicit testimony. When it's over – it's over. But, now and then, I do find in my heart the ability to forgive, and it costs me nothing to do that, except some loss of pride, which is maybe my problem.

So, maybe I wanted to put things in the right perspective. It was a good plan for the future, but it doesn't change the past

So we beat on, Boats against the current, Borne back ceaselessly, into the past **F. Scott Fitzgerald – The Great Gatsby**

Chapter Twenty-Seven

1700 K Street
Washington, D.C.
Thursday, October 20, 1983

It has been a busy week preparing for the 11a.m. board meeting today. I have been working closely with the accounting department putting together the financial state of affairs for the operating company. Charlotte Boyer discreetly dropped off last month's report to use as a guide. It was quite apparent how Bitterman prepared last month's numbers. I could trace expenses like rent and utilities back to the disbursement journal but the so-called accrual entries were set up to impress the board members with the numbers they wanted to see, with limited consideration for loss possibilities. I did the unfeigned numbers first and I was not totally shocked with to whom the checks were written and the excessive amounts.

I suppose, in a sense, I had seen only its demise. Yet in my mind, I could imagine the excitement and the great days in the beginning. If only the other eleven directors who, for all intents and purposes, sat in ostensibly treasonous but ultimately loyal comradeship today had acted sooner and removed PGC, they might have steadied the ship, changing its course. And, I would not be here today about to do my sullied deeds.

If only this board would have marshaled their forces. On this board were generals, admirals and seasoned business executives. But they were totally blinded by greed. If only Joe Neverson had kept his anger, resentment, and rudeness under control. If he would've stepped up and said, *there may be trouble ahead.* If only ten minutes had been devoted to wisdom and hindsight, all of this

could have been prevented. It's the sort of thing I tend to special-
ize in, but, as usual, I was sitting on the wrong side of the table.

It was 8 a.m. when I walked into the board room to find
Charlotte Boyer and her assistant S.G. laying out the pewter, silver and china. At each station was placed a leather notebook and a
Mont Blanc fountain pen, replete with ink wells. Inside the notebook was an agenda for the meeting, along with my Treasurer's
report.

"Big day, huh, Jack." Charlotte says.

"Is Bitterman here, yet?" I query of Boyer, with a knowing
smile.

"I'm sure he'll be along any minute, Jack." She replies, while
sliding an ashtray the length of the conference table.

I didn't trust Charlotte Boyer any further than I could see her.
However, she intrigued me and I wondered about all the crazy
things that must go on in her mind. Four years as PGC's paramour
had more than likely driven her insane. But, she was a top producer and very good at her job.

Recently I lay awake at night trying to place all the if-onlys
in some kind of order. I can think of a dozen or more, if-onlys,
each one as cringe-makingly- awful as the last. I look down the
conference table where Charlotte had slung the ashtray. I see the
blue livery of Atlantic States Surety displayed proudly on the wall.
Now it is simply the symbol of an imposter, a pale substitute for
the swashbuckling banner it was supposed to represent.

It was here where it all went so catastrophically wrong, the
room that housed the royal court of King Charles and his minions.
Here he had formed a house of cards or a row of dominoes, which
can only be kept apart until history repeats itself; and, now it was
about to end. The pieces were now pressing one against the other
and history would inevitably repeat itself.

Mr. Charles might have stepped out of a suburban cocktail party
staged on the set of *The Graduate*. "Insurance and surety bonds – financial and performance, that's the future!" He was obsessed with
business. For me, this was life as I had never imagined it.

With the conference room set I walked back to my office only to find Jerry Bitterman sitting in one of the chairs directly across my desk. Bitterman was bouncy and seemingly very nervous as he said, "They're all ready to sign. I have talked to each of them, it's a done deal. I assure you there will be no problems."

I just listened to Jerry ramble while staring into his eyes. "Let's write our checks now, Jack. You know, and then we can just mingle after the board meeting."

Again, I just listened to Bitterman. Then, after a moment, I ask. "Why do we have to write the checks today?"

"I need the money," Bitterman replies, excitedly. "And," he added. "So does Henry Fleck. "Don't you need your *fifty*?"

"I don't like it, Jerry. But, if it's okay with PGC I guess it will have to be okay with me. Let me ask you something. Once you cash this check all Gordon will have to say is he knew nothing about it. I think it is dangerous, but if you need the money you need the money."

"You're right, Jack. If those checks ever have to be explained he'll deny his involvement." Says Jerry Bitterman, he was really uneasy now. "He really will! But, he knows we have enough on him."

I opened my top left hand desk drawer. I pull out the C&B checkbook and spread the three ring binder across my writing table. I take out my Mont Blanc pen and say, Jerome Bitterman. What's your number?"

"PGC approved 3%. We agreed to pay you fifty thousand. The original deal was one- hundred-fifty thousand to Hank and one hundred fifty thousand for me. Hank won't budge *saying it wasn't his idea for me to quit my job,* so my check should be for one hundred thousand and Hank's one hundred fifty thousand. And, of course, fifty thousand for you." Bitterman says, dejectedly.

I wrote the checks, and handed Jerry's and Hank's to him.

"This ain't shit for all the work I put into this undertaking. It was my idea and I get a measly hundred grand." Bitterman preaches, while studying his safeguard.

"Not a bad day's pay for committing major fraud, Jerry." I reply. "And maybe you shouldn't have quit your job until this deal was done?" I add.

"Yeah, yeah," says Bitterman. "Best I go meet the directors in case any of them have questions."

They start to arrive around 10:30 a.m.. I was busy making mental notes on the Treasurer's report, nothing in writing, about the inadequate reserves, undisclosed credit-quality problems, aggressive accounting, and substantial unconsolidated indebtedness contained in offbalance-sheet special-purpose vehicles. Although the company claim it underwrote risk to a so-called zero-loss standard, its recent performance hadn't been free from error. The high leverage meant A.S.S. had virtually no margin of safety. The company's underwriting, transparency, accounting, and track record all had to be beyond reproach. I was seeing problems with every one of these issues.

Suddenly my door flew open and Jerry Bitterman introduced an older man donning a *Hickey Freeman* suit. "Jack Oleson meet Admiral Carl Wilson." I stood up and we shook hands.

"Jack is my replacement, Carl. Carl is one of the senior directors and board members. He's semi-retired, but still enjoys dabbling in construction and real estate."

I had skimmed through the board of director files. Carl didn't stand out from the others. Rather he raised a question. Why the military guys? In fact all of them appeared to be standup men with good credit and reputations. However, I was certain each one's personality and business acumen somehow fit in to Gordon's master plan.

"Do you have any questions?" I ask of Carl Wilson.

"No!" he says. "I think Jerry has answered everything. Very nice to meet you and I'm sure we'll be getting together again. I'm surely going to miss this fellow here," he adds, while slapping Bitterman on his back.

"Come on, I'll introduce you to the others." He motions me forward with a big smile on his face. Today is his moment. Tomorrow - he'll be yesterday's newspaper. Just another one who had come with nothing and virtually left with nothing.

With everyone seated at the long conference table I tested the seating arrangement in my mind. Paul Gordon Charles, of course, was at the far end of the table directly across from me. Madeline Haycock on his right; Tom Harvey on his left; Richard Corrigan was next to Harvey; on the other side Matt Ferrone sat next to Haycock; Ned Larson sat on Ferrone's right; and, Doctor Ralph Sandusky sat directly across from Larson. Ray Bertrand sat on Sandusky's left and General George Jurgens sat directly across from the doctor. Admiral Carl Wilson was next to General Jurgens and Colonel Roy Hampton sat across from Admiral Wilson. Cliff Hill, who was up for approval as a board member and director at this meeting, was sitting next to Roy Hampton. Charlotte Boyer sat directly across from Cliff Hill, batting her eyes at the prospective new member.

I looked down the long table and saw PGC looking at me. He had almost sinister features: hair turning silver at the temples, and eyes so black they were like the tinted windows of a sleek limousine - he could see out, but you couldn't see in. He told me during our first meeting he loved living like an aristocrat without the burden of having to be one. Blue bloods are so inbred and weak, because of all those generations of importance and grandeur, to live up to. No wonder they lack ambition. *I don't envy them.* It's only the trappings of aristocracy that I find worthwhile – the fine furniture, the paintings, the silver – the very things they have to sell when the money runs out. And it always does. Then all they're left with is their lovely manners. He's a southern chauvinist, very much a son of the region. I don't think he cares much for Yankees.

Charlotte stands up and calls the meeting to order. She explains the agenda and the meeting begins. When it came time for the Treasure's report I am introduced by PGC, himself. He must have memorized my resume as he recited my credentials like he was my father. Each director introduced themselves and gave a brief dossier of what they brought to the table. After which I went through my report and was surprised there were so few questions. When the new guy, Cliff Hill, who was a real estate developer and owned a large construction company, asked about claims – PGC piped up.

"The bonding business is simple. In exchange for receiving an up-front insurance premium, the surety agrees to cover financial commitments and performances of the contractors over the life of the bond if the insured defaults. The beauty of bonding is the surety doesn't need capital guarantee. The surety collects the insurance premium up front in exchange for guaranteeing the bonded and may invest the premium dollars over the long term.

"Of course," he says, "that doesn't mean the bonding business requires no capital. To get into this business we had to prove to regulators that the company had the wherewithal to make good on its guarantees. A bond insurer doesn't really have to pay claims so much as advance money, for brief periods during times of extreme financial distress. Still it's a business that requires extreme caution. It has to be written to a no-loss standard, otherwise the leverage is deadly. That's why, to expand, we're signing this loan agreement today. It's the capital needed for expansion."

He's so good, I thought. The rest of the table, however, looked like they were falling asleep. I'm sure they'd heard this pitch many times before. When PGC was done he introduced Cliff Hill and regurgitated his credentials. The vote was taken and Hill was unanimously approved.

Charlotte Boyer gave a report on new business. She told us Kansas and Nebraska were about to be approved pending the results of the annual report. She looked at me asking, "When do you think they will be ready, Jack?"

After the meeting everybody milled around in the massive lobby. Some went to lunch; others back to whatever they had scheduled. When most had cleared out, Joe Neverson and Maggie Little approached me. "So," Joe asks?

"Archibald's," suggests Maggie.

"Yeah," I agree. "I could use a drink."

We found a corner and ordered beers. "Bitterman says the money will be available tomorrow, is that true, Jack?"

"That's what he says." I reply.

"We need some checks, Jack. Like tomorrow." Maggie confirms.

"Can't I have a beer, without you putting on the pressure, already?" I say, agitated.

"Jack, you're right. Let's give it a 24-hour break." Joe Neverson agrees to, very relunctantly.

"Thanks!" I reply.

"You know Gordon has been in the insurance industry for years, and no one has ever questioned his reputation. No one has ever gone to his regulators without his permission. Let's put it this way he has friends in very high places. They are at the very top!" Joe reports.

"You're still a young guy, Jack. You should think long and hard before issuing reports." Neverson cautioned.

We ordered another round before we retired from Archibald's.

The past is history. Make the present good, and the past will take care of itself. **Knute Rockne**

Chapter Twenty-Eight

Jenkintown, PA
Friday, October 21, 1983

When I arrive at our Glenside home, about 1 p.m., I find Ellen sitting at the kitchen table, looking lovely, neatly dressed in a white ruffled blouse and brown pin-striped skirt. She was smoking a cigarette and sipping on a coca cola.

I tossed my briefcase on the table asking, "So, you want to buy a house today?"

"I really do, John. And, I can't believe you are going along with my dream to have my gingerbread house." She smiles, stands up, and puts her arms around me. "What a tangled web we weave, huh?" She says.

I kiss her on the forehead. She suggests, "Let's go early so I can show you around the neighborhood and the schools. We're suppose to meet Sally at two o'clock and I have to be back to work at 3 p.m."

On the short drive to Jenkintown she asks me about my week. I tell her about the board meeting and its cast of characters. "Of course," I say, "before and after the meeting, I was asked to disburse some checks." Ellen looks at me with a furtive grin. "And," she mouths.

"I cut C&B Leasing checks for three hundred thousand dollars."

"Let's put it this way, I got fifty thousand for my efforts."

"Nice," Ellen replies. "And,"

"Hank *the bank* received a check for one hundred fifty thousand from C&B. Bitterman received one for one hundred thousand, which covers the one hundred thousand he stole out of his mother's estate.

"You surely consort with a sordid cast of characters, Johnny, but I'll take the fifty." She polished off her Coca Cola and laughed. Don't ever tell me how you made fifty grand that quickly. It does spend, doesn't it?"

Ellen and Sally, the realtor, seem to know each other as friends. Ellen had met with her several times about the house, according to what I was told. I supposed they maybe even had stopped for a drink or two on an occasion. I never pried into Ellen's business affairs or friends. I was gone so much I didn't feel I had a right. Also, Ellen was the type who insisted on opening her own mail and living a private life. Close friends were important to her, whereas acquaintances just existed.

We walked around the house into the backyard first. Actually it was a relatively small with a single detached garage at the end of a long paved driveway. There was a very nice screened-in porch. What I liked most was the tall oak tree centered in this miniature back yard.

After perusing the perimeters we entered the house through the screened porch and back porch. Here we entered the kitchen, which had been modernized with a long bar with stools, where Ellen was now pointing and saying how perfect it will be for the kids to have their breakfasts and suppers. To the left of the kitchen was the dining room which continues into a large living room.

A set up of winding stairs ascend to the second floor from the living room. After taking a right angle, halfway up the stairs, three bedrooms line up on the west wall with a full bath separating the master bedroom from the other two. Ellen grabs my hand squeezing it looking for my approval. Meanwhile Sally keeps on chattering about the house and the excellent school system in the one square mile hamlet.

I don't know why I did it this way, but I just came right out with an offer. "We'll buy it for ninety-nine thousand dollars, seller pays all closing costs."

"I don't know, John. They think one hundred ten thousand is too low." Sally says, looking somewhat despondent. "May I offer them one hundred thousand?"

I looked at Ellen. "Okay, if you have ....." Sally interrupts me. "I'll try ninety-nine, but if it takes a hundred at least you've given me a negotiating tool."

"Whatever it takes, Sally. Ellen and I trust you. Okay?" I say, holding Ellen's hand.

"Okay," Sally looks at Ellen, radiating happiness for her. "Let's get to work on the mortgage. I've several mortgage brokers ....." This time I interrupted her. "We don't need a mortgage, Sally."

"What? You are paying cash?" She seems bowled over. "Ellen, I, I didn't know you were rich people?"

"We're not," was my wife's reply. "But John is always full of surprises. Aren't you? She hooks her arm inside mine. "I suppose I am." I confirm. "And, Sally I'm buying this house for Ellen. Title it in her name. I want her to always have her own home. I owe it to her for all the hell I've put her through. Yes, I'm paying cash."

There was an interlude as tears popped out of Ellen's eyes. I put my arms around her and she leans her head on my shoulders. For once she is speechless. Then, Sally starts to cry and puts her arms around Ellen. It was a great moment for Ellen.

Ellen checked her watch. "My God, it's five after three. I have to get to the office."

"Just call old Harvey and tell him you can't make it, *E.* Tell him I'm home." I suggest, kiddingly.

Ellen discretely kicked my right shoe with her left foot. "I'm in the middle of a project. I have to get back. Harvey," she said. "John, you're such a bastard. I haven't had a chance to tell you yet, but I don't work for Harvey anymore."

Sally told us she'd contact the sellers and meet us at the piano bar in Rudi's around eight o'clock. I dropped Ellen off at Jenkintown Plaza, only a few blocks away. She gave me a kiss and said, "Thank you, Johnny."

Love the moment and the energy of the moment will spread beyond all boundaries. **Immanuel Kant**

What Is Past Is Prologue

7012 Emerson Avenue
Minneapolis, Minnesota
Super Bowl V
Sunday, January 17, 1971

I had been procrastinating all weekend about going to the mall to purchase a new pair of shoes. The soles were literally peeling off both shoes and I didn't have the time to take them to a shoemaker, if I could find one.

It is Sunday afternoon and the game between Baltimore and Dallas had been tied by the Colts midway through the fourth quarter, 13-13. When the clock ticked down to five seconds remaining, Baltimore's Jim O'Brian kicks at 32 yard field goal to win Super Bowl V. Simultaneously Ellen punches off the television set, saying, "Let's go get those shoes before it's too late."

Without further adieu we left our apartment and jumped in our 1970 Ford Maverick and headed toward the mall. However, where I should've taken a left I took a right. It put us on Emerson Avenue and there it was: a *For Sale* sign on a lawn where this perfect little house was sitting.

Ellen was approximately four months pregnant with our first child. "John, let's stop!" she suggests, vigorously.

I pull along the curb. The house is pinkish-orange and white. The yard is well manicured and it looks to be in impeccable shape. "It's my dream house," Ellen says. "Let's take a peak."

It was always one of Ellen's favorite stories. "We went out to get a pair of shoes and bought a house. Ironically the realtor was the same man who had sold Beth and I our first house. He remembered me but I could tell he was having trouble placing Ellen.

I say nothing about the first house he sold us in St. Paul. He also sold that house for us when we were transferred to South Dakota. I could see the wheels spinning in his head.

Time is of the essence, Alfonse, I mouthed. "Yes," he said. *Time is of the essence.*

It was a phrase he used often when he sold Beth and I our first house in St. Paul. We had laughed about it. Now Alfonse Richardson was scratching his head about my wife. *I'm sure she was a blond. She could be wearing a wig, but why?* He was probably puzzling. Beth was such a beauty no man would easily forget her.

When I told Ellen the story she became slightly angry. "Why didn't you tell him I was your new wife?"

"He didn't ask?" I told her. "He only met Beth twice. His dealings were always with me. I suppose it's why he remembered me. Plus, she wasn't there today. He was confused though," I snickered.

"Do you really think we'll get the house, John, twenty thousand dollars is a lot? What did he say; the payment would be $70 per month?"

I laughed. "It'll be a walk in the park."

Ellen smiles at me, "It always is for you, Johnny."

"Not always, but getting this mortgage will not be difficult. Hell! I work for the bank."

She smiles again, saying, "Indeed you do. Does that make a difference?"

"It better," I acknowledge.

The bad news is time flies. The good news is you're the pilot.
Michael Altsbuler

Chapter Twenty-Nine

1700 K Street
Washington, D.C.
Veterans Day
Friday, November 11, 1983

The past three weeks I've had the opportunity to settle into a routine. PGC is in Fripp Island tending to his personal affairs. First, he'd purchased an extravagant vessel fit only for a King. Of course he has grandeurs to make. Ned Larson is the ram-rod on this expensive project. Meanwhile Matt Ferrone is busy a short way down the seaboard, in Charlestown, South Carolina, bargaining for a Lear jet. Larson and Ferrone had been on the telephone advising me to get financing ready for both luxury stuffs.

What a great training ground for real life in the sense that you're taking something that is essentially very perfect and perfecting it. Perhaps it is just a metaphor for life. If you're not perfectly balanced over the keel of the boat, it will wobble and slip through your fingers. There was once a song on Hit Parade ... it was called, *Enjoy Yourself (It's Later Than You Think)*." I summarize for Joe Neverson when he asked what Gordon was doing.

"It's amazing how quiet it has been the past couple weeks with him gone," I add. "I've really been busy getting the bank accounts and the general ledger balanced, trying to get ready for this audit. However, I don't know how any CPA could certify to these numbers."

Joe Neverson lights up a cigarette and paces around the conference room where I'm working so I have plenty of room to spread out the paperwork. "Jack," he asks. "We need some money now to pay claims. I need a million dollars to put a dozen claims on the back burners. *Damnation*," he shouts. "Skull and Bones didn't tap us, but I have a hunch a society a lot more mysterious than one of Yale's secret clubs may be about to."

"Joe, what's the protocol? Who authorizes claims to be paid? Internal control doesn't seem to be in place here. If there are any controls they're certainly a well kept secret. So, who says *yes* pay that claim? Huh, Joe?"

"That's the problem. We'll never meet to discuss claims. He'll meet with me. He'll meet with you. Then you and I will meet and I'll tell you the checks to cut. That's the protocol.

Anything else could be classified as a conspiracy. Remember he never signs a thing and will deny he ever talked to anybody about whatever. PGC has no witnesses."

The good old RICO (Racketeer Influenced and Corrupt Organizations) act, I thought. *Any act of bribery, counterfeiting, theft, embezzlement, fraud, obstruction of justice, money laundering, murder-for-hire.* He's probably done it each and every one. So goes one, they go all. He'll try blameworthiness on one or two and when he does a stool-pigeon will come forth.

"So, then, Joe, you simply tell me who to pay and I'll cut the checks." I say. "You know we have the money."

Joe Neverson laughs. "You're really not afraid to write those checks are you Jack?"

"Should I be, Joe? I'm simply doing my job. Why do you ask? Should I be afraid?" I ask.

Joe said, "He'll probably be back today. He's has a lot of irons in the fire, so he'll be back early. It's Friday and he loves to screw up everybody's weekend. I'll try talk with him as soon as he gets back. He'll probably try to avoid me, because he doesn't like talking claims. He won't avoid you, Jack, if he's looking for millions to finance a jet and a yacht. In fact," Joe says, "it might be more opportune for you to say I'm hitting you up for claims money."

"I'll do my best if I see him before you, Joe." I say with a smile.

Joe gives me a half-assed salute, smiles and walks out of the conference room leaving me with my work papers and thoughts.

I look at my watch, it is approaching noon. I'm supposed to meet the commercial loan manager of the savings and loan on the first floor of our building. His name is Jason Simpson, who I met at the Library Lounge bar at the St. Regis. He was talking through his beer goggles but I checked him out the next day and he is the commercial loan manager of the savings and loan. Today I was explaining what I needed from him and, in turn, what I was willing to give.

The savings and loan is trying to grow their business and I could certainly give him a considerable amount of business. At first, I could give him the collateral accounts which were joint checking accounts. This was, of course, in violation of what I'd promised Henry Fleck verbally. Instead of putting these collateral accounts with his bank I'd put them with Simpson's savings and loan, if he was able to finance the jet and boat.

I put my work papers in my brief case and head for the elevator. En route I tell Mary Robinson where I'm going and whom I was meeting in case PGC arrived unexpectedly. As I entered the savings and loan I met Jason Simpson in the lobby. "Are you ready," I ask.

"Jack," Jason Simpson said, looking embarrassed. "I thought it was next Friday. Did I fuck up?" He said, trying to apologize. "I'm going out to Arlington Cemetery to honor my Dad. He was killed on D Day. He never made it out of the boat as his group was in the first wave."

"I'm sorry, Jason." I reply. "We'll make it next week."

"No. Jack, do you want to go with me? I mean ….."

I interrupted Jason. "Yes, I would like to join you. My Dad was flying B 17's over there that day. They were looking to pick up wounded and bodies. He was with the Army Air Corps Transport Command. He was a navigator. He survived the war and went back for more a few years later in Korea."

"Okay," you understand. "Let's go, Jack." We walked and talked.

"You know, because of guys like our Dads, the American way of life hasn't been all that bad for millions of Americans, especially when you see how the rest of the world scrapes by." I say to Jason, trying to pick his emotions up.

He surprised me by saying, "Human experience is too complex and too inconsistent to be explained by any one war, law or truth. I never knew my Dad. He never met or knew anything about me. I just had to accept he was killed in WWII for a good cause. I was told my Dad was simply a hero, and he belonged to the ages.

We walk the distance to the top of the hill. We stop at President Kennedy's grave and move slightly northwesterly passing below the Custis-Lee mansion. "Where's your Dad," I ask.

"I come here on Memorial Day and Veterans Day. I come to the Tomb of the Unknown Soldier. Here a sentinel of the third U.S. Infantry maintains the vigil around the clock. The sentinel paces 21 steps down the mat before the tomb, pauses 21 seconds, and returns. The changing of the guard takes place every hour or half hour depending on the protocol."

"Dad is here," Jason said, while pointing to the inscription on the sarcophagus of the WW I soldier entombed here in 1921 and joined later by comrades, unknown servicemen from World War II and Korea, who lie in crypts beneath slabs flush with the terrace paving. The inscription reads:

Here rests in honored glory an American soldier known but to God

Looking out from that hill or from the nearby amphitheater, and whether watching the precision of the sentinels or not, the surrounding scenery and just being there is so awesome. It is clearly symbols of human struggle and sacrifice, the stones and monuments that lay in place at Arlington National Cemetery is steeped in history. In their time, all buried here, taken from many walks of life, creeds and races, have answered their country's call. Their stories will be remembered.

Σ

Mary Robinson greets me when I walk through the doors of Atlantic States Surety. It is nearly three o'clock. She points toward PGC's office and mouths in a well enunciated whisper, "He's back!"

I walk toward her desk and mouth back, *When?*

"He arrived just after you left for lunch. He told me to tell you to report to his office when you returned. I'll buzz Charlotte." Mary Robinson said anxiously and in a hurry.

"Give me ten minutes to get organized before you call Charlotte. He's probably in the middle of something anyway." I request.

"No, Jack, I can't wait. I'm going to call Charlotte and tell her your back. I'm going to throw the ball in her court. Okay?" Mary urges.

"Mary, I understand. Make your call." I relent.

I go in my office to find some papers on my desk chair. The rest are in my brief case. I suspect Charlotte has been tending to my affairs again, for my benefit, of course. There are pink telephone messages on my spindle near the phone. I page through them and find a message to call my wife. I looked at my watch, it is three o'clock. I reach for the telephone to dial Ellen, when my door is pushed open by Mary Robinson.

"He'll meet with you at four o'clock in his office. Don't be late." She cautions.

I asked Mary to close my door, which she does with a smile, and I dial my wife's office number. Her office put me right through to her. "What time will you be home tonight, honey?" She queries.

I had not been home for two weeks. "I don't know," I say. "Mr. Charles just got back from Fripp Island and he wants to see me at four o'clock. I should be able to get out of here by say, five or six. So, I suppose I'll be home by eight or nine."

"That will work. Sally wants to meet us at the piano bar tonight to discuss the house closing. Also, she needs some earnest money. So, Jack, bring your checkbook. Okay? Oh, I'll meet you at the piano bar. She's picking me up around 8 p.m." Ellen suggests, elatedly

I laugh, asking, "Is that all?"

Ever since our big weekend three weeks ago nary a word had been said about Harvey. Fienstein. Ellen was very excited about the house and tonight was post time.

I put my leather legal binder and Mont Blanc pen in my brief case and headed for the inner sanctum. When I arrived Charlotte Boyer was sitting in her swivel chair with her legs crossed, her skirt was pulled up to her pussy. She looks at her legs then looks at me, winking. Her desk was void of any working materials and she wore a big smirk.

"How's Ted," I ask with a sardonic grin.

"His wife is handling it well. She tells me she was going to leave him anyway. In fact, she's had several affairs. She has a beau now she is quite fond of so she just has to catch Ted, *red-handed*, with his cock in the cookie jar." Charlotte says, while unraveling her legs. She gets up from her office chair and motions for me to follow her.

PGC is at his desk. The overhead lights are hitting his face just right illuminating his dark tan. "Charlotte, fix Jack a drink." She gets me a tall Jack Daniels and a splash of club soda. "Now," he orders. "Push the doors together when you leave, Charlotte."

PGC gets up from his desk and motions for me to sit on the black leather sofa. He sits down in his heavily cushioned black chair. He loves all his trappings in his well organized office. There wasn't a speck of dust or anything out of place. His graphite black eyes seem to be blazing. PGC lights up one of his Dominican cigars. He seems to be studying the end of his cigar while he is gathering his thoughts. He is calm and proscribed. He always speaks with an unruffled detachment. His incongruity is startling.

"Jack," he finally addresses me, "When I gamble I know how to improve the odds. Come on I'll show you. I think you can influence events by mental concentration. He pulls four dice from his vest pocket and tells me to concentrate on two numbers for thirty seconds. When thirty seconds has passed he instructs me to roll the dice. I roll them and the dice show two twos and two fours.

"What were the numbers you concentrated on?" He said with excitement.

"I concentrated first on the twos and then on the fours. I say a little prayer and my rolls came up with twos and fours." I comment. Actually, I had concentrated on nothing but thirty seconds passing.

"Dice have six sides," he says, so you have a one-six-chance of getting your number when you throw them. If you do better than that you beat the law of averages. Concentration definitely helps." He exclaims with more enthusiasm I'd ever noticed in his personality.

He fixed me with an impenetrable look. He said, "You see, the same concentration that makes dice work can make most things in life work. For instance, I've never been sick a day in my life except for a common cold once in a blue moon. I just can't be bothered. I don't have the time. Being sick is a luxury. I concentrate on being well."

I was tempted not to let those remarks pass but it was late. I just wanted to get the business done and get on the road for Philadelphia. I drank my drink and when I was finished Charlotte brought me another, as if on cue. It was moments like these I wondered if there were surveillance cameras and microphones everywhere in PGC's office.

"Jack, as you know I've spent the past few weeks on Fripp Island making decisions concerning several situations. First, I've decided to renovate the house. I'm estimating; say three hundred and fifty thousand dollars to complete this project. He held up a tube. These are an architect's rendering of the project. So, you'll need to find a mortgage for this property.

"Second, I've found the right yacht. He held up another tube. The sales contract and the proposed enhancements are in here. The estimates are approximately one million. It's a steal, Jack. She's a long range cruiser. It's fitted with extra fuel tanks and capable of travelling trans-Atlantic. She has a cruising range of 4,000 nautical miles, and her dimensions make her extremely sea worthy. She is 66-feet long from her bow pulpit to her stern swimming platform and her beam; her widest point is 19-feet-six inches. She has four staterooms, crew quarters, and five heads, with showers. The owner's cabin is large enough to accommodate a king size bed. She has a sitting area and a bath outfitted with a shower and a Jacuzzi.

"The galley or kitchen is enormous sporting a double-door

refrigerator, microwave, double convection ovens, dishwasher, and, to top it off, the counter tops are made of granite. The saloon is large enough to entertain twenty people at sea and up to 35 in port. She has a marble bar and all the best furniture, which is custom made. Thick luxurious carpet flows through the yacht creating an ethereal pastel cocoon. It feels like one is walking on a giant pillows.

"The flying bridge, besides having the helm with all its electronics, has a bar and just like the rest of the yacht, it has piped-in music. When standing on the flying bridge, one feels like they are on an ocean liner. The water line is some twenty feet below and it gives off a feeling of power.

"She is supplied with all the toys a man would ever want; twin wave runners, a 25-foot ski boat, twin dinghies, and so much scuba and snorkeling equipment an entrepreneur could open a dive shop.

"She is made for the open seas; she is outfitted with protection. The manufacturer equipped her with two high powered 306-caliber rifles, one UZI, four .45 caliber hand guns and three .10 gauge automatic shot guns. The ammunition goes along with the hardware.

"Third, I've found the perfect jet. It's a Gulfstream with all the amenities. He held up another tube. The sales contract and the proposed enhancements are here. The estimates are approximately two million. This one is a real steal, better than the boat. Jack, make the financial arrangements so we can get the people in place to get all of this rolling." He handed me the three tubes and say, "Just make it happen, Jack. Just remember when you are dealing with banks or mortgage brokers you tell them what you want – never ask them."

"Mr. Charles," I say, "I was meeting with a banker when you arrived back this afternoon. His name is Jason Simpson, he is the commercial loan officer for the savings and loan on the first floor of our building. We met at the Library Lounge bar the other night and he was telling me how they needed demand deposits in the worst way. I, of course, responded with the fact I could supply him with all kinds of demand deposit accounts, if he would be willing to make some concessions." I could tell I had PGC's attention now. "We agreed to meet for lunch today." I said, before stopping abruptly.

"And," Gordon motioned categorically with his arms.

"Our meeting went well. It went much better than I thought it would. When I met him at the bar last Monday night he seem to be quite inebriated. He also seemed like a blow hard. Today I found a much different person. He is one who is quiet, subdued and focused. It's Veterans Day today. He asked me to join him on his annual pilgrimage to Arlington Cemetery." I paused to take a drink. PGC, after the pause, asked me to please continue.

"His father was with the US First Army, USV Corps, U.S. First Infantry *Division; 116 Regiment,* which hit Omaha Beach. He told me he was told that before the ramp went down they were getting direct fire right in their craft. Some men climbed over the side. The craft was still bucking with the waves, and some slipped under the metal ramp and were crushed when the craft crashed down. Some men leaped off the craft found the water over their heads. Many did not know how to swim at all. The majority who were in the water stripped off their equipment to survive. But whether good swimmers or not, many were hit in the water. Jason thinks his Dad was killed in the water and washed out to sea. That's why we were at the Tomb of the Unknown Soldier today."

It seemed I'd struck an emotion in PGC, with my story. If I didn't know better I swear I could see tears well up in his eyes. "I was touched too," I said. "My Dad was there too, he was an aviator with the US Army Air Corps. He was a navigator. Their job was to pick up wounded to transport them somewhere safe. He was with the Air Transport Command. So, Jason and I bonded, while talking about our fathers."

"Good work, Jack. When do you meet with Jason again?" PGC asked.

"Monday," I say.

"Good," he replies. "It seems we have what they want, and they have what we need. Good work, again, Jack."

I thank him, saying, "It will happen. I really like Jason and he likes me. We're the same age. This deal could really get him where he wants to be. I have something else to discuss."

PGC nodded. "Go ahead."

"Joe Neverson says he needs a million dollars to pay claims. What is the protocol? Who authorizes claim checks?" I ask a question which I was certain I already knew the answer.

"Only me," PGC says, forcefully. "Only I sign claims checks, Jack!"

"So," I agree. "I'll defer all Neverson's requests to you. You will tell me who and when I may pay a claim."

"That is the protocol, Jack. I'll be talking at Joe Neverson the first of next week." Paul Gordon Charles says, with a tone of aversion in his voice. "Is there anything else, Jack?"

"Yes, Tom Harvey has been bugging me about that Cessna he said you promised him. And, he wants a raise in his director's fee. And, his girlfriend says there are problems with her new Mercedes we bought her. And, Charley Rivers wants to know why he didn't get his last commission check."

"Enough already," shouts PGC. "Enough already," he reiterates again.

There was a pause and Charlotte Boyer showed up on cue with another drink. I thanked her and she left. Gordon asked, as I took a sip, "How's your wife and family?"

"They are all doing well, Mr. Charles. However, I wanted to ask you one more thing. She wants to purchase this little house in Jenkintown, Pennsylvania. It's perfect for us because it is in a small community with an excellent school system."

"How much," asks PGC

"One hundred thousand," I reply.

"You just received fifty, correct?" Gordon confirms.

"Yes," I reticently inveterate. "Should I get a mortgage from Jason?"

"No, no, no! You want to look strong. Take an advance from C&B. Then, if you need furniture or whatever, set yourself up a lease. Okay!"

I was overwhelmed at his solution. Money used to be so difficult to come by. Now it was just too easy, even though, from my end of it, it was all a ruse anyway. And sometime I forgot my reality, really thinking I was somebody else with such opportunity. Or, again, was I? I stood up to shake his hand, saying thank you.

"Jack," he said. "I might suggest you go ahead and look in this area for a home. Meanwhile, go ahead with the house in Pennsylvania. You'll need to be spending more and more time working weekends as fast as everything is developing. Are you going to Philadelphia tonight, Jack? PGC queried.

"Yes, I need to be leaving soon."

"Go ahead! Oh, ask your wife if you and her could join us for Thanksgiving on Fripp Island. You and I will take a day to begin the 1984 budget. Have a good weekend, Jack."

"Thank you sir," I reply, accepting wisdom that he really thinks he has me under his wing now. In ordinary circumstances, he would have accomplished just that. *Take fifty from C&B.* Then, when it matters, *I never told you to do that.* Ha Ha!

Facing it–always facing it–that's the way to get through. **Joseph Conrad**

What Is Past Is Prologue

Pierre Airport
Pierre, South Dakota
Super Bowl IV
Sunday, January 11, 1970

The Western Airline prop jet hovers over the state Capitol of South Dakota. I had spent considerable time here the past two years and never thought about what little space it occupies on earth. It was a one horse town built along the Missouri River, in the middle of nowhere, not that long ago. As the airplane circles for landing my cerebrum is racing.

We had come to South Dakota with such high hopes of moving up the corporate ladder by paying our dues for a few years of service in this uninhabited, isolated country. It was like getting sent to the North Pole, where there was no sunlight, with hopes of time spent leading to something superlative. That was the way it was suppose to play out. But, it hadn't.

We left here in August, 1969 with our skates on. I had hopes of working it all out by returning to Minnesota and starting a new career. It didn't happen. We were divorced and I agreed to let her keep the children. We had our differences at this juncture: music, food, drinks, attitudes toward people, position of the toilet seat, and so forth. Who killed JFK? Who kidnapped the Lindbergh baby? Why did my wife dump me? I don't know. No one believed it and everyone believed it. I believed it and I didn't believe it.

The cabin is silent, except for the ambient sounds of the aircraft. As I peer out the window I see the small airport terminal. I don't see Tommy Gooch's pick-up truck or any sign of Beth and our children. As we taxi to the terminal thoughts began entering my mind that maybe they wouldn't show up. I had not seen my children since November. I had talked with Beth and she had agreed to meet in Pierre so I could see the kids. We settled on January 11, 1970. Of course, I had no idea that would be the day the Vikings would be playing the Kansas City Chiefs in Super Bowl IV.

The Captain kept everyone on the plane posted as to how the game was going. It was a rout and Minnesota fans gave up hope early on, including me. My mind was wondering about more important matters.

I had taken a loan at the bank so I could buy the plane tickets for the trip. I had taken a job with a CPA firm in Minneapolis, but I certainly didn't make the kind of money to afford an unplanned, precipitous airplane ticket. But, I did it anyway. I waited for a half-hour and when nobody showed I called Beth from a pay phone in the airport. There was no answer. When another half-hour passed I meandered over to the one airport attendant working. She was an older lady and she had noticed my activities I'm sure. I asked when the next plane was leaving for Minneapolis. I told her my story and this kindly lady felt so sorry for me.

She told me a plane was coming in about an hour that would be flying to Minneapolis. I tried calling two more times, but no answer. Actually the flight arriving was the one I was schedule to be on anyway. I leaned on her counter, nobody else was in the small airport, and listened to the rest of the Super Bowl with her. Kansas City won, 23-7.

As I returned to Minneapolis my mind was racing with all kinds of thoughts. Beth's presence had stretched half way across the country. The image of my ex-wife lay over my feelings. Our two small children – a daughter and a son were heavy on my wits, too. Every month they had grown further from me. The family tie had become mainly their shared name. What had been shared living space had become shared documents. Legalities.

I became angry. Having extramarital sex should have been exciting enough for both of them, but I suppose she didn't see it that way. For her, cheating on me was only worth it if the sex, romance, and excitement were better than at home. So, I'm thinking.

For him, the taboo of having sex with another man's wife was the turn on. For him, safe sex meant having it with a married woman. Suddenly, I realized I was driving myself crazy for no reason.

I had found myself dwelling on the past more and more, in recent days. I was living in the past. A 1960s song playing on the radio, on the way to the airport today, made me yearn for my hometown. An old movie I'd seen on television brought on nostalgia so acute that my heart ached, recently.

Because of all this turmoil, I had abandoned a promising career, a wife, who did love me, but had a strange way of showing it, and two lovely children who most certainly kept me on a pedestal. I was thinking, as the lights of Minneapolis-St. Paul appeared outside my window, I realized I might never see my children again, unless I struck it rich somewhere down the road. I came here to find closure; instead it played out there may never be any closure.

But I knew better because, I'm just not the *whither thou goest'* *type*.

When life kicks you, let it kick you forward. **E. Stanley Jones**

Chapter Thirty

Rudi's Restaurant
Glenside, Pennsylvania
Friday, November 11, 1983

I arrived around 9 p.m. at Rudi's. Ellen and Sally were at the bar receiving all kinds of male attention. Ellen spotted me as soon as I walked in the door. I peered left and then right toward her position in the saloon. She nudged Sally and motioned me to come forward.

Ellen looked stunning and seemed content and relaxed. She threw her arms around me and gave me a sexy kiss on the lips.

"Wow," Sally said. "Two people in love!."

Ellen and I laughed thinking, *right.*

I was having a difficult time understanding Ellen's mood swings. She could change her moods very quietly, without notice. My position, for the most part, when it came to women was simply to be agreeable. For convenience sake, I determined to just let these emotions and moments play out.

When Ellen released me from her lip lock I extended my right hand toward Sally. "It seems so," I said. "Nothing like a new house to lighten the mood," huh, Sally. We're in love, indeed. I pronounced, with Ellen looking on showing a very satisfied smile.

I bellied up to the bar, ordered a Jack Daniels with a splatter of club soda and sat down between two good-looking women, Ellen and Sally.

"Just back from Washington," Sally asks, with a sexy spangle in her eyes.

"Yep, it seemed like a long drive tonight. Good to be home, though." I respond, watching Ellen's expression as she grins at me. Her beam seems genuine and warm.

"What exactly is your position with the company?" Ellen says, "You have a very busy and responsible position." What's with all the questions, I'm thinking. I like to ask them but not answer any inquiries, especially about myself. It's too much work.

"My biggest challenge on the job is deciding what to do next. Somebody once told me the problem with doing nothing is not knowing when you're finished." It is simply one of my confusing answers to a routine, not sure what-to-say question, I'm thinking.

"Ellen takes me off the hook by saying, "John is the Controller. He is in charge of the accounting and financial affairs of the company."

"Hmm, I'm impressed." Sally replies, with wheels apparently spinning in her head.

I would have said surveillance, which actually was what most FBI agents keep busy doing. Not much grand standing here, I'm thinking quietly with a devious grin on my face. The two words surveillance and FBI would have made for an interesting rest of the evening for Sally.

We made small talk until old Milt, who looks more dead than alive, begins playing the piano. He starts by playing *A Good Man Is Hard To Find*, and to my surprise Sally gets up, grabs the microphone and belts out the lyrics with real zest.

With all the prelims out of the way, I ask Sally why she sells real estate when she can sing like a pro.

"My husband hates when I sing," Sally says.

"Too bad," I say, while the three of us clink glasses.

"So," I propose. "Let's get the business out of the way. I extract a folded C&B check from my shirt pocket.

"Okay, they accepted the $99,000 offer, as is." Sally adds, reluctantly.

"What's *as is*? I need to arrive at questions before I arrive at answers." I ask just to ask.

Ellen looks at me saying, with her piercing green eyes, *knock it off*. She is very good at communicating, without speaking.

"Depends on who you ask, right Sally? We'll take it at $99,000 *as is*."

"Okay," Sally replies. "I mean, I was expecting you to ….."

"Negotiate," I query. "Give you a punch list. No, we're doing neither. We want the house plain and simple." I say with a big smile.

Ellen adds, "Sally, John is a skeptic, cynic, realist, and a bubble-burster. I've been around him now for fourteen years. About a lot of things he builds a solid wall of silence. But you can absolutely trust him when it comes to the things that matter most in our travel through life's experiences."

"Especially when it comes to matters of the heart, like you, Ellen?" chides Sally.

"I suppose," Ellen grins. "I suppose one needs to believe in what one's doing, and know why you are doing it."

"Wow," Sally rings out. "But it works for me," Sally confirms, now beaming.

Now it was my turn. "Sally, I do the right thing for the wrong reason, but the bottom line, truth and justice get done. If you want me to do the right thing for the right reason, I simply don't share that idealism." I was really tossing the malarkey tonight.

My remarks silenced Sally for a few minutes. I took the C&B check, in the amount of $50,000. I handed it to her. She looked at it and said, "We can work on your cynicism another time, John."

While Ellen and Sally were giving each other congratulatory hugs I was stewing privately. I don't like it when someone, especially women, invade my hard-won cynicism. I know what makes me tick and I have a lot of ticking to do in the coming days, weeks and months. But what the hell, grin and bear it for the cause.

Sally gives me a hug and a peck on the cheek while bidding me so long. After she leaves Ellen says, "Well, thank you again John. I know where you got all that money, but don't understand why. I'm sure it's better I don't know. Like you say, when it comes to business women are on a need-to-know basis."

Ellen looked at me, grabbing my hand, she says, "John, you have that faraway look you get when you're thinking about something objectionable."

"I've seen and done a lot of stuff, Ellen, but for some reason what I'm doing now scares the hell out of me. I mean I just put a fifty thousand dollar deposit on a house." I exclaim softly as Milt, the piano man, cranks up, *It Had To Be You*. Remember our first house? We barely came up with the $500 down payment.

Ellen didn't respond, instead she lights up a Winston and takes a sip of her drink. I ask, "What are we doing for Thanksgiving?"

She gets a crooked smile on her face, asking, "What?" She looks at me, strangely, asking, "Are you okay, John? What's with Thanksgiving?"

"He wants to do a working Thanksgiving Holiday in Fripp Island. He wants you and I to be there together. Sounds wonderful, doesn't it," I say with tongue in cheek.

Ellen says nothing for a moment, but then doubles over. She asks, "So what do we do with the kids? What will I do while you're having your meetings? No, thank you. But, tell him thank you for the offer."

Of course, I could have predicted her first response. I ordered us another round to give her time to digest current events. I wondered what she is thinking and can't even imagine what she might think are my thoughts.

"It's finally happened, huh," she says, in a whisper.

"What happened? I come back with.

"Now we're criminals. Congratulations, John." She snaps a little bit louder, attracting some attention. "We have our education. We are married, with children. And, then, we go to jail. Wonderful, John, it's just wonderful." She says. "Should I call Sally and tell her to stick that check up her ass?" Ellen whispers, snidely.

"Call nobody, Ellen. Everything is going to be alright." I assure her.

My words calmed her as she looks at the piano man, who is looking at her. He tickles the ivories with the introduction to *Here's That Rainy Day*. Simultaneously, Ellen takes the microphone and sings it beautifully as I admire her beauty and talent. When the last verse is sung the growing crowd gives her a round of applause. She does a slight curtsey and sits down next to me as Milt signals for another applause and for Ellen to stand again. She did waving her hand to the crowd.

"What would I do without my music?" she mouths at me, while squeezing my shoulder. I ordered another round of drinks for us.

When the drinks arrive Ellen looks at me in the eye, asking, "How bad is it?"

"Nothing that bad or I can't handle. I just feel guilty about that fifty thousand on the loan deal and the other fifty I was told to take from C&B that I just gave to Sally." I was sick of not being able to share anything with anybody. Ellen couldn't handle this stuff anymore, yet I brought up another scenario to upset her. No, more. "Ellen, everything is fine. Every job is different and seemingly more complicated at first. Remember I'm on the right side of the fence. I'm one of the guys with a white hat."

"Oh, what the hell," Ellen says. "What's a hundred grand to the big boys?" She laughs nervously, something she always did when she thought things weren't just quite right."

She had me laughing now. I tell her, "I'm meeting my handler Monday. I'm going to slide him twenty thousand and see if he takes it. You know it was his idea to up the ante."

"I see," says Ellen. "So that makes everything okay. But just maybe you are going to throw fuel on the fire by kicking back to your boss. I see! Jesus," she said, incuriously.

"He's not my boss, and let me tell you, my handler has every intention of keeping that money. I'm going to enjoy putting him in the squeeze box. There are very few of us that are not crooks at the Bureau. It's how it works." I tell her.

"Oh, that makes me feel better. Where are you meeting him, at the Ellipse?"

"Yep, right in front of the White House. President Reagan will be probably be looking out the window with binoculars, waiting for his share." I suggest.

Probably having noticed the up and down tension between my wife and I, Milt announces, "Let's get John up here," playing the intro to *Kansas City*. While singing the bridge I noticed somebody I'd seen before. He was wearing a navy double-breasted blazer, gray slacks with a razor crease, a pale blue shirt and a solid burgundy tie. He wore a perpetual smile. He seemed to be studying me as I sang. Then, he looks at Ellen. It was just a month ago I'd seen him right here. I was suspicious of him then, and certain he was tracking me or us now.

I ended the song with, *I'm going to pack my bags and I'm leavin' at the break of dawn, to find my Kansas City baby and my Kansas City home, Oh, but you know now...*

I thought about confronting the guy, but I had no reason to question him. Maybe he was just a local who came here every weekend. Instead I asked Pete, the bartender, if he knew who the man was? Pete told me he'd been there a few times, but no one seems to know him. "That he just drinks, smiles, keeps to himself and minds his own business."

We left the bar at closing time, 2 a.m. While walking to the car, Ellen asks, "What about Thanksgiving?"

"It won't happen," I told her. He was just testing me again. He doesn't like his players to be around their women. He thinks they're distracting. They take away from him. He likes women in their place. So, he'll change the date for Fripp to a non-holiday time."

"You're pretty sure of yourself, aren't you?" Ellen says.

The parking lot for the restaurant is in back of the building. Most customers walked out the front door and down a small paved hill to the parking lot. When we reached the car I went to the passenger side to open the door for Ellen. As she got in the car I saw the stranger from the bar amble down the hill. I closed Ellen's door slowly and kept my eye on the man who was approaching a lone vehicle across the parking lot from our car. Normally when I go around to my side of the car I approach the rear. Tonight I went around the front so I could see what was going on across the way.

I watched the stranger get into the passenger side of the lone vehicle on the other side of the parking lot. The car fires up and heads rapidly toward the hill. At that moment I know I'm being followed, but by whom and for what purpose I can't quite imagine.

"Is everything okay, John?" My wife asks, reaching for my hand.

"Yeah, fine," I say.

"Good," she says. "I can't wait just to crawl into bed."

"Yeah, me too, It's been a long day."

If I have made any valuable discoveries, it has been owing more to patient attention than to any other talent. **Isaac Newton**

Chapter Thirty-One

The Ellipse
Washington, D.C.
Monday, November 14, 1983

The meeting was scheduled for 1:30 p.m. I arrived fifteen minutes early and started walking the Ellipse. I had a lot on my mind, especially the ten thousand I would soon be giving my handler. I had worked it out in my mind, if he did anything but accept my gift. *Just follow the rules; any excess money goes to your handler.*

He arrived early as well. It was 1:25 p.m. when I saw him enter the Ellipse. We made two passes before we caught up with each other on the Constitution Avenue side. "What do you have?" He mouths softly.

"There's a lot happening. The loan is in place and he's buying and improving airplanes, homes and yachts. He must understand the RICO, because he doesn't discuss business or personal affairs with a group. Everything is one on one. Other than frivolous personal spending and ignoring what should-be-adhered-to business practices I'm working on reconciling the bank accounts and getting the general ledger in balance."

My handler tells me he wants a complete status report during Christmas week. Is there anything we can do for you? When I tell him no, he asks if I had something for him. We made one more trip around the Ellipse where at Constitution Avenue I set down my attaché case on a bench, tied my shoes, while he set his down next to mine and sat on the bench. I picked up his case and he took mine. He said he'd be in touch as he turned left in the direction of the Hoover Building.

I walked around the Ellipse two more times, taking a right on Constitution Avenue to grab a cab for the return to 1700 K Street. I was so sick of this life of cloak and dagger. Who was this so-called handler? He never had anything to say. It seemed his job was simply to keep track of me and I imagine several others. If he took that money for himself, why would he do it when I could trace it so easily back to him? This job gets crazier by the minute. It seems like the powerful are all in cahoots. And, I'm glad I gave him ten rather than twenty. Fuck him!

I had the cabbie drop me off at *Archibald's*. I ordered a cheeseburger and drank two beers waiting for the food to arrive. I stayed about an hour, paid the tab and walked back to the office. The day was just beginning for me, but my brain was elsewhere. *The Feds come on like gangbusters, cause a shit storm, and then try to wipe up the shit with money.* I'd been informed so many times. Even now, what is all the commotion about Atlantic States Surety?

So far I have enough evidence to put them all away for a good period of time. Yet, I meet with my handler and he asks no questions. Instead, he takes a ten thousand dollar payoff and doesn't mind I made an extra forty thousand. How fucked up is this Federal Bureau of Investigation? What's really going on I'm thinking as I enter 1700 K Street.

While waiting at the elevator Jason Simpson taps me on the shoulder. He says he talked with his boss, who knows of my boss, and would very much be interested in doing his financing in exchange for demand deposits. "Jack," he asks. "When can you get me the financials? Also I need this loan application filled out."

I look at Simpson. "How about within two weeks?" I suggest. "Thank you for your quick response, Jason. Let's have lunch tomorrow?" I ask..

"Let's, "Jason Simpson agreed. "Meet me in my office." Jason recommends. I agree.

I step off the elevator and some little guy, with a badge on a uniform, is trying to throw his clout around by threatening, Mary. "What's going on here?" I ask, Mary?

"This gentleman wants to serve some papers on Mr. Neverson.

I told him he wasn't here, but he's telling me I'm obstructing justice. "Neverson," I scratch my head, "isn't he that attorney that used from time to time and then fired?" I recall for Mary's benefit?

"Frankly, Mr. Oleson, I think he used to be employed here. He might do some consulting work now. The only thing I know is what I'm told. He's not here right now."

The constable growls, and then attempts to make a mad dash in the direction of Neverson's office. I clothes line him and chop him on the top of his head, when he tries getting up. He hits the floor in a daze, while I tell him it would be best for him if he left. He tells me he is going to call the FBI, the sheriff and the MPD if I'm kicking him out.

"Hey, it sounds like a party. Go ahead and call. I'd start with the FBI!" I stood my ground knowing full well he would be back with a posse.

A few minutes later Neverson comes into my office. "Jack, you're crazy man. You can get in trouble screwing with a constable. I'll call him and tell him he can serve me. Thanks anyway, I love the way you gave him the clothes line, though."

Neverson walks out of my office laughing raucously. I sit at my desk holding my head, thinking how I'd enjoyed the action. Now was the time to get back to all the trivial bullshit.

Live from miracle to miracle. **Arthur Rubenstein**

Chapter Thirty-Two

1700 K Street
Washington, D.C.
Tuesday, November 15, 1983

I spent all day pouring through the journals of the operating company. The journals were kept accurately making it easy to trace each entry directly to a bank statement. Each and every banking debit or credit was duly recorded in these journals just waiting for somebody to post its results to a general ledger. However, as mentioned before, there was no general ledger. Knowing there was no one in the office, besides me, who even knew the purpose of a general ledger I decided to post it myself. First, of course, I'd have to go to an office supply store to purchase general ledger sheets and binders.

I told Mary Robinson where I was going and would return in about a half an hour. When the elevator door opened there stood the constable I'd clothes-lined. I nodded at his glare and let him get off the elevator before I got on. Joe Neverson had made good on his word. He had called the constable, after my altercation with the little weasel, and told him to come into Atlantic States Surety's offices and he would accept their service of documents.

I suppose I was lucky Joe honored his word, or that constable could have filed charges against me. I had to get better control of my temper to keep out of awkward situations. However, controlling my hot temper had never been easy for me. The narcissistic personality does stupid things.

It was a lovely autumn day. Its golden beauty made me reflect on the cycles of the seasons, with corresponding thoughts about the cycles of life and death, and what we are doing on this planet in the first place. As a little boy I wondered about life after death a lot.

I enjoyed my walk to G Street where I had noticed an office supply store before. I had become aware of the place from the backseat of a taxi cab a few weeks ago. It was the kind of office supply store I liked, filled with all kinds of unique, old-style journal and ledger sheets. It was a store for real accountants, and I enjoyed browsing for fifteen minutes or so looking at the various selections.

I purchased a standard, black, hard cover, general ledger binder replete with 100 ledger sheets. Then, while checking out, I decided to double back and retrieve three more general ledger sets for the other companies. I added three thirteen column pads and a box of Ticonderoga number two pencils. Everybody now seemed to be using mechanical pencils, preferably a Pentel .005. Whereas I liked the wooden pencils, the ones you need to sharpen every ten minutes, but you sharpen a dozen when you went to the pencil sharpener. Go figure. I've always been weird about things like that, including still using my slide rule when there are calculators and computers so readily available.

I enjoyed the walk back to 17th and K, even though carrying four sets of ledgers was an annoying task. When I got to the door of 1700 K a gentleman held the door for me. I thanked him and moved toward the elevator, nodding at Jason Simpson while waiting for its arrival. Then, for no reason, I looked back toward the door somebody had just held open for me. There he was again, the guy that had shown up in Rudi's Restaurant I had inquired about. It was the one who had disappeared into the night, in a waiting car. Who is this guy, I'm thinking, as the elevator arrives. If I wouldn't have been so loaded down I would've walked over to him right then and there. Then suddenly, from out of nowhere, a tall attractive young woman with dark black hair dressed in black jeans and a black sweater shows up. She gives him a peck on the lips.

There is not a single mystery in this world that doesn't have a solution, if you live long enough to find it. *J. Edgar Hoover, 101.*

This fellow is maddening. I determine during the ride up the elevator I have to talk with the guy. I decided to lay my purchases down in my office and go right back down the stairs, knowing full well, however, that he and the woman in black would be gone. I wonder if the woman in black is the one who was driving the getaway car that night. But when I entered my office Charlotte Boyer is sitting behind my desk waiting for me.

"Hello, Jack," she announces herself from my office chair. "I see you have been doing a little shopping. Did you find what you were looking for, sweetheart?"

"Cut the crap," I shout. "What do you want and why are you sitting in my office?" I ask, sharply.

"I want you, Jack. How's your wife doing, up there in Philadelphia?" She mouths slowly, while riding her skirt up to the bottom of her shapely ass.

"Like you really care, Charlotte, about how my wife and children are doing." I respond, motioning for her to move out of my office chair.

"I'm certain your children are fine, but I wonder about your wife?" She says nattily, while getting up from my chair.

"You amuse me." I say, rather offhandedly. "Your trepidation is so comforting."

"We'll keep an eye on her, Jack. You can count on us." Charlotte replies, while winking, and heading toward the office door.

"Wait," I ask, but not too loudly. "How are you going to keep an eye on her, and for what reason? And, who are we?"

"Not your concern, Jack. Don't get mad, honey. Your face is getting red, like a bull, or should I say a baboon's ass." She adds.

"If I ever find out you or anyone else is bothering my family I will ....."

"Kill whoever," she interrupts, finishing my sentence. "Don't threaten, Jack. It's unbecoming of a gentleman."

I was beyond pissed off, but calm, cool, collected, for the moment, and looking for revenge. But, Charlotte Boyer dealt with abstractions, conjectures, and analysis, which are the main ingredients of bullshit. She was good at it. Maybe she was the best. She didn't go away. But why was she trying to get to me? What was her secret agenda? What were her motives? How about insanity? The definition of insanity is doing the same thing every time, and expecting different results.

I sat down at my desk to put my ledger sheets together with the hardback binders. While keeping busy with this little responsibility, I kept thinking about Charlotte Boyer. Was she one of us? I have wondered about her that first night we met. She was indeed an attractive woman, in her mid-thirties. She has light brown hair, which she wears now in a pageboy cut. She has light brown eyes with soft facial features. She seems aggressive in nature, but I sense that belligerence really isn't her way. She is engaged in reckless behavior, but she is really not that out of control in real life. In fact her actions are controlled and very premeditated. I wonder what the rewards are to take on such danger.

I wonder if she really knows about my real charge. There is always ambiguity in an assignment. I can only use my own philosophy. That, life is a continuing series of compromises, disappointments, betrayals and what-ifs. Only two words can accurately describe her bizzare behavior, they are conspiracy and a cover-up. But, who is the conspirator and who is covering up what?

With my ledger books put together I take the cash disbursement journal and start posting. I want to get this task done so I can get the true financial picture of the operating company. In particularly, it is the movement of funds downstream to C&B Leasing and upstream to the management company that intrigues me. Once I start posting I become engrossed with the project. I tell Mary Robinson I do not want to be disturbed, absolutely no interruptions, including telephone calls. Mr. Charles is back in Fripp Island and he will be there through Thanksgiving.

As I figured my Thanksgiving in Fripp Island was off. We'll work on the budget between the holidays was the message I'd received from Madeline Haycock, the company's so-called auditor. And, there was no mention of including my wife either. I was actually relieved. It would be a lot easier dealing in a semi-social situation with PGC alone. And I was also thankful to have

Thanksgiving with my family. I made a note to call Ellen to tell her Thanksgiving would be in Glenside, Pennsylvania, at home. I knew she would be happy, although her inquisitiveness about Fripp Island and its occupants tickled her fancy.

I checked my watch, it was nearing four o'clock. I had not stopped by for *Happy Hour* in some time so I decided I would post another forty-five minutes and join the daily drinkers to get the latest scuttlebutt. I was certain Joe Neverson must have heard something regarding payment of claims by now. I returned to my posting assuring myself I needed to talk with the troops to see how business is really doing.

It's not where you start, it's where you finish, I'm thinking. The words of my father to me as I was standing in the front yard leaving for my first year of college. Dad was making a big effort, seeming to want to make amends for things in the past, and we got closer. I guess I started to like him more, as I have done ever since. When we talked it was usually about academics and sports. I had excelled in sports and was going to college on a football scholarship, but academically I was a B student. Dad only required *A's* in mathematics with *B's* and *C's* in everything else. I suppose that is what he was referring to when he said *it's not how you start, it's how you finish.*

So, I wonder why I am still posting general ledger. Posting general ledger was my first assignment, in 1966, when I went to work for the bank in Missoula, Montana. It seems like I'm taking Dad's mantra and working it in reverse. Or, perhaps I was still just starting and the big finish was just over the horizon. The last time I checked I was thirty-nine years old. No, I shouldn't be posting general ledger any longer, but what the hell. Age doesn't matter.

I miss my younger days when I would just barge or lie my way into situations, or make my entry in disguise. I was an electric person, a specialist in cunning deviousness, and subterfuge. I was the master of *Dirty Tricks.* Some of my tactics were so preposterous it was all I could do to prevent myself from falling over with hilarity. Many were amused by my chutzpah, a Jewish buzzword meaning brass balls.

Winners never quit. Quitters never win. More words of wisdom from Dad. He would say just keep posting until you find the answers you are looking for. *It's the mundane everyday jobs that lead to the bigger picture.* I could hear Dad's scolding, barking voice. So I kept posting until I was through the March cash disbursement journal. I check my watch, it is nearing five o'clock. I close the ledger book, exit my office and make my way down the hall to *Happy Hour*.

"Jack," Richard Corrigan belts out when I enter the room. The *Silver Fox* shakes my hand and gives me a hearty smile. "I've been hearing glowing reports about you." He says while giving me another enthusiastic grin.

"Who from," I ask readily, "my mother."

He laughs, asking, "How are the books coming along? Do you think you'll be ready for the auditors?"

"They're cooked so I wonder if the auditors will be ready for me. From what I've looked at they didn't examine the numbers too closely last year. It appears they didn't have a general ledger to work with so, instead, they must have taken Jerry's reports and found some support for a bogus balance sheet. The net changes in their balance sheet then would force the desired profit and loss."

"Jack, all that crap is way over my head. Just do what you have to do to get the auditors to give us a good report."

The smile disappears from Corrigan's face when I ask. "Did we pay those auditors off last year?"

"You mean did Jerry Bitterman slide them a few bucks to massage the numbers?" Corrigan quickly responds, trying to cast any possible wrong doing in direction of the past controller.

"I don't think so, but it would be something to contemplate over if a situation would call for a tactic or two. Jack, what are you drinking?"

While Corrigan and I walked to the bar area he whispered sympathetically, "Have you got that damn airplane lined up for Tom Harvey?"

"We just need to write a check or finance it. He's already picked one out at Friendship Aviation, in Baltimore. What do you want to do?"

"How much, Jack," lipped Corrigan, covertly?

"It's a 1972 Cessna 402B, which means nothing to me. Tom says it is what he wants, in mint condition, and we can steal it at $150,000." I say, with a kind of a scoff.

"Fucker," Corrigan says. "This fucker thinks he's the *Red Baron*."

"Should I write a check and close the deal?" I ask Corrigan as he fixes a gin and tonic for himself. "Jack and Club," he asks. I nod as he pours my drink.

"Buy it tomorrow. Use a C&B check and I'll approve a transfer of funds from the Management Company. How about his girlfriend's fucking Mercedes?"

I took a swig off my Jack Daniels. As usual the first swill burned all the way down to the pit of my stomach. It's an awful tasting drink – first quaff anyway. "It's in the shop. Mercedes is analyzing and correcting every problem she's complaining about. And," I add, "We are upping his Directors fee by $200 a month."

"That fucker," Corrigan repeats. "Let me tell you something, Jack, PGC isn't going to put up with his shit much longer. That, *I'm just a white man in a black body* is wearing very thin."

As Richard was protesting over Tom Harvey's requirements, I caught the eye of Charlotte Boyer. She looked bored listening to Ted Masters whining. I suppose there were questions about Ted's uncertainty about their so called love affair. Ted was such a fine lawyer, but he knew nothing about dealing with women and understanding their wants. After a few moments I shook my head at Boyer, while she reeled off one of her evil laughs, surprising her lover Ted Masters. I was certain he didn't see his situation as anything hilarious. It appeared she had excused herself from Masters when she started walking toward me.

Quickly I fixed another drink, after which I joined Corrigan, who was chewing out the head of the casualty insurance department, Larry Leopold. "I'm sorry," I said, realizing I was joining a heated conversation. "Give me a few minutes, Jack." Richard requested. I turn and walk into Charlotte Boyer, who is standing right behind me. She asks, "Are you trying to put me out of sight, Jack?"

"And, out of mind." I say, asking, "What's going on between you and Ted? He looks very somber."

"Wouldn't you like to know, Jack?" She lisps, sexually.

"Jack," a voice rang out from behind me. It was Joe Neverson. Maggie is standing by his side and is wearing a frown. I kind of excuse myself from Charlotte and walk toward the *A Team*. "Did he call?" I ask.

Maggie spoke right up. "He said see what you can do with a million."

"What will a million dollars do, Joe?" I ask.

"It will keep the dogs away for a few weeks, maybe. How fast is he spending all the money, Jack." Joe asks.

"Well, tomorrow I'm buying Tom Harvey an airplane. PGC probably has another three or four million out there to spend before Christmas. And, we have ....."

Joe interrupts me saying, "Let's go somewhere so we can talk."

"Name it," I concur.

"Anna Maria's, it's not far from here. It's a great Italian restaurant and quiet. We better talk earnestly now or this house of cards will be falling much quicker than anybody might suspect."

Interesting information will be coming, I'm thinking. But in this game one has to think long-term. You rack your brain. Then, you do it again. All will end when the FBI wants it to end. The Feds come on like *gangbusters*, cause a shit storm, then try to wipe it clean with money. Smoke and mirrors is what it's all about.

"Let me close my office and I'll be ready. Italian food, that really sounds good." Now is the time, I'm thinking, we'll talk about what Joe wants to talk about. But, in the end, only the promise of anonymity in exchange for cooperation closes this case.

I return to my office to lock the journals and ledger books in my safe, which had just been delivered today. I had stuck the code in my wallet and was looking for it when Ted Masters appears at my door.

"What's up, Ted," I ask.

Ted remained silent and seemed somewhat distant; giving off

the impression he has something weighty on his mind. In fact ever since his affair with Charlotte Boyer Ted has not quite been his boring self. He's been worse, appearing to be in the dumps.

"Who am I?" Ted asks, looking like he is about to cry.

"You're a fine lawyer, Ted. You need to pick yourself up and dust yourself off. You know what they say."

"I simply feel like a failure." Ted says, looking like he is coming mentally coming apart.

"I hope this isn't all over Charlotte Boyer!" I say.

"No, it's about me. I threw away my marriage and children for no good reason. This is not me. I don't do things like this and I don't know why?" He seems like he is pleading for an answer or forgiveness.

"I think there may be a slight inconsistency in your story, which it makes it somewhat unbelievable, Ted. My first impression of you was to be a strong individual with a lot character. This Charlotte Boyer story makes no sense. What do you know about her? Do you discuss business with her? Do you think she tells you the truth about everything, or is there a possibility she might be using you?" I state and query.

I continue, asking, "Is it her moods, her sullenness, and her general nuttiness that attracts you most. Or, is it her arms, legs, the fair skin, and the big brunette bush of pubic hair that drives you to be a changed man?"

He smiles enigmatically. "Thanks, Jack. I'll let you go as I know you're going to dinner with Joe and Maggie."

"How did you know that?" I ask.

"I asked Maggie to join me for a drink, and she declined. I thought maybe she was giving me the run around too. She told me to verify her plans with you. I feel like an ass now." Ted Masters replies.

"Time to re-evaluate, Ted, you have to make intelligent decisions."

Ted was silent again. I state, "I have to go. Maybe we'll see you for a drink after dinner."

Life is what we make it. Always has been. Always will be.
Grandma Moses

Chapter Thirty-Three

Anna Maria's
New Hampshire Avenue
Sandwiched between Washington Circle and Dupont Circle
Washington, D.C.
Tuesday, November 15, 1983

The taxi cab pulls up in front of the Italian Restaurant. It is located in what looks like a row home in a block replete with row homes. We walk up seven steps to arrive at the entranceway. A beautiful woman, with jet black hair and olive skin, greets us. She is dressed exotically, like she is going to read our palms. She takes three menus and shows us to our table. It is a small and very homey room. She sets us up in a back corner for privacy, acquiescing to Joe Neverson's request. Before we can even look at our menus she is back with hot breads, three wine glasses, and a bottle of red and a bottle of white.

I pour Maggie a glass of white and me a glass of red. Joe had ordered his usual in advance, a scotch with a splash of soda. Joe slugs down his drink and orders another by signaling to a very sexy looking bartender. "Jack," Joe says. "So what do you mean PGC is going to be pissing away three or four million before Christmas?" Joe was acting like a man on fire!

On a personal note I was annoyed I had given the government nearly 15 years of my life. I'd seen the other side of the moon and I liked the action, and the opportunity to make easy money. This job is changing me day by day. I am no longer the nice guy I always thought I'd be, knowing full well I probably never was a really nice kind of guy. My grandmother Austin told me I was an egomaniac when I was in high school. Of course I didn't know what she meant, until she explained an egomaniac as one who always puts his cares and concerns first. I suppose she was right. I do always think about myself first.

"I'm buying Tom Harvey his plane tomorrow. I'm arranging financing for a mortgage on his Fripp Island property for a million dollars worth of improvements, a jet airplane to be improved considerably and a luxury yacht fit for a King. Oh, I almost forgot, two million is needed for enhancements at the Potomac Mansion. He wants all this by Christmas. The more I can finance or mortgage the more we should have to settle claims. And, I have two new sources of funds."

Joe orders another scotch while I pour Maggie and me another glass of wine. Maggie queries, "Jack, do you really believe he has any intentions of paying these claims?"

Joe stares at me waiting for my answer to the question. This is the most difficult part of my job, working both ends of the stick. Silence is either meaningless or portentous. Silence usually means nothing, except for the times when it is ominous. What silence means for an FBI agent is time to reflect about a nagging doubt that something is being missed, some questions are not asked, a clue is overlooked. Time gaps are always important, because things happen during those times. Be careful, I'm thinking, you are who you are and just play the game. Just follow the course and gather information.

"I'm not sure." I say. "He must know the claims situation, doesn't he? Why would he be doing all this spending to lose it all in the near future? There must be a master plan nobody knows about," I protest with a confused, wondering look..

With my answer Maggie sips her wine thoughtfully saying we need to get our stories straight. Joe Neverson adds, "Federal prisons are full of people who lie about something that is not a crime." You see I should have been the one to say what Joe just said. Instead, he assures, "When the Feds get on your case, you are toast."

With Joe's last remark, thank God, our waitress came to take our order. I had no interest in talking about the FBI. Maggie and Joe select veal dishes and me the spaghetti and meatballs.

The food is delicious and we enjoyed our meals without speaking about the need for more money for claims. We talked about Joe's declining marital situation and his concern and love for his children. Maggie was raising her two boys successfully and mentioned she'd been out with Ted Masters a couple of times for drinks. She informed us his affair with Charlotte Boyer, which prompted Ted's wife to file for divorce and sole custody of the children. I told them I'd just purchased a home in Jenkintown, Pennsylvania, which really surprised both of them.

"It's probably a good idea." Joe acknowledged.

I followed, "It might be. I can't see moving my family here with your prognosis of what is about to come. I do need to find a place to live here, however. I'm going to rent an apartment in Maryland come the first of the year. If things look better in 1984, we'll probably look for a house in Northern Virginia. We'll see how it goes."

After dinner Joe ordered another scotch while Maggie and I stuck with the wine. "What scares me the most is the not so distant future?" Joe says. "The million dollars will put the immediate problems on the back burners. However, if he spends all that other money I'm afraid he'll start hitting the collateral accounts to pay claims. If so, here will be real criminal problems for those of us involved. We're talking conspiracy, fraud, destruction of evidence, misappropriation of trust funds, and 101other charges, including the obstruction of justice."

Maggie gulped, then took a large swig of her wine and reached for the carafe of white to refill. Her hands shook slightly as she was pouring. I ask, Joe, "Who are the *us* involved?"

"Come on, Jack. It would certainly involve the three of us here." Joe said, assuredly.

"Sounds like we should all resign." I suggest. "And," I say, "especially the directors who sit in ostensibly treasonous but ultimately loyal comradeship with PGC. They should have marshaled their forces sooner. Do any of them even know about the claims and PGC's ludicrous spending?" I query, incredulously.

Maggie pipes up, "Maybe, Tom Harvey."

"Makes sense," I say. "He's getting everything he wants right now."

"They'll kill him!" Maggie chimes in.

"Kill him?" Asking for clarification, "They'll kill Tom Harvey for asking for too many perks."

"Yeah, yeah, yeah, who cares?" Joe chortles, with hostility. Once evidence is destroyed, it can never be retrieved, and people do not often take that irretrievable step. They tend to hide evidence. So let's get back to the embezzlement of collateral again.

"What do you want me to do, Joe?" I ask, sincerely.

"Jack, there is simply nothing you can do. Only PGC can release the money."

It was a cool, clear night, and we could see the stars shining brightly and there were no black helicopters hovering over us. And, right now there was no *wet stuff*, which is CIA jargon for killing someone, threatening us. "So let's walk back to St. Regis," I suggest.

Just then a yellow cab pulls up. I step over to the window. "We're walking," I say.

"To the St. Regis," the driver asks, while I step away. His remark stops me in my tracks. I turn, bend down and looked right at him. He was writing something on a pad. I ask him how he knew we were going to the St. Regis.

He looks up, saying, "I know everything about you sport." He spins off, quickly. I stand there slightly dazed. Neverson comes up to me asking, "Something wrong, Jack?"

"No," I deny. "I thought I saw somebody I knew, but it wasn't that person."

Perhaps it was a good thing. I was much less paranoid now that I had just discovered there really were people following me and maybe even wanting to kill me. The cab driver was the same guy I'd seen at Rudi's a couple times, holding the door for me today at 1700 K and now asking me if I wanted a ride to St. Regis, and as far as I knew he didn't know I was going there.

Maggie asks, "Is everyone in authority off their guard and giving you an opportunity to commit mokay, Jack?"

"Okay, yeah, I can use another drink, though."

"Library Lounge, here we come." Joe Neverson announces, with a ready to drink kind of smirk.

Always acknowledge a fault. This will throw those in authority off their guard and give you an opportunity to commit more. **Mark Twain**

Chapter Thirty-Four

Traveling on Amtrak, crossing the Susquehanna River
Twixt and between Baltimore, Maryland and Wilmington, Delaware
Friday, November 18, 1983

It had been a confusing but interesting week at Atlantic States Surety. I did more accounting work than I had done in years and successfully posted the general ledger through September 30, 1983. The actual results were what I'd expected. Most of the distributions were not for justifiable expenses. How about that? And, who was I going to question about the transactions? Nobody, that's who, my job was just to gather evidence for later questioning by somebody else. No fun at all for me.

Madeline Haycock called telling me the Fripp Island trip would be Thursday, December 8th thru Saturday and returning Sunday morning, December 11th. She said Atlantic's travel agency was making the arrangements. I agreed by saying nothing as to whether the dates fit into my plans or not. However, I couldn't imagine what a weekend would be like spending it with PGC and whoever. I snooped around a little and couldn't find anybody who had ever been there. I was certain, however, Charlotte Boyer had spent some time at Fripp, but I didn't want to solicit any information from her. As it turned out, I didn't need to.

I had been trained to pry if I wanted answers, but this situation I knew, intuitively, was dissimilar. In fact every situation was poles apart.

"Well, you must be somebody really special, Jack? You're the first one to join him at Fripp, other than his paramours and errand boys." She announced the following day after Madeline's call.

"Is there anything I should know," I ask Charlotte, being very general because I was looking for information. She knew what I was up to as she gave me a sardonic beam.

"I suppose I could give you a clue or two, Jack. That is if you're interested in some juicy details?"

I laugh, asking her to spare me the sexual exploits. She smiles while I'm thinking don't lie and don't pretend, Charlotte. Never tell anybody more than you have to; never tell the truth if a lie will suffice. So what was she up to? She was always smooth as marble. And, he destroyed things for money. A taut silence has descended momentarily between us.

I suspect Charlotte Boyer has never been a femme fatale, never sparking hidden flames. She had been a dutiful employee and a confused paramour. Or, had she? I wondered again, is she really an FBI agent? Don't let her good looks fool you, and she's no dumb bunny, I'm thinking during our pause. What if she is in love with him, and she probably is. He s not a man who plays by the rules. Maybe he blows up churches for fun. But, I can see an untamed intermittent light in her eyes. To her, PGC is the master of disguise. That his high IQ and natural charm enable him to blend into almost any situation and captivate people's minds, especially her wits.

"Well," she says. "He can't stand to be alone. He maintains at least one high-profile female companion at all times. I was one of them, which I'm certain you already know."

"You were the high profile one, correct?" I ask seriously.

"Yes, I know how to fit in, how to be successful, and how to make people like me." She replies with a serious message in her attitude

"And, how to make people not like you. You are pretty good at that too, Charlotte." I reply.

She gave me a knowing smile. While positioning herself so I could see her legs clearly. The way her thighs curve into rounded kneecaps, which give way to slender calves, which tapered to delicate ankles. I love her ankles. There is just something special about her exposed ankles and bare feet. Feet can be incredibly sexy, especially small, dainty feet sporting red-painted toenails.

She warns, "Be careful, Jack. He's charming, outgoing, and very self assured. On the other hand, he considers himself outside of societal norms and above anybody he meets. He lies easily and is obsessed with appearance."

"Sounds like my kind of guy, but I wonder why you are telling me all this, Charlotte Boyer," I ask.

"I hate Madeline Haycock, she's an opportunistic double-crossing whore!" Boyer was quick with her answer. "She's a snake in the grass, watch her Jack."

Boyer continues, "He's highly materialistic and image obsessed. To him you just exist as motion. That's the zone. Once you are in it you are trapped. To him extreme performance is not a physical game but a mental one. To him it's about focus and concentration. It is finding that zero zone."

I raise my brows but shut up. She is a good listener. What she is telling me is a pure verbatim of PGC's rules of engagement. I have already heard him say the same things. Perhaps she knows him like a book.

"Charlotte, who are you?" I ask calmly.

"I'm Charlotte Boyer. Who are you, really, Jack?"

"I'm really just a shirt sleeve accountant. That's who! Is there anything else I should know about going to Fripp Island?" I ask Charlotte, who is now backing away from me.

"Just keep your eyes and ears open, Jack."

As she walks away I wonder if she loves him so much she can even be nice to me. Or, who is she?

Suddenly the train slows down and grinds to a halt, while crossing over the Susquehanna River. Five minutes or so passes and it is eerie a feeling sitting in the train suspended high above the mighty river. There is no explanation why the locomotive is not moving so I walk back to the club car to get a drink and hit the buzz mill.

The club car is full. Most of them present I'm certain are regular travelers on this Northeast corridor run. I squeeze up to the bar and ask for a Jack and club soda. "What's up with the train stopping over the middle of the river?" I ask. The bartender is an older black gentlemen who grins and says, "Something across the river is going on with the switch boxes, it happens all the time."

His assurances make me feel better, until I see the guy again with the woman in black sitting in a booth drinking their drinks. I walk near their table to confirm my sighting. I see their eyes tracking my movements. There were two, who looked like regular businessmen, sitting across from them. I didn't want to cause a disturbance, but I was determined to talk with those hound dogs. I made my final approach, watching them attempt to leave.

I met him chest to chest and nose to nose. "Who are you two characters?" I ask, while sinking my right fist into his gut. He doubled over slightly, but did not make a sound. The woman in black made a move toward me, but backed off when I stepped on her foot and held it down.

"Jack," the protagonist said. "It's not what you think. We're around everywhere to protect you. We've been watching you since you started this assignment. In case you don't know, you are dealing with very dangerous people. They are the rough element of the populace who will do anything to accomplish their goals. They will eliminate anybody who causes problems without questions. Do you follow?"

"No, but if you are watching my back I'm sorry for the sucker punch. But, I don't believe you without some confirming evidence. I won't interfere with you if your job is watching me, but I don't want you to bother my wife and family in any way. Stay away from us this weekend. I'm serious. I'll try to check your story out, but if you are who you say you are you know I'll never get a confirmation. So, please stay out of our way. By the way," I ask, "what are your names?"

"The man looks at me, saying, "I'm Dick and she's Jane."

"Original," I say. As the train starts to move forward, I ask, "May I buy you a drink."

"Definitely," replies Dick as I back off Jane's foot.

Half the club car clears out once the train starts moving so we sit down in a booth with me facing the two of them. I study the two of them and they examine me while we wait for the drinks to arrive. They appear very uncomfortable. I'm not ill at ease, but very angry. I now despised all the government games played with its citizens. Or, was it the government's game?

"Where do you guys work out of," I ask, breaking the ice as the drinks arrive.

"Wherever they send us," answers the so-called Jane.

I laugh, saying, "What a great conversation. Look at the sun setting and how the moon illuminates the fields as far as the eyes can see. It's one of those evenings that will stick in our minds forever. Agree?"

Thankfully the conductor broke our attempt to communicate by shouting, "Wilmington, Delaware is our next station stop."

I was surprised when Dick and Jane got up and stepped off the train in Wilmington, or did they? I tried to get a glimpse of them out the window, but I couldn't locate them. They probably walked to the other end of the train. I thought about making that walk to see if I could find them but what the hell? Verbal volleyball would accomplish nothing. But I was wary of them, very wary. This whole case was driving me crazy.

I was torn between action and inaction, between waiting and doing. My training had taught me to be patient, but I was really tired of all this shit. I'm getting older and the world is wearing me down. I want a beer. I was coveting it like a man lost in the desert.

Maybe I had a plan of my own. *There is a time to sow and a time to reap.* Miss either of those times and you're fucked. As the train moved toward Philadelphia, a middle-aged man with a New York Yankee baseball cap walked into the club car with a folded umbrella, in his hand, which partly shielded his face. He was broad shouldered and wearing sun glasses. He appeared to be wearing an afro and actually reminded me of a colleague and friend. But, no, it couldn't be. Not on this fucking train!

"I had your ass covered a few minutes ago, but it looked like you were handling yourself pretty well."

Now I definitely recognized the voice. It was him and I couldn't believe it. He looked awful, but I smiled in recognition of his voice. "Richard Richards," I announce. What in the hell are you doing on this coach?"

"What the hell are you doing on this train," Rich queries, in response.

I stand up; we shake hands and hug each other like long lost brothers. "Really, what's going on Richie? Why are you here?"

"I managed to get your phone number; I still have some friends, and one heard you lived in Pennsylvania. I searched the area code and came up with a listing in Ellen's name. A telephone number, but no address. When I called Ellen answered and told me you'd be on this train. I told her what was going on with me, Bobbi and my family. I'll tell you later. But, they cut me loose."

"Bobbi," I ask.

"No," he said, "the fucking FBI."

"What, you, after all you've done," they put you out to pasture?"

Rich shook his head, "It was drugs, buddy. It was too many drugs and too much booze. It's my fault, not theirs. I fucked everything up." He said, as I saw tears roll down his cheeks.

"This way of life finally got to me. Every morning I poured whatever booze I had left from the night before, and poured it into a hurricane glass. A little bit of gin, scotch, vodka, whiskey, wine or whatever I could find. I threw a few cubes of ice on top, gave it a spin with my fingers and I drank the elixir down like we used to chug beers in college."

"Philadelphia is our next station stop. Philadelphia is next." A conductor shouts from the rear of the club car.

"Where are you staying, Rich?" I ask with a snicker.

There was a pause, before he said, "Your house. *Big E* suggested it when she found out I was broke with no car, and no place to go."

"Are things really that bad, Richie? I mean it's hard to imagine.

They said goodbye, leaving you with nothing. What, didn't you have eighteen plus years? And, they wouldn't let you finish your twenty year commitment. After all you've done, risking your life for the country and the good of the Bureau?" I whisper, softly, searching for the truth.

Everybody, except the bartender, has moved out of the club car. "Come on, we have to go, unless you want to spend the night in New York."

"New York sounds good to me, if you got the money." Richie assumes as we move forward to the exit door. When we walk up the stairs toward the main terminal, I was surprised to find Ellen at the top of the stairs. She hugs me and it takes her a few minutes to recognize Richie. She exclaims, "Richie, you – you look awful. It's good to see you though," reaching for a hug.

Ellen takes the wheel and drives our Chrysler New Yorker to Glenside. We were pretty quiet in the car, while en route. Richie kept looking at the City lights, especially Boathouse Row. Boathouse Row is the University of Pennsylvania fraternity houses that are outlined in white lights sitting alongside the Schuylkill River.

"As you know I worked South Jersey in the *sixties*. Bobbi and I were happiest here, with all the dreams, hopes and promises of the future. They pushed CIA on me, right out of William and Mary. But I didn't want to be a spy, work overseas, and all the shit they do. Like in killing people."

Ellen hops in there with, "So they send you and your family to Norfolk, Virginia and put you undercover. Yeah, they're assholes with no regard for their agents and their families."

There was another pause, after Ellen ended her speech. Finally, Richie, says, "You've changed haven't you, *E*?"

"You better believe it," she says, as she turns left on Waverly, heading the short distance to Berkley Road. "Stop," I command." Ellen pulls alongside the road after she turns onto Berkley. "What," she asks.

"Do you have a babysitter?" I ask.

"No shit, Dick Tracy." She responds. "What are you thinking?"

"Let's go to Rudi's. I need to talk with Richie and I'm sure we could all use a drink and something to eat. Plus when Joe and Dan see Richie they'll want to talk him to death."

"I told the babysitter we'd be back around 11 p.m. I'll call her and tell her you're coming on a later train and we'll be home about midnight."

"Okay, Rudi's here we come." I say, feeling guilty I wasn't going home to see the children.

We had become creatures of habit. When we arrived everyone who saw us acknowledged our presence. "See you after dinner," I snicker as we are seated by the hostess. All our friends were at the piano bar.

When our waitress brings us our first round of drinks, Richie says, "I'm happy, it seems like you guys have a great life going."

Ellen and I don't respond, while Rich slugs down his drink. I signal and she brings him another.

"Actually we've never been so uneasy." I said.

There was another silence between us. I finish my drink and Ellen finishes hers and when the waitress returns with Richie's second drink I ordered another one for us. "Menus," she asks. "Not yet," I reply.

"I'm the one that got the heave-ho. Are you guys, okay?" Richie asks.

"Things are too good, Richie. Everything I do seems like I'm making all the right moves. *Good job, etceteras.* It's never worked this way before, I feel like I'm being set up. It's very unsettling – unnerving. I have this crazy woman, who shows up in my office nearly every day offering advice while riding her dress up to her crotch. She's very attractive, but I can't get a handle on her purposes.

"Today was really confusing as she was imparting advice to me on what to expect on my long weekend at the boss's home in Fripp Island. I'm sorry, Ellen, I have a lot to tell you."

On that note Ellen orders another round of drinks and asks for the menu. Meanwhile Richie says. "John, you sound bewildered?"

"An honest man has nothing to fear, right?" I say, with a smile.

"Who ever told you that you were honest, my friend?" Richie asks, laughing.

All of a sudden I found my friend, Richie, coming back to life. He was the one who had told me you're not brave if you're not scared. How can anything not stressful, be rewarding. I always found Rich Richards to be extremely knowledgeable and competent, and dedicated. I was so young when I met him, and although he is only five years older, he is really street smart.

He had grown up in north Jersey. His idea of a great day, as a kid, was getting a ride across the George Washington Bridge, and finding his way to Yankee Stadium in the Bronx. Mine was sitting on a stack of Minneapolis Tribune papers and reading the box scores, paying extra attention to what the Brooklyn Dodgers had done and dreaming about seeing actually seeing Ebbets Field sometime in my life.

Ellen interrupts my reverie, saying, "So may we enjoy the rest of the evening? Richie you'll be with us this weekend, terrific! John you two can talk your asses off tomorrow. I'd like to enjoy dinner and sing some music before we go home. Please order me surf and turf. I need to call the babysitter."

"Maybe I'm just contrary, stubborn, and an ornery prick, but you haven't told her much, huh?" Rich asks.

"Real men don't join support groups. They keep their problems to themselves; didn't you tell me that, Richie?"

Richie gave me that killer smile he possesses that he used to persuade or con a lot of unsuspecting people with. "We're the *unkempt bunch*, John!"

I see Ellen approaching. "Do you want a job?" I ask discreetly.

"Me?" he says, as Ellen sits down. "You know I need one, buddy!"

A human being is only interesting if he's in contact with himself. I learned you have to trust yourself, be what you are, and do what you ought to do the way you should do it. You have to discover you, what you do, and trust it. **Barbra Streisand**

What Is Past Is Prologue

Virginia Beach, Virginia
Sunday, July 4, 1976

It was the big day we'd been hearing about since 1969, when President Richard Nixon created the American Revolution Bicentennial Commission. Initially, the Bicentennial celebration was planned as a single city exposition that would be staged in either Philadelphia, Pennsylvania or Boston, Massachusetts. But, it became much more that.

It began on April 1, 1975, when the American "Freedom Train" launched in Wilmington, Delaware to start its 21-month, 25,388-mile tour of the 48 contiguous states. On April 18, 1975 President Gerald Ford came to Boston to light a third lantern at the historic Old North Church. The big City harbors were all filled with a great fleet of ships and the celebration of fireworks, especially in Washington D.C., lit up the skies.

So it was fitting this would be the day I'd rendezvous with Rich Richards at the *Dirty Nail*, a bar I would often frequent during the next couple years.

I followed the directions I'd jotted down on a piece of scratch paper, and was now taking the Lynnhaven exit off the Norfolk-Virginia Beach Expressway. I followed Lynnhaven Road to Virginia Beach Boulevard, crossed over and turned into a large shopping center. I turned right at the Giant food store and followed the parking lot to the end where I found *the Dirty Nail* resting atop a modest incline.

It was a sunny day and it took my eyes a few moments to adjust to the darkness of the bar. It was the same feeling I had coming out of a Saturday matinee movie, when I was a kid, blinded by the light of a Minnesota afternoon sun. At first I thought the place was empty, but then I saw the bartender talking to what appeared to be a lone customer about three-quarters of the way down the long ingot.

He looked at me and I could tell he knew I was his appointment or vice versa. He continued talking to the barkeep as I moseyed toward his position. When I sat down right next to him, he finally acknowledged me. "Hey," he said. I nodded in rejoinder.

"Linda, get me another and whatever he wants. Put it on his tab."

Linda is a very sexy looking blond, a curvy figure replete with ample bosoms. She looks at me, and I say, "Jack Daniels and club soda. Put it on his tab."

She laughed and so did Rich Richards. When Linda came back with our drinks, Rich asked her to get him a pack of Marlboro. When she headed toward the vending machines Richards showed me his credentials and I showed him mine. "I've heard you're the best." I said.

Rich laughed again, asking, "The best at what? Drinking or fucking?"

"Does it matter," I ask?

"I like you, already, Jack, is that what your name is today?"

"What is it today, Sunday? My name is usually Jack on Sunday." I replied.

Linda came back with the cigarettes and Richards slid her a dollar bill and lighted up. "Give us another drink, honey." Were the next words out of his mouth?

"I need an accountant, Jack. And, I'm told your opening a new office right across the street from here. Good! I can get you a bunch of business as I know a bunch of people in this neck of the woods." Rich said, while motioning for another round of drinks.

My brain started to race as I watched, but couldn't hear, what Richards was negotiating with Linda the bartender. Rich was a man in his mid-to-late thirties, polished and smooth. He wore a short afro haircut mounted on top of a ruggedly handsome face. He had an athletic build, narrow at the hip and broad at the shoulders. He would be a formidable foe if anyone was stupid enough to start an argument or a fight. He simply had a good presence.

The phone rang and Linda said, "It's for you, Rich."

He reached for the phone mouthing, "Yeah." After which there was few minutes of break in his what seemed to be non-stop chatter, when I assumed he was just listening to somebody's orders. Suddenly, he said loudly, "Do have a problem with me, punk? Then, you fight like a man; you take me on if you think you can. But don't go spreading lies, punk. That's the way a wuss fights, a weak, pussy-mama's punk."

I just sat there making an observation, like a typical FBI man who wouldn't give anybody a heads up even if their ass was on fire. Richie punched the phone off and handed it to Linda. "Bring us another round," he orders.

"Here's the play," said my new acquaintance. It was an expression I'd hear a lot during our coming working relationship. "I'm working this case and I have to get some accounting information, mainly an analysis of gross receipts. These guys are using their place of business as a laundry for a rather big time drug operation."

Rich Richards lights up another Marlboro while I cogitate about how this would work. From my end it was relatively simple. And, I wouldn't want to be involved in his end. Agents hear about other agents, and undercover agents, who are referred to as the *unkempt bunch* have the best stories to tell. I'd been told Rich Richards was not only a legend in his own mind, but in the minds of agents who were not part of the *unkempt bunch.*

"When are you moving into your new offices?" He asks after ordering us yet another round of drinks.

"The construction is supposed to be completed by June 30th, but I agreed to move in July 10th, in exchange for a free month's rent. So I'll in there next Monday, with the supposition I'll be able to do the actual moving over the weekend. "Good, I'll see you at 9 a.m. on the 12th."

Rich slugged down his drink and left me sitting there with one half full and another fresh imbibe. Three more people were sitting at the end of the bar now and Linda was getting their orders. I wondered if that was why Richie had left so abruptly, or was it the phone call. Anyway I just wanted to get home to be with my family and to watch some of the Bicentennial festivities' on the tube. Linda came back asking if Rich had left. "I think so," I said.

"I suppose I get the tab," I posed.

"I expect you do, how well do you know Rich?" She inquired.

"Let's see, maybe fifteen years." A safe answer, for a certified impostor

"Then you should know he never picks up the check." Linda laughs, while sliding the tab in front of me.

"I haven't seen him in a while. I thought maybe he had changed." I whisper. "Don't tell anybody he hasn't. It wouldn't be good for his reputation."

"Ha!" Linda tittered. What reputation are you talking about?"

I care not what others think of what I do, but I care very much about what I think of what I do. That is character! **Teddy Roosevelt**

Chapter Thirty-Five

1700 K Street
Washington, D.C.
Monday, November 21, 1983

We had a nice weekend - Ellen and I and our boys, with Richie. Ellen made a pitcher of Bloody Marys on Saturday morning. She and I had one, while Richie drank the rest of the pitcher and offered to make another.

Heavy drinkers don't realize how people observe their activities and obsession. Ellen and I certainly did our share of drinking, but watching Richie knock back made us feel like teetotalers. He was always great with our children, and today was no different. He took them to the park to teach them to fly the kites they had received from their grandmother last summer. Richie loves kids, probably because he is still a kid, at heart, himself. The boys had a splendid day and we topped it off by taking them and Ritchie to a *Chuckie Cheese Restaurant* in the evening much to their delight.

We arrived home around 9 p.m. Ellen put the children to bed and joined Ritchie and I at the dining room table when she came back downstairs. We talked about his family, whom we knew as well as he knew ours. Richie was blatantly honest with us, saying none of them were doing too well since his departure. Or, he added, just before his going away. That he had had multiple affairs, but his drinking and drug use is why his wife, Bobbi, insisted he leave. Then, the FBI cut him loose. Or as his supervisor had suggested, you are just *taking an early retirement*. While telling his story he seemed unfazed, but he was trained to be that way. Or, the reason he was hired was because he could project that kind of image no matter how he truly felt. To most, perhaps, he lived in a constant state of randy.

When Richie had made his speech, Ellen commented that his case sounded way to familiar. She told him, and she was talking to me too, that we are sweet, caring, loving, gorgeous, funny, smart, and attentive men. But, we are not allowed to show the first-class side of us. It is too bad you have to work so hard at having everybody trying to underestimate you guys. However, when you studs are walking down the other side of the street, you bring flamboyant to a whole new level.

Ellen excused herself around 11 p.m., and Richie and I talked the night away. We all went to a movie Sunday afternoon, ate a good old-fashioned beef pot roast dinner, with carrots cooked where they were soft as melted butter, with mashed potatoes and gravy. After which we enjoyed cherry pie-alamode and felt like we were ready to burst. We helped Ellen with the dishes and then plopped into chairs in the living room to enjoy a snifter of brandy. My wife sat down at the piano and played some Beethoven and Mozart.

At five o'clock Richie and I jumped into the 1983 Cadillac Eldorado, I had bought for Charley Rivers, and then took back, and headed south for Washington D.C. Now I was back in my office posting general ledger and waiting for Richie to arrive for his eleven o'clock job interview with me. I had told Mary Robinson to be on the lookout for him. She had given me that look requesting just a little bit more information, but she knew better not to push.

I had given Richie five hundred dollars last night and told him after he dropped me off at work this morning to go clothes shopping. I told him to get a sports jacket, a nice pair of pants, a long-sleeved white shirt, tie, socks and a pair of black wing-tip shoes. Do not be late. I'm certain the receptionist reports all events through the long chain of command.

At eleven o'clock sharp my buzzer buzzed. "Mr. Oleson, your eleven o'clock is here." I told her I would be right out. I shuffled a few things around on my desk to make it look like I was burdened with work, killing three or four minutes. I opened the door and there was Richie talking away with Mary Robinson. He looked very sharp. Nobody would have guessed he was having all kinds of personal problems.

His six foot plus and 180 pound body fit perfectly into a bespoke blue sports blazer, tan slacks, expensive loafers, and a white button-down oxford shirt. The outfit and his good looks and presence suggested the image of an upper middle class man who probably attended the right schools and was now a man in full.

"Mr. Richards," I said as I approached to shake his hand. "I see you met Mary Robinson."

Richie stood up and shook my hand. "I'm Jack Oleson. Thank you for coming on such short notice." He picked up one of my brief cases, which I'd given him this morning. I said to Mary, "We'll be in my office. Hold all my calls and take messages."

I sat down behind my desk and Richie sat facing me. "Well, Mr. Richards, please allow me to look at your resume." He opened the briefcase and took out two blank sheets of typing paper, which were stapled together and folded lengthwise in half.

I had briefed Richie during the weekend about my qualms. Thank God, he knew how the game was played, because his knowledge saved me a lot of time. I told him I thought everywhere I go and my communications were being watched or bugged. That Charlotte Boyer, PGC's ex-paramour, is a complete mystery as are most of the other characters that make up the company. I told him everything, even though I privately questioned the anonymity of him showing up at this particular time. It certainly seemed an unlikely, fortunate twist of fate.

The nature of my job is to not trust anyone. So, I was very circumspect and I would watch his movements more closely than anyone's. On the other hand, in this case, I had to trust somebody. I didn't know my opponent, whether it was PGC or the Bureau itself. And, if I could trust anybody, it would be Richie. Or, could I? He and I had rules we shared, but they were informal. They were free of the bureaucratic crap that keeps a job from getting done. And, I wanted this job finished.

We had worked out an interview scenario, fearing my office was bugged. I acted like my questions were coming from his resume. His answers were what we agreed upon in my backyard, both realizing once he was hired I would become a double agent of sorts. I was bringing him in as a senior accountant, but really he was a spy for me. He was to watch everyone and find out what they were doing. I was putting him at a desk in the accounting department. As a senior accountant he would be allowed at Happy Hour get-togethers, where he could do a significant amount of surveillance and close watch. After forty-five minutes of a pre-determined bullshit interview, I suggested lunch to make him an official offer. Right!

Mary Robinson had her ears perked, like a German Sheppard dog that had just seen a rabbit run across the yard. "Lunch," I say, as we passed by her desk.

"Enjoy," Mary acknowledges, waving with her fingers. Richie waved back.

We walked to Archibald's where we were seated in the corner at my usual table. Richie was immediately distracted by the topless dancers. He loved women with nice figures. Here he could have a drink and hopefully we could discuss our next moves. We both ordered a beer and when the brews arrived I had his attention.

"Rich," I say. I'll pay you a $36,000 dollar salary, medical benefits and wheels, a Plymouth *K* car. I've rented an apartment in Maryland, just off the Cabin John Parkway. My move in date is December 1st, but it is empty right now so I'm certain I can move up the date. There, now your financial woes are on the back burners. Now it's your turn to help me out."

Over a cheeseburger and three more beers, a piece, I brought Richie up to date on my situation and what I thought was transpiring. That there was actually an insurmountable amount of work to do and doing the work would provide the link needed to shut down this company. This, indeed, would be a working assignment, including the nosing around after hours getting the rest of the story. As I paid the tab Richie asks a good question. "What makes you think they want you to shut this business down?"

It was one-thirty when we walked by Mary Robinson's desk. She is on the telephone which saves me from answering any questions. Of course, when I opened my office door and I didn't remember closing it when we left, I found Charlotte Boyer sitting behind my desk.

She crosses her legs and her skirt rides up to her crotch. Charlotte Boyer looks into Richie's, eyes with her penetrating glare. She smiles and suddenly I wonder if they know each other, if she is in fact one of us. God, I hope not! Here's where Richie is good. He states, "You're sexier than Jack said, Charlotte Boyer."

She stands up saying, "Welcome to Atlantic States Surety, stud." Richie smiles at her as she exited my office. I put my pointer finger to my lips, and then quickly dropped it to the general ledger setting on my desk. I'm thinking about who told her Richie was working here? *Welcome to Atlantic States Surety*. Fuck it!

"Before we get started I'm going to take you around to introduce you to a player or two. We'll start in the accounting department, where I'll show you your desk."

I was somewhat concerned about Richie sitting still at a desk for any extended period of time, like two minutes. He hated paperwork, although he understood accounting well, but didn't like the idea of pushing a pencil for any reason. He didn't like paper trails, which were always the source of audit trails.

There was a private office inside the accounting department where Jerry Bitterman hung out when he was around. I could have used it for my office as well, but I preferred not to be located with everyone else around and where people had easy access to what I may or may not be working on. My feelings were just an auditor's mentality.

After introducing Rich to the accounting personnel, as the senior accountant, everyone seemed anxious to know what he'd be doing. I said he'd be working with me and with the computer firm Jerry Bitterman had hired, to finish the bond program. Also, I added, to set up our general ledger. With outward grins and smiles, I showed Richie to his private office.

"Perfect," Rich says, sitting down at his desk with me directly across from him.

"You won't really be working with them, other than to have them help you locate information you need to review for your projects. Just be yourself and make special mental notes on who walks in and out of here. And, I'm sure Charlotte Boyer will be giving you special attention in the name of *just trying to help.*" I warn him, cautiously.

"I look forward to her games," taunts Richie. "For her the killing is secondary, and her rituals are primary."

"Yes," I said. "Perhaps the element of her surprise is gone, but for her it only makes the game more interesting." I walked over to a supply cabinet and slid out a 13-column and 4-column pad. I slid them across his desk along with a couple of pencils, saying, "These supplies will make you look very accountant-like."

"There is nothing like a set of well organized working papers to make my dick hard," Rich whispered.

"Remember," I said. "I think there is a cover up going on right here. Your conclusions can not be based on assumptions and probabilities. Even though," I added, the verity will probably remain elusive."

I showed Rich the office, going down the halls from one end of the building to the other. Most private office doors were closed, but we met a few of the players. My plan was to take him to happy hour at five o'clock to give him the opportunity to talk with lead players while a drink was in their hands. Richie was a natural born showman. Hell, he was a show off. And, like a lot of psychopaths, he enjoyed taunting the authorities. Bringing him in could be my greatest move, but I wondered how he suddenly appeared on an Amtrak train just when I needed him the most. Was it just coincidence? I doubted it.

Richard Corrigan was the first to meet Richie at Happy Hour. He introduced himself with that used-car salesman smile. "So," he said. "You're an accountant. As fast as things are moving around here we can use more accountants. Jack really has his hands full with all the activity. Tell me what exactly will you be working on?"

With his natural good looks, Rich cleaned up nicely. He had changed into a dark gray suit and gray tie that he said he usually donned for special occasions, like weddings and funerals, plus a silk shirt and diamond cufflinks. His shoes were real Italian Gravatis and his watch was a Rolex Oyster. In this room, I was the only one who suspected he bought it on the street for forty bucks. It looked like the real McCoy, but I never doubted the piece's validity. Why share information, nobody else does.

"I'm going to be working with Jack and the auditors so we can get the annual report together as soon as possible. From what Jack has told me it will be an extensive project getting all the numbers in the right position." Richie replies.

Corrigan still had that smile pasted on his lips when Ted Masters introduced himself to Richie. "I didn't catch your last name, Rich?" Masters indirectly queried.

"Richards, my name is Richard Richards. My parents were in kind of a rut when I was born. It's funny, my best friend is named Allen Allen. How do you like them apples?" Richie questions, with a smile. Richards quick wit even amused no-nonsense Ted Masters to a slight grin.

"Where do you hail from, Mr. Richards, asked a smiling Joe Neverson. Joe and Maggie had just appeared from around the corner, curious as usual when circumstances seemed centered around me.

"North Bergen County New Jersey," Richie says, proudly.

"Where?" asks Maggie, introducing herself. She, of course, had been checking Rich out when she got that first glimpse. *Nice ass*, I knew she was thinking. Her next move would be to find out if he was married or involved.

"Bergen County is in North Jersey, right across the George Washington Bridge. *The Bronx – Yankee Stadium* – it doesn't get any better than being from there." Says Rich Richards, proudly.

I stood off to the side watching all of them gather around Richie like he was the pied piper. He was telling everyone you are supposed to let your mind wander while driving in New Jersey. That the drivers are crazy in New Jersey, insane, weaving in and out, hitting their brakes for no reason, and signaling the opposite of what they are going to do. He has everybody laughing. He looks over at me and I grin while giving him a thumbs up.

Rich was a good guy, with bad personal habits. He, like me, had found himself in a different world than he had ever expected. His Dad was a cop in East Patterson, New Jersey. Richie found himself with the FBI, thinking he'd taken criminal justice to a higher level. He, like me, had wished for more than a paperwork assignment. Again, be careful what you wish for. Supposedly we were never asked to do something that was questionable. As part of our job we just did them on our own. We were warned, of course, not to do things on our own or be brought up on charges. We did it anyway so we could get results.

Richie and I were a part of the unkempt bunch. The unkempt bunch got things done and never got any credit for doing so. The FBI supposedly is concerned about their agent's personal lives, to lead a life of exemplary rectitude. They like their agents to be married with children but be cool, detached, and narcissistic and ambitious. This kind of attitude doesn't make a marriage work, it just gives off false impressions which is the only bylaws of the Bureau's workings.

People like Richie and I are good impersonators. If somebody asks the other what he or I do, he or I might suggest, *he and I smokes camels or rides them.*

"Who is he?" asks Joe Neverson, with a voice coming from behind me.

"He's an accountant." I reply, surreptitiously.

"Where did you find him?" asks Joe. "And what is he going to be doing for us?"

"Joe, take it easy." I say. "I've known him for a long time. He's a fine accountant who knows his stuff. He is down on his luck right now, like everyone else around here I'm beginning to surmise. Hey, I need him with the audit approaching and the annual reports. PGC has me running everywhere getting stuff financed and mort-gaged to the hilt. You will like Rich!"

"I already do, that's what scares me, Jack. Where's he staying?" Neverson asks.

"Tonight, he's staying with me at the St. Regis. Tomorrow I hope to get him in the apartment I rented in Maryland. The lease starts December 1st, but I thought you might be able to persuade them to let us in early." I suggest, with a grin.

"I was going to talk with you about that apartment. I need a place to stay since I agreed to leave my house at the end of the month. I'm wondering if I may rent a room too." Joe asks, with a simper

I laugh saying, "Why not? I have three bedrooms and I'm only there four nights a week. It's fully furnished. Why not? I could use the company. Okay. You get us in right away and we're set. I don't know how long Richie will be there, it really doesn't matter to me. My home is in Pennsylvania. Hey Joe, are you really going to pay rent each month?" He gives me that devious grin, asking, "What do you think?"

"You don't want to know what I'm thinking. I chide him..

"See you at St. Regis!" Joe says, laughing.

I caught Richie's eye as he was just finishing another drink. I gave him the high sign and he made his way towards me while saying his *see you tomorrow's*. "Let's head over to the St. Regis. You'll stay there with me tonight and tomorrow we will try getting into my apartment early. It will happen because Neverson is making the arrangements. Believe me, Joe doesn't take no for an answer."

"I like these people," Richie admits.

"I knew you would," I assumed right again. "They are all here because of bad breaks. I'll give PGC one thing, he gives those who deserve it another shot. Of course, it is all for his benefit. For a fair sum of money his stables are filled with able, smart, and willing folks. That's what makes it so difficult." I whisper. "Taking him down will fold the whole house of cards."

Richie put his arm around my shoulders as we walked into the elevator. What happened to that Charlotte Boyer?" Rich asks.

"She's around," I say, grinning. "She's around, but who knows where or why? Hiring you has certainly thrown her a nasty curve ball. We'll probably see her tonight."

When the elevator doors opened there they were again. It was my shadow and the woman in black. Richie pushes me by them without expressing a word. He keeps me walking, while saying, "I'll get the scoop on them, Jack. I've got your back now!"

When we walked into the St. Regis I direct Richie to the elevator, even though I see Joe and Maggie sitting at the bar. Richie's stuff was in my car, which was parked in the parking lot. He had carried in a hanging bag earlier when he changed clothes. That bag was slung on my bed, rather carelessly, and opened with all kinds paraphernalia exposed. Only a night, I'm thinking.

I hung his bag in the closet and told him his was the other bed. "Yeah, yeah, yeah," he mouthed, slighted irritated by my command. "This place is really small, Oleson." There were two Queen Beds with a dresser housing a television set and a chest of drawers. A sitting room with a desk and three chairs was just off the bedroom. There was an efficiency kitchen set up with a small bar near a front window just above the entranceway. Here was a stocked refrigerator and a small microwave oven. Richie, with no concern of cost, poured a Canadian Club. He used no ice or mix, simply straight booze.

"Nothing for me, Rich, we are meeting Joe and Maggie at the bar." I suggest while Rich hands me a Jack Daniels on the rocks. "Okay," he says. I take the drink, which I really did want and Rich knew it, but it made me think of our past together. Richie was an in charge kind of guy, right or wrong. I was more laid back and observant, basing my decisions on drills by others and judging what they were about to do next.

"Thanks, Rich, let's take our drinks and meet Joe and Maggie at the bar." I command.

He toasts me saying, "Let's go!" Richie had changed into a white suit with bell bottom pants and an open lavender blue *(dilly-dilly)* shirt showing off his chest hairs and a heavy gold chain wrapped around his neck.

"Wow," I say. "You look like Don Johnson." I laugh at his get up.

"*Kool, you gotta be Kool*, Oleson," he says, as we approach the elevator.

I couldn't really imagine how the rest of this night would go. Neverson would want to talk about business and drink. Maggie would be working on Richie to have a romance. I wasn't sure what Rich would be trying to accomplish. His favorite activity was fucking, and didn't like striking out. I wondered, seriously, if I'd made a mistake bringing him aboard the sinking ship thinking he still had the skills which made him so effective the past years. It was like rolling a pair of dice, hoping for snake eyes.

When we entered the bar Joe and Maggie were pounding drinks and Charlotte Boyer had joined them along with Ted Masters. "Shit," I thought. Maggie quickly moved a chair over and touched the seat next to her while pointing at Richie to sit down. He smiled and strolled to where she was pointing. I took Maggie's chair which was adjacent to Joe Neverson, who appeared to be talking to Charlotte and Ted.

"The material found is absurdly prejudicial," Neverson says, angrily."

As usual, Masters seemed unfazed with what Joe was talking about. It was obvious he was more apprehensive with Charlotte's mood. Now Boyer was looking at me. She winked, asking, "Why is your little helper sitting at the other end of the bar, Jack?"

I studied her while she smiled faux sweetly. "Why don't you ask him," I said.

"When you cross certain lines you can't go back, Jack." Charlotte Boyer said sarcastically. Meanwhile I noticed Ted Masters watching a couple break dancing to a song Michael Jackson was singing, *Billie Jean ... she was more like a beauty queen for a movie scene ... she told me her name was Billie Jean and she caused a scene... Billie Jean is not my lover...* I could tell Ted was ruminating over these lyrics as he stared blankly at the dancers. He was in pain watching Charlotte on the prowl, thinking, I'm sure, he had given up his wife and family for one night of indiscretion. Actually, his wife had given up on him two years before. Ted was convinced, however, everything was completely his fault.

"Go after her, Ted," I said. "Don't let her do what she wants." I nodded my head toward Maggie , Charlotte and Richie. Just then Joe Neverson returned from the bathroom and so Ted Masters picked up his drink and walked toward the motley three.

"Jack," Joe queried. "What's really going on? You never mentioned hiring another accountant."

"Everything is in its timing." My dismissive response took Neverson off guard as he smiled coyly at me.

"Okay, you know what you're doing and what you need. Just be sure you apprise him of what's going on here with payment of claims." Joe Neverson said, with tongue in cheek.

"Joe, for now, Rich is on a need-to-know basis." My tone must have seemed haughty, superior, and well, just plain sanctimonious. "So, Joe, what are you doing for Thanksgiving?" I asked, tired of the business argot for the day.

Joe laughs, "Not a fucking thing! Tell me, Jack, do you really care?"

"Now I was laughing, "No I don't. I don't care one damn bit." I reply.

"Then let's drink and talk about something else," Joe Neverson says.

"Well, here's something." I nod toward the end of the bar. Charlotte is moving in our direction with Ted following close behind. I see Rich slug down the rest of his drink and Maggie putting together her pocketbook.

"Look at Charlotte wearing that scoop top that's just begging for ogling." Joe snickered.

"You boys are drinking kind of slowly tonight." Charlotte comments as she sits down next to me. "Say your buddy has opted to spend the night with part B of the A team. I could have changed his mind but, what the hell, huh?" She laughs her high pitched witch's have hysterics.

When Joe got the word Rich was going home with Maggie he was infuriated. "Who the hell does your boy think he is," asked Joe.

"He probably needs some laundry done; it's just his way, Joe." I reply.

"Well, she's a big girl and doesn't do anything she doesn't want to do." Joe is acquiescing, but not liking Maggie getting involved with a stranger.

"Rich is harmless. He loves people and he is lonely. She'll be fine with him and they both will be at their desks at 8 a.m. I promise." I say, slapping Joe on the back. Meanwhile Ted Masters is dominating a rather heated conversation between Charlotte and him.

It is nine o'clock and I am tired. "Joe, are you hungry?" I ask.
"Starved," he chortled.
"Let's get something to eat and call it a day." I suggest.
"Okay," Joe says, slugging down the rest of his drink.

It is only when we forget all our learning that we begin to know.
Henry David Thoreau

What Is Past Is Prologue

Virginia Beach, Virginia
Monday, September 26, 1977

I'm coaching the Kings Grant Steelers, a Virginia Beach Junior High school football team, during a scrimmage against the Plaza Bears when I got the word: "Coach, your wife is on the way Norfolk General Hospital."

I smiled, knowing full well why she was going there. "Thank you," I said. "Mitchell," I say to my quarterback. "This is our last set of downs, keep running the ball. I have to leave."

"Everything okay, coach," asked Mitchell.

"Just fine," I yell back. "I'm just fine!"

I did a sprint to my car leaving players, parents and assistant coaches wondering where I am going. When I arrive at the hospital I ask at the information desk where the maternity ward is located. I run down the hall and take the elevator to the third floor. I go directly to the nurse's station to inquire about my wife?

"Are you Mr. Sletten," a nurse asks, with raised eyebrows. After my affirmation, she says. "Sir, there are complications. Your son is doing well, but your wife has had some problems."

"What kind of problems, this is our third child and she never had any complications before. Is she okay?" I ask, feeling somewhat defeated by the bad news.

"Listen, young man," an older nurse took over the conversation. "You have a beautiful baby boy and the doctors are with your wife. Why don't you go with Miss Wilson, here, and see your son, then she'll bring you back to meet the doctor. I'll let them know you are here."

"Okay," I agree. Miss Wilson smiles and I follow her to the nursery.

"A carbon copy," I said, when I saw him. Nurse Wilson was very young, it seemed. She went into the nursery, picked up the baby and brought him to the window. "Christopher Austin," I mouthed. It was the name we'd picked out if he was boy. I smiled at Nurse Wilson and nodded. She put him back in the bassinette and came out of the nursery. "A carbon copy," she asks, "What does that mean?"

"He looks exactly like his two brothers when they were born. It's a good thing. Now may we check on my wife?"

I was anxious waiting for the doctor, especially when I saw him arguing with another doctor, whose hands were flailing until he saw me. The doctors quickly parted and the obstetrician came directly in my direction. "Mr. Sletten," he says. "Congratulations! You have a fine son, healthy as a horse."

"Thank you, I saw him. He's beautiful. How about Ellen, how's my wife?" I ask, slowly, with wariness.

The doctor cleared his throat then told me Ellen had a stressful labor. That it was so stressful her heart stopped during delivery. That her cardiologist was in the delivery room and he saved her life. The baby came quickly and arrived just before her heart stopped. She had a difficult time delivering the baby and her heart wore out after the birth.

"She's resting comfortably and I expect she will return to normal soon enough. What happens in the future will be between her and the cardiologist."

I thanked him and he patted me on the back. "You can see her now. Good luck Mr. Sletten." He walked to the nurse's station, leaving me speechless.

Ellen was in a recovery room. Her gurney was just behind a curtain. There was a tube inserted in her right arm and a monitor beeping and a display screen showing a graph of her heart beating. She forced a smile when she saw me, but I could tell she was groggy. I sat on the edge of her bed and held her left hand.

"This was different," she mouths, while grinning. "I think I was dead for a second or two. It was so peaceful for a second or two. What did the doctor tell you, Johnny?"

"He told me we have a healthy, beautiful son and you're going to be just fine." I say, "All's well that ends well. And yes, we do have another good-looking son and I still have a beautiful, wonderful wife." I whisper.

"Yeah," she said. "We all have each other, and there's five of us now. Isn't that something? Hey, where are Joe, Dan and the dog?" She asks, then saying, "Jeez, I just want to go home."

"Judy is at the house. I called your mother, she's flying down tomorrow. She told me she would stay as long as you need her."

"Good," Ellen said. "Sometimes you need your mother."

"Sometimes, I suppose you do." I reply.

"Don't be so enthusiastic, Johnny."

"Right," I reply. "Isn't she the one who gave me a box of nails for my birthday a few years ago? And, for you an umbrella and a heating pad when you graduated from Penn State?"

Suddenly a nurse appears and tells me she needs to do a few tests. I tell Ellen I'll see her in the morning, give her a kiss and depart. It was nearing ten o'clock when I entered my car in Norfolk General's vast parking lot.

When I arrive home I find Judy, from across the street, sitting on our sofa watching television with our German Shepherd dog, Lady, guarding all. She had put Joe and Dan to bed and the house was as peaceful as it could be. Judy was my age and her husband was perhaps a few years older. He was home with their two kids and she was manning our fort. "Well," she queried.

I told her the story and she got tears in her eyes. She and Ellen talked back and forth nearly every day. They shared a few drinks and caught each other up on the neighborhood gossip. Since I was gone so much and her husband was a traveling salesman, Ellen and she had really bonded. "Do you want me to stay," she asks.

"No, I'm going to be just fine."

When Judy left I felt so alone and I wondered if Ellen felt so unaccompanied every time I left. But, for me, it was the silence I didn't like. I don't like silence, and I never did. I even feel like waking up the kids. But I know that would be a mistake. So I pour a glass of Black Jack Daniels over ice cubes only, light up a cigarette, put in an eight track tape at low volume and listened to Sinatra. The solitary times, with all my vices, is when I do my best thinking.

I intuitively knew all was going to well for it to last. We had a beautiful home and a good-looking family of five. My FBI assignments were going well, especially since we had moved to Virginia Beach. My office was just a few miles down the road and most of my real work was done in those confines. Actually it seemed like I was really just a self-employed accountant. But I was constantly reminded, at least once a week; my assignments and life could all change at a moment's notice. I often speculated about such a transition. It was just something I had to live with, while Ellen refused to think about changing friends and lifestyle.

Me? I always have a need to keep something to myself. But, how bad, really, was her heart condition? My understanding of it was limited. She has an enlarged heart that is so strong it beats so fast that a wall builds up on its perimeter. If this wall becomes too large the heart could just stop. Frankly, when this first came up a few years ago I didn't concern myself too much. I just didn't know enough about the condition and Ellen never really spoke about the problem. Today the heart stopped during child birth. It really leaves so much room for supposition. I wonder what might happen next and when?

That Ellen could die at age 32 seemed impossible. But Elvis, at age 42, was found dead at Graceland just six weeks ago. With that depressing thought I fixed another drink.

Make the most of yourself, for that is all there is of you. **Ralph Waldo Emerson**

Chapter Thirty-Six

1700 K Street
Washington, D.C.
Tuesday, November 22, 1983

The negotiations for access to my apartment didn't go well. They wanted a half-month's rent, which didn't make sense to me. When I told Richie we couldn't get in until December 1st, he laughed and told me he would continue to stay with Maggie until whenever. In fact he told me Maggie wanted him there for Thanksgiving.

I had no difficulty with his decision as I wanted to have alone time with my family. When Rich Richards was around he needed as much attention as the kids. I was now looking forward to the long weekend and Rich could cover the accounting department on Black Friday.

Rich has been a productive employee today. I put him on posting the general ledgers and asked him to jot down who is doing what in the accounting department. He is a good accountant so the posting was probably a refreshing assignment, but what he enjoys most is the eavesdropping duty. Richie loves surveillance and counter surveillance. And, he found out some information. The people in the accounting department don't like me because I'm kind of a mystery man who basically ignores them. Before they would just do things for their former boss, Jerry Bitterman, and he would slide certain people sums of cash. *It was, to put it simply, more fun working for Jerry.*

Also, it seems Charlotte Boyer is planting seeds that I may not be who I seem to be. She, of course, stops by to check with Rich Richards several times a day; fishing for information. Boyer's main interest seems to be me. Who is Jack Oleson? Who is that cowboy from Montana?

None of this surprises me, especially the part about Charlotte Boyer. I figured she is trying to get something on me to report to PGC so she could get back in with him. Or, maybe Charlotte was one of us and who knew what the Bureau was really up to? I ask Rich to make Happy Hour everyday to see if any other concerns about me might be in the rumor mill.

Once again, my thoughts were not to trust Richie either. He certainly could see a lucrative situation here. He would have no trouble working his way to the top, if I wasn't around.

Meanwhile Madeline Haycock has been pressuring me to get the loan for the Lear jet and the Yacht approved. The work crews are ready to go and the money has to be available immediately. I spent a couple hours with Jason Simpson today and he is certain both deals will be approved, but it might take another week to get the board's approval and the money together. *It's a done deal, Jack! Both of them!* Simpson has assured me. I told Jason I needed a closing date to get Haycock off my back and he understands the exercise. We looked at the calendar and he points to December 12th.

"Perfect," I said. "PGC and I are going to be in Fripp Island on the 8th through that weekend."

"Why are you going there?" Jason asks.

"We're going to work on the budget." I say.

"Sure you are," Jason mouths with a grin. He too has an eccentric boss, I remember.

When I'd given Madeline Haycock the closing date I knew I had her off my back until after the Thanksgiving weekend. But, it better close on that date or there would be hell to pay.

The monthly board meeting was scheduled for Tuesday, November 29th. I had to have the Treasurer's report ready for that, but since it is all a bunch of bullshit there wouldn't be much time spent on it. *Just make it consistent with the last one.* Is what echoes in my mind? Tomorrow I have a meeting with the auditors to schedule the scope and time. I've decided to keep Rich Richards out of the auditing scam. And there was a new project stewing, a French Café in Bethesda, Maryland.

Madeline Haycock, told me to, *Tell Ted Masters to start working on the liquor license applications and procedures. After the board meeting, make sure Tom Harvey hangs around. We're going to the Club for dinner, which is where the Chef works. We are going to hire their chef for our French Café. PGC wants Tom Harvey at the Club.*

I couldn't wait to get into my apartment. Living at the St. Regis, I couldn't get away from Atlantic States Surety. After normal working hours, the activities and some of the players just moved *the venue* to the St. Regis. I was just so glad that Richie chose to stay with Maggie Little for the time being. Tonight I would have dinner, alone, at some remote location and get to bed early. I had a big day tomorrow and wanted to get away early to get home for Thanksgiving weekend.

Do what you can, with what you have, where you are. **Theodore Roosevelt**

Chapter Thirty-Seven

1700 K Street
Washington, D.C.
Wednesday, November 23, 1983

I woke up early and felt full of energy. I gathered my briefcase and the Washington Post newspaper and headed for the restaurant off the main lobby. I was seated at a table for two near a window and ordered coffee. I was reading about the scene at JFK's grave yesterday commemorating the 20th anniversary of John F. Kennedy's assassination. How could that be twenty years ago already I'm thinking when a waitress comes to take my order.

"Two eggs, sunny side up with white toast and sausage." I ordered as she refills my coffee cup.

While I look at the pictures and skim the articles I think back to that fateful day in 1963. I was taking an accounting exam at Concordia College. My roommate, Phil, finished the exam early, handed in the test and left. Ten minutes later, I heard someone open the door in the back of the classroom. It was Phil, who had just left. He said: *someone shot the President.* We were all stunned. The Accounting professor said, "What's the punch line, Phil?"

"They say he died at 1 o'clock Central Time."

I look at my watch, it is twenty minutes after 1 p.m. The Professor says: "Turn in your tests. I'll give consideration for what you didn't finish. There's a television in the cafeteria. I'll see you over there."

The cafeteria filled up quickly. When we got there Walter Cronkite was summing up the events leading up to the President's assassination. I remember the next three days being glued to television set with my fiancé, Beth, in her apartment. We went outside only a couple times that weekend. What I remember most about that weekend was the stillness everywhere. Nobody was stirring. When we went finally went to the grocery store on Saturday night, the store was filled with Kennedy pictures and other paraphernalia regarding our President. How could they have so much on hand so quickly? I wondered. It almost seemed somebody had planned to have this merchandise ready. We were in Moorhead, Minnesota and all this stuff was here. What about New York, Philadelphia and Washington, D.C.? Where did this entire product come from?

It's a conspiracy, I thought. The so-called lone assassin, Lee Harvey Oswald, had been bush whacked this morning, by Jack Ruby, while they were transferring him to another location. Nothing was making sense, yet everybody seemed to be buying the scenario being thrown out by the media. Nobody seemed to want the real story or to take the time to assess the facts. Knowing what I know and how the government works I'm completely convinced it was a *black ops* tactic that killed the President. Older and wiser now I'm convinced of a conspiracy and it's what I am thinking when my breakfast arrived.

When I was finished eating, I walked down to my office building. I arrived at eight o'clock and Richie was already at his desk drinking coffee and talking with the head bookkeeper, McKenzie Gillen. We all said good morning and Nancy Sullivan went to get me a cup of coffee. "Just black," she asks. "Am I right?"

Richie gave me a general ledger progress report and said there was no other news to report. I asked him if he was going to spend Thanksgiving with Maggie and he confirmed those were the plans. I told him I had a very busy day ahead and was going to try get a jump on the traffic around three o'clock. I told him if he needed anything to just call me.

"Mr. Oleson, you have an interview at 10 a.m. I'm just reminding you. Her name is Mary Shanahan. She's a bookkeeper and a secretary. She seems very professional."

"When she comes for her interview just bring her to my office. I'll tell Mary Robinson the same. Thank you McKenzie."

I leave the accounting office to stop by Mary Robinson's desk to tell her what to do when my interview arrives. I also want to remind her about the auditors coming at eleven o'clock. She smiles, makes a written note, and asks me if I am going home for Thanksgiving. When I tell her I am she says - *Good.*

A ten o'clock sharp my phone buzzes. Mary Robinson tells me my appointment is here. "Show her in, please," I say. Shortly there is a rap on my door. Mary opens it and shows a young woman into my office. She sits down across from my desk.

I study her for a second. She has these big green eyes and this cute, wide-open face. She reminds me of Ellen, and I find her tantalizing. "So you are here for the bookkeeping and secretarial position."

She had graduated from Gettysburg College, in Gettysburg, Pennsylvania, earning a Bachelor of Arts degree in Business Education. She was going to teach but went right to work as a bookkeeper at a new car dealership instead. She was now looking for a better paying job with possibilities of advancement.

I told her about C&B Leasing and some of the other things we had going on. She could start on Monday, December 5th. After she left I felt like an asshole. I had a great job to give this young lady and so I did. I didn't mention, however, it probably wouldn't last too long. But, on the other hand, she'd probably be better off having worked here. I always found a way to rationalize my guilt.

The auditors showed up on time, eleven o'clock sharp. We met in my office for about 45 minutes. They told me what approach they used last year and the scope of their examination. They said they would have four people involved and they could get started as soon as I could give them a trial balance as of December 31, 1983. With the formalities out of the way I suggested we have lunch and our claims attorney would be joining us.

I had recommended Joe Neverson to meet with us and he had agreed. I think Joe Neverson to be the most knowledgeable about the business and he probably knew about any deals that might have been in place a year ago. Although, I didn't think Joe would ever admit to knowing anything about anything, I thought he would be an asset sitting on my side of the table.

When we were done I buzzed Mary Robinson to ring Joe Neverson to meet us near the entrance door in about five minutes. I wanted Joe to get a long look at these guys before we sat down face to face. It seemed by conversation one of the auditors was on the job last year. When we all met Joe said, "Hey Matt," and then shook hands with all four. Matt was the lead auditor a year ago. I noticed how Matt's eyes were locked on Joe's. Suddenly, I thought, Matt looks very edgy.

Immediately I could obviously see what a great fiasco was coming about all for the greed of basically one man. If the truth be known there would be heavy losses with no profits, caused by lousy management, half-crazed losers trying to be businessmen making grotesquely unrealistic estimates of future successes.

When I first started this assignment it was like walking into a nuthouse for the purpose of walking out with a king's ransom. It was simply a bubble. From what I first saw, it could not possibly be either real or sustained. Soon enough a mighty crash would happen. In the rubble would be those who had gambled, won, and then lost. My strong suit was to anticipate such an upcoming disaster. I had already determined PGC was way ahead of his time. His whole company was structured to bamboozle people.

What these auditors should be doing is delving into Atlantic States financial papers and statements, studying them night and day, until they could pinpoint the water downed assets, and the real debts and losses that do not appear on the balance sheet and related statement of income and expense and cash flows.

Of course nobody had ever seen a real balance sheet let alone a general ledger. This is where the company would unravel from: the fraud, the false accounting designed to inflate revenue and minimize bogus expenses. I knew with my interference all would come tumbling down and would be glaringly into the spotlight soon enough. My efforts, supposedly on behalf of the government and for the good of the people would just speed it up. Whether the illusions are in the millions or billions, the colossal deceptions are so convoluted that it creates profits when there are none. My job is not to prove it, rather just gather information so somebody above me can work it best to their purpose or advantage.

Once again my thoughts were running rampant as I wonder what the Bureau really wants to accomplish in this particular undertaking. And as usual I'm curious about the ultimate purpose and who is really the benefactor. But, that is none of my concern. I was just to take all the risks, bury the audit trail, pay off the auditors and keep my mouth shut.

Over lunch we didn't talk much about the audit, rather it was about the Redskins; Joe Theisman, John Riggins, Art Monk and the *Hogs.* Would they win their second straight Super Bowl? We did talk some about claims and the recognition of revenue. Of course I knew how Bitterman worked it. He recognized all the revenue even if was an account receivable, which shouldn't exist in an insurance company. Claims – only a small percent had been reserved for and none paid. Expenses? What a joke. PGC was taking fifty thousand dollar checks and they'd been charged to prepaid travel advances, a current asset, to be counted as cash equivalents on the balance sheet.

During lunch I noticed Joe Neverson and Matt seemingly communicating with their eyes. Finally Matt asks the question, looking at me. "Are you okay with last year's fee, Jack?"

"What part of it," I ask, while lighting up.

There was an uncomfortable silence at the table. Joe broke the peace. "Everything is good, Matt. I'll go over last year's billing with Jack and how it works. If he has any questions I'll be in touch."

The tab arrived just when Joe Neverson finished his speech. The auditing firm picked it up and the meeting had concluded with me saying, "I'll be in touch on the dates."

It is never too late to become what you might have been. **George Eliot**

Chapter Thirty-Eight

Thanksgiving Day
240 Berkley Road
Glenside, Pennsylvania
Thursday, November 24, 1983

I would have never thought this Thanksgiving would be our last as a complete family unit. I'd left my office the day before, at 2 o'clock, with Mary Robinson wishing me and mine an enjoyable holiday. She said nothing extraordinary but I sensed words unspoken in her eyes. What does she know that I don't? I wondered as I got in the elevator.

I arrived home slightly after 5 o'clock to find Ellen in the driveway, loading the kids, in the Chrysler New Yorker, to go food shopping. She looks very frustrated when I pull the 280 Z along the curb in front of our house. Joe and Dan came running to me announcing they are going to the grocery store and ask if I'm coming with them. Christopher is staying close to his mother as she shrugged her shoulders and smiled, showing a sense of relief at my arrival.

"Hey," I input. "Pennsylvania always feels like home! It's good to be home, and it's for four whole days."

"Home is where your family resides," Ellen confirms.

"Yes," I voice. "Home is the most excellent place to be! Neil Diamond, right?"

Joe sounds off, *Turn on Your Heart Light*. "Remember, Dad, how you had me play that over and over again on our trip to Minnesota last fall?"

"Okay, now that we got that straight, Johnny, let's go food shopping." I motion everyone toward the car. I'd never heard the term *food shopping* before I met Ellen, for the second time, in 1969. In Minnesota we just said *going to the Red Owl*. Everybody knew what you were going to do there. It's where everybody bought their groceries. But, I suppose the term food shopping implies you may be going anywhere to by your food because there are several choices out of the ordinary in the big Eastern cities. It is good to be thinking about something so innocuous, rather than who is doing what to whom.

Actually I always did enjoy food shopping. So much so Ellen spends more time putting back stuff I throw in the cart then she does putting what she needs in the basket. When the push cart is overflowing with groceries we moved toward the check-out line. The children are excited and rambunctious as we unload the hand cart. When everything has been totaled Ellen and I can't come up with our Pathmark card.

"Forget it," I said to the checker

"But you'll lose the discount," the checker replies, in a panic.

"It's okay," I assured her, "We're kind of in a hurry.

"I can check with a manager," she says.

"No, we're in a hurry. Really, it's okay." I guarantee her again.

"I can ....."

I interrupt the lady, saying, "We'll survive," I say, while writing her a check for the full amount of the purchase.

"So, big shot, how much more did we pay because we didn't have our card? Ellen laughs, covertly.

"I don't know," I soften. "But, who the hell cares?"

"Right", my wife mouths, "Who the hell does care? I know the FBI sure doesn't. Money doesn't matter to them or to you, does it? *Easy come, easy go!*"

"It surely came in handy for that house we just bought, didn't it?" I answer back.

"I suppose it does," says Ellen as we all piled into the car to head home.

Ellen has a way of making a confrontation out of everything. Women, I simply didn't understand them.

The boys were raising hell in the back seat and I could tell they were driving Ellen crazy. At a red light I turn and give them a clenched fist, which quiets them down until we pull into our driveway. I told the boys, including Christopher, to haul the stuff in the house and put it on the dining room table. While they were toiling with that project, Ellen and I watch them, while smoking a cigarette. Afterwards we go into the house. Once inside, Ellen proceeds with putting groceries into the right places. I turn on some music and fixed us each a drink.

"So they're good for something," she whispers.

"I suppose everything does get smaller with age," Ellen says. "Remember Thanksgivings in Virginia Beach? There were all the traditions, rituals and people. I prepared enough turkey for fifty people. Richie prepared Bloody Mary's for the entire community. We had so many friends. I looked forward to every holiday." She reminisces with a haughty, superior, and sanctimonious tone. Then, she smiles faux sweetly, saying, "Fix me another drink, Johnny."

The five of us had a delicious Thanksgiving dinner and we spent a great day together. I had football games playing on the television in my home office, but I just checked in on the scores occasionally. We had turkey and dressing sandwiches, while the five of us watched a Thanksgiving Special on the television during the early evening.

Finally, about 9 o'clock, Ellen and I had some time to spend together. We put some music on and sat down at the oval dining room table, with a fresh white table cloth. We each had a glass of wine, Ellen a white and for me a red. We clink glasses as Ellen smiles, saying: "Today is what I'd always hoped it would be like. Thank you, Johnny, for trying so hard to make things work."

"Tokien wrote, it doesn't do to leave a live dragon out of your calculations if you live near him." I answer while pouring another shot of wine.

"I see," she replies. "You never mentioned Tokien before you went to seminary. Maybe some good came out of that maneuver after all? So, who's the dragon?" She asks.

"Dragons," I said. "There seem to be many. I feel like I am surrounded by enemies and things are at work. I'm starting to be-lieve that there is as much corruption in this country as there is the perception of corruption, and it is that perception that guys like PGC uses to demoralize and ultimately corrupt accountants, businessmen, judges, lawyers, police, and politicians. We do the same thing."

"We, I'm assuming, is the FBI?" Ellen queries, calmly.

"Ellen, every day is hallucinatory. The days of the erstwhile Elliot Ness are over. Evil is very seductive. PGC is self-centered, self-indulgent, narcissistic, and aloof. It's what they all say, but their opinions are based on pure hearsay. He has such primitive instincts. I don't dislike him, but he is a criminal. Our world is shrinking and changing around us. His Board of Directors are socially progressive, who with their snooty, iconoclastic behavior become the keepers of the traditional values. Which is all show, but it makes PGC look sane."

"Remember the bigger the lie the more people will believe it. There is white and there is black, and there are a hundred shades of gray in between."

"It's that bad, huh?" Ellen says, pouring herself another drink. "I have a feeling this assignment might go on beyond your estimates. So, we'll just try to raise our children as if our past experiences are not important for their future, but you and I know they really are of great consequence."

"I'm going to make this whole fiasco end as quickly as possible. I just need to correctly figure out who's who. I honestly do not trust anyone, including Richie. But, the reason I brought him aboard was because I know how to read him. If he's working for me he'll find out what I need to know. If he's against me, I'll know within the next two weeks. He won't stab me in the back."

"How do you do it, Johnny?"

I pour us both another glass of wine while I was thinking of a response, different from the old standard. "A cover story is being put in force, by the corridors of power in Washington." I speculate.

"What," she asks. "What do you foreshadow?"

"Politics is power, no more." I proclaim while pouring me another full one.

"Johnny, you are scaring me." Ellen says.

"Stir the shit storm," I voice. "I still believe the truth is on my side."

Ellen says nothing, probably thinking I had too much to drink. She, by all accounts, was a precocious, snotty little bitch who everyone thought was bright and beautiful. But, the extroverted young woman I first met has become increasingly moody and withdrawn the past couple years. Time, however, marches on. We all change.

"Our obsession with wanting to freeze a moment in time, I suppose is true, save any moment in time except tomorrow." Ellen says, emptying the bottle of white in her glass.

"Keep your friend's close, but your enemies closer." I recall, emptying the bottle of red in my glass.

We were both tired and I for sure was not making any sense. "He's smart," I say slurring my words slightly. "He is also more complex than I imagined."

"Johnny, let's go to bed. We had a wonderful Thanksgiving, okay?"

"Hey," I said, getting up from the table. "We're just typically middle-aged suburbanites having alcoholic fun."

"Right!" Ellen adds. "Sure we are. Typical? Yeah, right."

Remember that there is nothing stable in human affairs; therefore avoid undue elation in prosperity, or undue depression in adversity. **Socrates**

Chapter Thirty-Nine

1700 K Street
Washington, D.C.
Monday, November 28, 1983

Everybody seems to be moving around and working in slow motion. As I am going through the mail Rich Richards raps on my door lightly. He is dressed in a dove-gray suit that is expensive and surprisingly tasteful. His shoes are not only real, but they are lizard.

"Wow," I say. "You're looking pretty snappy."

"I'd be more comfortable if I was in an awful gray poplin cotton suit, the sort of thing that prisons issue when they set you free. That along with shoes that actually have gum soles, and the uppers are made of a miracle synthetic that could be safely cleaned with a Brillo pad." Rich fired back with zest.

"Has anything extraordinary happened since I left for Thanksgiving?" I ask, shrugging my shoulders.

"It was pretty quiet here Friday. The place was operating with a skeleton crew. Let's see, Maggie was here. Half the accounting apartment was here and working. Joe Neverson was off somewhere with his kids. Oh, Ted Masters was pining in his office. He looked terrible. It was his first Thanksgiving away from his wife and family and Charlotte Boyer had disappeared somewhere. Man, old Ted really fucked up messing with *Hush, Hush Sweet Charlotte.*"

I contemplate for a minute while Rich lights a cigarette. "Let's go downstairs and get some coffee. As we walk we talk. "I have to move this thing along," I suggest.

Rich nods. "Okay," he agrees. "What's the game plan? Everyone who works here seems to be like *Stepford* employees.

You know, they are programmed to do what they are told to do and do it now."

I smile at Rich Richards, saying, "You are a quick study, my boy."

"That's why I get the big bucks, Oleson." It is his quick witted responses, I like.

"That's why I get the big bucks." He repeats.

"Yeah, yeah, yeah, I hear you!" I scoff.

"Listen," I demand. "I want you to handle all check requisitions. I will ask McKenzie, who currently receives these call for's, to direct them to you. You and I will evaluate their various applications together, at 1 o'clock every afternoon. I'm certain there is a trend. When you receive the requests I want you to chit-chat with the bearer about the content of their petition for's."

We sit down at a table with our coffee. "I want to chart all current events. The past transactions will take care of themselves." I say.

"You're certainly the wordsmith and the chart man boss. I'll gather the data and you can graphically represent it the way you want." Richie barked.

"Then," I said, "I want to look at the collateral. First, I want to see if it is there and, second, I want to see where it is stored. Thirdly, does the collateral agree with the bonding contract?"

Suddenly I noticed Rich's eyes are concentrated on the other side of the room. I look in the same direction and immediately pick up on whom he is peering. There they are again, the one I'd sucker-punched on the train and the lady in black.

"Who are those guys?" I ask, parroting lines in the movie, *Butch Cassidy and the Sundance Kid?* "Hire a couple of thugs and get them off my back, Richie."

"I know who they are, Jack." Rich Richards says, calmly. "They work for PGC. The guy is a private *dick*, and she is his diversion."

"How do you know this?" I ask Richie.

"Maggie tells me PGC has all key hires followed and researched until he is convinced they are not plants. He'll drop the shadow soon, so goes the rumor mill. Maggie has been having drinks with Ted. Ted is forlorn over Charlotte Boyer, and when he gets drunk he says things to Maggie to make himself look good. He told her: *He has people watching Jack Oleson for Mr. Charles.* That these spies report to him and he reports gathered information to the Paul Gordon Charles, his own self."

"His own self; I love your attempt at the southern vernacular." I say, and then asking, "Are they still there?"

"You bet." Rich answers. "Like flies on shit!"

"Okay," I say, now that you're talking like a Norwegian. "I'm not doing anything suspicious, so let them play their game. Hopefully they'll go away soon enough. Of course that doesn't mean we can't fuck with them a little." I asked our waitresses to order them each a large stack of pancakes. The waitress seem to think it is strange I was ordering for another table, but when I slipped her a twenty dollar bill she showed no further concerns.

Rich laughs, saying, "Let's see if Ted Masters reports this maneuver to Maggie."

"Seriously, Jack, remember no matter where you see them ignore them, but always assume they are watching, even if you can't see them." Rich Richards proclaims.

We order another cup of coffee to keep the spies at their table. When the pancakes come there is all sorts of action and commotion at their table. When the waitress points at me, I nod and give them the Italian salute. Rich and I get up from our table and walk out of the restaurant with smug looks on our faces.

I learned a long time ago there is no such thing as a normal life, rather there is just life. Like who could have forecasted this morning's exploit, at my age. Sometimes, though, you just have to wait for the other guy to make his move, and when he does something will come to pass. Consequently, I had the feeling this morning when nothing happens that something is going to come about. For instance, after eating their unordered pancakes, the lovely couple might change their course of direction, or they may simply stay the course. That's why there is nothing normal about any life.

It was 10 o'clock when I sat back down in my office chair. The office is starting to bustle, people are moving about and telephones are ringing. I don't know quite what to gather for the budget meeting in Fripp Island. I looked around to find last year's budget but couldn't find it. I walked into the accounting department and asked McKenzie if she knows where last year's budget is located. She just shrugs her shoulders, saying, "Jerry Bitterman never shared those kinds of things with us."

Good old Jerry I think. I wonder if he'd spent his one hundred thousand already. Joe Neverson told me Jerry had stolen a like amount from his mother's estate. The scuttlebutt was he needed to replace those funds pronto.

Meanwhile I was thinking about all the financing I had to get done before December 8th. I had to solidify the commitments and closing dates with Jason Simpson, regarding the PGC's yacht, houses and airplanes. I needed to meet with Henry Fleck's colleague at Maryland National Bank in Baltimore to set up lease arrangements for new vehicles. There were so many things going on it was difficult to remember everything, especially in sequential needs, of what I needed to accomplish next.

Next Monday Mary Shanahan would be starting and I was resolute about getting her to take over the day-to-day operations of the leasing company, inclusive of the bookkeeping. There was so much to do it was overwhelming, for the first time in my undercover agent career I felt like I belonged to whom I was pursuing rather than to the Bureau. I had no idea what to do about the truth. Or if an authenticity did subsist.

The remainder of the day passed in predictable fashion. It was a very busy day at work and for the first time it seemed like I had control of the accounting department by having my overseer, Richie, present inside the department itself.

At 1 o'clock sharp Richie and I met to review the check requisitions. There were none that stood out. I left the office at 1:45 and ambled toward the White House taking a meandering route. I approached the ellipse at exactly 2:12 PM and began walking clockwise. After the second pass my handler showed up on my left shoulder, saying, "Anything of significance?"

"Yes," I said. "He's having me followed."

"I know," my handler said. "Go to the top of the Washington Monument."

My handler turned left on Constitution Avenue, while I made a couple more passes around the ellipse. I bought the Washington Post and sat down on a bench across Constitution Avenue at The National Mall near the Washington Monument. After waiting ten minutes I bought a ticket and traveled to the top. There is not much room on top of the monument but enough room for the guy I was to meet. He nodded and whispered, "Let's take the stairs."

He showed me his credentials and down we went talking softly all the way. Things were getting squirrely now. Yet, I still couldn't get a read on what exactly was happening on this mission.

I updated handler number two, who appeared cool, slightly smug, the way any cop is when he knows he has the full weight of the law in his badge case. Yet his shirt, his tie, socks, watch, even his haircut, were all bargain basement, and I found myself irrationally offended by the air of sensible frugality about him.

We shook hands without playing crush the cartilage and I exited the monument while he stayed. I wonder if he was going to walk back up to the top. He probably did and I'm glad that I didn't make such a smart-aleck reply. I meandered over to the Smithsonian Institute and hailed a cab for the trip back to 1700 K Street.

No trumpets sound when the important decisions in our life are made. Destiny is made known silently. **Agnes DeMille**

Chapter Forty

The past ten days had passed in a hackneyed method. Everyone at Atlantic States Surety was busy doing their jobs to protect the company's coffers. Bonds were being written in abundance all over the country. The company had licenses and offices in eighteen states by December 1st, which was only two short of PGC's goal. So far Kansas and Nebraska had yet to yield for licensing wanting more explicative's concerning the validity of Atlantic State Surety's financial statements. Who would have thought it would be the Jayhawkers and the Cornhuskers, who would've been the sticklers for the truth? Anyway Corrigan told me that PGC had told him to tell me to fix the problems. I imagined I would get an earful when I met with him during the next three days.

I had departed Washington's National Airport at 8:30 a.m. today on Piedmont Airlines. It was a roundabout milk run to Newport News, Virginia – Norfolk, Virginia – Charlotte, North Carolina – Columbia, South Carolina to my final destination – Charleston, South Carolina. We arrived five hours later on the 50-seat, four-engineered, Dash 7 aircraft with a soft landing and Piedmont's in good spirits faces.

I had never been in this section of the country before and I was surprised how undersized the cities were that I'd seen in movies and heard about all my life. Everything seemed so rural, which made me think of where I grew up in Minnesota. The big dissimilarity was the Atlantic Ocean, which lies majestically just a few miles in the near distance. Of course where I grew up we had Lac qui Parle Lake where one, on a good day, could catch Bullheads, Carp or Sheepheads. So in the Mid-west the splendor of even seeing the extraordinary Atlantic Ocean was just a daydream.

The Municipal Airport in Charleston is diminutive. It is built like a three-ring horseshoe. The outside ring gives access to boarding and for de-boarding airplanes. The passengers walk to or from the planes, going up or down rolling stairs off the runways. The inner ring is the terminal and the upper ring is where the air traffic controllers kept their eyes peeled on all the goings-on. The car I have reserved is not available, but I'm told it should be here shortly. I have to drive south on U.S. Route 17 to Beaufort, South Carolina and follow the directions to Fripp Island from there. I figure maybe an hour plus travel time to PGC's mansion by the sea.

While I wait for my rental car to arrive, I sit outside the terminal ring and soak up the warm December sun. A large round thermometer reads 75 degrees, some thirty degrees warmer than Washington had been when the airplane took off this morning. The flight here had been relaxing even though it seemed we were taking off and landing every half-hour, which we were. But the trip had given me time to think about my situation and what might lie ahead on this impenetrable undercover assignment.

From the get go Paul Gordon Charles reeked of the old, familiar scent of cronyism, corruption, and cover-up. Thinking about my job I supposed I was to root out the waste, fraud, and abuse in the federally regulated programs, for the benefit of protecting citizens; instead, I felt like I was participating in a game of damage control. For whom and for what purpose, I didn't know?

My first cursory reading of the 1982 certified financial statements pointed out a lack of internal control, but I found no management letters suggesting how to correct this problem. I wondered if anyone in the various Insurance Commissions even read the reports, especially the footnotes. Since there had been no claims reported, and, only a minimum reserve set, I supposed not too much digging had been done with all the other numbers being reported in conformity with insurance company conventions.

The game playing, rank politicization, and stonewalling messages heard loud and clear didn't seem of interest to anyone, strangely enough. Only a significant claim not being paid maybe would get an insurance commission auditor's attention, and then those held accountable would go into a cover-up mode so not to get egg on their faces.

And what this man, PGC, was doing in broad public and right under political noses was outrageous, unprecedented, and disturbing. Yet the dissent-stifling and hardball games keep piling up. It is obvious to me, and from what I'd already been told, they've been on to this guy for some time. Oh where, oh where, are the watchdogs? Or, are those so-called watchdogs being paid off?

"Mr. Oleson ... Mr. Oleson ... your car is ready," a sweet, young lady shouts and points toward me. I followed her inside to her work station and signed the contract. She told me where the car is parked and I took my suitcase and walk toward the lot.

The car, a 1982 Ford *Galaxy 500*, was dirty on the outside and filthy on the inside. PGC wouldn't be caught dead in this car so I ran it through a car wash and vacuumed, including the filled ashtrays. I was told to dress casual so I had worn jeans and a black golf shirt under a black wool sports jacket. The kind a preacher wears. It was a good thing because I got a little bit dusty cleaning up the car. Then, I headed south on U.S. Route 17.

It seems an excursion travels swiftly when you're going somewhere you don't want to go. I couldn't imagine spending three nights in Gordon's habitat with no scheme of what to be expecting. I conjured up his penetrating dark eyes, like night, but nevertheless seeming to burn like coal, bearing down on me. For him, only money is God. He lives in the moment without history; he is arrogant and thinks he is invincible. And, he will pay any price to be unconquerable.

How can anything so stressful be rewarding, I'm thinking as I drive in silence watching the countryside go by outside my window. Again it reminds me of Minnesota, where the living is easy and carefree. Living in Washington – Norfolk, Virginia – back to Washington – Philadelphia, Pennsylvania has given me an extreme ridged structure, and pecking order that has all gone against my home grown instincts. What a paradox?

I've watched how people work against each other and how the unique styles, visions, energy, optimisms, and idealisms soon fall to the wayside with the new guys. Soon enough the suffocating influence of the old root out the new and they become pessimistic, isolated, and divided with internal conflicts and squabbles. However, the system chugs on, unsinkable and without purpose. I've learned about how it works and it really takes the wind out of the sails.

Me, the master of the equivocal phrase, and expert at the meaningless sentence, a scholar of the ambiguous word survives because of being an undercover agent. I didn't have to work with these assholes who were trying to maneuver each other to get on top. The center of power in any place was by definition a haven for lunatics and lunatic behavior. I didn't have to deal with all the crap because I was on my own, out of sight.

Through it all I remained unfazed, by getting people to underestimate me. My motto: to never tell the truth when a good lie will do, or, don't ruin a good story by telling the truth helped me survive because nobody knew me. How could they I didn't know myself so how could they know me.

I improvised a lot and didn't worry about crossing the so-called line. I always ignored the FBI aphorism proclaiming *we don't do revenge – we do justice.* I knew better, any such axiom was pure unadulterated bullshit. So, I learned that nothing ever goes the way you imagine. No, never! But, my hesitation was now gone. I knew what I had to do, I thought, as I crossed into the city limits of Beaufort, South Carolina.

I followed the sign to the business district and as I approached the area I saw the Beaufort post office on the right side of the road. It was a rectangular brick building, which reminded me of the post office back home in Minnesota where I grew up. Per the postal clerk's instructions, I drove to the first light and turned left. I followed a boulevard for about three miles, turned right and made a quick turn left. I saw the bridge he was talking about to my right and crossed over to what he said would be a series of islands.

The view of Beaufort from the bridge is breathtaking. The town itself appears quaint and I can see the Marine Corps base – Parris Island located just south of Beaufort. Once on the other side it doesn't seem like anything spectacular exists here. It is just a two lane road traveling between the trees and little hamlets where gas stations and convenience food stores are the only signs of life. After traveling exactly four miles, I was monitoring the odometer, I saw a sign: *Fripp Island – 3 miles.*

As I approach Fripp Island I see a bridge to cross over. I pull over to the side of the road to take a few pictures. The island appears beached in its entirety around its perimeter. White silver sand glistens from the sunlight as I snapped two or three pictures. It was simply a picturesque setting. When I arrived on the other side of the bridge there is a gate house. They ask for identification and whom I was visiting. I show the woman a Pennsylvania driver's license and tell her Paul Gordon Charles is expecting me. She smiles, saying, "Wait here for a moment," and walks into the gate house. I see her pick up a phone, talk and hang up. She points at and tells me to pull over to a parking location. She says, with a smile, "Someone will be here shortly to meet you."

Soon enough a black Rolls Royce rolls up and encircles the gate house, pulling up just ahead of me. I almost wanted to laugh, but I was also pleased I had washed and cleaned the rent-a-car. I wondered if PGC would even allow it in his driveway. Ned Larson steps out of the Roll's. He smiles as he looks me in the eyes. He looks like Clint Eastwood with his ruggedly handsome face and lean body.

"Welcome to Fripp, John…I mean Jack." Ned said, looking around to make sure no one had heard his greeting.

I laugh. Commander Ned Larson is a good friend from my Virginia Beach days. We'd had a lot of long talks. He had even built my parents house in Virginia Beach. He is a Navy F-14 pilot, who did two tours in Vietnam. He hails from Bowman, North Dakota and graduated from St. Johns College, near St. Cloud,

Minnesota. St. John's is in the Minnesota Intercollegiate Athletic Conference as was Concordia, my alma mater. Ned and I had a lot in common, especially our roots.

"Hey, Jack, follow me in your car. We're going to park it. Gordon wouldn't allow a *piece of shit* like that to be seen on his property." He points out a garage in the near distance. I laugh again, but I was so happy to see Ned Larson. "Are you going to be here all weekend," I ask him.

"You bet," he says. "This is a pretty big weekend for PGC. He has a lot for you to do." Now Ned was laughing, while noticing my lack of enthusiasm. "Let's go," he said.

I jumped in the front seat. Ned, who I remember as a horrible driver, put the Roll's in gear and we started to crawl into a noteworthy society.

Before we get in the car, Ned tells me not to talk or respond. He is going to give me a little tour of the island and if I respond do so positively about the scenery. "Surveillance man," he says.

We drive by the golf courses that offer magnificent panoramic views of the Great Salt Marsh and freshwater lakes. The courses boast dramatic views of the ocean and inlet. I thought it was a most unique place, with all its subtle blues and greens. Suddenly PGC's mansion came into view as Ned Larson made the turn onto a titanic driveway lined with palm trees. The house is magnificent, with three entrances in the front. The first floor rises up to large picture windows across the second floor. A portico is centered on top of the roof. From the outside, the house looks like a maze of sumptuousness.

We didn't go in the front entrance. Ned walked me around the house where more than an Olympic swimming pool was surrounded by pooling white lounge chairs occupied by beautiful, topless women. The back of the house had four stately columns going across a back porch. An opulent bar was centered between the two inside pilasters. There was a working bartender and two waitresses serving the guests.

I hadn't brought a swimming suit, nor did I even own one. The women were beautiful and Ned had the good sense to walk me to the bar for a drink. The people there were puzzling because no one acted like they knew each other. Ned and I each took a beer and walked the perimeter of the pool, which had a subtle rise as we walked toward the ocean.

Ned and I sat down on the highest point, on a bench facing the sea. After a few moments I suggested we sit facing the pool, which gave us a more interesting view of the women flopping in and out of the pool. There is nothing better than watching a nice set of tits floating in clear blue water. I was enjoying myself and my mind was wandering when I received an unexpected tap on my shoulder.

It was Madeline Haycock showing off even more cleavage than I'd seen in the pool. She was the best yet.

"Welcome, Jack Oleson. Were your travels relaxing," she asks with her sexy English-Australian accent. Are you enjoying the scenery?" She asks, with a cunning smile.

"Indeed," I say.

"Mr. Charles is in conference, but he wants you to continue to relax and enjoy yourself. Ned will get you anything you need, Jack, I mean anything." She looks at Ned like he better service my wants. Ned nods and toasts her with his beer. Madeline leaves twiddling her fingers like a Southern Belle fanning herself.

Ned and I are mute, until Madeline Haycock disappears from sight. Ned, asks, "Is there anything you want?"

"Yeah, Ned, would you call Ellen to see if it is okay if I fuck each one of those women in alphabetical order."

"Done," he says. What's her number," he asks. "Why alphabetically?"

"So, I can honestly tell Ellen they meant nothing to me." I reply.

"I see." said Ned. "I see!"

"Come on, let me show you your room. Gordon won't be available until we go to dinner tonight. I have something I want to show you."

We strolled through a back entrance into the house. We totter up a spiral staircase to a second floor landing. Here we walk outside on the second deck which is lined with white, wooden rocking chairs under port holes used as windows from old ship's relics. We take a right and Ned walks me to my room. The bedroom is furnished with a Queen sized bed and a solid oak dresser. There are a few nautical prints on the wall, but the bedroom is relatively austere. The room has a panoramic view of the deep-sea and its own bathroom replete with a shower for two.

I set my room up, while Ned was on the balcony looking at the ocean. "Okay," I say. I was so relieved he was here. I couldn't even imagine what might go on while traveling with Mr. Charles. Ned knows and I sense he wants me to know as little as possible at the goings-on with Paul Gordon Charles.

"Jack, let's have another beer and then I want to show you something."

"Where did all the women come from," I queried.

"If you want to fuck one of them all you have to do is point one out. They are expensive call girls, Jack. He pays them well whether they do anything or not. Pretty women can get most men to do what they want. Gordon says." Ned Larson scoffs at the notion.

"Why are you always whispering," I ask.

"Surveillance," he says again, pursing his lips.

We take our beers and I follow him toward the back of the property. As we walk I see a dock where a large boat is moored. Next to it is a small boat with a Johnson motor. To the right and to the left are other large boats, some with empty sails and poles towering into the wind.

Ned walks to the small boat and motions for me to get aboard. "This is mine," he says. "It gives me something to do when he is with his whores." Ned charges, whispering again. "Come on," he says. "We'll take a little ride."

I don't like big bodies of water, even though I'm an excellent swimmer. But Ned, a Navy man, sped his boat out into the ocean with ease. The sun was going down and the most bravura view appeared in the Western sky. It was bright yellow against an orange back drop, showing the poles glistening off the vessels lined up against the beach.

"Jack this is going to be a strange weekend for you. Everything will be available to you. First, I have to take you to a store to get you proper sailing attire. If the weather holds were going boating to Savannah, Georgia. Tom Harvey and his paramour will be joining us. We have a crew as well. It's a new bunch, so I'll be busy watching them. Just enjoy yourself!"

"Man, this guy really ….." Ned interrupts by pursing his fingers to closed lips, whispering, "Wait until we get further out, up around the bend. Sound carries well through water."

We sit in silence for maybe ten minutes. Then, Ned said, "It's okay now."

"Ned, how do you live this way?"

"It's not so bad, Jack. I live well, but I don't know for how long. I guess this will all end when they figure out whom or what they want."

"Yeah, *they*, who are *they*?"

Ned shut down the motor and we just drifted in the water for a half hour or so. We talked about everything and everyone. We stayed away from what we were really doing here today. It seemed Ned and I didn't really trust each other anymore. At least there seemed to be an uneasy tension between us, a feeling that never existed before.

"What is this really about, Ned?" I ask. "I mean this is crazy!"

The hardest thing to learn in life is which bridge to cross and which to burn. **David Russell**

Chapter Forty-One

Money makes you do things you don't want to do. It's like you can't get a little bit pregnant. Who am I? I'm wondering, watching PGC spending money like there was no end to it. What in the hell am I doing here?

What I'm learning is evil and viciousness is only fully understandable in anecdotal form. I'm wondering why a man like me would be associating with an asshole like PGC. I forget sometimes, in my crazy situations, I'm an FBI agent. I wouldn't, under normal circumstances, even say hello to such amoral fiber because there are consequences in dealing with such people. Danger is indeed precarious and evil is seductive, while virtue is boring. But, again, evil pays better than high merit.

As my mind wanders I'm hardly observing what's going on around me, but I'm certain PGC is scrutinizing me. As a special bottle of Champaign is opened and poured into PGC's glass, for tasting, he speaks, "This is the best selection of the Yacht Club – Dom …" something or other, he announces. I couldn't understand the second word of the selection. As he nodded with his approval, Ned nudged me, whispering, "Drink it slowly, and savor it."

When everyone's glass was poured, PGC raised his crystal toasting his perfect evening. And, it was splendidly done. At our table was PGC with Madeline Haycock, the company's auditor and current paramour, on his left. Moving clockwise and on her left was Kurt somebody, who was introduced as the yacht's Captain, and on his left was a young blonde gal with a dynamite figure, pouty lips, and seemingly brainless. Her name was Annabelle. Those two were the Crew, I would find out soon enough. Next to her were me and then Ned. Tom Harvey was sitting on PGC's right and his paramour, Angelica, was between Harvey and Commander Ned Larson.

The night had begun with two Rolls Royce's caravanning us to the Yacht Club which, of course, was located right on the ocean front. . It was so close to PGC's house we could have walked, but if you have a Roll's you must use it, especially if you have two.

After we were seated it seemed our table had the best vista in the Yacht Club with its sweeping, spectacular view of the ocean and its inlets. PGC grinned at Tom Harvey, then, says, "I understand you have you've been flying your Cessna we bought you, Tom?"

Looking around the table I start to make mental notes as to why each of us is here. I am certain my presence had nothing to do with the 1984 budget. And I wondered about Tom Harvey. Richard Corrigan told me PGC wasn't going to put up with Harvey's continual wants, demands and whining. So, when he seemingly went right after Tom Harvey I could see where this was going, and I definitely didn't want to see it go there.

"Finally," Tom says which he delivered with a negative attitude.

A good sociopath had to learn how and when to be polite and charming. PGC was the master about knowing when to be gracious and enchanting. "And Angel," he asked. "Did you get the problems resolved with your new Mercedes?"

Angel was not drunk, like her beau, Tom Harvey, and complimented me by saying, with a smile, "Jack took care of everything very nicely for us." While she was responding, I noticed Tom Harvey's head bobbing much to PGC's amusement.

PGC was wearing tan slacks, blue blazer, a golf shirt and penny loafers. He always wore the right clothes for each occasion. When Tom Harvey nodded off and spilled his drink on the table and down his shirt and pants, PGC apologized to the waitress and told her to clean it up. Then he ordered Ned Larson to get Tom Harvey squared away.

Once again Tom Harvey had been manipulated into one of PGC's schemes. He should have understood what was going on because he had been there before; but even so it was not a guarantee that he was going to get it right this time. In fact, experience should have told him it was just baggage. And memory carries the bags.

I took a long swig of my Jack Daniels, keeping my eyes wide open and watching everything that was going on. I was thinking we were at the threshold of another great folly as I watched Angel, who seemed emotionally distraught and vulnerable since Tom Harvey had been removed from the table.

What I didn't know, until later, that Ned Larson had taken Tom Harvey into the locker room, skinned off his clothes and hosed him down in a shower. PGC's purpose was to always humiliate. He had had a fresh set of clothes placed in a locker and Ned pointed them out in a rented cubbyhole so Tom could get squared away. Of course, I could see now this had all been scripted in advance.

When Tom Harvey walked back into the club he almost looked fresh as a daisy as Ned Larson walked him to his chair adjacent to PGC. Another drink was ready for him and he seemed somewhat coherent until he took his first sip.

I watched Angel and she seemed somewhat disturbed by the events. She was a beautiful chocolate-brown-skinned lady who had a beautiful figure and striking facial qualities. Tom Harvey had put her on the map and she hated the way PGC controlled her man. She intuitively seemed to know Gordon had his eyes on her and when the time was right he would fuck her. The last time on the boat PGC had caught her stark naked, with one hand covering her bush, and the other one over one breast. He had looked, then, said, "Excuse me Angel."

She had told Tom about it, but he just laughed telling her PGC wanted to fuck her. "For Paul Gordon Charles," he said, "you are no different than screwing the IRS out of money." Tom wouldn't have seen the humor, if he knew to PGC that screwing his gal was no more than getting even for all Harvey's demands and requests. And that it would happen, Angel would be enter-taining him soon enough.

So adversity builds character, I'm thinking as the evening becomes more disgusting than entertaining. There are certain un-written rules and privileges. When we finished our drinks it was time to go, because it was PGC time. But time stopped momen-tarily when Tom Harvey ordered another scotch whiskey. Gordon nodded his approval and a Chives Regal was placed in front of Tom.

"Angel, may I get you another drink." PGC asked, caringly.

She smiled, saying, "I'll have one when we get home."

She was wearing a frilly pink blouse that accentuated her brown skin, and a black silk skirt that didn't reach her knees. She had wavy chestnut hair that she wore shoulder length, nice big brown eyes, a nose with slightly fared nostrils and lush lips that now and then flashed a slightly amused smile. Yes, as Tom Harvey was bobbing his head again, she was a good-looking woman with a cultured voice and manner.

Paul Gordon Charles stood up. Ned Larson led Tom Harvey away from the table and Madeline Haycock attended to Angel. I imagined she told her it would be a threesome tonight. I did an eye-recon of the room and moseyed to the second Rolls Royce under the portico of Club's entranceway.

As the car moved toward the mansion I checked my watch, it was 8 P.M. and I wondered what else would transpire during the evening. It was early.

Most people spend more time and energy going around problems than trying to solve them. **Henry Ford**

Chapter Forty-Two

Flying High
Fripp Island, South Carolina
Thursday, December 8, 1983

The name of his estate is *Flying High*. There is a gold plate centered above the entrance gate making known his manor house. When we arrive everyone seems to have out of the ordinary guidelines in mind. PGC, Madeline, and Angelica disappeared in the bearing of the master bedroom suite. Ned Larson was leading Tom Harvey to his designated loft. I couldn't help but chuckle when I saw Tom leaning on Ned, while stumbling along in a complete state of unconsciousness. The boat crew vanished somewhere out back, while I went out to the bar, now void of people, and fixed myself a drink.

I wasn't sitting at the saloon long before Annabelle, the lovely boat's mate, sat down next me, with a Corona beer. "Hi, Jack," she says. "What are you doing here all by yourself?"

Majestic trees were casting long moon shadows over the grassy fields. Soft, balmy breezes were rustling the palm trees and night birds were beginning to sing. I was becoming mesmerized by such a magical moment when pretty Annabelle had sat down next to me. I grinned when her eyes seemed to fix on mine.

Kurt, the ship's Captain, is a large powerfully built man, and in the moonlight he appears as imposing and menacing as a stone god, like, say, Neptune. He waves and I nod in his direction. He shouts to Annabelle saying he would be on the boat studying the navigation charts for tomorrow's trip. She yells back that she'd be at the bar for a while. "See you later," she shouts, affectionately.

When I ask Annabelle how old she is she doesn't lie, "Sixteen," she says.

"And you're drinking already," I ask., "I've been drinking, fucking and smoking since I was twelve years old." She whispers, softly.

"This place is bugged and he has spies everywhere," Annabelle adds.

"You know a lot for a young lady," I tell her. "Why would he bug his own place?"

Annabelle gets off her stool and moseys behind the bar. "Jack and club soda," I order. She fixes me a drink and takes another Corona for herself.

"I've been around rich people all my life. They covet everything. If folks are trying to get a notch up on them they make certain they find an opponent's plot." Annabelle spoke with a hush-hush in her voice and a sense of scrutiny in her mannerisms.

"I see," I said. "Overt surveillance to the max is the word."

"What did you say," she queries.

I could tell she didn't understand my response and Ned Larson saved the moment, arriving just in the indentation of time so I didn't have to explain what I'd just commented about. Ned motioned for Annabelle to follow him. She put her beer down and followed Larson into the house. A few minutes later Ned was back, picking up Annabelle's half-drank bottle of Corona. He poured it out and fixed himself a scotch whiskey and water.

Ned had no more than sat down when I heard this loud rumbling noise. Suddenly steel bars descended from the top of the house, covering windows and doors. "What the hell," I said, while Ned just chortled. He told me, "It's just the security system sealing of his master suite."

"Come on," Ned says. "Let's take a walk."

We meandered to the benches atop the rise and sat down facing the sea. "Jack, he told me to tell you Annabelle is off limits, for now anyway."

"I've made no move on her, Ned." I respond with an irritated tone.

"I know," he said. "What you should feel good about though is that he thinks you could."

"He's insatiable, isn't he?" I say. "He's fucking insatiable!"

"Jack, you haven't seen anything yet. Tomorrow we're cruising to Savannah, Georgia. Don't be surprised if Tom Harvey falls overboard and is left for the sharks. Tom - just doesn't get it – he's no long important to PGC. As I'm sure you could tell at dinner, Tom Harvey was being punished. But actually tonight was just the set up. Tom Harvey was to be shown as an uncontrollable drunk to everyone present, including those at the surrounding tables in the Yacht Club. Why? It's easy to say the drunk, Tom Harvey, fell off the boat and drowned. *You know, it was too bad about Tom.* People will say. *He was a successful black businessman with all the right connections."*

"Are you sure this spot is not bugged, Ned?" I was feeling somewhat anxious now.

"I'm positive, Jack. There is nowhere to hide microphones at this location. Plus only gossip, rumor, and small talk go on here. Stuff he would just find pedestrian. Even he needs a place where all won't be recorded. Remember the Nixon tapes? He does. Plus he trusts me without reservation."

"But," I say, "Never say never and from my point of view, can I trust you?"

"You better," Ned says. "You had better trust me."

Just then we heard a door open, Angelica and Annabelle walk to the bar to fix drinks. They were wearing long white, silk gowns. As they approach us Annabelle gives me another drink and Angelica gives one to Ned. It is clear they have nothing on under those gowns. They sit back to back with us and sip their drinks. Whatever we are all thinking was being unsaid.

Finally Angelica pronounces, "Evil is seductive and virtue is boring."

"But evil seems to pay better than virtue," adds Ned.

"But virtue is its own reward, isn't it? I ask. After a pregnant pause, I continue, "No, I don't think so." Rethinking my quip, I say, "There are consequences either way. There is jeopardy in both conducts. Any kind of danger is dangerous."

Watch it now I say to myself. I don't know how much education people have around here. I know Annabelle has none, but Angelica seems first class and well read by conversation.

And, well read means everything to me. I think about the two beautiful women behind our backs; why would they live a life or even associate with a man like PGC?

Money never sleeps, they say, and these girls sleep for money. While I was chewing everything over in my mind, the women slugged down their drinks saying they'd see us in the morning.

"Ned," I ask while the women are sashaying back to the house. "What in the hell just happened here?"

"Tom Harvey is being punished, how severely we won't know until tomorrow. Tom will drink until the drinks stop coming. So, when he was unconscious Madeline Haycock slipped a couple pills into Angelica's drink to make her insentient, but functional. Annabelle cut a deal with PGC to do whatever for the opportunity for Kurt and her to be his crew for the summer. So, based on my past experiences, I can speculate what happened."

"Yeah," I say, sucking Jack Daniels off an ice cube now.

"When he's with Madeline Gordon doesn't screw other women. They like to have two strange women in bed with them, in the 69 position, doing each other. First he has them get naked and put on those white gowns you saw them wearing. Then, just use your imagination, Jack. It doesn't take long for PGC to cum, he's very selfish, and I've been told by Charlotte Boyer. It takes him less time to become satisfied than to cook a 3-minute egg. Then he kicks them out after they make Madeline cum. Then they fall asleep, totally content."

The door opens in the back of the house. Annabelle walked out in a pair of jeans and a halter top. She stops at the bar and grabs another Corona. She walks by us like we weren't there and goes directly to the yacht.

"Sweet Sixteen," I say. "What a shame. My daughter, Kincaid, is seventeen. My worst nightmare would be for her to be in Annabelle's situation."

"Yeah," Ned says. "Here we are two Midwest boys, who don't

even think about such perverted scenarios and look at us now. Were all grown up and corrupted.

"What's up tomorrow?" I ask.

"First I'll buy you some put-out-to-sea clothes. We'll get on the yacht about noon and cruise away. What happens once aboard is capricious." Ned says, with a laugh. "We'll see, Jack. We better hit the sack."

We are continually faced by great opportunities brilliantly disguised as insoluble problems. **Lee Iacocca**

Chapter Forty-Three

Wet Dreams
Tybee Island, Georgia
Friday, December 9, 1983

Ned Larson and I were riding in one of PGC's Mercedes Benz's en route to Beaufort, South Carolina at eight o'clock in the morning. When we arrived at Beaufort's Nautical and Seafaring Store, Ned starts laughing inwardly.

"This won't exactly be needful things for a Minnesota lake fishing excursion," he says. "But," he continues, "I'll point out what will be required today. He suggests Bermuda shorts, golf shirts, sandals and other things to carry while cruising on the vessel. I even had to pick out special toe-nail clippers to get my feet ship-shape. I tried everything looked-for on for size. Larson paid the bill, which I mentally calculated at several hundred dollars, and we headed back to Fripp Island.

It was nearing noon when we were all aboard PGC's 1982, 70' Lanphere yacht. First we were given a tour by Madeline starting with its massive foredeck with tender, then up to the Skylounge cockpit, and the Skylounge seating area with day head behind. She pointed out Lanphere's signature curved window seating. We went back downstairs where she showed us the dining room, fully equipped galley, and the open and airy salon. Then she showed us the matching guest cabins port and starboard side with a full beam master stateroom. Last she showed us a 2 bunk crew's stateroom, with its own entrance. She said the engine room was below. I was impressed.

"Her name is *Wet Dreams*," Madeline added, with an acerbic grin.

The temperature was eighty-five degrees and the women aboard were donning black itsy-bitsy bikini bottoms with fire engine red halters on top. The women were barefoot and temporarily gathering in the Skylounge seating area. Whereas the men, including me, wore white Bermuda shorts and sky-blue golf shirts. We wore what they called *Jesus* sandals on our feet. I looked like the others, but I didn't feel like myself.

Captain Kurt, had pulled the craft out of its tie-up and glided southeasterly by the Huntington Island Lighthouse and the Parris Island Marine Corps Recruiting Depot. I stood at the helm with the Captain as he elucidated our course and final destination. He said the travel time to Tybee Island should be two hours plus. That, we would be pass by Hilton Head Island, Savannah, Georgia, Fort Pulaski and to the point at Tybee.

While Kurt was talking I noticed his eyes kept shifting, especially when the women removed their tops. They were now lying outside on the topside of the boat just below the captain's Skylounge cockpit. We had a splendid view and I'm sure the ladies were enjoying showing off their stuff. Meanwhile, Annabelle was serving drinks and snacks to all while keeping her top securely fastened.

I decide to go below so nobody is thinking I was hanging in the *catbird* seat just to watch the women. As I moseyed I was surprised to see PGC talking with Tom Harvey. They each have what appears to be a Bloody Mary and were smoking what I guessed were Havana cigars. I doubted PGC had any vodka in his drink, especially if he was going to throw Tom overboard today.

"Where's your drink, Jack?" shouts Paul Gordon Charles.

"I'm getting one," I answer with a smile. "Thank you. What a beautiful trip. I'm really enjoying it."

Tom Harvey toasts me. "A great day, indeed," he said.

I shuffle around the corner to where I found Ned Larson nursing a beer. He looks like he is in deep thought.

"What's up, Ned," I ask.

"I just get sick of this crap, sometimes. I just got off the phone with my wife and she's tired of being alone all the time. We've got the baby coming, and, I'm twenty years older than her. I don't know when I'll be home next." He is shaking his head as he speaks softly.

Ned gets up and fixes me a drink. "Try not to be seen without a drink, Jack." Larson kind of cautions me. He wants you to have a good time. But never play into his hands. He wants everybody to get drunk, hopefully to loosen their tongues." He is whispering now.

Larson pours himself a scotch whiskey and leans on the bar, looking me directly in the eye. "Jack, did you ever fuck my wife?"

I motion for another drink. He fixes an extra strong one, I notice, while I speculate on what had precipitated this request for information. And, I recall, the mother of evil is speculation. I need somebody now to interrupt us so I could postpone my answer.

Ned had met his wife in my Virginia Beach office, in the late 70's. Brenda had worked for me for approximately two years when she met Larson. Ned and I knew each other in two different roles. He as a successful contractor, and I was his accountant. Also, we were undercover agents for the FBI.

Brenda and I were close for different reasons before Ned entered the picture. I was fifteen years older than her, and she flattered me by being so interested in my life. She, on the other hand, had come from Georgia with only a few dollars in her pocket. She had a high school education with little work experience, but she was an excellent typist. She was also very attractive with a pleasant personality. I gave her an opportunity and we had a great working relationship.

When she and Ned advised me they were dating, I told them both to just date and have a good time. I explained to Ned, for the obvious reasons, he should wait and let his recent divorce settle. For Brenda, I said just wait. That true love will stand a test of time. He's the same age as your father and he has kids nearly as old as you.

"But, he's an Navy aviator. I came to Norfolk to find a fly boy. I found him. He's tall, handsome and a very nice man. I don't care if he's older. I know what he's all about." She pleads her case with me.

"Do you know what's he's all about," I ask. He has a whole other life before he met you. Brenda, sometimes there are things you don't know about. Things are not always what they seem. The older people get the more they want to forget about what happened before." I told her to be circumspect. And she didn't know what that meant so I said, *cautious.*

A few months later they were married despite my sage advice. The net result for me was losing a very good employee. Ned Larson immediately told her to ask me for a raise. Since I have never been one who liked suggestions leading to threats, Brenda and I parted ways.

A few months later they were married, and I wasn't invited to the wedding. Around the same time as their wedding I was told my current assignment was ending. They gave me *the you did a great job* routine, of course, but for my own safety and the safety of my family I needed to *get out of Dodge.* That, I would be transferring out of the Tidewater area soon. I didn't figure I'd ever see Brenda, Ned or anybody else I had known the past eight years again.

Ned filled our glasses again as I answered him with a smart but firm question. "Did you ever fuck my wife?"

Taken somewhat back, he smiled, saying, "Of course, not. I'm sorry. You know how things go around here." Ned slapped me on my back.

"No, Ned. I never fucked you wife. Who suggested that I did?"

There was a long pause as we passed by the City of Savannah, Georgia in the near distance. I didn't think Brenda would have ever told Ned, if we had sex with each other.

"PGC said you had fucked her."

"PGC," I questioned, with a laugh. "For God sakes do you believe everything he tells you?" There was a pause again, "He never lets up, Ned?"

"Jack, I had to ask. Do you understand?" Ned catechizes, apologetically.

I did understand. And, Brenda and I did have a few reminiscences, but those retentions were before they were married.

And not as an excuse, those remembrances exist because we were drinking and angry at our life's situation. The present-day is a sum of calling to mind of bygones and how we dealt with it.

We heard stirring on the stairs and Annabelle appeared with her big tray giving Ned the drink orders. Up to this point I didn't know Ned was the bartender on this voyage. Or, why I was on this journey at all? Not a lick of work had been done so far. What the hell?

Ned primed drinks for everybody, while Annabelle gathered some more snacks. "Gordon wants everybody top side," she told us.

I wondered why she was already calling PGC by his preferred middle name, Gordon. Evidently she was doing something correctly. "Let's go," Ned said. "He wants everybody topside when he comes into port."

It was Tom Harvey with Angelica; PGC with Madeline; Ned Larson and Annabelle; Captain Kurt at the helm and me next to him as we approached the dock. I thought about how great it would be to have Ellen along, if all these people had some semblance of status quo. I was sure Ned was thinking along those same lines.

When the Captain pulled into the slip a crew was there to tie us off and take care of those boating details everybody dreads. When we walked off the boat two limousines were waiting for us. PGC and Madeline rode in the lead carriage, while the rest of us piled in the other. The drivers were dressed to the nines and opened doors for everyone.

Tybee is a small community featuring one main street by the seaside. The houses and churches appeared to have been built a long time ago and were very weather worn. We wound around a few blocks with locals stopping to look at who might be in these ostentatious automobiles. A few minutes later we turned into a wooded area where an old building, which looked like it was about to collapse, was still standing. A weather worn sign announced: *Harry's Place.*

"When he goes slumming, here's where he goes." Ned Larson

said as we walks toward *Harry's Place*. The place is wide open, no screens or glass on the windows. They had set up a big round table, which appears to be one hundred years old, for us to sit together on the deck. Somebody had to know we were coming. I wonder who made the arrangements.

"For those of you who haven't been here before, it is beer only at our table." announces Madeline Haycock. Ned and she did seem to be executing all the shots with PGC sitting next to Tom Harvey, who he was getting an earful about something.

I studied the bar's décor. It seemed as if everyone who had ever been here had left something nailed to the wall. There were car license plates from every state in the Union. The decals were from all the years of the twentieth century, starting with the *Roaring Twenties*. There were snap shots of people going back in ages just as far, and, of course various celebrities who had been there. I spotted Sinatra, who seems to be on everyone's walls in the country. Fish nets and other paraphernalia hung on the ramparts as did a picture of a smiling Jimmy Carter. I wondered if any of this could have been staged. I decided not, though, because of all the dust and filth. I wondered if Ned had sprayed Lysol on everything PGC neared. He didn't like germs.

After three rounds of beer PGC called for hot chicken wings, french fries and onion rings. We had arrived at three o'clock and had been informed we were leaving at five o'clock. I was surprised; it really was a good time. It was another side of PGC that I didn't think he would ever expose. Meanwhile, off and on, I saw Ned Larson communicating with two tough looking guys at the bar. My curiosity was keen.

We caravanned back to the docks and we were ready to cruise at five-thirty P.M. However, Kurt was not present. The captain always stayed with the vessel, during a stop. When word passed to PGC that the Captain was unaccounted for, he said, "Fuck him!"

Meanwhile, the women had changed from their bikinis to skin tight black designer jeans with ruffled red blouses. The men changed to designer black jeans with long-sleeve white shirts. All of us were issued a transparent wind breaker. Ned stepped to the helm, with me by his side, and pushes the yacht out into the water.

Everybody was now sitting at an oval table in the Skylounge. The temperature had dropped to fifty-eight degrees and there was a soft breeze blowing as we saw the lights of Savannah in the distance. Annabelle kept the drinks coming and the cruise back to Fripp Island was very enjoyable and relaxing. Everybody was talking about ordinary things while Tom Harvey nodded off and slept most of the way. Nobody, save myself, seemed to be bothered about the disappearance of Captain Kurt.

I kept watching Tom Harvey and what was going on around his position. Annabelle was rearmost tending bar, while Ned was guiding us home. So I didn't bother Ned concerning Tom's fate and when and if he might be thrown overboard. I didn't think he would now, especially since the Captain had vanished.

The lights shining from the shore was romantic, but there is no one to be quixotic with. The women all looked beautiful donning their expensive clothing. Annabelle, of course, had been spoken for last night. And, supposedly, she had belonged to Captain Kurt, who now was missing. As we approached home base, near Fripp Island, I was happy that nothing had occurred that couldn't logically be explained. In addition, tomorrow was Saturday, one day closer to me flying home to Philadelphia for a crack at normalcy?

You cannot plan the future by the past. **Edmund Burke**

Chapter Forty-Four

Flying High
Fripp Island, South Carolina
Saturday, December 10, 1983

After the voyage I helped Ned close down the yacht. Everybody else seemed to disappear as it took us an hour to clean everything up. Annabelle joined us about fifteen minutes before we were done, putting dishes away for us and other stuff women do better than men. "Where have you been?" I ask. She motioned toward the steel bars descending its path covering PGC's master suite.

"Any word on Kurt," I ask Annabelle?

"Are you kidding? We won't see Kurt again." She says, seemingly knowing more than what she was letting on.

"What do you think happened?" I ask trying to withdraw some information from her.

She was too savvy to give up any cloak-and-dagger gen. The course of our lives can change so quickly if something is said or not said.

"I'm so tired," she says. "I just want to get some sleep. Are you guys through here?" She asks.

Ned Larson encourages her. "Go ahead, Annabelle. We'll give you some space. Let's go, Jack." Ned heartened me, motioning to a gangplank that led to the dock.

We walked to the top of the rise and sat down on the benches facing the water and the boat. Ned seems emotionally distraught and vulnerable. "He plays for keeps, Jack, and should never be trusted. His xenophobic personality towards all is exhausting and irksome. His behavior is completely against my religion. And, I suppose you want to know what happened to Kurt?"

I said nothing as I watched Ned Larson stew, perhaps he was trying to reconcile the past with the present. Again a man has to make intelligent decisions.

"Okay," Ned said, reticently. "He likes Annabelle. He wants her to be part of his entourage. He wants her to finish high school and go to college. He wants to make something out of her so she will worship him. He'll never change."

"That's not her, Ned. I've communicated with her for less than an hour and I would bet an education is the last thing on her mind." I laugh, quietly.

"Well, Kurt didn't work into the program. He's been banging Annabelle for a short time now and it was him who got her away from home with the lure of travel. But, don't underestimate her, Jack. She knows how to get around in more ways than one."

"Oh, I'm not taking her too lightly at all. I just don't understand why she is so important to Gordon. He has everything else he wants. What role is he playing, Elvis?" I ask.

"He liked Elvis." Ned said. "He liked him a lot."

"So what happened to Kurt?"

"You won't see Kurt anymore, Jack." Ned assures me.

"That's what she said. What? Did you pitch him overboard?" I ask.

There was a pregnant pause, while Ned fiddled with a set of keys.

"You don't need to know, Jack. Believe me." Ned cautions.

I didn't sleep at all. I got up early because I couldn't watch the ceiling fan go round and round anymore. Nobody seemed up and about. Not even Ned, but he was probably tired. He had captained the boat back to Fripp Island, like a professional. However, he was always up at the crack of dawn. I walk toward the bench beyond the swimming pool where Ned and I had perched last night, everything now seems extraordinarily quiet.

I had a lot going on in my mind with the disappearance of Captain Kurt. During the trip back Ned hadn't spoken a word to me, which was strange. Ned liked to visit, like all North Dakotans. And, I wonder if it had something to do with that strange question he'd asked me?

I looked out at *Wet Dreams*, which was moored nicely against a rising sun in the East. The boat was so beautiful just sitting in the water rocking back and forth. I wondered if Annabelle was aboard, wondering about Captain Kurt.

I decided to walk out to the yacht to reconnoiter the situation. When I walked up the gang plank all was quiet. Suddenly, I heard commotion and a rumbling. I recognized the guy right away. He was one of the tough looking guys Ned had been talking with at Harry's Place on Tybee Island. How did he get here I'm thinking. And, where or where is the other guy. Ned was talking to two of them at Harry's Place.

"Hi," I said. "Where did you come from, or are you a friend of Annabelle?" I ask with a friendly smile, while walking directly to the gun cabinet PGC had shown me the day before. I open the middle drawer of the cabinet and pull out a loaded Smith and Wesson *Saturday Night Special*. It was a *10*, a weapon I'd been trained with. It was six shooter with rapid fire. I flipped open the cylinder and the ammunition looked good to go. The speed in which I'd taken the weapon evidently surprised the interloper, because he just stood there watching my maneuvers.

"What are you are doing with that gun?" The young man queries, while pissing his pants.

"I'm going to shoot you right between the eyes. One shot only," I warn. "If you answer my questions, I'll be kind and just shoot one of your big toes off."

There was dead silence and I had the middle of his forehead lined up in my gun sight. He said nothing. But, I did.

"Where is Annabelle," I ask. He stuttered something inaudible. "Where is Kurt," I follow up.

There is a stillness, when I ask, "Who the hell are you?"

So many people think they are important and powerful until they meet somebody like me, who doesn't give a shit. I hadn't given a shit since my first marriage broke up. I'd rather shoot this guy dead than listen to a bullshit story.

He was sweating profusely, when stuttering out his name: "Vin…cent."

Vincent said no more before I heard Annabelle running up the stairs. "Jack," she shouted, "what are you doing?"

"I'm ready to blow Vincent away unless you explain to me what he's doing here? No, Annabelle, no, go find Ned and tell him to come here immediately."

I continue pointing my gun, the *38 Saturday Night Special,* at Vincent's forehead.

"Where is Gordon," she asks?

"Hopefully for you, he's still in bed. Annabelle you better find Ned quickly." I mean now, if you want to save what you have working here." I whisper in her ear.

"Don't move, honey." Another voice comes from behind Annabelle. When I see him he's wielding a switch blade. I laugh, yelling out, "Are you bringing a knife to a gun fight?" I moved my gun from Vincent to him back to Vincent again.

"Are you going Annabelle?" I shout.

"I'll find Ned. Please don't tell Gordon, Jack."

"You've got five minutes before I shoot one of these guys." I respond.

She ran out the door and was back with Ned Larson in less than five minutes. Evidently she knew his secret spot where he sleeps with a Mexican gal.

"What's going on here, Jack?" Ned asks, weakly.

"Look around, Ned. You recognize these guys, don't you?" I ask.

"Yeah," he says.

"I don't know what you are doing and I don't want to know. Just clean this situation up and I was never here. Do you understand, Ned?" I shout angrily.

Ned was a little slow to respond and the asshole on the steps moves behind Annabelle. When he clicks open his switch blade, a street savvy Annabelle sidesteps to her right and I fire one round just as a natural response. The bullet appears to go through his right hand and the knife falls to the floor. A few seconds later the culprit starts to whine and cry. I shout at him, "Shut up or I'll shoot a hole in your head."

"Jack, who are you?" Annabelle asks, in shock. "Who taught you how to shoot like that?"

"I'm the accountant, so be careful." I reply. "This never happened, do you hear."

Ned studied me, while shaking his head. I handed him the pistol.

My whole brashness changed as I walk away from the yacht, looking for that good old fashioned southern breakfast I'd heard so much about.

If you are distressed by anything external, the pain is not due to the thing itself, but to your estimate of it; and this you have the power to revoke at any moment. **Marcus Aurelius**

Chapter Forty-Five

Flying High
Fripp Island, South Carolina
Saturday, December 10, 1983

The geometry of judgment is a circle, with all reason temporarily having deserted me. At the moment I didn't know who, where I or what I was doing. That in time, anything that was something becomes nothing and existence itself has no ultimate purpose except cessation, leaving each of us being shaped by our own life's experiences.

I thought things would be different when I joined the Bureau. To date they have done nothing to me but they have done nothing for me, either. Consequently, now the Bureau means nothing to me. What put me here was boredom. Boredom is a state of mind akin to an emotion. Perhaps the emotion to which boredom most often leads to is despair. Yes, despair, misery, desolation and hopelessness are my present state of mind.

Are you ironed means are you carrying iron, are you packing a gun? No, I handed it to Ned Larson when I exited the yacht. I walked into the ground level of the mansion and stopped in the bathroom on the left just after I entered. I washed my hands and face and brushed my hair, thinking it was time for brunch. It was nearing ten o'clock.

I had already experienced one moment of transcendence this morning, when my mind was enabled to raise no barriers of self-doubt and therefore allowed my talent to be expressed more fully than has ever been possible previously, while with the Bureau. A tremulous consequence had filled me, but my hand had remained steady and swift. It's what psychologists call a *flow state* and what I was told as an athlete was *being in the zone.*

People want discipline, rules to follow and live by. The happiest employees, it has been articulated, are governed by gentle bosses who quietly but firmly demand respect. So, it has been spoken. All kinds of thoughts are racing through my mind as I enter the kitchen area. PGC is sitting at the head of the table reading a newspaper. Madeline Haycock is on his right. Tom Harvey is seated to his left, with his friend Angelica to his left. There is an open space next to Madeline.

"Good morning, Jack." Madeline greets me, pointing out my place next to hers. Her face is imperturbable, her voice soft. Always she is lithe, graceful, with no telltale twitch of tension in her stride of gestures.

"Good morning, everybody," I say with a nod and a compulsory smile.

PGC keeps reading his paper as two very pretty African-American girls began serving us. They start with coffee and then suggest a drink from the bar. Tom Harvey orders what appears to be at least his second Bloody Mary. The rest of us veto, which immediately draws the boss's attention.

"Jack," where's your drink?" Gordon queries with an attitude.

"Bloody Mary," I request from one of the servers.

With my order, Mr. Charles grins.

"Yes," he said. "And, you're drink, Angelica?"

She orders a screwdriver, while Madeline motions for a refill. Paul Gordon Charles looks pleased now and I'm certain there is no vodka in his orange or tomato juice. I also find it interesting that a place had not been set for Ned Larson. I wonder if that whole scene had been staged this morning. Certainly, not the shooting, I thought. But then again, PGC wouldn't care if anybody got shot as long as it wasn't him. In fact he might even enjoy a shooting.

The breakfast, brunch or whatever the official PGC name for it was excellent. There is course after course each one leading to the next selection. The house is full of silence. The food is so tasty there is no room for idle talk. And, of course, unless Paul Gordon Charles spoke all talk was considered work-shy.

Tom Harvey kept pouring down Bloody Mary's as I noticed Angelica getting more repulsed with each one. Thunders of silence pervaded the house. It was the kind of silence that quakes through you and breaks your sweat and promises lightening. I was thinking that through the silence moves a predator, making the quietness uncomfortable.

As I look around at the beautiful setting and think of the delectable courses we had just gobbled, I'm conjecturing what it is that PGC enjoys the most. He seems to like the seductive despair of his landed gentry, the deeply settled hopelessness, the corrupting bitterness that gives no quarter to any optimist who might wish to debate dark world interpretations. He wants those around him to see the world as hopeless, and to believe it will remain that way unless it is he *the great one* only who can sustain them in the way in which they see slices of his luxurious corporeal. He will quote T.S. Eliot, as he often does: *Life you may evade, but death you shall not.*

He understands the necessity of understatement but the value of hyperbole. He is perspicacious enough to order high-ranking military officers around. He proclaims for all the beauty and joy of life, but the world is nonetheless a war zone. It will be he alone, with his all-knowing wisdom that can make the save. His gaze is sharp now with sinister calculation. At precisely eleven thirty A.M. he dismisses the table, asking only me to remain. He raises his eyebrows quizzically as everyone else departs.

"Jack, we will meet at one o'clock to go over the budget. I expect we'll be busy until four o'clock. You'll need my input, but then you can take it from there. Also, I want to discuss the status and timing of the financing you've arranged for my projects."

I wander out back to get some fresh air, thinking tomorrow at this time I'll be home with my family. In a way I was losing touch with reality. I felt totally compelled and controlled by this man. He was constantly telling me to do this and that to move his criminal activities forward to meet his goalmouths and opportunities. Guilt is a tireless horse. I'd been harboring a lot of onus moving forward with all this against-the-law goings-on.

The bar was open and six gorgeous young women had just arrived in their scanty bikinis. I ordered a beer and walked out to the bench atop the rise on the other side of the pool. There I could see the yacht, but there was no activity. Strange, I thought as I directed my attention back toward the pool area. The girls were getting their drinks, talking and getting squared away in their beach chairs. I wondered why? Ned and I were the only men here without a companion.

Since I began this assignment I had been surrounded by the type of passive, fearful people who'd chosen to stay in school to avoid conflict and consequences of real life. Avoiding going to Vietnam by continuing to pursue a higher education came to mind, a little game played out by the richer and smarter. For the most part, Vietnam was a poor man's war and for those not pursuing a higher education. I always felt guilty that I'd been held exempt from that ghastly duty, but not guilty enough to volunteer.

But now I was on a different stage and I could say or do anything I wanted, without worrying about anyone being able to talk over me, save PGC. Like this must be what narcissist heaven is like?

I peer across the pool and looked at the fine-looking females out there hiding from the real world in all their splendidness. I started classifying women by type years ago. Some were simply insecure and fearful; there were the super serious and so brainwashed by the unreality of academe they were hardly human anymore; and those you would take home to mother, the girls who were just looking for their Mrs. degree; and the slut jackpot, those who not only wanted to fuck you, but they also wanted to take care of you, like wash your laundry, etcetera's. Most men preferred the latter group. But they weren't the marrying type. This bunch makes life more interesting. But, you couldn't take them home to mother. And being cautious, especially when it comes to ladies, is the greatest risk of all if guy wants to be happy.

In the midst of all my crazy contemplations I see Madeline

Haycock walking toward me. I check my watch; it is 12:44 P.M. She has on her bikini and moseys over to me, while trying to keep her resplendent breasts holstered in her tit-sling.

"Jack," she says with a smile. "Gordon isn't feeling up to par. He's taking a nap so he is postponing your meeting with him until three o'clock. Hopefully, he'll feel better so he can meet with you and we can still make our dinner engagement at the Yacht Club tonight. Have another drink and enjoy yourself." She pans her arms toward the pool's circumference and all the pretty women.

I wait until Madeline disappears into the house and walk to the bar, nodding to each one of the gals on the way. If this was a work weekend, I'd never quite seen one like it. And, it's what I expected. PGC would set some scenarios, give me a feel for his extravagances and try set me up to see how I would role play on his platform. And, there would be a woman. Someone he thinks might get to me, or at least he might get some suggestive pictures he could use to blackmail, if that kind of day should present itself. And I had already fired the gun at the perpetrator in the yacht. He could turn that panorama into anything he so sought after, if that extortion setting was necessary. Was he sly? Yes, but I was way ahead of him.

This time I ordered Jack Daniels with a splash of club soda. As soon as the bartender set it down, one of ladies approached me, saying, "Hi Jack. I'm Carole."

"May I buy you a drink, Carole?" I ask.

Everyone has dirt, I'm thinking. But PGC's scams are legendary. I knew he was working on reeling me in right now. I'd passed all his tests, which made me feel more secure with him not thinking I am a stoolpigeon. There is an art to making something difficult look easy, seemingly I had done it once again. Again life can only be understood backwards, but it must be lived forwards regardless of the situation. Just cover your ass. Always cover your ass.

"Where do you live, Jack?" Carole asks.

"Washington D.C." I reply. "Where are you from?"

"I'm from New York. Brooklyn," she says.

As she was telling me her history I was looking over her boda-cious figure. She was displaying a large set of tata's. She articulated her sentences well and seemed to be educated. So, I asked. "What college did you graduate from?"

She smiles, thinking I was trying to embarrass her.

"Pace University." She says. "I have a major in Communications Arts and Journalism."

"Really, do you want a job?" I ask.

"You couldn't afford me," she replies, being charming with her answer.

"May I have a copy of your resume!" I say, to throw fuel on the fire.

"I'll do you one better, I'll show you my resume. Of course, if you can afford to look at it." She says, winking her left eye."

I like her. She has savvy. She is beautiful and can talk the talk. I say, "I have a meeting at three o'clock and dinner scheduled for the Yacht Club tonight. So, I don't think I'll have time."

"Your three o'clock will be cancelled and I'd love to have dinner with you at the Yacht Club tonight." She says, with a mind-blow-ing beam on her face.

Carole stood perhaps five feet tall but has a presence bigger than her height and weight. Her voice is mellifluous. She makes common words sound like spoken music. She is a petite dynamo. She is a carbon copy of Ellen. PGC has done his job well, match-ing me up with one like my own. Not everyone sees the tiger, but I do. The tiger is always there. I'm thinking as I watch Carole sip her drink with a Machiavellian straightforwardness about her aura.

It is not the strongest of the species that survive, nor the most intel-ligent, but the one most responsive to change. **Charles Darwin**

Chapter Forty-Six

Beaufort, South Carolina
Sunday, December 11, 1983

My bag is packed and I'm sitting on the bench, at the rise, on the far side of the pool. I am facing the seaside waiting for PGC, Madeline and, if I understood correctly, Annabelle to get ready for the drive to Charleston for their flight to Washington National and mine to Philadelphia.

The sky is still dark, although a red rising sun is starting to appear on the Eastern horizon. I notice a winking light moving across the stars, but I know it is nothing more than an airliner, too high to be heard, bound for some port that at least some perceptive passengers will discover is identical to the place from which they departed. I check my timepiece, it is five o'clock a.m. Our scheduled departure for Charleston is exactly 5:15 a.m.

A magical night had brought forth a procession of capering lost excitements. Albeit somewhat reluctantly. Carole had total discipline of her body and her intellect. She had no discipline of her emotions. She is, therefore out of balance, and balance is a requirement for sanity. Her words meant a sense of longing and loss. Her voice had a clairvoyant quality. Then came the questions and inadequate answers and gradually a new kind of awfulness: the recognition of lost promises and the bitter cost of vows not kept. She imagines herself to be a victim and instead blames another, and not just another but also the world.

Her predictions had been correct. My three o'clock appointment with PGC was cancelled as was our dinner engagement. Carole and I had taken a long walk on the beach, drank three or four bottles of wine and eaten tasty hot hors d'oeuvres served by the waitrons. Afterwards we went to my room, with two more bottles of wine and talked the night away.

Of course she would have satisfied me in any way I requested, but we just kissed, petted some, but mostly I just held her as she told me of her sad state of affairs. She didn't obtain any information about me, and she didn't try. But I sensed how she was extending her emotions because she had needed to talk with somebody for a long time. We exchanged telephone numbers and the evening ended at midnight when she disappeared into the hours of darkness.

With my thoughts running widespread I made my way toward the front of the mansion. I really didn't realize how big it was until I walked around it. When I got forward-facing one of the Rolls Royce's was idling with its lights on.

The trunk was open and I put my suitcase aboard. At the same time Annabelle, Madeline and PGC came out of the house. I had noticed their bags had already been loaded when I put my single piece of luggage in the stem. Madeline sat in the passenger side of the front seat with Annabelle right behind her. I sat behind PGC, who was driving this morning. I had heard the scuttlebutt and stories about his driving. When he was behind the wheel he owned the road.

Once we were out of the gated community PGC started driving like a mad man. It's a two lane road across the bridge from Fripp and all the way to Beaufort. Again it was just two lanes running between the trees lining the road and through small hamlets. There was no traffic since it was so early in the morning and Paul Gordon Charles was cranking his Rolls Royce to a high speed. Madeline sat frozen in the front seat and Annabelle kept eyeing me like I might do something about this maniac. I cringed at every coming intersection as we raced through these small communities I suppose at one hundred miles per hour. Where oh where are the cops?

Obviously, like everything else he did, PGC probably knew their schedules and who to pay off if something went wide of the mark. Then it happened as I figured it would. Somebody pulled out in front of us and PGC had to slam on the brakes to keep from rear-ending them. There was another vehicle coming from the other direction which was going at a good clip as well. Rather than just keeping behind the vehicle in front of us until the on-coming vehicle passed on by, PGC pulls around the slower sedan ahead and pours the cobs to it.

It was a game of chicken. PGC was flooring his car and the oncoming pickup truck was being driven just as hard directly at the Rolls Royce. Madeline pissed herself and told PGC she had as he kept the accelerator mashed to the floor. Annabelle grabbed my hand as it appeared it was going to be a head on collision. I closed my eyes thinking it was end of my time, holding Annabelle's hand as tightly as I could.

Suddenly I feel a G-force pull to the right and a whoosh noise to my left. I opened my eyes and I see what happened. The people in the slow moving sedan, in front of us, had braked and came to a rolling stop, which allowed PGC to pull back into the right lane. The pickup sailed by untouched because PGC had pulled out of his way. He was probably drunk or he certainly would have backed off before the near crash. Or, the driver probably was on a suicide mission.

As we crossed the bridge into Beaufort PGC says, "That was excellent driving. It was safe driving."

No one responds to his preposterous statement. When we ar-rive on the other side Madeline says I not only peed my pants but I crapped them too. We need to stop at a motel so I can get cleaned up. Annabelle says, "I crapped my pants too."

We pulled into a Holiday Inn. PGC told me to rent a room so the women could get disemboweled. It felt so good to get out of that damn car and I couldn't believe what a feeling of lack of restrictions had come over me. What made this asshole revel in tormenting everyone? I mull it all over while renting a room so the women can wipe their asses and shower up.

"We all have a destiny," PGC says, as we stand outside the Roll's while the women are taking care of their glitches.

"But," I say challenging him for the first time ever, "I don't believe we should try making our destiny the destiny of others. That's less than sophistry."

"Jack, I'm still feeling a little under the weather. Do you mind driving us to Charleston?"

What a relief, I'm thinking as he hands me the keys. He sits down in the back seat. When the women come out of the motel Madeline gets into the back seat with PGC and Annabelle sits up front with me.

The trip to the Municipal Airport in Charleston was uneventful. Madeline and PGC slept the whole way while Annabelle kept asking me questions about living in Washington D.C. Her questions helped pass the time. When we arrive Ned Larson meets us at the door. I hadn't seen him since the shooting. He unloaded their bags and I grab mine. His job, I guess, is to bring the Rolls back to Fripp Island. I had a nine o'clock flight so I thanked PGC and said I'll see you tomorrow to Madeline and Annabelle. For posting such a tough exterior Annabelle looked like a scared child when I left for my gate.

Madeline had upgraded me to first class on a non-stop flight on an Eastern Airline's *whisper jet* to Philadelphia. The plane took off on time at nine o'clock. My scheduled arrival time was eleven o'clock in Philadelphia. I had called Ellen from Charleston and she sounded excited to meet me with the boys.

I told her I had a lot to tell her. She said she had a lot to tell me. I hoped her tales were not as peppery as mine. She assured me she doubted it. I told her I really missed her and the boys. She said they missed me too.

Once on that *whisper jet* I ordered a glass of tomato juice and two mini vodka bottles. The first bottle I drank straight down and the second I mixed with the tomato juice. As we winged toward Philadelphia I couldn't believe what had happened the past few days. The most incredulous was the seven mile road trip this morning with PGC. I promised myself I would never get in a transportation genre with him again. He was simply cracked.

"Two more vodkas," I say to a stewardess passing by.

She looked me in the eye, smiles and says, "It's Sunday morning."

I smile back, saying, "I'm going to church when we reach Philadelphia. I gave her a twenty dollar bill for the two vodkas. She said, "I'll be back with the change."

"Keep it," I said.

She said, "I can't."

"Sure you can," I reply. "I won't tell anybody."

The fourth vodka put me in a daydream.

People are always blaming their circumstances for what they are. I don't believe in circumstances. The people who get on in this world are the people who get up and look for the circumstances they want, and, if they can't find them, make them. **George Bernard Shaw**

What Is Past Is Prologue

Concordia College
College football game
Saturday, October 13, 1962

It is a bright, clear, sunny day in Moorhead, Minnesota. We're beating up on the Augsburg *Augies*, 28-0. It's late in the fourth quarter so some of us promising freshman are playing the game out. The colorful autumn leaves are scattered everywhere and bunched up along the sidelines and end zones. I look into the stands and I see my Dad and his brother, Norris, making their way down the bleachers. I have been looking forward to seeing them after the game. I haven't been home since I arrived here in August for the first two weeks of football training. I was feeling kind of homesick.

I haven't been finding football much fun in college. I had been a star fullback in high school, rushing for lots of yards and scoring a bunch of touchdowns. I found my position much different when I arrived here. Everybody was a star and there wasn't much difference in talent between each player's position. I had put on ten pounds during the summer and the extra weight had slowed my speed. Concordia had invested a tidy sum in me so I was moved to the center position on offense and nose guard on defense.

"You played a good game, John." My uncle, Norris, says.

"Thank you for coming. It was a pretty easy game. We really have a lot of good players in our freshman class."

Dad slapped me on my back, saying, "Well, you still have your hands on the ball, John."

I suspected Dad was a little disappointed I wasn't running the ball and scoring touchdowns. There was a lot more glory doing that, but frankly I didn't care. I was playing football now for my education. I had the girl I was going to marry and had no burning desire to impress anybody else. Dad intuitively knew how I felt and simply appreciated me hanging in there for the real purpose of this college business, an education.

We went to Warren's Café in Moorhead for an early supper. We each had a steak and I caught them up on what was going on other than football. As we visited Dad asked me if I wanted to ride home with them so I could see Beth Ann. She was planning to visit and do some ironing while she was there.

I really wanted to see her but I had to be back for practice on Monday afternoon, so there wouldn't be enough time. "I'd love to come but I have an accounting exam Monday and I need to study for it." So, I declined the offer.

We said our goodbyes with me saying I'm really looking forward to Thanksgiving vacation. They dropped me off by my dormitory and I ambled up to my room. When I reached the 7th Floor there were a bunch of people in the hall. Willmar people, I'm thinking. I was told two senior players from their high school were visiting to watch our freshman team play. The two visiting plus the two who lived on my floor were gathered. We had all played against each other in the West Central Conference the past few years.

"Sletten," a carrot head shouts. "What are you doing centering the ball?" he asks. "Hell, you were our All-Conference fullback the past couple of years."

"That's what happens when you go away to college. You are not the best anymore. College ball is a real equalizer." I reply, smiling.

"Hey, you want a ride to Benson. We have room for another. Mike is going back with us." The tall carrot head queries.

They talked me into it and I called home to see if they would pick me up at the Benson train station, which was only twenty some miles from our house. I put a couple of items in my half-full laundry bag and met them in the parking lot outside the dorm.

The tall carrot head was driving a brand new 1962 Oldsmobile Cutlass. He told us his Dad owned the Oldsmobile dealership in

Willmar. So, we started out driving south on U.S. Route 75 to Breckenridge, where we veered off onto Route 9 which would take us through a small town, Doran, then straight ahead to Benson.

It seem that carrot head just kept going faster and faster, barely slowing down when we reached Breckenridge and nearly rolling the car over when he entered onto Route 9. He was scaring the hell out of me. I was sitting directly behind him, which was good, because I couldn't see the speedometer. I saw the lights of Doran coming up on the left where he said he was going to stop for gas and for everybody to be ready to ante up.

I closed my eyes. Suddenly, I heard the screeching of tires followed by sounds of crashing. The radio was still playing Jimmy Clanton singing, *Venue in Blue Jeans* and I was alone in the car. I pushed open the door and looked at the demolished Olds. The only place that hadn't been wiped out was where I had been sitting. I began to panic standing in the middle of the road with car beams shining in my direction. I started vigorously flagging down the approaching lights. As the car slowed I heard Mike shouting, "My brother. Where's my brother?"

"I'm okay," his brother shouted. There was a dead silence as I calculated they both were alive and in opposite ditches.

Two guys, who were dressed like hunters, approached me asking, "What happened?"

I told them I was okay and two of the guys were in the respective ditches. "I don't know about the driver." I said.

Two other cars had arrived now and somebody had called the police in Breckenridge as squad cars started to arrive. Soon enough ambulances and the Minnesota Highway Patrol were present. A patrolman took me into Doran where I could call my parents. My Dad had just arrived home and answered the telephone when I called. He said Mom, Beth and he would get right in the car. I told him to come to the hospital in Breckenridge because the Highway Patrol officer wanted me to get checked for internal injuries.

We all survived. Carrot head was found in a corn field some twenty yards from the automobile. He was all broken up and was hospitalized for nine months. He never played football again.

Mike and his brother spent several weeks in the hospital. I was really sore but I was at football practice on Monday.

What I didn't know then was that this event would be the beginning of a lifetime anxiety. My irrational fear was caused by simply riding with some asshole that was driving a car like a crazed zealot.

Luck is what happens when preparation meets opportunity.
Darrell Royal

Chapter Forty-Seven

Philadelphia, Pennsylvania
Sunday, December 11, 1983

The *whisper jet* touched down in Philadelphia on time. It is so good to be home after such a bizarre trip to a rich man's island off the coast of South Carolina. So much has happened; and so much didn't happen. But every journey has to end and the end of the journey is always called home.

PGC and I didn't even look at last year's budget. Instead he told me who to talk with, including the department heads and to put the numbers together according to their forecasts. When I had the budget completed, *before the end of the year*, we would sit down and review my prognostications.

I was surprised to see Ellen alone at the gate. She raised her eyebrows when she saw me wearing a blue blazer, over a black silk shirt, with tan pants. I waved and gave her an exultant smile. She is a natural beauty, uses little makeup, and doesn't spend forever in front of a mirror. I'm always so happy to see her no matter where we meet. Ellen is so beautiful, charming and witty. She makes the past go away, giving me everything to look forward to.

"So, what haberdashery did you come from?" She asks. "You look maybe mid-thirties, worldly, cheerful, wildly successful in business, confident, and content." Ellen suggests, reaching around my waist while I kiss her on the lips.

"You are a liar, Ellen." I say.

"Well, you are a liar's liar my dear." She retorts;

"Where are the boys," I ask.

"The girl next door is watching them." Ellen replies with a

sort of a naughty grin on her face. She and most women examine things on levels men don't even think about.

Before I could ask why? She tells me, "Because I want to be alone with my husband, for a few hours. Why? Just because I love your boyish charm, your sarcastic wit, you're very annoying habits and your stubborn unforgiving nature and, because I'm never afraid when I'm with you. You have character and guts despite your lies."

Talking with Ellen is where I usually get in trouble and sometimes without even knowing it. So I just respond with a *WOW* as she retreats into a pensive silence as we enter the baggage claim area. Ned Larson purchased me a new-fangled travel bag for my new duds. The portmanteau I'd brought along, he advised me to never be seen with it around PGC again. A bag like it gives him indigestion.

"You have a new valise too." She asks. "Life is not easy without money," she adds.

"You know how it works, *E*." I say, with a lark.

"Do I?" She questions, with a mixture of haughty indifference and a naïve belief she is a member of the victim class. She looks at my brand spanking new loafers, which were made out of some sort of reptilian leather.

I gather the two bags and walked over to where Ellen is standing. "We bring nothing into this world, and it is certain we carry nothing out." She states with that mischievous grin on her face again.

She nods at the doors across from the baggage claim area. When we walk out a limousine driver opens the trunk to his vehicle and takes my suitcases. Ellen's pleasing smile turns to a laugh. We are going for a short stay at the Ben Franklin Hotel in Center City. I gave her a romantic kiss before she suggests we better get into the car.

"What are people going to think, giving each other a sexy kiss?" She asks as I slide across the seat and she follows sitting right next to me. She leans forward, clutching and handing me a Jack Daniel's and club soda. Then, she seizes her gin and tonic and asks the driver to take the scenic route.

"What an unexpected, pleasant surprise." I say to Ellen as we touch glasses.

"God only knows what we'll have to give up paying for it, but we deserve a few hours alone." Ellen says, without a doubt.

"Forget about it," I say, while taking my company Diner's Club out of my inside jacket pocket. I show her the credit card.

"Ellen beams, saying, "That trumps me!"

The limousine had come up South Broad Street to City Hall, it went around City Hall to the Ben Franklin Parkway to the Art Museum. The driver went up a backside way around the museum and perched atop the steps where *Rocky* had made his run. Ellen and I got out of the vehicle and walked over to the top step. We sat down and looked at the City. We held hands. Ellen says, "I'm never going to be helpless again."

The silence between us now was comfortable. I thought about in the end we are all helpless, if you want to get to the hard truth of things. But I didn't want to dispute anything while she was in such a good mood.

"I've got money in the bank and it's my *when-it-falls-apart* money." Ellen whispers, while lighting up a Winston. I light up a Kool 100 and we sit for ten minutes. I'm wondering why there were no tall buildings in Philadelphia. Ellen explains it to me that nothing could be taller than the William Penn statue atop City Hall. She told me that might be changing soon, according to what she was hearing at the CPA firm where she worked.

"Hey," she says, "Let's get to the hotel. We have things to do there before we go home. Right?"

"Right," I agree. The awkwardness would come later when I brought her up to date on the goings-on with the Atlantic States Surety assignment. She couldn't even imagine how bad it was, at least according to me. However, I couldn't speak the truth or my concerns. I could only tell her when I thought this job might end. And that would be a lie. She had the children and one hundred and one more important things to be concerned about. I would just go about my business, secretively.

It's not the having, it's the getting. **Elizabeth Taylor**

Chapter Forty-Eight

1700 K Street
Washington D.C.
Tuesday, December 13, 1983

Ellen and I got home shortly after five o'clock p.m. Sunday. The boys were excited to see us when we got home. Jeanie, the babysitter, had been pestered by each one of them asking how long it would be before we got there. We ordered a pizza and all of us sat around the kitchen table eating and visiting. After I helped Ellen clean up the kitchen the children went upstairs to put their pajamas on with the bribe of popcorn and television for a couple of hours. I loved these family times.

Monday I had a few things to do so I called Mary Robinson and told her I was taking the day off and would be in the office first thing on Tuesday. I'd told her I was renting a U-Haul truck to move a few things from Philadelphia into my new Maryland apartment I'd rented effective December 1st. Joe Neverson was already living there. I had purchased two queen sized beds, one for each bedroom, a sofa and two chairs, and a kitchen set. Ellen had packed up an old set of dishes, pots and pans, towels, sheets other stuff I would have never thought about.

I arrived at my Maryland apartment around 8 p.m. Neverson is sitting on my sofa watching television, eating a chili dog. His presence instantly annoyed me, but I figure I'm just tired and don't want to get into it. I asked him if he could give me a hand and he does. When we were through unloading he follows me to a U-Haul dealer where I drop off the truck. When we get back he helps me put things away and make the beds.

He tells me he is going to New Orleans for the balance of the week and he'll be staying in a nice hotel. He says he'd steal some towels, shampoo, lotion, and the works while he is there. We talk for a couple hours about my trip to Fripp. There is nothing I say that seems to shock or astonish him. Not even the scene on the Yacht Saturday morning. We conclude our talk with Joe warning me to be careful and judicious. That it seems like PGC has something up his sleeve.

"What did you think?" Charlotte Boyer asks, while entering my office like Loretta Young does while sweeping down the stairs in the opening scene of the *Loretta Young* show in the *50's*.

"It's a pretty impressive place, Charlotte. Did you go there often?" I inquire with a pleasing chortle.

"Maybe I did, maybe I didn't. I'll talk to you later, Jack." She gave me a finger wave and she was off.

I had a ton of work to do and hoped I wouldn't be bothered by a lot of nuisance stuff today. But, next Mary Shanahan stood in my doorway. "Mr. Oleson," she says.

Good God, I'm thinking, how could I have forgotten about her. "Mary, how are you doing?" I ask. "Has McKenzie been keeping you busy?"

"Yes, she has but she told me to check with you about what you want me to do today. So here I am." She says, reverently.

"Let's have lunch together at *twelve-thirty*. I can discuss with you where I want you to begin. I really have a lot for you to do. Okay?" I suggest with a coy look. When she walks away she looks so perfectly proportioned.

I check my watch, it is nine o'clock. I'm wondering if PGC and his entourage are coming in today. I decide to wait until 10 a.m. to check with Mary Robinson. I needed to check with Rich Richards to see how he is coming along with the general ledger postings. When I walk into the accounting department everybody is listening to Rich tell a joke. When they see me they turn their heads and go back to work.

"Good morning, everybody," I say. They greeted me back. I told Rich to go ahead and finish his story. Then, I needed to speak with him in my office. He nods and I leave the accounting department kind of shaking my head. Rich, I'm thinking, a wild and crazy guy.

I peer out my office window waiting for Rich to arrive. The sky is an odd orange hue, as if the day could go either way. The morning is turning sour, I'm thinking as Rich Richards walks into my office. When I see him he still has a bigger-than-life quality about him, a star power that draws people to him, makes them want to just touch him. He gives me an engaging smile and slaps me on the back.

"How was the trip, boss?" He asks before I can get out a word.

"It was all bullshit but an interesting trip." I say. "You would've loved it. Let's catch a drink tonight so I can tell you about it. You know, it was bizarre. All of it, the whole thing is so odd."

Rich, always the professional, says, "Okay. We'll have that drink tonight."

"Rich, how are the general ledger postings coming along?"

"Good Jack, I'll be finished today with the operating company. I'll pull a trial balance and we can go over it in late afternoon if you have time."

"Just lay it on my desk when you are finished, then move on to the management company. Good, thank you Rich." I say, with some gusto now that I see things are getting completed.

"Everything okay, Jack? You seem distracted this morning." Asks Rich?"

"I'm fine. I just have a lot going on. We'll talk later, my friend." I reply.

I thought back to being in PGC's office Saturday for that meeting we didn't have. The den was very masculine pervaded with mahogany, brass, leather, a wet bar and a big television. What was he trying to say to me that last day in his lair? He spoke in riddles wrapped inside an enigma. He's a confidence man and a walking parody of the spirit of capitalism. To live in a democracy you have all or nothing at all, he had told me as he panned his office. He had gained it all with the right formality, ritual, and procedure. So were his posers. There were no rings around his collar.

I checked my watch it was ten o'clock. I dialed Jason Simpson to check on the status of the loan closings. When Jason got on the line I asked: "Closing is on Thursday, right?"

"Jack," he queried, while stammering. "Where's my calendar," he mutters as I hear him shuffling paper around on his desk. He yells for his secretary. For the first time today, I laugh while listening to Jason. "Are the Charles'closings scheduled for Thursday?"

The 15th, Joyce says. I know Joyce pretty well now, and she takes care of all Jason's promises. Simpson perhaps was the most scatterbrained, unorganized man I've ever met for having such a responsible position. He was great at selling a deal, but lacked sorely in paperwork assignments. Life is a parade of fools marching to no purpose, or was there a virtuous single-mindedness for Simpson and to just appear like a chump. Or, is he just dumb like a fox?

"Jack does it have to be Thursday the 15th." Jason asks in a flurry.

"He's coming here today just for the closings. We've given you millions of dollars in demand deposits. I promised him the closings would take place on the 15th. I was in Fripp Island with him this past weekend. He's counting on everything being closed Thursday." I say with a real sense of earnestness.

"I know. I know. My boss is an eccentric too. What are we doing?" Jason shouts at Joyce again. "Let's get all this done and the paper work typed, Joyce. Free up Thursday, say closing will be 1 P.M." Jason talks, more calmly now.

I say, "Joyce, *who was on speaker phone with Jason now*, we're closing on the Potomac property, Fripp Island property, the new jet airplane, and the new yacht. I gave all the paperwork to Jason a month ago. I assume he gave it to you. Right, Jason? Because you told me a couple of weeks ago everything was approved."

"It is Jack. Believe me it is." Jason responds assuredly. "Be sure to convey to Gordon we appreciate all the deposits."

Joyce says goodbye telling me everything would be set for Thursday at 1 P.M. Jason took his phone off speaker. "Jack, let me ask you something."

"You said you were with him this past weekend. What's he like?"

"Why do you ask, Jason?" I query.

"I've heard some things." Jason says.

I thought a moment and then said. "You know there is nothing funnier than disproportionate and overwrought anger. You know, when someone really fucking loses their cool and completely explodes over something small. That's PGC. It's his way or the highway."

"One o'clock, Thursday, Jack. And, thanks." Jason says anxiously.

I'm beginning to feel like I've worked for and known PGC for twenty years. I'm constantly explaining him to bankers and others what he is all about. He was so close but yet so far away. He had an aura of limitless potential, he projected America incarnate, and his darkness was concealed by a sunny, coltish smile and a euphonious name. His aura had an aura. His aspiration is neither voyeuristic nor wide-ranging. But, what really matters to him are his calibrations of clout.

I check my watch. It is eleven o'clock. I walk out of my office to check with Mary Robinson about PGC's arrival. She tells me she hasn't heard a word. I ask her to tell Madeline Haycock, if she calls, the closings are for Thursday at 1 P.M.

Mary smiles at me saying, "You've had a busy morning, Jack."

"Actually," Mary says, "I don't think he'll be here until tomorrow. That's what Charlotte Boyer told me."

"Tomorrow would be better." I say, walking across the room toward the Claims department. I thought I should check with Maggie about pending claims and find out how Rich Richards and she are doing living together.

Maggie was yacking on the telephone about a claim when I arrived at her desk. She made the yack-yack motion into the mouthpiece of her phone and then quickly cut the caller off by saying she would check it out.

"The traveler returns," she says to me, smiling.

"How is the claims situation, I feel like I've been gone for six months." I inquire.

"Not much changes in a few days, Jack. Joe, I guess you saw him last night, is flying to New Orleans this morning to negotiate that mess Charley Rivers got us involved with." She says leaning back in her chair.

"Refresh my memory, Maggie." I ask.

"Charley used his powers to issue a performance bond and took a forty thousand dollar cash premium, say two years ago. The builder has now defaulted on the job and is looking for us to ante up." She follows my question with her answer.

"So, what's the problem?" I ask, knowing full well it will be all about some uncommon transaction that doesn't make any sense.

Maggie says, "Charley stole the premium money. He used his powers but there never was a bond issued. Of course the builder can't prove he ever paid a premium, and Joe will try to negotiate something with the builder's lawyer."

"Christ," I say. "Does PGC know about this problem?"

"Are you kidding," the deal was probably his idea. I'm sure he received two-thirds of the forty, Charley took ten and you bought him a new Cadillac. Am I right?" Maggie questions me.

"And the Cadillac is sitting in my driveway in Pennsylvania. Swell," I said disgustedly.

Maggie is giving me that sneaky grin of hers when I ask. "Where is Charley?"

"Oh, you won't see Charley again." Maggie says, lighting up a cigarette and crossing her legs.

"You know I keep hearing that I won't see somebody again. It happened twice this weekend by two different people. What's goes on here, Maggie?"

She throws me a curve ball by asking about my weekend in South Carolina. I throw her a knuckleball back by asking her how Rich Richards and she are getting along. "I'm meeting him for drinks after Happy Hour." I said.

"I know," she says with a wily tone in her voice.

"Let's have lunch at Archibald's," Maggie suggests.

"I'm taking Mary Shanahan to lunch today." I respond.

"Oh, you are? Are you? Are you going to Archibald's? She laughs, guilefully, saying, "she'll like a big set of tits dancing in front of her face while eating a cheeseburger."

"Shrewd Maggie, you are very sly." She had me laughing now. "So, why don't you join Rich and I at the Library Lounge tonight." I ask, in a scheming way.

"Clever," Maggie says. "You are very clever, Jack, indeed. I'll see if I can make it."

I leave Claims laughing about taking Mary Shanahan to Archibald's for lunch. I check my watch it is11:45 A.M. I stop at Mary Robinson's desk thinking about the truth that remains so elusive.

"No word," Mr. Oleson.

"Mary for all the information you keep track of for me, well, I'm going to take you to dinner."

Mary smiles at me and bats her eyes. "Mr. Oleson do not make promises to a lady unless you plan to keep them." I stopped in my tracks, saying, "I mean what I say. Would you like to have dinner with me next week? Say, next Tuesday evening."

Mary smiles again. "I'll check my schedule and confirm tomorrow."

"Good." I say, walking back into my office and closing the door behind me.

The way to develop self-confidence is to do the thing you fear.
William Jennings Bryan

Chapter Forty-Nine

1700 K Street
Washington D.C.
Tuesday, December 13, 1983

When Mary Shanahan knocked at my office door, I checked my watch, it is 12:29 p.m.

"Come in," I call out, softly.

God, she is pretty just standing there. Her proximity and her literal and figurative presence is causing me some conflict.

"Ready for lunch," I ask, getting up from my desk and putting on my suit coat.

"Let's go to the Mayflower. They have a nice lunch. We'll take a cab."

"Am I dressed enough?" She asks.

"You're perfect." I say, with a smile.

We stop at Mary Robinson's desk and I tell her we will be gone for about an hour. Upon request the Bureau made the arrangements for me. I love the irony of going there. It would be the last place anybody would look for me. I'd been told J. Edgar Hoover used to go there nearly every day for lunch. It was he who said the best place to hide is right under their noses.

"The Mayflower," I say. "Eleven-twenty-seven Connecticut Avenue Northwest," I add as I let Mary slide in ahead of me. You learn fast to tell a cab driver where you want to go and then follow with an address in Washington D.C. or any large Eastern city. If you don't they spin you around the block a few times in the name of one-way streets.

The hotel is close to Cathedral of St. Matthew the Apostle and the National Geographic Society, as well as the White House and Ford's Theater. I point these places out to Mary as we pass by. She is impressed and I can tell she has probably never been here before.

When we entered the lobby of the Mayflower, with all its glass and marbles, Mary Shanahan eyes were all over the place. When we approach the maître d' station Mary is still looking around at the beauty of the insides of the hotel. Once again the Bureau didn't let the old team down. My reservation was there along with a plain white envelope addressed to Jack Oleson.

As we were ushered to our table we walked by a lot of expensive suits, ties and dresses. In the center of the rather large restaurant is an impressive four-point salad bar. It is surrounded by tables and chairs, mostly set for four but others for two. Our table is set in the back, in a very private location. I have never sensed I belong in these kinds of places, but I adjust well and do not like going to a greasy spoon any longer. So, I intuitively knew how Mary must be feeling. Dumbfounded, perhaps, is the most accurate emotion.

"Who are all these people, Mr. Oleson." Mary asks. "They seem to just appear from nowhere."

"Well, I'll tell you, Mary, but you have to stop addressing me as Mr. Oleson. Just call me Jack. Okay. Look straight ahead. There is Senator Lowell Weikert and Senator Ted Kennedy. We could go around the room and spot many celebrities and politicians but that would be tacky. You have to pretend you don't see them, if you want to be *cool*."

"Jack," she said reticently. "I can't believe I'm sitting here with all these people. This is the most exciting thing I've ever done."

She was beside herself when our waiter approached the table. He said, "May I get you something from the bar." He looked at Mary, with his pen ready to write. She didn't know what to say so I said. "Give the lady a glass of Chardonnay and I'll have a Merlot."

"I really don't know what you ordered, but I'm sure I'll enjoy it." Ten minutes later he was back with the wines and glasses of ice water. "Are you having salad and soup for appetizers," he asks. I nod in the affirmative. "Any time you're ready. Help yourself."

I walk Mary to the salad bar and she doesn't really know what to do there, either.

"Just do what I do, Mary." We made our way through the salad bar line and returned to our seats. I noticed her watching me to the extent of what forks and spoons I was using for the salad and soup. I was told to do the same after I first started way back when. *Just do what I do.*

She seemed to like the wine. I think it took the edge off. While we ate and drank we discussed what she would be doing starting when we got back to the office this afternoon. My first priority was the budget. I told her she would be setting up the work papers and entering last year's balances. In addition, she would be taking care of all C&B Leasing records. And coming up soon we would be opening a restaurant in Chevy Chase, Maryland. That she would also be keeping its books. Once again she seemed overwhelmed but I could tell she excited about and up for the challenge.

When the waiter came back for our lunch order, I said, "I'll order for the lady." The waiter directed his attention towards me. "She'll have the Chili Dog with extra mustard."

He gulped and then replied, "Sir, I don't believe we have that on our menu today."

"Oh shucks," I said. Then the waiter cracked up. "No one's ever had the guts to ask for a Chili Dog since I've been working here." Then, he composed himself.

"We'll have the petite filets. One of them cooked medium and the other medium well."

Mary said, "I didn't quite get that. Why was he laughing so hard? Don't they sell Chili Dogs here?"

"You are such a breath of fresh air, Mary. Always just be yourself." I encourage her, popping the up end of my spoon, sending it end over end into the middle of a woman's soup bowl at the next table. It's the old element of surprise. Fun stuff exercised to simply piss somebody off.

We enjoyed our steaks and passed on the desert menu. I told Mary not to tell anyone where we had lunch today, assuring her nobody would understand. When working for me I alone need to know where and what we are doing. So, if anyone asks you where we had lunch just say the *Library*. Okay.

While we rode in the cab she asked me if anybody would believe she had lunch in the library. "Yes," I assure her. "Just listen and do what I say. You'll know about the *library* soon enough."

I check my watch as we wait for the elevator. It is 2:20 p.m. When the elevator door opens there stands Ned Larson.

"Hi, Jack." He says, motioning me in. I introduce him to Mary Shanahan, and he is cordial as usual.

"Is he here?" I ask.

"Nope, he won't be until Thursday. Madeline called to talk with you, but she got your message the closings would be one o'clock on Thursday. He congratulated me for finding you." Ned says, with a smile. "Good job, Jack!"

"Ned, we have a lot to discuss, but I have to get Mary working on the budget. I'll see you at Happy Hour. Are you going to make it?" I ask with an, *it would be a good idea tone.*

"I'll be there," Ned pledges to me. Good God, I thought, he seems to have lost his way. He's acting like his supreme commander, PGC.

Mary and I get off the elevator and make our way toward my office.

"Hello, you two." Mary Robinson greets us. "Nice lunch?"

I give Mary a thumb's up as we pass by. She gives me her crafty grin.

I usher Mary Shanahan into my office and tell her she will be working at my partner's desk, directly across from me. They had moved the new desk into my office when I was in South Carolina. I showed her how it worked and that her new high back chair was to be delivered today.

She asks, "Jack," again reticently, "why are you being so good to me?"

"If you listen and learn and don't question me, I'll see to it you make more money than you ever dreamed about in your wildest imagination. More importantly what you learn while working for me will make you successful the rest of your life. There are no strings attached, Mary. Hard work and watch my back side, like I'll watch yours. There are going to be a lot of people very jealous of you. There are going to be people accusing us of having an affair, only because of your quick assent to the management team. It will be a transformative experience."

"Mary Shanahan you wanted a challenge. You've got it. Why am I being so good to you, because I see in you what others saw in me fifteen years bygone? I, too, grew up in a small town America in Minnesota. It's about the same size as Gettysburg, Pennsylvania. The best athletes, the best students and the best people hail from these kinds of places. Frankly, my dear, I believe in you. You are the one I've chosen to help me with all that is going on here. Okay?" I say.

"I'll do my best," she replies, with a tear seeping from her right eye.

"Your best is all I ask. Remember I'll be sitting directly across from you so you'll have an advantage most don't have. I'll answer every question as they come up."

I push my chair around to her side of the desk. I reach into my left drawer and pull out last year's budget, which is an extensive set of work papers. I set them on her side of the partner's desk. Then I hand her a full thirteen column pad, saying, "Set up the same sheets we used last year. Just copy the headings. Then we'll go to work. Do you understand what to do?"

I could see the wheels spinning in her head. Then, she nods in the affirmative. "Okay," I caution her. "Don't ever say you understand if you don't." I smiled at her so she didn't think I was reprimanding her.

Just then the office door opens and her chair is rolled into the office. I had her push mine back to my spot and I pushed hers to her sector.

"I'll be around. It's the way it is here for me. Mary Robinson always knows where to find me, if you need me. Oh, do you have a boyfriend?" I ask.

"Why do you ask?" She probes, showing a little tone of dynamism.

"I don't want you to commit to something, if you cannot do the time." I alert her. "This is not a forty-hour-a-week job. It's an opportunity."

"He goes to Yale. He's a sophomore, a younger fellow. I never see him so I think he might be sowing his wild oats. I don't know what we have together. He writes once in a while." She tells me.

"Thanks for sharing," I say, with a staid tone. "Good luck, Mary. I'm counting on you!"

"Oh," I stop and say before I leave the office. "I want to introduce you at Happy Hour tonight. It's at five o'clock. I'll pick you up. See you soon."

The mind is the most powerful aphrodisiac. I take the elevator to the street, thinking about what an asshole I am. I start walking slowly down K Street in the direction of G. En route I pull the envelope I received, at the Mayflower, out of my vest pocket. I read it; it's in code: M W 1 E R b x it translates: *meet ... Wednesday... 1 o'clock ... ellipse ... report ... briefcase exchange.* This was different. I usually received my instructions in the want ads of the Washington Post.

When I arrive at G Street I go into the office supply store. I bought a 13 column pad. On the way back I stop at Archibald's, drink two beers and returned to the office. When I enter the elevator, I check my watch. It is a quarter to four.

I'm an optimist. It doesn't seem too much use in being anything else.
Winston Churchill

Chapter Fifty

1700 K Street
Washington D.C.
Tuesday, December 13, 1983

I returned to my office about 4:45 p.m. Shanahan was busy setting up work papers and she grins when I plop down in my office chair, looking directly at her.

"Has anybody been looking for me?" I ask.

She took out a yellow legal pad where she had made some notes. "There was a Charlotte Boyer, a tall pretty woman stopped by twice. During her first visit she kept staring at me and asked me a bunch of questions. I answered some of them, but most of the time she just interrupted my responses with other questions. The second time she told me to be careful, because you are a hot item. *Honey you don't want to get burned*, I think she said. She told me to tell you she would see you tonight."

Mary shrugs her shoulders. "Who is she?"

"Basically it's a long story, which I will tell you all about on another day. But, one word says all regarding Charlotte Boyer. *Crazy!*"

"And, Ted Masters came by. He said you were looking for him. What does he do? He's very dapper and nice." Mary asks.

"Ted is our general counsel. We'll probably catch up with him during Happy Hour. Why don't you wrap up here and we'll head out." I suggest, while making a mental check list of things to do.

"I'm not connecting the dots here, but I'm sure once I get the people straight everything will start making sense." Shanahan says, saying she's ready.

I couldn't help but notice when she bent over to get her purse that she has a curvy ass with slender, shapely legs. I estimated her at five feet two, one hundred ten pounds, petite, with a nice chest, accentuated by a skin tight sweater. She has a cute face, big green eyes, high cheekbones, a wholesome pretty girl.

"So, Jack, where's Happy Hour?" Shanahan asks, seemingly enthusiastic and excited.

"Just down the hall," I answer. "It happens every day from five o'clock until six. Sometimes it goes until seven, but it's rare. It's an opportunity to catch up with each other and find out what's going on. It's a good thing, but it is restricted to office heads and certain key assistants."

When we neared the crowd the noise of laughter and talking went up decibels. I don't know if Mary was nervous or not but she reached out her left hand and grabbed my right hand. Realizing what she had done she apologized quickly and she pulled her palm down to her side.

"Jack," Richard Corrigan greets, loudly. "And this must be your new assistant, Mary Shanahan. This is Matt Ferrone, Risk Management. Mary smiled at each of them as she shook their hands. Matt extended his hand toward me and I toward him. Corrigan slapped me on the back, saying, "Good to have you back. I hear through the rumor mill your trip went well."

"Yes, it did. Gordon has a fabulous place down there." I reply. "I don't know how he keeps up with it all."

"Jack, he's somewhat eccentric but he's a brilliant man. He makes things happen. Hey, get you and that young lady a drink. We'll talk later."

"Mary, stay close by tonight. I don't want you to get trapped into a conversation with some of these people who are always up to no good. Like this one, who you've already met, Charlotte Boyer."

"Jack, where have you been hiding out all day? I hear you were quite a hit down in South Carolina this past weekend. I mean kind of a big shot, huh?" She says on the sly.

"You must have been visiting with Ned Larson today, huh?" I say to divert her. "Well, if you will excuse us, I understand you've met Mary, we're going to have a drink."

"Tootles, Jack," she says, with her feminine finger surf.

Mary looks at me with raised eyebrows. "You don't like her very much, do you Jack."

"Trust is the word; do not talk with her, other than yes – no answers. She's very smart and knows the game better than most."

"What game," asks Mary?

"The games of *Deceit*, dishonesty, treachery, trickery, sham, pretense, cheating, duplicity the works. Don't worry. You'll learn about what goes on here as you go along. Just keep your ears and eyes open and trust no one." I say forcefully.

"Don't trust you, Jack." She says quietly.

"Oh, you can trust me. I'm the guy with the white hat." I laugh and so does she as Ted Masters joins us.

Ted looks forlorn as always. He seems so stressed out and it's like he is ready to blow. I discuss with him mainly two situations. He will have to read over the loan documents tomorrow for the loan closings on Thursday. He needs to be at the closings Thursday in case PGC has any questions. And, we have to give PGC an update on how the liquor license is coming along. Now Theodore Rex Masters looks even more frazzled.

Ted's problem is he's a straight shooter. I'm sure what's running through his mind is he is never investigating anything that has to do with the insurance company. It's always about PGC and his personal stuff. He was a career professor, at the University of Virginia in Charlottesville, a quiet academic life with many friends, and an opportunity to enrich the lives of students. His family was settled in the beautiful, quaint little historic setting. What was so perfect to him was a living hell for his wife. So, he took a job with the Virginia Insurance Commission and then onto Atlantic States Surety. It is the dark nautilus of her heart. His wife's heart, who wants the good times that only big money can bring.

"I'll take you downstairs in the morning to introduce you to Jason and his assistant, Joyce. Having those closings go off without a hitch is priority number one for PGC." I told Ted when Mary came back with our drinks.

"Good. Maybe Friday I can get with you to finish the paper

work for the liquor license." Ted says while looking up and seeing Charlotte Boyer heading in our direction.

"How's it going with her?" I ask.

"So ... so ... so, eh ... " He says, while doing the wave with his hands.

I saw Ned Larson talking with Richard Corrigan. Just as Charlotte arrives I nod in Ned's direction. We walk to the bar, where I refilled my drink. Mary is still working on her glass of wine. The crowd has thinned and we just stand there and talk waiting for Ned to get away from Corrigan.

Mary reminded me of the beauty of innocence, humility, and gentleness. But everybody needs to make money. And in the end all things work out for the best, hard as that is to believe. Because miracles happen that nobody sees, and among us walk heroes who are never recognized, and people live in loneliness because they cannot believe they are loved.

Ned Larson cut in on my contemplations, while Mary is refilling my drink. "When did you get back," I ask.

"Last night." He says.

"What happened down there, Ned?" I ask, carefully, and in a whisper.

"Unforeseen problems had to be resolved. Nothing you have to concern yourself with." Larson says.

"Are you okay?" I ask.

"Jack, I'm not made for this work, I nonetheless have fallen to it as naturally as an acorn falls from a branch. No lessor man could have been as successful at this job and I do not believe that any man exists who is my equal at it. But it goes against everything I stand for and this way goes against my Catholic religion. I can see in the mirror my own vulnerability. It's a cacophony of self-dismantling."

Mary handed me another drink, while I noticed she'd refreshed hers. I smiled at her and she grinned back. I saw Maggie Little coming our way and I motioned her over. I properly introduced her to Mary and said, "Ned and I have a couple things we need to finish up. Maggie can you keep Mary company for a few minutes."

Ned told me his wife, Brenda, wanted a divorce. He kept his head down, as if in thought. Fate plays with loaded dice and a wise man expects the unexpected. Appearances are not reality, but they can be a convincing alternative to it. You can control appearances most of the time, but facts are what they are. Appearances are the currency of my profession.

Ned Larson was burning like pitch in perdition, when Rich Richards appears. He had been talking with Corrigan, who Rich said, was trying to talk him into selling bonds. *Leave the accounting to Oleson, Rich.*

Ned Larson excused himself, saying he'd talk to me tomorrow. I told Rich, that sales has always been his game. "Go ahead, Rich, you might be able to watch my back on the street better than from behind a desk in the accounting department."

"Thanks Jack. I finished your general ledger postings. I never want to post general ledger again and I never will post general ledger again. No sir! No sir! I will not post general ledger again."

"Let's take the girls to dinner, Rich." I suggest. "But go tell Corrigan first."

I stepped over to where Maggie and Mary were laughing. "Would you two ladies like to join Rich and I for dinner?" They looked at each other. "I don't know about Mary, but I'm going." Maggie says.

"Me too," says Mary Shanahan. "I don't know how I'm going to get home, though."

"We'll get you home, honey," Maggie assures her.

Just happened doesn't just happen, sometimes it does. There is such a thing as good luck.

Borrow trouble for yourself, if that is your nature, but don't lend it to your neighbors. **Rudyard Kipling**

What Is Past Is Prologue

Clarkfield's Lutheran Church
Wedding Day
Clarkfield, Minnesota
Saturday, February 1, 1964

Life pivots on the smallest hinge of time. I was about to walk out of the life I knew so well and was in search for a new life that I could not know and I might come desperately to regret. But Beth Ann Harper's unflappable calm continues to intrigue me. She has psychokinetic magic, a power of mind over matter. This is what I'd been telling my friends when they'd ask why I had abandoned my circle of friends for this gal. On the morning of our Wedding Day my world seemed kind of upside down.

Sometimes I saw the world as hopeless, but she believed it did not have to remain that way. She had an annoyingly hopeful heart. But, for all the beauty and joy of life, I insist the world is nonetheless a war zone. I realize my analysis is a cold equation, especially on our Wedding Day.

I can love February in January. February doesn't care. But, can I love March in April? Maybe April will care. I wonder can we, Beth Ann and I, love each other twelve months of the year until *death do us part.* My head says no, my heart says maybe, and my dick is saying yes. Dick wins every time.

We have a beautiful wedding on a very cold winter evening; a wind chill of 29 below zero is raging and blowing snow from its drifts through the hamlet. In the church I stand proudly at the alter waiting patiently for Mr. Harper to walk his daughter down the aisle to give me her hand.

Beth looks so beautiful in her pure white dress and veil. I had never really noticed how small her waist is as her gown is pulled tight around her curvilinear physique. She looks like a *Sparkle Plenty doll* and I am so full of pride.

Several of my friends from high school and college are here, which is important to me. Most of her friends from high school are present along with family, relatives and friends whom make up more than 300 people.

We say our vows, *until death do us part*. And, then, walk the walk and talk the talk with our guests.

After a tasty pot luck dinner in the basement of the church, we cut the cake; shield ourselves from raring-to-go invitees throwing rice, which is difficult to discriminate from the blowing snow. It is so cold but our 1955 Chevrolet starts right up like it always does. But when I put the car in reverse, it doesn't move. I put it in drive, it doesn't move. That's when I see my high school buddies standing at the curb laughing.

They had physically lifted the car off the ground and suspended the axel off the pavement. They picked up the car again and removed the block. It was a good and harmless trick which made me laugh for miles afterwards. Beth and I were finally off into our new life, with ten dollars in our pocket. I am a sophomore in college, nineteen years old. She works in a bank, she is eighteen. We were way too young to be married, but we were certain we loved each other and no one was going to tell us differently.

If we could turn back the clock, we wouldn't have done anything different on our Wedding Day. We both felt our share of luck had come to us early and today culminated the greatest thing that ever happened to us. The good times ahead would be even better than the old. What could possibly go wrong, with such a perfect union? Absolutely nothing, right? I was the guy who always put two and two together. Right?

I always thrive on purpose. I thrive on commitment. But, in actuality, I didn't want to live a life of repetitive work, innocent pleasures, and with as little reflection as I could manage. I had things I wanted to do. I truly believed our marriage could stand up to the assay. And if it couldn't, well, maybe Longfellow was right when he summed it all up: *Let the dead past bury its dead.*

Worry a little bit every day and in a lifetime you will lose a couple of years. If something is wrong, fix it if you can. But train yourself not to worry. Worry never fixes anything. **Mary Hemingway**

Chapter Fifty-One

1700 K Street
Washington D.C.
Friday, December 23, 1983

I t's December the 23ʳᵈ are the opening lyrics from Irving Berlin's
White Christmas, I'm thinking, as I write the date on a check
I'm going to send for January's rent on my Maryland apartment.
There's nothing like starting off a new year with the rent on time.
I paste a stamp on the envelope and continue to get ready for an
early leave-taking Christmas departure.

The past ten days I'd really been involved with the accounting
department getting the numbers organized for the up-coming audit. The best crusade so far had been the hiring of Mary Shanahan.
She is intelligent, loyal, and seems to comprehend and understand
what I am trying to accomplish. Additionally she is taking excellent care of C&B Leasing's operations.

Rich Richards is doing well in sales and I'm happy I don't have
to deal with him on a day to day basis. His living conditions are
working out well, so far, according to Maggie. She told me he is
very attentive and good with her boys. Also, with concern in her
voice, she told me he never stops drinking. He never gets notice-
ably drunk or nasty, but most of the time just passes out around
nine o'clock and sleeps on the sofa.

Joe Neverson is spending most of his time in Louisiana putting huge claims on the back burners. When he came home last
weekend he brought some really nice towels, bath robes and
other hotel paraphernalia he had stolen from the hotel. Joe just
likes stealing stuff. He gets a real kick out of it, whether he needs
the trappings or not. He's been telling me he's been looking for

Charley Rivers, but he seems to have vanished without a trace.

Charley returned the Cadillac I'd bought for him; it was sitting in my driveway in Pennsylvania. *You won't see Charley no more!* Neverson knows what happened to Charley and I suspect he wants me to push him, but I do not want to get involved in that one. And this phrase you won't see so and so no more is becoming an often heard idiom I'm hearing lately. I should have asked somebody the one word question, *Why?* But I don't. There are all kinds of shit going on here, but I'm just concentrating on the accounting. The interpretation of the numbers is what always brings these cases close at hand.

As I study the results of the bookkeeping I know I can bring this case to closure sooner than I might want. Actually, I am enjoying the action. The position gives me a lot of power and I enjoy having so many people counting on me. I'm almost putting behind me why I am here in the first place. And, I really don't care. I guess it is my last hurrah? And, I am making an exciting amount of money with plenty of perks.

Joe Neverson has been talking to me about Christmas. He wants to spend it with his children, but not necessarily his wife, Linda. I suggest he and his family join us for Christmas in Pennsylvania. He thought about it for a moment and told me he'd ask his wife. I'd met her once. She is petite with a cute face and big blue eyes. She looks Midwest wholesome, but Joe warned me she was a complete bitch. A real viper! *So, they all bitch.* What's that have to do with Christmas?

Joe nods his head and smiles. *For some reason, my wife still loves me,* so he didn't think she would object to being with us. Our children were all the same age. We each had three. My invitation seemed like a great adventure for the children and alternative for him and his wife.

Joe had been traveling, riding in airplanes and working weekends the past two Saturdays and Sundays. He did not feel rested at all. His mood was gloomy, even foul. Before my invite, he thought the coming holidays would be a chaotic mess, a frenzy of events, some which were anticipated and others wholly unexpected. He would feel like a visitor in his own home.

The clock had not stopped. It was still ticking, louder and louder. Joe had spent all his money, burned every bridge, alienated almost every friend, and driven himself to the point of exhaustion. He had blown the trumpet for so long that no one heard it anymore.

With his duties defined, tasks distributed, responsibilities clarified, he tried to appear upbeat, hopeful, confident that a miracle was on the way. But he knew better. And, there wasn't much to fight over, at least not in assets. They were all gone. He told me it's late in the fourth quarter and the game is almost over. He told me this morning his family would be at our place mid-day Christmas Eve.

As I'm loading up my briefcase Mary Shanahan asks me what time I'm leaving. I told her now. It was strange when I saw tears in her eyes.

"What's wrong," I ask.

"I'm going to miss you." Shanahan says.

"I'm going to miss you to," I say back, reaching into my attaché and pulling out a Christmas card for her. It is simply a card with two tickets in the fold to the Kennedy Center; *Woman of the Year* is playing, starring Lauren *Bacall*.

"It's Saturday, January 28th," she says.

"Take your boyfriend, or if he can't make it we'll go together." I suggest.

Shanahan gives me a hug and apologizes for being so emotional. I caress her cheek as she moves her mouth toward mine. I give her light contact on the lips, and exit my office.

Mary Robinson is sitting at her desk. When she sees me, she smiles.

"I keep wondering what goes on behind those closed doors, Mr. Oleson." She asks.

"Nothing but work, work, work, work," I tell her.

"Huh, huh," She says, "I got you covered."

I hand her a card with fifty dollars in it and wish her a Merry Christmas. She smiles and thanks me again for taking her to dinner last week. We did have a nice time. I learned a lot about her and, of course, she learned nothing about me. But that's the way it works with a guy like me.

"Take care of that family, Jack. And, all of you have a Merry Christmas. See you next Monday."

As I wait for the elevator I think about what President John Kennedy once said about problems. *When written in Chinese, the word crisis is composed of two characters. One represents danger, and the other represents opportunity.*

1984? It could be dangerous or opportunistic. Or, maybe it will be both? Successful danger usually breeds opportunity.

Keep your fears to yourself, but share your courage with others.
Robert Louis Stevenson

Chapter Fifty-Two

1700 K Street
Washington D.C.
Monday, January 16, 1984

A pall of gloom seems to be hanging over the office when I arrive at 9 p.m.; it seems everyone has already heard the bad news. Tom Harvey, a senior Board of Director's member had been killed in a plane crash Saturday morning.

I hand greeted Mary Robinson, who was fielding telephone calls, and went into my office. Shanahan was busy working on her side of the partner's desk when I entered. She smiled at me while I sat down on my side. Mary was busy writing checks out for C&B Leasing.

I checked my calendar confirming the auditors would be starting today. I had made arrangements for them to start working in the conference room. They were scheduled to arrive at eleven o'clock. I was ready for them, but I couldn't get Tom Harvey off my mind. Alcohol helps when I'm depressed, and a fifth of Jack Daniels was in my bottom drawer. It was a gift from Shanahan when I returned from Christmas. So, I thought about filling a jigger, but no, it was too early. And, what would Mary think? And, I didn't need another bad habit.

I felt terribly guilty because the threatening signs had been there. I thought he was a dead man in South Carolina, when Ned said Tom might be thrown overboard. All the sarcastic remarks made about his complaining and whining when perquisites weren't coming fast enough, he was peeving the higher ups. They were plainly disgusted with him. Corrigan had indicated on several occasions PGC was tired of Harvey's insatiability. Gee, I wonder where he acquired those dearth neediness skills. But, caveat cryptograms were usually more bullshit than reality.

"*Here's looking at you kid*," I say to Mary Shanahan, breaking my daydream.

"*Casablanca*," she answers. I'm amusing myself with a little trivia game I play with her every day.

"Hey, how did you know that one?" I ask, amazed with her answer.

"I have nearly twenty years to catch up on." She says. "I'm working on it."

I take my leather bound notebook and Mont Blanc pen from my left hand desk drawer and started making notes for my upcoming meeting with the auditors. I make an outline: 1) valuation of insurance company assets; 2) liabilities and policyholders' surplus; 3) insurance companies revenues and expenses; 4) insurance company financial analysis and solvency surveillance; 5) the annual statement and general interrogatories.

A half an hour passes with both of us diligently working in quietness. Shanahan breaks the silence by asking, "Did you know Tom Harvey well, Jack?"

I lean back in my chair and peer out the window with a feeling of an unaccustomed sense of anxiety, though not fear. This was going to be messy, but not dangerous. Whereas I should be confused, devastated, furious, and frightened beyond reason, I wasn't. My heart had been hardened by the observation of the many rumors and resulting actions of crimes moreover salacious to leave alone.

This was a rascally bunch of hard-drinking, hell-raising people that did diligent and professional work. I wonder if fatalism is simply an inheritance. Everything is so close and yet so far away. My mind had drifted again. Back to reality, I say.

"I didn't know him well. He and his girlfriend, Angel, were at Fripp Island when I was there in December. He seemed to always be around and was an active board member. No, I didn't know him well." I reply.

The intercom buzzes. Shanahan answers, listens and put the phone on hold, whispering, "It's Madeline Haycock."

"Debauchery, Jack," she shouts into the phone. "The Washington Post, the Federal Aviation Commission, Tom's lawyers, insurance companies ... everybody is fucking calling. I'm forwarding the calls to you. The plane was owned by C&B Leasing, I'm told. Right?

"PGC says, *get rid of them.*" She hangs up.

I check my watch; it is 10:45A.M. Shanahan looks me directly in the eye. I shake my head, saying, "It's time for the auditors."

Matthew Wilson is a tall, lanky and resolutely thin man. He is wearing a three piece pinstripe suit and a slightly dusty pair of black wing tip shoes. His insecurity is palpable. He seems frazzled with his assignment at hand, probably because he'd done the job last year and I'm sure there were things he overlooked or ignored that were now playing back in his mind. He seems more fragile then I remember. Perhaps his feelings run deep and any type of failure makes him cantankerous. He shakes my hand, weakly, and forces a smile.

Next he introduces the second guy on the audit team, Bernard Goodman. Everything about Bernard is round. He seems to be made of a series of balls piled one atop the other. His buttery cheeks and jowls seem to rest, without benefit of a neck, upon the two balls of fat that comprise his chest, which in turn rest upon a grate swollen paunch. His arms and legs, which look too short, appear to be made of spherical parts. Yet he seems proud of his entire physique, his massive neck, his broad shoulders, his prodigious forearms (to short or not). His back is like a Jersey bull. "Jack," he says, while extending his right hand and putting me in one of those bone crunching handshakes. "I'm very pleased to meet you."

Bernard Goodman then introduces the third member of the audit team. She is a sexy little number, donning a pair of brainy spectacles. She has soft skin, a great mane of light brown hair, big sensual lips, and a chest she makes sure you see. "I'm Emily Harding. It is nice to meet you, Mr. Oleson. I'm looking forward to working with you." She's wearing a brown skirt a good two inches above the knees, revealing her legs, and emphasizing her tiny waist. She is wearing a white ruffled blouse; open down to the top of her breasts. The swollen curve of her hips, her creamy flan breasts, her shimmering shanks, so insouciantly crosses when she sits down. I like her and she loves the attention she is receiving.

"The fourth member of our team will be with us tomorrow. He's finishing a job in White Oak." Matthew Wilson announces like he was making a great addition to our conversation. When there is no one else to introduce or absorb I suggest we move into the conference room where there will be plenty of room to work. "This is magnificent," Bernard Goodman say, upon entering.

"It is," I reply. "No briefcases on the table. PGC would have a fit if the wood gets scratched. Make me a list of what you need, and I'll make all journals, ledgers and documents available to you upon request. First, let me show you the location of the coffee chamber and the rest rooms."

The race is on when I give them the general ledger and all the related journals for the operating company, Atlantic States Surety Company. I give them the bank reconciliations and bank statements for all accounts. "What else?" I ask.

"We have enough for now," Matthew Wilson regurgitates.

It is 12:30 p.m. when the auditors were off to lunch. As I watch them exit through the main entrance my eyes are tracking Emily Harding. I don't think I'm in trouble, I know I'm in trouble. I was thinking as she disappears into the elevator. It was guilt on top of guilt. But, if you're already in trouble, and you haven't done anything, then you might as well do it.

Matthew Wilson couldn't be budged, unless it was money. But, it would take lots of money. I expected Bernard Goodman could be contrived, if there was money and his ego was massaged. Emily Harding? I could get to her. She was full of herself. And, all women like money.

"Okay!" I say out loud. Mary Robinson has been watching me cogitate and leer at auditor number three..

Mary is shaking her head as she hands me a stack of messages. "You're a popular man today. And, I saw what you were looking at, Jack Oleson."

I smile, asking, "Are most of these about Tom Harvey."

"Mostly," Mary says. "Your wife called, Jack. She said it was nothing important, but if she called it's important. Go ahead now; call her before you go to lunch."

"Thanks Mary," I said. "I'll call her right now."

When I walked back into my office Shanahan was quiet. I dialed my wife, Ellen, up at her office and they put me right through.

"Oh, thanks for calling. You didn't need to call me back right away. Mary Robinson said you're having a busy day." Ellen says.

"I thought something might be wrong. Ellen, you may call me anytime you want. You're my number one priority, you know that." I assure her. It is so good to hear her voice. It is so good to be talking with a real person, who is dealing in realities and not the constant life of games I deal with.

"I don't know what's up with my schedule. Tom's funeral will probably be Friday. Jesse Jackson is doing the eulogy. This week and next week will be day-by-day. I'll call you each evening."

It was a pleasant conversation, but I sensed words unspoken. I suspected she might be feeling me out. Was I coming home this weekend? For the moment I felt my life was falling apart and my world was upside down. Justice has many definitions.

"Are you okay?" Mary Shanahan asks.

"Yeah, yeah, I'm fine. I'm just very tired. All this stuff about Tom Harvey and with the auditors here, plus the regular routine makes for a long day. How are you doing today, Shanahan?" I ask with a smile.

"There are more leases every day. I have a heap here for you to approve and execute. We have that new bank over in Baltimore, *Suburban*, who wants to fund leases for us. He says he met with you and Henry Fleck. He wants you to call him." Mary tells me like I should be excited about all the new business.

"Give me the stack of leases, Mary. We'll go over them to-gether now." I tell her.

We spend the next hour reviewing the leases she had typed and the related credit reports. Most of the leases were for employees at branch locations. The others were from automobile dealerships and legitimate folks who have good credit. Of course, we dealt with all types of customers to not raise eyebrows. The bogus company leases were many covering toys like airplanes and yachts. As long as the payments were made the leases appeared genuine. Of course, I knew better and Mary Shanahan didn't.

When we were done I ask Mary if she is going to have more time to help me with the audit and the annual report. Of course, she says, and that she is certainly willing to work overtime and weekends. "Whatever it takes, Jack."

"Will that work for your boyfriend?" I ask.

"I think we are over, if there ever was anything. And, I was going to ask you today if you will take me to the Kennedy Center on the 28th. But I know you're really busy right now so you can tell me later." Shanahan says, with hope in her eyes.

"I'll tell you now," I say. "I will be proud to take you on the 28th. Just remember, tell no one."

"Thank you," she says, smiling. "You know I've become love-struck with you, Jack."

"I know," I said. "I know. But it's not what you think. It's not puppy love, either. Just give it time."

"I'm trying, Jack." She said with tear drops rolling down her checks.

"Life is not to be trusted, and it gives us a temporary loan. The days of one's life are simply installments against the loan." I reply, walking over to her desk. I put my arm around her. "Come on, let's get to work. Everything will be okay."

The telephone buzzes. Shanahan answers, whispering it's Madeline Haycock.

"Madeline," I say. "What can I do for you?"

"Gordon is really pissed off. People are calling. And, what about the restaurant, has that liquor license been approved yet?" She's keeping her voice at a mild roar.

"Madeline, calm down. I understand funeral arrangements are being made for Thursday or Friday. Ted and I are meeting this afternoon to put the final touches on the liquor license. Do you know the auditors started here today? There is really a lot going on. I've talked to our insurance company and they are putting everything on hold until after the funeral." I told her with a growing attitude in my voice.

"Okay, Jack. I understand. Have you heard from the police or the FBI?" She asks.

"Why would I hear from them?" I ask, quizzically.

"Oh never mind." She says. "Talk to you later."

After I hang up I told Shanahan to take copious messages. I told her I would have Mary Robinson forward all my calls to her. I said I had to spend some time with Ted Masters about the restaurant. I had to talk with Joe Neverson to discuss the claims situation. I check my watch, it is three o'clock.

"I'll return around five o'clock. We'll do Happy Hour at five and I would like you to go dinner with me at *Blues Alley* in Georgetown. I'll arrange for your car to be parked at the St. Regis this afternoon. You can stay at my place in Glen Echo tonight. Do you want to think about it?" I ask.

"No," she says. "I don't need to think about it." She handed me her car keys. Saying, "Oh, I need my suitcase. It's in the trunk of my car."

I smile, thinking I would've never thought of carrying a suitcase around in my car. A spare tire, why not a spare travel case? Women think of everything, but I should have asked the question.

The best way to ask a question is to already know the answer. Perhaps she acted impetuously, but so did I. Life is what happens when you are making other plans.

If you are lucky enough to find a way of life you love, you have to find the courage to live it. **John Irving**

Chapter Fifty-Three

Georgetown
District of Columbia
Blues Alley
In the alley at Wisconsin Avenue below M Street
Monday, January 16, 1984

After meeting with Ted Masters and Joe Neverson I arrive back at my office at exactly five o'clock. There were several messages but nothing urgent. I put the pile of pink slips in my middle drawer directing Shanahan with a, "Let's go."

She is ready. Her overnight case has been moved from her trunk to mine. Shanahan confirms the mission has been accomplished by showing me her keys. "How," she asks, do you make all these things happen?"

"I left our office at three o'clock, spent an hour with Ted Masters, and an hour with Joe Neverson. So, what did I make happen?" I query, while locking my office door.

"I didn't see you make anything happen, yet, Jack. I saw absolutely nothing." She acknowledged, with a knowing tone in her voice. Mary Shanahan was a quick study. What she didn't know is reservations had been made for us at Blues Alley, which is essential. Between our first and second drinks I was to meet my handler in the *Men's* room to hand him a tape describing what I knew about Tom Harvey's airplane crash.

It was quiet at Happy Hour. Richard Corrigan approached Mary and I.

"The funeral is Friday, Jack. Gordon told me to tell you to pick Jesse Jackson up at National Airport and take him directly to the church on Friday morning. Mary Robinson will give you the details and the directions. PGC wants you to take a Rolls Royce to pick him up."

"Are you in a lot of pain, Richard? Bereavement sometimes takes a grave toll on a person. If there is anything I can do just ask." I follow.

Corrigan gives the impression he's bewildered. He stammers to say something when he sees my grin. "Get the fuck out of here, Jack. Shit on it, I'm not bereaved? Shit." We laugh heartily. Richard Corrigan suggests another drink. As we walk to the bar he asks me how the audit is going. "It's like two heavyweight fighters just feeling each other out." I say.

"They won't be asking any interesting questions, other than general ones, for at least two weeks. It will be a relatively long process to agree on any numbers," I assure Corrigan.

"Why me," I ask Richard. "Why do I have to pick Jesse Jackson up at National Airport? I don't even know where the church is located. What if I get fucking lost?" I protest.

"I don't even know if I can drive that Rolls Royce."

Corrigan was hooting now, saying, "Just start it and steer, pal."

We made small talk and finished our drinks. He asked me a few questions about Mary Shanahan and I asked him about Rich Richards. He told me Rich was a crackerjack salesman and will be the top producer in January, if he keeps up the good work. "I'm sending him to New Orleans and Dallas for a month to see what he can drum up."

"He is a great hire, Jack." Corrigan says, slapping me on the back.

"So, is Mary Shanahan." I say.

Everybody has pretty much left and I tell Corrigan I have to get Mary on her way. It is six o'clock when we exit 1700 K Street. We jump in my car, which I keep parked at the St. Regis, and we drive through relatively light traffic and park near our destination, Blues Alley. It's 6:45 p.m. Our reservations are at seven o'clock.

The street is dark, deserted, and kind of creepy with nobody around. A row of cars are parked along a chain-link fence and the scrubby banks of the Potomac River just beyond. I had wedged my Chrysler New Yorker between a black SL Mercedes and a white panel van.

"Are you sure you know where we are going, Jack?" She asks, looking at the ugly street scenery. "It's kind of scary here." She says.

"We are going to D.C.'s oldest and most prominent jazz club. Dizzy Gillespie, Nancy Wilson; all the great ones have performed here." We are greeted by a host who checks his reservation book. He smiles, saying enthusiastically, "Mr. Oleson, we have your table ready."

We follow him to what appears to be one of the better tables. He seats Mary Shanahan. I sit directly across from her. She smiles saying, "Once again I'm, well, I'm rapt."

Lola, our server, interrupts our thoughts, asking, "What may I get you from the bar? We order wine and she says, "Let me get you your drinks. When I come back I'll explain our Louisiana Creole cuisine.

"Jack," Mary asks, "What is this all about? It's kind of overwhelming for me. Listen to the music. A gifted piano player and a gifted saxophone player and a gifted drummer are playing jazz music so beautifully. Everyone in here appears rich and sophisticated, like they have it altogether. And at this table, which appears to be the best one in the house, I'm sitting here feeling like I don't belong at this juncture of my life, except that I'm with you, who must be somebody important. Yet, I really don't know anything about you. And, you are so unassuming."

I wonder if Shanahan would've kept talking if the drinks hadn't arrived. We clinked glasses and took a sip. "I think that's the most you have ever said to at one time," I say, grinning.

"I'm sorry." She speaks, softly. "If I ever date anybody else how are they going to measure up to the times we have spent together?"

"No, no your concern is legitimate. Everything is moving fast. You are young and haven't been around the block too many times. I promised you an opportunity and maybe this is too much for you.

If it is, tell me, and I'll transfer you to the accounting department. But I think being my assistant is the best thing for you right now. I take up a lot of your time right now, but you say you can handle it. So, just enjoy all of the perks. This may never happen to you again. And, you are safe when you are with me." I assure her, being interrupted by Lola, who brings us another round of drinks.

She nods at the bar. I see him. "I haven't finished the first one yet," says Mary.

"Take your time, Shanahan, just relax. Excuse me for a minute, Mary; I need to use the facilities. I'll be right back."

On the way I tell Lola to bring us a shrimp cocktail for two. Then, I proceed to the Men's room. There are two other men in the restroom; my handler is washing his hands in one of the sinks while I go to one of the urinals. When the other two leave I walk over to an adjacent sink and discreetly hand him the tape. He says absolutely nothing and leaves. Two minutes later I return to my table. I notice the restaurant is full.

Mary Shanahan has finished her first glass of wine and is half way through her second. When I sit down she asks: "Everything okay, Jack."

"Couldn't be better," I assure her as the shrimp cocktail arrives.

We had a tasty and interesting dinner. Louisiana Creole really tangs the palate. When we finished eating we drank wine and enjoyed two more sets of music. Mary Shanahan is feeling pretty cheery when we depart *Blues Alley*. When we sit down in the car sshe asks me, "Where we are going next?" I tell here, "To my place in Glen Echo, Maryland." "Where's that?" She asks with a slight slur. "Did you get me drunk to take advantage of me?" She asks.

I was amused at her condition, when I queried, "Do you want me to take advantage of you?"

"Yeah, I guess so." She whispers and repeats as she slowly falls asleep

While driving along the Potomac on the Cabin John Parkway I get off at Glen Echo, Maryland. The drive from *Blues Alley* has taken about twenty minutes. Mary Shanahan is sound asleep when we arrive. I gently wake her and help her out of the car. I take her suitcase out of the trunk and walk her into my apartment.

Joe Neverson had honored my request and was staying at Maggie's place. Mary quickly plopped in a chair. She apologizes for getting drunk. I ask her if she wants a cup of coffee. She just wants to go to bed. I walk her back to my bedroom and tell her she may sleep here tonight. I put her suitcase across a chair and tell her I will wake her up at six o'clock. She starts stripping down and I leave the room.

I pour a glass of Jack Daniels over ice and go out on my wooden porch. I light up a cigarette and put Sinatra on my tape deck. I play it at a really low volume. It is the first time today I'm alone and can really relax. I like being alone, especially when I'm trying to figure something out. Although I don't like being completely alone, it is good to have company in the other room. It is comforting just to have somebody here.

I had a gut feeling and my hunches are somewhat reasonably exact. I had PGC nailed to the cross with all his nefarious business dealings. I suspected him of murder, but I hadn't investigated my suspicion. My assignment here was financial only, but, I knew now there was a lot more going on.

Crooked FBI agents are bribed with cash, jewelry, and wine. FBI informants are bribed with much more, including protection. In reviewing PGC files and what I'd observed first hand I found it strange that something always seems too happen when the law gets too close. Wiretaps get compromised, bugs are discovered, cops who are hot on the trail find themselves demoted or transferred; witnesses disappear, or recant, or forget.

This was about an agent gone badly, or an informant gone badly. Of course, the bonding company had major problems, but they were problems that could disappear once the fix is in. This case was abysmal, who really was PGC? He is a man who pontificates, in the background, but never talks on the phone. Why do so, if you don't have to especially if you have to keep what's said very vague. He doesn't talk in the car because someone could easily put a new door on it with audio equipment.

All kinds of thoughts are racing through my mind as I fix another drink. As I sit back down out on the porch I wonder, what does this guy do? I suppose nothing, PGC is simply a delegator. He has his staff take care of the details. He totally relies on his staff to prepare 3x5 index cards with all the details for meetings. He will often quote Ronald Reagan, *Government is not the solution to our problems; government is the problem.*

My contemplations are broken up by Shanahan. "Jack, are you coming to bed?"

"Do you want a drink, Mary?" I ask.

"No, I want you to come to bed." She pleads.

"I'll sleep on the sofa, Mary." I reply.

"No," she barks. "I'm afraid. I've never done this before. I just want you to take me in your arms and hold me."

I thought about it. "Okay," I agree. "I need to cuddle with somebody too. I'll keep my hands to myself, though, Mary."

"If you can do that I'll really feel bad about myself." She says with a smile.

Courage is doing what you're afraid to do. There can be no courage unless you are scared. **Eddie Rickenbacher**

Chapter Fifty-four

Calvary Baptist Church
755 Eighth Street Northeast
Washington D.C.
Friday, January 20, 1984

M ary Robinson gave me the marching orders from National Airport to the church, saying, "Give Jesse Jackson a big hug from me."

It's 7 a.m. I'm sitting in the driver's seat of a Rolls Royce looking over the orders before leaving for the airdrome. Jackson's Piedmont flight will be landing at the airfield at 9 a.m. The marching mandates are for me are to meet him in front of the North Terminal and then transport him directly to the Calvary Baptist church. The directive states it is a six mile expedition and will take approximately twelve minutes.

I arrive at the north terminal of National Airport, thirty minutes early. It's amazing how much respect you get if you're driving the right car. I park in front of the main entrance of the building. I engage my emergency flashers, waiting for a policeman stop by to move me along. Rather everyone just looks at the ostentatious automobile, admiring its beauty and uniqueness. Twenty minutes pass as I make a few phone calls I didn't have to make. I just wanted to use the phone, playing *big operator*. Of course the calls were vague and unformulated.

"Sir," a deep voice speaks. I hang up the telephone and turn toward the vocal sound. Here is a giant of a man masquerading as a security officer, who looks like *Big Daddy* Lipscomb of the old (*1957-58*) Baltimore Colts

"You are going to have to move your car." He says, politely.

"I'm waiting on the Reverend Jesse Jackson, who is scheduled to do a eulogy at 11 a.m. In fact, I'm wondering if maybe you can give me directions to 755 Eighth Street Northeast. It's the Calvary Baptist Church." God, I'm thinking privately, do I ever stop trying to outsmart the other guy. If I can just stall him for a few more minutes Jackson should appear and I won't have to circle the terminal.

"Tom Harvey's funeral is there today. He was a great black man. Sure, I can help you with directions, sir. Just take South Smith Boulevard about a tenth of a mile, and then take the exit toward the GW Parkway north. Merge and cross over the Potomac into the District of Columbia. Take the Massachusetts Avenue exit, then straight ahead to 2nd Street Northwest. Turn right onto 2nd Street Northwest. Turn right onto H Street Northwest. Turn right onto 8th Street Northeast. You're right there. Cavalry Baptist Church is on the left."

"There's Jesse," he says pointing across the way toward Reverend Jackson, who is standing right there with two suitcases and a beautiful young woman. "Sir," he says, "Allow me to get Jesse Jackson's bags and escort him to the car."

"Sir," I ask. "How do you know these precise directions by heart?"

"It's where I go to church." He replies as he makes a bee-line for Jessie Jackson and his companion.

During our fifteen minute ride to the church Jesse Jackson really has nothing to say. I'm thinking he thinks I might be one jump ahead of a cab driver. And, what does he have to say to a guy like me. So to show him I have an intelligent mind, I ask two hackneyed questions and he gives me two very hollow and throwaway answers. When he and his friend exit the car he thanks me while gathering his two suitcases. I nod, thinking he was one of most, recognized, well-known men in the United States. Yet, I didn't know any more about him other than his being with Martin Luther King the moment the black leader was shot.

The longstanding Baptist church has an air of holiness to it. It is definitely old-style and beckons an observer to come worship. When I walk into the sanctuary and mosey toward the alter

I see two large golden urns, side by side. I stop and look around the church. The atmosphere makes me feel safe. Yet, there are the remains of Tom Harvey and his son. Tom, I'd just recently taken a luxurious yacht cruise with off the coast of South Carolina and Georgia. During that ride Ned Larson warns me Tom Harvey might be thrown overboard on our voyage. My God, why was all this so behind closed doors? All everyone had been talking about all week was how PGC must have had Tom's airplane sabotaged. The story was the plane had just exploded in mid-air.

About 10 a.m. people started to come. The first six pews were roped off for family and dignitaries. There was standing room only when the personages entered single file and took their seats. They filled all the pews except the first one. The mayor of Washington D.C. was present, along with several Congressmen and Senators. The last bunch to enter, which seems rather strange, is PGC and his entourage. Along with the *god himself* is Corrigan, Larson, Ferrone, Masters, Boyer, Haycock, and the entire board of directors. Finally comes Angelica, Tom Harvey's current paramour, as she enters she raises the eyebrows of those who knew about the relationship between Harvey and her. She is followed by Tom's daughter, Nadine, who appears not so bereft, but just thoroughly pissed off.

Me, and I don't know why, I'm sitting in the first pew, in front of the pulpit, on the right side of the church. To my left are Jesse Jackson's friend, to whom I've not been introduced, and Jesse sitting on the aisle. This is crazy – bizarre, I'm thinking.

I notice the huge gap between Nadine and Angelica. I heard during the week Tom had recently signed a new will giving Angelica fifty percent control of his real estate empire, worth some twenty million dollars. Nadine is the only surviving family member. Her mother and Tom Harvey's only wife had died mysteriously a few years back. I sensed Nadine just wanted the funeral over with so she could get down to business.

Angelica, a softer gentler person, was trying to be grief-stricken by the demise of her significant other, but I figured she was in it all along for the money. When I see this beautiful woman I now think of Fripp Island. After PGC liquored Tom up and then dropped a pill in his last drink, which I pretended I didn't see him do, PGC and Haycock had taken Angelica and Annabelle, who is a sixteen-year-old boats mate he picked up while I was in South Carolina, to bed with them. These two, Angelica and Annabelle, 69ed each other for PGC and Haycock's amusement. This is what I'm thinking about as the funeral is called to order. The service is moving along with its meaningful, religious, sacred, pious and holy music. Then it's Jesse Jackson turn. I'd done a lot of preaching while in seminary and always came to the pulpit with outlines and notes. It was much like politicians come to lecterns with monitors and placards. Jesse Jackson, on this day, took nothing to the pulpit but himself. He was awe-inspiring and I hung on his every word. So did everybody else, save Nadine Harvey. Jesse Jackson is a magnificent orator.

Funerals are so different with the absence of a body. When the words have been spoken the funeral observance is over, when there is no body to cling to or bury in a final resting place. It is simply over, whereas, really the interment is just a psychological stratagem. *Come visit and bring flowers*, a family might do it once or twice before realizing there is no point.

PGC thanks me for getting Jackson to the church on time and he tells me to go back to the office. What a relief! There is so much to do and I want to just get it done and get away from all this madness. With my orders carried out, I shake some hands with people I know and make a quiet exit.

Courage and perseverance have a magical talisman, before which difficulties disappear and obstacles vanish into air. **John Quincy Adams**

Chapter Fifty-five

1700 K Street
Washington D.C.
Friday, January 20, 1984

"How is your day going?" I ask Mary Shanahan as I walk into my office. Fortuitously, Mary Robinson was busy on the phones when I walked by her perch. It had already been a long day and it was just approaching two o'clock. I sat down on my side of the desk and shuffled through a dozen telephone messages. As instructed Shanahan had the pink slips sorted by order of the call. The last call was at the bottom of the stack. In the middle of the stack was one from my wife. I slipped that one out of the pile, asking Shanahan, "What did she say?"

Mary smiled at me, "She said to call her at her office as soon as possible."

Mary went back to work as I dialed Ellen's office. She answered on the first ring, saying, "Thanks for calling me back right away. How are you?"

"I just got back from Tom Harvey's funeral. I was the designated chauffeur for Jesse Jackson. I picked him and some young lady up at National and drove them to the church. It's been an unusual day. I'll tell you all about it later. So, what's up with you?" I ask.

"I wanted to know if you are coming home this weekend. I have to work tomorrow and I was wondering if you could watch the kids. Or, should I arrange for a sitter? You know, maybe you can take them to a movie. They miss you, Jack." Ellen said.

"I miss them too." I said. "Okay, I'll be home tonight. I don't think anything will come up. With PGC in town I never know.

But, I'm pretty certain with Tom Harvey's funeral today he'll keep out of sight. In fact he might already be headed back to South Carolina. So, unless you hear differently I'll plan on being home around eight o'clock tonight. And tomorrow, while you begin another tax season, I'll take the boys to the mall and to a movie. Tomorrow night I'll take you to dinner."

Ellen was very pleasant and I really wanted to go home today. I felt myself wearing down as there was constant activity and new surprises every day. Working here is really tough. The hours are long, and sometimes the demands are incredible. Everything has to be done yesterday. It can be rough-and-tumble at times. The place is like a stop-and-go movie. Everyone races through moments of intense activity and then becomes motionless and distant.

"So, you're going home tonight." Mary Shanahan says, interrupting my musing.

"Yeah, its tax season and she works Saturdays the next three and a half months. Plus I'll be here next weekend – we have a date at the Kennedy Center. Remember?" I probe, with my soliloquy being crisscrossed with fond memories.

"I'm looking forward to it, Jack. I think you might want to check with the auditors as soon as you can. Matthew Wilson and Bernard Goodman keep checking with me about when you are returning from the funeral." She says, "They both seem unequivocal about the necessity of you communicating with them A.S.A.P."

"Alright, I'll go see what they want. Keep me posted if you hear any news about Tom Harvey. I am certain all of this action is not going to simply spin into the wind."

"Jack, I think they want to discuss the Advances account. I analyzed it for them and it contains twelve checks in the amount of sixty thousand dollars each drawn on the first Monday of each month, payable to and endorsed by PGC. The total is seven hundred twenty thousand dollars." Shanahan cautions me with a tone of skullduggery, but manages to give me the information in an air of innocence, like a parson's monologue.

"That's a nice round number," I say, while I hesitate in the doorway waiting for Mary Robinson to get really busy so I can sneak by her to the conference room without interference. "Thanks for the head's up, Mary." I duck out the door and walk behind Mary's desk while she is directing people to the waiting room. I'm in deep thought while en route, on a slow walk, to the conference room. Fraud is the crime of voice and every accounting fraud damages the economy, costs jobs, and hurts the retirement funds of every citizen. Crooked executives know that their chances of being caught cooking the books are minuscule. At Atlantic States Surety there were no books to cook until I arrived and put the numbers together. It's the job of the independent CPA firm to find material fraud, but most CPAs would not recognize fraud if it hit them square in the face. The why is so simple? It is the lack of experience of the auditors and the false expectations about the clients. The intricacies of accounting fraud are the use of accounting tricks to fool investors. CPA firms, instead of acting like watchdogs, boost their revenues by morphing into advisers and consultants to their clients.

The conference room is busy when I walk into the boardroom. Matthew Wilson is sitting at the head of the table, with Emily Harding sitting to his left in the center of the long conference table. Bernard Goodman is sitting at the other end of the table, facing Wilson. Next to Goodman, and directly across from Harding, is the Yale kid I hadn't met. He appears to be taking a crack at the bank reconciliations. He stands up and introduces himself as Jerry Hamner as if he was the *Man of the Hour*.

"Mary Shanahan tells me you have been looking for me." I say, looking first at Wilson, then my eyes shift to Goodman.

"Emily will you pass me the *Advances* schedule." Wilson requests, with a look of mischief on his face.

He looks at the four-column accounting sheet, and says, "Mister Charles takes a sixty thousand dollar advance each and every month. Can you tell us how this works, Jack?" Matthew Wilson asks, handing me the schedule Mary Shanahan has prepared for them upon request.

I look at the schedule and there it is in black and white. I stare up and fix my eyes directly on the good-looking Emily Harding. She winks at me which makes me beam.

"Here's how it works. We accrue a fifty thousand dollar a month salary for PGC and five thousand a month for payroll taxes. We accrue an additional five thousand a month for incidental expenses. He draws down sixty thousand a month against the accrual. The entries are not done until year's end." There I'm thinking. Bullshit covers bullshit very effectively. "How did you handle it last year, Matt?" I ask.

If looks could kill, I'm thinking, as Matthew Wilson glowers at me. I was not trying to act coy, just properly cautious, but I noted the curiosity on the auditor's faces. I sense Emily Harding was wondering just who I was. I was wondering the same thing as the seconds passing seemed like hours.

"Okay, Jack, thank you. Please give me a copy of the entries when you make them." Matthew Wilson asks, showing signs of frustration by repeatedly rapping his pencil on the table. He reminds me of Ichabod Crane, gangly and mysterious, but extremely loquacious. He speaks endlessly around the subject at hand. Meanwhile Bernard Goodman nods at me and the young Yale boy puts his pencil back to his work papers. Emily Harding looks at me as if she is lusting, while flashing signals with her mannerisms.

"Anything else," I query, looking at Wilson.

"Not for now," says Wilson.

"Oh, Matt, I'm ready to sign that engagement letter and firm up your fee. When you have time to direct your attention to the matter, I'll make myself available." I add, wincing at what I was seeing, Wilson's obsequiousness. With my last remark he was showing a meekness, fearfulness and passivity that make this all work. Seven hundred twenty thousand of advances will remain a current asset as a cash equivalent.

I stop by to tell Mary Robinson about the funeral and meeting Jesse Jackson. She was all ears, but the telephone kept ringing so I made my way back to our office. It was 3:30 p.m. and all I wanted to do was get out of here. I sense something is really wrong. Who is Paul Gordon Charles? He's more than who I think or what they are telling me. He pulls strings. He runs a one-man empire as a total recluse. He is more secret than the CIA and perhaps more powerful than the President. What makes him so powerful, with his aluminum personality and being a self-perpetuating paper monster, *never his name in print*, with a brain liking to a computer's memory bank? He's a man who leans on others to accomplish his wants and whims. Who is this guy? How does he get away with what he does? Questions! Questions? And more questions?

His machinery has been cranking through his halls toward a scandal that will grind him down, or will it? Now I feel part of the machinery, but I'm working for the other side. We, the good guys with the white hats, will get everything squared away. Or, are we the good guys really the bad guys? Just make it all innocuous, bland, and safe in a harmless way. But why does he get a pass? What's really going on here?

Atlantic States Surety's upward and downward paths seem to be diverging, yet joined, like prongs of a tuning fork pitched to a note of expediency. Slowly, steadily, I am climbing into the moral abyss of the inner circle until I finally fall into it, thinking I had made it to the top just as I'm beginning to realize I am actually touching the bottom. But I'm a FBI man, I wonder if I'm being set up by PGC and the Bureau. It is all about who is expendable.

I have survived my first minor roles on the front lines, with PGC. I have risen in the confidence of his closest aides. I understand to get along with him you must keep what he tells you to yourself, unless he tells you otherwise. And don't ask questions unless you have a good reason. Above all keep your mouth shut. All loose talk about the boss is dangerous to him and forbidden to his aides. The loyal soldier is silent, and he does not pry.

It's four o'clock when Mary Shanahan returns to the office. "I took a late lunch today. I wanted to wait until you came back, in case an important call came." Mary said.

"Thanks," I say. "You take good care of me."

"Jack, is anybody staying in your Glen Echo apartment this weekend?"

"No, why do you ask?" I reply, curiously.

"My ex-boyfriend told me to get my stuff out by Friday."

"The Yale guy," I ask, surprised.

"Yep, the Yale guy," she confirms.

"Do you need help with moving your stuff?" I ask.

"I don't have much, but I could use some help. My only alternative is to get the stuff and go to Gettysburg to stay with a friend for the weekend. I really don't want to do that. I'm sorry, Jack. I know you have to go home to your family." She apologizes with tears coming to her eyes.

"I'll call Ellen and tell her I'll be home by nine o'clock tomorrow morning." It will work for her and she knows that I won't let her down. Let me make that call right now."

I made the call telling Ellen PGC was calling a meeting at 7 p.m. and I would be too tired to drive home afterwards. She was okay with it, but I'm not too sure she believed me.

Mary and I left the office at 4:30 and drove to the place she has been staying in Silver Spring, Maryland. It was a very small house owned by her ex-boyfriend's grandmother. I followed her to the location. She had a lot more there then she had remembered. We boxed dishes, pans, pots, and silverware, lamps, books, magazines and bed clothes. She put all her clothing in two suitcases and we departed for Glen Echo. On this trip she followed me.

She is moved into one of my bedrooms by eight o'clock. Actually it was good to have someone there. Joe Neverson was there for a few weeks but he moved into the apartment I'd rented in November the first of the year. Joe promised to pay the one-year lease I had signed. I figured I'd be buying a house in Northern Virginia, if this assignment was going to go on much longer, so I rented this apartment in Glen Echo January 1st when I found the advertisement in the newspaper.

The small two bedroom apartment was actually located in single, forty-year-old woman's house. The rent was dirt cheap, which was plenty good enough for me. In addition to the two bedrooms it had, a full bathroom, a small kitchen and a smaller living room. I took Mary out to dinner in nearby Bethesda, Maryland. We went to bed early as I wanted leave by 5 a.m.

Before we went to bed we shared a bottle of wine. I told her she could she could stay with me as long as she wanted. *Always remember you are more important than your problems.* I told her I had no idea how long I'd be there that life was day to day for me, at best.

Courage is like love; it must have hope to nourish it. **Napoleon Bonaparte**

Chapter Fifty-six

1700 K Street
Washington D.C.
Friday, January 27, 1984

It had been a menacing week dealing with Nadine Harvey.
PGC had demanded she return Tom's Mercedes SL and make
arrangements for C&B to pick up his yacht in Fripp Island. Also
he demanded I contact Angelica to make arrangements for this
woman to surrender her Mercedes SL. Neither of the women was
being cooperative. It was ugly, but there was no mercy coming
from PGC, through Madeline Haycock. Only demands, like turning over Tom Harvey's Atlantic States Associates stock certificates, which he owned a good portion of Atlantic States Surety.
Of course no mention was made about getting Harvey's estate released from the recent bank guarantee on the twenty million dollar loan with Henry Fleck's bank in Baltimore, American State.

I had an interesting weekend with Ellen and the boys. I arrived
home last Saturday about 8:45 a.m. Ellen was happy to see me as
were the children who were sitting down at the breakfast nook in
our recently purchased home in Jenkintown, Pennsylvania. They
were thrilled when I walked in the door having already heard from
their Mom (Ellen) the plans for the day. She gave me a quick kiss
and it seemed she couldn't wait to get out the door.

I took the children to the mall and bought them a few unnecessary things. At one o'clock in the afternoon we went to the movie
theatre. I picked the movie out; I thought it was about Al Capone,
Scarface. Instead it was the vilest movie I'd ever seen, with people
getting their arms and legs sawed off and Al Pacino saying the *F*
word three times in every sentence. There was virtually nobody in

the theatre and the kids didn't want to leave so we stayed until the movie ended. Actually the boys and I really enjoyed the action in the movie and I hoped they didn't really understand the cursing and other innuendos. But, I should have known better and I asked them not to mention the movie to their mother.

Ellen and I had plans to go to dinner that night, but she didn't get home until 11:00 p.m. The boys were in bed and I had drunk most of a fifth of Jack Daniels by the time she arrived. I was perplexed, but didn't ask any questions. I could tell she'd had a few herself, because she was in a first-rate mood. "Sorry," she said. "We went out for a couple drinks after work and time just got away from us."

"Who are we?" I ask.

"Johnny," she says. "I'm here seven days a week. I never get out. You come home for a weekend – is it so wrong for me to spend a night out with my friends?"

She made a good point. "Do you have room for one more," I ask her.

"I sure do," she said.

We had several more and went to bed and made passionate love. I felt very content on Sunday when I left for Washington. Yet, there was something in the back of my mind that seemed different.

I arrived at my Glen Echo apartment about 6:15 p.m. on Sunday. Mary Shanahan was talking to my landlord when I drove up. It was a good thing in my absence Miss Vick, the property-owner, had approved Mary as a co-tenant saying there were all kinds of situations with people who worked in the District. "Just pay the rent on time."

Miss Vick had given Mary a history of Glen Echo, which was quite interesting. It was so good to be somewhere that had more than four barren walls. Mary was good company and we were getting along splendidly. She even convinced me to load the refrigerator with groceries. And, she knew how to cook. I wondered how long this was going to last?

PGC was back in South Carolina and Madeline Haycock

was barking orders at everyone. Madeline had told me today that Annabelle was on board and I was to look into a private school for her to attend. A high school, obviously. They would be here next week and Gordon wanted to discuss the progress of the audit and several other things with me.

Mary and I had been driving to work together with the agreement that nobody would know anything about our living arrangement. I mean nobody. We stopped going to lunch together, unless somebody else was with us. We had kind of created our own prison, but we were surviving.

Suddenly Joe Neverson taps on the door and walks into our office. He says he needs one hundred thousand dollars to stave off a major glitch. That PGC approved the payment. He looked very lost in thought and worried. I told him he would have the check as soon as I could confirm PGC had OK'd payment.

"Who do you want the check payable to, Joe." I ask.

"Red Bertrand Construction." Joe said, shamefacedly. "No, make it to RB Construction, Inc."

My eyebrows rise, Mary Shanahan told me later, when I queried. "For the restaurant in the name of claims, correct?"

Joe says, "That's one way to put it, good guess, Jack."

I call Madeline Haycock to confirm the payment. She tells me to give the check to Joe, straightaway. I ask Mary to have McKenzie draw a check, and charge it to claims in favor of RB Construction, Inc. in the amount of one hundred thousand."

Shanahan returns with a check request form for me to initial. She says, McKenzie wants back up for the call for when you get it." Good ole McKenzie Gillen I'm thinking, all she's doing is ensconcing for me. I sign the request form and Mary brings the check back in ten minutes, ready for signatures.

I told her to have Corrigan and Ferrone sign. I knew they were both in and they never question signing any checks. Mary took off for the signatures. Meanwhile I buzz Joe Neverson. Maggie answers. Can I buy you two lunch at Archibald's. Maggie put me on hold, then comes back. "Do you have the check, Jack."

"Yes, Maggie, it's ready to go." I answer.

"If it's okay I'll ask Ted Masters to join us. He gets the check." Maggie says.

"Of course, we'll see you there in a half hour." I respond.

When Shanahan returns with the signed check I tell her we were going to Archibald's for lunch with Joe, Maggie, and Ted Masters. I warn her that she might see some things that might shock her. "Like a big set of tits." She reproaches.

"Can you handle it," I ask her, with a grin.

"Can you handle it, Jack?" She counters, with a striking smile.

"Let's go," I say.

Mary Robinson studies us when I tell her we are going to lunch. Neverson and Maggie Little meet us at the door by pure coincidence. While we were waiting for the elevator Ted Masters joins us. We all ride down to the first floor together. Nary a word is spoken as we pass by the St. Regis and enter Archibald's a few minutes later.

We had a beer at the bar while our corner table was cleared. We were well known there now for our excessive tips. I loved this style of life, and wished it was really real. All of what I'd done in the past dozen or so years sometimes seems like I'm on temporary vacation. I always know it will end quickly, though. When it's over it's over.

Mary nudges me saying she has never drank a beer. "Just sip it I told her. If you don't like it just leave it."

"I can do that," she rejoinders.

A woman in full took us to our table. I watched Mary Shanahan's eyes with each of our movements. Once seated, Ted Masters asks if Mary is privy to all information. I told all of them she is to me what Maggie to Joe. That settled it; all responsibility had been transferred to me.

We ordered another round of beers with cheeseburgers all the way around and a bowl of onion rings. "Ted, tell us about the restaurant, I ask, handing him the check for one hundred thousand dollars. Masters examined the instrument, folds it and put it in his shirt pocket.

"PGC wants the restaurant opened on February 1st. I'll have

the liquor license on Monday. The balance of the construction work will be done by this weekend." Ted announces very
unenthusiastically.

Joe Neverson asks, "How much more will it take to get
opened?"

"He's having a big party opening day; all in attendance will
simply sign the tabs, giving Atlantic States Surety the opportunity
to pay the damages. PGC is estimating fifty- thousand-dollars in
tabs. I'm seriously considering resigning," says Ted Masters.

I laugh. "Really, Ted. And miss out on all this fraudulent
activity."

Joe laughs, "Really, Ted. What good would it do? Where we
go one, we go all."

Just then the food comes and saves Ted Masters from making
any other stupid remarks. We move paraphernalia around on the
table and started eating our cheeseburgers and onion rings, while
a naked woman is seemingly dancing right on top of us. Masters
was through with his speeches as was everyone else while we were
eating. Maggie Little was the only one who spoke, ordering us
another round of beers.

When we were done eating Ted Masters excused himself. He
was clearly upset, distraught over the possibility of losing his license if all this shit hits the fan and a cover up begins. *"It's worse
than Watergate,"* he thinks out loud.

We ordered and drink one more round of beer before I pay
the bill and walk back to the office. As we walk I hope I'm doing
the right thing exposing Mary to all this information. Maggie is
hard core, but Shanahan seems to have a certain toughness about
her as well. Mary did have an advantage by spending so much time
with me.

Mary Robinson tells me Matt Wilson has been looking for
me. "That little twirp," she adds. Also that Madeline Haycock had
called a couple of times. I knew what Haycock wanted. I needed
to talk with Wilson.

I told Shanahan I'm going to the conference room to see
Wilson. I walk to the boardroom doors on the double quick. When

I entered they all seem busy at work. I don't even look at Harding. I walk directly to Wilson's station. "I'm ready," he said. "Is there somewhere private?"

I motioned him toward the door and we walked directly to my office. I ask Mary to check with McKenzie in the accounting department. She put the papers she was working on in her middle drawer and exits.

Shanahan had put the engagement letter front and center on my desk. It was three pages long. I spent a few seconds paging through it. "I sign here," I ask.

"Right," Wilson says.

"And the retainer," I query.

"Fifty thousand - cash." He says, knowing full well I know how it was handled last year.

"Done!" I say, "I'll have an envelope for you Monday."

Ichabod Crane got up without any further ado and exited my office. What a piece of shit, I thought.

I buzz Mary Robinson asking her to page Shanahan and tell her to return to our office. A few minutes later she arrives and I ask her to call Madeline Haycock.

When Haycock comes on the telephone I tell her all has been accomplished. The audit and the restaurant were on schedule. She wished me a pleasant weekend and reminded me to check into schools for Annabelle.

"Let's call it a week, Mary," I say.

She gave me a kindly smile, "Let's just go home, Jack."

"Yes," I said. "Let's go home."

It is the function of creative man to perceive and to connect the seemingly unconnected. **William Plommer**

What Is Past Is Prologue

Thanksgiving
Rome, New York
Thursday, November 27, 1969

We had been back and forth for seven weeks. It all began when I had flown to Syracuse, New York on October 3rd. When I returned to Minnesota a few days later, I did the old two-week-notice trick of quitting my job. However, I requested, I'd prefer to leave at the end of the week. Since my father-in-law was a large client of the firm they agreed I could leave on Friday and wished me well. Now I just needed to, in earnest, start tightening up my affairs.

Our divorce was scheduled for the 24th of October. I told Beth I would be returning to New York on October 13th to look for a job. That I would be staying with Ellen until I flew back for the divorce proceedings. We divvied up and tagged our property. She said she would stay in our duplex until the 24th. She, too, had made arrangements to move back to South Dakota to be near her boyfriend. When I was ready to leave she hugged me, unexpectedly, asking if we were doing the right thing. "Absolutely not," I said, "But it's too late to do anything else." It wasn't, of course, but I'd had enough.

"We had agreed to divide the children too. Kincaid would stay with her mother and Charley would go with me. She said she would make arrangements with my mother to drop Kincaid and Charley in Montevideo. After divorce court proceedings I was to pick up Charley at my parent's house, which was only forty miles away from Willmar, Minnesota where the divorce action was being held. We were so young and foolish and actually thought we could pull this magnum opus off without anybody knowing about it. We were laughingstocks, immature, inconsiderate assholes. The both of us were all of the aforementioned.

I returned to New York on Monday, October 13th. By the end of the week I'd found a job as assistant to the Controller of Lenox Industries in Syracuse. My starting day was November 3rd. Ellen agreed to travel with me to the divorce proceedings and help me with my son while traveling. I had arranged for a U-Haul trailer, to pull behind my 1966 Mercury, to transport my stuff to New York. I had an electronic Thomas organ, two amplifiers and guitars to load. I didn't have much else except Charley's junk and two suitcases full of clothes. There were a lot of assurances and pledges to keep before the 24th of October.

We met all the commitments and arrived at Ellen's apartment early Monday morning in time for her to go to work. I spent the rest of the week finding an apartment for my son and I. The place was relatively close to work. The address was 1025 James Street in Syracuse's downtown area. After this triumph I arranged day care for Charley, which I did nearby to our newly rented apartment. Everything appeared to be set.

On October 23rd Ellen and I flew to Minneapolis. The next day we met my brother and his wife outside the court house in Willmar. Rick and Jackie had agreed to be witnesses to the breakup of the marriage. Without my sister-in-law's testimony the judge would not have granted the divorce. Beth, of course, was a no show. Once the hearing was over Ellen and I began our grueling journey.

With everything seemingly arranged I started my job as scheduled on Monday, November 3rd. It was good to be back to work, but it was difficult getting Charley to and from day care. And then the trek to Rome to be with Ellen, and the marathon back again was very taxing. Even though we took turns driving, Ellen to Syracuse after work and I driving to Rome the next evening, dividing up the burden.

To give us a break, I arranged for child care on Saturday night, November 8th. The Irish Rovers were playing in a night club on

Onondaga Lake. We had an excellent dinner before the show, but more importantly we agreed Ellen would write her husband a letter, he was stationed in Okinawa with the Air Force, about her state of affairs with me. The Irish Rovers were fantastic. Ellen wrote her husband and after he received the letter he took leave and returned home a few days later. I had created a superfluous sticky situation.

Ellen's husband arrived Griffiss Air Force Base in Rome, New York on Friday afternoon, November 21st. After work I picked up Charley and we went to our apartment. I was eager for Ellen to call. But, the hours passed slowly and her call never came. I was upset but figured they needed time to talk.

The next day, Saturday, Charley and I had breakfast, lunch and dinner and there was still no word from Ellen. After I put Charley to bed I had plenty of time to think. What had transpired the past 120 days had turned my world upside down. Without my son, Charley, lying in bed on the other side of the room, I was totally alone. I felt panicky and concerned that when Ellen had seen her husband she fell in love with him all over again.

She called the next day, Sunday, apologizing she'd not been in touch with me but they needed time to talk everything out. Rather than express my wounded ego, I told her I understood, even though I didn't. So far, she told me nothing has been resolved. He does not want a divorce, even if you and I are having sex. He asked me to wait until he was discharged from the Air Force in March.

"He actually believes we are not having sex?" I had asked, incredulously.

"Why should he. He thinks I'm a Saint, and I've been giving him good sex since he has been home." She stated, incontestably.

I was flabbergasted. "You're having sex with him, Ellen. This is outlandish." I said.

My statement had backed Ellen into a corner. "He is my husband. And to be certain about anything you must face your doubts. Plus, I don't want to be charged with adultery. He can't do that now because I didn't refuse his sexual advances. Doesn't it make sense, Johnny?"

"None," I said. She hung up on me.

I didn't get a chance to tell her my problems. I was fired Friday, while she evidently was busy having sex with her husband. My boss had been really pleased with my work. But, he was constantly questioning me as to why a young man like me, with a family and good job references, would come to Syracuse, New York from Minnesota? He had warned me not to hold anything back, but I was just too embarrassed about how my life was going.

He'd called my ex-father-in-law and didn't receive a glowing report. The only thing he probably heard was I left his daughter and granddaughter in the cold for another woman. He wasn't told the whole story. Anyway I was fired not for what I had done, but for covering up my real story. My only error was one of omission.

This changed everything, but I hadn't had a chance to talk with Ellen about it which was probably just as well. I had already made a decision about what I was going to do. It was what would be best for the children in the long haul. Through my mother, I obtained Beth's telephone number and told her I thought it would be best if she would fly east and take Charley back with her. And, if she came, could she please bring Kincaid so I could see her. Then, I told her I was fired because of what her Dad had reported to my employer. She said she would call me back. And, she did, saying they would arrive in Syracuse at noon on Tuesday and return at noon on Wednesday.

Ellen didn't call again until early Tuesday morning. I told her what was happening unswervingly and she seemed self-possessed. She asked, "What are you going to do, Johnny?"

"Ellen you and your husband seem to be getting along well. I need to pack my bags. I'm going back to Minneapolis."

I had recently purchased a new 1970 Ford Maverick. Ellen had been driving it. I had been driving her Volkswagen *Bug*. Why? I don't know, it was just one of those stupid things that happen in life's experiences.

She said, "Jim has agreed to a divorce. He just wants me to wait until his discharge, which will happen the first part of March."

Ellen says, with composure. I knew for sure now, the subject of divorce hadn't been brought up, or she had told him I was no more than an old friend. Of what I'm certain, she left unsaid any plans concerning me. Whatever had been written, spoken or become known she sought and sensed where would be a safe harbor. I wish Beth would have been so prudent.

"Johnny, when you pick them up please come to my place. I'll fix dinner and the four of us will play cards or do something tonight." I'll go with you to the airport tomorrow. We'll stop at your place after we leave Charley, Kincaid and their mother at the airport and I'll help you pack your stuff. While we're there we can make up for some lost time. You'll come back here and the three of us will go out for a little bit. Then you'll spend the night. We'll have Thanksgiving dinner here on Thursday."

I agree, thinking but not saying, *you have it all figured out don't you. And, you'll be fucking us both while making sure Beth and I don't have an opportunity. Good for you.*

Thanksgiving was unique this year. Who would have guessed that last year's would be our grand finale? Tuesday night had been even more matchless with Jim, Ellen, Beth, and I having dinner together that Jim and Ellen prepared. The four of us played cards until bedtime.

Ellen and Jim went to their bedroom. Beth and Kincaid took the sofa and Charley and I hit the floor. Charley was between Ellen and I in the portable crib.

Ellen and I did take Beth and the children to the airport on Wednesday morning. I remember Ellen leaving us alone while Beth Ann, Kincaid, and Charley and me said goodbye at the gate. I knew this was finally the end of us as a family. And that life just doesn't work out the way you think. It was unfathomable.

Ellen and I made love several times in my apartment Wednesday afternoon. We also managed to get the little I had boxed up so I was ready to go on Friday morning. Ellen said Jim would ride over with me Thursday morning to help me load the electronic Thomas organ. Wednesday night Jim, Ellen and I went to a pizza joint in Rome, New York and ate pizza and drank beer.

It was a good night and we actually had some laughs. After this hellacious week I needed a crease up or two. Once we got home they went to bed and I was on the sofa, which was the way it should be. It put me in a stormy mood, though, when Jim came out for cigarettes. Ellen liked to smoke a cigarette after sex. But, then, I shouldn't have known that.

Today, Thursday morning, Jim and I drive to Syracuse and load up my stuff. The apartment is empty and I hadn't even lived there a month. While Ellen prepared for Thanksgiving dinner, Jim and I watched some football. After dinner the three of us cleaned up the dishes. Around five o'clock Ellen suggests she and I take a ride. We drive up to the Delta Reservoir, just north of Rome, and park along the water and make passionate love. It is an emotional time. Our plans just were not working out like we thought, but we still loved each other.

When we went to bed that night, I was lying on the sofa wondering how she really did it. She loved us both and she was servicing us both. She didn't want to lose either of us. Me? I was just going home to Minnesota. I would be okay no matter what happened. And now, I couldn't wait to leave for Minneapolis in the morning. I wanted to get on with my life. There was too much confusion going on here and I had so much to do. I had to get a job and find a place to live. I had no money and I was feeling bitter about the way these whole shenanigans had worked out for me. I was especially worried about my children.

Failure is only the opportunity to more intelligently begin again.
Henry Ford

Chapter Fifty-seven

I t was a busy day. First I had to meet up with Ned Larson to get the cash for the restaurant and the auditors. We met at Tysons Corner Center, under the clock entrance, at 1961 Chain Bridge Road in McLean, Virginia which is just off the Capital Beltway.

We walked into the mall, bought a cup of coffee and sat down at a table in the courtyard. We made small talk about how it was going with PGC, but it was nothing about nothing. We exchanged meaningless pleasantries such as asking about each other's families, which neither of us could care less about. We stayed away from anything negative. The truth was Ned and I simply didn't trust each other anymore.

When we finished our coffees Ned pulled a paper bag from under his winter coat and handed it to me. I hesitated a few seconds, scanning the perimeter to see if anybody was paying any particular attention to us. Satisfied nobody was looking, I glided the package between my winter coat and V-neck sweater, wondering from what slush fund these moneys were unearthed.

"Good luck," Ned said, with a smirk. His long legs strode to the mall exit on the double quick. He didn't look back. I whisper to myself, under my breath, *nice seeing you too.*

My next stop is in Bethesda, Maryland, around where the Rockville Pike meets Wisconsin Avenue. It's a small building in the downtown area, wedged between rows of edifices, located at 4921 Bethesda Avenue. It's PGC's new French restaurant, Café Sebastian.

A wide cement ramp leads to the entranceway. Once inside there are circular dining tables wall to wall occupying the entire area. There is no bar, but drinks of choice are served before, during, and after meals. This is an eating establishment. In the center of the restaurant, but located in a nook, is PGC's private table, with seating for six. Six is his favorite number. Only Paul Gordon Charles is allowed to use this table. Only Paul Gordon Charles and his selected guests for the evening may sit in this location. *What a crock of shit*, I'm thinking as I wait for Sebastian.

Sebastian is the only name I know him by. He is young, maybe mid-thirties. He has been the chef of the Bethesda Country Club, a nearby prestigious establishment. It is a place, I understand, PGC frequents often for fine dining. The night I first met Sebastian was when Richard Corrigan, Matt Ferrone, Ned Larson and I met PGC with Tom Harvey. Tom Harvey was drunk and spent most of the evening nodding off. The guest of honor was the Louisianan Charley Rivers. After a wonderful dinner, and before Matt Ferrone yanked Charley Rivers out of the Club to the 18th green, which was totally visible from our table, I was introduced to Sebastian who was to be the chef, operating officer and part owner of Café Sebastian. After which, Matt Ferrone gave Charley Rivers the beating of his life for everyone in the Club to see.

"Jack," Sebastian says, shaking my hand like an old friend.

I suggest we sit down somewhere where we'll have some privacy. He pointed at PGC's table, which cannot be seen from the entranceway. We sit down and I take the paper bag out from under my coat where it remained stashed. I set the package on the chair next to me and pick five ten-thousand-dollar bundles from it. In each bundle were five two-thousand-dollar straps which were rubber banned. Sebastian fanned through the bills and thanked me. He said: "Are you coming to the grand opening on Wednesday, February 1st?"

"I hope so," I say, less than enthusiastically.

Sebastian gave me a forced smile. "Good luck." I say. "I'm sure you'll do well."

I feel haggard and drained from long hours of pressure, watching able men reduced to "gophers" and errand boys, breaking their necks, whenever PGC has a whim. Even though I'm a FBI agent I don't feel like one anymore. This man self-absorbs everyone around him. Now I'm a bag man, delivering money to whomever as directed. And money is no concern; the excessive expenses have been safely buried in inconspicuous budgets. His presence is everywhere. He orders everyone around like they are deck hands. Every action and reaction is cloak and dagger.

I arrive back at the office around noon. Most everyone has left or is leaving. Mary Shanahan is working diligently preparing schedules for the auditors. I quickly count and transfer the balance of the money into my brief case. There is fifty-five thousand dollars in the bag. I consider the extra five thousand and determine it is reparation for being the delivery service for this set-up. I would give fifty thousand to Matthew Wilson Monday morning and keep the extra five thousand in my briefcase waiting for further instruction. Although, I doubted any further instruction would be coming. PGC liked to think he had you by the balls.

We worked for another hour and I told Mary to wrap it up. We left the building and had lunch at the Washington Hilton. We drove to Glen Echo, relaxed for an hour or so, showered and began getting dressed for the Kennedy Center. It didn't take me as long to get ready so I fixed myself a drink and started telling Mary a few things about where we were going.

"The Kennedy Center is located on the banks of the Potomac River near the Lincoln Memorial. It opened in September of 1971, *about the same time I arrived in Washington to work for the Bureau.* I was thinking. It is the nation's living memorial to President Kennedy, who was a lifelong supporter and advocate of the arts. The Kennedy Center made its public debut on September 8, 1971, with a gala opening performance featuring the world premiere of a Requiem mass honoring President Kennedy, a work commissioned from the legendary composer and conductor Leonard Bernstein.

"In the Grand Foyer is a three-thousand-pound, eight-foot-bronze bust of President Kennedy. It is a magnificent piece that sets a mood of veneration. Nearby is the Eisenhower Theater where we'll see the play, *Woman of the Year*, starring Lauren Bacall.

She was married to Humphrey Bogart. Our seats are Orchestra, section A, at center stage. They are really great seats." *Thank you FBI*, I whisper under my breath.

While I was reciting all of this background information about John Fitzgerald Kennedy and the Kennedy Center she suddenly appears from her bedroom. She is absolutely stunning. She is wearing a Navy blue above-the-knee sheath. The V-neckline adds an extra hit of interest. She has matching pumps which appear to be on two or three inch heels. A short string of pearls is worn around her neck and partially covered by a white scarf. Her flaming red hair matches her lipstick, making her look like she was born on the 4th of July. Her makeup sets off her beautiful green eyes and open face. "How do I look, Jack?" She asks with a smile, leaving me temporarily speechless.

"Very Irish, Mary Shanahan, and, you are simply beautiful." I say, smiling.

"You clean up very well yourself, Jack Oleson." She says, with a wide grin.

"Would you like a dry Riesling," I ask.

"Yes," she said. "Why do I feel like Cinderella, Jack?"

"Because you are a princess," I say back to her.

"You know what I mean, Jack. I just keep waiting for all my dreams coming true to end."

Just as I was about to respond, a white limousine pulls into the driveway. She asks, "Is that for us, Jack?"

"That's for us, Mary Shanahan."

There is one thing that gives radiance to everything. It is the idea of something just around the corner. **G.K. Chesterton**

Chapter Fifty-eight

The winter is moving along quickly and everything is working out according to PGC's master plan. Tom Harvey's estate is all knotted up with his daughter Nadine contesting her father's will because he named his significant other, Angelica, a fifty per cent beneficiary. I'm certain she would have been happy to take a million and hit the road, but Nadine: I don't want that gold digging bitch to get a solitary cent. The insurance company has C&B in flux for the cost of the airplane, but so far has not made any offers or settlement suggestions pending a criminal investigation.

It seems like any accusations against PGC for arranging Tom Harvey's death lack evidence. So far all concerns are conjecture and rumors. Neither Nadine nor Angelica has made any overtures to return the property they are holding in the name of C&B Leasing. Paul Gordon Charles isn't pushing them either, allowing the status quo.

The audit was completed on the first of March. Matthew Wilson is an experienced, sharp, underpaid auditor who knows how to put numbers in the right viewpoint, if it is worth his while. Most insurance accounting principles can be useful in achieving regulatory objectives. The general framework of statutory insurance accounting is based on concepts of valuation, continuity and realization. The plan is simple, according to the gospel of Matthew Wilson. He asks for what he wants to see. He wants nothing more and not anything less.

Shanahan is busy, on the opposite side of our partner's desk, making the entreated reconsiderations on the1984 budget. PGC didn't want the budget completed until the audit was absolute so we could put sagacious increases in the revenue projections. Meanwhile I'm jotting notes on a legal pad, in shorthand, about the existing state of affairs. I look across the desk and Mary is smiling at me. I ogle back.

"Statutory accounting principles concentrate on conservative valuation rules for balance sheet items. The concern about operating results has always been of secondary importance to analysis of financial position. Generally, a liquidation view of the company has been adopted in the formulation of statutory accounting principles. What may appear to be unorthodox and inconsistent accounting practices become understandable when placed in the context of the solvency goal."

"What did you say, Jack?" Mary asks.

"Oh, I'm just thinking out loud." I say. "Listen you may learn something about insurance accounting.

She goes back to her numbers and I start my shorthand, announcing, "Statutory accounting imposes an unusually harsh valuation rule by excluding some assets from the balance sheet altogether. A conservative measurement of surplus results when the lowest of several possible values is selected for assets and the highest of several possible values is selected for liabilities. So the majority of assets admitted to the balance sheet are monetary items. These admitted assets are cash or can be converted to cash quickly without loss of value. I don't know from whom PGC had received this advice, but he has set his companies up perfectly.

"PGC would claim it was all his idea, and once presented, it was approved by Certified Public Accountants and Lawyers. But, the more likely scenario is he only followed the directions of his advisors. Of course, he never signed or agreed to anything nor did he ever see any documents. According to him, a man who brags he has1,500 hundred expensive suits hanging in his closets, doesn't really know the difference between an admitted asset and a non-admitted asset."

"Jack, what are you rambling about?" She asks, now smiling with a tongue-in-cheek look.

"Mary, just listen. I'm making notes about the Annual Report and Audit. Okay?" I beseech her.

"Stating assets and liabilities in terms of a monetary unit is the valuation process. Valuation rules of statutory accounting have been designed to state a conservative statement of policyholders' surplus. Valuation should also prevent sharp fluctuations in policyholders' surplus. For example non-admitted assets are furniture, fixtures, equipment, supplies, automobiles, computer software, uncollected premiums over ninety days due, and loans to shareholders and certain personnel. The admitted assets are cash or cash equivalents, with limitations on investing too large a portion in portfolio assets like in stock exposing surplus to market price fluctuations. My God, we made Matthew Wilson's job so easy.

"The only assets showing are cash in checking and savings with the latter bearing a reasonable rate of interest? And what Mathew Wilson considered as cash includes the collateral and joint accounts, quadrupling the value of admitted assets. What a hoodwinking, you think Shanahan? The property, furniture and equipment are not balance sheet items because they are owned by C&B Leasing, who leases these assets back to the operating company. The liabilities and other monthly expenses reside in the management company, leaving the operating company clean as a whistle. The operating company, on the audited report as of December 31, 1984 looks stronger than the electric chair.

"The term realization is used by Matthew Wilson to mean the recognition of revenue and expenses. Even though premiums have been paid they are not completely recognized into income until the contract provisions are completed. So he creates a liability for unearned premium, which is based on the schedule you prepared, Shanahan. Then Wilson requested back up for 10% of the schedule, telling me in advance which ones he wanted to see. He, of course, agrees with our calculations of unearned premium. For fifty *large*, who would argue against our computations? Certainly not Matthew Wilson, a white collar criminal extraordinaire.

"The real issue is loss and loss expense estimates. In the bonding business Risk Management estimates the amount of the loss and loss adjustment expenses. The estimates are made by Risk Management and then reviewed by the Claims examiner to make sure the estimates are sound and consistent with company guidelines. Or, should I say, this is the way it is supposed to work. Atlantic States Surety runs their *good cop–bad cop* a little differently. Risk Management makes their assessments and estimates, but when it gets to the Claims Department it is put at the bottom of a pile until somebody yelps for help."

"Jack, you are on a roll. And, I can't believe how much I understand. Why are you reviewing everything? Isn't the audit over?" Mary asks.

"Life has a way of making nothing ever over." I reply. "So bear with me."

"Details on losses incurred are kept on the gross and net basis. The gross basis provides for the loss cost before reinsurance, subrogation, or salvage recoveries. The net basis provides for the amount of loss incurred by the company after reinsurance, subrogation, and salvage. Financial statements show losses on a net basis. The amount of any subrogation or salvage receivable is not recorded until the cash is received.

"Atlantic States Surety claims are kept in the heads of Maggie Little and Joe Neverson. Although meticulous files are kept by Maggie Little they are carried around in attaché cases or locked away in a fire proof safe in the collateral storage area. PGC does not want any records available that somebody could sabotage. He's a paranoid son-of-a-bitch and runs his empire like the old Nixon White House, only more carefully.

"From day one all I hear about is how Joe Neverson needs money to pay claims. I'm never given a number other than he tells me, after the loan closing, a million dollars might put a few claims that are pending on a temporary hold. Since 27 March 1983, a claim has never been accrued or paid. No entry has been made in the general ledger since inception because there was no general ledger maintained for 1983. A fact I left alone for Matthew Wilson not to have to explain. *How the hell do you audit a company with no general ledger?* I thought about asking for a copy of last year's work papers, but I didn't for obvious reasons. On the other hand, if there had been a general ledger there still would've been no entry made because these types of goings-on's non-ledger assets and liabilities.

"So when Matthew Wilson asks me about claims I told him there were three pending and I gave him the purged files. He creates a minimal reserve and that is the name of that tune. Soon enough Matt will be in for the jolt of his life and nobody deserves it more. I wonder if he is splitting the *kitty* with any of the others. Maybe Bernard Goodman, the sexy Emily Harding, but not the Yale kid Jerry Hamner. Three of the four might be on the take. I really doubt it though, Matthew Wilson is too greedy. He's a gluttonous motherfucker!"

"Jack, who are you?" Mary asks. "You really trust me, sharing all your thoughts. Especially, since I'm starting to understand so much. Sometimes you scare me."

"What did God tell Moses at the burning bush? *I am who I am.*" I voice in a deep, husky vocal sound. Mary, I will always take care of you. Just trust me and don't try to understand me."

I keep drawing circles on the legal pad, connecting them to a stick man, looking desolate and forlorn. "Look," I say to Mary Shanahan. "Obstruction of Justice is lying to investigators. Such lying could carry a separate count of bank fraud. Matthew Wilson is crazy, Mary. He is given to emotional outbursts or flights of temper. He speaks deliberately with the caution he once knew when he was a good accountant working for Arthur Andersen early in his career. Do you know about Arthur Andersen?" I query of Mary Shanahan.

"I think so," she said. "Isn't one of the Big Eight firms named after him?"

"Very good," I say. "Many years ago, the story goes, in modern day accounting, no one embodied the ideal of a scrupulously honest auditor better than Arthur Andersen, a hard-driving Chicagoan who founded his own firm in 1913.

"In a story that is famous within the profession, the head of one of Andersen's largest clients, a rail company, visited the young man at his office and threatened to fire him as auditor unless he signed off on some fudged numbers. Staring down the president of the railway company, Andersen declared, *there's not enough money in the city of Chicago to induce me to change that report.*"

"The head of the railway company fired Andersen, but within months, the company was in bankruptcy. The incident crystallized Andersen's reputation for honesty, and Andersen's accounting practice flourished because of its founder's integrity, not despite it. The firm's unofficial motto, which Andersen learned from his mother, said it all: *Think straight, talk straight.*"

There was a long pause by me. Mary went back to her working papers and began posting her adjustments once more. Finally, she asks, "Where are you going with all this rhetoric, Jack? Are you reflecting about the audit results? Are you dissatisfied?" She queries, beginning her posting once again as I continue my interpolation.

"The mandatory audit is designed to guarantee the credibility of earnings statements. But when the company is salted with executives who are willing to use every arcane bookkeeping technique imaginable to claim they are hitting their profit numbers, it just doesn't matter. The thinking behind this kind of risk is that the accounting so-called magicians will always rescue the company even though a series of accounting maneuvers defy gravity. And, although they really don't hit the numbers, they say they do and everyone is happy."

"Accounting rules are challenges to be overcome through ingenious financial chaos. For instance, by using simple accounting tricks to inflate the company's income, by disguising the amount of debt on the balance sheet pumps up cash flow. All this can be achieved by forming a series of private partnerships or *S* corporations, known as special purpose entities, and engage in business transactions with those special purpose entities."

"Like leasing and management companies," interjects, Mary Shanahan. She smiles at me while putting her right pointer finger to her lips, whispering, "Are you sure our office isn't bugged?"

"I hope this office is bugged. Then they'll know what I'm thinking. PGC wants this to look like a lean, efficient company to its banks. By foisting large chunks of debt into these special purpose entities he makes the operating company's balance sheet strong and the income statement convincing." I declare, while Mary interrupts me.

"I don't understand." She wonders out loud.

"The scam is very simple. Depositing the proceeds of a bank loan and recording it as premium earned is dirty business. The company can hide its debt in a special purpose entity, which makes the operating company appear healthier than it really is showing the appearance of growth. With the special purpose companies millions can be produced in phantom revenues."

I say, somewhat exhausted. Although, I love thinking out loud and there were two purposes to my discourse. First, to teach Shanahan and second I'm hoping PGC might be listening to this session. I would like to see him squirm.

Mary looks at me strangely, like what has happened to the old closed mouth Jack Oleson. Frankly, I didn't care about my job or what PGC was all about. When I was in college I was told accounting and auditing was a gentlemanly profession. That accountants and auditors didn't poach clients from each other, it was unseemly. But in the 1980s, with anti-competitive restrictions removed, the accountants and auditors courted each other's clients aggressively.

I say, "Too many corporate managers, auditors and analysis are participating in a game of nods and winks. Competitors cooperate in the gray area between legitimacy and outright fraud. A gray area where the accounting is being perverted; where managers are cutting corners; and where earnings reports reflect the desires of management rather than the underlying financial performance of the company."

"Me, I'm just an old-fashioned, green eye-shade accountant who takes pride in getting numbers right, whether or not they please whoever. I suppose I'm just laced with wariness and caginess, which doesn't make sense in these 1980s."

Mary keeps on working away, but I know she's listening. I check my watch it is nearing six o'clock. "The Securities Act of 1933 spelled out, for the first time, a list of conditions a company had to meet in order to be able to sell shares of its stock to the public. Among those conditions the company had to file accurate financial statements. In order to assure the accuracy of these financial statements, companies had to hire an auditor to check their numbers at least once a year, for the annual report. The laws were a great boon to the accounting industry."

"Mary, you've just been through you're first audit. Do you think justice was served?"

She studies me. "No!" She says. "It doesn't seem like you do."

She pauses, looking directly into my eyes, then says, "Tomorrow is St. Patrick's Day."

"So it is. Here ends the lesson. Let's go to the St. Regis."

I don't know the key to success, but the key to failure is trying to please everybody. **Bill Cosby**

Chapter Fifty-nine

Lafayette Square
Washington D.C.
Memorial Day
Monday, May 28, 1984

I t had originally been called President's Park, but now that title encompassed the White House grounds, Lafayette Park and the Ellipse, a fifty-two-acre parcel of land on the south side of the White House. Lafayette Square is a seven-acre public park located directly north of the White House on H Street between 15th and 17th Streets, Northwest. I stood near the center of the park, looking at the equestrian statue of Andrew Jackson, the hero of the Battle of New Orleans and America's seventh chief executive. I'm remembering that song, *The Battle of New Orleans, sung by Johnny Horton*, released in 1959. The lyrics didn't make sense to me then, but nothing made sense during my teenage years, especially song lines.

Jackson now sat on a pediment of majestic Tennessee marble. It was the first statue of a man on horseback ever cast in the United States. Hey, I learn something new every day, I'm ruminating. The monument is surrounded by a low wrought-iron fence, with a scattering of ancient cannons inside this space. Four other statues memorializing foreign Revolutionary War heroes anchor its corners.

It is nearing our meet time, when I hear helicopter blades chopping through the air on the south side of the White House. I suppose it is Marine One carrying President Reagan back to the White House from Camp David. He is scheduled to speak and give remarks at Memorial Day ceremonies honoring an unknown serviceman of the Vietnam Conflict this afternoon, according to the newspapers and television reports.

I turn my head and see a man sitting on a bench near the oval-shaped fountain on the east side of the park midway between Jackson and the statue of Polish General Thaddeus Kosciuszko, who'd helped the fledgling English colonies free themselves from British rule. The man is dressed in black slacks and a white shirt. He has a large attache next to him. He appears to be dozing. I laugh, knowing what he's really doing, surveillance. He isn't the only person in the park. I look toward the trees on the northwest side of the park where I spy a woman in a pinstripe pantsuit wearing white sneakers carrying a briefcase. Her back is to me. She stops to examine the statue of German army officer Friedrich Wilhelm von Steuben, who also helped the colonists kick Mad King George's royal ass more than two centuries ago.

Then I notice a pregnant woman entering the park from the northern end where St. John's Church is located. She is wearing jogging attire, though she looks incapable of even walking quickly without collapsing. She appears to have a yellow Walkman clipped to her belt and she has ear phones plugged into her ears.

And there is a fourth inhabitant of the park. He looks like an infantryman, dressed in camouflage fatigues, dark bandanna, and a muscle shirt. He's donning a camouflage jacket and wearing combat boots. The man is walking slowly right through the middle of the park. This guy causes my eyebrows to rise because wearing this kind of attire doesn't work in highly patrolled Lafayette Square. There is a heavy police presence. And that presence is always strengthened when the President is in the area. But, I had not come here to think about these kinds of things. I'd come to Lafayette Square to meet my handler.

I glance around and notice the man was now awake, going through his attache. The woman in the pantsuit is still lingering around the von Steuben statue with her back toward me. The jogger is nearing the statue of Jackson. The infantryman is still dodging and weaving through Lafayette Park, although the Square isn't that large. He should have managed it by now. It was like the man was traveling in quicksand, moving but not getting anywhere. Now I see a gun and holster showing under his jacket when he moves a certain way; I can see the awkward but familiar bump in the camouflage. He must be a ballsy cop, I'm thinking. You don't come here armed, unless you want a rooftop counter sniper to assume the worst, with the result that your next of kin might receive an official apology after your funeral. Something just didn't feel right.

I let my gaze drift to the woman in the pantsuit at the northwest corner of the park. The lady was still examining the statue, an act that normally would take at most a minute or so. I eyed the briefcase she was carrying. Because of the distance I could not see it clearly, but it appeared bulky enough to contain a small bomb. I was frightened as I didn't understand what was possibly being timetabled.

My handler was already fifteen minutes late, which had never happened before. Then, I spotted the jogger once more. The pregnant woman was looking in the direction of the lady in the pantsuit. My attention next shifted to the man. He had risen too, slipped the attache over his shoulder and set off to the north side of the park toward St. John's Church.

He was tall, I noted, but his clothes hung well on his narrow frame. I gauged his age at closer to thirty than forty, though I never got a clear look at his face because of the poor visual angle with the many trees in the park.

My gaze swiveled again. On the other side of the park the lady in the pantsuit was finally moving, heading northwest toward the Decatur House Museum. I looked behind her. The infantryman seems to be watching me now, not moving at all. I see the man's index finger twitch as though on a trigger pull.

Suddenly I hear the sounds of muscular engines, flashing lights and sirens, putting me on standby alert. What I think is the Presidential motorcade makes the turn onto Pennsylvania Avenue. These types of limo exits tend to happen fast for obvious reasons. The motorcade, I suppose, is on its way to Arlington National Cemetery.

The lady in the white sneakers and the tall man in the business man's suit are gone from my line of vision. The pregnant woman seems to be retreating from the park. And then she simply disappears from my view. She vanishes.

The infantryman comes up behind me. "Jack," he says, reaching inside his jacket for what I thought might be his pistol. I instinctively blocked his movement with a hard left-handed chop and a right handed upper-cut to his jaw. I kicked his gun between the wrought iron surrounding the Jackson Monument. I'm wondering where the cops are, when the man mouths, *FBI.* I keep one eye on him and look around for any witnesses to this action. There are a few groups of people taking pictures of the White House, but nothing significant is going on. I see no uniformed police officers, which is highly a strange sequence of events.

The man shows me his credentials. "I don't know you sir." I say, while walking off toward H Street. I stop, reconsider, turn around and the man is gone. I don't have a lot of answers but what I did had been the correct thing to do. If you don't know who or why, never play your hand. Simply go into protection detail. Remember what you've been taught, you are always being tested. Life is a gut check. When in doubt never give yourself up, even if you think your ass will be in the professional wringer.

Do that which you fear to do, and the fear will die. **Ralph Waldo Emerson**

Chapter Sixty

Glen Echo, Maryland
Memorial Day
6 P.M.
Monday, May 28, 1984

I couldn't believe I had cut short my weekend with my family to meet my handler for no avail. And, what was that fiasco all about at Lafayette Square? Was it a hoax? Or, was it the continued mysterious workings of the Bureau. Maybe it was PGC playing his games?

I was watching the six o'clock news on television. It's showing President Reagan's motorcade coming to a stop at the Amphitheater at Arlington National Cemetery. The scene then flashes to him speaking at the Amphitheater:

Memorial Day is a day of ceremonies and speeches. Throughout America today, we honor the dead of our wars. We recall their valor and their sacrifices. We remember they gave their lives so that others might live.....

We're also gathered here for a special event – the national funeral for an unknown soldier who will today join the heroes of three other wars.....

Not long ago, when a memorial was dedicated here in Washington to our Vietnam veterans, the events surrounding that dedication were a stirring reminder of America's resilience, of how our nation could learn and grow and transcend the tragedies of the past.....

And the veterans of Vietnam who were never welcomed home with speeches and bands, but who were never defeated in battle and were heroes as surely as any who have ever fought in a noble cause, stage their own parade on Constitution Avenue. As America watched them – some in wheelchairs, all of them proud – there was a feeling – that as

*a nation we were coming together again and that we had, at long last,
welcomed the boys' home.....*

*The Unknown Soldier who is returned to us today and whom we
lay to rest is symbolic of all our missing sons, and we will present him
present him with the Congressional Medal of Honor, the highest military decoration that we can bestow..... Today we pause to embrace him
and all who served us so well in a war whose end offered no parades, no
flags, and so little thanks. We can be worthy of the values and ideals for
which our sons sacrificed – for their courage, and for their noble service.
Let us, if we must, debate the lesson learned at some other time. Today,
we simply say with pride, "Thank you, dear son. May God cradle you
in His loving arms?"*

The excerpts from Reagan's Memorial Day address gave me
the chills. The delivery was exquisite and the message long over-
due. But it is too little, too late to be effective. I compare it to my
service, which is also a war with no definable purpose. Just do what
you are told and keep your mouth shut. Maybe you will make it
out of here alive, if you're lucky.

I flip off the television. Mary Shanahan is sitting on the sofa
looking through a magazine. I don't like to talk about things. It is
just my way, but I say to Mary, "We need to talk."

"What," is Mary's response? "Did you say we need to talk?"
She asks, staring at me with her bright green eyes.

We need to talk are perhaps the scariest four words in the
English language.

We live on Princeton Avenue and I suggested we take a walk.
We ambled to University Avenue and turn left and make another
left on Yale Avenue. Then we take a right onto Columbia Avenue,
where we slow our pace.

"Mary times will be changing soon enough. I'm getting pressure from PGC to move my family here. I'm plenty content with
the way things are and so is Ellen. But, our boys deserve and need
more than an every- other-weekend father. This won't happen until September. But, it will happen then because we want to start
the boys in their new school in Virginia on time." I say, feeling
beleaguered and somewhat depressed.

"Jack, I knew this day would come. This has been all too good to be true. I just feel I let you down somehow. I mean we've kissed, but it has never gone any further. We've slept together, but I sensed we both just needed to be by each other. I'm attracted to you, but you have Ellen and your children to think about. You never talk about your life. I know nothing about you really. You've shown me a great time and taught me the accounting trade. Yet, what is most important is you are my best friend. And, for me that's enough." Mary says, showing tears now.

I grab her hand and we start walking again. We remain silent until we get to Harvard Avenue. We turn right on Harvard and amble to University, where we walk past Byrn Mawr Avenue toward Wellesley Circle.

"I never wanted to hurt you Mary. The whole thingamajig is more than complicated. But, I justify to myself what we are doing is for your long range benefit and mine. I told you from day one you would get an education that should set you up for life. You've proven what a great asset you are on the job. You are my best friend, too. I'm going to explain a few things to you tonight that you might be better off not knowing. You deserve to know, however, because I care so very much about you. But what I tell you tonight cannot be repeated or acknowledged to anybody for the rest of your life. I think you can handle it. Can you?" I say, squeezing her hand and moseying around the circle toward Cornell Avenue.

I tell her everything as we turn right on Cornell Avenue to Vassar Circle, turning left around the halo and exiting the maze via University Avenue. I talk without stopping all the way back to Princeton Avenue and to our house.

"Do you think your IQ has gone up, while walking through all those Ivy League and Seven Sisters streets?" I ask Mary.

"Mine can't get any higher," she guffaws. "How about yours?"

It seems fitting that we had picked this small community as a place to live. It is a real community, its residents celebrate with and care for each other, and the town retains a real small town spirit despite the many changes over the years. Glen Echo has become widely known as an unusual enclave, an extraordinarily desirable place to live and yet an easy commute to the rest of Metropolitan Washington. And as has been the case throughout its history, once people move here they want to stay.

"I want you to sojourn here, Mary. I'll continue to pay the rent until you want to leave. This is our place." I sincerely promise her.

"And you, Jack. How long will you be with me?" Shanahan asks.

"Forever, in spirit, but not always physically present. We have until September. If Ellen doesn't join me, I might be with you forever." I say, encouragingly.

"I'm not counting on forever, but I'm going to stay the course, Jack. You've taught me to be patient." She said, smiling, coquettishly.

We open a couple bottles of wine, one red – one white. We play a Neil Diamond tape and enjoy each other's company. She invites me to sleep in her bed. We hold each other tightly and quietly fall asleep.

A man does what he must – in spite of personal consequences, in spite of obstacles and dangers and pressures – and that is the basis of all human morality. **John F. Kennedy**

Chapter Sixty-one

220 Runnymede Avenue
Jenkintown, Pennsylvania
Wednesday, June 13, 1984

The past few months have been pretty unadventurous. We received the Annual Audit reports and the Certified Financial Statements for the year ended December 31, 1983. In addition we received the tax returns for Atlantic States Surety Associates, a partnership; Atlantic States Surety Company, a C Corporation; and, C&B Leasing, a partnership.

Paul Gordon Charles was pleased with the results, with all the ratios exceeding the A.M. Best Company ratings. The five factors used to measure a company's stability and strength are (1) underwriting performance, (2) management economy, (3) reserve adequacy, (4) adequacy of net resources, and (5) soundness of investments. All things considered we were given a B rating, which is a good score.

PGC had penciled the budget numbers for 1984 next to the line items on the 1983 report. I'm having Shanahan adjust the reports and told Gordon I'd have the new budget ready by July 1st. He was content and first mentioned to me that we would be taking his new corporate jet to Dallas, Texas to attend the Republican Convention in August. That ten of us would be attending the Presidential luncheon on August 20th. *So mark your calendar and include your wife.* He'd told me.

I'm forty years old today. I'm leaving about one o'clock for Philadelphia to celebrate my birthday with my family. I'm looking forward to it, having taken the rest of the week off as well. Ellen and I have much to discuss regarding so many subjects. Neither of us has been angry at each other for a couple of months, probably just indifferent. Our life has been very comfortable for both of us this year. It's probably because I don't know a lot about her day-to-day life anymore, and she doesn't know about mine. When we are together, however, we act madly in love on the outside. We certainly enjoy each other's company and sharing the boys together. Being a family for them is important to both of us.

It is Mary Shanahan's birthday today too. She is twenty-eight years old. I gave her a card before I left and she said we would have birthday cake together on Sunday night when I get back. She is going to Gettysburg, Pennsylvania to visit her parents for the weekend. I kissed her goodbye and left the office around one o'clock.

It's a hot day and I'm blasting the New Yorker's air conditioner as I barrel ass North on 95. I have it so cold in the car I can see my breath. As I pass through Wilmington, Delaware I give fleeting thoughts to it being forty years since I was born at Wilmington General. But I keep moving along, arriving home around 4:30 p.m. Joe and Dan are excited when I pull into the driveway. They both tell me, at the same time that Mom and Chris will be home soon.

"We're going to Rizzo's for pizza." Dan exclaims.

"Dad, then we are going to open your presents!" Joe calls out, with glee.

"Great," I say, enthusiastically. "Will one you guys get me a beer?"

We sit down at the picnic table in the back yard and they tell me some new stories since the last time I was home. As they talk non-stop I start feeling so guilty because I am missing so much of their youth. I hardly know Christopher at all. What a terrible job I have to sacrifice so much for such a worthless purpose. But the job really isn't to blame. I could quit the damn job. It is really all about the life style I enjoy and the freedom it gives me. I am a selfish man. I should have never been married in the first place. I should have never been allowed to have children. In fact, if you want to be a father you should have to pass a test. One has to take a test to do anything else.

I also live other lives, a life of puzzles in the form of funny stories. When I tell my stories, which never meet with family approval, I am always the leading character but not the hero. The beginnings of my stories sound like factual reporting, but after I put a spin on them the end result is what fits the occasion best.

The boys hear Ellen's car in the driveway and they run to meet her. First, I see Christopher running up the driveway. When he sees me he slows to a walk, peers at me and waves his right hand, like he's not quite sure just who I am. I wave back, while the other boys come around the house in advance of their mother, who now appears with a smile on her face. She looks terrific, good looks and gorgeousness. I mean nobody deserves such luck, especially an asshole like me.

"Hi, Johnny," she greets me with a wholehearted upsurge. She walks directly toward me as I stand up from the picnic table. She sets a handful of stuff on the table and gives me a huge hug and kiss. "There," she says, "we've got that covered." She laughs and wiggles her ass.

"Hello, old man," she says, with a teasing voice, sitting down at the end of the table.

"Lordy, lordy look who's forty." She laughs.

I jibe back. "Don't laugh to hard, you're next up for forty."

Suddenly, Danny appears with two beers, one for us both. Ellen and I smile at each other. "Isn't he a chip off the old block, Johnny." Ellen scoffs.

"Thanks Dan." I say.

"When we going, Mom." Joe shouts as he is tosses a ball to Christopher.

"When I finish this beer, is that okay?" Ellen replies with a *give-me-a-break* attitude.

I watch Ellen's body language. When she was in her twenties men's eyes followed her everywhere, then she would settle into her seat or on a bar stool with a practiced hair-flip. When she left a room, there was a moment of deflations when all returned to normal life. While it seemed apparent to everyone Ellen was headed somewhere more important, her path and presence always left something of her guise behind.

Ellen doesn't have many friends, but those she has are very

close and Ellen was one who could always be counted on. If one of her girlfriends was in a crisis, Ellen would rush in, offer tidal waves of concern. She could sooth or incite in the name of support. Like: *Just get over it*, or, conversely, *just get even*. Either bit of advice was inspiring.

The emotions of men, however, were a different order. They were pesky annoyances, small dust devils at her feet. Her knack for causing heartbreak was innate, but her vitality often made people forgive her romantic misdeeds. Now, however, she's nearing forty and not so easily forgiven as when her skin bloomed like roses.

The first time I slept with her I was on the rebound from my first marriage and her marriage was in trouble. But her sense of fun enchanted me, and once I had sufficiently armored myself against her allure, by viewing her always as a good friend first, I was able to enjoy the best part of her without becoming ensnared. She was so complex and difficult to understand.

So her story, which is a huge part of mine, is my recollections. But in real life – imagination sometimes has to stand in for the total experience. This is okay, especially if you want to spin her yarn to suit yourself best.

We went to Rizzo's, a place we used to take the boys when they were smaller. We ordered a large pizza, coca cola's and beers for Ellen and I. We spent a couple hours drinking, eating and sharing lots of laughs and conversation.

It was still light out when we got home and we enjoyed birthday cake and ice cream together. I opened my cards and presents. Everything had *Forty* printed on it. I didn't feel old at forty, it was when I turned thirty that I felt old. When it turned dark the boys tired and I helped Ellen get them to bed.

Afterwards I fixed Ellen a gin and tonic and me a Jack Daniels and club soda. I told her she looked good and seemed to be in a better disposition. She told me the same. We asked no more questions of each other. We enjoyed my special Day and shared a lot of adult stories and laughs.

During our nightcap I told her PGC wants us to move to the Washington D.C. area. I told her I had done some investigating with Gordon's realtor and I found some new townhouses going up in Vienna, Virginia. "They're beautiful," I said. "Not far from Tysons Corner, right off Chain Bridge Road. I've already been approved for a mortgage. I just need you to look at the property. The one I like is on a corner lot. The address is less than three miles away from a new elementary and middle school. It will be perfect for us." I expound on.

"Would we have to sell this house," Ellen asks.

"No," I reply. "It's great rental property."

"And, when does this job end?" She asks.

"I have no idea, but when it does, no more FBI." I assure her. "I can get a good job as controller or with a CPA firm in D.C. or the surrounding Metropolitan area." I answer, with confidence.

"Go ahead, Johnny. Buy the place, your taste is excellent. Send me some pictures." She said, but rather apathetically.

"Okay, I will. But are you going to join me? I mean this is an opportunity to put our family back in order, Ellen. It's what I want most of all." I say, unambiguously.

"You think you do, but I'm not so sure. Our marriage has been nothing but new starts. And I'm not sure what I want any more either. I know I love you. You are the most interesting character in my life. But simple love is not good enough anymore."

I felt her sense of honesty. I also sensed her need for more adventure. But in the past I could always make her see it my way. "Let's give it one more chance, Ellen," I pleaded.

"What? And, quit my job? Sell my home?" She said with a broached tone in her voice. "I'm sorry," she apologized. "Johnny, just go ahead and buy the house. Do it for you. We'll see what happens. Every day is different from the next."

"Ellen we have two new companies, a restaurant and an automobile dealership. We need an accountant for both places. I could also throw C&B Leasing to you rather quickly. I could trump your current salary by $1,000 a month." I tell her, unreservedly.

"I'm having one more drink, Johnny." She decrees, while going to the counter and pouring one for me and one for her.

"It's not so easy for me. I love my life here, but for the boys I'll consider the move as long as we don't have to sell my *gingerbread* house. Go ahead, Johnny, buy your house. I like it when we calmly make the best decisions for both of us." She said, so serenely.

"Done," I said. "It will get everybody off my back, too. It's kind of a win-win situation. Those properties are going to climb in value, quickly."

"Johnny, I have to work in the morning. How long are you going to be home?" Ellen queries?

"I'll be here until Sunday. Is that okay?" I ask.

"You have no idea how I miss you. It's just that times are changing for us. I love you. Are you coming to bed?" She asks, with an alluring smile. "Happy Birthday, honey," she says, throwing me a kiss.

Our lives' have paralleled each other's since 1959. In the twenty-five years I've known her she has reinvented herself several times. When we first moved to D.C and I had just started my job with the Bureau, she showed up for drinks with me and my Dad at Fort McNair in a summer dress so transparent that when she passed between us and a bay window hot with sunlight, the dress seemed to incinerate like flash paper. Her auburn hair was clipped back with a polka-dot plastic barrette, which knocked about five years off her age. She looked like a teenager again.

"Jeez, Ellen, you look fabulous," my Dad had said, smiling.

"Do I now, Warren? How am I supposed to dress and look when I'm meeting a Bird Colonel and his up-and-coming son for drinks? I'm so proud of you both." She said, with her beguiling grin. She had the Colonel's undivided attention. "Thank you sir, I got the job at the Pentagon."

Ellen talked on, oblivious to the salivations that her dress was causing. She had to know of its effect, but it was as though she'd put it on in the morning, calculated what it would do, then forgot about it as it cast its spell. Her eyes and attention never strayed from Dad or me, which was part of her style.

She would even take time to let one of Dad's jokes sweep over her, as though she needed a moment to absorb its brilliance, then laugh her face falling forward and give you a look of quizzical admiration, as if to say, *You are much more complicated and interesting than I ever supposed.*

Funny, Ellen was just as happy alone as with company. When she was alone she was potential; with others she was realized. Alone, she was self-contained, her tightly spinning magnetic energy oscillating around her. When in company, she had invisible tethers to everyone in the room: as they moved away, she pulled them in. She knew who was doing better than she was, what man she would care to seduce just to prove she could. And get out of it by saying *I just want to get off.*

I swallowed the balance of my drink, while thinking about Shanahan for a moment. I climbed the stairs and crawled into bed with Ellen. She turned toward me and pulled herself close. Well, well, well, what a tangled web we weave, I lip to myself.

The strongest of all warriors are these two – time and patience.
Leo Tolstoy

Chapter Sixty-two

Independence Day
Princeton Avenue
Glen Echo, Maryland
Wednesday, July 4, 1984

"It's the Fourth of July." I declare to Mary Shanahan. Since the holiday is in the middle of the week I elected to spend it in Maryland with Shanahan. Very few people have to work on Independence Day. It is a day of family celebrations with picnics and barbecues, showing a great deal of emphasis on the American tradition of political freedom. Activities associated with the day include watermelon or hotdog eating competitions and sporting events, such as baseball games, three-legged races, swimming activities and tug-of-war games. I'm thinking I should be home with my family, but it's not practical.

"You know I never liked the Fourth of July, Mary. Summer baseball had just ended and the weather was always so hot. Our hometown was like a ghost town, it seemed, because everyone else was at the Lake. We didn't have a lake home, nor were we invited as extras to anybody else's place. Fortunately it was a one day holiday so it was just an ordinary non-eventful day." I speak out, feeling slightly lonely like I did yesterday when I was young.

"Like today, Jack." She says, unsympathetically.

"I'm nervous about what I've told you, but I'm gratified I've told you everything. I'm uneasy not for me but for you. During the rest of your whole entire life you can never tell anyone what you know. I feel so badly for you. It's a difficult thing to do, to deny a certain period of time you have spent with somebody you care about as time that didn't exist." I caution her, apprehensively.

"I thank you for giving me time to prepare." Mary says, fretfully. "However, I don't think we will ever be completely apart. I love you, Jack, and I owe you so much for bringing me happiness. Never fear, no matter what happens; I will not give away your secrets. There are so many things, I have learned from you. The most important phenomenon is patience." She states, earnestly.

There is a long pause. I look at my watch, noting it is one o'clock. "Listen," I say. "Let's have a drink. I have a lot more to update you about. Like one hundred and one complications." She fixes me a Jack Daniels and club soda, while I open a bottle of white for her.

"Well," she says, as we sit down on the outside steps.

"What are we supposed to do about paying Café Sebastian tabs? What do they total, fifty some thousand?" I ask, Mary.

She laughs. "My, oh my, he sticks it to everybody. Poor Sebastian, he's running around like a chicken with his head cut off thinking PGC isn't going to pay."

"How about claims, how much are they asking for?" I ask.

"Jack, I talk with Maggie every day. We're friends. I think it's millions. She doesn't tell all. I don't think she thinks PGC will let this cash cow go." Mary says, with trepidation.

"Okay, Mary, you know who I am and what my job is all about. I mean thank God I hired you and we have the relationship we do. I'm going to ask you to do one more thing for me. I'm going to put my *302s* together and give you a copy to put in a safe deposit box. It's asking a lot, but they're not getting away with this one." I say, with a great sense of angst.

"*302s*, aren't they FBI reports? I'll take care of anything you want, Jack. I work for you. I'll do what you tell me to do. And with my limited experience and knowledge, I know something is terribly wrong here." She says, showing great mawkishness.

"Yes, a 302 form is used by FBI agents to report or summarize the interviews that we conduct and contains information from the notes taken during the interview by the non-primary agent. It consists of information taken from the subject, rather than details about the subject themselves. The *302* is a form for reporting information that may become testimony. I don't want what I know deep-sixed, if something happens to me unexpectedly."

I spilled my guts again to Mary Shanahan during the next few hours. I told her we just received a B rating from A.M. Best based on the bogus financial statements we just had certified. This, of course, will lead regulators to believe we have adequate reserves, but, in actuality, have inadequate reserves. Actually Atlantic State Surety has many undisclosed credit-quality problems, which do not reflect the aggressive accounting, and the substantial unconsolidated indebtedness contained in off-balance sheet special-purpose egresses.

PGC's contention that zero-loss standards are free from error is just another bullshit tool that has virtually no margin of safety. The company's underwriting transparency, accounting, and track record should be beyond reproach. The bond insurance business is simple. In exchange for receiving upfront insurance premiums, the bond insurer agrees to cover all interest and principal payments over the life of the bond if the issuer defaults.

The beauty of bond insurance is that the bond insurer doesn't need capital to buy the bonds. The bond investor puts up the capital. The insurer collects the insurance premiums up front in exchange for guaranteeing the bonds and should invest the premiums over the long term.

That's not to say bond insurance requires no capital. To enter the business, the bond regulators have to prove that the company has the wherewithal to make good on its guarantees. That means the bond insurer doesn't really need to pay claims so much as advance money for brief periods during times of extreme financial distress. Still, it is a business that requires extreme caution. It has to be underwritten to a no-loss standard, otherwise the leverage is deadly. PGC's no-loss standard is simply to not pay the claims, and spend all the collected premium dollars for his personal caprices. Paul Gordon Charles has been in the insurance industry for years, and no one has ever questioned his reputation. No one has ever gone to his regulators without his permission. Yes, he has friends in high places, very high places.

Shanahan is like a sponge, absorbing everything I'm talking about. During my lengthy discourse she is asking all the right questions. She is totally getting my heads-up advisory. Maybe she and I had done too good of job. We obtained the results PGC was looking for very quickly. We understood and could prove the deceit, duplicity, and fraud I thought the Bureau was out to authenticate, but evidently not. There's more to it and maybe I'm being set up. Now, I'm wondering about the why?

Mary fixed me another drink. When she sat back down on the steps I tell here the most confusing thing is what happened at Lafayette Square on Memorial Day. I was told that he was in Fripp Island, but that really tells me nothing. He is never where the action takes place. All I know is the FBI would not have left me hanging out there. My handler must not have scheduled the meet, which leads me to believe PGC has inside information and knows more about me than he's acknowledging. The other possibility is Ned Larson. Ned's the one who recommended me for the job and he knows a lot about me. And where, oh, where is Charlotte Boyer?

Mary is studying me when I say, "How did Rich Richards just happen to be on that Amtrak train in November? Rich was one of their most treasured undercover agents. He immediately got rid of those two people dogging my family and I with dispatch. I hired him and nobody asked any questions. He didn't work long for me before Corrigan confiscated him to sell bonds. He was the top producer for two months and he's gone.

"Maggie said they had pretty much a platonic relationship and he was good to have around her boys. After maybe a month living with her, he was gone. Richard Corrigan told me Richards had come to him saying he had to go back to his family. Corrigan said he was crying when he resigned from Atlantic States Surety. It doesn't sound like the Rich Richards I know. I can't imagine him crying about anything."

"Let us not forget about Rich posting the entire general ledger." Adds, Shanahan, "He did a great job!"

"Yeah, but I just don't know what or who they're after. You

never do know with these guys. But I'm becoming convinced the operations of Atlantic States Surety are a small part or a stepping stone to a much larger picture. I'm starting to believe PGC is an out-of-control agent or an informant. I'm certain he knew who I was the day I was so-called hired. However, I have been useful and he's using the Bureau, through me, to achieve his personal goals." I say, assuredly.

"Do you think the truth will reveal itself?" Mary Shanahan asks.

"No one will ever know the complete story, they never do. That's the way of criminal politics. But we'll know enough to make us keep wondering the rest of our lives. That is why I'm putting it all down and giving it to you. If something happens. Send it to the Washington Post."

Now I'm studying Mary, thinking about what she just asked me as being out of context and balderdash at this juncture. And she is so unruffled and unbothered with what I was telling her. Does she have ice in her veins? I'm wondering now if they had annexed her or worse yet where had she really come from in the first place. I had not made any phone calls to verify her resume or check her out. I realized she had to go either way. If she was working for them as an informant, Mary had to go. If she is simply Mary Shanahan, which is what I believe, she has to go too soon. She can't go down with this ship.

"Mary," I say. "Let's go over to Conduit Road to Trav's and get a bowl of chili and drink some cheap beer." I suggest, the name of being careless and for some breathing space.

"Okay, I've been waiting for you to take me out to an old-time saloon, with an ambiance of roadside-type seediness."

It felt ordinary to be at Trav's and away from the day to day annoyances and disappointments. Mary Shanahan looks comfortable chatting with the other convivial patrons. It is good to see how well she fits in with this friendly bunch. Trav's had a long *L* shaped bar where people seemed to congregate at the intersection of the two legs of the *L*. We had several beers and enjoyed the chili as people talked with us. They had seen us many times before and it seems we had been causing quite a stir. Like, *who are these guys?* They were able to get out of us we were not married to each other and we worked in Washington.

At six o'clock the news came on the television set at Trav's. It showed President Reagan in Richard Petty's winning circle. Petty had won his 200th race at the Firecracker 400 at Daytona International Speedway. Ronald Reagan was in attendance, he was the first sitting president to attend a NASCAR race. Reagan had celebrated the milestone with Petty and his family in victory lane.

Every time I see President Reagan or hear him speak I get the *willies* wondering what he knows about Paul Gordon Charles. Or, does he have a clue about what's going on with Paul Gordon Charles. Or, does he care?

A plump, fiftyish-sixtyish woman, with her hair pulled back into a perfect bun, who resembles my mother, sits down next to me. Her likeness startles me. "Are you buying," she asks.

"Absolutely," I reply, introducing myself. "I'm Jack."

"Jack or John," she queries?

"Jack," I affirm. "Didn't I tell you it was Jack?"

I didn't really want to talk with this stranger and especially did not want to satisfy this woman's curiosity. I remind myself I will get through it all. That I will do the right thing, like my mother taught me. I drink the last of my beer and look to my right. It's Shanahan with a big smile on her face. "I just ordered us one more." She said.

"Did you see a rather plump lady, who was sitting here, leave?" I ask.

"I've had my eye on you the whole time, nobody but me has sat here since we arrived." Mary assures me. "Are you okay, Jack."

"I'm fine," I say, "Everyone has a dream."

Shanahan looks at me again. "Jack, are you okay? What are you talking about, *Everyone has a dream?*

"Second thoughts are contagious." I say, "Don't worry about it. We had another beer before we headed back to Princeton Avenue.

En route I determined I was going to start slowly distancing myself from Shanahan. I would not give her my *302s*. I would pursue my home purchase and until I'm able to move I'll travel home every weekend. I will show no signs of doubt, but I'll keep my eyes peeled on her movements and concerns.

Of all the liars in the world, sometimes the worst are your own fears. **Rudyard Kipling**

Chapter Sixty-three

1700 K Street
Washington D.C.
Friday, July 20, 1984

A new nuisance comes into play as I'm trying to get to the bottom of this whole fiasco. It seems like there is always a diversion from just studying the state of affairs as a whole. Annabelle Bergman, who I met during my trip to Fripp Island, has been living at PGC's Maryland mansion the past six months. During this time she has been going to high school and servicing PGC when he sends Madeline Haycock off on her so-called auditing missions.

During PGC's last trip to Fripp with Madeline, Annabelle drove to Georgetown and got drunk at the Crazy Horse Saloon, a hangout for the younger crowd, and drove her Mercedes SL convertible into a parked car on M Street. She was totally drunk and MPD found a loaded pistol under her front seat with no license to carry.

Paul Gordon Charles retained a prestigious lawyer who made a deal for damages, eliminated the gun charge and settled everything for the surrender of Annabelle's license and mandatory attendance to school for drunk drivers. My part of this deal was to take her to class and give her a ride home every Thursday night for eight weeks. It was not too bad a deal. Her class was conducted near the *New York, New York* restaurant on K Street. It is a popular place for Congressman and Senators. I'd sit at the bar and watch the comings and goings. I am still a hayseed from Minnesota and never want to outgrow my roots.

I'm missing my closeness with Shanahan. I put my new plan in force the day after Independence Day. I'd been home, in Philadelphia, the past two weekends, leaving Mary to fend for herself. During the working day she just does her job and I spend most of my time out of the office searching for answers by talking to other employees. I am putting a few things together, slowly but surely. Mary hasn't pushed me for anything like she would've had she been looking for any information. I hope it is that simple because I really care for her. I also want to keep her aboard as long as I can, but if it gets dicey I will protect her future first. She is doing most of the accounting work where I am mostly dealing PGC's wants.

I told her my son was flying in with my parents on Saturday morning and we are going to take a quick auto tour of D.C, and then drive to Philadelphia to spend the night with my family and then back to D.C. on Sunday so they could make their return flight to Minnesota. She seemed genuinely happy for me. I hadn't seen my son Charley for five years.

I told Mary to give Sebastian a check for $25,000. He was really becoming a pain in the ass, and rightfully so, I gave him money on my own say-so. It was chump change to PGC and if he continued to dine there, with his entourage, money needed to be laid out so Sebastian could buy food.

The closing on my Vienna house is scheduled for Thursday, July 26th. I hadn't told Mary yet, because I figure she'll be upset. But, on the other hand, maybe she won't be. She seems to handle everything extraordinarily well.

"Let's you and I go somewhere mindboggling, for dinner, tonight, Mary?" I ask.

"That would be wonderful. Where do you suggest?" She queries.

"The *Hayloft*. It's a dinner theatre, in Manassas, Virginia. It's only about twenty miles from our apartment.

"I've heard of it, Jack. Sounds terrific, what's playing." She asks.

"It's a mystery. You know where everybody present is a suspect. It's a fun evening and the food and drinks are good. It starts at eight o'clock, so we have plenty of time."

I see her face light up for the first time since the Fourth of July. I knew and I think she sensed this would be our last hoorah. Everything would really start changing beginning tomorrow. I hadn't told her yet about the house closing and the application I'd made for my son, Joe, to go to Randolph Macon Military Academy in the fall. There are a lot of things I haven't shared with her, recently. So tonight we will enjoy and hope for the best for both of us.

Ask yourself, what's the worst that can happen? Prepare to accept it. Then improve upon the worst. **Dale Carnegie**

Chapter Sixty-four

1700 K Street
Washington D.C.
Tuesday, July 31, 1984

It had been an eventful month. My son, Charley, arrived with my parents on Saturday, July 21st as scheduled. We had done our quick auto tour of Washington and then traveled to our house in Jenkintown, Pennsylvania. My parents and I were enjoying Charley's wide-eyed stares at everything he was seeing. From Washington D.C. to Baltimore, Maryland to Wilmington, Delaware to Philadelphia, Pennsylvania all the way to Jenkintown his eyes were fixed out the window. We just knew he wanted to be under these City lights for the rest of his life. And, he was only sixteen years old.

We spent Saturday night in Jenkintown so my parents could see Ellen and our three boys, Joe, Dan and Chris. Here Charley would meet his three brothers. He had met Joe and Dan in South Dakota, but not Chris. Our boys took Charley around to meet some of their friends. When they came back we had a cook out in the backyard and everyone visited until it was time for the younger boys to go to bed. My parents were worn out too and hit the sack as well. Ellen, Charley and I sat on our porch and talked for a couple hours. Charley would've talked all night if I hadn't suggested we get some sleep.

I'll always remember tears welling up in Charley's eyes when he said goodbye to Ellen. Seeing his tears, Ellen started to cry herself. Looking back a year later, the scene that day seemed to be an augury of the near future. I believe in divination, prophesy and second sight.

When we returned to Washington I had reserved a room at the St. Regis for Charley and I. My parents were going to stay with my sister and her family in Springfield, Virginia. When Charley asked me where I lived I told him I would show him. That I was moving into my new house the first part of August, until then I was staying at the hotel. He told me how excited he was to be staying in the heart of Washington D.C.

There was a lot going on so I arranged for a limousine to take him where he wanted to go. I suggested all the regular tourist traps. He couldn't belief he was getting to do this, especially in a limousine. It was one of those magical moments made possible by the right timing in life's sequence of events. The past two days Charley has been staying at McKenzie Gillen's house in Silver Spring, Maryland. She has a fifteenyear- old daughter who has instantly fallen in love with my son. Charley is a good looking young man, but nobody should have as much luck as this trip has brought him. He has enjoyed himself.

"What's the scuttlebutt about Charlotte Boyer," I ask Shanahan.

"Nobody knows," Mary says, looking at me with a shrug of her shoulders. "And, there is more, Jack. After Corrigan fired Larry Leopold, Charlotte dumped Ted Masters and Sandy Adams, St. Elsewhere's (Larry Leopold) capable and pretty Harvard assistant moved in with Charlotte Boyer. They're saying Charlotte and Sandy are lesbians. Although I'm certain Boyer goes each way. Anyway they're saying Charlotte and Sandy are living in Australia, and, living like queens. And, that, St. Elsewhere is flat drinking himself to death."

"Why do they call him St. Elsewhere?" I ask, laughing."

"He watches the television program, *St. Elsewhere*, religiously" Mary says, returning my guffaw.

"Has anybody else vanished?" I ask, curiously.

Mary shakes her head negatively. "I do need to talk about C&B Leasing. The lease payments going out exceed the leasing income. With these airplanes, houses and yacht's expenses, it's becoming horrendous. Not only are new leases not set up for these additions, dollars are constantly being issued for gold plated spigots, etcetera's. What are you going to do, Jack?"

"I've spoken to PGC. He wants me to set up joint ventures for the airplanes, houses, and yachts to cover the short falls. What is the monthly shortfall?" I ask Shanahan.

"That depends," she says reticently. "Just to make the payments we need an additional $24,000 a month. His constant request for ten thousand here and twenty thousand there seems to be a bottomless pit. What are we going to do about coming up with that money? AAnd, what are joint ventures?" says Mary, outrageously.

"A Joint Venture Agreement provides a contract for two or more individuals or entities to form a business relationship suitable for a single project or purpose. A contractual joint venture is tax transparent where there is no pooling of profits or losses and no formal registration requirements. Further, there may be limited liability provided the joint venture is not deemed a partnership. It's a perfect vehicle to accomplish his goals.

"First, he gave me a list of ten players who are to put an equal sum of money into the Joint Ventures on a monthly basis. Each one of these players is to get a salary increase for net payroll to pay each Joint Venture a certain sum to pay leases. Say, twenty-two hundred per month for each player. The $2,200 will be paid $800 per month to each Joint Venture.

"Second, he wants me to refinance the real leases. Perhaps we can raise three or four hundred thousand by doing that number.

"Third, he wants me to write some bogus leases and assign them to the new bank in Baltimore, which would bank us another half-a-million.

"Fourth, he wants me to take the big ticket items: Rolls Royce's', Mercedes's, New Yorker's and finance them again. Illegal, yes, but who will question what we're doing."

"Does it matter what you do, Jack, because of who you are?" Shanahan asks.

"No, I suppose it doesn't. It doesn't as long as I get the job done. But in this case, I haven't figured out what the job is all about. But I'll play it to the end, Mary. I'll figure it all out. It might take me another month or so to put everything in place. Are you with me?" I query, asking?.

"I am, Jack, until you tell me to leave. I trust you will tell me the right time. And, I hope you trust who I am. I've had a sense you have some reservations since Memorial Day. I was having a hard time keeping my feelings for you silent, while you continue talking business.

"Hey did you enjoy Charley's visit. I'm sorry I didn't get to meet him." Shanahan asks.

"You will meet him. We're taking him to National at one o'clock. His flight to Minneapolis is scheduled at 2:20 p.m." I tell her.

"Another month in the books," I say as we're walking out of National Airport. I check my watch, it is nearing four o'clock. We saw Charley off on time and stopped at a bar for a drink as the Northwest Boeing 727 was on the runway set to go.

"He certainly is a handsome young man," Mary tells me. "He seems very confident and intelligent too." She adds. "Where does he want to go to school?"

"Princeton, I hope. I've been encouraging him to go Ivy League. I ask him if he knows what he wants to be. His answer is direct and very simple. *I want to be rich.*" I make known his announcement.

Shanahan gives me a good roar, saying, "Maybe I should wait for him, Jack."

"Maybe you should." I state.

"You know I'm closing on my house tomorrow. The closing is just down stairs at the Savings and Loan. My furniture will be delivered Thursday and Ellen and the boys are coming down Friday evening. So we have tonight, tomorrow night and then we will officially be apart. Are your plans to stay here?" I ask Mary.

"Most certainly," she says. "Where else would I go with everything so up in the air?"

"I feel the same way. The new house and having my family under the same roof seems exciting. But me, like you, with what I'm predicting will happen with Atlantic States Surety is pretty unsettling. Hopefully, we can figure all this out in August. I have some ideas that might work. God, I'm starting to feel like I'm a double agent." I tell Shanahan.

"Are you," Mary Shanahan asks, with an adroit tone in her voice.

"I'll tell you a month from now," I say with a snicker as I turn my New Yorker into the St. Regis valet parking cosmos.

"Let's go to our office, and catch the infamous Happy Hour. I need to start asking a lot of questions. I'm going to devote my time with some different subjects, like Arthur Aamot. And, why don't you try finding out more about Charlotte Boyer. Maggie Little would be a good place to start." I hint.

"Okay! I'll be looking forward to that drink at five o'clock and maybe a nice dinner afterwards". Mary puts forward.

"Here's looking at you kid!" I agree, with a grin.

Shanahan rejoinders "Play it again, Sam."

Even if you are on the right track, you will get run over if you just sit there. **Will Rogers**

Chapter Sixty-five

Money is flying out of Atlantic States Surety like it is going out of style. PGC is balls to the wall with Ned Larson about getting the *Gray* car market scotching. It was just talk before August 1st and now it has become reality when Gordon signed a huge lease with an option to buy on a building in Chevy Chase, Maryland. Of course the first step is to get Matthew Ferrone in there to refurbish and make improvements, PGC style.

The building is over a hundred years old. PGC just being PGC had to coddle and indulge it. The idea, of course, is to add layers of luxuries to his new landmark. He begins by fortifying it, sealing doors and windows and hiring armed guards to protect it and its occupants. He is adding elevators, electronic surveillance, security codes, closed circuit television, a weight room, a steam room, locker rooms and an executive dining room on the second floor, inclusive of a 25'x25' luxury suite for himself. Secrecy is his passion. Most of the building is carpeted, but in a few spots the wood was not damaged and the hardwood floors are being re-done and donned with expensive oriental rugs. Since August 3rd, $300,000 has been advanced for building improvements and furnishings out of C&B Leasing.

Per the Czar's (Paul Gordon Charles) instructions I had Shanahan draw a lease between German Imports of Maryland, a newly formed Maryland Corporation with PGC as a one hundred per-cent shareholder, and C&B Leasing for equipment, furniture, and leasehold Improvements in the amount of $300,000. I assigned this lease to Metro Bank in Baltimore, an arrangement made possible by Henry Fleck and his friend, Bubba Mooney, to replace the funds paid out of C&B Leasing for same.

At the outset, I sensed no personal danger in what I was doing. I especially felt that way because I was an undercover agent with the FBI. I took considerable satisfaction from knowing that I had no criminal liability and I consistently sought to keep it that way. But even Shanahan looked at me sometimes with a puzzled, scolding silence, making me feel like a guilty school boy in the principal's office. Even though she knew, almost all, we still seemed to be playacting, pretending, testing each other as if the other knew something scandalous the other didn't. But I never gave it all up, never, nobody was better at stonewalling than me. And I never wanted PGC, me and some other minion seen together in the same room alone. Conspiracy time, racketeering (RICO), and fraud were words of pallor that hung over our every conversation.

Although I sensed fear from everyone I was talking with, I started seeing cover-up personalities emerging. Some adopted an enthusiastic know-nothing posture, unabashedly declaring their innocence. Some exuded confidence, almost as distant from the mess as PGC intended and pretended to be. Neverson brooded and stewed quietly. Richard Corrigan, sensing danger, moved in shrewdly behind a screen of fact-finding agents whom he maneuvered like chess pieces. It was also ad hoc, developed in small reactions to the flurry of each day's events.

I'm not sure when I crossed the line into criminal culpability, when I failed in my efforts to protect myself, but I know that certain crucial events took place on park benches in meets as covert as the microfilm exchanges in the spy movies. It was the same when I met my handlers exchanging briefcases. With surprising aplomb, we were adopting mannerisms of amateur spies.

I sensed no one was going to budge. Each player waited for the other to confess and shoulder the cover-up alone. The war of leverage was dragging on day to day. My adult life had been calculated blindly and shrewdly, I had always thought. I was now reaching the pinnacle. I was not the source of authority for the cover-up, yet I became its linchpin.

Shanahan had made a list of the collateral for the current leases. For some reason we were holding the titles to all the vehicles, including the Rolls Royces and the Mercedes, even though the leases were not fully paid. I told the new banker at Metro, Bubba Mooney that here were a million dollars-worth of vehicle leases I'd promised Henry Fleck I'd give to you. His eyes lit up like he was making the deal of the century. He was young but still should've received the *sucker of the year* award. Young fellows are given responsible jobs and because they have no business savvy they can be taken advantage of so easy. This was the first move where I could be culpable in major league fraud, but again I was only a federal agent doing my job. Right? Right!

I walked out of Metro Bank with a cashier's check in the amount $1,212,007 dollars payable to C&B Leasing.

I can't tell you how I thought about putting that check in the C&B account and drawing one out to myself for one million and hitting the road. It would have been so easy.

"My God, Jack, what are you doing? Have you gone crazy?" Mary asks, generally concerned for me.

"Mary, give Sebastian twenty-five thousand. I feel sorry for him. I guess the new has worn off that Chandelier, huh?" I laugh. "That poor guy is going to take a PGC bath. God, I hate this job"

"I never heard you say that before, Jack," Mary teases. "Is it really that bad, huh, Jack?" Mary asks.

"Depends on you look at it. If you need a million or two just write a few bogus leases or double finance somebody else's collateral. Depends on how you look at. I'm a fucking FBI agent, supposedly a man of honor deceitfully fucking descent, good, hardworking people out of their money for PGC and his dirty little secrets. Depends on how you look at it, Shanahan."

"Ellen has reticently agreed to move to Vienna, if we keep the house in Jenkintown. She's really not sure she wants any part of this life anymore, or, me anyway. Ellen has decided she can't handle our son, Joe, anymore. He stayed out all night last Friday and worried her to death. He just won't listen to her. I'm working on getting him enrolled in Randolph Macon Military Academy in Front Royal, Virginia. It's only an hour away from Vienna. Joe is willing to go, which is the biggest problem I understand. Danny has been coming back with me the past two weekends, he loves his beloved Virginia. Ellen wants me to enroll him in school here." I tell Mary, with some trepidation.

"Wow, it sounds like she might want you to take the children so she can run." Mary says.

"It does, doesn't it?" I say to Mary.

"I'm moving forward, regardless. If she really wants out I will give her that. I will be happy to take the children. Although, I do not believe she'll let Christopher go. And, there is another facet. PGC wants her to take care of the Café and the new car dealership's books. I imagine that will include C&B too, if anything survives."

"But you know they won't, Jack. And, you're in control for the most part. Right?"

I laugh. "I don't know what I'm doing here, Mary. We'll all know soon enough, I do believe. Based on my past experiences the Bureau has to make its move soon. Too many people will be losing their shirts. I can't believe it has gone on this long. There has to be something big at the end of this rainbow."

"What's next?" Mary asks. "He wants Ned Larson and I to fly to Munich, Germany to buy some cars. Ned knows what he wants. Me, I just have to bring the C&B checkbook. He's thinking a million for cars."

"Where is this money coming from. He told me to talk with Art Aamot. I did. He told me PGC wants him to draw down on some collateral accounts, turn the money over to me to put in C&B." I say.

"This is crazy, Jack. You can't get out because....oh well.,,,, yeah." She says. "And, what's my role?"

"You might want to get out, Mary. You have your whole life ahead of you. Think about it." I tell her.

"If I'm safe from prosecution, I wouldn't miss the end of this deal for anything. Am I safe, Jack." Asks Mary?

"I really don't know. If I was you, at your age, I wouldn't take a chance. I'd get out." I suggest.

"Are trying to get rid of me, Jack?" She asks kiddingly. Tear drops were coming from both eyes, now. "If you tell me it is best to go, I'll take your advice. But give me two weeks to get things together for you. As you know, I do most of the work."

"Look, it's four o'clock. Cut that check for Sebastian and we'll have an early dinner at the cafe. My son, Danny, is spending the night with Maggie Little's two sons at their house. I told her I could use some time with you. She agreed. I told her we would be staying in Glen Echo if she needs to get ahold of us."

"Maggie's a good egg. She cares about everybody. Hey you're pretty cock sure of yourself, Jack. *We're staying in Glen Echo tonight.*

"Let's go make Sebastian's day." I say.

Mary Shanahan writes a check for $25,000, and I sign it. She puts it in her purse and we're off.

Become so wrapped up in something that you forget to be afraid.
Lady Bird Johnson

Chapter Sixty-six

1700 K Street
Washington D.C.
Friday, August 17, 1984

"Your flight is leaving Sunday morning at 7:10 a.m. from Dulles on Delta Airlines, with a stop in Atlanta and then a non-stop to Austin, Texas, arriving there at two o'clock. Monday morning, at 6:15 a.m. you have a non-stop flight to Dallas, Texas. You are to rendezvous with PGC's crowd at the hotel for a $10,000 dollar a plate luncheon with Ronald Reagan. I wish you were taking me, instead of your wife." Shanahan says, with a twitter.

"My sister lives in Austin. I haven't seen Chrissy and her family for a few years. I'm looking forward to it. Well, thank you Mary, I have to call Ellen to give her the itinerary. Ellen's mother is watching Dan and Chris in Hershey, Pennsylvania. Joe is going to Ocean City, New Jersey for the week with a friend's parents. Maggie is giving Danny a ride to Gettysburg to meet my mother-in-law on Saturday." Shanahan interrupts me.

"Jack, I'll take Danny all the way to Hershey. I need to see my parents and grandmother in Gettysburg anyway. Don't worry about it, I'll talk with Maggie and make the arrangements."

"Danny will talk your ear off. He should be a good lawyer. He always has a hundred and one questions and he won't let you slide anything by him." I laugh. "He's very persistent."

"Like father like son?" She questions.

"He's a very intelligent young man." I add.

"Like his Daddy?" She queries, with a grin.

"More like his mother, she's the smart one in this family." I say.

"Hey, Neverson, Little, and I are meeting at the St. Regis at five o'clock. Ellen is going to meet us there. She's taking a cab from Union Station when her train gets here. Why don't you join us? I would like you to meet Ellen. She knows Joe and Maggie and has talked with you on the telephone a number of times. I think you will like her, Mary. Okay?" I ask.

"But she knows nothing about me. That's amazing, Jack. Sure, I would like to meet her." Shanahan says, uncannily.

"I'm good at undercover work, except when it comes to you." I laugh, without explanation

We all arrived about 5:30 p.m. at the St. Regis. The four of us sit down at a round table, squeezing an extra chair between the four. We are telling our usual war stories, devouring hors d'oeuvres and drinking when the one-man-band fires up his first song, *All Night Long … Well, my friends, the time has come … raise the roof and have some fun … throw away the work to be done … let the music play on …* I check my watch, it is eight o'clock. I look around the lounge and then ask Mary to dance. Of course she jumps right up and leads me to the small dance floor. The next song is *Rainy Night in Georgia*, a slow dance, and about half way through the tune I get a tap on my shoulder and its Ellen standing there.

She's says tersely: "So this is what you do with your time when you're not at home?" I knew she was kidding, but Mary looked alarmed. Ellen smiles and gives me a kiss on the lips. "And with whom are you dancing, Jack? Let me see, she's beautiful and she's young. Good choice, same old Jack."

"May I cut in?" Ellen asks Mary. Shanahan nods in the affirmative and Ellen and I finished dancing the ditty. Afterwards we ordered another round of drinks, including a gin and tonic for Ellen.

Ellen knew Joe from Christmas when he and his family joined our family for the Holiday. She knew of Maggie because Danny had been staying there off and on during the summer. We all got along splendidly and had a nice dinner at the St. Regis. And as the lyrics of the first song sung tonight suggested, *throw away the work to be done*. We did and had a grand evening telling funny stories and laughing.

When we left for our room, Joe said, "Say hello to Ron for me."

Ellen had a big smile on her face in response, whispering and pointing at herself, "Can you belief I'm going to have lunch with the President of the United States?" Everyone laughs at her giddiness. "Oh, Ellen says, "Thank you, Maggie and Mary, for seeing to Danny. He's a handful."

As we walk away I put the rabbit ears above Ellen's head and turn around to see the three of them laughing.

A pessimist sees the difficulty in every opportunity; the optimist sees the opportunity in every difficulty. **Harry S. Truman**

Chapter Sixty-seven

Dulles International Airport
Chantilly, Virginia
Saturday, August 18, 1984

It is a bright, sunny day when Ellen and I arrive at Dulles International Airport early on Saturday morning. Dulles is a 26 mile drive from downtown Washington D.C. There was very little traffic today and we arrived an hour before takeoff. We checked our bags, and bought coffee and donuts to fortify us.

Ellen is in a pleasant mood but something doesn't feel quite right about this trip. At first PGC wanted the whole team to fly down on his corporate jet. I didn't want any part of flying on its virgin flight, especially since he wasn't going to be aboard. Fate intervened, however. Matt Ferrone had hired two former Marine Corps pilots to fly PGC's aircraft. All was well until Annabelle Bergman mouthed off to one of the pilots when he refused to lug a bunch of her stuff onto the aircraft. The pilot is a retired Lt. Colonel and was not about to take marching orders from a sixteen-year-old foul mouthed tramp. So Matt was told to fire both pilots for not showing the proper respect.

I check my watch; it is six-forty a.m. We walk to the gate and en route I see a familiar face lurking around a corner. He's looking at me. He seemingly wants me to notice him and the lady in black, who had just joined him. *What the hell*, I'm thinking out loud, softly. I wave to them as we enter the plane. We have First Class seats, on the left and in the first row. After we sit down I quickly order a Bloody Mary, one for each of us. Ellen raises her eyebrow when the drinks are put in front of us. The stewardess says there is going to be a slight delay so we may go ahead and use the seat trays.

Ellen always was partial to an aisle seat and I enjoy sitting by a window. We had placed ourselves in the harmonizing positions. Ellen was sipping her drink, while I busied myself staring out the window trying to figure out the reason for the delay.

I'm wondering if I'm being set up on this thing. That if something goes wrong I will be the fall guy. Or did I know too much and they had decided to eliminate me. It seems that PGC had taken me into his confidence beyond my wildest expectations. I have always appraised my performance and chastised myself for having seemed naïve and guppy like at times, but I know I was learning more about the arm-twisting and back-room politics than I ever expected. In fact, it seems every time I walk out of his office I am in a good frame of mind. It seems like everyone else walks out of there looking like a pallbearer who has just taken a great fall. The hostile side of PGC's personality fits him like a glove, much more than the compliant side..

I look at Ellen. I'm thinking; just give my lovely wife a cigarette, a drink, and something to read and she is happy. I need to tell her that there is a slight chance of rough sledding in the near future, but I have minimized her fear in the past and have failed miserably to prepare cover for what might lay in store this time around.

I check my watch. It is 7:30 a.m. I ask the stewardess for another round of Bloody Marys. She brings them. She no more than sets them down when the Captain, I think he's the Captain, emerges from the cockpit door. He has broad shoulders, narrow at the hip, standing about six feet tall and weighing maybe 225 pounds. He is bald on top but has a good mane of salt and pepper hair flow on the fenders of his head. He wears neatly trimmed side burns, like Elvis did. He just stands there for a moment, like he is collecting his thoughts. He is wearing a sharp blue uniform, which covers a white shirt with a deftly tied cravat tightened around his décolletage. I guess him in his late forties or maybe fifty. A name plate displays: *Captain Andrew Orr.*

A flight attendant hands the Captain a microphone. He announces there is a delay because of late arriving VIP passengers. This remark gets every ones attention and eyes rise.

"Once they're on board, we will be in the air and should land in Atlanta pretty much on schedule."

"Mr. Oleson – Mrs. Oleson the passengers will be here any moment. They will be sitting directly across from you. They are people with the Republican National Committee. That's all you need to know."

"Why are these people flying to Atlanta, isn't the convention in Dallas? And, do you know their names?" I ask.

Ellen looks directly at Captain Orr, then at me. I smile, and then look at Captain Orr, asking. "What are you really up to Captain? And, who do you really work for? Maybe it's the CIA. Is it the *Company*, huh?"

The sounds of people walking down the gangway, saves Captain Orr. And, I know who it is before I see them. It is the fat man and the lady in black. As they enter the First Class section they fix their eyes on Ellen and me sitting in our First Class seats. They look drawn and haggard, not particularly happy, acknowledging our presence with mechanical smiles before minding the motion to be seated by Captain Andrew Orr.

"What in the hell is going on, Jack," asks Ellen? "You're so pensive."

"You got me," I say, not wanting to put any more doubt in Ellen's mind. The other passengers in First Class look up slightly when this couple is escorted to their seats, but when they don't recognize them as celebrated people they ignore them.

Meanwhile Captain Orr has disappeared into the cockpit. I supposed he's hiding out in there while the real pilots are busy getting the aircraft to the runway for takeoff. Once we were in the air we were served breakfast and one more Bloody Mary. En route the ride was as smooth as glass and my fears had subsided, at least while flying at thirty thousand feet.

I whisper to Ellen. "I'm going to the bathroom. When I come back, slide over to the window seat so I can sit in the aisle seat. I want to talk with the late arriving guests of honor. Who knows they might be movie stars."

"Okay," says Ellen, in an undertone. "I know not to ask any questions. Keep your ears open and your mouth shut. Right?"

I was gone for five minutes and when I came back Ellen sashayed over to the window seat as the aircraft started its descent. The lady in black was looking at me. I could see her gawp from the corner of my eye. I turned my head quickly to the right and asked, "Are you guys following me today? I thought Rich Richards got you two out of my life."

The lady in black smiled. "Whatever are you talking about, sir?" This exchange jarred the fat man awake.

"Hey, how the hell are you big man? Where are you meeting PGC? What a coincidence we're both riding First Class on this plane. I hear you are a VIP with the Republican National Committee?" I suggest. The last time I was this close to the man I sucker punched him on an Amtrak Metroliner, while traveling across the Susquehanna River betwixt and between Maryland and Delaware.

"Are you looking for trouble, sir?" The fat man asks, with brashness.

"No, but I think you are Fatso. And, I've had enough of your cloak and dagger exercises. And, if I see you again after I get off of this plane be assured you're going to get hurt."

"Is that a threat," Fat boy asks.

"No, now I'm supposed to say, it's a promise, right?" I query, abysmally.

I hear the gear go down as a stewardess announces the usual stuff before landing. When the jet touches down and taxies to the terminal a man comes out of the cockpit dressed like a cowboy, donning a ten gallon hat. He's wearing tight-fitting jeans underneath his leather chaps and his footwear is a pair of fancy cowboy boots. He looks at me and I start to laugh. He looks annoyed, with my all-knowing bit of fun at his expense.

"Nice flying," I say. "Say hello to PGC for me at the rodeo, Captain Andrew Orr.

"Asshole," Orr charges, with a look of ... *if eyes could kill.*

Ellen and I stand in the corner of the gangway nearest the plane watching people pass by. Fat man and the lady in black are followed by Captain Orr. They are just about in the terminal. The other departing passengers appear guarded and uncomfortable. Long worried looks are exchanged, but little is being said. It is like no one wants to recognize, or talk about, the gravity of the situation. But what situation do we share with all these other people? Absolutely none - zero, I'm thinking. Or, is it my wild imagination, or, guilt by association that is eating at me. "To hell with it," I say in a mutter. Do what you usually do. "Stonewall it!" I say murmuring, softly, like I'm a crazy man on an illusory mission. Ellen and I go back to our seats. I check my watch. It's 9:25 a.m. I order Ellen a gin and tonic and me a Jack Daniels and club soda. I'm pretty sure I knew what is going on now both by instinct and by osmosis. I find it true that power's property is an aphrodisiac, which seems like just compensation for the lonely burdens of undercover work.

Without me even knowing it PGC has switched me into the citadel of an executive mess, where I spend an increasing amount of time with the other select potentates. They no longer question my request for air-travel expenses or limousine service. I am now above all those bureaucratic hassles.

On the other side of the fence my handler is emphasizing finding the source of PGC's income in order to find some tax deficiency, for which he might be prosecuted. If successful it would produce a counter scandal to divert attention from the realistic issues. I have not been told about the quantifiable primary, but I have a few clues now and I will go to the twelfth of never to unravel this case. It's personal now.

I check my watch. It is 11:15 a.m. We are scheduled to take off in ten minutes. I request another gin and tonic and a Jack and club soda. I'm back in the window seat now. Ellen looks at me, smiles and says, "You are certainly a man who glances frequently at your watch, Jack."

I grin back, saying, "Someday this precision will earn me a place in the Certified Public Accountants' Hall of Fame."

Do not anticipate trouble, or worry about what may never happen. Keep in the sunlight. **Benjamin Franklin**

Chapter Sixty-eight

We had a very nice flight from Austin to Dallas on Monday morning. We took a taxi from the airport to the Renaissance Dallas Hotel. It was around nine o'clock when we were settled into our room. Our schedule was to rendezvous with the rest of our party at eleven o'clock in the hotel lobby for the Presidential luncheon.

My sister picked us up at Austin airport when we arrived on Saturday afternoon. Being in the beautiful Capitol City of Texas gave off the impression we were out of harm's way. Nevertheless, I kept imagining somebody lurking around a corner keeping their eyes on my every move. But as time passed I saw nobody acting or doing anything idiosyncratic. Saturday night we went to a crazy restaurant that served delicious food, while the waiters and waitresses cracked insulting remarks and played dirty tricks. I loved it because nobody liked playing practical jokes and tossing insults at folks better than me. Sunday we went to church with my sister and her family and afterwards they showed us around Austin, including the Capitol Building and the University of Texas. It had been a long time since Ellen and I had done just normal day-to-day things. It was a well-needed time out. It simply felt good.

I am sitting in a comfortable chair, in our hotel room, sipping a cup of coffee and smoking a cigarette. I'm waiting for Ellen to do the things women do before advancing to an occasion. I'm racking my brain trying to figure out why we are here for a ten-thousand-dollar a plate luncheon. If it was two of us or three of us it might make some sense, but ten of us makes a team. Are we his team? What's the game and who's the opponent, I stand up and gaze out the window in awe.

Likewise I'm thinking about even being at the 1984 Republican National Convention which is convening today, August 20th at the Reunion Arena in downtown Dallas, Texas. Their purport is to nominate the incumbent Ronald Reagan of California for President of the United States and incumbent George H. W. Bush of Texas for Vice President.

It seems every day gets more confusing than the day before. I check my watch. It's 10:18 a.m. I tap on the bathroom door and Ellen announces she'll be ready in ten minutes. I pick up the paper which announces on the front page it's the thirty-third GOP presidential nominating convention, the first Republican convention held in Texas and the only convention of either party ever held in Dallas.

I put the paper down and gaze at the Dallas skyline. My thoughts drift back to another time, it was nearly twenty-one years ago. John Fitzgerald Kennedy's presidential motorcade was winding through downtown Dallas on Main Street, when it made an unexpected right turn onto Houston Street and then a quick left onto Elm Street at Dealey Plaza. During this last turn the motorcade slowed to a near crawl before going by the Texas Book Depository. Moments later, before Kennedy's presidential parade reached the Grassy Knoll, gun shots rang out.

"Jack," Ellen said. "Are you okay?" She startled me out of my concentration.

"Ready," I ask? "I was looking at the Texas skyline, thinking about JFK's motorcade passing between those tall buildings, some twenty years ago." I voiced mellifluously to her.

"The buildings were probably not so tall then, Jack. I'm ready." She assures me.

"You look lovely, Ellen," I say, with a meaningful smile.

I suppose the FBI used their magic, but somehow all the people in our bunch were cleared for security purposes. We had a good table three rows back from where the President was to be seated at the head table, along with nine other notables, elevated on a platform slightly above us. We were all seated at the same time and a host arrived quickly to pour our Champaign.

Our table was oval-shaped with ten chairs placed around its perimeter. Name tags were placed where we were designated to sit. PGC was centered where he could look directly at the President. His two women friends, Madeline Haycock, at his right and Annabelle Bergman at his left were looking giddy. Richard Corrigan, Ned Larson, and Ellen filled out his right side. At his left, sitting next to Bergman, were Matt Ferrone, Ray Bertrand, and Jason Simpson. I was sitting directly across from Paul Gordon Charles, which I found unfathomable.

I check my watch, it is almost noon. Suddenly President Reagan enters with the playing of *Hail to the Chief*. He was moving quickly, majestically and waving enthusiastically to a roaring throng. During the next forty-five minutes everyone chatted and glanced up, periodically, at Ronald Reagan methodically eating his lunch.

I was thinking about the original plan which had everyone present, excluding PGC, aboard the corporate jet. Then there was the fiasco with Annabelle Bergman and the consequential firing of the Marine airline pilots. The change was made to fly commercial. I made separate arrangements because I didn't trust what he might do after the Tom Harvey airplane crash.

So here we all are, each of us sitting in an order of importance. I still didn't understand why we made this trip, but I'm sure it will come to light soon enough. I look at Ellen and notice she is having a good time talking with the others. I look at PGC and he is looking back. He nods and gives me a horselaugh and I nod back, with a guise of sanction. Then a nobleman sitting next to Reagan's right stands up and goes to the microphone to introduce the President.

The President gives a ten minute address and he's given a resounding applause. And that's what you get for spending $100,000 at a Presidential luncheon, I'm thinking as I notice Paul Gordon Charles go off with, what looked like, two Secret Service agents.

Secrecy is his passion, everything is confidential. Salaries, perks, advancement and most especially with whom he does business. He continually warns about the evils of the loose tongue. I study the group he has assembled. Good looks dominate. Neatness is mandatory. The dress code is strict, dark gray or navy wool suits, white or blue cotton button-downs, medium starch, and silk ties. No beards, mustaches or hair over the ears.

Work is a pressure cooker. Everybody overworks, eighty-hour work weeks and lots of time away from home. It's not easy and he knows it. The bottom line is the money, no matter where it comes from. Profits, lots of profits! Everyone is supposed to look and act affluent. We are supposed to take pride in our wealth. Our social life revolves around him, where everybody, except him, drinks like a fish and some become plagued with alcoholism. He does not like turnover ... *owe your soul to the company store.* Right, Tennessee Ernie?

He hates *Fibbie*s, because the FBI doesn't play fair and they cheat and play dirty. They shadowbox, so beware. First, he says, comes the shock about what they know, then the burst of dutiful activity to prove they're wrong, then it's the wariness and stonewalling, and finally the frayed edges begin to show, and then the cover up. Beware, he has told us. If we let them in, he repeats time and time again, all we will have are worries, because of their shady habits and evasive solutions. Is that calling the kettle black, I'm musing when Ellen taps me on the shoulder?

"Let's go see Dallas, Jack." My wife asserts, with a galvanized big smile on her face.

The people who get on in this world are the people who get up and look for the circumstances they want, and, if they can't find them, make them. **George Bernard Shaw**

Chapter Sixty-nine

Kingsley Road SW
Vienna, Virginia
Labor Day
Monday, September 3, 1984

Ellen and I had just returned from Front Royal, Virginia where we had enrolled our oldest son, Joe, in Randolph Macon Military Academy as a 7th grader. I had just paid for first semester which was safe harbor considering my shaky employment situation and the a bit too much cost of the academy. There was another reason I only paid for the first semester, PGC had given me a cash bonus for $6,000 to enroll Joe, and, as usual, I saw an opportunity to pocket an extra three thousand for contingencies. All things considered the extra cash reserve, I now carried in my left front pocket, made me feel more secure. Of course, my wife knew nothing of these details. In these kinds of matters, for her own good, she was always kept on a need-to-know basis.

Ellen took the week off to help me and the two boys get situated. We are going to enroll Danny in Vienna Elementary School tomorrow. He is all excited about being back in Virginia, recalling his commitment to do so, when we moved from the Commonwealth of Virginia to the State of Pennsylvania. I couldn't get my mind off leaving Joe at military school. Although he seemed excited about the change, it was still difficult for me as we had been so close when he was younger. He excelled in football, basketball and baseball and at the time he was playing as little leaguer I was very much involved, even as a coach. I was happy, too, Danny was living with me now as Ellen was going back to Pennsylvania to work until the end of September and then she would be coming here to live and work on October 1st.

Ellen prepared a quick supper consisting hot dogs, macaroni and cheese, with baked beans. When we were through eating Danny and Chris went upstairs to watch television. After we cleaned up I fixed Ellen a gin and tonic and me a Jack and soda. We sat down at the kitchen table to discuss finishing the basement of our new split level townhouse. We are to meet with the contractor tomorrow night so Ellen sketches out her plan, including my Chicago Bar. I'm satisfied with her blueprint and confirm by saying, with some enthusiasm, "Okay, let's do it."

I sense something is amiss here as I watch my wife sip her drink. When something new is happening she usually is ecstatic, but not today. It's like her mind is wandering, like she's picking up signals from somewhere else.

"Johnny, what's really going on here? We had that wonderful trip to Dallas – saw the President – saw Dallas, Texas; Ned and PGC, himself, kept asking me take over the accounting for the dealership and the restaurant. *We'll pay you double what you are making now.*" They are enticing me, especially PGC, that Don Quixote in a three-piece suit." Ellen voices, rather boisterously.

"A Don Quixote in a three-piece suit, huh?" I repeat, laughing. "Ellen that's one of the reasons I love you so much. You are such a natural lexicologist." I laugh again and so does she, while lighting up a Winston.

"But Ellen, I don't trust him or the FBI. With the assistance of the Bureau his crimes have been covered up. Eventually, though, even with their help, covering up all traces is not always successful. And when they want, the FBI can get to anyone, anywhere. Regardless for now, though, I think the best thing is to simply play this hand out. I do believe this house of cards is about to fall.

"Financially we've had a good year, which we needed desperately. We own two nice houses and have two household's full of furniture. We have two new vehicles and sometimes three. I forget, most of the time, I even work for the FBI."

"Yeah," she says. "What about the fucking FBI?" She probes. "What exactly is there role here?"

"I don't know." I say. "But, I have a theory. On paper it seems

PGC and what he is doing might be right on tract. The trouble is we don't know exactly what he is doing or where he's going. We need to see more unless he breaks his story to somebody or all of us. From what I hear and see, he thinks he has the right people in place. His so-called *Home Team*. I really believe he's setting up a new place and scenario. He can do it, too, if we all help."

"The *team*," Ellen asks, "Like the knights at the oval table in Dallas. Is that the team you're talking about?"

"It's a variety of talents. It's an existent bunch filled with compulsory experience that he mandates badly. He really doesn't know how to do much himself. However he's the best at analyzing the results. I'm sure he has a master plan. And, I have a few clues coming from his recent whereabouts.

"Remember what I'm about to say comes forth thru my own speculation, suspicions and investigations. I do believe he's about ready to put to sea." I say, with frenetic sureness.

Ellen gets up, picking up our glasses for a refill. "Please continue, Johnny."

"I believe his strategies are to move his whole show to Sydney, Australia sometime in early 1985. His whole extravaganza includes his self-proclaimed *team*. The *team*, again, is probably the most important part of his adventure. He knows what he wants but he needs the *team* to make it all happen. PGC knows how to interrupt reports and judge if everything has been done to his orders. The problem is, at least the way I see it, other than the women and maybe Ned Larson, the rest of us won't budge for such soi-disant preposterousness. Which is basically for services rendered and once accomplished, he promises the almighty life of luxury. There is a price: all we have to do is give up our wives, families, children and our whole way of life." I say, going bottoms up with my drink. Ellen takes my glass to fix me another.

"The banker might enlist in the program. What choice does he have, with millions of dollars' worth of loans going bad and all of the collateral sold or double collateralized; he would really have to get out of Dodge quickly or go straight to jail. He would never get another job in the banking industry or any other industry when the facts are disclosed. Plus he doesn't like his wife and cares very little about his children. He hit on me when we were in Dallas. He's no friend of yours, John." Ellen warns.

"Well, with what I've done to him, I guess I'm no friend of his, either. And, you're right Ellen, maybe Jason Simpson will stay on the *team*. And, looking at the others, what else is Richard Corrigan going to do? He'll bring his wife. Ned Larson, the same thing. He just retired from the Navy reserves and does not have a good relationship with his wife. She's twenty years younger than him. Matt Ferrone was a military helicopter pilot. He spent most of his life away from his family. Why wouldn't he go? Ray Bertrand. He would go if Corrigan goes, and Ray would take his wife with him. That leaves you and I, Ellen."

She laughs out loud. "There's a hole in the plan, alas!" She says, before laughing again. "Tell me, Johnny, where is all this money coming from?" She asks, quizzically.

"Again this is just my theory on what I've seen occurring and conversations I've had with many, and especially PGC. It is my deductive reasoning about what his imaginings might be and what could be done. He will put out a dictum to generate any type of premium dollars without any regard to risk. These monies will funnel through partnerships to PGC. At a designated time another aphorism will be made to completely clean the operating company out of cash and cash equivalents. He will do the same with the management company because all its funds will be immediately siphoned to the operating company, let's say *twenty million* here.

"Next, he'll dictate to cash out all the significant cash collateral accounts in the name of claims. This might take some time; let's say *seventy five million* here.

"He's already mortgaged all his properties, airplanes, boats, and cars to the hilt. He should have raised *ten million* here, because most of the proposed work for which the money was for hasn't even started and for what has been done the contractors haven't been paid. So, let's stiff them!

"Use as much credit as possible, including food purveyors, beer and liquor sources. With the product available have some parties and push sales until they cut the food and liquor off. Stiff them all. Then load up on credit cards and run the limits through the cash register as sales. Pay nobody and collect up what you can without upsetting Sebastian, too much. Then, torch the restaurant and collect from the insurance company grounded on actual damages and loss on future earnings established by the inflated sales figures from day one. Let's say, *three million* here.

"So, give or take a few million, PGC, has approximately one-hundred-million dollars to play with in the building of a new empire." I announce, like I have convinced a jury the man is guilty as hell.

"Hmm," says Ellen. "I had no idea this is what's going on here. How does the Bureau feel about PGC? And, what do they want you to do about it. And, what is their purport in the whole scheme of things."

"That's exactly what I've been asking myself for a year now. I have enough evidence to indict him on almost any charge. But there's more to it. I think he might be an informant and he has certain information they want. He bribes them and they let him do what he wants for the information he gives them. He is now out of control and must be stopped. But how is he stopped? What does he know? He likes to doodle on his leather note pad. One time we were sitting in his office, around the coffee table, and he got up to answer a ringing phone near his desk. I noted he had doodled in penciled-in-squares:

HOSTAGES FOR ARMS ISREAL TO IRANIANS US RESUPPLY ISREAL $$$ TO US CASPAR THE FRIENDLY GHOST GOES NORTH TO ALASKA

When he came back to his seat he noticed he'd left the pad where I could see it. Then he scribbled on the exposed page and turned to a new one. With my photographic memory, which is a curse sometimes, I mastered what I saw, but didn't think too much of it at the time. I still don't. My only thoughts were, really nothing. However, now I'm thinking it might be the one thing he knows about, as an FBI informant that higher ups want to know about. And if they did, they would probably make him disappear. So, instead he might use his own leverage to make himself disappear," I shrug my shoulders.

"Jesus, John, you're scaring me." Ellen says, with a apprehensive look on her face.

"John, fix us another drink. It's awfully quiet upstairs. I need to get those two in bed. Remember we have to be at Vienna Elementary at eight o'clock in the morning." She smiles, but does so nervously.

I tuned in an *oldies* station playing out of Washington D.C. and fixed Ellen and I another drink. Ten minutes later she came down the stairs, with tears in her eyes. "Danny put Chris in his pajamas and he put his on too. They both are sleeping in a twin bed together. God bless them." She hugs me around the neck and sits down.

"What do you think he plans to do?" Ellen asks, like she wants to know.

"He told me in his dimly lit office, not long ago, about his castles in the air. First, they are to live like Kings and Queens. Second, they are to build a City, replete with banks, insurance, and utility companies. Third, they are to expand horizons concentrating on health care and medical research. He wants to live forever.

"We'll have our own church and we will provide jobs for those we allow in our selected community. *We'll need butchers, bakers and candlestick makers.* We'll live in a perfect world, near Sydney, Australia. It is renowned as a dynamic and cosmopolitan city of three or four million. It combines excellent business and education facilities with great leisure. Sydney is Australia's oldest and largest city set on one of the world's most stunning harbors, fringed by easy-to-reach, sandy beaches. Our City will be born on one of those sandy beaches not too far from Sydney, but far enough. He said, with the only feeling of emotion and excitement I ever saw in the man." I say, but looking at Ellen with an expression of doubt that this all could happen before the Bureau would shut him down.

Ellen finished her drink, saying, "Johnny, this is a story with surprises. Let's stay the course. And, let's go to bed."

We are all in the gutter, but some of us are looking at the stars.
Oscar Wilde

Chapter Seventy

Mayflower Hotel
Washington, D.C.
Friday, October 5, 1984

My suit was a three-piece, navy in color, made out of one hundred percent wool. I wore a brilliant white shirt, button-down all-cotton, pinpoint, with a small, dark silk bow tie which bestowed upon me a look of extreme intelligence and wisdom. It seemed appropriate for the occasion.

I had been in a meeting since nine o'clock this morning with the Virginia Insurance examiners. They had arrived Atlantic States Surety offices at two o'clock yesterday afternoon. They announced their business by saying the Bureau of Insurance licenses, regulates, investigates and examines insurance companies, agencies and agents on behalf of the citizens of the Commonwealth of Virginia.

According to Mary Robinson, Richard Corrigan and Ray Bertrand walked through the front doors just after the auditors arrived. Mary had given them the high sign and they'd come directly to Robinson's desk to see what was going on. When the auditors explained their business, both Corrigan and Bertrand pointed to my office door. Mary Robinson buzzed me and I met them at the front desk. After being introduced, I suggested we go to a small conference room adjacent to the coffee bar. They agreed.

There were two of them. First, was a woman who was rail thin and kept lighting one cigarette after another during our conversation? She had a severe rattle in her chest and coughed during most of our meeting. She looked like she was in her seventies, and ready to expire at any moment. She was actually only 54 years old. Second was a man, who appeared emaciated, undernourished and already dead. His skin color was an ashen gray. He was nearly bald, but had a few wisps of gray hair dangling in his right eye. He smoked cigarettes faster than the lady. He, too, had a severe rattle coming from his chest and he coughed louder than his counterpart. He looked like he might be in his late eighties, if he wasn't dead, but it turned out he was 56 years old.

I told them this conference room would be their work station. They thought that was wonderful, seemingly more concerned about being near the coffee bar. When I asked them the purpose of their visit they gave me a laundry list of items they would like to examine. First, the Commission has been receiving an inordinate amount of complaints about claims not being paid timely or at all. Their mission is to work toward a resolution of these complaints. Mainly, they wanted to ensure the business practices of Atlantic States Surety are in compliance with Virginia's insurance laws and regulations. Therefore they would be reviewing policies and contracts to ensure they are in compliance with statutory and regulatory requirements.

While they coughed away I faked coughed to cover up my laugh just thinking about Joe Neverson dealing with these two assholes. Second, they said they would be reviewing the recently submitted 1983 annual report and subsequent events. Based on the telephone calls and written complaints the loss reserves seem to have been understated. So, these two clowns, they would be examining Atlantic State's accounts, records, books, and operations for the purpose of assessing the solvency of the insurance company. Another round of coughs covered a hysterical laughing fit again.

On first sight, I was thinking it would take these two people five years to conduct such an audit scope. If they didn't add some competent help they would more than likely die on the job before it completion. I asked them when they wanted to start their examination.

"Tomorrow," said the man. Through a series of coughs, he introduced himself again as the lead auditor, Jacob Johnson from Indiana.

What purpose *from Indiana* had to do with anything I didn't know? Then, he reintroduced the woman as Judith Holmes. "Just call me, Judy," Holmes piped up.

I nodded, saying, "Judy."

"Call me, Jake." Johnson rang out.

"Jack," I said, with a grin. "Jack Oleson."

I wondered if that's the way they ran their *good cop – bad cop routine.* Both were the good cops?

We set it up to begin at nine o'clock Friday morning. He wanted to start with a few claim's files. I told him to make a list of what he wanted to examine, which I figured would take him all day tomorrow. It would take them half a day just lighting up, smoking and putting out cigarettes. And, that didn't include eating donuts and drinking coffee. Although I was sure they didn't eat much, by the looks of their physiques.

"Hey Shanahan," I say. "Are you ready for lunch?"

"Wow! You look sharp today with that cute little bow tie?" She raises her eyebrows, in search for an answer.

"It gives me that scholarly and sagacious look. Don't you think?" I request for information.

She grabs her coat and we wave to Robinson as we mosey toward the elevator. Mary Robinson seems to know everything about everybody and I sense she approves of our relationship. She doesn't know any more about it than we do. Or, does she know more?

"You know a lot more about me now than the first time we came here. Do you remember, what was it a year ago?" I ask Mary, once we were comfortably seated at the restaurant in the grand hotel.

"Remember, are you crazy?" She said, wiping a tear from her cheek. "It was the greatest day of my life, Jack."

I smile at her, asking, "Mary are you okay? I mean, why are you crying?"

"It's ending, isn't it Jack?"

"It's probably the best time for you to go, and it's the worst time for me if you leave." I reply.

We just sat there looking at each other.

"You know, J. Edgar Hoover ate lunch here every day for more than twenty years, so we agents are always told about the run of the mill things he did. His daily menu choices never varied, so I was told, and they were even considerably blander than his personality – buttered toast, cottage cheese, grapefruit, salad, and chicken soup. Ha!" I laughed.

"I wish he would've known what he had in you, Jack." Mary said, with pride in her voice.

"I'm sure he thought I was a good draft pick." I reply.

"Jack, you have told me who you are. But it's not really who you are – no, not at all. If you tell me to leave, of course, I will. I want to stay the course. Maybe, I can help?"

I ordered us the same drinks I did last year, asking for time to look at the menu. "Shanahan, what's going to be happening here in the next few months is dangerous, extremely dangerous. We're not on a level ground. PGC does not play fair, and the Bureau doesn't either. You'll learn soon enough that most of feds don't play fair. You think nobody knows about the two of us? They know everything about us both. We've played it straight, very straight. But it doesn't make any difference to PGC or the FBI. We're just checkers on their board and they'll play us the way it will do them the most good."

"I can deal with your wife and children. In fact I fell in love with Danny when I took him to Hershey. He's you all over again, Jack. I just love him. But what I can't bear is the thought of losing your humor and the way you deal with life. You've given me such strength the past year. No, I want to stay to the end. The next time you tell me to go, I will trust you. I will go the next time because I know it is getting really dodgy."

I saw the waiter patiently hanging on for her speech to end. When it did I ordered the same as last year plus two more glasses of wine. "Okay. But do not trust anyone. There's not a single person you can confide in, including Maggie. Just always remember that. It will become so important later on. Also, every word you utter, whether at home or in the office or anywhere in the building, is likely to be recorded. They might even listen to you in your car. And, the less your say to anybody the better off you are."

We finished our lunch and noticed the crowd was thinning. "Ellen is taking Dan and Chris back to Pennsylvania tonight. She has some things to take care of and she needs to check on the house. Or, I feel she might have some other agenda. I don't ask questions. I promised I'd go to Front Royal tomorrow, Joe has a football game. Would you like to go with me? Tomorrow night will be ours."

"When is Ellen leaving?" Shanahan asks.

"When Danny gets out of school, today." I reply.

I motion for the maître d' to get us another drink. He brings it swiftly.

"Ellen tells me there is all kind of weird shit going on with this so-called luxury car dealership. Those purchases are being made and Ned Larson is making payment for these expensive vehicles but they never arrive in Chevy Chase. She said she received a strange call the other day from a shipping company saying ten vehicles would be arriving in New Zealand in two days. She asked for the description of the vehicles and the serial numbers. They were the ones Ned Larson had just paid for in Munich, Germany." I tell her, with a worried tone in my voice.

"My God," Mary said. "Do you think Ellen might be in danger?"

"Funny you ask. She thinks she already knows too much and she's not good at hiding her emotions. I told her to make copies of everything. She told me she already thought of it and had made the copies. She's taking them with her to Pennsylvania. She's really scared. Ned and Ellen have known each other a long time and now she doesn't trust him at all. She catches him in one lie after another, Ned isn't good at lying either."

"I told her to take her job back in Jenkintown and get out of this deal here. So that is why she is really going to Pennsylvania this weekend. We are all afraid of what's coming next. Are you sure you still want to stay?" I ask, Shanahan.

I motion for our check. I pay it and the maître d' leads us to the door.

Nothing is exciting if you know what the outcome is going to be.
Joseph Campbell

Chapter Seventy-one

Ellen's last day working, indirectly, for PGC at the car dealership was as uneventful as the first day. Ellen put it so deftly, telling me, "It's a joke, but it scares the hell out of me just to be in that big building alone. There's not a damn thing going on there. He must have spent a fortune remolding the place. Everything is beautiful, but I'm the only one there. It's just me, a telephone and the file cabinet.

"The most exciting thing happening is the mailman coming maybe to deliver a single piece of mail. There is no bookkeeping to do because there are no transactions. There are proposed sales contracts, but they never seem to materialize. Ned, supposedly, is flying back and forth to Munich, Germany delivering money for the purchase of cars, which apparently are being shipped to New Zealand. Go figure."

I hadn't received any feedback about Ellen giving her two-week notice. PGC was playing it cool like he didn't give a shit she was leaving. I knew better, though, nobody quits on him without some repercussions. I wondered if Ellen had observed and knew too much. She didn't know the source of funds for these purchases. But, she did have evidence the vehicles purchased in Germany were being shipped to New Zealand. She did know the large building leased, to be used for automobile sales, had been improved with another undisclosed source of funds. There were large sums of money coming in and large sums of money going out for auto purchases and leasehold improvements. So what did she really know? Nothing really, she could only speculate about it all based on what I'd been telling over the past year's events. But she knew what she had seen.

The partnerships and joint ventures, I'm thinking. Had Ellen seen or been involved with any of these income tax evasions? Yes, on her first day, she had been told to draw a draft of a joint venture for the automobile dealership. He had given her a copy of the Mississippi Joint Venture. She had told me about this but I didn't pay it much attention at the time. I was too busy with the contractor getting the first level of our split level finished. Then she did mention that PGC had told her to get the details from Ned Larson and put together a prospectus, and an agreement to form a partnership, letters of intent, disclosure statements and the limited partnership agreement itself. Once drafted, he told her to give it to Ted Masters for fine tuning. This assignment had been given to her on her first day of employment. Ellen hadn't mentioned anything about it since.

Letters become words, words become sentences, sentences become paragraphs and paragraphs become agreements. Drafting a partnership was really a contentious issue and nothing out of the ordinary, I'm musing. I needed to find out if any of the blanks were chockfull with specifics. I knew there was more, but Ellen probably didn't see that much out of the ordinary. The whole thing was shrouded in mystery, but if I asked her certain questions she may realize she saw more than she thought.

Ellen was rehired by her old firm and her start date was on Monday, October 29th. So, she was going to be here one more week and then Danny, Chris and she were moving back to Pennsylvania. It was the best thing for all concerned with so much uncertainty in the winds. We had been going to Front Royal, Virginia nearly every weekend to visit Joe. He was doing well and it seemed the regimented military discipline suited him. Danny wanted to stay in Virginia with me, but I had no idea what my schedule would be day to day. So, I told him he would have to go back to Pennsylvania. Christopher just wanted to be with his mother.

Before I left the office I asked Shanahan if she had made

copies of the C&B bank statements, leases, journals and general ledger. She pulled the attaché case I'd given her this Monday past and tapped it three times before handing it to me.

I smiled, mouthing, "Thank you."

I told her I wanted her to do the same thing next week for the joint ventures and the other partnerships.

"I'll bring you a new attaché case." I say.

"It's not so easy, Jack. I feel somebody's watching me. I know it's probably just my imagination, but it's kind of an eerie feeling." She said, with some misgivings and trepidation in her whisper.

"I know, Mary. Just be careful, again trust nobody. And, if you want out all you have to do is say so." She knew I always meant what I said.

I picked up the briefcase and wished her a good weekend. She reached for my hand and I squeezed it while leaning forward to kiss her lips.

When I walked by Mary Robinson's desk she smiled, saying, "Have a good one, Mr. Oleson." I waved and walked directly to the elevator doors.

Driving west on Route 66 my mind was racing. I hadn't even seen PGC since the Republican Convention at Dallas in August. Almost two months ago, I'm thinking. I haven't seen him or heard from him directly. Something crazy is going on and I'm becoming more certain about my suppositions. He's slowly, but not so slowly all things considered, liquidating and moving his operations to Australia or is it New Zealand. Oh where oh where is Charlotte Boyer and *Harvard girl*, Sandy? I'm betting they are the front runners for PGC and probably setting up office and living quarters.

As I take the Vienna exit I'm looking forward to being with my family. I also am anxious to ask Ellen about a few things, hoping I can jar her memory. I'm convinced somebody has to know something.

Another mystery, I'm discerning, are the two Virginia auditors. I check with them a couple times a day and they seem to be spinning their wheels, smoking cigarettes, and taking their time. McKenzie Gillen told me they tried interrogating her but she deferred their questions to me. I told her she had done the right thing. I wanted every question or request to come through me and for her to pass the word in case they sneak around trying to get information from someone other than me. They've been there two weeks and have not come up with a question yet.

Suddenly I feel I'm being maneuvered, by PGC and whoever at the FBI. It seems I am being pushed toward something awful. I began to feel I was given this assignment because they didn't think I would get the job done. I hadn't heard from my handler since the fiasco at Lafayette Park. I was confused as I pulled my car up in front of our house.

We took the boys for pizza. After we ate we let the boys play some video games while we had a beer and kept our eyes on them. I was happy we were going to Front Royal to visit Joe in the morning. It's always important to have something to look forward to. We didn't talk about business or anything concerning the goings-on with PGC. We kept it pleasant simply enjoying our time with the boys. I decided, in lieu of tonight, during our driving time to Front Royal tomorrow, I would ask her a few questions about her two weeks in the automobile industry.

The ride back from the pizza parlor was quiet. The boys fell asleep in the back seat and both Ellen and I were quiet thinking about our own life's resolutions. Things had changed so much in the passing of a little over a year's time. In retrospect, the year these events transpire is of no consequence. Where they occur is not important. The time is always, and the place is everywhere.

You cannot solve the problem with the same kind of thinking that has created the problem. **Albert Einstein**

Chapter Seventy-two

1700 K Street
Washington D.C.
Monday, October 29, 1984

Ellen and I had enjoyed our week together in Vienna. She had composed the house nicely, with clean sheets on the beds and another set in the linen closet. Towels were hanging on towel racks with additional ones folded neatly on another shelve. Suits and shirts were hanging in our walk in closets and shoes were lined up on the floor. The dressers were filled with other daily essentials and to say it simply, everything was in its place. The kitchen had pots, pans, silverware and dishes.

I hadn't spent much time in the office the week Ellen was here. I'd fought the Beltway traffic and drove into D.C. on the George Washington Parkway every day. When I arrived at the office I would talk with Shanahan and make a few rounds assuring everybody, except Neverson, the Virginia auditors were moving along surely but slowly. All one had to do is look at them and know they were moving along at a snail's pace.

***

On Monday, a week ago, McKenzie Gillen requested a meeting with me. McKenzie had been the backbone of the accounting department since the company's inception. She told me she was giving her two weeks' notice. "Mr. Oleson, the money is almost gone." She got tear in her eyes saying, "I can't believe it. I don't see how we're going to cover payroll next week, unless you know something I don't. And those damn auditors are a nuisance. I keep deferring them to you." It was strange, I thought, they ask me nothing.

"I understand McKenzie. It's not your fault. PGC is trying to grow the company too hurriedly. If you're uncomfortable you may leave today and I'll give you two week's severance and your vacation pay. You've done a great job for the company. If you need a recommendation, simply write your own letter and I'll sign it. Or, better yet have whoever call me."

McKenzie smiled and gave me a hug. "Good luck Mr. Oleson. I just have a bad feeling about what's going on here. And that is no reflection on you, sir."

"Good luck to you, McKenzie, I'm certain you will leave your work papers with Nancy so somebody knows what they're doing." I said, with confidence in her.

"Yes, Nancy can do all my jobs. But, I think she might be giving her notice soon, too." McKenzie stated. "I hope not too soon." I reply, with a reproachful smile.

As McKenzie exited my office Shanahan returns as if on cue. "Same old back and forth," I say. "McKenzie just resigned. I can't blame her. She's a smart gal and she knows the monkeyshines that go on around here."

Mary just shook her head. "I suspect there'll be more, if the paychecks start bouncing."

Mary must've been talking with McKenzie, I'm thinking. Why would Shanahan think the paychecks might be bouncing?

I sit down in my chair and I begin making notes. I had so much to do I felt frozen in time, because something else was bothering me. I had come in at this juncture as a FBI undercover agent to gather evidence about what was going on here. Like I'd done a dozen times before, I was performing a task by being the simple tool of the higher-ups. I never knew their extant goals, which were none of my business or concern. I just gather the facts. But, somehow I had gotten involved with the people and the nefarious ways of Atlantic States Surety. Now I feel like I'm walking a tight rope between the Bureau and the Company I'm investigating. I'm suspicious of both and the hurdle had become the most difficult to jump.

I checked my watch, it was noon. I told Mary Shanahan I had to go, but I could be reached at home if she needed me.

"Home, like in Vienna," She asked, smiling.

When I arrived home Ellen is sitting on the front steps smoking a Winston. She waves when I drive up and I shout to her, "Come on, I'm taking you to lunch."

She locks the front door and gets in the passenger side front door. "Where are we going, sport's fan?" She queries.

"A nice little spot I know in Fairfax." I tell her.

"Are they still around, Jack?" She laughs, curiously.

"Dino's Den? I remember the night you auditioned there. You were so afraid you wouldn't get the gig." Ellen laughs again.

"I was? I don't remember being scared about any gig. I'm the best, remember?" I speak so self-assuredly, with a degree of braggadocio. "Plus, I put that joint on the map."

"That's what you told everybody." Ellen mimed, while smiling. She seemed to be enjoying herself reminiscing about thirteen years ago, when we were filled with so much hope and promise.

"Hey, remember that night I got home late. Everybody was buying me drinks and time got away from me. I was so tired when I arrived home I left the keys in the trunk, after taking my instruments into the house. As soon as I shut the trunk I knew I'd locked my keys in there. *Fuck it*, I said and I just went to bed.

"The next morning I wasn't feeling too well, but I had to get to a meeting in D.C. so I took the tire iron out of your trunk and just beat the hell out of my trunk until I could squeeze my arm inside to fish out the keys." I say, laughing somewhat hysterically as was Ellen.

"After you left for work two neighbors, who had witnessed the car pounding, came over and asked me if I was okay. That they had never seen such an exhibition of anger." Ellen recalls, with both of us thinking back now on how traumatic it was at the time.

We pulled up in front of Dino's Den. We walked into the restaurant. The place hadn't changed one bit in ten years. We sat down at the bar and I ordered a gin and tonic and Jack and club soda from the bartender. Just then I saw Dino carrying two boxes of beer from one room to the next. A few minutes later he came walking toward the bar. "Dino," I rang out.

He looked at me, then he squinted his eyes giving me the double take. "Johnny," he said. "Johnny JASCO." He shouts. "From under what rock did you crawl?" He gave me a big Italian hug. Then, he looks at my wife. "I remember you too, you're Johnny's wife, but I don't remember your name."

Ellen said her name and then he went into a dissertation about me being the best entertainer he'd ever had in his place. I had played there about a year, before I was transferred to Norfolk. He told the bartender to give us anything we wanted and it was on the house. "I've got to go but things are coming back to me, Johnny. I heard from somebody after you left here to go to Norfolk that you joined the FBI. Is that true?"

"You know the rumor mill, Dino. That's the craziest thing I've ever heard, though. FBI? Come on!" I reply. "They don't use guitar players. I mean, it's like me going to the Seminary."

"That's what I told those assholes, not Johnny. Listen, Johnny, come see us again if I miss you later." Dino says, while walking out the front door.

"*Glory Days*, huh, Johnny. Good old glory days." Ellen says, with qualms in her voice. "And there is nothing you like better than spinning a good lie, huh?"

She hated talking about my glory days. Ellen and I spent two hours drinking and eating *French Dips*. My wife was relaxed enjoying her drinks and enjoying my company and began talking about what was on her mind.

———◦((◦))◦———

"Jack!" Shanahan shouted.

"Yeah," I said. "Why so loud?" I ask.

"Telephone," she said. "It's line 4."

"Who is it?" I ask."

"It's your wife." Shanahan says.

Ellen was in a good mood, saying she can't believe it was a week ago we had such a good time at Dino's Den. She told me it was good to get back at her old job where things seemed so safe now. She told me she hoped what she had said would help me, but she was so frightened. That, she was still in a state of flux over our relationship as she was as sure I was too. *But let's keep all our options open. I still love you so much.* She told me she would not be down this weekend, but the plans were still firm for the holidays. We would have Thanksgiving and Christmas in our new home in Virginia.

When I hung up the telephone Mary asked me if everything was okay. I check my watch it one o'clock. "Shanahan, let's take a walk."

She looked at me strangely, replying," Okay, Jack."

We walked to the Washington Monument and talk about everything but Atlantic States Surety. We talk about us and what we mean to each other. We talk about everything except PGC.

We walked toward the Lincoln Memorial. En route we found an empty park bench. We sat down. There was a chill in the air and I put my right arm around her shoulder. She leaned her head on my shoulder. I started to cry. I lost it and cried hard. She threw her arms around my neck and started patting me on the back.

"This insanity just keeps growing and growing. I know it's bad, but I'm telling you it's even worse than you know. It's bigger than big. It's the power fix, the high which I have pursued all my life that is wearing off now. I don't want it anymore. I just want to come down off my high horse. Sometimes I think I've raised so high and fallen so low. I've been rolled over by the power and deceit I've seen everywhere on this power fix.

"I have never been an emotional person. But, I find myself trembling at odd times for a few seconds, feeling that I might be on the verge of a nervous breakdown, and then I swing back to a lucidity and calmness I have rarely known.

"I have a curse. I remember every fact, every small detail like what people were wearing on certain days, where everybody was seated at a meeting. My mind locks on facts, and I can recite them as easily as people recite their own names and birthdays. I have no problem keeping cover stories or complicated lies straight. Perhaps it's why I've been so good at this fucking job of mine."

Shanahan turned my face toward hers and kissed me. She said, "I love you, Jack."

"I'm going to tell you something really scary, Shanahan. I told you Ellen, because she worked a few weeks at the car dealership in Chevy Chase, and she made some astute observations. She was directed to write checks totaling nearly a million dollars for car purchases in Munich, Germany and also for leasehold improvements. During her last week working there she started getting telephone calls from a shipping line confirming the vehicles had been shipped to New Zealand. Ned Larson is supposedly handling the movement of all this money on his midnight runs to Germany. But the amount of money spent doesn't match the shipping orders of the automobiles supposedly purchased. Not even close. Do you get the picture, Mary? And, she asked me, where in the hell does this money come from to cover the checks she has written. When she asked Ned, he told her: *Cash.* And, not to ask that question again.

"During her lunch break, one day last week, Ellen heard a bunch of yelling and screaming in the display room. She was scared and took a peek to see what was going on. It was Ned Larson and Mike Ferrone standing toe-to-toe with two, who looked Iranian, big guys in suits. They were wearing scarfs or turbans around their heads. Ellen heard Ned Larson explain, four vehicles were on the way to Israel with the arms. And, once delivered, those vehicles were to be dispatched to Sydney, Australia. *You have 72 hours,* said one of the perpetrators."

"My God, Jack, this is illusory." Mary says.

"Ellen told me Ned Larson stayed behind. He asked her if she had heard anything. Ellen replied, how *could I have not heard it all. I'm not sure what it means, if that counts,* she told Ned Larson.

"This was on a Tuesday and Ellen told me Ned told her two days later to give her two-week's notice. He said there are serious rumors there may be an attempt on her life."

Mary and I sat in quietude watching people walk by. She was stunned and I couldn't believe I told her.

Finally, I said. "I'm putting an ad in the Post to set up a meet and hopefully my handler will respond. If he does I'm telling him I have to come out of cover and why. Frankly, I don't know what he will do. But, if he does nothing then he'll have another problem. Me! And, anyone who knows me at the Bureau has knowledge of what a hot head I am if pushed. And, we unkempts are capable of anything. If I get no satisfaction, I need to talk with a lawyer because this may be bigger than I think. You know, Mary, no one likes a squealer, a Judas, an informant, a tattletale, especially one who is also guilty. Every base motivation, well, I can attribute to me. I played along for the money, for old-fashioned publicity, for spite because I am an unscrupulous character. I suppose that's why they chose me. All I want now is to be a good, descent and honest man. A law abiding citizens who teaches school and coaches football, basketball and baseball. It's all I ever wanted in the first place."

I grabbed Mary's hand and helped her off the park bench. "Here's looking at you kid."

She smiled and squeezed my hand as we walked away from the Capitol Building on the National Mall. We walked silently side by side, holding hands. In a sense I felt as if I were being led to the electric chair. It was alternately pleasant and excruciating. They, whoever they were, certainly had me on a tightrope, and knew how to shake the wire.

A few paces ahead I saw a street vendor. "Let me buy you lunch, Shanahan."

"Two chili dogs with mustard," I shout. There was a man in front of us picking over his chili dog, like a health inspector, before daring a bite or willingness to move.

"Pardon me," I say, extending a ten dollar bill to the vendor, who in turn extended the chili dogs. The health inspector threw his dog in the trash basket, while Mary and I sat on a curb and nailed ours off. "Sometimes there is nothing better than the simplest things in life." I said to Mary, while licking my chops.

"How about we have dinner at Blues Alley tonight? I suggest, while wiping a glob of mustard off the bottom of my necktie.

"Perfect," she mouths. "I love Blues Alley, Jack. Do you have another shirt and tie in the office?" She asks, expressing amusement.

I slip off my tie and throw it in the trash basket where rests the health inspector's chili dog.

"Yeah," I said. "Blues Alley will be perfect for us tonight, Shanahan."

"Hey Jack," she asks, "Why couldn't they put *Humpty Dumpty* together again?"

"Because he fell from such a high place." I answer.

"Right on," she says. "Right on, Jack."

The willow which bends to the tempest, often escapes better than the oak which resists it; and so in great calamities, it sometimes happens that light and frivolous spirits recover their elasticity and presence of mind sooner than those of a loftier character. **Sir Walter Scott**

Chapter Seventy-three

PGC's mansion sits off the 495 Beltway on River Road very near the banks of the Potomac River. I had taken the River Road exit off the Beltway and had driven to a corner bar where Persimmons Tree Road meets up with Oaklyn Drive. The bar is named Bozo's. It is small but plush, like everything else in this neck of the woods. The building is long and narrow, with an elongated bar facing a sparkling, lengthy mirror. On the other wall is the same thing. Between the two bars there is enough area to walk back and forth to the bathrooms and front door. When I amble into the bar I see Neverson standing at the end of the saloon on my left. He smiles when he sees me, then waves me toward him as he toasts me with his scotch and water.

"I knew traffic would be a bitch today so I took an early leave. I just got here ten minutes ago, though," Joe says. "Jack and club?" He asks.

"I came up the Cabin John, it wasn't too bad." I said. "Well, what's going on, Joe? He's never had you and I together at the same time in the same place. Things must be changing?" I guess.

"Jack you haven't been around on Saturdays, lately, but the last three or four have been interesting. I think he's moving out," Joe says. "The two whores and a couple of his Potomac slaves have been hauling boxes out of there like there's no tomorrow. I've really been the only one around to notice. Everyone who comes in on Saturdays, leaves at noon. I'm the only one around in the afternoon. I guess we'll see if his house has been cleaned out when we meet there tonight." Joe Neverson adds.

While Joe orders us another drink, I spot a Washington Post lying on a barstool next to me. I notice a headline on the front page stating, *Business Executive named in a multitude of fraud charges*. Joe starts laughing as he sees me glancing at the article. I shake my head with a grin and say, "We're next, huh, Joe."

"They are a quiet bunch of auditors," I say. "It doesn't seem like their even fishing around. They just sit there and smoke cigarettes." I put forward in astonishing amazement.

"They asked me for some claims files about two weeks ago, and I gave them three. I haven't heard from them since. You're right, they just sit there." Joe alluded to their out of the ordinary techniques, while ordering another round of drinks.

"It seems you and I will have to put this dog down. There is no money left and I have a feeling you have millions in unsettled claims. You know, Joe, it seems like they simply don't know what questions to ask. It's like they don't want to find problems. Or, maybe they don't know where to begin. I can't figure either one of them out, but why try. Everything is always a mystery here. And, what do you think he wants with us tonight?" I ask Joe, who appears deep in thought.

"I've known the man for years," Joe says, "he probably wants an update about the auditors. Or, you would think he would be interested in how it was going. But, I don't think so watching all his stuff being removed from the inner sanctum. I don't know Jack, actually it kind of scares me. I know things about him I would never repeat to anybody. Remember when we spent Christmas at your house last year and my wife and I got into an argument? She was threatening me and I told here to be careful what she was threatening to do. And she yelled, *Are you going to have him kill me too?*"

"Yeah I wondered what that was all about, but I figured it was just words out of anger?" I use body language by shrugging my shoulders."

"Well my wife knows a thing about a thing or two, as she keeps reminding me." Joe emphasizes.

"I haven't seen the man since August, when we were at the GOP convention. I haven't talked with him since then, either. I talk with his whores, mainly Haycock. I see Annabelle every Thursday night. I take her to drunk school. While in Dallas he promised my wife the moon, talking her into working for his big time gray-market Mercedes Benz dealership. She worked for a few weeks and heard and saw a lot that didn't make any sense. He was never around there either, after spending hundreds of thousands fixing up his offices. Ned Larson was running the show for him. I, personally, think he's ready to book. He should have enough money." Then, I gave Joe my thoughts about what I did know. "And, how about the collateral accounts," I ask.

"Art Aamot has been unloading rather large joint accounts supposedly to pay claims. Of course, we all know better. Aamot has been issuing checks to Ned Larson, who is cashing them all over the place. He's bailing, Jack, and he's setting up somewhere else. But where? Does Ellen have any clues," Joe asks, with a serious tone in his voice.

"Australia – New Zealand. He seems to be doing business there, Ellen thinks."

"We've got time for one more," Joe says, ordering another round from the bartender.

We pause for a few minutes, before Joe asks me what I'm going to do with the rest of my life. "It's over here, Jack. We're yesterday's newspaper. I say he'll be wherever he's going by Thanksgiving. He'll leave you and I to settle with the authorities, whoever they are: although, I am sure even the FBI will be in on this before it's over.

"Jack, whatever he says tonight let's just say we'll do it but, of course, we won't," Joe says. "I don't even trust having a drink there. Let's simply get out as soon as we can. I'm scared," Joe acknowledged.

I'm just listening as Joe Neverson continues to ramble. I have no idea what PGC is really capable of, other than the disappearing people on the boat and Tom Harvey's mysterious airplane crash, but I'm betting it's horrid. I would simply like to shut it down tomorrow, but the FBI doesn't want it done now. Of course, they have another agenda.

I check my watch; it's twenty-to-seven. "We better go Joe."
Joe checks his watch, saying, "Yeah."

We set our drinks down on the bar and each throw down a
twenty dollars bill. Joe and I agree to drive together and return
here afterwards. It's a short drive and we arrive at 7 p.m. sharp.
The mansion is completely surrounded by an eight foot high stone
fence. The large steel gates are usually closed and opened only
after you identify yourself. Of course, surveillance cameras are everywhere. I pull alongside the speaker and press a green lit button,
which has always been red in the past. Absolutely nothing happens. The place seems abandoned. Joe says, "Let's get the hell out
of here."

I push the button again, and nothing happens. Joe encourages
me again to just leave. I back away from the speaker and put the
car out of sight along the wall. I look around the development. It's
rolling hills and the houses are staggered a half mile apart. Joe is
very nervous, but points out Jimmy Hoffa's house in the distance,
kitty-corner from PGC's. There are no lights on there and few
everywhere else. The lights showing on the properties are mostly
ground lights.

I pull up again and turn right into the mansion's huge circular driveway and swing around under the portico that centers at
PGC's front entranceway. "Let's go ring the doorbell, Joe."

Joe, hesitates but exits the car when I did and we meander
toward the front door. I ring the doorbell and nobody answers. I
ring it again, and nobody answers. Joe and I look at each other and
we both shrug our shoulders.

"Let's get out of here, Jack. Something doesn't feel right."
Neverson says.

"Okay." I agree. Both Joe and I had never known Paul Gordon
Charles to miss a meeting without calling to cancel. We got back
in the car and when we reached the straightaway to the gate we
heard a rumble and watched the gates close in front of us.

"Shit!" Announces Joe Neverson. "What the hell is he up to."

"Let's get out, Joe, and take a look around." I reach under my
seat and pull out my Smith and Wesson, which is holstered. And,

I clip the holster to the left side of my belt. Joe asks, "Where the hell did you get that gun?"

"Have gun will travel, Joe." I looked serious now, having no idea what might happen next. "Come on. Let's have a look around." I say, resolutely.

We exit slowly out of the car. Joe walks over toward me and stands off my right shoulder as we look around. There were lights shining on the bottom floor but nobody seemed to be stirring. The cars were probably in the six-car garage, but the doors were all closed. Joe and I look at each other, like *Dragnet's Joe Friday and Frank Smith*. We both just want to leave, but can't. Also, we knew somebody is fucking with us.

We walk toward the front gate to try separating the two pieces of rot iron by hand, but it won't budge. I reached through the holes in the gate and pressed the button to access the speaker. I pressed the button three times and there is no response.

"What shall we do, Joe," I ask. "Start walking?"

"Gordon," Neverson yells out. He roars two more times to no avail. There is a dead silence that pervades the whole area. It is such an eerie feeling because we know somebody is there.

"Let's get our stuff out of the car and get out of here. We can walk back to the bar and get your car, Joe." I say, in desperado.

"How are we going to get over that wall, Jack?" Joe twitters.

I thought for a moment and said, "I'll pull the damn car along the wall and climb." I'm laughing and hoping to draw the attention of whoever might be watching. I was hopeful the security system was on so we could get some police action to the property. So I moved the car and absolutely nothing came to pass.

"I'll go first Joe, when I get on top I'll wait for you." I climbed to the top of the car, leaving a few dents along the way, then I easily pull myself up to the top of the wall. Jim did the same thing and once atop we shook hands like Batman and Robin. We had two options; (1) climb down and start walking, (2) sit on our perch and try flag someone down. Then, all of sudden, a light blinked three times from the turret. PGC has built a tower rising 66 feet, another one of his favorite numbers, above his house. It looks like a lighthouse.

The flashing continues for about five minutes. I wonder, whoever it is, if they are sending a Morse code message. I'd heard Gordon knew the code and loved to play with the ins and outs of the secret language. Then a spotlight beams from the turret. It lights Joe and I up like Christmas trees. "Let's go!" I shout. I drop down to one knee and then hang over the side before dropping about three feet to the ground. Joe does the same thing. Safely off the wall, we hear another rumble and watched the gate open.

I upholstered my gun and we wait to see what happens next. Then we hear footsteps approaching. I position myself in a shooting stance ready to fire, while the footsteps stop. "Jack," I hear the approaching voice. "Jack, its Ned, Ned Larson." The voice says, cautiously.

"Ned, this is Jack Oleson. I am with Joe Neverson. I also have a Smith and Wesson in my hand, ready to fire. And, you know I will fire at first sight if you don't come out through the gate with your hands up." I warn, with vigor.

I hear his footsteps start up again and get closer. I look at Joe who is positioned on the opposite side of the gate with what looks like a boy scout's jackknife. He is in an attack position as well, but looking anxious. Anxious men can be very dangerous, but they also do stupid things. Suddenly, Ned Larson appears with his hands in the air. He smiles at me, and then at Joe, asking, "What's going on here?"

I laugh, still holding my gun on his chest. "You tell me, Ned. We were summoned by Madeline Haycock to be here at seven o'clock to meet the boss. When we arrive the gate is wide open and nobody answers the security system or the doorbell. We decide to leave and the gate closes. Then, the Morse code starts flashing from the turret, once we climb the wall to get out of here. When we're on the other side the gate opens. It is definitely not a typical PGC operation. No, Ned, you tell us what's going on." I say pithily, with my gun still pointed at Ned's chest.

"Gordon, Madeline, and Annabelle are all fucked up. Its alcohol and cocaine. Gordon went for his annual physical this morning and found out he has herpes. He caught it from Madeline, who has been fooling around with her scuba diver instructor in South Carolina. She gave it to Gordon and Gordon gave it to Annabelle. They all have herpes.

"Gordon went crazy today, after everything was confirmed. He was going to kill Madeline. He shot holes in all her luggage. Then they all made up and continued drinking and sniffing. When I reminded him Jack and Joe were coming for a seven o'clock meeting he went to the top of his turret with weapons. Mike Ferrone and I kept him away from the guns and convinced him safe harbor was to send an S.O.S. Then we told him to shine a full spotlight on the yard. He didn't see you, but I saw you go over the wall." Says, Larson.

"Why did you lock the gate, and not just let us go." I ask.

"He locked the gate; I'm the one who opened it so you could get your car. I didn't want him to see it in the morning, hoping he'd forget the whole night." Ned preached.

"Joe," I nodded toward him.

"The story is so bizarre it's has to be true, let's get the hell out of here Jack." Neverson said, pointing at the vehicle.

"Okay, Ned, good luck with the rest of your evening." I said, making my way to the car and opening the door. God, I couldn't wait for all this to end.

Joe and I were happy to be back at Bozo's ten minutes later. We had a lot to talk about.

Bravery is the capacity to perform properly even when scared half to death. **Omar Bradley**

Chapter Seventy-four

Paul Gordon Charles has not been seen or heard from since Ned Larson's message to us in mid-November at the Charles' Potomac mansion. In fact nobody has seen Ned Larson or Matthew Ferroneb either. Madeline Haycock keeps in touch via the telephone, but has no specific orders. Her conversations with me are simply to ask how the auditors are progressing and the cash balances. When I tell her we're barely meeting payroll she says it will get better soon. Right!

I'm sitting in Joe Neverson's office waiting for him to get off the telephone. He's arguing with someone, nastily, trying to stall the inevitable. Joe always makes me laugh because he gets so worked up talking I think he is going to throw a chair or something else through a window. What is so hyperactive about his antics it's all a performance. He knows the claims payments being requested are never going to be disbursed.

After he hang up he says, "I'm going to miss mind-fucking with all these people." Then he laughs, like he usually does. Laughing is simply a way of covering up the pain of lying, cheating and stealing. It's his way to cope and exist.

"Let's get Art "the fart" Aamot in here to see how much collateral has been stolen," I tell Joe.

Joe nods and punches Arthur's extension. Neverson tells Art to report to his office. A few minutes later Aamot arrives looking very anxious and jumpy. "Art," I say, commandingly, . "How much collateral is missing and where did it go? And Aamot, who doesn't play games, I caution to give it to me straight."

"At least a million in joint accounts," he says. "Probably more because his signature trumps all. The joint accounts I'm talking about are the ones with large amounts that are being held until jobs are complete and punch-lists are over and done with. These are the accounts least likely to be noticed because it could be months or years before anyone queries about their existence or closings. In fact, it only takes three of these accounts to make up the first million."

"Art," I say, "the auditors are about to examine the collateral. I need you to make me a list of the security that exists, just in round numbers, and the collateral accounts that are missing. We have to try to get the bloodhounds off the track. I need the list today. And, concerning the missing collateral, I need to know dates, to whom it was given and if it has been liquidated."

"Today," Aamot asks, softly. He looks at Joe Neverson for help, but Joe says, "Today, Art. It's important, or you could be ousted for fraudulent activity. You better get moving. We need to see you by three o'clock with the answers." Joe mandates.

Arthur Aamot's departure leaves Joe and I staring at each other. "It's Nancy Sullivan's last day today." I tell Joe. "I haven't even looked for anybody to replace her because I don't think the company will make it to the end of the year."

"What are you going to do about cutting checks, etcetera, etcetera." Joe queries, saying, "I never thought it would come to this. One year ago this was a cash cow. I knew it was all about him, but I never thought he'd shoot the cash cow." Neverson shakes his head in disgust, while moving things around on his desk.

"I keep thinking about the Board of Directors. Nobody ever questioned PGC's numbers or where they came from. He picks his members carefully. They are powerful and wealthy men who, unfortunately, don't understand balance sheets, income statements or cash flows. Even after the big loan they all guaranteed, not one of them ever questioned the figures. They are kind of like the auditors; they don't see the indicators sitting right under their noses." I say.

"It's amazing how PGC created this company attitude that everybody working for him are simply better than all those who don't. And to this day, as much trouble as the company is in, they have no reason to believe the company is in trouble. How could it be with everybody pulling such a nice director's fees, salaries and the company apparently having an open spigot from the banks?" Joe opined.

He is a genius having set up an interstate operation. The dirty deals are spread around the country and never catch up with each other. By design he knew they never would because when and if they did he would be long gone with the money. Each state commission is supposed to scrutinize the annual reports and certified financial statements, especially its footnotes. And if they don't understand something they certainly have the leverage to get more information. But, they don't. Because, they don't understand how the business works. Where oh, where are the watchdogs. Instead they send in a couple of imbecilic assholes like those from the grand Commonwealth of Virginia to audit." I say, not quite believing myself it's really over.

The telephone buzzes and Joe picks it up which gives me more time to weigh up the situation.

I don't believe it is ever in Paul Gordon Charles mind to fail. In fact it isn't he who has failed. The company has failed. He has seized the opportunity for himself. The demise of Atlantic States Surety has only confirmed he is truly indispensible, where everyone else is expendable.

As he tells everybody who works for him: Atlantic States Surety isn't a job – it's a mission – it's an opportunity. The mission, of course, is nothing more than the cover story for a massive fraud. It's a story of human weakness. It is greed and rampant self-delusion; of ambition run amok; of a grand experiment in the deregulated world; of a business model that doesn't work; and of canny people who believe their next gamble will cover their last disaster – and who can't admit they are wrong. The opportunity is there for the taking.

PGC doesn't know it but it has cost him. He has destroyed his marriage, ignores his kids and has destroyed three other relationships with other women, of which, three are still with him. At least two of them are for sure. And they all have one thing in common - they share herpes. But, according to his rules, people didn't just go to work for PGC. Rather he become the most important part of their life, more important than their own family because he is the best thing for them to support so their family can maintain the living standard to which they have been accustomed.

"I'm sorry," Joe apologizes for the interruption.

"We will see what Arthur Aamot has to say, when he gives up the numbers at 3 p.m. I have a feeling it will be bad. I don't know why the auditors don't have a clue. All this stealing is going on right under their noses. PGC has flown the coup. I think we should give them enough ammunition to shut it down after Christmas. However, if we could securely depend on our paychecks it might be worth sticking around. But, there's no guarantee there will be money to pay the rent come January 1st." I say, looking at Joe who doesn't move or say anything.

"I have a bunch to do. Think about it." I say, while walking out the door.

I check my watch, its 10:20 a.m. I walk toward my office and it seems strange not to see Mary Robinson at the reception desk. She quit on Black Friday, the day after Thanksgiving. She told me she'd had enough. That she couldn't take Madeline Haycock and that little high school snot barking orders at her anymore. She suggested I bail before it gets any worse.

I didn't even know the new receptionist's name. She was in her thirties, I guessed, and seemed overwhelmed with her job. I knew she wouldn't last long, one way or the other. I nodded as I walked by. She gave me a little hand wave.

When I walked into our office Mary Shanahan was busy sorting through Nancy Sullivan's work. I sat down at my desk to call my son, Joe, who I had picked up from Randolph Macon Academy yesterday. I told him to pack everything when I arrived, and I'd explain later. En route to Vienna he told me he liked the school, but looked forward to being back with the family again.

Emotionally he seems to have matured considerably during his time at the military school. I think when he answered I woke him up. I told him there was plenty of food and soda in the house and I'd be home about six o'clock. I told him I'd take him out for a nice dinner tonight. He seemed happy and content.

"Hi, Mary Shanahan," I greeted.

"My, my you seem like you are in a good mood today." She said to me with a smile.

"It's Christmas, Mary." I mouth softly, at her.

"I promised you I would tell you when it is time. I met with my handler last week and he told me to shut it down after Christmas, if I see fit." I say, shrugging my shoulders.

"So that's it," she asks, hoping I'm kidding. "Will I ever see you again, Jack?" she tears up, grabbing a Kleenex from the top of her desk.

"I certainly hope so, Mary. But, I don't know. My life seems totally upside down right now." I say, flicking my number two Ticonderoga pencil against our door.

"You always do something stupid like that to make me laugh. It's not fair, Jack. I've been dreading this day and your flicking a pencil against the door." She says, while I flick another one against the wall.

"Here's the play: 1) I'm talking to the auditors late this afternoon. I want to feel them as to where they are going in their meaning-less investigation. You know if the boss didn't bail we could've stuck some money in the company and lasted maybe another year or so. But PGC has another agenda; 2) 26 December, we'll start purging files and making copies of what I want, hoping the auditors will still be smoking cigarettes and making zero progress; 3) 27 December, purging files and making copies of journals and ledgers; 4) 29 December thru 1 January, I'll be in Pennsylvania getting my family settled; 5) 2 January, Neverson and I will evaluate and make the call. We'll get any and all personal stuff out of our office and draw our paychecks; 6) 3 January, I'll solve the auditor's problem about noon and then we'll go to lunch and never come back; 7) 4 January, The marshals will arrive to take over the business."

Shanahan is speechless. "That's the prelim, Mary. But I hope that's it. Other than being with you every day, I'm sick of this place. It's time to move on." I say, quietly.

"What's next for you, Jack?" Mary asks, really wondering.

"I'll go back to Pennsylvania and disappear into the woodwork. I'll do some per diem work for CPA firms during tax season. I'll be testifying probably once or twice a week for a year or so. I'm going to look into an early retirement and start my own firm. My life will be changing."

"How about you, Mary, do have any plans?"

"For the past year my plans have revolved around you. My God we've worked together and lived together. I'm going to be terribly lonesome. I know I am. So what can I do? You have given me the best experience ever. I want to stay in accounting, and I've even been thinking about the government: The GAO or the Internal Revenue Service. I've also thought about Intelligence. I don't know, but I hope you'll be able to advise and help me. First, I'm going back to Gettysburg to spend maybe a month. I'm going to keep our apartment in Glen Echo. As you know it's a month-to-month deal and I'll probably be back in Washington to work, soon enough." Mary tells me, like her plans have been well thought out.

There was a rap on the door. It is Ted Masters. He nods in Mary's direction. "May we have a few works, Jack?"

"Sit down, Ted." I say. "Mary can hear anything anybody wants to say to me. She's my right arm."

"Jack, you know I resigned as Secretary of Atlantic States Surety the week after Thanksgiving." He reached with his right hand into his left vest pocket and extracts an envelope. He extends it towards me. "It's my resignation, effectively immediately, from Atlantic States Surety as general council. When I told Haycock the company needs a Secretary to execute documents she conferred with him, I presume, and she told me to make Annabelle Bergman Secretary. I cannot make Annabelle Secretary, under my signature."

"You are doing the right thing, Ted. This nonsense has to end.

I will keep this on file and duly note the place and time of your resignation. Mary Shanahan is your witness."

We exchanged pleasantries and I knew I'd never see Ted Masters again. During his tenure here he lost his family and pride all because of a crazy relationship he had with Charlotte Boyer, who I'm sure is part of Gordon's harem again.

I check my watch; it is 11:30 a.m. I say, "There's not much sense in getting any work done. Put all that stuff on your desk in order and let's go to lunch. The only two left now are Bertrand and Corrigan. I can't remember the last time I've seen them either.

"I want you to give me a resignation letter with last day being December 28th. I'll put it with Ted Masters' letter of resignation letter. I'm beginning to think we should all draw our checks, key people anyway, and submit our resignation letters on the 28th of December in unison. Then hang a *CLOSED* sign on the door. When the auditors arrive on 2 January there is the final answer in black and white, or red will work. Can you imagine those idiots making that telephone call to Richmond? There's a *CLOSED* sign on their door. I'll run that by Neverson."

"You are crazy, Jack. Do you think you could actually get away with insulting those auditors like that?" Shanahan asks, while laughing it up.

"That would be the beauty of it, Mary. The problem is I wouldn't be able to see the look on their faces. It's a good plan, especially considering how bad it really is with this company. Unless we help it will take them years to sort it all out." I answer.

"Jack, let's go to lunch before you get any more zany ideas." She suggests.

"Hey, Shanahan, I like your skin tight, black leather skirt." I say, with a wolf call.

She smiles. "Let's go to lunch, Jack."

"Hey, Shanahan, I like your skin tight, black leather skirt." I repeat, in a whisper, as we head for the elevator.

We decide on Archibald's for beers and cheeseburgers, and for old times' sake. When we arrive Joe Neverson and Maggie Little are frantically waving us over. We spent the next two hours with

Joe and Maggie drinking, eating and revealing my *everybody re-signs* idea. Actually, we all thought it was a good conception. But, it was more than a good inkling. It's what the auditors deserve and PGC would appreciate. We all thought it was sidesplitting. But, not so far-fetched that we decide to think about it.

When we go back to the office it almost seemed like a ghost town. The new receptionist, again I couldn't remember her name, was gone. No explanation. Ralph Arthur Aamot was sitting in my office. He handed me two lists. The first one was the collateral inventory, which amounted to approximately thirty-three million dollars. The second list what PGC had already swiped. It totaled exactly three million dollars. There were five checks made out to Ned Larson and had been cashed by Ned Larson at various banks. I thanked Ralph for his quick response and had Mary file Aamot's report with the resignations, which now included Mary's.

I called my son, Joe, who answered the phone and said he was playing Pac Man, eating and watching television. He assured me it was like being in Heaven, after being in military school, and not to worry if I'm late. I thanked Joe and told him I'd be home between eight and nine o'clock.

"Mary put everything away. We're going to Glen Echo." I stated in a commanding tone.

I followed Mary to our house, as we call it. She fixed me a Jack Daniels and club soda. She opened a bottle of dry Riesling and poured herself a glass. We both sensed this might be our last time together and maybe we were determined to make it our best. We did so with more emotion and passion then I would have expected to experience with my dear friend.

"It must have been the skin tight black leather skirt, Shanahan." I said, as I headed for my car.

"It must've." she said.

"Merry Christmas," I shouted.

"Merry Christmas," she called out, wiping her eyes with a napkin.

En route to Vienna it really hit me. This marathon in a rich man's world was really ending. My relationship with Mary Shanahan was over. We had spent more than a year together and other than some kissing and petting we had just been good friends. That had all changed tonight, but it was only tonight. Tomorrow Ellen, Dan and Chris will arrive and we would have our family of five back in tack. It's what I had hoped. On December the 23rd Mom and Dad were arriving for Christmas Eve. Christmas Day they would be leaving for my sister's in Charles Town, West Virginia. Christmas would pass and the grand finale would be next week. What finale was still to be determined.

Imagination is the highest kite one can fly. **Lauren Bacall**

Chapter Seventy-five

1700 L Street
Washington D.C.
Wednesday, December 26, 1984

On Christmas Eve I almost told my Dad my secret. After enjoying Christmas Eve dinner we opened presents and watched the children revel in their gifts. I could tell Ellen's mind was preoccupied but she made it through the evening with a smile on her face. She didn't want to explain the why's and why not's of the way we were living. It was slightly after ten o'clock when I asked my Dad to join me downstairs for a drink.

I fixed him a Johnny Walker Black with club soda and a Jack Daniels and club soda for myself. Dad wasn't the type who pressed for answers because he didn't like being pressed or harangued for information himself. We made some small talk about football and who might get to the Super Bowl. We both agreed the 49ers would play the Dolphins (Montana versus Marino). Then, Dad asked me what was going on. Why we had two houses, one in Pennsylvania and one in Virginia. I told him we were going to sell our house in Pennsylvania because we like the Washington D.C. area better.

I fixed another drink and he asked me how the job was going. This was where it got steamy. I told him everything was good and about all the new businesses PGC had set up. I told him 1985 should be a banner year. Actually I felt so guilty telling him these falsities when I knew by the end of the year everything was going to change completely, but in the other direction. Actually I was scared to death with what was about to happen. I wanted to seek Dad's advice in the worst way, but I couldn't put him through it. Nearly fifteen years of my life had been a mystery, although he could handle it, I could tell him all that had happened over a few drinks on Christmas Eve.

On December 26th the day pretty much went as planned. Mary and I purged files and made copies according to our agenda. I filled four briefcases full of information and walked it to my car, one case at a time. I unloaded the briefcases into a footlocker I had arranged in the trunk of my car. These were copies and the originals were neatly filed in the file cabinets in our office. Next we refilled the briefcases with C&B Leasing bank statements and leases. We left nothing behind regarding the leasing company. We worked on this project from eight o'clock a.m. until four o'clock p.m. With very few people around and with no receptionist the task went from impossible to doable – and, it was done.

At four o'clock I stopped by to see the auditors. They were in there smoking cigarettes and contemplating with each other about what they should do next. I asked them if they needed anything and they said more cooperation, but there didn't seem to be anybody around this week. I replied by telling them we are operating with a skeleton crew until the first of the year. But, if they needed anything I would be happy to find it for them. They nodded with a smile and I told them I'd see them tomorrow.

Next I went to the claims department to check with Joe and Maggie to see if the auditors had been harassing them. "We haven't even seen them today, Jack." Said, Maggie Little.

Joe's office door was open and I walked into his working quarters. He motioned for me to sit down in the chair in front of his desk. I did and waited for him to get off the telephone. When he did I smiled. He did the same asking me how the purging was going.

"Done," I said. "Tomorrow I'll get the pay checks out, including your monthly fee and make a transfer from A.S.S. Associates into the payroll account. Tell whoever to go directly to the bank and cash them."

Joe told me Corrigan had called him today and wouldn't be back in the office until next Wednesday, the 2nd. He said Richard sounded strange, like he was upbeat and his old energetic self. Corrigan didn't ask about the auditors or anyone else. He just wished everybody a Merry Christmas and a Happy New Year.

"I've done a lot of thinking and I keep asking myself why I should give the auditors any help. Here are all the resignation letters, including mine, and I'm leaving at noon for Pennsylvania tomorrow. And, yup, that's the way I'm playing it. Fuck 'em all!"

"You've got more guts than I do, Jack. But, good for you if that's the way you play it."

"I don't know if it's guts, Joe, or stupidity. And, I might have an advantage you do not. I'm not sure, though. Anyway, I've had enough of this shit!" '

"How about Mary, is she okay?" Joe asks, with disquiet.

"She's already resigned, like me. Her last day is Friday, too." I report.

Joe shakes his head. "God, I'm going to miss you guys. We've had a lot fun."

"Ellen took the three boys to Pennsylvania today. Between you and I that is where I'm going to be living too." I tell, Joe, because somebody has to know how to get in touch with me. "I have a secure line there, you know the number."

"Mary and I are going to the St. Regis." I announce to Joe Neverson. "We'll see you there?"

"I wouldn't miss this farewell for anything," Joe says. "Hey, tell Maggie to come in here on your way out. See you shortly."

When I walked into my office Mary was busy as hell, putting everything where it should be. She looked at me with those bright green eyes. "Your wife called. She said they arrived safely at home in Pennsylvania. She said no need to call – see you on Friday." Mary's voice cracked at the end of her message.

I put my arms out and she fell into my chest hugging me profusely. I whisper in her ear, "Come on we're going to the Library. Joe and Maggie are going to meet us there. This is our night."

Shanahan perks up, "Yes." She said, "Let's get out of here."

We were shocked when we arrived the Library Lounge. They had a table for six in the middle of the lounge. Along with Maggie and Joe were Ted Masters and a smiling Richard Corrigan. "Jack and Mary, welcome." Corrigan greets us. "Ray Bertrand hopes to join us later."

"Say nothing," says Corrigan. "Joe told me your decision. Ray and I aren't going to Australia or anywhere else either. You've done a great job and all of us appreciate it. Especially since you came here from outer space a year ago, it was outer space wasn't it Jack or whatever your name is?" Corrigan gave me a devious, knowing smile. So did, Neverson.

Two hours later the table looked like a sea of glasses. Ray Bertrand had arrived and joined in the festivities. Maggie had Mary drinking her ass off and laughing. I was so happy to see her cheery. And I took a moment to realize these were the best friends I have ever had and probably after tonight I would never see them again. And that tonight is a magical moment in my lifetime.

We had dinner right at the table, petite filet mignon for everybody. Afterwards the drinks started to flow again. I had Maggie get us a suite for four, telling her I'd pay for it. I didn't know how Richard and Ray were going to get home but when Bertrand's wife showed up it all fit. What a great lady, that Peggy Bertrand. So, we kept drinking until last call, except Masters, he had the sense to go home after dinner. It was great of him to come after his year of personal disaster at Atlantic States.

Our stay at the Regis was nice. Joe slept with Maggie and I slept with Mary. Our beds were separated by a reading lamp. A suite was not available, which Maggie failed to mention, but she did get us a room. And when we got to the room we all kind of passed out. Everybody was sound asleep when our heads hit the pillow.

It was a great night to end a life-changing exciting activity with people who love me as much as I love them.

Great men are they who see that spiritual is stronger than any material force, that thoughts rule the world. **Ralph Waldo Emerson**

What Is Past Is Prologue

Central High School
Montevideo, Minnesota
Saturday Night, February 10, 1962

I always like the beginnings of things. The pure white snow, the first kiss, the first swipe at cheating on a test, most people, I guess, never think about those kinds of things. And endings, I like endings, too. Even if it is the smashing of a glass, a tearful goodbye, or the last awful word which can never be unsaid or unremembered. The beginnings are sweet, the endings usually are bitter, but the middle is the tightrope you walk between the one and the other. In the middle, things always happen you hadn't planned on, and it is these things, the possibility of these things that haunt and trouble me.

I was running late for the game. We are playing the Granite Falls *Kilowatts*, a yearly rival because they are only twelve miles away from our town. We play them in football, but they are no match for us. We are a much larger school. But, in baseball and basketball they always gave us a good run. Mom started nagging me to get ready to go, but I was watching something on television and had lost track of time. When she handed me my gym bag and she said, "Come on now, *don't let the team down Johnny.*" I headed for the door realizing she was right. "Go team go."

Yeah, yeah, yeah, I'm thinking I'm a cool teenager, but deep down I know I'm not. I'm totally uncool, but I am a good athlete. I don't know why I don't feel like playing basketball tonight. My girlfriend is going to be there and I love showing off for her. I get to the gym a few minutes late and Coach gives me the eyeballs. He doesn't say anything, but I'm not the type of kid that tries to show anyone up or make a statement. Im just a player.

The game starts at 8 o'clock. Our tall center tipped the ball to me and I dribbled to the top of the key and shot. *Swish.* No big deal, it's the way most of our games start. I'm a shooter. Granite Falls came down the court and I intercepted a pass and drove down the court and laid it up. I did that three more times, all of sudden it is 10-0.

Granite takes a time out and comes down the court, afterwards, takes a shot and misses. Our center tosses me the ball off his rebound and I dribbled to the top of the key and gun. Swish, it is 12-0. I score ten more consecutive points and the first quarter ends, 22-0.

Everybody is going crazy with my performance. I like the beginning. And then the second quarter starts. The Kilowatts started triple teaming me, which I couldn't understand. I couldn't move. Where oh, where are my teammates. At the end of the half it was, 30-20. I had scored six of the last eight points, giving me 28 points at halftime. The middle is a bitch as was the ending in this case. We lost the game, 65-60. I had scored forty-four points and we lost. I was pissed off beyond pissed off. Former Coach Herm told me after the game it was the most incredible outside shooting he'd ever seen. And after knowing me since I was a kid, he said *he always knew I would have a game like this. You are a shooter, son.* And that coming from the former head coach, who I never thought even liked me, especially after I'd beaned his son with a screwball playing a scrimmage game in baseball.

"But, we lost," I told him." He grinned and slapped me on the back.

When Beth and I went to the sock hop afterwards, my English teacher, who was chaperoning, stopped me. He said. "Don't get the big head, John."

He was the guy who tried teaching English by telling us how his Dad used to take him to the woodshed, when he did something wrong. And his father announced, as he wailed him, *this hurts me more than it hurts you.*

So, anyway, some endings turn out successfully and some don't. The one I just recalled was disappointing, but December 27, 1984 was excellent.

Life is day to day at best and an everlasting learning experience.

Epilogue

220 Runnymede Avenue
Jenkintown, Pennsylvania
Sunday, April 14, 1985

I'm sitting on the sofa watching the Phillies play when Ellen comes walking in the front door. It is 3:10 p.m. She looks completely worn out, which was unusual for her.

"Another tax season bites the dust." I say to my wife with thumbs up. I had finished mine on Friday and we had gone out for drinks after work. It is something we did and always looked forward to when a long winter's work was complete. But on Friday we had one drink and Ellen told me she needed to go home. She said she just wasn't feeling well, that it was nothing in particular, rather just a nauseas feeling. We left the bar and went home. She fiddled around with a few things and told me she was going to bed.

Since the first of the year I'd become John Austin Sletten again. I started working as a per diem accountant for three different CPA's, who shared the same office on Walnut Street in Philadelphia. I'd take the SEPTA train from Jenkintown to Center City on Mondays, to pick up work from each CPA. The following Monday I'd return the assignments and they would give me another set of jobs. It became quite a routine and I enjoyed the train rides into the city.

I met with the FBI at 6th and Arch in Philadelphia twice a month for depositions. Although they pretended to be interested in what went on at Atlantic States Surety during my tenure there I could tell they really were indifferent. They were more interested in PGC's life style and the monies he spent then the contemptible fraudulent acts and thefts he was making on a day-to-day basis. What bothered me though was the constant quizzing about my wife's employment at the so-called car dealership and what paperwork she might have seen and comments she overheard.

I had a feeling they were debriefing Ned Larson, but I didn't ask any questions about anything regarding the gray car market. *I don't know*, was my word for word answer when it came to anything about that hoax. I did appreciate the FBI keeping me out of the cleanup of Atlantic States Surety. Although I heard through my meeting with the Bureau the Commonwealth of Virginia was sorting out that mess. And, that it would take years if they just didn't give up first. Giving up meant the claims would just be paid or settled upon on a one by one basis. They found the coffers emptied, but there was some collateral money that could be used if any of those particular cases ever came up.

I was told there would be a new assignment soon but for now, and for my sake they wanted the waters to still. In other words until the next shitty assignment came up I could do my per diem work and still receive my FBI pay.

During the winter Ellen and I had been getting along well. Although we were both so busy that we really didn't have much time to see each other or visit. The children had adjusted well and all three were in the Jenkintown school system. It was like going to Heaven coming back to Pennsylvania, but I missed the action. And, I think Ellen sensed I missed the pandemonium of being involved with the bizarre activities of the greedy and fraud-laden financial world.

I hadn't heard from or seen anyone since our last hurrah at the St. Regis that December night. It had been particularly difficult for me to not call Mary Shanahan. But I didn't, and she hadn't called me. It was like the past sixteen months never happened and I knew it was best for it to stay that way. It was best, but a problematic obsession to let go. Shanahan was a big part of my life.

I'm seasoning up steaks to cook on the grill when Ellen kind of shuffles into the kitchen. She is white as a ghost. She then does something she rarely does, reaching out to me and putting her arms around my shoulders. "I don't know what's wrong with me, Johnny. I'm so weak. Would you draw me some water and carry it upstairs for me. And, will you make sure the kids are fed and look over their homework."

I walk Ellen back up the stairs and help her get into bed. I prop her pillow up so she can sip her water. She smiles at me and says, "I'll be alright. It was a long tax season. Just take care of the children, John. I love you."

<hr/>

Sunday, April 28, 1985

It was the day after Ellen's funeral. Everybody else had departed after the luncheon we'd had in Hershey, Pennsylvania the day before. Now the three boys and I had assembled on our front lawn to wave goodbye to my parents, who were headed to Boston to visit friends.

Ellen had woken up at six o'clock in the morning on April 15th. She was having a difficult time breathing as she was gasping for breath. I started to panic and I couldn't find the telephone in our bedroom, so I ran down the stairs and grabbed the one in the kitchen. My fingers were shaking so badly I could hardly punch out 911. A few minutes later the paramedics arrived and helped Ellen walk down the stairways. The boys and I watched what was going on, probably in a state of shock, all of us. I ask Joe, if he would make sure to get his brothers up to school. I told him I had to go to the hospital to be with Mom. He assured me he would take care of his brothers.

When I got to the hospital they already had Ellen in an intensive care room. A nurse told me she had expired in the ambulance, but they revived her with the paddles. "Do you have a priest, we can call for you sir?"

"I'm Lutheran," I said. "Is it that bad?" I asked.

Fortunately, she didn't have to answer the question. A doctor came out saying they had her stabilized. He shrugged his shoulders assuring me it was touch and go. He could promise nothing, but he hoped to have her in a room if she remained stable within the hour. He then left abruptly.

"Mr. Sletten, a voice from the past comes from behind me. "I'm Chaplain Adelaide Harrington."

I turned around and we both just stood there and looked at each other. I hadn't seen or heard from her since the program we shared together at Allentown State Hospital. "Ade," I query. "What are you doing here?"

"I work here, John. Maybe God put me here today. This is my first day on the job. I can't believe what is happening." She answers, while extending me a book. It's a small paper back with Lucy (Charlie Brown) on the cover. *Good Grief* was the title.

"I'm glad God doesn't take a day off, Ade. I'm happy it's you, a friend." I say, with meaning. "But, Ellen's still alive." I wave the book and say, "Hopefully, I won't have to read this. But, thank you."

She gave me a hug and a peck on the cheek and told me she'd be checking in on Ellen and I as time progresses. "Here's my number, John," call me anytime or any place if you need somebody to talk with."

"How's it with you Ade," I ask.

"Okay, I guess, I received my Doctorate of Divinity. What about Edward and I? We're divorced."

"I'm sorry." I reply.

"I'm not," she said. "I have to make my rounds. I'll see you soon."

Ellen fought the good fight. On the third day of her hospitalization she slipped into a coma and never recovered. She had tubes running in every parts of her body. For nine days she battled an unknown problem. The doctors tried everything including sending tissues to the National Centers for Disease in Atlanta. They could not figure out what was wrong with her.

I spent every night with Ellen at the hospital. During the time I read two novels and visited with Chaplain Harrington every day. When Ellen passed away on Wednesday, April 24, 1985, from a massive heart attack, Ade was there to comfort me. It was about

5:30 in the afternoon when Ellen took her last breath. Her last words to me were that night before she was hospitalized. *Take care of the children, John, and I love you.*

Ellen was from Hershey, Pennsylvania. We as a couple were from nowhere because of my occupation. Her mother had six plots in Hershey Cemetery, which overlook the hamlet. It's a beautiful setting and it's where we originally met. In her case her final resting place was where she began.

As my parents pulled away I couldn't quite believe what I was seeing. They were simply leaving their oldest son, who knew nothing about raising children, alone with three lovely grandchildren to fend for ourselves. Oh, I knew we'd survive. I would do what I had to do so we would all survive. But, my life now had to be a lot different than the good times of the past. At least I knew what the first step had to be: Resign my job with the Federal Bureau of Investigation. Then, more importantly, learn how to be a real father and find out what really happened to Ellen.

To Be Continued
In Book II
CHAOS

Bibliography

Secret Agent Man (song)
Written by Steve Barri and P.F. Sloan
Performed by Johnny Rivers

Quotes for Copying
Compiled by Janet Alexander Pell
Copyright @ 2003

Quotes for Living
Compiled by Janet Alexander Pell
Copyright @ 2001

Quotes for Writing
Compiled by Janet Alexander Pell
Copyright @ 2001

CPSIA information can be obtained at www.ICGtesting.com
Printed in the USA
BVOW010122220812

298510BV00001B/28/P